How to Date a Puckboy

Rush Hockey Books 1-3

Elise Faber

HOW TO DATE A PUCKBOY
BY ELISE FABER
Newsletter sign-up

HOW TO DATE A PUCKBOY

Print ISBN-13: 978-1-63749-107-2
Ebook ISBN-13: 978-1-63749-099-0

Rush Hockey

Big Puck Energy
Filthy Puckboy
So Pucking Over It
Love, Pucks, and Other Stories

PART 1:

BIG PUCK ENERGY

Prologue

Billie Rose

Billie Rose waded through a graveyard of beer bottles.

Chairs were overturned, glasses were broken, pool cues had been reduced to splinters. Even the door to the bathroom had been torn off one hinge, the cheap wood hanging lazily from the bottom one, swaying gently in the breeze that came courtesy of the shattered window just to the right of the bar's entrance.

Suffice to say, the bar was trashed.

Absolutely trashed.

As was Axel Finnegan, the captain of the Rush and ringleader for all the antics that had left one of the two bars in River's Bend in such a state.

He was propped up in a booth, his big, bulky hockey player's body pinned between the table and the wall.

And he was singing.

Loudly and off-key.

The song of choice?

Diamonds by Rhianna.

Unfortunately for Billie's ears, he wasn't nearly as talented as RiRi.

"Shine bright like a—" He belched, stepping on the gemstone

in the lyric, and then resumed singing. Even louder, and somehow even more off-key.

Good lord.

The man might be talented on the ice, but his singing skills rivaled nails on a chalkboard.

And the nails would win the talent competition.

Wincing, she glanced over at Barry, the owner of the bar, and somehow heard his sigh over the noise. He was polishing what looked to be one of his few remaining glasses.

"I'll get you sorted, Bar," she said, stifling her own sigh as she crossed to him and held out her hand. "Keys?" she asked.

He put down the glass, tossed the towel over his shoulder, and reached into his pocket, slapping the set of bronze and stainless steel into her hand. They were each topped with colored rubber covers. "Blue still for the front door?"

A nod, anger drifting into his eyes. "Not that it'll make much sense to lock up with that window."

"I'll get you sorted," she repeated.

And she would.

Before she kicked some hockey player ass.

"I know," Barry told her, patting her on the shoulder. "You're a good woman, Billie Rose."

She smiled and then made it her mission to shoo him from the bar. His night had been long enough, what with the entire Rush hockey team deciding to go on a tear through River's Bend. Which, unfortunately for Bar, meant they hadn't had many places to "tear" to. They'd started the night at Monroe's, the other bar in town, and when they'd gotten sloppy, they'd strolled down to the other side of Main Street and came here. To Haggarty's.

Where havoc was wreaked.

Barry dragged his feet, and she knew that part of him still saw her as a little girl, still worried after her, especially when he peppered her with offers to stay, or to come back in the morning, or to call someone to come assist her. Knew it when he paused at the front door and asked, "You need help with *him?*"

But she was an adult now, no longer the shy, quiet girl who had been picked on at River's Bend Elementary, or the wild child teenager who'd pranked and drank—and, *cough,* other illicit things—her way through River's Bend High School.

She was a grown-ass woman—one who had absolutely no patience for bullshit, no matter the form it came in. But she *especially* had no tolerance for bullshit if it came courtesy of a pretty boy hockey player.

The Rush were the scourge.

A *necessary* scourge.

But still a scourge.

Her lips curved, thinking her English teacher of a grandmother would have given her a gold star for using the word *scourge* three times in as many sentences.

Hell, probably not.

Billie Rose's English teacher of a grandmother would have told her to expand her vocabulary.

Bane. *Eh, no.*

Pestilence. *Better.*

Curse? *Best.*

Because the Rush were both the life's blood and the curse of River's Bend.

A curse she was determined to break.

She spoke, and if her tone was deadly, if it made Barry shudder; made him pale slightly, grab his coat from the hooks just inside the door, and slip out said door; if it made him realize that the rest of him knew her as a grown-ass adult who took no shit from anyone when she said, "No, I'll take care of him," then so be it.

And if it made him cross himself...then heaven help Axel Finnegan.

Because she was done with Axel's particular brand of bullshit.

She'd been born in this town—*literally* in town, along the side of the road, her parents not having even made it to the highway that led to the next city over, where the only hospital around was located. She'd been too impatient to wait, too grounded to River's Bend even then. The town was in her blood. She ate and drank, slept and bled and cried to make it the best it could be for everyone who lived here. River's Bend was the most important thing in her life, and she *would not* allow these...these...

"Fuckboys," she muttered.

Right. She wouldn't allow the fuckboys of the Rush to continue their reign of terror.

She wouldn't let them ruin it.

Not *her* town.

If she'd had her way—and she had to be frank, as the newly elected mayor, she got her way a lot of the time (and if she had to be truthful—*blegh*—she'd gotten her way most of her life)—she would have gone along with the Chamber of Commerce's recommendation to not renew the Rush's contract with the town.

She'd reclaim the ice rink, take the town back, kick the fuckers out.

But the Rush were a large income source for the town (including taxes that had just funded a new elementary school), and that wasn't even taking into account that the organization employed hundreds of River's Bend citizens.

No jobs.

No income.

No *good*.

Which meant River's Bend needed the Rush.

But they didn't need them like *this*, didn't need them drinking, fucking, and smashing their way through town. Hell, she knew for a fact that Barry had struggled to get insurance after being dropped from his previous provider.

If he had to pay out of pocket for the repairs...

If the town continued to bear the brunt of the team's antics...

If the gamble she was taking didn't pay off...

River's Bend wouldn't survive.

She blew out a breath, turned to that drunk, singing hockey bastard, and battened down her resolve.

Billie Rose was just going to have to take the team in hand.

Axel Finnegan was the ringleader.

The problem child. The poster boy for fuckboys everywhere.

So, her lips curved, she would begin with him.

And she knew exactly where to start.

One

Axel

I groaned and tried valiantly to open my eyes, but my head was pounding, so the moment light passed my lids, I slammed them closed again.

"Fuck," I muttered, running a hand over my face—

Or trying to.

Because it was impossible.

No, not *impossible*. I frowned, forced my lids open, ignoring the sunlight stabbing at my brain.

Only *one* was impossible to move because...it was handcuffed to some sort of rail above my head. The other hand was at my side, pinned half under my ass. *That* one was just numb, and I moved it carefully, nerves prickling, tingles shooting up my arm.

What kind of freaky shit had I gotten into last night?

I squinted, trying to remember, but not able to recall anything more than swatches of noise and things breaking and booze going down smoother and smoother.

Until it had tasted like water.

That's probably why it hurt so much to open my eyes today.

A foot kicked mine, and not lightly either.

"Ow," I muttered, glancing up and squinting at the sun.

Someone was standing there, not that I could see more than a wavering black silhouette.

"Whatcha doing down there?"

Female.

My mind perked up. My brain focused enough for the wavering shadow to steady, to turn into something...delicious.

Small. Curvy. *Delicious.*

"Depends," I said, curving my lips into the smile that had successfully gotten me pussy from the time I was fifteen. "You coming down here to experience it?"

Silence.

Long and quiet enough that I could hear the birds chirping and the insects buzzing, and seriously, what the fuck time of the day was it?

I hadn't been up this early in...

I couldn't remember. Or maybe I *could* have remembered if the woman standing over me hadn't started laughing. Not a gentle, quiet, tinkling laugh like so many of the puck bunnies that hung out at the rink and wanted a piece of me before I hit it big, but a loud and hearty guffaw that shouldn't have been sexy and yet somehow was.

Roughened velvet.

I wanted to fuck her, and I hadn't even seen her face.

But hell, the way the shadows had coalesced into something curvy and petite paired with that sexy unhindered laugh, and I was hard.

"Baby—" I began.

The *click* of a shotgun cocking had my mind rocketing well away from my dick.

Okay, this wasn't nearly as amusing.

Or sexy.

"Hold on a—" I tried.

The laugh had disappeared, taut intensity had surrounded him. "I'm going to talk." Deadly words. "And you're going to speak when I give you permission to do so."

Ice. Orders.

They both began prickling down my nape, curling in my

stomach like a venomous snake prepared to strike.

Meh.

Just call me Steve Irwin.

Of course...there was also that sting ray.

And I had a shotgun pointed at my head.

So...right. I kept my snark locked (albeit loaded, *heh*). The sun, on the other hand, was a total bitch, and since I was tired of squinting against it, I dropped my gaze to my feet.

The woman nudged me with her foot again—this time hard enough to hurt. "I'd advise that you keep your eyes on mine."

"I would," I said, getting frustrated now, that snake darting forward and baring its fangs as I stupidly reached out to grab it, "if I could fucking see you instead of burning my fucking irises by staring into the *sun!*"

Silence.

Shit.

I clenched my teeth against an apology and waited, trying to hold back a wince, expecting the shotgun to go off.

Instead, she surprised me by stepping to the side so that I could look up at her and see something besides blinding white light.

Blinking a few times to steady my vision, I felt my cock get even harder.

Fuck.

She was a porn film star come to life.

A cowboy hat on her head, a low-cut white tank covered by a flannel only halfway buttoned up, skintight jeans, and boots.

Not cowboy boots, but sturdy, brown leather boots with bright red laces.

They were well-worn. They were dirty.

They did *not* fit with the curvy little woman in front of me.

"Baby—"

The gun leveled at my chest.

"I don't believe I gave you permission to speak," she gritted out.

Probably, I should shut up, but I'd never been great with authority or people telling me what to do. "I don't believe I asked *you* to wake me up and point a shotgun at me," I snapped.

Slowly, she lifted one hand and tilted back her hat.

That snake coiled again.

Only this time, I could admit it was coiled in the corner in fear, hoping to not be provoked, because it wasn't sure it would survive if it struck again.

"Well," she said lightly, "I normally point shotguns at people who show up unwelcome on my porch, but I *especially* point shotguns at those who show up unwelcome *and* spend their free time tearing up my town." The gun didn't waver, not in the least. "So, what the fuck are you doing here, Axel Finnegan?"

Come to think of it, I didn't *know* what I was doing here.

Last I remembered, I'd been cuddled up to a rather tall blonde, and her hands had been sliding beneath the waistband of my jeans.

Had I fucked her?

I couldn't remember.

And it hurt too much when I tried to, so I just let it go. The blonde wouldn't be the first girl I didn't remember sleeping with. If I was being truthful—something I despised—she also probably wouldn't be the last.

"I don't know," I said, squinting against the sun and trying to actually see where I was. I should also probably be sorting out how I'd become handcuffed to the railing, but...meh.

I'd been in stranger scenarios.

One time I'd woken up floating in a pool, naked, sunburned to hell and precariously perched on one of those inflatable rafts shaped like a giant pineapple. Another time, I'd woken up naked and with half a watermelon (half-eaten to go with the theme) over my junk. Still once more, I'd peeled back my lids and woken up between three nude people—*people* because only two of them were female.

The common theme was nakedness.

Yeah, yeah, I liked to take off my clothes.

But I had a nice body, and *people* didn't seem to mind.

Not to mention, I grew up in locker rooms, grew up with stall showers where shyness and covering my junk wasn't necessary. I'd seen more dick than most porn stars, but it was part of the game—well, not the game so much as the cleaning up process afterward.

As was the partying and the waking up naked—and sometimes still drunk.

Not much fazed me. Not the dicks or the nakedness or the women and booze. Every time I'd ever woken up in a pesky scenario, I'd just shrugged, dragged my sorry ass out of there, and stumbled home.

Sometimes remembering (the watermelon had been a joke by my linemate). Sometimes not (like not remembering if I fucked the blonde from last night).

But I'd never woken up like this.

First, I wasn't clothed—which I supposed, wasn't the unusual part.

Second, I was handcuffed. This was out of the norm, but not unheard of.

Third, I was staring down the barrel of gun, the other side held by a gorgeous woman who appeared to be looking for any excuse to pull the trigger.

That was a little strange.

"You don't know," she said slowly, as though I were an idiot.

And maybe I was. I hadn't gone to college. I'd barely graduated high school. I was good at exactly three things—hockey, fucking, and drinking.

The middle skill was what prompted my next reply.

"Do you have a bondage fantasy?" I asked, rattling the cuff. "Because I'd be happy to oblige."

The gun dropped further...pointing at my dick.

I watched her finger tighten on the trigger, and I felt fear—*real fear*—for the first time in a long, *long* time.

But I couldn't even push out the request for her not to shoot me.

All I *could* do was sit there and watch and cringe and...*wait*.

Just when I thought she was definitely going to fire, she spun on her heel, stomped back across the porch, and disappeared into the house.

The door slammed.

And silence descended again.

Two

Bailey

This was some bullshit.

Some complete and utter bullshit.

First, I'd been up half the night dealing with a cow in labor because the baby had been breech and mama cow had needed assistance—which meant I'd been armpit deep in said mama cow's uterus (or I suppose, if I were being technical, I had only been *elbow* deep in her uterus. The rest of my arm had become intimately acquainted with mama cow's birth canal).

The second piece of bullshit?

The man on my front porch.

Axel Finnegan.

Player—both on the ice and off. But, more importantly, Axel Finnegan was trouble.

Trouble that had somehow ended up on my porch—*handcuffed* to my railing—after I'd gotten approximately two hours of sleep.

I let the front door slam behind me, stashed my shotgun on the rack in the hall, and stomped over to my phone charging on the cradle in the kitchen. There was one person who would know—read: who was *responsible*—for Axel Finnegan being handcuffed on my porch.

My aunt.

One Billie Rose.

I jabbed at the screen, pulling up her number, and hit the green button to connect the call. It began ringing...and then immediately went to voicemail.

"Fuck," I hissed, dropping the cell on the counter.

I did *not* have time for this shit.

Grabbing my jacket off the hook—and leaving my shotgun in place, much to my chagrin—I shoved my cell into my pocket and headed back across the porch, clomping loudly and not giving two shits when it made Axel lurch up to his feet.

I kept walking.

"Hey! Where are you going?"

Not bothering to answer, I kept walking, heading to the barn where I dropped a leaf of hay into each of the horse's feeders, and then prepped the rest of the animals' food—pigs, goats, and a couple of sheep.

All were rescues.

The only working animals on the farm were the cows, and they were out grazing, the mama who'd given birth to the last of the few off-season calves that had been born the last couple of weeks having joined her brethren (or sister-ren?). Thankfully, though, there weren't any more pregnant cows who'd be keeping me from my bed.

I'd trudge through, like I always did, and tonight, I'd get some rest.

Right.

Because running a dilapidated cattle ranch on my own meant that I got *loads* of rest. Sighing, I waited for the horses to finish eating then let them out to pasture before beginning one of my many tasks that meant rest was truly only for the weary—mucking stalls.

Which meant it was a good hour before I emerged from the barn and headed toward my truck.

"Hey!" Axel called again, still handcuffed to the porch railing.

Did I feel a tingle of guilt?

Yeah.

Did I let that tingle change my plan?

Nope. The petty in me was happy to make him pay.

He scrambled to his feet again, crouching since the cuffs meant that he couldn't stand fully erect—

And hell, I did *not* need to think about Axel and erect things.

Not when he was the town bicycle.

Town hockey puck?

Town—?

"You can't just leave me here!" he shouted. "I have practice and—"

I yanked open the door, turned on the engine, drowning out the sound of his further protests, and drove off to fix the section of downed fence I'd spotted the previous day.

That took a couple of hours, and I was hot, sweaty, and cranky as fuck by the time I got back to the house.

I wasn't a breakfast girl, so I usually ate an early lunch, and as much as I was hoping that whatever fucked-up fairy had dropped off Axel on my porch—and my suspicions pointed to only one person, good ole Auntie Billie Rose—had picked him up, alas, it was not to be.

He was still there. Still handcuffed. Still naked.

He stood, as much as he was able to anyway, when I pulled into the drive.

Was silent—miracle of fucking miracles—as I got out and walked up to the front porch. *Stayed* silent as I moved back into the house, made myself a damned sandwich, and called Billie Rose. Well, I don't know if he stayed silent as I was in the kitchen, making that sandwich and phone call, but if he *did* talk, he wasn't loud enough for me to hear him.

Also—no surprise—Billie Rose didn't pick up.

Which was probably why I did what I did next.

I made the man a fucking sandwich.

Maybe someone might think it was a nice gesture.

It wasn't.

Neither was me grabbing him a bottle of water from the fridge. I didn't have keys to the handcuffs, and Billie Rose wasn't picking up her phone. I was fully aware that at some point I was going to have to call the sheriff to come get the trouble off my porch, but I'd rather not have everyone in River's Bend knowing what had happened, and everyone would know if I let the man die of dehydration on my porch.

The teasing alone would be unbearable.

Or not.

Because, smiling darkly, I thought that some of the townspeople might trade teasing for cheering, but...sigh. Neither of those was the point. I needed to make sure he didn't expire while I waited a little longer, crossed my fingers, and hoped that Billie Rose picked up.

But I *couldn't* have him dying of dehydration on my porch.

Too much paperwork.

"Then why the sandwich?" I muttered. It wasn't like Axel Finnegan was going to starve to death after a few hours. Or of dehydration, for that matter. It was just...my grandfather had ingrained a certain set of skills in me while growing up.

And one of those was being a good host.

Okay, so maybe being a good host didn't leave someone handcuffed to the porch railing, but...meh.

My hosting skills only went so far.

I pushed out the front door.

Axel was sitting on the porch, looking dejected, and I didn't feel a pang of remorse for leaving him there. I *didn't*.

I set the sandwich in front of him, the bottle next to it.

Silence.

"Is it poisoned?" he asked.

Amusement bubbled up inside me, but I didn't let it show. Instead, I turned on my heel, headed back into my house, and ate my sandwich, drank *my* bottle of water while staring at my phone, willing Billie Rose to call me back.

And then calling her two more times, just for good measure.

Then losing my temper on the last time and hissing out onto her voicemail, "You are so dead, Billie Rose. I cannot believe you would do this to me."

After jabbing at the button to end the call, I tossed my cell on the counter, sighed, and got back to work.

"Wait!" Axel called as I pounded down the stairs again.

I spun slowly and turned to face him, lifted my brows.

"You're really going to leave me here?" he asked, voice small. "Again?"

"You got a spare set of keys for those cuffs?" I countered, rolling my eyes at the innocent look.

He froze, frowning up at his arm. "Nooo," he said, drawing out the word.

"Exactly."

I began walking again, heading to the barn to bring the horses back in when Axel spoke again.

"But...you got a saw?"

THREE

AXEL

She was going to kill me.

Or I was going to lose an arm. Or—I lurched back—my dick.

"Jesus, watch where you're aiming that thing!"

"What?" she asked loudly, flipping the switch so the saw revved, drowning out anything I might say. Then she lifted it, holding the sharp, spinning blade casually, like it wouldn't just slice to shit anything that got close. "Sorry, I can't hear you."

And then she brought the blade down.

"Fucking hell!" I scrambled away, trying to get my feet under me, knowing it was a fucking lesson in futility since the saw was descending.

A loud whirring noise. A sharp, piercing sound.

Heat.

"Oh fuuuck," I groaned.

The wood vibrated, the cuffs heated, tiny metal shards flew into the air, swirling around me like snow, burning my skin as they landed on it—dangerous, probably, but it wasn't like she'd provided me with eye protection—and then—

I was free.

The saw turned off, dropped to the porch, too fucking near my leg—and my femoral artery—for comfort, and then the woman, whose name I still didn't know, dropped a pile of clothes next to me—sweats, a T-shirt, and a pair of socks—headed to the barn. I jumped to my feet, scrambled into the clothes that were a bit tight but fit reasonably well, and trailed after her, my entire body stiff from being chained to the railing.

"Wait," I called. "I have to get to practice."

She kept walking.

It took me a few strides to get my legs to loosen up, but then they were ticking, and I caught up with her just as she pushed into the barn, snagging her arm and dragging her to a stop.

"Get your fucking hand off me," she gritted, eyes flashing.

"I have to get to practice," I said again, not letting her go.

Which was a mistake.

"*Don't* touch me."

My fingers tightened. "But I need to go, otherwise I'll be fucked."

I might be a mess, but hockey came first.

Always.

"Fucked?" Her eyes narrowed, and she snorted. "Yeah. I know the feeling. Now, *let go.*" She grabbed my thumb and yanked it back, sending red-hot pain splintering up my hand and arm. I had to drop to my knees so I didn't break the digit, and then she shoved me back.

I ended up on my ass.

"You're free." A wave of her hand. "So get the fuck out of here."

Except I had no shoes, no car, no phone, and no clue where I was. I only knew that the apartments I lived in were nowhere in sight and that Main Street was real the fuck far away. "I—"

"Road to town is a mile up the road," she said, pointing and effectively interrupting me before I could really get going.

And then turned away.

What the *fuck?*

No one interrupted me. When I spoke in the locker room or at the bar or anywhere, really, people listened. They didn't try to break my thumbs or turn away from me. They certainly didn't leave me handcuffed to porch railings.

"How far out of town are we?" I asked, standing up and rubbing my sorely abused thumb.

She stopped, spun to face me. "*We* are not out of town. *You* are out of town. And including the mile you need to walk to the road," she said, "*you* are six miles from the ice rink. If you start running now, I suspect it'll be the perfect warmup for practice."

"I don't have any shoes."

"You're a big, tough hockey guy. You'll survive."

"I—"

But she'd given me her back again.

I'd said it once, I would say it again. People did *not* ignore me.

"Look, baby," I said, moving in front of her, forcing her to stop. "If you give me a ride, I'll make it worth your while."

Silence.

A long beat of quiet.

A long, slow breath.

Two things with this woman that I was coming to realize would bring nothing good.

Though, I supposed this scenario was different from before. It didn't involve a saw or me being handcuffed, so one could argue that it was actually *better* than the previous times.

Go me.

Plus, instead of pulling a shotgun out of nowhere, she just snorted and went back to walking away, sidestepping me and moving farther into the barn, moving across the space and entering a room at the far end without another look back.

Less, *go me.*

"Fuck," I muttered, knowing that I wasn't going to walk six-plus miles into town.

Maybe I could find a phone inside the house?

There had to be one.

Right.

Except, I'd taken exactly one step back toward the exit when the woman stuck her head out of the room and said in a cool, dead tone that had the hairs on my nape prickling, "And if you're considering what I think you're considering, know that I have shotguns in many more places than my house."

I froze.

Then I remembered myself.

I was Axel *Fucking* Finnegan. I wasn't scared of anything, least of all a tiny, curvy female with brown curls and a body that was dwarfed by a plaid flannel.

Straightening my shoulders, I strode to her, not stopping until my toes were lined up with those incongruous brown boots, and absolutely willing to sacrifice a few toes if need be.

And my pride might make that a necessity.

"You got a shotgun in that room?" I nodded toward the space she'd previously disappeared into.

Her brow furrowed. "No."

"Good."

"Why?"

"Because it means you won't shoot me when I do this." I moved into her, bodies brushing close as I pushed forward, herding her into the room, forcing her to lift her chin in order to continue looking at me.

Which she did.

Because *of course* she did.

I caged her in against the wall, putting one hand by her hip, the other by her head. She was tiny, so I had to bend pretty far in order to meet her eyes, chin lift or not.

"Do what?" she asked, markedly calm.

I leaned closer. "What's your name, baby?" I asked, staring deep into her eyes.

Her lips parted and need exploded through me. Tons of curves to worship, pretty brown eyes to watch as I made her come. I felt her breath on my mouth, so damned close and yet not nearly close enough. I wanted to taste her, to get my tongue in her mouth, her pussy. My cock twitched and I leaned a little more heavily against her until my pelvis was lined up with hers, my chest only a hairsbreadth away.

White teeth digging into a pink bottom lip.

Pupils dilating.

A body softening.

And...

Then she started laughing. At me. *Again*.

What. The. Fuck?

She shoved me back and slid to the side. "Does that actually *work?*" she asked between giant guffaws, bending at the waist. "Oh, my God. *What's your name, baby?*" she added in a poor approximation of my voice. "That can't actually work on women. No fucking way."

It did work.

It *always* worked.

And I'd thought it before, but seriously, I was thinking it again. What in the actual fuck was wrong with this woman?

"Here," she said, straightening and coming back over to me. "Let me save you the trouble, Lothario."

Her hands clamped onto my face and...she kissed me.

Fuck, how she kissed me. Her tongue slipping into my mouth, sleek, hot darts making my cock go instantly hard. Her lips pressing into mine, a little rough and all too tempting. Her body and those fucking curves coming flush to mine.

She kissed me until I forgot that I was trying to kiss *her* into submission—or at least into a ride to town.

She kissed me until my cock ached and my hands found their way to her body.

She kissed me until I forgot all about practice and six miles to the rink and the fact that I'd woken up handcuffed and naked on her porch.

She kissed me until—

I reached for her, and she broke away.

"Phone's in the tack room," she said, voice so fucking neutral it sliced right through the haze of arousal. My cock deflated. My lungs seized. "You've got an hour to get off my property, or I'm introducing you to my other shotgun."

Then she was gone.

Four

Bailey

Oh hell, I thought as I stormed away, leaving Axel Finnegan and his problems behind me, but—unfortunately for my psyche—not leaving behind the feel of his lips, the brush of his tongue, the way his hard body had felt against mine.

"I shouldn't have done that," I whispered, channeling my inner Hagrid. "I should *not* have done that."

It was a quintessentially stupid thing to have done.

Kissing the sluttiest man in River's Bend?

Enjoying that kiss more than I'd enjoyed perhaps any other kiss in the entire entirety of my life?

See? Really fucking stupid.

I hadn't slept with anyone in a long time, *too* fucking long, clearly, as I'd wanted to jump the bones of *fucking* Axel Finnegan.

But it wasn't like I wanted to be in a relationship. I didn't. I was unattached, not because of a lack of attention—not to sound cocky, but I'd had steady company when I wanted over the years, hookups when I hadn't, and interest expressed when I wasn't down for either of those two. However, running a ranch was exhausting work, and now running *this* ranch, slowly digging it out from the financial hellhole my parents had left for me—a double fuck you because I hadn't even wanted the ranch in the first place, and the debt on the land had been so *freaking* astronomical, that I hadn't been able to sell it and pay off those debts.

I knew Russet Ranch could be profitable. It had been when my grandpa had been in charge, but my parents weren't for hard work, and they'd slowly eaten away at the cushion until my inheritance had been less influx and more trying to get out from beneath this giant boulder with my credit score intact.

That had been two years ago.

Now, I was another year away from being clear and free, and...I kind of liked ranch work.

Okay, the last shouldn't be a surprise. I'd loved the summers I'd spent here, getting up with the sun and spending the day on horseback with my grandpa. He'd tell me stories of his younger days. He'd listen to me about my kid-to-teenager related problems (*e.g., "Sarah isn't talking to me anymore!" and "Mr. Watson is the meanest teacher EVER!" and later, "Bobby Mulligan is the biggest asshole on the planet!"*)

Then Gramps had died.

My parents had decided to sell their house and live on the paid-off ranch, not realizing that the profits from that property couldn't all go straight into their pockets, not if they wanted to keep enjoying those profits.

But...money flowed through their hands like water.

They didn't invest in a new roof for the barn, and the hay got moldy and rat-infested, so they had to buy more hay at a premium. The fences weren't kept up as they should have been, and we lost several heifers due to auto accidents. The vet was too expensive, so we couldn't afford to call him out if a mama was struggling to give birth.

And pretty soon the business was floundering.

That was what I'd inherited.

That was what I might have sold, even despite the hit I'd take to my credit.

If not for...this.

I sighed.

Because *this* was the horseshoes nailed to the front door. Openings pointing up, held there by Gramps as I'd hammered them in place one scorching summer evening. *This* was the wine barrel planters lining either side of the porch we'd made one summer together. *This* was the tack room and the door to the barn with scratches from Gramps's knife, marking my increasing height year after year. *This* was the fences on the west side of the property we'd built together, the tractor with its peeling green paint he'd taught me how to repair on a whisper and a prayer and a roll of duct tape and a can of WD-40. *This* was the heavy gate that had given me more than a few splinters over the years as I'd opened and closed it to allow Gramp's big, old Chevy truck through.

History. Mine. Gramps.

Right here on this land.

Still, I probably should have let it go when my parents told me they were moving on when I'd bought them out. It certainly would have been easier than these last two years of working, hardly sleeping, and worrying about worrying myself into an early grave.

But all the worrying about worrying had brought forth a light at the end of the tunnel.

I could see it on the horizon—a time when I might be able to breathe, to not work every moment of every day. Where I might be able to hire back some ranch hands instead of relying on the type of trading help all of us ranchers relied on.

Eli's roof caved in? We all dropped everything to go over and repair it.

A fence at Tommy's was down? We brought supplies and got to work.

It was shipment day (read: my cows became someone else's steaks)? I had more spare hands than I knew what to do with.

My neighbors were the only reason I'd survived these last two years.

I would just like to...not need them quite as much.

Not have to worry about calling Eli away from his sick wife, or Tommy from his kids, or Hank from his preferred solitude.

They'd probably show up anyway because they were good guys and they'd been close to Gramps. I just...wanted to be able to do it by myself, to not be like my parents and mooch everyone into oblivion.

Which was why I didn't have an ounce of time for someone like Axel, who'd had everything handed to him, and he didn't even understand how precious that gift was. Instead, he kicked that gift horse in the mouth, knocked out the poor animal's teeth—like the fucking hockey player he was—and terrorized the town of River's Bend.

I didn't have time for his special brand of bullshit.

I had a mama and baby cow to check on, hay to plant, and hopefully dinner to eat and sleep to get.

Which was why I went straight to the counter for my keys, grabbing my coat on the way back out, because although I was sweating now, the moment the sun went behind the mountains in the distance, it would start to get chilly really quickly.

Axel was sitting on the fence as I pulled out, his ass on the top rung and his bare feet on the other.

He looked good.

Too damned good.

And unfortunately, now I knew exactly what was beneath his clothes, with confidence to declare that he looked good *everywhere.*

My lips tingled.

My fingers gripped the steering wheel tight, some insane urge encouraging me to pull over and offer him a ride, no matter how big of an asshole he was, no matter that his special brand of bullshit would bring me no little amount of trouble.

Luckily for me, Gramps always said I was more stubborn than a turtle wanting to stay in its shell.

Because that stubbornness had me hitting the gas pedal instead of the brake.

It had me zooming by Axel Finnegan, leaving a cloud of dust in my wake.

It had me concentrating on mama and baby cow, on checking to make sure the field and equipment were ready for planting tomorrow, and it had me…looking for Axel when I eventually made my way back to my house.

He was gone.

That was *not* disappointment.

Fuck me, I was kind of worried it was.

Five

Axel

Fuck, I love hockey.

The speed, the rush of scoring a goal, the roar of the crowd, the thrill...of spying a pretty girl in the stands and knowing that she was going to go home with me.

Case in point, the gorgeous redhead smiling at me every time I went near the far side of the boards.

And considering that she was gorgeous, both in face and body, and that with every loop I made toward her side of the ice, her top seemed to move a centimeter lower, I figured it was a damned good bet she would be in my bed that evening.

I smiled in her direction.

Her top slid another inch lower, revealing navy lace and the tops of dusky pink nipples.

My cock twitched in my cup.

Not super comfortable, for those wondering in the peanut gallery. But damn if it wasn't worth it. My mouth—

"Ow!" I hissed, jerking my focus away from the woman and rubbing the side of my neck as I glared at my teammate.

"I think you focusing on tits too much is why you ended up naked on that farm this morning," Joel, my left winger, said on a smirk, having shot the puck—albeit without much more force than to make the impact sting—at me.

"Fucker," I muttered, shooting the puck back—only a *little* harder since Joel could really let it fucking rip, wasn't great at letting things go, and I didn't want to get a harder puck in return. "And technically, I wasn't naked when you got me."

Just had been naked *previously*.

And had been wearing too tight, borrowed clothes that had screamed about my previous, unclothed state.

Not ideal.

Which was why Joel grinned as he caught the puck easily on the end of his blade and messed around with it on the ice. "Just saying, keep being an asshole and next time, I won't pick your naked ass up."

"Not naked. Plus"—I waved a hand at myself—"Not too many people have been gifted the naked goodness of all *this*."

Joel froze for a heartbeat.

Then busted out laughing.

"Dude," he said through his obnoxious chortles, "half the fucking planet has seen your naked ass."

"Or at least half the fucking *town*," Ryan said, his tone dry. Ry was the right winger on the line I centered of him, Joel, and myself.

And also, *such* a fucking comedian.

Talented player.

But total douche canoe.

Mainly because he was the only guy on the Rush who acted like he was too good to hang out with the rest of the team. Probably couldn't wait until he got out of this Podunk town and had his chance at the big leagues.

Fucking loser.

Or maybe that's you.

I blinked, started to push the thought away, but then Coach blew his whistle and yelled, "Quit talking and fucking skate!"

Aw.

That brought forth such good memories over the years. So many old, slightly overweight, white men yelling at me. And yeah, I was white, too, but I wasn't old and definitely wasn't slightly overweight...my body was a temple of liquor, meals at 7-11, and a shit-ton of hard work in the gym—in other words, I was hot as hell.

Bam.

Take that strange, curvy ranch woman with the shotgun and balls of steel.

"Finnegan!"

Right.

The point was that I'd gotten so used to my coaches yelling at me over the years that I didn't much give a shit when they did it now.

I just rolled my eyes and started skating.

One, to impress that redhead with her tits hanging out.

Two, because I didn't want to play on this fucking team forever.

I wanted to make it in the big time, and I was getting too fucking old—sad that at twenty-five I was getting too old to get a real shot at the NHL, but true—to find myself permanently on a roster of an NHL team. I was tired of this bouncing up and down bullshit like the last two seasons had been—one game in the minors with the Rush, one game up with the Gold. I worked my ass off on the ice both here and there, but I wasn't ever going to be one of those flashy guys leading the league in points.

Grinding, fighting for an ugly goal, *that* was my style.

And funny story, most of the big-league teams wanted goal-scorers.

Still, being here was grinding on me—no pun intended—and the only way I knew to blow off steam was to play hard and then drink and fuck harder, to blank out the memories, the disappointment...and then to get the hell back on the ice and do it all over again.

So that was what I did.

I blanked the woman, the naked, handcuffed shenanigans, and I worked my ass off.

We ran through drills as a team and then broke into smaller groups for more drills, more personalized attention (read: more getting yelled at), but through it all I worked my ass off and was dripping sweat by the time I smiled at the redhead through the glass one final time and made my way off the ice.

I went to the workout room, did my cooldown, stretched, met with the trainer, talked to Coach briefly (I'd probably be playing a game up with the Gold the following week if I continued having good showings in *our* match-ups). Then I took a shower, not bothering to hurry.

I knew the redhead would be waiting.

And I wasn't disappointed.

She was standing outside the back door, along with a brunette and a buxom blonde—a trifecta of femininity that any straight male would be hard-pressed to ignore. The last one, the blonde, had been around a lot, so much so that the guys called her Glitter Tits because her lotion left sparkles behind.

Her personal calling card as she banged her way through the roster.

And one I wasn't going to play with.

Fucking glitter. Herpes of the craft world.

And also of the hookup world.

"Oh, thank you, Jesus," Joel muttered, coming up behind me. "I call—"

"The redhead is mine."

Joel grunted, clearly not as perturbed by the glitter. "I wanted Candi anyway. Bitch sucks like a fucking Hoover. But I'll take two." He moved toward the blonde and brunette. "Ladies," he said smoothly, wrapping arms around their shoulders. "What are we doing tonight?"

"Haggarty's?" the blonde offered.

Joel winced. "Don't think we're allowed there for a while."

The blonde, Candi apparently, giggled.

And that was as much as I heard. Because I sidled my way over to the redhead. "Hi, honey," I murmured.

She blinked up at me, her lips curving as she stepped up to me, close enough that her breasts rested against my chest. They were large, but not natural and soft. Instead, they were hard globes.

Good thing I was an equal opportunity breast man.

Fake. Real. Big. Small. Barely there.

I liked them all.

"How about Monroe's?" she asked, nibbling at her bottom lip.

She shifted and trailed a finger down my abdomen, heading for the waistband of my slacks. "Then my place?" A beat. "*With* my girls?"

I grinned.

"And your friend?"

My grin faded as I wrapped my fingers around her wrist, stilled the movements. "I like Joel, but I don't share."

Much, anyway.

Or rather, any*more.*

And as gorgeous as the redhead was, she wasn't pretty enough for me to be sharing a pussy or to start fucking sword-fighting.

Been there, done that.

I preferred my own All-I-Could-Eat Buffet.

She smiled up at him. "Okay. Monroe's. My place. No sharing." She rose on tiptoe and pressed her lips to my ear, tongue flicking out. "Unless I can convince you otherwise." A beat. "And I bet I can."

I laughed, slid my hand up her side, my fingers grazing the underside of one breast. "I'll take that bet."

Groaning, my head pounding, my ass sore as hell, I started to roll over.

Then stopped.

Or...I *was* stopped.

By—

I peeled my lids back, the morning sunlight blinding me, and groaned again, this time louder and filled with fury.

I was handcuffed to a railing.

Again.

I was naked. *Again.*

I was—

A door opened. Footsteps echoed across the wood, started to fade as they moved by me.

Then stopped, echoed again, this time louder, and they came close.

Then, "Seriously?"

I glanced up at the brown-haired woman from the day before, her legs encased in tight denim, her curvy ass on display, her breasts pushing against a blue tank, revealed by a half-zipped hoodie, her hair tucked under a worn baseball hat.

"Um, hi?" I said, going—and failing—for casual.

She closed her eyes, tilted her head back, staring up at the ceiling of the porch, her long, drawn-out sigh raising and dropping her shoulders.

My gaze followed hers, saw nothing aside from wood panels with a few recessed lights and peeling paint.

Then she dropped her head back down, her nostrils flaring on the sharp inhale she took.

She whirled on her heel, started for the barn.

"You're not going for the shotgun, are you?" I asked, my free hand unconsciously covering my dick.

Her eyes went to the ceiling again.

Then she sighed again, shoulders slumping.

"I'm getting the fucking saw."

Six

Bailey

I was resting the blade on the cuff, Axel's wrist angled away as far as possible, and suddenly I realized something I hadn't the day before.

I could end the man's career with one wrong move.

Yesterday, I'd been furious, not thinking, whipping the saw around like it was a fly swatter.

Today…I was resigned.

And a little terrified that I might saw someone's hand off.

Saw *his* hand off.

A flick of the switch to turn it on, fingers on the trigger, and…

I sighed.

Dropped the power tool.

Blue eyes, dark brows gathered tightly together over them, confusion forming a frown.

I spun on my heel, headed to the barn, and went to the tack room, beyond the saddles and rope and other horse paraphernalia, all the way to the back, where my grandpa's tool bench had been moved.

By my mom.

Who'd turned the garage into a craft room.

Another thing Gramps would be turning over in his grave for.

Lace and gingham where there had once been steel and gasoline? He'd have lost his ever-loving mind.

I searched through the ancient, heavy drawers, the wood so worn that it was decades out from being able to give me a sliver and smooth as butter, until I found what I was looking for.

Then I closed the drawer with my hip, left the barn, and returned to the mini-hockey god on my porch.

He was pretty.

He was talented.

He was...totally out of control.

Luckily, the last wasn't my problem to deal with.

I just needed him off my porch so I could continue digging myself out of my financial hole, get myself into a position where I could sell the ranch...or, if I kept it, where I didn't have to work seven days a week, twelve hours a day, just to prevent it from sinking to the bottom of the ocean and dragging me down with it.

Maybe get laid.

Maybe spend a few months without my arm up a cow's—

I stepped out of the barn and saw those blue eyes on me, felt a shiver down my spine.

Dangerous. *Stupid.*

Fucking hell, I should have just risked the dismemberment—*his* dismemberment.

Instead, I'd gotten worried about ending a man's career...and maybe his life, since it was a decently long drive to the hospital, and I wasn't all that good with tourniquets.

And yet, I still carried the pipe saw across the yard, up the steps, and knelt next to Axel.

"You smell like you bathed in whiskey," I grumbled.

A flash of straight white teeth.

"*You* smell like shit."

That shouldn't have sliced.

I'd just been in the barn, after all.

And I'd spent the last two years elbow deep in shit.

It was probably bonded directly to my cells, my DNA. My perfume might as well have been called Manure. So, Axel had given me less of an insult than an observation...and it was an *observation* I was going to ignore.

Ignoring made the hurt go away, right?

I lifted the pipe saw, placed it on the cuff, and began sawing, its thin metal teeth struggling to find purchase on the cuff for a few strokes before getting into a groove.

I ignored the bitter tang of alcohol emanating from his pores, ignored that I was probably inundating him with the smell of *shit*, and kept working. This was a lot harder than just using the Sawzall, and I was wondering what in the fuck-all I'd been thinking, worrying about the man's arm when my own were on fire.

My arms were just as important.

My wrists, my elbows, my aching shoulder (that I'd had surgery on just before I'd inherited the farm). They were my livelihood, too.

He shifted, and my eyes slid down, and I...nearly sawed off both of our arms.

I should have gotten him pants first, I realized, steadying myself.

The man's cock was...well, I hoped to fuck for the girls he boned that he was a *show*er and not a *grow*er because...sweet baby Jesus.

Axel cleared his throat.

Probably because I was staring.

Probably because—fuck me—*No.* Not *fuck me.* No *fucking* me. There would be no *fucking*, period.

"Baby—"

Right. The man didn't know my name, immediately defaulted to endearments, had a big dick...and I unfortunately knew that because he'd blacked out and ended up on my porch. Twice.

I went back to sawing.

Luckily, the sound drowned him out when he tried to talk again, and I sawed faster...because avoidance was a great strategy when a girl had been caught drooling over a penis.

Saw. Saw. *Saw.*

Saw. Sawing. *Sawing* some more.

I was *all* about the sawing and thinking about sawing and sawing was life and—

Thunk.

The blade made it through the last of the metal. I caught it before it did damage to his leg...or his cock...or any of *my* respective parts, and...

He pulled his arm free, wincing as he rolled his wrist. "Thanks."

Right. Stop staring. *Focus.*

I hopped to my feet, and if it was fast and abrupt then...it was fast and abrupt.

Shit.

He dropped his arm to his lap, drawing my eyes down and—

"I'll get you some clothes," I said quickly, whirling away and thinking that if this kept happening, I needed to invest in more sweats...or bigger sizes or...more obviously, to get the clothes I was loaning this man back. It would probably also be prudent to invest in lock picking classes, or maybe a skeleton key for handcuffs.

Did they make that?

I hoped so. Because Billie Rose was relentless and the Rush didn't seem to be inclined to stop partying, and a skeleton key would save my saw...*and* my arms.

Fingers on my elbow, a big, strong body hovering over mine.

"I—" he began.

I jerked away, spun, and walked into my house. Was it fast? Yes. Did it border on running? Yes. Did I stop to lock the door behind me? Also, yes.

I wasn't stupid.

I knew Axel's reputation.

And I knew my own...or rather my own *body*. A body that had experienced a serious lack of orgasms over the last few years. Yes, it was sad that my life had gotten so exhausting that even the act of pulling my vibrator out of my bedside drawer and using it had seemed like too much effort.

But that didn't mean I was going to leave my front door unlocked and risk tripping and falling onto Axel's dick.

Unlikely? Maybe.

Unlikely when I'd gotten a glimpse of that dick and my body had gone all puppy-wiggling-as-I-waited-desperately for a treat? Nope.

Hence the door-locking.

I hurried to my closet, yanked out my final pair of fat-time-of-the-month sweats, a T-shirt that I wore as a nightshirt, and then I headed downstairs...

To find a naked Axel standing in my entryway, back to me, gaze seemingly on the door.

That I'd locked.

I *knew* I did.

I must have made a noise because Axel spun...and sweet Jesus... my eyes slid down again.

Seven

Axel

The door hadn't latched properly.

I'd heard the lock *click*, turned to the door wanting to get a glance at that lush ass encased in tight denim, and then...the wind had picked up, and the panel of wood that had seen better days about two decades before had swung open...

Like a gift from the hockey gods.

So...I'd walked in.

It was like stepping into another world.

The eighties had exploded. Hell, the seventies and the sixties had exploded right along with it. The kitchen was that avocado green, and gold shag carpeting was in the family room, and pale blue curtains patterned with roses hung over the windows.

It was a visual assault on the senses.

The keyword being: *assault*.

Then my gaze had caught on a picture. Of the woman, of the woman whose name I still didn't know wearing a white dress and heels, her arms around an older man. Their eyes too similar to not be family. Her eyes filled with warmth, her smile wide. None of the shadows present in her chocolate brown gaze that had glared down at me.

And I'd frozen.

Beautiful.

Young.

Warm.

And where had that woman gone?

"What. The. *Fuck?*"

My eyes darted up to the stairs, and seriously. Where. Had. That. Woman. In. The. Picture. Gone?

There was no makeup on her face—not that she needed it. She was fucking breathtaking without that crap slopped on like so many of the women I interacted with wore. It was just...like something had changed from the woman in the picture, and not just that I'd seen her twice without a stitch of makeup on. But there wasn't any time to pinpoint exactly what had made the change, nor truly how it manifested in her eyes and face currently. Because she was bearing down on me, her expression furious, those eyes...they were about as far away from warm as I had ever seen.

Glacial.

Icebergs.

No, shards of ice hanging from the ceiling, preparing to fall and impale me.

I turned, watched her come down the steps holding a pair of cream-colored sweats and a tie-dye—yes, seriously, a *tie-dye*—shirt in her hands. She walked right up to me, slammed them against my chest, and snapped again, "What *the* fuck?"

Then she shoved me.

Hard enough that I stumbled back a step.

Luckily, I was used to skating around the ice with blades on my feet.

I could take a shove and keep on ticking.

"What the fuck, *what?*" I asked, glancing down and seeing that she'd provided a pair of socks, too. Thick and wooly, something that would protect my feet better than a thin strip of cotton. I tugged on the sweats, the socks, started to pull the shirt over my head when she spoke again.

"What the fuck are you doing *in my house?*"

I shrugged and yanked the shirt down, my head popping free, the material tight on my torso. "Wind blew the door open."

"The wind," she began in disbelief.

I stepped closer. "Yes. The wind."

A huff. "Right." She strode for the door, strode *out* the door, boots slapping on the front porch.

I was bending, tugging on the socks when I heard it.

A sharp inhale of breath, the absence of footsteps.

Straightening, I headed for the porch, pushed out the screen door, hearing it slam behind me. I didn't bother with the wooden one that had blown open earlier, just went to investigate that sharp breath.

And found it.

Or rather, found *her*. Because she was down on her knees, fingers wrapped around the narrow-bladed hand saw...and not moving.

"Baby?"

She jerked, and I heard that noise again, realized what it was, why it sounded familiar. Because I'd made that sound before, many times over the years. Because I'd heard countless teammates make the same noise.

In pain.

She was in pain.

Why did I care?

I *shouldn't* care. She didn't give a fuck about me. She'd nearly sawed my nuts off, for fuck's sake. But...she'd gotten me clothes twice and made me a sandwich the day before. She'd freed me from her railing without dismemberment—or undue attention from the sheriff.

And there was sad in her eyes.

I'd seen the happy in that picture, and I was curious. What had happened to *that* woman? Why did I have the prickly beast in front of me?

I dropped my hand to her shoulder.

She jerked again; the hiss of discomfort more audible.

"Let me help you."

Her fingers wrapped around the saw and with a grimace that had pain shooting through *me*, just in solidarity, she pushed to her feet. "I don't need help."

I raised a brow. “Oh?” I eyed the other saw that still sat by the railing. “So you can grab that one, too?”

She’d been turning for the three stairs that would lead to the path to the barn, but my question stopped her.

Slowly, she spun around, her gaze going to the porch—presumably to the saw—and then back up. I wasn’t so self-centered (and look, I was *plenty* self-centered) to miss the agony that crept into her eyes. I *was*, however, enough of an asshole to call her bluff.

Evidenced by me staying still as she moved stiffly back to me, not saying a word as I watched her brace herself and bend.

Slowly.

Stiffly.

Painfully.

A hissed-out breath...then her fingers closed around the saw, and she straightened. Just as slowly. Just a stiffly. Just as painfully.

“Call your ride,” she said, making her way to the stairs.

Both the saws in one hand.

The other on the railing.

A slow step down.

Another.

One more.

I moved, trailing her, some instinct inside me telling me not to grab the saws from her hands. Even though the urge was real, which was more than a bit disconcerting.

I didn’t have a chivalrous bone in my body. I wasn’t going to start now.

I did, however, walk next to her, and no, it wasn’t because her stiff gait as she made her way down the path to the barn had me worried that I might need to catch her.

It was...because it was easier to annoy her that way.

“What’s your name?”

“Fuck off,” she snapped.

“Baby,” I began

“Not *that* either.”

I caught her arm, and, fuck it, I took the saws. Just to annoy her, not because I’d reached my limit of watching her uneven and painful stride and *had* to take the saws because I couldn't watch her limping again.

She glared.

Nope. Definitely *not* struggling to watch her in pain.

I stepped out of reach, tightened my grip on the saws.

That glare intensified.

I kept walking, into the barn, into the room where I'd used the phone before. It sat on a squat workbench in the back, several of the drawers open and rifled through. I saw the one that seemed to have other similar tools in it, shoved the little saw in, then turned and noticed the hooks on the wall, found the spot where the other electric saw belonged.

Then I should have used the phone, should have taken the shit-giving Joel was going to dish out and call my teammate.

I *should* memorize the number for the taxi company in town.

River's Bend, California was a small town, adjacent to several bigger ones in the Sacramento Valley. It had boomed during the Gold Rush (hence my team's name...and its convenient association with the NHL team the San Francisco Gold), but River's Bend was tucked more into the foothills of the Sierras and hadn't seen the same growth as some of the other cities in the area.

The people of River's Bend preferred it this way.

Hell, they'd probably prefer it if the town had never built—and then subsequently retrofitted and modernized—the rink, thus drawing in the Rush...and all the trouble the team brought.

See?

I wasn't unaware of the ill feelings the town had for the team.

Yeah, we'd broken a few glasses, the occasional pool cue, and one window. But we needed to let loose, and there wasn't much to do in River's Bend except for drinking, carousing, playing pool, and fucking on the Ridge.

We were just doing our civic duty.

Supporting local businesses.

Plus, I always cut a check for any damage done.

Which was probably the only reason we were allowed back in town—and in the few bars that were in residence on Main Street.

I was an asshole.

I drank too much, fucked too much, lost my temper too easily.

But I paid for my mistakes.

And I was good at ignoring the voice that said, maybe if I drank less, kept my temper more, focused on my game, then I might make it out of the minors.

I'd tried that before.

It hadn't made one fucking bit of difference.

Now I was going to make it *my* way—and that included plenty of booze and pussy and living the small part of my life that I could control my fucking way.

It didn't include curvy, acerbic brunettes.

Or feelings.

I reached for the phone, considering the distance to town—I knew my way now thanks to the pickup yesterday—and how fucked up my feet would be if I walked.

I had the rest of the day off.

I could ice them, pop the ibuprofen.

And save myself the trouble of Joel and his smirks.

That was so tempting that I actually stepped away from the phone, walked out of the room, and—

"What. The. Fuck?"

Eight

Bailey

I'd hauled my ass up the ladder, each step more painful than the last...because I was an idiot who didn't pay attention to my tweaky back, because the lightbulb overhead was out, because the farm was barely in the black, and I still had a shit-ton of debt to pay off so I couldn't hire any hands to help.

Because...I'd overdone it with a hay load six months before and had strained something.

Then had continued irritating it, over and *over* again, because I couldn't stop working.

Repairing the fences on the west side near the highway. Trying to change the oil on Gramps' ancient trunk. Pulling out the Halloween decorations from the attic.

Bending over to pick up a saw, or to put on my socks, or to snag something I'd dropped, or to shave my ankles, or—

Bending over.

Period.

It hurt like hell. Which was why I tended to assume the squat and commence with activities stance.

Unfortunately, Axel Finnegan had the annoying tendency to scramble my brain.

So I did things like look at his penis (again, dammit!!). And, hell, it wasn't just his penis either, which sucked. It was...all of him. His body was gorgeous. His face, which came in regular contact with sticks and pucks and other hockey players, was even more so.

I wanted to write an ode to the lines of his jaw, so defined, so crisp, so...nibble-able.

Which wasn't a word, but I was hauling my broken self up a ladder, changing some bulbs that had gone out the day before, after having dragged the old wooden ladder from the corner and painfully wrestling it in position...

So, I was giving myself a break when it came to making up words.

By climbing up a ladder and reaching uncomfortably to unscrew the bulb over my head.

Ah, the life of a rancher.

Some girls liked to get pedicures and their hair done.

I was a stickler for LED bulbs, which meant I wouldn't be changing this damned thing in six months or a year or however long normal lightbulbs lasted.

I was just screwing the bulb in when—

"*What the fuck?*"

And *that* was the moment I lost my grip on the bulb...and the ladder.

The bulb miraculously stayed in the socket.

My body, however, didn't stay on the ladder.

My fingers scrabbled at the step, nails breaking off—and *that* was why I didn't splurge for manicures. Splinters jammed up into my skin, and, in the absolute worst-case scenario, despite all my scrabbling, I didn't manage to stay on the fucking ladder.

One second of free fall.

One second to know that no matter how much my back had hurt before, it was going to hurt a hell of a lot more after hitting the ground.

I watched the ladder teeter.

Felt the ground get closer.

Knew I'd hit it, and then the ladder would hit me.

Joy.

I closed my eyes, braced, and—

Impact.

But not with the hard, compacted earth of the barn. With a set of strong arms and a muscular chest.

For a moment, my brain locked onto the fact that his exhale was louder than made a girl feel good. Because, seriously, was it really necessary to "*Oof!*" that loudly?

I wasn't filled with cotton candy, but hell, I wasn't made of bricks either.

And then I wasn't thinking about the volumes of *oofs* or what I was filled with, whether that be cotton candy or bricks or bowling fucking balls because pain radiated up my back, down my legs, burned all through my body.

It was much less pain, I knew, than if I'd hit the ground without Axel below me, taking the brunt of my fall, but it still took my breath away, had tears forming in my eyes.

His body jerked.

He *oof*ed again and then…we were moving.

Faster than I could track.

I caught a glimpse over his shoulder of the ladder wavering, tipping over before he moved again, hopping to his feet and—

"Fuck," he hissed, jerking again, the ladder having hit him square across the back.

"Are you o—?"

He began shifting, moving the ladder off him.

But he didn't move fast enough.

Because the bulb that I'd been screwing into place chose that moment to fall out of the socket, dropping down, and hitting Axel on the shoulder.

Glass exploded, tiny shards shooting outward and slicing us both. He cursed again, kept walking, and then we were out in the daylight, the sun blinding me as I bounced in his arms.

"What—?" But I stopped when his gaze jerked down to mine, eyes blazing.

And for the first time in my life, I didn't say anything, didn't come up with something snarky or sarcastic or bristly to say in response. I just clamped my lips together and let the man carry me up the porch stairs and inside.

He didn't stop until he'd entered the family room—an uncomfortable combination of blond wood and pale blue with shag carpet that my grandmother had decorated the space with before she'd died.

The only reason that Gramps had never changed it.

It was my grandma to a T—soft and warm, but on closer inspection, loud as fuck.

Case in point, the couch that looked blue, but when we got near, the solid blue became a tangle of azure flowers—bluebells, roses, irises, tulips, more that I couldn't identify.

Axel set me on the couch.

Gently.

Gently enough that I was surprised, shocked really, that a man of his size could be that gentle. "Stay," he muttered, slipping his arms out from underneath me. Then he straightened, whipped off his shirt.

Ho, mama.

I'd missed the tattoo before, but holy shit, that was glorious, a swathe of black lines twisting and folding together, starting in the middle of his back and wrapping forward, drifting around to his ribs. Those lines were strong and brash, inviting fingers and tongue to trace.

"Glass," he murmured, probably because he caught me looking —okay, *staring*.

Right.

I glanced down, lifted my hand to begin plucking the shards that had stuck to my shirt, were jabbing into my skin.

"Stop."

I froze.

He bent, carefully dug into the shag carpeting to extract a shard, then crossed to me, leaning close and doing it fast. So fast that my snark and sass and sarcasm stayed banked, that I just lay there staring up at him, my eyes wide.

An inhale, my lips parting.

But Axel didn't acknowledge the parting, my breathing accelerating.

He just leaned close and began picking the shards off, one after another, carefully folding them into his borrowed shirt. A couple of them stung, burning slightly when he tugged them free, and I knew I'd have a few places like he did, like the small cuts dotting his chest.

My hand lifted, touched the skin beneath it.

His eyes came to mine again, hot and warm and...gentle.

"I'm sorry," I whispered.

His brows dragged together. "For what?"

My brows lifted. "Um, the lightbulb and the fact that you've spent the last five minutes picking glass out of my shirt?"

Contrition across his face, trailed by fury.

Both of which confused me.

Until I heard his words.

"Um," he said sarcastically, albeit that sarcasm was coated with plenty of gentle, "how about I'm the one who says I'm sorry considering that I lost my fucking temper and made you fall off a tall ass ladder?"

I lifted my brows, a flicker of amusement sliding through me. "Just saying, my lightbulb is what made you bleed."

"Just *saying*." He smoothed back my hair. "My yelling at you is what caused you to fall off the ladder." His fingers brushed over my cheek. "I'm sorry," he whispered, his eyes drifting from mine. "It's lucky I was able to catch you."

A warm tendril in my stomach.

The silence stretched.

I stared into deep blue eyes.

My tongue darted out, wet my bottom lip.

He leaned in—

Oh fuck.

Fuck.

Then he froze, straightened. "Right." He cleared his throat. "Where's your vacuum?"

Nine

Axel

The vacuum was mostly metal, puke green, and it went without saying, was absolutely ancient.

It had also puffed out smoke when I'd first plugged it in.

But I dutifully did something that I hadn't done in a good ten years, probably since before I'd moved away from home, during the times that my mom cared enough to pretend that she gave a damn about me.

Usually when I had a new surrogate dad and he made some comment about needing to teach me responsibility.

Then I'd be running a vacuum, dusting, scrubbing toilets.

Days, weeks, months later, he would leave, and she would disappear into a bottle.

Sometimes that bottle was filled with pills, sometimes it was filled with alcohol.

Either way, it meant that she forgot about me, and I could do what I wanted. Which was to get the fuck out of the house, get to the rink and beg for as much free ice time as possible, and when no ice was available (or I couldn't smile, charm, or beg my way into it), I found any flat surface I could to practice stick handling.

With a tennis ball and a hand-me-down stick.

Then running or doing push-ups and crunches and squats because they were good for building strength, and I could do them without any extra equipment.

Without needing any money.

Boyfriend time had the side benefit that I could usually scrounge some money from the men fucking my mom and could squirrel it away so that I had enough when it came time to pay for the season.

Boyfriend time also meant that I might be able to get the next size of skates, usually used. Very rarely—*very* rarely—new. But those new times were...fucking chef's kiss. To not have my toes scrunched up, to not have skates that weighed what felt like one-metric ton when the rest of the guys on the ice seemingly had every bit of new equipment, was amazing.

None of them could run a vacuum like I could, though.

Even a bellowing, smoke-producing one.

And miracle of miracles, the woman—whose name I somehow still didn't know—had stayed where I'd put her on the couch, eyes still wide, watching me like she'd never seen a grown-ass man vacuum.

So maybe I hadn't vacuumed the entire time I'd *been* a grown-ass man (one of the perks of playing hockey—even if I wasn't in the big leagues—meant that I could afford a maid service to come clean my rugs and toilets and dishes once a week).

Best money I ever spent.

Though some part of me had to wonder if seeing her look at me the way she was might mean I was willing to trade vacuuming duty for sexual favors.

Newsflash, I was *totally* willing to trade vacuuming duty for sexual favors.

Especially if it meant that I got my hands on that hot ass of hers.

I finished the path between the door and the couch, glanced down to shut off the vacuum, then saw a shard glittering on the too-small sweats she'd loaned me. So, I clicked the back of the vacuum in place, hit the switch to turn it off, and tugged off the borrowed pants.

A choking sound had me whipping around.

She was staring at me again, this time in a hot way that told me *she* might be all in for trading those sexual favors for housecleaning.

Maybe I could dust the baseboards for a blow job.

As though reading the thought on my mind, she scowled and looked away, starting to sit up. Quickly, I shook out the sweats, ran the vacuum over a large enough area to ensure there were no more tiny little pieces of glass that might remain and hurt her.

Hurt *her*.

Huh.

That was a new concept.

Usually, I didn't care about that. *Usually*, I was all about protecting myself. I had to, after all. I was the only person in the world who'd ever done any *me-protecting*, and I couldn't trust anyone else to do it. Not if I didn't want to get thrown to the wolves.

Me first.

Always.

It was the only way to survive.

I shut the vacuum down a second time, wrapped the cord, and glanced back at the couch.

Sure enough, she was on her feet. Hobbling forward. *Hobbling*.

Fucking hell, save me from stubborn women.

I shoved the vacuum to the side, stifled a sigh. Then I walked over to her, scooped her up, and set her down onto the couch again, this time holding her in my lap.

"What the fuck?" she snapped.

"The cactus is back, I see." I bent, inhaled, noting that beneath the horseshit, she smelled faintly of apples.

That was a definite step up.

"Let me go you—" She started to struggle against my hold, pushed against my hands then immediately paused, her breath hissing out.

"And so is the pain," I added. Carefully, I hefted her, shifting and flipping her so she was face down on the couch.

"What the fu—"

My fingers found the taut muscles that had spasmed on her back, digging in and massaging them in the way that the trainers for the Rush always did. Just on the edge of too painful, but with purpose that would ultimately be for the better.

She groaned, every muscle in her body going tense.

And then she melted, relaxed under my ministrations—and fuck, I might actually be losing it if I was using dumbass words like *ministrations* when I was just kneading a few sore muscles on a woman's back.

And *then* I paid attention to what I was doing, what I was feeling—and it wasn't that I was stroking a woman's back who I was trying to get into my bed (though, no surprise, I wouldn't turn that down). Rather, it was that I was feeling a slew of tight muscles that were riddled with knots. Absolutely *riddled* with them.

Her trapezius muscle was clenched tight.

The space on either side of her spine, curving around her shoulder blades felt like bubble wrap, knot after knot after knot present.

Her middle and lower back weren't much better.

So instead of it becoming an invitation, a coaxing, my touch stayed focused, kept that trainer-esque purpose as I diligently worked on those knots.

She didn't move, didn't fight me, and after a few moments, I heard it.

The softest moan.

My dick twitched.

That trainer-esque purpose disappeared like a fucking puff of smoke from the cigars Joel snuck in behind the rink.

My hands began moving with a different purpose then, kneading gentling into caresses, fingertips grazing. I watched goose bumps lift on her skin, listened to her breathing speed up, and I leaned a little closer.

She smelled like sunshine and flowers on a warm spring day.

My dick twitched again.

"You know," I said, ignoring the slight husk to my words, attempting levity, keeping those touches going, hoping to snag one piece of information from the mysterious woman beneath me. "I still don't know your name."

She went still.

Stiff.

Fuck. Too fast. Too much.

You have your fucking hands on her, bro. Just take the fucking win.

Her head shifted, turning to the side, her chocolate eyes coming to mine.

Then she shocked the shit out of me by giving me something wonderful.

She burst out laughing.

It was...beautiful.

It...stunned me to stillness as I watched those walls fall, as I saw a bright, beautiful center I wouldn't have expected from the prickly, stubborn woman I'd known so far.

It was...the woman from the picture I'd seen.

Warm and open and...so fucking intoxicating.

And I got to soak in all that beautiful for all of one heartbeat before I heard,

"Yoo-hoo!"

The front door swung open...and I realized I was on top of her, of this woman whose name I didn't know.

Naked.

Ten

Bailey

"*Yoo-hoo!*"

Kill.

Me.

Now.

I bucked like a pissed-off mama cow, attempting to launch Axel off my back, but he was tall and strong and...heavy.

Which meant that he was firmly on top of me when my aunt made it down the hall and into the family room.

Naked and on top of me.

The key word being...*naked.*

Or maybe *on top of me.*

Or maybe—

Fuck.

"Get off," I hissed, bucking again. A pained grunt escaped my lips, but at least I managed to dislodge the brute. Except...maybe that was worse?

Because now the naked Axel, in all his glorious nakedness, had been knocked off me and—

"*Oh!*"

Billie Rose, my aunt, even though we were only two years apart in age, skittered to a stop and her mouth and eyes went wide, feigning shock at the sight of a naked Axel Finnegan. As if she hadn't handcuffed him to my freaking porch.

"I'm sorry to interrupt," she said, clamping her hands over her eyes and starting to turn for the front door. "I'll just—"

"Stay right where you are," I ordered, pushing up off the couch, biting back my grimace, and finding my feet.

I turned, found that Axel had procured a throw pillow—pale yellow with more of the floral upon floral upon floral design—and clamped it over his pelvis.

Somehow still sexy, even with an ugly as sin pillow held over his nether bits.

And *nether bits.*

Seriously, I was *losing* it.

Which was why I marched over to Billie Rose, wound my fingers around her elbow, and did some clamping of my own, holding her tight when she would have escaped, and guiding her into the kitchen.

"What the fuck, Billie?" I said once we were out of earshot.

"The door wasn't shut," she said, deliberately tugging her elbow free and making herself at home in my kitchen, opening the cupboards and pulling out mugs for coffee, filling the pot with water, adding grounds, setting it to brew.

"Let me guess," I muttered as she moved to the fridge, tugging the door wide, "it was the *wind*."

Billie Rose turned to me, her blond curls bouncing. "The wind?" Her brows drew together before her head whipped back to the fridge. "God, Bailey, it's like a wasteland in here. What do you eat? Do you need your Auntie Billie Rose to pick you up some groceries?"

"Ew, stop it, Bill," I muttered. "You know it's weird you call yourself that when you're basically my age." I sighed. "I'm fine. Just busy and haven't had time to go to the store."

So yeah, the pickings were a little slim.

It was tough to get to the grocery store when I worked so much and lived far from town. I'd used the last of my bread and lunch meat the night before for my dinner sandwich.

Which had been after my lunch sandwich.

And yeah maybe it lacked creativity, but sandwiches were easy and cheap and there were a ton of different varieties.

Last week it had been cheddar and salami.

Maybe this week it would be turkey. Or roast beef. Or PB and J.

God, it had been a long time since I'd had peanut butter and jelly.

Just the thought of it had my mouth watering.

See?

Variety. Delicious, delicious variety.

"Is there any fruit in here?" Billie Rose tugged open a drawer. "What about vegetables?" Plastic scraped as she opened another drawer. "Found— *Ugh*. I found *one*." The door slammed and she held up a carrot that, admittedly, had seen better days.

Just as Axel walked into the room. He was wearing the sweats I'd given him before, and I sent a prayer up to whatever gods were out there that a shard of glass would impale itself into his femoral when he headed for the coffee pot and asked silkily, "Do you want a cup...*Bailey?*"

Fuck.

He'd been listening to our conversation—or to Billie's prattling, rather.

And...hell. Why was a small part of me disappointed that he knew my name? That the weird little game we were playing at had ended, and—

"I had a dog named Bailey once," he said affably.

Except for the slice of devil in his eyes.

Fucker.

I narrowed *my* eyes, showed him the slice of devil *I* could have.

Axel put his palms up in surrender. "What? She was loyal." A shrug. "A bit dumb and slow, of course. But a good old girl." He grinned, ran his hands over his jaw, the bristles of his beard making a scratching sound that filled the kitchen. "I once threw a ball and it bounced off the fence, but instead of her stopping and turning around, she bounced off the fence, too." He chuckled. "Poor, dumb girl."

*Mother*fucker.

"I need to get back to work." I slanted my stare at Billie Rose, expressed every bit of displeasure I had for my *aunt* and her interfering tendencies in that one glance. "Enjoy your free coffee and then"—I widened my eyes deliberately—"take out the trash."

Not the slyest of insults, and as I turned for the front door of the house and caught sight of Axel's face, I knew he'd picked it up loud and clear.

Normally, I might feel a little guilty, especially when he'd stopped me from getting seriously hurt.

But he was grinning.

And an ass.

Loyal. Dumb. Slow?

He was the reason I'd fallen off the ladder.

Yelling at me.

Startling me.

So yeah, he could be *trash*.

Hell, he'd proved it time and again with his antics in town.

So, I held on to my fury, tucked that rage close to my heart—and admittedly, I'd become very good at that, at holding tight to my anger. Focusing on it. Living it. Breathing it in until it had burned its way onto my lungs, until it boiled its way through my veins.

Asshole.

He was an asshole.

And...I had work to do.

Starting with cleaning up the barn.

Ending with the planting.

There were always fences that needed to be repaired, stalls that needed to be mucked, horses that needed to be exercised and brushed down. Tack to be organized. The hydraulic fluid on the tractor refilled, the loose connection that was the cause of the leak and the regular need to refill changed out.

Then the sun would go down.

I'd summon the energy to go to town and shop for groceries, for the supplies for those peanut butter and jelly sandwiches.

Maybe I'd even treat myself to some ice cream.

See?

I'd really live it up. Peanut butter and jelly and ice cream. Quiet and solitude and peace.

What more could a woman want?

What more could *I* want?

Nothing.

I'd tried to have more once, and it had led me back here. That was the universe telling me to not reach for big dreams, to live and breathe small, to take comfort in the familiar, in this home, in this ranch, in the...

Peace.

But when I saw the ladder on its side, the shards of glass all around it...

When I remembered the gentle way that Axel had pushed back my hair...

When I remembered the desire that had weaved its way through my body when he'd been on top of me, hands moving over my body...

I'd felt alive.

Ever since Axel had showed up naked on my porch, I'd felt *alive*. More in these last few days than I'd felt over the last two years.

And that had me...worried.

What had me even *more* worried?

Part of me wanted to see what might happen if Axel appeared on my porch for a third day in a row.

Eleven

Axel

Billie Rose filled a mug with coffee, set it on the worn wooden table. "I don't know if I should be relieved or disappointed that you've put on clothes," she said, eyeing me closely, lips tipping up at the edges. "No one can say that you don't put the work in for your beach bod."

I picked up the mug, took a sip of the strong, black brew. "Can never be too on top of the beach bod."

A chuckle. Then, "I have your clothes in my car, by the way."

"I—"

I'd been prepared for another quip about beach readiness—maybe some reference to my pasty-ass skin since the majority of my naked time happened in the locker room or the bedroom—but that was the last thing I'd been expecting her to say.

"M-my c-clothes?" I sputtered.

Fuck.

Had I slept with *her?*

With *Billie Rose?*

Wasn't she...the mayor? And apparently Bailey's aunt, which was a weird twist of...weirdness because I was creeping on her niece, and while sober I could appreciate she was an attractive woman, I didn't want to fuck Billie Rose.

Not in the least.

Billie Rose lifted her mug to her lips, sipped. "Yup. Because when you're drunk and I'm taking you home, you like to get naked."

I couldn't lie.

That sounded like me.

Except...home meant that I'd—

And she was the mayor and Bailey's aunt and...*fuck*.

"We didn't have sex, if that's what you're worried about." My eyes shot up, hit Billie's. "You're pretty, but I don't fuck drunk guys." She huffed out a laugh before her expression went abruptly serious, eyes narrowing. "And I *don't* fuck drunk guys who seem to have made it their duty to fuck up my town."

"I didn't mean—"

"To deface public property and sex your way through town and to make it extremely difficult on the people whose livelihood depends on the team?"

Was that a trickle of guilt?

Fuck.

Ever since I'd spent two mornings getting splinters all up my ass, I'd been feeling too fucking much.

Guilt.

Desire. Okay, *that* was familiar.

But the guilt, the empathy...yeah, those weren't comfortable or *wanted*, really.

"Fuck," I whispered.

"Yeah," Billie Rose muttered, taking another sip of her coffee. "Tell me about it." She leaned against the counter next to me, sighed. "The council voted to not renew the Rush's contract."

That jolted through me. "What?"

If they cut the contract...

If the Rush couldn't stay in River's Bend and it was made known that it was because of the team's behavior, because of *me*...

Fuck.

As in, my career would be *fucked*.

She smiled, and it wasn't the least bit friendly. "You heard me. And the thing is, *I'm* the one who can decide to accept that vote and nix the contract." The mug hit the counter. "So, the way I see it is that you have two choices. I can get you your clothes, I'll drive you home, and you can stop being an asshole by fucking with my town." Her finger jabbed at my chest. "You can keep your focus on your career and the ice, and I won't terminate the contract. Or"—her voice went sickly sweet—"you can keep fucking around, keep fucking with the town, and I will make it so the Rush *never* have a home in River's Bend again."

A bright smile.

"Now"—she drained her mug, rinsed it in the sink, then set it on the drying rack—"shall we get you dressed and home?"

I thought I glimpsed Bailey atop a horse, but Billie Rose was turning out of the driveway, speeding like a fucking maniac, and by the time I got over my whiplash to look again, the horse—and rider—were gone.

Sighing, I sat back in the seat.

Clothed.

With another pile of clothes folded in my lap.

Both smelled like shit.

Obviously, Billie Rose hadn't bothered to run them through the wash—not that I'd expected her to (though I couldn't deny that it would have been nice)—so I'd chosen the slightly less fragrant option.

It was still bad.

Whiskey and stale sweat and the cloying odor of something female.

I should have kept the sweats and T that Bailey had given me.

Yeah, they were too tight.

Yeah, they were tie-dye.

But they smelled like Bailey—well, the Bailey beneath the horse shit. The Bailey I'd smelled on the couch. Soft and floral with a hint of apples.

That was much preferred to the manure version.

Billie Rose swung her little sedan so rapidly around the turn that I ended up plastered against the door, head banging off the glass.

"God," I muttered.

"Yes?" she quipped, winding the car the other way, so quickly this time that I nearly ended up in her lap.

"Hilarious."

"I do try." A shrug, one of her hands coming off the wheel and shoving me, none too lightly, back into my seat. "Now, I'm not saying that my problem with the Rush might be solved if you weren't around to froth the waters of debauchery, but...I'm also *not* going to tell you to be sure to buckle up..."

She let that trail off, a hint of malice hitting the interior of the car.

Not that I was fearing for my life—well, that wasn't true since apparently the woman drove like a fucking nut—but I also didn't think that she'd purposely kill me, if only because that would create bad press for the town.

I reached behind me and buckled my seat belt anyway.

"Froth the waters of debauchery?" I asked, going for cool and collected, because minus the whole being-launched-from-a-moving-vehicle thing, the woman was funny.

Inappropriately.

Meh.

That was the best kind.

A shrug. "If the bad descriptor fits."

"If you say so."

Billie Rose didn't seem to have a reply to that, and since I was concentrating on trying to stay in my seat, I didn't add any further snark. Just shut up, held on, and hoped I would make it back to my apartment in one piece.

"It's weird not having you undress yourself as I drive," she murmured as she turned down Main Street.

I glanced at her, lifted my brows.

"You don't remember?"

My gaze went back to the street. "I don't remember a lot of things."

"Including the window? And the glasses? And RiRi?"

"RiRi?"

"RiRi," she repeated.

I shook my head. "Still not ringing a bell."

"RiRi," she repeated, this time with a huff, then added, her disgusted eyes slanting toward me for a second before flicking back to the road. "*Rihanna*. Your rendition of my favorite song of hers?"

"No," I said. "Not ringing a bell."

A beat. "Pity. Your voice is..."

She let that hang.

Hell, I knew my singing voice was awful.

I frequently tortured the guys with it.

But I didn't recall singing to *her*.

So...what the fuck?

She passed through the one—and only—signal downtown and turned right into the driveway of my apartment complex. Which took my mind off any Rihanna renditions and brought me face to face with something I should have recognized earlier.

Billie Rose had driven me home.

Except, Billie Rose *hadn't* driven me home.

She knew where I lived, but she'd driven me to Bailey's ranch, handcuffed me to the porch railing, and left me naked on her niece's porch.

What. The. *Fuck?*

The car screeched to a halt. She threw the transmission into park and turned to face me. "Time to go bye-bye." A finger wave before she reached across me, threw open the door.

"You know where I live," I said, rather stupidly.

A roll of her eyes. "Um, yeah. Everyone in town knows where you live." She huffed out a breath. "You've brought a good ninety percent of the single women here."

Okay, maybe that was true.

Maybe it wasn't.

Probably because the number was more like ninety-five percent.

Not the point.

I shook myself.

"But if you know where I live, then why'd you take me to Bailey's ranch?"

Her brows dragged together. "Why do you think *I* did that?"

Now *my* brows dragged together. "Um, because you showed up at Bailey's place with my clothes and told me I like to get naked when you drive me home?"

White teeth into a pink bottom lip. "Ah. Right. The fatal flaw in my plan—giving too many details." A shrug, her shaking that off as casually as she'd whipped her car through back-country roads. "Yes, I dropped you at Bailey's."

Dropped.

Now that was a euphemism.

"Why?"

"I have my reasons." A shrug, her lips tipped up into a smirk that told me I really wouldn't like those reasons.

"And the handcuffs?" I pressed, deciding to let those *reasons* go for the moment.

She blinked, expression going innocent (and completely unbelievably so). "What handcuffs? Oh"—she glanced away—"that's my phone. Probably important mayor business."

"I didn't hear your phone ring—"

Hand darting down, she unclicked my seat belt, shoved me hard enough that I nearly toppled out into the parking lot. Then once more, and I was falling out of the seat, catching myself on the frame, my clothes hitting the pavement. I gave in to the inevitable, got out, and stood.

"Gotta run!" she called.

The car moved forward.

Paused.

"Can you shut that?"

Right.

Stifling a sigh, I closed the door.

The window whirred down and one shoe then another flew through the opening. "Don't forget these!"

"I...uh...thanks, I guess."

She started to pull forward again. Stopped. The smile faded.

"Seriously, Axel. Stop fucking with my town, or I'll do worse than handcuffs."

I faltered, having bent to reach for one of my shoes. "Wait, what?"

A wave. A beatific smile that didn't reach her eyes. "Bye! Have a great day!"

Billie Rose screeched out of the apartment complex.

I thought of the mayor and that beatific smile, of her hard blue eyes.

And I knew that handcuffs were the least of my worries.

Twelve

Bailey

Horses and cows. Planting and fences.

Shit. Lots and lots of shoveling shit.

Sandwiches.

And two weeks without Axel Finnegan on my front porch.

I was feeling strangely disappointed that he hadn't been there in all his naked glory.

No one had been to the ranch.

Not *one* person.

I'd come home from riding my horse, Data, to find my fridge and pantry stocked.

Billie Rose.

From the outside, it probably would seem like it was her way of apologizing for the naked delivery, but more likely, it was Billie Rose just taking care of me. Because she was nosy and pushy and used to getting her own way, and I knew it wasn't the last time she'd be interjecting herself into my life.

Regardless, she'd saved me a trip to the store *and* I'd had a variety of sandwich options that week.

Yeah, my aunt knew me.

Not all that surprising considering that, growing up, we spent most summers of our lives together on the ranch.

Billie Rose was my dad's much-younger sister. A native of River's Bend, she'd been a frequent visitor to Gramp's house. Even though Gramps and Gran were my maternal grandparents, they'd always been welcoming to everyone, whether they were biologically related or family through marriage or otherwise. More times than I could count, I'd come into the house to find someone from town in Gran's kitchen, eating her cookies, gossiping and laughing and—

I swallowed the bolt of grief, breathed it out through my nose, and knew I would probably always miss them.

Billie Rose had spent a lot of her time in the kitchen with Gran before she'd passed away when I was twelve. The two of them had been River's Bend's welcoming committee before, always fluttering around, always connected, always volunteering at school or organizing meal trains or raising money for a youth soccer team. Rooted in the town. And I was more at home with the cows and the horses and out in the field under the sun and sky with Gramps. Of course, though, it had been impossible not to be pulled into Billie Rose's orbit when I visited.

The poor girl with the crappy, disengaged parents who was dumped with her grandparents every summer while they went on luxurious vacations.

Not that I wanted to be anywhere else.

I just...I'd seen a few too many pitying looks during the summer months.

Well, before Billie took me under her wing, that was.

And, truthfully, the times I spent on the ranch were the best of my life. Mostly, because during the rest of the year, I was in the Bay Area with my parents.

Until I was a senior in high school.

That was when Gramps had gotten sick.

Then he'd died.

And then *they'd* spent the time while I'd been away at college nearly running the ranch into the ground.

So here I was, having just turned twenty-five, with a reverse mortgage hanging over my head—nearly paid off now, thankfully—and a college degree in English Literature.

Once I'd dreamed of being a high school English teacher.

Now I dreamed of cows and calves and fence repair.

And my diploma probably dreamed of being dusted off and put to actual use.

But...the ranch.

My legacy.

My family history.

And...I loved it here.

Sighing, I walked out onto the porch—where there was no Axel Finnegan, bee-tee-dub, just like every other day of the previous two weeks—and stared out at the horizon, the sun setting to the west, thinking about all the time in front of me.

I was tired.

Then again I was *always* tired.

But normally the tiredness didn't stretch out in front of me like a giant yawning chasm, threatening to take me under and choke me in the dark, tumultuous waters—

Dramatic much?

Not normally.

But tonight?

Yeah, I was.

Which was probably why I went back into my house, got my keys, hopped in my truck, and instead of going to bed early, like I always did...I drove to town.

It was Friday night.

Which meant that Monroe's, as one of River's Bend's two night spots (minus The Ridge, where all the kids went to get busy), was slammed.

Luckily, I was by myself.

Because there was a single barstool in the corner that I could squeeze myself onto, have a couple of beers, socialize in the least *social* way possible (being around people without actually having to interact with them much), and get this itching, prickling feeling that had been making its presence known between my shoulder blades for the last couple of weeks *go the fuck away.*

Then I'd go back to the ranch, to my solitude.

That was what I wanted.

Right?

I—

"Bailey?"

I blinked, glanced up at the woman behind the bar, and for a moment my socializing without actually socializing went by the back burner. "Dessie!" I squealed, so fucking happy to see her. "God, it's been *years*! When did you get back to town?"

Desiree shrugged and rolled her eyes. "When did the claws of River's Bend mafia drag me back in, you mean?"

I grinned. "Yeah. That."

"A month ago." She pulled a beer, pushed it toward a man two seats down from me. "Roger needed some help with the bar, and since I'm a glutton for punishment, I decided to move home for a bit and help."

"But I thought you'd just made lieutenant at the fire department."

Her face went strange.

Maybe sad. Maybe mad. Maybe—

She turned away, grabbed a chilled glass, and spun back around. "Still an IPA girl?"

I studied her face, but the strangeness was gone, and this wasn't the place to press anyway. "Is there any other type of beer?" I asked lightly.

"There is according to the dumbasses in the corner." She tilted her head and my gaze followed hers...

To Axel Finnegan holding court in the corner.

A blonde I didn't recognize sat on his lap. Two men who were big enough that they were certainly hockey players were taking up large portions of the booth around him, more women interspersed between them. Pitchers of beer sat among the group in various stages of emptiness, cups and baskets of food following the same pattern.

"They've given the order for the cheapest beer with the highest alcohol count." Dessie rolled her eyes, turned back to the tap, and began filling my glass. "Though, from what I hear, I guess we should just be happy they're not busting out windows." A snort. "Anyway, you would think grown men would get tired of just getting fucked up all the time."

"Unfortunately, I don't think there's anything grown about them," I muttered, fiddling with the coaster that Desiree had tossed on the bar in front of me.

"That's not what you said when I was naked and on top of you."

Dessie's eyes bugged out of her head.

I spun, saw that one Axel Finnegan had dislodged the blonde from his lap and squeezed next to me, leaning against the bar with a devil may care smile on his face.

"*You*," I snapped.

"Buttercup." He reached forward and tugged lightly at a strand of my hair.

Desiree choked.

I batted him away. "Back up, you—you—"

"Bastard?" One dark brown brow lifted. "Asshole?" He leaned closer, breath puffing on my lips. "Cock-sucker?" He leaned in farther, until his mouth was very near my ear. "Only once," he murmured, "and I found it wasn't for me."

Heat blazed through me.

Why was the thought of him sucking off another man so fucking hot?

Probably because I was imagining him with an equally hot guy, and then I was *imagining* both of those hot guys with me.

At the same time.

Yum.

I shivered.

Fuck.

Not *yum*.

Shit.

A flick of moisture. A flick of his *tongue* against my ear. And then a rough chuckle, the fucker seeming to know exactly what I was thinking.

I brought my hand up, pressed it against his chest...

Then dug my nails in.

Hard.

He winced.

Then covered my hand with his own, squeezed lightly, and murmured, "I *don't* mind a little bit of pain, though."

My thighs squeezed tight.

But I managed to get my shit together, shove him back, and spin forward on my stool.

Clearly, talking to him wasn't getting him to leave me alone. I turned back to Dessie, determined to ignore him. Her lips had tipped up in the corners, and her brows were practically in her hairline.

"He's pretty, but annoying," I stage-whispered. "And he's *not* getting fucked." I glared over at him. "Not by me anyway. Not now. Not before. Not *ever.*"

He smirked.

I lifted my chin toward the corner booth he'd previously occupied but deliberately kept my gaze from his. "And not by that pretty blonde in the corner if he keeps ignoring her."

He turned, spared a glance toward the booth. For all of a...*second.*

If that.

Then he was shifting closer, moving so that his leg was tangled with mine, so that his body was too damned near.

Hot and hard and...I knew *exactly* what he was packing.

"Newsflash, buttercup," he murmured. "I don't give a fuck about the blonde."

Why did that send my pulse skittering? My breath accelerating?

"Don't pretend that you give a fuck about me," I said, hating that my voice wavered.

Slightly.

But enough.

"I'm not pretending."

I sucked in a breath.

Because there was a vulnerability in his bright blue eyes.

Because...he might be telling the truth, and I didn't know what *the fuck* to make of that.

Except, that it made me feel...*something.*

I felt Desiree move away, and whether it was to give me the privacy she thought I wanted (since Axel was still there and close, and I hadn't kicked him in the big ol' dick I knew he had) or because she had other customers she needed to serve, I didn't know.

But I really, *seriously* missed the shield she'd provided.

Because it left me unable to ignore Axel, left me all too vulnerable to the heat curling in my belly.

Not that Axel had been much deterred by her with all his ear-licking and thigh-pressing. Not that *I* was deterred by his nearness or his yummy smell or those blazing blue eyes or the fingers drifting slowly down my throat—

Wait.

My *throat?*

Next, they'd be tracing along my collarbones, potentially sliding down beneath my bra, grazing my nip—

What the fuck was I doing?

Getting lured into complacency by the sexy smile and the spicy scent and hard body and the huge dick and—

Being a complete idiot.

Case in point?

The buxom blonde making an appearance.

"Axel," she whined, draping herself over him. "I'm *cold.*"

He turned to deal with her.

And I used the opportunity...

To run.

Thirteen

Axel

The blonde with the big tits, whose name I could *not* remember for the life of me, had turned into an octopus.

With like fourteen arms.

And giant-ass suckers.

And—

I managed to wrestle her tentacles free and turned back to Bailey—

Who was gone.

"Fuck," I muttered.

"Axel!" Another whine.

And I'd had enough.

"Take a fucking hint," I growled. "I'm not interested now, and I'm not going to ever be."

A wobbling bottom lip, but ineffective considering that I'd already witnessed her ability to produce tears on a whim multiple times that evening, including when Joel had accidentally bumped her arm and she'd let loose the waterworks. Oh, and when another of the girls had eaten the last mozzarella stick. And, come to think of it, when I'd asked her to get off so I could take a piss.

Tears weren't sexy.

Tears on command were even less so.

Even with the great rack and pretty face.

"But—"

I nodded to the booth. "Go find Joel. He likes emotional bitches."

A tear slid free.

"And I don't, so fuck off, Cassidy."

"I—my name is Candi."

"I don't care."

"I—" A sob hitched her chest, and I was too much of a man to not notice that the sob hitching through her chest also had her boobs jiggling.

Damn.

That was nice.

Not so nice?

The tears glistening in her eyes and those tentacles reaching for me again.

"Fuck. Off," I repeated, lifting her away from me. This woman had always struck me as slightly nuts, so there was no way I was letting her get any closer. I planted my hand in between those massive boobs when she reached for me again, held her off, bending slightly so I could meet those falsely watery eyes. "I mean it. *Fuck. Off.* Do you get me?"

I held her stare.

Finally, she nodded.

"Go find Joel."

Another nod.

Then she was spinning away on a huff, marching across the busy floor. I didn't spare her another look. Instead, I searched the rest of the space for the stubborn, pesky brunette who liked to laugh at my attempts at charm and pointed shotguns at my junk.

There was no sign of her.

"Maybe enjoy your beer on the back patio?"

"That's not my beer—" My gaze caught on the bartender's, who lifted her eyebrows and dragged her stare from the full beer on the bar to a door I'd never noticed before. "Right." I snagged the glass. "I'll just go...enjoy...um...*this* on the patio."

It was more question than statement.

Which was probably why she nodded and lifted her chin toward the door.

Since I wasn't a *complete* idiot, I shut up and hit the door.

The cool air tugged at my skin, making it tighten like it did when I first skated out onto the ice. It was a familiar feeling and one of my favorites—home and the only thing that had never let me down: the game.

But then I stopped thinking about hockey.

Because all I could think about was *her*.

She was standing against a wooden post, nearly hidden in the shadows of the pergola, only the hanging lights overhead and moonlight drifting through the clouds revealing her profile.

And she was beautiful.

And sad.

And there was something in her that drew me to her—a moth to the light, a bee to nectar, a big, dumb, horny hockey player to something steel...with something soft and vulnerable beneath.

That wasn't like me.

I didn't *do* vulnerable.

I didn't *do* women I couldn't do easily.

But...Bailey...

Fuck, I didn't know what it was about her. What had me moving across the empty space, the late fall air obviously too cold for most of the other patrons, especially without the outdoor heaters on.

"You forgot this," I said, holding the beer out like it was an offering.

For peace?

For mistakes?

For wanting something I shouldn't?

She jumped and spun around, her hand clamping to her chest. "What the fuck?" she snapped, her eyes narrowing. "Fucking hell, Axel"—she inhaled sharply through her nose—"can't you take a hint?"

"Cool."

That had her freezing, brows drawing together.

I took a long sip of the beer, felt the cool, bubbly slide down my throat. "*God,* that's good."

"Hey! That's my—"

"I'm taking a hint." I sipped again, turning away and moving across the space, stepping out from beneath the pergola and staring up at the stars.

So bright.

No smog.

Just cold, fresh air and the faint buzz of conversation and music and *people.*

There wasn't anyone out here—no one aside from me and Bailey, that was. But her presence was...unsettling. Muted and yet somehow still huge. An aura that sank into my bones, that quieted me, and yet something that also had my skin buzzing with awareness.

I didn't *like* awareness.

I liked to skate fast and crush people against the boards in pursuit of the puck. I liked to be surrounded by noise and activity and to let myself be swept along in it, to numb myself in sensation so I couldn't be quiet like this, couldn't. I liked to drink until I didn't remember, and I liked to fuck until it was all pleasure and no pain and—

My sigh bubbled up in my throat and I swallowed it down.

Awareness was something I tried to avoid at all costs.

But it was something that grew until it nearly encompassed me as Bailey stomped over, her rubber-soled boots clomping on the concrete.

One second, I was just listening to her footsteps.

The next her presence was *in* mine, scent tangling with that of the beer as she came close, her ponytail whipping me across the cheek as her hand swept down and snagged the glass out of my grip.

"This"—the beer sloshed over the rim, splashed along her wrist—"is *mine—*"

Whatever else she was going to say was cut off.

Because of me.

Mainly because that beer was dripping off her golden skin,

making it glisten under the twinkling lights overhead, the sheen calling to me.

To my mouth, my lips, my *tongue.*

I grasped her wrist, wrapping my fingers around the slender strength of her.

And then...I lifted it to my mouth, flicked out my tongue...and *tasted.*

Her skin. The beer.

The sweet, fruity taste of her.

The bitter hoppy flavor of the beer.

The soft, breathy sound of her moan in my ears.

My jaw flexed, and then I was dragging my lips along her wrist, up the inside of her forearm, pushing the loose sleeve of her flannel up as I went, pausing at her elbow, and then—

I couldn't resist nipping at the silken skin.

"Ow!" she hissed.

I soothed the small hurt with my tongue, was rewarded with the sweet, fruity taste of her.

It was better sans beer.

It was *better* when she moaned again, when that sound rippled through me and she didn't resist me pulling her closer, didn't protest when I wrapped her in my arms, dragged my lips from her elbow up to her throat, pressing my mouth to the spot just beneath her jaw.

She shuddered.

I moved to her ear, tasting that hanging lobe, dipping down to kiss the spot behind it that was pure *Bailey*. Apples and sweet, floral and just the slightest bit of horse.

No shit.

Just...nature and outside and quiet and the bright sun and the blue sky and...splinters in my ass.

I huffed out a breath, leaned back enough to see that her eyes were closed, her lips parted.

I had to taste her.

So...I did.

Slanting my mouth across hers, dancing my tongue across her lips.

She exhaled, moan rumbling up through her throat, along her tongue, into my mouth. That heat and need arrowed straight for my dick, making it throb and ache as it hardened against my zipper.

I groaned.

She stiffened, went ramrod straight in my arms.

Curses blared through my mind, but though I paused, I didn't lift my mouth from hers. Just held still and my breath and waited and hoped and hell, I threw up a couple of prayers to the hockey gods that she wasn't about to dump the beer over my head or my crotch or my—

A feminine sigh.

Then...she melted.

Her body coming flush against mine. Her moan rumbling through my mouth again.

Plush breasts. Strong thighs.

I heard a clink, felt cold liquid hit my shoes, soak into my jeans.

But then her fingers were gripping my arms and she was crawling up my body, lips fusing to mine, one leg wrapping around my waist. I reacted instantly, driving my tongue deeply into her mouth, grabbing that lush thigh, snagging the other so she was straddling my waist.

Short.

She was too short. I had to strain to reach her—

But fuck, I loved having her curves beneath my hands.

Loved it so much that I spun, pinning her against one of the pillars of the pergola, seeing the shadows from the lights overhead dance across her body, her face.

I wanted to see it glimmer all along her naked skin.

I *needed*—

Her hands moved, sliding to my middle, dipping beneath the hem of my shirt. I sucked in a breath when they skated over my stomach then up, fingers gliding along my pecs, nails dragging over my nipples.

Need reached a boiling point, and I started to reach for the button of her jeans.

Flicked it open.

I had a condom in my wallet. I always did.

It would be so easy to tug down her jeans, to yank open the fly on mine.

Her teeth found my bottom lip, nipped, sending a bolt of pain through me. It barely hurt, the slight sting sending my control splintering.

Yeah.

I wanted to fuck her.

Right there.

Right *now*.

Hefting her up, I kissed her harder, grabbed the tag of the zipper—

And it was like someone had gripped handfuls of my hair and wrenched tightly, dragging my mouth from hers, shaking me fiercely.

Not here.

I couldn't fuck her *here*.

Fourteen

Bailey

I was distantly aware of movement, of Axel taking his mouth from mine and carrying me somewhere.

Distantly because I was touching that chest I'd seen twice before, caressing the muscles, feeling them bounce beneath my palms, his nipples tightening under my fingertips. Then I was stroking across his stomach.

Hard abs.

Strong arms.

Down.

A hard—

Holy hell, the top of his cock was resting against his stomach and pushing out above the waistband of his underwear. Ignoring the fact that he was still carrying me—because his cock was like a hypnotist's pendulum, and my gaze couldn't go anywhere else—I licked my lips as I stared at the hardened tip, moisture beading at the top, the taut skin pulled tight over the blunt head.

If I was feeling insecure about what he wanted—or if he wanted *me*—the amount of precum currently making my mouth water, not to mention the hard dick, would have made that clear.

This man wanted me.

But I *wasn't* feeling insecure.

I was on fucking *fire*.

I wanted him.

I *needed* him.

Stroking down his stomach, I shoved my hand into his underwear, wrapping my fingers around his cock.

He cursed, choking on a groan.

My pussy clenched, an empty, needy bitch, and I needed him. *Needed*.

In my mouth. Inside *me*. In my hands. Between my breasts. Hard and pulsing on my tongue as his cum slid down my throat.

One touch had struck the match and I was burning, desperate, ready to fuck him right *freaking* then and there. His arms were still around me, his mouth on mine for another searing taste before drifting to my cheek, my jaw, my throat, nipping and licking and kissing as he continued leading me toward...somewhere I hoped would lead to his hands coming back to my pants, only dragging them down this time instead of stopping.

And the focus on my pants being solely a prerequisite to getting them out of the way so that he could push that giant cock inside me and fuck me into oblivion.

"Killing me, buttercup," he breathed against my skin, his lips and tongue working there and slowly driving me insane.

"Why?" I murmured, stroking my thumb over a throbbing vein on his shaft.

"Because I'm trying to get you back to my place when all I really want to do is fuck you right here and now."

My heart thudded.

My breath caught.

Then I said, "Okay."

He dropped his forehead to mine then huffed out a laugh, nipped my lips, and I tasted his smile. "Okay?"

"If I'm pretending this is a moment of insanity"—which I was, mostly because I was suddenly dying to fuck Axel, and my fingers were around his cock, and I couldn't make sense of *why* I was going to do something so fucking stupid, so...insanity—"then I could go for a little public sex."

I'd deal with the consequences later.

I'd deal with *all* of it later.

Axel froze, eyes blazing as he looked down at me.

"My apartment is around the corner," he murmured. "Public sex later."

"Late—"

My words were cut off by his lips, his tongue.

And then he was moving again, or maybe it was that we never *stopped* moving, and I was just so enamored of those bright blue eyes and the muscled body and the hard cock that was currently pulsing against my palm that I hadn't noticed that he could walk and carry me *and* talk, and then kiss me and carry me *and* walk, all without bringing us into the path of a speeding car or running into a pole or something.

That was probably mostly due to everyone in River's Bend being either in their beds or inside Monroe's.

No cars on the road to be hit by.

But he was kissing me, and I was ending a long-held drought, and he was sexy and a good kisser, and I held the man's cock in my hands and—

I wasn't going to worry about cars or the population's sleeping habits.

Instead, I was thinking about the feel of Axel's tongue as it stroked against mine, how his arms were so strong as they held me seemingly without effort. How the cool air on my skin did nothing to cool the fire blazing through me.

How...I just wanted.

So, I kissed him back as he ascended the stairs, held tight when he shifted me to the side to unlock a door.

And then, when we were inside, I tugged at his shirt.

But I didn't get far, didn't get it much more than an inch up before he spun us, pinning me between him and the door.

One long, heated draw on my mouth, his tongue probing deeply, his lips fierce against mine.

Then my feet hit the floor.

A big hand pressing my back and shoulders against the door one more time.

And Axel...oh fucking hell...Axel dropped to his knees.

Oh, *fuck*.

He was tall, much taller than me, but that height difference hadn't seemed so great when I was in his arms, my legs wrapped around his waist.

But when he was kneeling in front of me, his mouth even with my breasts, his hands coming to my jeans, dragging the zipper down, yanking the material to my ankles, and his size was...absolutely intoxicating.

A tug at one of my boots had it sliding from my foot. He tossed it over his shoulder and was on my next boot before the first even thudded to the ground.

Then the second was gone, my pants were whipped from my legs.

"Fuck," he growled.

I jumped, confused by the rumble of sound, even more so by the hands gripping my hips, spinning me so I was face-first against the door.

"This *fucking* ass," he rumbled, his hand smoothing slowly over my curves.

A yank had one side of my plain cotton panties tugged up, my cheek exposed.

"I've been dreaming about this ass," he rasped.

A bite of pain...no, a *bite*, I realized as the sting had moisture pooling between my legs, gathering at the tops of my thighs. But it was quickly soothed by tongue and lips and then he was tugging up the other side of my underwear, kissing his way over, fingers drifting slowly up my legs.

"Fuck," he murmured, hand moving around to my front, brushing over the damp material of my panties, pressing lightly on my clit. "I've been dreaming about *this* too."

I opened my mouth to say...something.

But then he tugged my hips sharply back, making me brace myself on the wooden panel, and the words caught in my throat.

My underwear disappeared, and my gasp turned into a moan and then a squeal when his mouth took its place. Long strokes of his tongue that built heat in my center, nips from his teeth that sent shivers through me, a press of one broad finger inside then two, causing my head to fall forehead against the door, my hips to arch back against his mouth, his fingers, his tongue.

"Oh, fuck," I breathed.

"Mmm." A rough groan, the sound vibrating through me.

"Oh, fuck," I breathed again.

Another groan, another finger slipping into me, and then his mouth closed over my clit, sucking deeply, tongue flicking, and—

"Fuck. Oh, fuck. *Fuck*. I'm going to—"

I didn't finish the sentence.

Because his tongue began working faster.

Because...I was going to come, and I was going to do it right then and—

Oh my God.

I was coming and holy shit, it was a brutal pleasure. No coaxing. No gentle wave flowing over me.

It was a nuclear bomb detonating directly over me.

Pleasure exploded through my body, bursting from my middle, flaming through my limbs.

And he didn't stop, not as the pleasure began to fade, not as my body went limp. He merely wrapped one big arm around me, holding me close, his fingers still deep and moving inside me as he began walking.

Long strides down a dark hall.

My breath shooting out of me when a soft mattress hit my back, when those fingers slipped from my pussy.

The lights flicked on.

I blinked against the sudden brightness.

Then Axel Finnegan was on top of me, spreading my thighs, his eyes absolutely on fire.

And I couldn't wait to be reduced to ashes.

FIFTEEN

AXEL

My hands trembled as they slid up her thighs.

Golden skin, strong legs...bare pussy.

That was a surprise, a good one, all those glistening folds on display for me.

Bending slowly, I pressed a kiss to one hip bone and then the other.

Then the area in between.

Then because she tasted like heaven and I needed her on my tongue again, I kissed her. Right on that bare pussy, avoiding her clit because I knew it would still be sensitive, delving into her folds and dragging my tongue through all that moisture.

Liquid heat.

Thighs trembling.

Her stomach clenching and releasing even as it was only halfway on display, because she still had her flannel and shirt and bra—I assumed—on. I needed to get to that, to get them off her, but how could I with the feast in front of me?

She hissed out a breath when I hit a particularly sensitive spot on her labia, so I focused there, sucking and licking until her moans came louder and faster, until she gripped my hair, until her thighs tried to close on me.

I pushed her legs farther apart, dipped my tongue deeply into her and redoubled my efforts.

A shudder. "Axel."

I kept going, using the pressure and pattern I'd learned that made her explode in my front hall. I kept going until she was shaking, until those fingers delved into my hair, dug into my scalp, held me to her.

I kept going until my name was a shriek on her lips, until she shook so fiercely that I half-worried she was going to fall to pieces.

Then she slumped to the mattress, her legs going limp around me.

I meant to keep going easy—or, well, not *easy* because I wasn't the kind of guy to fuck easy—but I'd intended to stay in control, to make this night the best ever for her.

To get her so addicted to me that she would come back and—

Wait.

What?

But before that thought could penetrate, Bailey *moved.*

Suddenly, I was on my back, and she was climbing over me, her hands on my shoulders and pressing me down into the mattress.

"Buttercup—"

Her mouth covered mine, tongue driving deep, hands gripping the sides of my face as she proceeded to kiss the fuck out of me.

I reached for the hem of her top, tugging it and her flannel off.

It bunched at her shoulders for a moment before she broke the kiss, and then she yanked the material over her head, tossing it to the side, leaving her in a plain beige bra that shouldn't have been sexy.

But it was.

Plumping those curves up until they threatened to spill over.

Then she was reaching behind her, arching back as she unsnapped her bra, and revealing...

Holy hell, she had great tits.

Big wasn't the half of it—because they *were* big, with perfectly-sized, puffy nipples. It was the way they bounced and hung and just fucking made my palms itch with the need to have them in my hands.

And my mouth.

I needed to taste her there, too.

She was reaching for my shirt, yanking *that* up, and since I wanted to be naked just as much as I wanted my mouth on her again, I let her.

And same went when she went for my pants.

I let her undo the zipper, drag the material down my legs.

She didn't get them far, but since my cock popped free, it was far enough, especially when she slid down my body and sucked my dick into her mouth.

Deep.

Wet.

A lot of suction.

A firm grip.

And...I lost my patience.

My hips jerked up, and I hit the back of her throat. Clumsy. Definitely an asshole move, since she wasn't prepared for it.

But...she was incredible.

She didn't cough or choke or push me away.

She just dipped down, sucked me deeper, gripped me tighter, and...*fucking* blew me.

Until my hips were jerking uncontrollably. Until sweat sheeted my body. Until my hands shook, and my thighs cramped and—

Fuck it.

I tore her off me before I exploded, tossing her up the mattress, barely having the presence of mind to stop her head from hitting the bedpost.

Then I was reaching for my nightstand, ripping the drawer open, rifling through the contents, desperate for a condom. Shit hit the floor, but I didn't care what it was, or that I heard shit shattering. *Nothing* was more important in that moment than getting inside her.

Finally, my fingers closed on the plastic square, and I lurched back, tearing it open with my teeth and rolling it down my cock.

Fuck.

It was hard.

I was shaking, my control on the precipice of snapping.

And...I was big.

And Bailey was small. So small that some of the need that had seized me waned. Because I was six-six, two hundred and ten pounds. She was...five-three? *Maybe* four. And though she was curvy, she couldn't have been more than a hundred and thirty pounds.

I was going to kill her, smother her, rip her to shreds, hurt—

"What?" she asked, chest heaving, breasts jiggling.

I wanted to not give a fuck, a worry. I wanted to shove her legs wide, to pound deep into her.

It was what I would have done with anyone else.

But...I was worried.

Which was why I snagged her and rolled to my back, bringing her on top.

Her lips parted, a gasp in the air.

I wrapped my hands around her hips, drew her down. "Ride me, buttercup."

Those lips went back together, curved into a smile, eyes dancing. "Yeah?"

I couldn't form words, so I just nodded, and thank fuck, she began to lower herself, notching my tip inside, and then, making my eyes roll back, curses litter the air, she sank down. Slowly, yes, but not stopping until her pelvis rested atop mine, until I was fully seated, until her tight, wet pussy was clasping my cock so fiercely that I nearly exploded before she even began moving.

"You're big," she whispered, shifting herself from side to side, making every single muscle in my body go tense, my orgasm already prickling at the base of my spine. "Fuck, you're *big.*"

She sucked in a breath, released it as a moan.

"Fuck," she breathed, lifting up and down slowly. "*Fuck.*"

Fuck was right.

She felt...perfect. Incredible. A fucking wet dream come to life.

I smirked, kept my hands on her hips. "Move, buttercup."

She *had* to move, or I might fucking die.

Dramatic? Yes. But she was clamping down on me like a vise and I was going to come, and yeah, she'd had two orgasms, but she hadn't had one with me inside her yet.

And I might be an asshole, but I always pleased my partners.

Which meant I didn't come without them. Or before them. Or—

"Fuck," I whispered as she rippled around me again.

But luckily, she started moving, and I got my hands on her breasts, on her nipples, rolling them lightly between thumb and forefinger, then harder when she moaned, arched forward, and demanded, "More."

Her head fell back, and she began moving faster, hips jerking, my name tumbling off her lips.

She was close.

Thank fuck.

I reached down between us, pressed my thumb to her clit, circling it firmly, grabbing at one of her hips when she bucked, holding her to me, making sure she didn't falter as she kept grinding me hard and deep and—

"Axel," she murmured, head snapping forward, eyes blazing when they hit mine. "I need—"

She was close.

But not *there*.

Flipping us, I started stroking into her.

"Yes. Oh, fuck," she whispered. "Oh fuck. Harder, baby, *harder*."

That I could do.

I positioned her beneath me until I was hitting the spot inside her that had her gripping me tighter, and then I fucked her hard and fast, her pussy convulsing around me, her nails digging into my shoulders, her moans coming in quick succession.

"Oh, my *God*—"

She arched her neck back against the pillows, hips rising up to meet mine.

My name tumbled from her lips, the slick sounds of us coming together driving me closer to that edge.

But that was okay.

Because, thank fuck, she was there, too.

Nails digging deeper into my skin. Legs locking around my hips.

Pussy gripping me tight and—

She came apart, but I could barely watch her because my orgasm had wrapped around my body and yanked me roughly under. It exploded out from the base of my spine, shooting into my limbs, my movements going jerky as pleasure burst through me.

Nirvana.

The best fucking *ever.*

No.

The best *fucking* ever.

I collapsed down, barely able to catch myself so I didn't crush her and rolled us to the side, fingers stroking small patterns on the skin of her back, sending them through the strands of her hair.

My head was spinning.

Panic was chasing those tendrils of pleasure.

I was rocked to my fucking core and didn't have a fucking clue what to say.

Which was probably why I blurted, loudly and roughly, "I'm going to clean up."

Her gaze came to my face, but I didn't let it connect with mine.

"Right," she whispered.

And if my gait into the bathroom was more walk than run, then it was only because she seemed as rocked as I was—her eyes wide, her face pale, no more words coming.

I took my time cleaning up, washing my hands and dick and hands again because that shit should be done in the right order and I was so fucked that I was doing it wrong and—

I gripped the edge of the counter, hung my head.

"Fuck, Axel," I whispered, gaze coming to the mirror.

Taking in my own wide eyes, my own pale face.

"What was that?" I asked my reflection.

Except, I thought I knew.

And it absolutely terrified me.

So much so, that it took me a fucking lifetime—or so it seemed—to force myself out of the bathroom, my hand shaking when I turned the knob, knees practically knocking together as I tried to steel myself.

I needn't have bothered.
Because Bailey was gone.

Sixteen

Bailey

I brushed Data's flank, her soft chestnut hair shining in the morning light.

It was beautiful.

She was beautiful.

And normally, I'd be able to appreciate those things. I'd made an effort to find the beauty in the small stuff after coming home to find that my parents had fucked up Gramps' legacy, after working my ass off for the last two years, after digging myself and the property out of the reverse mortgage hole.

Because I'd spent too long in the dark to waste any more time not appreciating the light.

But this morning, like every other morning of the last couple of weeks, I was...unsettled.

And I was spending all my extra energy trying to pretend that I wasn't, or at least trying to pretend that the reason I *was* so disconcerted wasn't one Axel Fucking Finnegan.

"Come on, Bay," I whispered to myself, running the brush along Data's side. "Head down, move forward. Meet your goal. Get the fuck out." Data whinnied angrily, as though she knew what I was saying and wasn't happy her built-in spa service was talking about leaving.

Either that, or all my *unsettled* was making me lose my mind.

Yeah.

Probably the second. Because I kept right on conversing with a horse.

"Or stay," I soothed, brushing Data in earnest now. "Maybe I'll stay when I can afford help and can actually live and travel and eat at the occasional fancy restaurant and maybe I can finish my teaching degree and get a pedicure or wear clothes that aren't at risk of getting covered in horseshit, or..."

I put down the brush, wove my fingers through Data's mane.

"Who am I kidding?" I whispered. "I would always come right back."

As much as I hated the burden of the farm, I'd always felt at home here. Even though I hadn't grown up in River's Bend, even though my parents had moved me all over the fucking Bay Area. So many schools that I couldn't count—or, rather, I *could* count (I'd been in ten of them). More places to live than that—and often leaving them in the middle of the night, our stuff shoved into the back of the car, searching out the next poor soul to mooch off.

River's Bend.

This farm.

Stability.

Warm. *Home*. A break from my flighty parents.

To Gramps and Gram and even fucking Billie Rose (though she'd been way less interfering back then).

Even without Gramps and Gran, the people in this town were more than just friends or acquaintances. They were my family.

They'd been there, a constant source of stability my entire life.

So, I might groan and gripe about having to put off getting my teaching credential, having to come back, to step in and save Russet Ranch.

But this was also my *place*.

Plus, it had been the perfect opportunity to escape from...

To forget about—

Gravel crunching.

I turned just in time to see a familiar little SUV tear into my driveway, spraying rocks in all directions—and I made a mental note that when it came time to spread fresh gravel in a couple of months' time that Billie Rose would be helping.

"I'll get her a fucking shovel with her damn name emblazoned on it," I muttered.

Of course, Billie would probably show up before the sun had risen with bells on and loving that she could help someone...which would make the punishment very much *less* like a punishment, at least in my mind.

Probably to truly have an effect on her, I should force her to sit and watch while the rest of us worked.

Which would defeat the entire purpose.

But then again, I often felt defeated when it came to Billie Rose.

Smothering a sigh, I braced myself for the hurricane that would be my aunt.

The mayor of River's Bend hopped out of her car, her curls bouncing, her slacks and blouse clean and crisp and yet, paired—some might say incongruously—with sneakers. This was only if someone didn't know her, because those who *did* know her, knew that any heels she wore were strictly for appearing put together and in charge during her daily meetings. *I,* for instance, knew Billie had a pair of pumps in her trunk for when she would head back to City Hall and start making her way through her agenda for the day.

So take that little tidbit and—

I shook myself, watched her approach.

Billie Rose *was* River's Bend, through and through, and that meant hard-working (and ever-ready to jump in with those sneaker-clad feet), down to earth, and with limited patience for fancy and high maintenance. It went without saying that my aunt was pretty and her makeup complemented that, but it wasn't heavy or overstated. Simple. Optimized for high performance.

River's Bend to a T.

This small town in one tiny woman.

"Bailey," she called, the door slamming behind her as she began to storm my way with all the grace of a cow being flung around a fictional tornado. "I need you!"

Okay, maybe I was wrong.

Perhaps her makeup and clothing style was actually optimized for pushiness.

Or demanding-ness? Or—

"Bailey!" Her sneakers crunched loudly over the gravel.

A smothered sigh as I set aside the brush, turned to face Billie. "What's up?"

Brows narrowing. "Don't take that tone with me," she clipped.

My own brows snapped down. "Don't take *that* tone with *me,*" I countered.

Her frown deepened. Then cleared, mouth tipping up at the edges. "You know normal people are afraid of me."

"You *know,*" I said (or rather, continued countering), "I once had to rescue you from a dress because you couldn't get out of it—"

"That was scary!" she exclaimed, smile dying. "It was too tight, and I couldn't breathe—"

"Or operate zippers?" I asked dryly

"It was *hidden.*"

I shot her a look. "Yup. *So* difficult." I lifted my arm, looked down at my rib cage, and mimed undoing the "hidden" zipper.

"Brat," Billie rose muttered.

"Yup." I smiled. "Now, what do you need?"

Billie's expression went down-to-business. "The harvest parade is coming up."

Oh, Christ. The harvest parade was hell in the form of orange and yellow and red leaves, plastic gourds, and leftover uncarved pumpkins (since our California heat typically turned the carved ones to mush in less than a week).

Was I a monster who hated Thanksgiving?

Fuck, yeah.

But there was nothing worse than sitting around with my parents on that holiday, especially when they usually failed to show up in the first place (which meant that I ended up sitting around by myself for hours), and on the odd times they *did* show up to the festivities, they created drama and then flitted out, none the more aware of the train wreck they left in their wake. *Or*—and this had been rare growing up—it was spent with my *other* family.

With Billie's lovely, well-adjusted, super sweet and rosy (*ha*) parents and siblings.

They didn't live in River's Bend any longer, her parents moving to Palm Springs because they loved the weather, and her siblings having scattered across the state and country for work, but growing up, and even on the rare occasions I saw them now, they made my parents look like...well, monsters.

So Thanksgiving.

I wasn't there for it.

But Thanksgiving in River's Bend was H-E-Double-Hockey-Sticks.

No. Not thinking of hockey, because that would bring thoughts of Axel and our night and—

Double no.

The point was that Thanksgiving meant there was a parade. I might be a monster who didn't enjoy the holidays, but parades were worse. They were basically writhing masses of snotty and screaming kids, parents who were determined to one-up each other with costumes and all too much togetherness for my isolated-ranch-loving heart.

But Billie Rose naturally liked—okay *loved*—parades. Because she loved all things River's Bend and togetherness and bolstering town spirit.

And never mind that I'd just been thinking about how much I loved it just before Billie had shown up.

I was a cranky rancher.

I didn't do parades or color-coded costumes and—

Billie Rose had been Miss Harvest Parade 2012.

I knew this because even though I hadn't been here for the parade that particular year, Billie had come down to San Francisco with her mom, and the three of us had gone shopping for her dress in Union Square. It was where the zipper incident had gone down and when I'd put my superior rescuing skills to work—here I mentally buffed my knuckles on my shoulder. *Go me.*

Of course—and this had nothing to do with my hatred of the Harvest Festival and its corresponding parade—but I knew about Billie's victory because I'd wanted to go.

Because my mom had promised to drive me up for the festivities.

And...

Then she'd flaked.

Surprise? No.

It was very much *not* a surprise and there was no point in being upset about it and—

Anyway, my past didn't change the fact that parades were the devil and I sincerely disliked that I was going to be helping with one. *Going to* because Billie was going to ask and I was going to say yes, and *yes,* there would be lots of grumbling and lots of sighing and lots of cursing under my breath so the snotty, screamy kids and their one-upping parents couldn't hear.

But I was going to help.

Because Billie Rose was going to ask.

"Horses," I said, focusing back on the issue at hand. "Is that what you want?"

Billie's curls bounced as she nodded her head, and then no joke —*no joke*—she pulled out a clipboard from her pocket. How? Where—? But Billie Rose was listing off more *wants.* "Friendly ones for pony rides. And I also need four dozen hay bales, three saddles, and a variety of farm implements—"

"Where did you get—?" *Wait.* "Farm implements?" Like pitch forks and shit that people might impale themselves on? I shook my head. "No, that's not happening. Yes, on the bales of hay and saddles," I added quickly as Billie's expression turned thunderous. "I can also provide a baby cow."

Yes, technically it was a calf (a steer, really, since I'd relieved him of his balls), but Billie was Billie, and a baby *cow,* even if that was the wrong technical term, would distract her from *farm implements.* God help me if Billie got it in her head to decorate the parade route with pitch forks or heavy tillers that might fall and smash into a toddler's head, or worse and yet still somehow in the realm of possibility for my aunt, rail posts with rusty nails in them.

Now *that* would be a theme.

This year's Harvest Parade—Tetanus for Everyone!

Okay, so it probably wouldn't be fencing. That was important to *me*, but it couldn't be to Billie. Plus, I didn't think she would categorize posts, nails, and barbed wire as farm implements.

So…what?

Those pitchforks? Corroded saw blades? Plows? Hoes? Horseshoes?

Okay, the last would be okay…unless one of those snotty, screamy kids decided to chuck one at my head and—

Right.

Enough with the snotty, screamy kids.

Luckily, my distraction worked.

"A baby *cow?*" Billie shrieked, making me jump. Her face lit up. "Really?" The last was somehow even louder, and I resisted the urge to clamp my hands over my ears.

"Really," I agreed, nodding toward the barn and the stall I currently had the late-season calf in. Mama cow had rejected him, and so I was the softie currently feeding Picard three times a day by bottle.

Yeah, I was a closet Star Trek nerd.

No, I wasn't going to tell anyone that his name was Picard.

I led the way inside, opened the wooden door, and revealed the black calf.

Billie Rose's squeals of excitement got louder. So loud that she startled Picard, his cute (which was the reason I'd brought him down and was feeding him three times a day—though thankfully, the vet had said I could stop with the middle of the night bottles) head shooting up, his *cow* (okay, easy on the pun, *steer*) eyes going wide and showing off the whites surrounding them.

I swatted Billie. "Have you forgotten everything about working with animals?"

She wasn't listening to me. Instead, she was already moving into the stall and kneeling at Picard's side, her arms going around the little steer's neck and hugging him tight. He was a love bug and ate up any attention I'd been able to spare him so far, so it was no surprise that he cuddled right up into Billie's lap, getting hay and dust all over her clothes.

But I knew that she probably had a change of them in her trunk, next to those heels. Billie Rose was nothing if not prepared.

Annoying.

A busybody.

But prepared.

And, I supposed, lovable, loyal, hard-working, and persistent.

I hated that I was finding good things in her. However, I also knew all of my hate and annoyance and frustration with my aunt and her busybody ways was because I was *unsettled*.

Because of Axel Finnegan and his magnificent cock.

Because—

"I love you."

I blinked, brows drawing together, fear coiling in my stomach, fear and something else. The possibility of something, the *need* of something, the longing and—

"I love you, my little smuffikins," Billie Rose semi-repeated, hugging Picard tight. "Who's my baby?" She glanced up, her blue eyes locking with mine. "What's her name?"

"His," I corrected. "And his name is..." Fuck. What was something that was sensible and rancher-tough and—right, the tough ranchers probably didn't even name their cattle. Just marched them right up onto the truck and—

"Cow," I blurted.

"Cow?" Billie Rose asked incredulously and decided *that* was the moment she'd begin remembering her animal husbandry skills and bovine terminology. Not when she'd been shrieking her way through the barn. *Now* she remembered that a cow referred to a female. "I thought you said he was a boy?"

Well, I couldn't admit to having named him Picard now, could I?

I had *one* secret.

Well...a *few*. But the least toxic of those was my closet nerdiness.

"Cow," I confirmed, more firmly this time.

Her eyes narrowed, fixed me in place. "This is one of your stupid nerd names, isn't it?"

Okay, so maybe Billie Rose knew most of my secrets.

Well, I wasn't giving her any more fuel to dig deeper, to discover the ones I'd buried deep.

"I don't know what you're talking about," I said innocently.

Too innocently.

Billie's brows lifted. "Bailey," she warned.

Shit.

I straightened my shoulders. "The steer's name is Cow."

A sigh. "*Bailey.*"

"It's *Cow.*"

She just stared at me.

Christ. I plunked my hands on my hips, and then I did the only thing I could—

"What kind of farm implements do you want?"

Seventeen

Axel

"Hey, man!" Joel called as I tossed my bag into my car. "They're finally letting us back into Haggarty's, and I've got a plethora of small-town girls who are bored and looking for a wild night coming."

"Go you."

Joel narrowed his eyes. "What's with you?"

"Nothing." I rolled my shoulders, the tension from the phone call that had premeditated me packing my shit already eating at me.

"Oh shit, you got a call up, didn't you?" Joel asked.

I nodded, went for casual. "Yeah."

A punch to my shoulder. "That's a fucking good thing, yeah?"

"Yeah," I muttered. "It's great."

Joel searched my face. "Doesn't sound like you think it's great. That's the call we all want to get, so why are you acting like someone cut off your dick?"

"I'm not. I just have a long drive ahead of me."

Silence.

Rightly reading that I was less excited and more...anxious, regretful, trying to sort out a fucking tangle of emotions inside my head that had me really wanting to stay in River's Bend with this fucker and the guys and drink my way into oblivion.

But...I didn't want to be like my mother.

"I need to go. They want me there for practice with the Gold in the morning."

"You got this."

"I know."

Penetrating green eyes then, "Right, man. Whatever you say. You know, if you talked about shit every once in a while—"

I sighed. "Just back off, okay?"

"Same shit different day with you, isn't it?" Joel shook his head. "Can't get out of your own fucking way."

"Fuck you."

"Fuck *you* right back."

God, Joel was an annoying fucker. Especially when he cracked a grin.

"Do me a favor," I said, tugging my phone out of my pocket and ignoring the smirk. "Don't trash Haggarty's, yeah?"

"Yeah, we already talked about that," Joel muttered. "After the mayor from hell paid you several visits." He shuddered. "That woman is a fucking menace."

Yeah, I'd had to cop to the kidnapping when he gave me a ride.

But I'd also shared later that the team's contract was at risk, that we might soon be viewed as fucking lepers in the hockey world.

He'd agreed to help me get the guys to cool it.

Mostly because we'd been the ringleaders and if *we* were cooling it, then the guys would cool it.

Still, I reiterated, "No broken glasses or windows. No being dicks to the locals."

A scowl, his legendary temper sparking. "Like I *said*, we've already talked about this. I'm on board with you getting the guys on track. But that doesn't mean I'm not going to go out and tie one on when the fancy strikes."

I started to sink down into the driver's seat. "Yeah, I know."

"You go spend four hours driving and fucking with your own head." He tilted his head toward Main Street. "I'll enjoy all the pussy you're missing out on."

"Great," I muttered. "Have fun with that."

A smirk, his temper already gone.

Probably, because I *was* facing a long drive with a fucked-up head.

"Oh, I will."

I leaned back against the wall of the locker room and watched the people buzzing around—players, media, support staff. The same as the Rush, except magnified to an nth degree.

Like comparing small potatoes to...bigger ones.

And that right there was my high school education.

The point was, more money, bigger back office, more...opportunity.

Though not for me.

I'd played two games at the Gold Mine, and now...I was heading back to River's Bend.

Same shit, different day.

Up and down, back and forth.

Not finding my place.

Cotton candy in your head, boy. No point in making dreams. Not for a Finnegan.

And God, I loved hearing my drunk of a mother's voice in my head.

Especially when I'd been told before I'd even had a chance to get undressed that I was being booted right back down.

I'd made it to the third line.

I'd thought...well, I'd thought that this time was different.

Good plays, more ice time. I'd even made it onto the scoresheet—and not for a penalty this time. Instead, I'd made a great pass over to Ben who'd managed to sneak it in for a goal that had tied the game. Total clutch. And...it didn't fucking matter. I was going right back to Bumfuck, California, where I couldn't even drink my way into oblivion because then I might fuck up the small sliver of a chance I had at making it back here again and then a scary, curly-haired blond woman might handcuff me to the porch of a woman who pointed shotguns at me and nearly sawed my balls off with power tools, and—

"Hey."

I jerked, cracking my head against the shelving overhead, and reminding me that—in this case, luckily—I was still wearing my helmet.

Ripping it off, I turned to look at Brit.

The goalie—and first female player in the NHL—had played her ass off and still looked fresh enough to play three more games even though rumor had it she was going to retire at the end of the season when her contract was up.

"Hey," I said, plunking my helmet onto the bench next to me.

"You played great tonight."

"Yeah, thanks," I muttered. "You did, too." I bent, started ripping the tape off my socks, waiting for her to leave.

She would.

They always did.

Instead, though, she sat next to me.

Waited.

I needed to get undressed—or at least to get my gear off then move into the private locker room to shower.

Another difference.

No press in the locker rooms in River's Bend, no need to worry about scarring some child who stumbled onto a sports blog's live stream.

I could just dump all my gear on the floor, get naked, and then—

"What's the deal with you, anyway?"

I glanced up from my socks, saw her brows had dragged together. "What do you mean?"

"Talented player. No fucking passion."

Now my brows dragged together. "I—"

She shrugged. "You see glimpses of it on the ice, moments of greatness, and then..." A flutter of her hand. "It's just...*gone.*"

I yanked my jersey over my head. "Well, thanks for the pep talk."

"I've never actually seen someone so skilled just...*not* have it." She leaned back and crossed one ankle over the other. "Or not maintain it anyway," she said. "Because that pass to Ben was sweet.

Same as your work in the defensive zone." Her eyes were considering. "So, the question is, where does that all go?"

I knew *exactly* where that all went, and that was down the fucking drain because I was a pathetic nobody who would never—

"Doesn't matter," I said, cutting the pity train off as I yanked my shoulder pads over my head, tugged my elbow pads down and off my arms.

"Except, I'd kind of think you'd be good on the roster."

One shin guard. Then the other. "Right."

She punched me in the shoulder.

Hard.

"Ow!" I exclaimed. "What?" I asked, getting to work on my skates.

A flash of white teeth. "You know what."

"I know that goalies are fucking weird," I muttered.

She snorted. "Original."

"And I know that I'm not ever going to be on the roster —permanently."

A pause. "Yeah? How do you know that?"

I sighed, but I didn't jump back onto the pity train, just shrugged, dropped my dirty shit in their respective spots, and then moved into the private locker room. I'd shower. Drive four hours. Get up at dawn to get on a fucking bus to drive eight hours—and basically right past this arena—to SoCal to play with the Rush.

Work hard.

Head down.

Not quite ever enough.

I reached for the waistband of my compression shorts, started to push them down.

"You know—"

I jumped, not realizing that Brit had followed me into the other room, and halted in my undressing, fingers clenching on the fabric.

She smirked. "You ain't got nothing I haven't seen a hundred times before, Axel."

Right.

A woman used to locker rooms and nakedness and—

Still, she turned away when she repeated, "You know, I think I've got a bead on what's going on in that pretty brain of yours."

"Look," I said, pushing down my shorts and stepping into the shower. "We both know that my brain isn't in the realm of pretty."

"Ah," she said after a moment. Her tone went dry. "Because you're just a big, dumb hockey player, do I have that right?"

I didn't comment, just pumped some shampoo into my hair, washed it quickly. Then took care of the rest of my body. By the time I'd finished and wrapped a towel around my waist, Brit had showered, too. She rubbed a sheet of cotton over her hair as we both walked into the locker room to get dressed, but she didn't immediately go to her stall as I expected.

Instead, she sat down next to me and sighed.

"So," she said. "I've been at this a long time, you know that, Finn, yeah?"

"It's Axel."

A grin. "No offense, but Axel is a stupid name. Finn is..."

"A good name for a rabbit?" I offered.

"...a strong, powerful—" Her face clouded, and I didn't blame her. A *rabbit?* No. A fish. A shark. A dolphin, but definitely not a bunny. She shook her head. "Wait, what?"

"Nothing," I said as I tugged on my underwear.

"Right," she replied and shook her head again. "Um, anyway, my point is that I've been doing this a long time."

"I know."

"So, Finn, I've seen a lot of broody males come through this locker room, and I know their moods."

I shot her a look as I pulled on my pants.

She just smiled, wide and bright. "And *your* mood says either you're upset about a woman or you're torturing yourself because you don't think you belong here."

I'd been buttoning my shirt, but her words made me freeze.

Her smile sobered. "Or...both," she murmured.

Clearing my throat, I said, "It's fine, Brit. Don't bother with"—I waved my hand—"all this. It's not worth it."

"*It's* not worth it? Or *you're* not worth it?"

Those words were a fucking punch to the gut, but after a

moment, I kept buttoning. "What do you think your chances are at the Cup this season?"

Silence.

A flicker of sadness in her chocolate brown eyes, but after a moment she said, "Good."

"Good," I repeated. Then I bent to shove my feet into shoes.

"Better, of course, with a full roster," she said, tugging the towel from her head and laying it across her lap.

I grunted, reached for my backpack.

"Right," she said and stood, but just when I thought she was going to finally leave me alone, she stepped close, dropped her voice. "Look, Finny. I'm not trying to be nosy here. Well, I mean, I'm *always* nosy, but in this case, I'm trying to restrain myself, so I'll just say that I don't bullshit about hockey, not to the media, not to my teammates, not to myself. If there's something that needs to be improved, I tell it like it is. And the problem with you—"

My heart began to beat a little faster.

"—isn't what's happening on the ice. It's what's happening in here—"

She tapped my forehead.

"The *only* thing that is wrong with you is that you need to get out of your own way." Her expression was fierce. "You do that," she said. "You figure out how to flush down whatever bullshit is swirling around in there, and you will be *here.*" A wave to the locker room. "Not just for a game or two. But *permanently*."

I inhaled, struggled to figure out what to say.

But she was already gone—striding across the room to her stall.

Getting dressed.

Getting on with her life.

And leaving me...to go back to mine.

Eighteen

Bailey

The knock on my door wasn't surprising.

The person on the other side of the wooden panel was.

I'd been expecting another assault from Billie Rose because I hadn't been to town for a few days and the planning for the Harvest Festival was reaching its fever peak. There would be more asks to be made, volunteer slots to pick up (or be voluntold for).

And I'd say yes.

Because Billie Rose was Billie Rose, and it was impossible to say no.

Because I was me and I *couldn't* say no.

Because the Harvest Festival meant a lot to this town, and I wouldn't let them down.

So, all that being said, I did *not* expect Dessie to be standing on my porch with a bottle of wine in one hand and a plastic bag hanging from the wrist of her other arm.

I sniffed when a delicious scent hit my nose. "Is that Danika's?"

A wave, the plastic crinkling. "Would I take a drive down to Sacramento for any other food?"

Scandinavian and Mexican fusion shouldn't be good.

Danika's didn't follow the rules of anything that *should be.*

It was part bakery, part restaurant, part shop, and all tiny hole-in-the-wall, non-credit-card-accepting vessel of deliciousness.

"Tacos?" I asked.

Or maybe begged.

A nod. "Pork. And that smørrebrød you like"—an open-faced sandwich on homemade rye bread that was already making my mouth water—"*and* that beet salad you like, and—"

Lagkage.

Please let it be *lagkage*. I needed three layers of sponge cake, fruit, and pastry cream in my mouth, and I needed it now.

"Lagkage."

I did a happy dance, and I wasn't shy about showing it as I pulled open the door farther and let Dessie—and, it had to be said, *the food*—in.

"Did you just only let me in because I have Danika's?"

A grin. "Yup."

"Rude," Dessie said, moving down the hall, but she only made it a few feet because then she halted.

Presumably spying the mess that was my family room.

I'd hauled Gran's old couch to the back porch and would eventually get it into the back of Gramps's truck so I could take it to the dump. The carpet and some of the subflooring would be joining the party, along with some of the sheetrock I'd cut out to investigate the leak.

Investigate, try to cobble together a repair, and knowing that I was going to need more help.

"Told you I was busy," I said dryly, hitching my head toward the kitchen, considering that was the only place I currently had more than one place to sit.

"Yeah, I see now that you weren't lying." She set the bag on the counter, started pulling out takeout containers.

I moved to the cabinet and snagged two wineglasses, then snagged the opener from a drawer. Dessie had been here often enough to retrieve a couple of forks and paper towels (I hadn't bothered to buy napkins in years) and then we were both sitting down and digging in.

No polite offerings.

Just two forks going at it.

We'd dug into the lagkage before Dessie hit at the real reason she was there. "Axel Finnegan."

One name.

Not even phrased as a question.

"I'm not going to sleep with him," I said, not quite lying—since I'd *already* slept with him and wasn't going to make that same mistake again.

"Hmm."

"What?"

"He wasn't giving me that vibe."

I shoved a huge bite of cake (and it was extra delicious because they'd put a layer of dulce de leche in amongst that yummy pastry cream), mostly to buy myself time to come up with a response.

"What vibe?" I asked.

That wasn't much of one, but...Danika's food coma had my brain moving sluggishly.

Probably why Dessie had brought it in the first place.

Feed me.

Interrogate me.

They went hand in hand.

"You know you could use him to unwind a little, to get some unhindered adult contact, and hopefully a couple of orgasms and a hard dick."

I'd gotten that.

I'd gotten all three. *Fuck*, had I gotten all three.

And it had left me with...unease.

"I love you, Dessie," I said, "but this isn't a conversation I want to have."

My friend's eyes locked with mine, and I knew she was thinking of my past, of why I might not want to have this conversation. And...I held my breath, expecting her to push.

To my surprise and relief, she didn't.

"Tell me what Billie has commandeered you into doing for the festival," she said before taking another bite of the cake, lips clinging tightly to the tines in order to get every last bit of pastry cream.

I knew the feeling.

I was doing the exact same thing with every bite.

"What *doesn't* she have me doing?"

I was on setup Friday morning, and stations Friday night and Saturday, and cleanup on Sunday.

My weekend was living and breathing the festival, the parade, the snotty-nosed kids.

And...I was semi-looking forward to it.

Or at least, I was getting swept up in Billie's excitement, so it felt less like a chore and instead something fun I was doing for the people of River's Bend...and if I happened to be one of those people...

Then I was trying to embrace it.

"Word," Dessie said. "She got Barry and Roger to donate kegs and wine, so I'm on the first shift of adult beverage distribution, and then I'm doing something with candy corn, something with turkey feathers, and something that involves confetti."

I sighed, held up my fork. "Fucking Billie Rose."

"Fucking Billie Rose," she muttered, clinking her fork to mine.

Then I thought of my fridge filled without asking, how my aunt always showed up for River's Bend. I thought of the kids' excitement and the happy memories that would be made during the festival, and a tendril of guilt coiled through me.

I'd volunteer at a hundred festivals if it meant that I could play a small role in what Billie Rose had built.

So I sighed, shoved another bite of cake in my mouth, chewed, swallowed, and said, "But we love her though."

"Yup. We sure do."

"She might be annoying, but she's our special brand of it."

Dessie clinked my fork again. "Damn right she is."

Nineteen

Axel

I moved to the door of my apartment, a giant thermos of coffee in my hand.

My attempt at getting rid of the fuzziness in my brain.

But not from alcohol for once.

Okay, not *for once*.

It had been weeks since I'd been to the bars in town, weeks since I'd organized any time out with the guys, had allowed myself to be coaxed away from the rink or my apartment to hang with the puck bunnies, weeks since Bailey, since the games with the Gold, since...Brit.

It had just been me and the puck and the ice...and Brit's words.

Just me and *all* of Netflix and not making my way back up to the Gold.

Just me and the bus (and the team...and it went without saying, my noise-canceling earbuds) as we'd been traveling for a shit-ton of games. But even then, it still had been me and DoorDash and going to bed early in my hotel room, earplugs in place because the fucking rookie I was paired with, Bennie, snored like a goddamned chainsaw.

But none of that was the cause of the discord in my mind.

Instead, all that spinning and feeling like I was on my back foot came from...a woman who'd gotten me off my game.

No.

Two women.

Though thankfully, that game had not been my *hockey* game.

I was playing the best I had in years—probably because I wasn't fucking and drinking and staying up all hours of the night. Probably because...Brit's words had stuck in my fucking head.

As much as I tried to ignore them.

And anyway, not staying out, not tearing through town, not drinking...none of that was rocket science. It was something I should have been doing. It was just...

What was the point of trying that hard if I wasn't going to hit my goal?

Stupid, right?

Defeatist for sure.

But I'd spent too many years on the bus, on this team, on others, getting called up for a game or two, enjoying those five-star hotels and the chartered flights and the food and trainers and all the perks that come from being in the big leagues. Then getting bumped back down to the minors, back to the hours on the bus and midlist hotels, the bringing lunch and dinner from home or stopping at some fast-food joint if our order got fucked, or splurging for DoorDash because the food the team provided for us wasn't enough. Then add in a dash of an occasional commercial flight—and all that limited leg room—if we were traveling far enough that the bus travel wasn't going to do it.

But that was rare.

Bus life was where it was at.

My biggest perk in years was that I'd finally been on the team long enough to score my own double seat.

Yup.

I was most excited because I had two bus seats to myself and didn't have to share an armrest.

Go me.

But...I'd been holding on for a while, battling and working my ass off...and for what?

A game with the Gold, maybe two. Hanging on the fourth line, and if someone was injured creeping up to the third, and then right back down with the taste of my dream on my tongue...

And—

The only thing that is wrong with you is that you need to get out of your own way.

Those words. Brit's fucking words.

"There's no point in continuing to try," I muttered, taking a huge sip of the caffeinated brew. "There's no fucking point because I'm never going—"

I froze, those words echoing through my head, the spinning and discord becoming a full-on tornado.

Because I'd heard them before.

Just not from my mouth, but...from my mother's.

Bemoaning the shit hand she'd been dealt. Blaming the universe for not getting what she wanted.

Acting like the world owed her something just because she had been born.

And yeah, I could get behind the world owing everyone equal rights and respect and universal health care and housing, but the world didn't owe me a spot on the Gold, didn't owe me a spot on any NHL team.

And for me to think it did...

Fuck.

That meant I was becoming like *her.*

Soothing the hurts, the disappointment, the hole inside me with booze and fucking.

Blaming everyone else. Being angry.

Being fucking *mean.*

You're a fucking failure, Axel.

You ruined my life.

You're pathetic and—

I Was. Turning. Into. My. Mother.

Letting the disappointments turn me into someone terrible, someone mean, someone...pathetic.

I'd never believed those words then.

But here—*now*—sitting in this empty apartment, feeling like *this*, reflecting on the last years with the Rush...what I'd done to this town, what I'd done to the women I'd been with, how carelessly I'd treated them.

Taking what they offered and then sending them on their way so I could move on to the next and the next and—

My feet slid to a stop, my lungs filling in one sharp inhale, and I blinked back against the sting of that...

That...

Fucking painful truth.

What I'd done to *myself.*

My mother.

I was turning into my *mother*.

I sank to my knees, yanked out my cell, fingers fumbling as I jabbed at the screen. Not her. Not her.

I might be an asshole.

But I couldn't be *her.*

The call rang—once, twice, three times—

And, fuck, what was I doing.

Calling my *mom?*

Sick as fuck.

I started to lift my cell from my ear to end the call when she picked up—

"Hello?"

Her voice was the same—a complete glimpse into her emotional state and...that of our relationship.

"Hello?" she asked again. A male voice in the background, coming closer. My mother's tone growing somehow even more chipper, a teenager-esque giggle coming across the airwaves. "Hello? I—" There was fumbling, like she was going to hang up.

"Mom," I said.

Silence.

That fumbling stopping.

"Axel."

Giggles gone. Icicles in every syllable.

"Mom," I repeated, and then, somehow, because I couldn't hang up, "How are you doing?"

Calculating.

Her voice immediately went calculating, "I've really been struggling."

Fuck.

"I'm sorry to hear that."

"*Really* struggling." A sniff. "I-I—" A wobble in her tone I was well familiar with. "I've been struggling to even buy groceries in this day and age."

"I can send you some."

"Really?" she exclaimed. "I think six hundred should cover it. Just the essentials, you know—"

I closed my eyes as she prattled on, letting my head fall back against the wall.

"So, when are you going to send it, baby? I've got Venmo now and my handle is—"

"Groceries, Mom," I said. "I'll send you groceries."

"What?"

"I can have groceries delivered to your apartment. Do you want 2% or fat-free milk?"

"I-I—*Axel.*"

Little daggers of ice flying toward my eardrums. I'd stopped sending her money seven years ago because she'd lit a fucking stick of dynamite and tossed it at my career and hadn't given one fuck. And because it had never been enough. She'd wanted me to become some version of The Boyfriends, giving and giving until I was sucked dry. Because...it was always about her.

"I'm fine, Mom," I said dryly. "Thanks for asking."

Silence.

Then she sighed. "Is that what this is about?" she snapped. "That I like to live my own life? I put *everything* on hold for you. *Everything* and you've never been grateful. *Never.*"

"I know it was hard to be a single mom," I said.

A scoff. "*Do* you?"

"I do."

"So, you'll send it?" she asked. "A thousand to make it a nice round number?"

I bit back a sigh. "No, Mom."

"I saw you're doing your same shit again. Never quite getting to the finish line, huh? Never good enough to—"

The male rumble grew in volume.

"What?" Noise through the airwaves, fumbling, and I knew the query wasn't for me.

Knew what was going to happen next.

"Useless."

A click.

Silence.

I sat there with my eyes closed and my head back against the wall and the thermos in my lap and—

"Fuck," I sighed, opening my eyes and shoving my phone into my pocket.

Same shit.

Different day or month or year.

But the phone call had done what I'd intended, had reminded me, fucking slapped me right back into reality. I couldn't allow myself to become like her. No fucking way. And that resolution, the absolute certainty that I was now desperate to cling to, had paired with the dizziness, the tornado. Brit and Bailey and my mother. The juxtaposition of a woman from my past and the good ones from my present were fucking with my brain.

Which was probably why I didn't realize I'd started moving again, had actually opened the door.

To *her*.

Another woman of my present.

Another good one—a blonde, curly-haired, meddling kidnapper who liked to handcuff me to porches.

Maybe that said something weird about me, that I thought she was good with all that baggage, but I couldn't deny that Billie Rose had a strong sense of conviction and loved this town.

So good, despite the kidnapping.

"The Harvest Festival and Parade!"

It was yelled.

Straight up *yelled* in my direction, and after the phone call and brutal truth I'd just come face-to-face with and the dizziness in my brain from these fucking women who kept making me feel shit that I didn't want to...

I jumped like a scalded cat.

"Fuck!" I cursed as my coffee sloshed out through the open top of my thermos and burned the back of my hand.

Billie Rose *tsked*, and the kidnapper extraordinaire quickly took action, pushing the door to my apartment fully open, moving with astonishing speed that I rarely saw any place outside of the ice and would have been thoroughly impressed with if it hadn't come with a side of *Burning My Fucking Hand Off.*

But it did come with a side of that, so instead of admiration, I just followed her cursing and muttering as she hustled into my space, heading unerringly for the kitchen.

As though she knew without a doubt where it was.

And considering this woman appeared to have super speed, maybe she also had X-ray vision.

Either that or she could see that my apartment wasn't huge and there weren't too many places for a kitchen to be located.

So, I didn't ponder on superpowers too long, just headed into the kitchen and stuck my hand under the faucet that Billie Rose had "helpfully" (yes, I mentally gave that air quotes) turned on for me, ignoring her when she grabbed my thermos, dumped it, rinsed it, and turned it upside down to drain.

She snagged the canister of coffee, brewed another pot, and, after drying it, refilled my mug. It also didn't miss my notice that she'd put in black, just like I'd taken it at Bailey's house.

Good God.

The woman had a mind like an elephant.

Then she turned to me. "So, as I was saying—"

I snorted. "*Saying* isn't screaming." A beat, my gaze locking with hers, watching hers fill with a scary sort of determination. "Just saying," I muttered.

She held my eyes, that steely, flinty focus locking me in place.

Then she smiled. Brightly.

And *that* was almost scarier. "As I was saying," she repeated, opening cupboards and grabbing a mug. She filled it before rummaging through my fridge and cabinets until she turned up some milk and sugar. Making herself at home, as though she hadn't startled me into spilling my coffee and injuring myself, hadn't then barged inside and helped herself to my fridge and pantry. "As I was *saying,* the Harvest Festival and Parade is coming up."

Another bright smile.

Yup. That was definitely more frightening than the steely determination.

"I have no idea what in the fuck-all that is," I said, still salty as I pulled my hand from the water, the back of it bright pink and aching.

"I had a meeting with Edward"—Eddie, our GM, because no one called him Edward...except, apparently, *Billie Rose*—"yesterday afternoon, and now that you've stopped leading your hooligan crew in wreaking havoc through my town, I want the team involved in the festival." She smiled, digging into the purse hanging from her elbow and pulling out a tube of burn cream which she plunked onto the counter. "And *he* wants the team involved, especially considering my decision on whether or not to renew the team's usage contract of city properties will be coming up shortly." A casual shrug...that wasn't casual in the least based on the look she slanted my way. "So"—a clap of her hands—"you're my Harvest Festival and Parade buddy."

Wait, what?

I turned off the water, grabbed a paper towel, and dried my hands, putting the buddy thing aside for the moment and asking what I thought was the most pertinent question to start, "What's a Harvest Festival?"

Her mug had almost been at her lips, but my question had her freezing and slowly lowering the mug, plunking it onto the counter before *plunking* her hands onto her hips. "*Excuse me?*"

"Um..." I cleared my throat. "What's a Harvest Festival?"

"What's a *Harvest Festival?*" Her sound of disbelief prickled down my spine as I picked up the burn cream. "Axel Finnegan, you cannot seriously tell me that you've been in this town for three years and you don't even know what River's Bend's biggest annual event is."

Fuck.

"Um..."

There didn't appear to be a right or wrong answer to that.

Only wrong and...*wrong*.

So I didn't answer. Just stood there like a lump and stared at her.

Her brows lifted to form sharp rainbows on her forehead. Then she sighed. "The Harvest Festival begins on the weekend after Thanksgiving"—her gaze held mine, pinning me in place—"coincidentally, a weekend during which the Rush have no games—"

And if she didn't orchestrate that, I'd eat my glove.

And since I didn't let anyone wash them if I scored in a game (and because I'd been scoring a lot lately, that had been a while), that would be disgusting.

But then again, hockey superstitions often were gross.

"It kicks off with the festival's pie-eating contest on Friday evening," she went on, gesturing energetically with her free hand, her excitement for the event in every syllable. "That is followed up with bingo, face painting, a cake boogie, and a local arts and crafts fair, and other fun events that will last the entire weekend, including a parade."

I rubbed the ache that was beginning to form at my temple. "A cake *boogie?*"

She smiled. "Yup."

"I'm—" That ache intensified. "I don't know what that is either."

Her blond curls bounced as she shook her head in disgust. "A cake boogie is quite simply an event where everyone dances until the music stops, and whoever freezes last gets to go get a slice of cake."

That ache intensified. "Doesn't that mean everyone wants to be last?"

Her smile widened. "Yes, *if* the prize for winning the cake boogie wasn't the most coveted trophy in River's Bend history." She pulled out her cell, swiped at the screen, and showed him a truly horrific trophy. Vaguely cake-shaped, half of the gold finish wiped off and...was that duct tape holding it to its base?

I didn't understand these people.

Truly. I did *not.*

"People want to win *that?*"

A nod sent those curls bouncing. "Yup." The P at the end was a *pop*. "Just like they want to visit the petting zoo on Saturday and the kids want a pony ride and the adults want to win the limbo contest and take a turn at the dunk—"

My brain had gone from spinning to tornado again. "Wait," I said, putting my hand up.

Miraculously, she shut up.

"So, the festival is a mashup of…" I trailed off, not wanting to insult her when she was armed with coffee, had handcuffed me to porches, and held the team's future in those tiny palms.

"Awesomeness, fun, and town spirit?" she supplied.

"Right," I said. I cleared my throat. "*That.*"

"Exactly." Her eyes sparkled. "And it all culminates in the"—and no joke, here she did jazz hands—"Harvest Parade!"

"Wow." My tone was neutral. "That sounds amazing."

See?

That was perfect. Supportive and not insulting and—

Very *not* perfect.

Because Billie Rose said what she said next.

She clapped her hands together. "Great! I'm so glad you said that."

Okay, it wasn't *that* sentiment that was imperfect.

It was what came out of those pink lips next.

"So that means, you'll have no problem being my co-chair on the planning committee!" Her mug went into the sink as I processed the words that might as well have been in another language.

Co-chair?

Planning committee?

I—wait, what?

She turned, was heading toward the door by the time they *did* click.

"Wait—" I began, moving after her.

Her hand closed on the knob, began turning it, tugged open the wooden panel. "Our first meeting is this Thursday. I'll pick you up at six." A finger wave.

"I—*wait*—Billie Rose—"

She paused in the doorway. "Oh, and don't worry," she said. "Edward gave me the entire team's schedule of practices, events, games, and travel. We'll work around it to make sure you don't miss anything!"

"I—"

Shit. Why did that sound like a threat?

I didn't have time to process whether it truly was or not.

Because the door slammed, and Billie Rose was gone.

Twenty

Bailey

I slid through the crowd—it was Wednesday night Happy Hour at Monroe's and that meant the place was packed—and waved at Desiree as I pushed through a cluster of women near the bar.

Puck bunnies and fuck boys.

Those fuck boys being *puck* boys.

Not that I was looking.

In fact, I was deliberately keeping my gaze from that corner booth, from the cluster of big, brawny, and it had to be said, sexy men sitting at the table.

Heaven help me if I saw Axel again.

I might...do something stupid.

Something *else* stupid.

Something else really *fucking* stupid.

A girl tottered toward me, and I knew with only a glance that she wasn't from River's Bend (because I pretty much knew everyone—small town and all). She was in full going-out mode—which, more power to her for being able to rock those heels and the crop top and the sheer amount of sparkles on her body in a small-town bar. The thing I *did* have a problem with was her tottering toward me unsteadily, two pitchers of beer in her hands, both filled to the brim, and small splashes overflowing with each step she took.

"Whoa," I said, instantly moving toward her, intending to take one and help her with the burden.

"Back off, bitch," she snapped, jerking them away from me, another splash hitting the floor...and my shoes.

And my jeans.

Fucking hell. Now I was going to smell like cheap beer all fucking night.

Glitter bitch marched by, and I bit back a retort, shaking my head as I continued to the bar, and took a seat on an empty stool on Desiree's side of it.

"We've got to stop meeting like this," my childhood friend said. "Especially when you only come in for Happy Hour and not for my precious good looks." She fluttered her lashes at me. "I'm pretty to look at, even when drinks aren't half off."

I rolled my eyes. "You know it's been busy at the ranch."

"I *know* that you've avoided me for weeks now. Ever since one hot hockey player trailed after you onto the patio—"

My eyes narrowed. "Tell me what happened in San Bernadino, you know, at the job you were supposedly incredibly happy at and had just gotten a big promotion and—"

She spun away, grabbing a pitcher, glaring at me after she'd turned back and started to fill it.

Point to me.

Now, hopefully, she'd leave all conversation about the hot hockey man to die in a small, empty grave...or handcuffed to my porch—

No.

That wasn't right.

Neither was me being a snarky bitch to one of my friends.

"Sorry," I muttered.

"Me, too," she muttered back.

"Avoid talking about topics we've been avoiding?" I offered.

"Seems wisest," she said, after passing the pitcher off to a waitress.

In truth, I'd been doing my best to avoid everyone—including hot hockey players—and the ranch had helped me accomplish that. Downed fences, sick animals, a barn door that had needed repairing. The leak in the house that had forced me to pull up the carpet in the family room and throw away Gran's blue floral couch that had gotten wet too and ended up damaged and musty.

And there went me moving into the black.

House repairs and new furniture were expensive.

But the expense—and even the smell—weren't why I'd resisted the repairs. That was the couch Gran had picked out, her curtains and throw pillows, and it was the carpet Gramps had installed.

The only gift my parents had given me was to have not bothered spending the money to update the rooms they considered useless in the house.

The master bedroom and bathroom? Freshly updated (the new pipes freshly *leaking* inside the wall and all along the floor of the family room).

The kitchen, the family room, the guest rooms? All had been left untouched when they'd dumped the ranch into my lap. Including the room I stayed in—because I couldn't stay in *theirs*. Their fancy-ass mattress had nearly killed me—and my back—and I'd taken the next best alternative.

A rock-hard, ancient bed in a rarely used room.

Of course, if I'd been staying in the master bedroom, I probably would have noticed the leak and thus, would still have the couch and the ugly carpet.

I couldn't decide if I was sad or relieved.

It was bittersweet, but...circling back to extremely ugly.

"So, avoiding the topics we've been avoiding," Dessie said, wiping up a spill before pouring cocktails. "How are you?"

"Fine."

Desiree narrowed her eyes. "Uh-huh."

"Seriously."

"I know you, Bay. I know when you're busy. Which is always," she added. "Or at least that's what Billie Rose says and how you were before I left town."

"That was years ago."

"My point," she said, dropping a coaster onto the bar in front of me, "is that I knew you then, and I'd like to think I know you at least a bit now because that expression you're wearing is classic Bailey." She turned away before I could muster a response to that, and when she turned back, my IPA in her hand, the glass plunking onto the coaster. "And it's classic Bailey because it tells me that you're putting on a brave face, but something is tearing you up inside."

Got it in one.

But fuck it all, I wasn't going to cop to it.

"This is us avoiding topics we should be avoiding?"

Dessie grinned. "Well, you know me. I'm a stubborn pain in the ass."

Sighing, I said, "Nothing's tearing me up inside." Then added, after taking a swig of my beer when her expression didn't relax, "I really just *am* busy. Especially, since Billie Rose is on a rampage about the Harvest Parade."

"Not just the parade," Desiree muttered. "It's the entire festival."

Another sip. "You're right about *that*."

Someone hollered for Desiree, and my friend slid a menu on the counter and started to move away. "I'll take care of Mr. Impatient, but figure out something to eat. It's on me tonight—"

"I'm fine—"

A glare cut my words off. "It's on *me*, Bay. And you'll shut up and accept it."

Dessie was gone before I could finish my protest. "Right," I whispered, taking another sip as I studied the menu. I was lowering the glass to my coaster when someone shoved into the space next to me, bumping my arm, sloshing my beer, and making it so that I was going to smell like beer two times over, though at least the second time around it was with better beer.

Gasping, I set the glass down and shook out my hand, turning to see who'd bumped into me.

It was another woman—this one with long, blond hair and wearing a crop top and sparkles that mirrored the first one who'd bumped into me. She didn't apologize, tell me to back off, or even spare me a look. Instead, she just glared down the bar and began muttering about the bartender ignoring her.

Given that Desiree had about as much patience as I did with rude assholes, that *was* probably the case.

Another bump.

Though this one, thankfully, didn't end up with me being covered in more beer.

Because it was safely out of reach when another woman squeezed in. "I can't believe Axel isn't here."

His name was...

Heat.

Sinking into my bones, prickling down through my spine, gathering between my thighs.

Fuck, even my pussy convulsed, remembering how good it had felt to have him inside.

Pathetic.

I'm not pretending.

His words from that night. Tickling across my nape, sliding down my spine—

"He *never* comes out anymore," the new girl complained, thankfully drawing me out of my memories, stopping me from turning into a puddle of sexual need.

A lie.

Because I'd seen his face when he'd realized what he'd done.

When he'd realized he'd slept with *me.*

I'd seen the disgust and the remorse and...

I'd lived through that for two years. I wasn't going there again, least of all with a fucking puckboy who had slept with half the damned town.

The girl huffed and waved at Desiree. "Well, I don't know why he doesn't come out anymore. It's boring without him." The last ended on a whine and was punctuated with another rude wave toward Dessie.

Dessie's gaze glazed past the woman and locked with mine. She rolled her eyes.

Biting back a grin, I lifted my beer in salute.

Or maybe commiseration.

Then she turned back to the customers in front of her and began pouring drinks.

Meanwhile, I was stuck next to twin Crop Tops and trying to ignore their conversation, to ignore all mentions of Axel Finnegan. Hell, I was trying to ignore all mentions of any of the team, of hockey in general.

And I was failing.

Because I was listening to the gossip.

How Axel had apparently been killing it on the ice but avoiding any of the post-game celebrations, at least according to the Crop Tops and his teammates.

"We're probably just not at the right place," the first girl said. "I mean, not even half the guys are here."

"I've gone to three of their road games," the girl who had squeezed in said. "He didn't go out after those either. And some of the other guys have stopped going out, too. And the ones that *do* go out, end up going home early."

Silence.

From the women, at least. The background noise of the bar was the only sound, for a few moments anyway.

Then the first Crop Top huffed and waved at Dessie again. "God, this bartender."

Meanwhile, I was kind of obsessing over the fact that Axel had stopped partying...and he'd done it after we'd slept together. I mean, that probably had nothing to do with me. He'd already been slowing down after the whole naked and handcuffed incidents. Or more likely, Billie Rose had gotten to him and threatened him with more kidnapping and splinters in his ass if he didn't get his shit together.

Or maybe...I had a magical pussy.

One that turned a man from playboy to hard worker.

Ha.

My magical pussy with the rainbows and glitter and pheromone-producing clit that drove men *wild* was totally why he'd run from the room the moment he'd come, why he hadn't been out to the ranch or seen me since that night.

I'd told him to not pretend that he cared about me.

He'd told me he wasn't pretending.

And he'd proved that over the last weeks.

I needed to take his actions at face value.

He'd gotten what he wanted.

He was done with me.

It was sick—*I*—was sick in being so unsettled—in thinking about him all the time, dreaming about him—

Fucking hell, desperate for another night with him.

The sex had been good. Hot. The best fucking *ever*. But that was all it was, so I needed to stop hiding at the ranch, stop worrying about running into him in town, stop avoiding my life just because he might be around.

And I was doing that.

Hence, Wednesday night at Monroe's.

"Did you decide what you wanted to eat?"

Blinking, I glanced up at Dessie. "What?"

The Crop Tops next to me huffed.

"Food, Bay," she said, her brows drawing together. "Do you want something to eat?"

"Sorry." I laughed, tucked my hair behind my ear. "I was thinking about..."

Now Dessie's brows lifted.

"Fencing," I finished lamely.

Dessie shook her head. "I'm going to get you something so that you stop thinking about fencing."

How about something to stop me from thinking about Axel Finnegan?

Luckily, I managed to hold that back and just told her, "I trust you to take care of me."

A grin.

No. A *smirk*, mischief creeping into Dessie's eyes.

Uh-oh.

"I trust," I added quickly, "that *you'll* get me home at a reasonable hour and that you'll only bring me one more beer so I don't end up hungover and—"

Dessie tossed her head, her long black hair shining as it cascaded down her back. "Oh no, Bay," she said, lips twitching. "You said you trusted me to take care of you." There was that mischief again. "So I'm going to—"

"Dessie," I warned.

A pat to my hand. "I'll take care of you."

"*Des—*"

"I wish someone would take care of *me.*" From one of the Crop Tops.

Dessie glanced from me to the women, that mischief grew, and...I knew.

I was fucked.

Twenty-One

Axel

"Go, go," Joel called. "Take it."

He let the puck slide through his feet, leaving me to pick it up.

Unfortunately for him—or me, really—he hadn't considered what was happening behind him.

Unfortunately for *me*, he was a big fucker and I didn't see the opposing player barreling toward me until I was picking myself up off the ice, moving my tongue around the inside of my mouth-guard-protected teeth, half expecting to find several out of place or floating around out of their sockets.

They were all in place.

And I was moving again, chasing down the fucker who'd laid me out, who was streaking toward our net.

I hauled ass.

And...didn't catch up in time to disrupt his shot.

Goal.

Cool.

Sighing as the whistles blew and the red light turned on, I rolled my shoulders and tried not to glance up at the scoreboard as I skated back to the bench.

Because it would reveal...an eight-goal deficit.

Insurmountable.

Shitty as fuck.

But that was the breaks of professional hockey.

"Sorry, man," Joel muttered, squirting some water in his mouth and promptly spitting it on the skate mat in front of him. Pointless habit. Not hydrating and probably gross, but fuck if I didn't do that same damned thing when he handed me the bottle.

Needed to wet my mouth.

Didn't want a lot of water sloshing around in my stomach when I tried to skate.

Though tonight that didn't matter.

Skating hard, working hard, trying hard, not one was going to make a bit of difference. This game was in the books. The best we could do was try to pull some decent plays together, something we could focus on going into the next game.

Joel snagged the bottle back, dropped it into the holder on the inset shelf in front of us. "How bad is it going to be?"

"Coach?" I asked.

Another line jumped on the ice, and we scooted down as we spoke, eyes on the ice, moving into position to get ready to take our next turn at getting beat the fuck down.

"Yeah," he muttered once we ran out of scooting room.

I slanted a glimpse at our head coach, noted the apoplectic expression on his face. "Bad," I muttered back.

"Shit."

"*Same* shit. Different day."

A half-grin. "Yeah," Joel said, sliding down again.

I followed suit, along with the rest of the guys on the bench, and said, "So, we're gonna do what we always do."

"There isn't any pussy on the ice."

Fucker. Albeit a funny one.

"No, asshole." But my lips were twitching, and I tried to channel Brit when I said, "We're gonna go out there and do *one* good thing before we get reamed in the locker room."

"Same shit," Joel said lightly, lifting his fist.

I bumped. "Different day."

And, nearly as one—since he was a big fucker and took up more than his fair share of the boards—we jumped onto the ice.

And...eventually, we managed to do one good thing.

I slung my bag over my shoulder, tugged on my beanie, and slammed my car door.

It was late. My legs were on fire. My eyes were bleary.

Yeah, we'd played like shit that night, yeah we'd lost...because of the aforementioned playing like shit. And yeah, as expected, we'd gotten our asses reamed, Coach screaming at us, and look, I got that sometimes some yelling worked. The keyword being *some*.

It snapped our dumbasses to attention.

Refocused us.

But when we already knew that we'd fucked up majorly, and yelling for that long, after that shitty of a game...

Wasn't going to make one fucking bit of difference.

Me staying after the game, trying to focus on that one good thing Joel and I had cobbled together and failing. So instead, I spent hours trying to fix my fucking hands that hadn't done what I'd wanted them to in the game, might. If I practiced enough, maybe I could play better, pass better, shoot better.

Be fucking better.

Unless the problem was in my head, like Brit had suggested.

Like I was starting to agree.

Like—

"Enough," I whispered, bleeping the locks and letting my head tilt back, roll back and forth to ease the throbbing muscles in my neck.

The parking lot for my apartment was being repaved, so I'd parked on the street a couple of blocks away, and if I cut through the patio of Monroe's, it would only take me a few more minutes to get home, soak my aching bones, and drink...some water since I was no longer self-medicating with alcohol and fucking.

Not going to be my mother.

No fucking way.

Sighing, I started walking, and in my sober state, I couldn't miss that the moon was high in the sky, shining through the clouds like a horror film, making me half expect a fucking werewolf to jump out of the bushes and take me down. Maybe that would make me a better player.

Werewolves were fast, yeah?

I'd just strap on four skates, let my tail be my rudder, and—

A rush of noise startled me, and I jumped as the back door of Monroe's flew open, nearly wiping me out.

But hockey skills.

I dodged, danced back...and just missed being flattened as I snagged the edge of the door, catching it before it slammed back into the brick wall, intending to just close it and continue on to my apartment.

Except...

"I'm totally fine," Bailey said on a giggle. "I'll just walk to Billie's and get her to give me a ride."

The slender bartender with shining black hair and deep brown eyes who'd encouraged me to follow Bailey onto this patio a few weeks back said, "That's not going to happen, Bay. You're going to sit your drunk ass back at the bar and then I'll close up and drive you home."

Bailey shook her head. "I'm fine to walk a couple of blocks—"

She turned, threw an arm out, and promptly proved that she definitely wasn't fine to walk a few feet, let alone a few blocks, stumbling backward and nearly ending up on her ass.

Dropping my bag, I lurched forward, caught her.

She smelled like sunshine and apples, like dry grass and cool summer evenings.

She—

Blinked up at me, and then she smiled and—

Fuck, she was beautiful.

Warm and soft and woman. Hot and uninhibited and incredible in bed. Spicy and fierce and could wield a shotgun. Tough and strong and worked her ass off.

I'd been sober a lot lately.

Which meant that I'd been listening.

And I'd heard the talk, how she'd dug the ranch out of a financial hole, how she hardly accepted help, how she barely took a break and was always working and...how she'd always been like that.

Even as a kid.

Earning her keep, working her ass off.

To prove herself? To prove that she belonged?

All that listening meant that it was getting harder to ignore the emotions blossoming in my chest, to stop thinking about her, to ignore the voice in my head that said I could be different with her, that I *was* already different because of her.

That I wasn't going to be my mother and could have something good in my life without fucking it up.

Bailey blinked, her brows drawn together as she started to sit up. I snagged her arm, popped her up to her feet, not missing that she wavered when I got her onto them, so I left my fingers there, trying and failing to ignore how good it felt to be next to her, to hold her.

"I'm fine," she said, trying to pull free.

My fingers tightened before I realized it. "Easy, buttercup," I murmured, catching a glimpse of warmth in her eyes before she turned her gaze back to her friend and repeated, "I'm fine."

"Nope. You're drunk," the bartender said. "After two beers," she added. "Which is a sad state of affairs about your social life, I think, but not the point at this moment. Come inside, Bay. Last call is in a few minutes, and then I'll get you over to Billie Rose's or drive you home."

"I don't *want* to go home."

"Okay, I'll take you to Billie's."

She made a face, and fuck, it was cute. "I don't want to go to Billie's either."

"You just said—" The bartender sighed. "Bay. My place, yours, or Billie Rose's. That's your choice."

"Fine," Bailey muttered. "I'll go home. You always complain I never come out, but then when I try to have a good time—"

"You don't come out," the bartender said. "And it's not a complaint of you tonight, sweetie. I just can't have you going on an adventure when I'm trying to close down the bar."

Bailey pouted.

She was still cute, even though I didn't normally like drunk bitches, even though I definitely couldn't stand those who pouted.

Except, for Bailey.

Which was probably why my mouth worked before my brain caught up. "I'll drive her home."

Two female heads swiveled in my direction.

"We've got it," the bartender said, moving forward and peeling my fingers from Bailey's arm. "Thanks for the save, but you can go about your evening."

An argument was on the tip of my tongue, a protest that *I* was going to take care of her, dammit. That she was mine to protect and get home.

But...

Down that path led...

"Okay," I said, stepping back and picking up my bag, slinging it over my shoulder. "Night."

A hand on my arm, breasts pressing into my back. "Don't go."

Apples and flowers in my nose.

Warm, soft woman against me.

Need burning through my veins. It had been weeks since I'd had her, had anyone, and I wanted—

Gently, I dislodged her, started to step away.

"I miss your dick."

I froze, air stuck in the back of my throat, making me choke.

The bartender chuckled. "I thought you weren't going to sleep with him."

My gaze shot to hers, eyes narrowing. "It wasn't like that, don't try to insinuate that she's—"

Bailey stumbled, and I caught her against me.

The bartender's brows lifted, almost in challenge.

And all I could do was finish lamely, "...that she's like *that*."

"I *am* like that," Bailey declared. She lifted a hand to her mouth, as though she were whispering to her friend, but the words were loud as hell. "But only for Axel."

I inhaled sharply.

The bartender laughed as she glanced up at me. "She's going to hate herself if she remembers saying that in the morning."

"But Dessie! He's got a big cock."

It was still an attempt at a stage-whisper.

As thus, it wasn't a whisper at all.

And paired with her burrowing into me, with her arms sliding around my waist, her breasts hitting my chest, and that need burning through me? It transformed my need into a fucking inferno, blasting through the trees, flaming high and hot, incinerating everything in its path. I was a pile of ash, being blown in all directions, not sure which was the right one.

Run, be scattered like the pieces on the wind.

Stay, and be burned all over again.

Run, like I always did, like my mother always did.

Stay, and fight for what I want, for what might be.

"Okay, never mind." Dessie's brows were nearly in her hairline. "She's going to hate she said *that* in the morning."

My fingers traced along the sides of Bailey's arms until my hands could dip in, cup the indent of her waist, and I embraced the only part of me I knew how to embrace.

The cocky, arrogant asshole.

But I didn't run.

Instead, I grinned up at Dessie. "Can't hate the truth."

"Oh, honey," Dessie said. "You can *definitely* hate the truth. And this one"—a nod toward Bailey—"saying all that"—she waved a hand in the direction of my pelvis—"she's going to have a ton of hate for these *truths* coming out of her mouth right now."

Bailey ran a hand down my chest. "He's wearing a suit." Still stage whispering. "He's yummy in a suit. I've only seen him naked and in a T-shirt. A suit is better." She smiled up at me dopily, and fuck, that was cute, too. "Well, naked is best," she said, ticking off on her fingers. "Jeans are yummy. A T-shirt is great. But a suit is the best."

"That's two *bests*, buttercup."

A shrug. "Meh."

Burn.

I was going to *burn*.

Forcing myself to not taste that dopey smile, I caught Dessie's eyes. "I'm taking her home."

Bailey smiled, nodded jerkily.

Dessie's amusement cooled. "That's *not* happening."

"I'm a dick," I said. "A dick who's slept with a lot of girls, but I don't do unwilling, and I don't do drunk."

Dessie's lips pressed flat, her eyes going fierce. "I'm still not letting you—"

Bailey wove her fingers through mine. "I'm going home with him, Desiree."

That felt...right. Her fingers in mine, her body close. The words.

I lifted my free hand, rubbed a spot over my heart that was twinging—fucking sore muscles from too much hockey. "I'll get her home safe and in bed. *Alone*," I added when Desiree frowned even more fiercely. "I promise."

The bartender's brown eyes locked with mine, but a shout coming from inside had her turning away. She called out that she'd be right there before whipping back to face me, lifting a finger and pointing it in my direction. "It goes without saying that if that changes, I'll cut that big dick of yours off."

Bailey giggled.

I glared down at her. "I thought you liked my dick," I told her. "It getting cut off should make you sad."

She blew me a kiss. "I'll tell you a secret." She leaned close, but the volume didn't decrease. "Dessie seems scary, but she's a big softie."

"I'm not," Dessie said.

"Noted," I told her, holding her stare. "And there will be no reason to cut off my dick."

"See, that is another truth spoken," she muttered, spinning on her heel and heading back into Monroe's, pausing only to toss over her shoulder, "Because don't forget that I have a kitchen full of sharp knives available for my use."

Bailey's hand dipped into the waistband of my slacks the moment the door banged shut. "She's all bark." A beat. "I promise."

I highly doubted that.

But considering I was fending off a woman who'd turned into an octopus as I shepherded her to my car (an octopus who was trying in earnest to get her hands down my pants), I didn't have any more mental energy to spare for Desiree the bartender.

Into the passenger's seat.

Belt buckled.

Door closed.

Her *eyes* closed.

Thank God.

I got into my side, quietly closing the door behind me, and turning on the engine, taking off along the quiet street.

A sleeping Bailey was a lot less dangerous to my fortitude...and the *thoughts* swirling through my mind.

"They said you don't come out anymore."

The words came as I'd pulled out of downtown.

Were said so quietly that I barely heard it.

When I chanced a glance at her, she was still, those lids still closed.

"What, buttercup?" I asked softly, turning onto the dark road that led out to her ranch.

"The women."

Sleepy words.

Ones I should have left to lie.

But I couldn't.

"What women?"

"The ones from the bar," she said, head rolling, those lids peeling back and her eyes hitting mine. "They said you don't go out with your teammates anymore."

I hadn't.

Not since that night.

My fingers clenched on the steering wheel, and I focused back on the road. "I don't."

"Why not?"

Because of you.

Because of *me.*

Because of that night and all the feelings I'd caught but was pretending I hadn't.

Because...I didn't want to be like my mom, avoiding hard work and drinking myself into a person I couldn't stand to look at in the mirror.

Because maybe I could be the man Brit talked about, the man I wanted to be.

I didn't tell her any of that.

"It got old," I said instead. Which was the truth. The barest bit of it. But still the truth, since I couldn't bring myself to lie to this woman. "And at some point I have to grow up."

She was quiet.

Then her lips curved, lids dipping again. "And Billie Rose got to you."

I chuckled. Because that was also the truth. She'd given me the shove up the mountain, before the push had come from Brit, bringing me to the cliff's edge, before the jolt of courage this woman was giving me to jump off and let the wind rush over my skin, the ground come up faster than it seemed possible, the trees and bushes and rocks flying by.

The better to impale me? To end me? To—

Maybe I'd have a parachute.

Maybe Bailey could be *my* parachute.

"Billie Rose *is* pretty fucking scary," I said quickly, pushing the thoughts aside.

A wobbly nod. "Yeah. And knows too much."

Now I laughed outright. "She does at that."

Her eyes opened again, and I had to force my gaze back to the road. So fucking pretty and captivating and...

I wanted her.

A *fucking* lot.

"Axel?"

"Mmm," I said, deliberately concentrating on driving.

"I want you."

The mirror of my thoughts had my dick going hard, my stare slanting to the side. "You're drunk."

A shrug. "Drunk *and* horny."

"I meant what I told Desiree. You're too drunk, buttercup. It's not happening."

Bailey made a face, reaching over the console, squeezing my thigh. "Dessie worries too much."

I returned it to her lap. "Dessie is a good friend to you," I said. "And I won't break her trust."

It was an excuse.

But it was also the truth.

And look who had fucking morals for the first time in my life.

A fucking miracle that was.

So was the silence that fell, the silence that was then followed by agreement. "Yeah," she whispered. "That's fair."

Thank God.

"But *I* never promised Dessie anything."

My gaze shot back to hers—

Just in time to see her whip her shirt up and over her head.

TWENTY-TWO

BAILEY

I rolled over in bed, my head pounding, the light shining through the window like tiny spikes that were cheerfully driving themselves into my brain.

For a moment, I thought I was sick.

My throat was sore, I felt like I'd been run over by a truck, and then there was that headache.

But then I rolled over and encountered...

Naked skin.

Tattoos I recognized.

Muscles I'd stroked with my fingers and my tongue.

I jerked my gaze up and fell right into deep blue eyes.

A handsome face. Hair that was just on the right side of long. Dark brown hair that had clearly been mussed by fingers. Scruff on a square jaw. Lips that were clearly meant to be kissed.

Axel Finnegan.

And all at once, the night came back to me.

The bar.

Too many beers. No. *Two* many beers.

I'd said...

Oh fuck. I'd said a lot. Too much, and I'd—

Axel was in bed with me.

Naked.

And *I* was naked.

And I'd—

A squeal welling up in my throat, embarrassment threatening to swell up and choke me. Violently.

Until it unalived me and the horror of reliving the events from the night before just freaking *stopped*.

"Buttercup," he murmured, reaching out a hand and—

I panicked.

Lurching back from that hand, even as I wanted it on my face, my skin, my body. It was need and danger wrapped up in a single body part.

"I-I—"

I scrambled away from him, getting tangled in the sheets as I tried to escape and...

That strong hand caught me before I ended up on the floor, fingers wrapping around my wrist, yanking me away from the edge of the mattress, stopping me from falling out of bed.

I was naked.

I'd been drunk.

He was naked.

The last thing I remembered was taking my shirt off.

"Not so fast, buttercup," he said, drawing me across the mattress, the tangle of sheets, the comforter bunching up between us, between my naked body and his.

"I need to go. I *have* to go." The arm he'd grabbed was trapped between us, but I used the other to push against him.

Fuck.

That was his *hip*.

All strong muscles and hard man and hot, bare skin.

Shit. *Shit.*

"I need to go," I said again. "I have to—"

He rolled us, his body pinning me in place, fingers still around my wrist, drawing that arm up and over my head. My other hand was somehow still on his hip, and with him over me, I found that instead of pushing him away, I was drawing him closer.

"First," he murmured, "you can't go."

My chin came up, and I jerked my hand away like it had been burned. "First," I snapped, starting to feel more like myself, even though he was still on top of me, making my body sing, my mind swim, "you can't tell me one fucking thing, Axel Finnegan. *One* fucking *thing!*"

His palm dropped to my thigh.

Hot and broad, squeezing a little roughly before sliding up, cupping my ass. Long, thick fingers drifting into the crack, dipping down, in, and brushing—

My breath caught.

"First," he said, swiping those fingers forward. "You're wet, and naked, and"—another swipe—"*that's* my favorite way to find you."

"Asshole."

Swipe. Dip.

"Correction"—one blunt tip traced my entrance—"*this* is my favorite way to find you—naked and wet and snapping at me."

A quiver ran through me. "You're sick."

His fingers released my wrist, coming up to cup my cheek, turning my face gently from side to side. "And you're beautiful when you're angry. When your eyes are full of fire and your cheeks go pink and—"

"Fuck. Off."

He dipped closer, brushed his nose against mine. "And I love to hear you say the word *fuck.*" Another brush, his lips drawing close to mine. "Especially, when it's in regard to me."

I glared at him. "*First,* I seem to remember you promising Dessie that you wouldn't take advantage of me, and yet, here I am, naked in bed, and you're—you're—"

"First," he said, interrupting me again. "You can't go because you're already home."

"I—" I stopped, glanced around, realized that we were in *my* bed, in my room.

In my...house.

Oh.

But that didn't change the other—

"Second"—he jerked me closer, wrapping my leg around his hip—"we didn't fuck last night."

"I'm naked and we're in bed together, I think it's obvious that—"

"I'd *think*," he said, shifting his weight and snagging my other leg, bringing it around his waist. "I'd think it would be obvious that you would be able to feel that I'm wearing pants, considering that *you're* naked."

Oh.

Now that he mentioned it, there was a bit of friction from his slacks rubbing against my...

"*I'm* still naked and—"

"Because you stripped down in my car, and when I tried to put your clothes back *on* you, you kept taking them off again."

"I—" Images of me taking my top off in his car, of unsnapping my bra, throwing it out the window. Then on the front porch, leaping up the stairs, yelling, "One, two, three, he, he, he!"

Like I'd done with Gramps when I was six years old.

Except, I hadn't gotten naked when I was six, hadn't kicked off my shoes, unbuttoned my pants, and dropped them on the porch.

Along with my underwear.

Hadn't then flounced through my house, tugged off a man's shirt he'd tugged over my head (twice), hadn't thrown myself at him, obviously (and *ew*), hadn't—

Begged him to stay in bed with me.

"Oh, God," I groaned, dropping my head back to the pillows and slamming my eyes shut.

"It was hot," he said softly, nuzzling my throat, lips pressing lightly to my skin. "Biggest case of blue balls I'd ever had in my life, having you rubbing against me, your naked body on display, you asking for me to fuck you." An inhale. "*Begging* me to fuck you."

My lungs seized. My thighs trembled—

Which he felt, if his smirk was anything to go by.

"But I promised," he said. "I promised, and I might be an asshole, but I don't break my promises."

A breath in.

A breath out.

Desire boiling in my veins.

His mouth dragged higher, drifting across my jaw, sending that heat boiling into steam, threatening to explode out through my skin. His lips reached my ear. "I've never wanted anything as much as I wanted you in that moment."

"But you didn't take me," I breathed.

"No," he whispered.

"Why?" I whispered back.

He stilled in my arms. Yes, *in* my arms because they'd come around him, had wrapped him tight, were holding him close.

"Do you really think so little of me?"

The question was so quiet that I barely heard it.

But I *did* hear it.

And it struck me hard, embedded itself in my heart, my gut... my tongue. Which loosened, my reply sliding off it, floating through the air even before I realized it. "In my experience, men don't care much for promises." A beat. "Or boundaries. Or—"

I clamped my teeth together.

Idiot.

I didn't talk about that. I didn't *think* about that.

His muscles bunched beneath my palms.

He was quiet for a long moment. Then, "What kind of experience is that, buttercup?"

Experience I wasn't going to talk about.

Not now.

Not *ever.*

I pulled my hands away from the warm skin and hard lines, dropped my legs back down to the mattress. "You should go."

Calloused fingertips on my cheek, drifting down my throat. "I *should...*"

I inhaled.

Silently, but sharply enough that it felt like a series of stab wounds through my lungs.

He lifted his head.

His eyes hit mine.

I didn't dare breathe again.

A thumb pressing lightly into my bottom lip, and the movement had my lungs unfreezing, the air trapped within them slowly hissing out.

His expression was gentle, those eyes soft and warm and—

Something unlocked inside me, and all of sudden there was a maelstrom of words swirling in my belly, crawling up the back of my throat, threatening to escape.

Too much threatening to escape.

Too many things that I couldn't afford to think about, that would tear me apart all over again.

And I'd just barely put myself back together.

That thumb slid to the side, traced the corner of my mouth.

His head dropped again, and his lips came close, near enough that I could feel the damp heat of his breath against my mouth… heat that inched closer, breath that kissed mine.

But his lips didn't brush over mine, didn't take mine, didn't coax mine wider, his tongue dipping into my mouth.

Instead…he kissed my cheek.

"I should go."

Then he was up and out of my bed, grabbing his shoes and bag and shirt off the chair in the corner of my room, heading for the door without a second glance.

I almost called him back.

Almost.

But, in the end, I let him walk right out of my room.

My house.

Presumably, my life.

Twenty-Three

Axel

I waited until I saw her come out of the house, fully dressed (sadly) and heading for the barn.

I waited until she disappeared inside, knowing that she was taking care of the animals, knowing that she wouldn't dare to do anything other than fulfill the responsibilities that came with having them in her life.

Pft.

It was insane to think that I knew the woman at all.

She was a fucking mystery, an enigma, and yet, I knew that if I trailed my lips down her throat, her breath would catch. I knew that she liked her clit stroked firmly with my tongue. I knew how her hips felt beneath my palms, the sound she made when she came.

I knew...

Sex.

I knew how to fuck her.

Why did that thought have my fingers clenching on the steering wheel as I navigated past the place she'd tossed her bra out the window?

Why did that thought have my foot hitting the brakes, stopping, retrieving it?

Why did the fact that I knew hardly anything outside of how to make her come sit heavy in my gut?

Why—

"It doesn't matter," I whispered.

I hit the gas.

None of it mattered.

I had practice to get to.

I had work to do.

I had to prove myself.

I had a life to live, and...that life didn't include a brown-eyed beauty.

Even *if* I knew how to make her come in at least a half-dozen ways.

The sweat was stinging as it dripped into my eyes, but I still pushed it on the treadmill.

I wasn't going to quit.

I wasn't going to end up like *her*.

I was going to flush the bullshit out of my mind, and I was going to do what Brit said and I was going to not be a total fuckup for the rest of my life.

My quads burned. My lungs felt like they'd been rubbed raw with rough-grit sandpaper.

But I wasn't. Going. To—

A hand reached over the top of the treadmill's control panel.

"Wait—"

It slapped at the red stop button, and I felt the machine slow down, the incline flattening out, the belt coming to a stop. I yanked the towel off the rail, swiped at the sweat pouring down my forehead.

"What the fuck?" I snapped, dropping my arm and glaring at...

Pierre Barie.

Shit.

My teeth clinked together so fast that I was surprised a few of them didn't immediately crack and drop out of my mouth.

This wasn't just snapping at my boss—one of my coaches or the head trainer or even the Rush's GM.

This was snapping at my boss's boss's *boss*.

Pierre Barie was the owner of the Rush. He was also the owner of the Gold, the much more successful NHL team, and the organization I'd been drafted by all those seasons ago (before I'd been traded to and played for the Rangers and their AHL affiliate and then traded back to the Rush). He was the owner of the team I'd been trying get a spot on for *fucking* years, and the owner of the team that I'd only gotten to play a total of eighteen games for *over* those years.

He didn't make roster decisions.

That was up to Charlotte Harris, the GM of the Gold.

But cursing out the boss's boss's boss (or maybe there should even be another *boss* in there) wasn't good form.

"Shit," I said, quickly stepping off the treadmill, wiping at my forehead again. Fuck. I was still cursing at him. "I'm sorry, sir, I—"

Pierre leaned back against the wall, his suit devoid of wrinkles as he crossed his arms and ankles and studied me. "I don't get you."

"I...well...there's nothing really to get about me," I said.

Silence.

Then a sigh.

"Talented young player," he said, pushing off the wall, uncrossing his arms and moving toward me. "Char was stoked when we picked you up, and that first season with the Rush? It looked like all the potential we'd seen in you was going to come to fruition."

Churning began in my stomach.

One season.

Then I'd crashed, burned, and been traded to New York.

Before that trade had gone through, I'd been eighteen, fucking stoked to have escaped the bullshit that was my life. And instead of flushing the bullshit down the drain, keeping my head up and moving forward, *I'd* been sucked in.

Sucked *down*.

The top, the pinnacle, every single thing I'd hoped for had been *right* there.

And then I'd been reminded of how easily it could all be torn away, how easily it could be reduced to ash and scattered in every direction on the wind.

"Something changed."

Not a question. A statement that told me he knew it as fact, and unfortunately...it *was* fact. I couldn't bullshit or bravado my way out of the truth, not with Pierre standing there, pinning me in place with his icy blue stare.

He didn't know that *everything* had changed.

I'd thought they'd wanted me, valued me as a player, had thought of me as—

I'd thought *I* was something.

In the end, it was the same old shit.

In an instant, the foundation I'd built was gone, revealed to have been built out of toothpicks and tissue paper, to be so fragile that it was almost laughable that I would have thought it might just hold its shape in the first place.

"The question is, where did all that potential go?"

I didn't reply.

What could I say?

My little house of toothpicks and tissue paper had fallen to pieces, and I'd lost it like a toddler having a hissy fit over being given the wrong color plate?

That I'd thought it would be easy?

After so long of having it hard, of fighting for every inch, I'd just hoped that I might get just a *little* fucking bit of easy.

But I hadn't gotten easy.

Same shit, different day. Same life. *Always.*

"Something changed, and the fire went out of you," he said. "That fire went out until..."

Until I'd fucked a woman who'd made me feel something.

Until Brit told me that I needed to be the one to see myself through this.

Until the fog in my head had cleared and I'd realized I was becoming my mother.

My. *Mother.*

Fucking hell.

"Now," Pierre finished.

I inhaled.

His head tilted to the side, studying me closely. "I saw a report, caught a game, then two and three, and even in the losses, I'm seeing that player Char had once been so excited for again." Pierre leaned back against the wall. "So, I'm wondering what has changed, and if it's here to stay."

My lungs were burning, the air held tight in them for too long.

I released it.

"I'm getting older," I told him. "I know it's do or die time. That's a great motivator." I shrugged, my eyes drifting to the side, unable to hold his any longer. "There's not any deep reason."

A long moment of quiet.

Then, "Is that also why you're pushing yourself into oblivion after practice when you should be at home or with your teammates relaxing with a beer?"

I couldn't go home, couldn't remember Bailey, remember the man I was.

I couldn't go out, couldn't keep hiding from the man I was worried I'd become.

Not just because I had a fucking Harvest Festival planning meeting with Billie Rose, but because I couldn't...be *out* again, couldn't let myself be drawn into that trap of hiding behind the alcohol, my teammates, the women.

Not if I wanted to be...

Not *her*.

"No," I said. "I have a meeting with the mayor," I said.

Brows lifting.

"I'm helping at the Harvest Festival thing."

Pierre's brows lifted even higher. "What's a Harvest Festival?"

See? Exactly what I'd been thinking when Billie Rose had first brought it up, and now I was going to be elbows deep in fall vomit festival "fun." The parade, pumpkins, kids, and me being roped in by a curly-haired blonde with a penchant for organizing...

And kidnapping.

And handcuffs.

Po-tay-to. Po-tah-to.

"I'm still not entirely sure," I admitted, and Pierre's brows dropped, his lips twitching at the corners.

"Yet, you're volunteering?"

"Well, I'm thinking of it more like voluntolding."

A pause. "How'd Billie Rose manage that?"

Well...fuck.

I couldn't exactly mention that she'd threatened the team (and had done so because I'd been the ringleader of getting the boys into trouble because I was so far up my ass it took me being threatened with the final nail in the coffin of my career and then being drunk-napped and handcuffed twice for me to realize that I needed to turn some shit around).

That wouldn't exactly help my chances of securing a spot on the Gold...or any other team in the NHL for that matter.

Nope.

So...I did the smart thing for once and shut the fuck up.

Pierre cocked his head to the side. "Billie Rose *can* be persuasive, and a bulldog when she wants something."

That was something I could agree to without giving anything away. "Yes."

"Hell, she single-handedly took on the organization's lawyers during the initial negotiation"—he chuckled—"I swear we were lucky to come out of that with our shirts."

"Yeah," I said, not really knowing *what* to say.

Blue eyes on mine. "So, what does your voluntolding assignment include?"

"Apparently *all* of my free time outside of the team."

If the schedule and spreadsheet she'd emailed me was to be believed.

And how she'd gotten my email was as much of a mystery as how she'd managed to arrange my schedule with Coach without my permission.

The Power of Billie Rose.

I believed in it.

I was leaving it at that.

Pierre's blue eyes twinkled. "She why you stopped terrorizing the town?"

Yes...and no.

Brit had been the guide to the top. Billie Rose the impetus to jump. Her *niece* the person that actually shoved me off the cliff and into the fog...that had cleared, just in time for me to realize that the reflection that was staring at me in the pool of water at its base wasn't my own.

Instead, it was...my mother's.

And *that* had been hard enough of a snap to make me recognize that this chance was my last chance and I'd better get my shit together.

So here I was.

On the treadmill.

After practice.

After some extra time on the ice.

But—at least the last, the whole getting it together finally part, realizing it was my last chance—gave me a convenient shield to hide behind. All that hard work meant that no one was going to look at me too closely and—

That hopefully included the owner of the team I'd once thought was going to be my free ticket to the big leagues, to the future that would finally fill that void inside me, would prove to the world that I wasn't a complete and total failure.

Unfortunately, he was standing in front of me.

Seeing me.

Unfortunately, he didn't have, wouldn't ever have that golden ticket.

He didn't make roster decisions—not that I was naive enough to think that he couldn't influence them—but more than that, he knew exactly what was going on.

He saw too much.

He saw *me*.

Which was why it wasn't a surprise when Pierre pushed off the wall again, straightened the cuffs of his suit jacket, and nodded. "Well, I'm off."

Then the man who'd once held my dreams in his hands left.

He'd seen right through me.

Again.

Twenty-Four

Bailey

The straw scratched my arms as I hefted it across the street, but I supposed I should feel lucky that Billie Rose was far enough removed from ranch life to not recognize the difference between straw and hay.

Hay—heavy as hell.

Straw—much lighter as I hauled bale after bale of it from the back of the truck and used it to line the street.

In what Billie would think were quaint lines of *hay* bales bracketing each side of Main Street, but what were, in actuality, straw bales that my arms (and back) were thanking me for.

Dessie—whose arms were full of plastic pumpkins—and gourds...yup, those were gourds—passed by me, slanting another curious look at me. *Another* because she'd been tossing them my way the entire time we'd been completing our Billie Rose assigned duties.

Me: hay bales.

Dessie: decorative gourds.

Me: avoiding my friend's curiosity post-Axel spending the night in my home.

Dessie: walking by at regular intervals, her expression saying that she was going to get it out of me.

Me: making those straw bales a perfect line.

Dessie: launching gourds left and right, losing patience by the second.

The only gift I'd received was that gourd-launching took less time than hale-bale-lining, so Billie Rose had commandeered Dessie for some other project.

A little relief.

At least for the moment.

Because straw bales were just the beginnings of my tasks.

Later, I was on twinkly light duty—and had express instructions to make sure they draped perfectly—before I needed to head to the auditorium to wrap treats for the cake boogie. Then tonight after the parade, I was on the face-painting booth for one hour, would be helping the kids make decorative frames out of candy corn (the only thing that blegh of a treat was good for, stale post-Halloween leftovers or otherwise) for the final two.

Tomorrow, I'd start early with chores on the ranch...and then I had a full day of volunteering.

Was I salty about it?

Outwardly, yes.

Inwardly, the little girl inside me who never got to come to the festivities was excited to be a part of everything—once I'd managed to swallow the bittersweet and moved on beyond my past memories, that was.

Because pouting about the parade made me...pathetic.

I couldn't punish everyone else just because my mom was a tool bag.

The kids deserved better, and their excitement made it impossible *not* to match their energy.

So, I would ignore what I missed out on and paint a bajillion pumpkins and butterflies and Batman symbols on adorable cheeks. I'd hot glue a shit-ton of candy corn to cardstock cutouts and use *all* the Polaroid cameras to take shots of the families and kids and cute little babies to fill those homemade frames.

I'd haul bales (of straw), and shake my butt at the cake boogie, and I'd—

"Whoa there."

My fingers clenched around the bale wire, the heavy-duty string that was keeping all the straw together, and it bit into my skin.

But that wasn't what took my breath away.

No, it was a male voice. Sliding down my spine, hot breath soaking into my skin, teasing fingers drifting up my thigh, dipping in through my silken, wet heat.

I spun and saw...him.

Axel Finnegan.

Standing there, black circles beneath his eyes, scruff on his face, short black bristles highlighting the strong lines of his jaw...and jumping back, dodging the bale of hay I was holding, lips tipping up when I gasped and jerked away, nearly toppling myself over in my attempts to not knock him to the ground.

One hand gripped the bale wire between mine, the other wrapped around my waist.

"Easy, buttercup," he murmured, his breath in my hair, his mouth near my ear.

I shivered, leaned into him, even though the straw bale was between us and he was bending over it like we were playing a weird game of reverse limbo.

I could swear that I felt his lips brush the top of my ear, but then he was slipping the bale from my grip, sliding his hand off my waist.

"This going in line with the others?"

My head jerked like a bobblehead doll. "I—"

But he was gone, walking across the street, his blue T-shirt straining over the muscles of his back, his biceps...

Holy hell, that cotton stretched to the max over his chest and arms wasn't *nearly* as good as his ass in those jeans.

That was a gift from the gods for women.

Two plump Christmas hams, strong thighs that I'd sat atop as I'd sucked his cock deep, legs that had flexed and contracted as he'd pinned me to the mattress, as he'd fucked me rough and hard...so that I'd come so freaking hard that—

"Need some help with the rest of these?"

I jumped again, spun to face Axel, and...braced.

To see *what?*

The sliver of hurt on his face that I'd put there the last time I'd seen him?

The slight hint of soft in his eyes that he'd given me that morning?

Panic? Derision? Anger?

Heat?

But none of those were present.

This was Axel Finnegan, star hockey player, former bad boy, but current town favorite because he'd been avoiding the bars, attending the Harvest Festival planning meetings, and because just two days before, he'd picked up Betty Harrison's unruly black lab who'd escaped the yard, returned Balthazar (yeah, really) home, and *then* had repaired the fence through which big, goofy Batty had slithered.

Pre-season—he'd been despised (and, yeah, that disgust had been warranted).

Today—he was revered.

He'd earned it, at least from what I could see, from what I'd experienced, from what the copious amounts—and it was *copious*—of town gossip had said.

Reviled to Golden Boy.

Quite the swing.

And yeah, so maybe I'd been paying attention to what he'd been doing, what was being said *about* him...because I was pathetic and maybe I'd sent him away...

But I was still—

Staring at him.

My mouth unmoving.

The hay—*straw*—bales in the back of my truck.

I had shit to do, and that didn't include drooling over Axel, even *if* his ass was squeezable and those thighs had my pussy clenching, and his *eyes* were so fucking blue and pretty and pinning me in place.

"Bailey?"

"Yes," I said, shaking myself out of the Fuck Fog and whipping around so I could grab another bale. "This is the last load." I cleared my throat. "I just need to finish lining the block and then I'm on twinkly light duty."

Silence—or as silent as it could be with the hustle and bustle of the setup—fell between us.

Then he stepped close to where I was standing at the back of the truck, leaned down, and—*dammit*—I sucked in a breath.

Because his mouth was near, and his body was close to mine, and I wanted...

Him.

But all he did was lean beyond me, snag a bale, and turn away, carrying it across the blocked-off street and placing it in line with the other bales. Perfectly so, in truth, nudging it slightly with his foot after a glance that had his head tilting from side to side.

Then he turned back.

And all *I* could do was clench the bale wire tighter and start my feet moving, bringing the straw over, scuttling beyond him, plunking it down onto the sidewalk.

Did it land straight?

No.

Did I fix it, even knowing that Billie Rose might go full Harvest Fesitivazilla?

Nope.

I just hurried back, giving Axel a wide berth, snatching another bale, not acknowledging that he was doing the same. Definitely not acknowledging that he was helping me, that his scent was in my nose as we crossed paths in the street, that my gaze kept drifting to his body, remembering, *needing.*

I'd told him to go.

I'd *told* him.

So, head down.

Avoid.

Move shit.

Lunch.

Then twinkly lights and cake slice wrapping.

Avoid like it was an art form that I'd mastered. Because avoidance *was* an art form I'd mastered, ever since Colt—

The name drew me to a stop in the middle of the street, my

empty hands—since I'd been heading back for another bale—clutching into tight fists.

I hadn't thought that name, hadn't allowed it to cross my mind, not since I'd signed the divorce papers. But today, his name whispering around my brain turned my blood frozen, set my heart to pumping tiny icicles through my veins.

His voice as frigid as a northern lake.

His fingers biting into my skin.

His fists lifting and then...coming down.

His body pinning mine into place, taking—

"Bailey."

I didn't jump.

Not that time.

Instead, my body reacted on instinct. I was back in time, during those two years with *him*. I was in my past, on that stormy night, firmly entrenched in the moment that *everything* had changed.

Where I'd reached my breaking point.

Where *I'd* broken—body and mind and heart.

Fists into my ribs, connecting with my skull, my jaw...my *soul*.

Pain tearing through me. Tears sliding down my face, a scream lodged in my throat. Trying to hold it together, to wait until he'd finished, until he'd gone, until...it was over.

Then running out into the night.

The heavy rain plastering my torn clothes to my body, my feet bare and cold, and then bare and cold and *bleeding* from the rough road.

All of those memories flashed through my brain like a slideshow of cruelty and violence and my body moved without my knowledge, without my permission.

I dropped to my knees, threw my hands over my head, and...

I braced.

Waited for the blows to come.

Silence again, only this time it held as the memories faded and the pounding in my ears settled to a faint drum of noise, as the street sounds drifted back in, and I became aware of the fact that I was on my knees, in the middle of the road, with my arms folded over my head.

Trying to protect my most vulnerable spots.

"Buttercup."

A whisper that shuddered through me with all the ease of a jackhammer.

But that wasn't what sent my heart hammering against my ribs.

I was on my knees. *Bracing*.

In the middle of the *fucking* street.

My eyes flew open—

And caught on Axel's.

Pity.

There was pity in those deep blue depths.

I pushed off the ground. I found my feet.

And...I ran.

Twenty-Five

Axel

One second, she was on her knees.

The next, she was up and running away from me.

Not toward her truck, not getting in and driving down the blocked-off street, but taking off down Main, making a sharp right, and disappearing into a narrow alley that was almost hidden between two brick buildings.

She'd dropped to her knees in a second, the move so rapid, it could only be instinctual.

Cowering, compressed into a tiny ball.

Covering her head and—

It's not your problem.

It wasn't.

She'd made it clear that it wasn't.

So, I should just let her go, give her the space to get herself together—and I had no doubt that she *would* get herself together because she was a total badass.

But she'd been cowering—

It's not your—

Fuck that.

I took off after her, not wanting to scare her, but also not willing to let her run off to who knew where, freaked the fuck out and—

It might not be my problem, but I needed to get my head out of my ass and stop pretending. I couldn't stop myself from caring about her, from thinking about her, from wanting her.

There was something about Bailey that...

We were connected.

We were...something that I couldn't just ignore.

Absorbing that, recognizing distantly that where that truth sat in my stomach and heart and mind was...terrifying.

Maybe it was.

But I was going after her anyway.

I hauled ass down the alley, turned to the right. *Nothing.* Turned left. *Nothing.* "Fuck," I whispered, pausing for a second and taking stock of my surroundings. The alley opened onto a narrow street, the backs of the businesses on the next street over close enough to create plenty of shadows, even in the sunlit afternoon. But the stretch of dark opened up beyond the buildings, the sunlight glowing through the end of another short alley ahead.

Old brick buildings.

Crisscrossed roads.

A small town that was full of sickeningly happy people who were setting up a carnival on steroids.

I shook my head.

Not the time, and anyway, I was trying to stay on the good side of this town, trying to not fuck my shit up for a change. *That* was why I was hauling hay bales and had crawled out of bed at six after being on the bus all night.

To get ready for the festival.

To spend the night painting faces and making frames out of candy.

Then tomorrow to tell fortunes if the fucking costume that Billie Rose had showed me earlier was any indication. And when the guys caught sight of me in that dumbass hat and robe, sitting in front of a crystal ball, making predictions for kids...

The shit-giving would be immense.

Worse? Somehow, I didn't care.

The guys were...

I knew they didn't get it—my sudden change in personality, the loss of interest in fucking and drinking, in working hard and playing harder. Why my life was suddenly all about hockey and the town and about doing my job on the ice and then spending every spare moment off it that hadn't been taken over by Billie Rose living and breathing the sport.

My life.

My past.

My...failures.

Swallowing hard, pushing that away, I moved across the narrow street, slipped through the alley, and left the shadows and buildings behind. To the left there was a wide-open park, its huge playground filled with kids and parents, the younger subset tearing down and around the slides and across the monkey bars and just having a freaking ball while the older people set up more tables...and a balloon trellis that guided people from Main Street over to the park (albeit through a wider alley than the one I'd just come through). It was chaos and bright colors, but of the happy variety, the large trees dotting the perimeter of the park and giving plenty of shade for both young and old.

But Bailey wouldn't be there.

Not with how her face had been, how she'd run.

I turned, gaze searching.

And when I saw it...I knew exactly where she'd gone.

I still approached with caution, though, like she was a wild animal ready to swipe out with her claws if I dared to get too close. A breath and I rounded the back of the dumpster, sank down beside her. "Couldn't pick a nicer-smelling place to run off and cry to?"

Her shoulders jerked, head lifting from where it had been pressed to her knees, turning to look at me, and fuck if her damp brown eyes didn't have my heart squeezing. But since they also had my stomach churning, my feet wanting to get to work, to turn my body away and run from what was probably going to end in disaster—

Because it involved me.

Because my whole goal was to get out of this town when she had firm roots keeping her here.

Because my whole fucking life was built on tissue paper and toothpicks, and it always collapsed and—

"You are such an asshole," she snapped, drawing me out of my mental tailspin.

I grinned.

I was that.

And being an asshole was a hell of a lot easier than being in my head, so I'd take it.

Same as I'd take her being pissed at me because that was better than sitting here being sad with her, letting her sit in the embarrassment and shame, letting it roll over her, suck her down—

I was already there.

She didn't need to join me.

Her head dropped back to her knees, voice muffled. "Just go away, okay?"

Tempting.

It was certainly the safer option to leave, perhaps the smarter one, too. I should focus on the shit I needed to do, to concentrate on getting the hell out of this town and the havoc it was wreaking on my mind.

But this fucking woman had me...addicted.

I couldn't leave.

Which was why I plunked down next to her, bent my knees, resting my elbows on them, and looked out on the park, to those kids playing and the parents setting up and the mature trees and open space and—

"This isn't you going away," she muttered.

My lips twitched.

Fuck, I loved it when she snapped at me.

"Nope," was all I said in reply, keeping my eyes on the park, on the kids running around. One of them was trying to corral a small dog who appeared to be determined to catch a squirrel running high through the branches of the trees overhead and failing miserably. The little pup had his paws up on the tree trunk and was barking like mad, its equally little human tugging on the leash and not making much progress.

Cute.

And hell, I didn't know what was wrong with me.

Or maybe I *did*. Maybe *she* was sitting right next to me.

Bailey sighed.

"You gonna cry or run?" I pushed.

Her head popped up, those pretty (and furious) eyes hitting mine. "You know, just when I was thinking that you might not be a *giant* asshole, you prove me wrong."

A shrug. "Well, you made that quite clear the other night."

Regret across her face.

A reminder of my weakness in asking her to see me differently than I see myself, than the world saw me, the town, my family—

Cutting that thought off right at the tracks, I glanced back at the park. "And anyway, being pissed at me is easier than being sad."

Out of the corner of my eye, I saw the stillness enter her body.

It called to a stillness in my own, one that had been there from the moment I'd seen her drop to her knees, her arms lifting to ward me off.

Fear.

Such solid, rigid fear that she'd been transported back to a moment in time, to a memory, to a darkness that engulfed her in just one millisecond.

I'd seen the horror on her face when she straightened, knew she'd forgotten where she was.

Forgotten *who* she was.

Or maybe that was just me projecting.

Or *maybe* that was what was happening to *me*.

"What are *you* pissed about, Axel?"

Or perhaps that was why her question threw me for such a loop.

Because I *was* pissed and hurt and scared and...

"Who hurt you?" I countered instead of thinking about any of the shit that was cycling through my mind.

Flush it down. Don't let it control me.

Move on.

"Bailey," I pressed, asking again, "Who hurt you?"

Silence was my answer.

Silence that was punctuated by the screams of kids, the conversations of adults, the hum of cars in the distance. I could *almost* hear Billie Rose directing people to finish setting up the hay bales.

Because she definitely wouldn't miss that it had been halted, that Bailey and I had dropped the ball.

The bale.

Whatever.

"Who?" I asked again.

Her voice slightly muffled again, head having returned to her knees. "What does it matter? It's over now."

Twenty-Six

Bailey

I realized I'd made a mistake the moment his hand came to the back of my neck, fingers threading up into my hair, lifting my head until I had to meet his gaze.

His *eyes.*

They were furious. "What does it *matter?*" he asked, completely aghast. "I touched your fucking arm, and you fucking fell to pieces in the middle of the street."

"It wasn't you touching my arm."

I shouldn't have said that.

Another mistake.

Kind of like fucking this man on an impulse, getting drunk on two fucking beers, and somehow ending up falling asleep in his arms, waking up naked, and wanting...

Idiot.

I should *not* have said that.

Great, now I was channeling my inner Hagrid.

"Who was it?" he asked, the question a shard of ice. "What happened?"

What happened?

Then or ten minutes ago?

Ten minutes ago, it had been me, remembering what it was like to want and need someone. It was my heart feeling vulnerable. The slight bite of cool in the air, clinging to my skin. A man who was bigger than me coming up behind me. The rumble of a male voice.

A male who was much, much stronger than me.

One who could hurt me—

"Nothing," I said, that fear beginning to churn in my stomach. "It *doesn't* matter. I'm over it and—"

His laughter was tinged with a sharp edge. "Yeah, sure you're *over* it."

The ridicule stung, I couldn't lie. But at least that helped me shove down the memories of the past. "Go fuck yourself."

"I'd rather fuck *you*."

Which was so ridiculous that I actually laughed. *Laughed* after making a freaking idiot of myself in front of half the town and what had most certainly been Billie Rose's watchful (and soon-to-be demanding) gaze.

I laughed because this man pissed me off so *freaking* much.

"Just like you're *over* trying to drown your worries in pussy and booze, so you don't have to think about how much of a fuckup you are?" The moment the words crossed my lips, guilt wrapped around me, tight enough to threaten my breath.

He reared back, eyes going wide for a heartbeat.

Then cooling, any emotion concealed behind thick, frosty ice.

"I *am* a fuckup," he said after a moment, shocking the shit out of me and making those ropes of guilt wrap even tighter. His voice dropped. "Or at least, that's the sentiment I can't get the fuck out of my head."

That was the last thing I'd thought he'd say.

Ever.

Fuck, I was an asshole.

"But that doesn't have anything to do with what happened out there." He glanced away. "What happened to you."

My heart began thudding, but I did my level best to cling to the topic at hand—that being Axel and not me. "You know that you're an excellent hockey player."

He snorted.

More guilt giving me fucking rope burns as it wrapped tightly around me. Part of me couldn't believe that this man was actually insecure. Except...I'd seen a glimpse of his insecurity in my bedroom, a glimmer of vulnerability before he'd left my bedroom. Oh, it had been there and gone quickly, masked by sexy words and a smoldering smile. But it had been there. "You are," I said softly. "I don't even watch hockey, and I've heard about how good you've been playing."

His gaze didn't come back to mine, but his tone had softened. "Who hurt you, buttercup?"

I inhaled, dropping my chin to my knees.

"My ex-husband."

I hadn't meant to admit that. To do more Hagrid-channeling and tell Axel about Co—

A breath. My eyes closing and then opening.

Swallowing down bile.

Pushing forward.

About Colt.

God, just thinking his name again had the bile threatening to rise once more, had panic itching down my spine, flexing and itching its way down my arms and legs.

A gentle hand settled on my nape, massaging lightly. "What's his name, social security number, and last known city of residence?"

I shouldn't have laughed.

Not after what Colt had done to me.

But, somehow, I giggled. "What are you going to do?" I asked. "You couldn't even take on Billie Rose."

"Well, I don't know who could."

"You have a good foot on her and outweigh her by like a hundred pounds."

"I have the same on you, and you scare the shit out of me."

I sucked in a breath. "Axel."

"And anyway," he said quickly. "I now can say that I both know your aunt *and* have experienced the Power of Billie Rose. A thousand pounds wouldn't make the least bit of difference in stopping her from getting what she wanted."

My lips twitched.

"No." I turned my head, resting my ear on my folded arms as I watched him. "It wouldn't stop her." Then I inhaled again, released it slowly. "The truth is," I whispered, "you scare me, too. I—" My eyes traced his profile, the strong lines of his jaw, his nose, the tiny scar at the corner of his mouth.

That moved when he asked, "Because of your ex?"

I nodded. "I trusted him, and he hurt me." His head turned, eyes blazing when they hit mine, and I struggled, not knowing if I wanted to be swept into the powerful whirlpools, to drown in Axel Finnegan's bright blue gaze, or if I needed to run, to throw up every barrier, cling to every bit of distance.

But I'd done that already.

I'd run.

And I was sitting next to him anyway.

"What's his name?"

"Colt," I said and sighed. "And that's more than I want to talk about today."

Another flash of blue eyes. "He hurt you."

He had.

Broke pieces of me into so many pieces I hadn't thought I would be able to move forward. But I *had* moved on. I'd healed and found myself, and did I still hide a bit beneath my protective layers?

Yes.

Did I still prefer my own company?

For the most part.

But not always. I might be more comfortable at the ranch with the horses as my only friends. I might use it as a shield. But I'd begun to inch out behind it. Coming to town more frequently, seeing my friends, rebuilding bonds I hadn't been capable of creating after Colt.

Opening up to this man.

Wanting him.

Sitting here.

I wasn't that broken woman any longer, and I was doing myself a disservice clinging to that notion.

"He did," I said softly. "But I'm not going to let him do it any longer." I released a breath, turned away from those blazing blue eyes, and stared out at the park. The scene of fun and togetherness, family and River's Bend, chaos and love settling me.

This was home.

And this man next to me...he wasn't a threat.

"Why do you think you're a fuckup?"

He moved—I felt rather than saw it since I was still watching the bedlam in front of me—but even as his hand settled on my back, fingers sifting through the ends of my hair, I didn't flinch again.

Because he wasn't Colt.

He was Axel.

Pleasure not pain. Respecting the boundaries I'd put in place. Coming after me, distracting me, going all growly and protective and—

He. Wasn't. Colt.

My chest rose and fell on a breath.

And when he didn't answer my question, I asked again, "Why do you think you're a fuckup?"

His fingers stilled for a heartbeat before moving again. "You know," he murmured, "you have the prettiest hair I've ever seen. I swear to fuck that I've dreamed about it sliding over my naked skin too many times to count."

Heat boiling up through my toes, skating up my calves, like roughened fingertips trailing along them, skating over my thighs, dipping between them.

My tongue darted out, dampening my bottom lip, remembering his kiss, how greedily he'd tasted me.

But he still hadn't answered my question.

"Axel."

A sigh, those fingers still running through my hair. "You're not going to give me an inch, are you?"

"No," I said. "That's not my style."

He went motionless again, and then to my surprise, he chuckled. "Fucking love that, too," he muttered. I opened my mouth to say...something, but his free hand lifted, thumb brushing across my bottom lip. "I am a fuckup. Not think it. I *know* it."

"I shouldn't have said that before. People make mistakes," I said, thinking he was referring to the town and his crappy behavior of the last months. "But it's the way they make them right that's important."

"Yeah," he whispered.

"You've changed," I said softly, not liking the thread of disdain in that word. "Seriously, I can see it. The whole town has."

He turned back to me. "Thank you."

My inner radar was pinging, a coil of unease settling in my belly. "Axel," I said, cupping his jaw, the bristles of his beard scrapping my palm. "I was feeling vulnerable before and trying to keep you away. I didn't mean it. It's just...easier sometimes to keep people at a distance so I can be safe."

A shift, his mouth coming to my palm, lips pressing lightly.

Making me shiver.

Then he gently set my hand back on my knee and turned back to the park. "It's okay, buttercup. I get it." Not a whisper this time, the tone almost cheerful, but I could still hear the disdain.

"No, I don't think you do."

Twenty-Seven

Axel

Her brows were furrowed.

Her eyes sparked.

She turned and poked me in the arm. "You are *not* a fuckup."

Tell that to the man with all the potential who couldn't make it to the finish line.

"Axel," she said, and fuck, she was pretty with all that ferocity on her face. "You are talented and smart and have a soft side."

I snorted.

Her hand came to my cheek again, and, fuck, I wanted nothing more than to kiss my way up her arm, stripping her naked as I moved, getting my mouth on her skin, her breasts, her pussy.

A hint of funk tempering the flowers and apples in my nose, and I was reminded where I was.

I wanted her...minus the side of dumpster.

"Admit it," she said lightly. "You have a soft side that gets you roped into helping a drunk woman who's stripping off her clothes and gluing candy corn onto paper frames later tonight."

"*That's* what I'm doing?"

She poked him. "Nice try, baby. You know exactly what each task entails because Billie Rose does a good spreadsheet."

I laughed.

Because it was the truth.

The mayor had given me an exceptionally detailed spreadsheet.

"So," she said, "why do you think you're a fuckup?"

"Besides my attempts at destroying the town?"

A roll of her eyes. "Yes."

"Besides—"

She stroked her hand along my jaw, down my throat, and rested it on my chest, just above my heart.

It was gentle.

It was the slightest bit possessive.

It...made me unstick.

Made the words inside me unstick.

"—being unable to make it out of the minors, especially when I got a chance I shouldn't have and couldn't take advantage of it, and—"

I clamped my teeth together, cut myself off before I revealed anything else.

Her fingers dug in slightly. "Axel," she breathed.

"Ignore me," I said. "We should get back to those bales." I started to peel her hand away, but she moved closer, her curves pushing into my side, her scent all around me, her mouth close to mine.

"What are you talking about?"

And...the truth just...came out.

"I might have believed you seven years ago when I was first playing, when I was fucking tearing it up," he muttered. "*Before* I found out that the only reason I made it into the league was because my mom fucked my way into it."

She jerked back, her head nearly hitting the dumpster, but I shot out my hand, slipping between her skull and the metal, cradling it so it didn't collide with the hard surface, protecting her even though my mind was a million miles away, was back in the past, back when I found out.

"I know I don't know anything about hockey," she said, "but that doesn't seem right."

I blinked.

"I mean, there are lawyers and contracts and stuff," she said softly. "Right? I mean, one person doesn't make the decision. Doesn't it have to go through a whole chain of people before they decide to sign a player?"

She...was right.

It wasn't something I'd ever thought of before.

But it didn't change the fact that, "The scout only came to watch me play because my mom fucked him."

"What?" she whispered.

"I never would have gotten seen, gotten an offer, made it this far if it weren't for my mom." I turned my head away.

Bailey's hand went to my hair, ran lightly through. "What happened?"

The truth had begun pouring out of me, and I couldn't stop it. "She's...well, the fucking *furthest* thing away from a mother that you would want, and she...is the reason I get to live my dream." I laughed, and it was bitter. Because I *was* bitter about it. "And she fucking *loved* telling me that. I thought I'd finally gotten away from it all, from all the bullshit and drama and drinking and lies and lording every fucking thing she'd ever done for me over my head, when she bothered to remember she had a son, that was. But no, she waited until we were heading into the playoffs, until it looked like a contract with the Gold was a real possibility and then..."

"She threatened to go to the media, and to sue the scout for sexual assault, the team for harassment unless I paid her off—even though I was already paying for her apartment, her phone and groceries, and had bought her a car." I blew out a breath. "I fucking gave her *anything* she asked for and she still threatened me, threatened to take every fucking thing away from me." I dropped my head back, and it collided with the dumpster, the sharp *thunk* reverberating through the metal. "I cut her off. I tried to push through... but every day, there was a call or a note or a threat. A-and my game started suffering and...next thing I knew, we were fucking knocked out in the first round of the playoffs, and I was traded." I clenched my jaw. "I had my shot. I fucked it up. *I'm* a fuckup. Even with a silver fucking platter in front of me, I couldn't hack it, couldn't make it. I still can't—"

"No."

I blinked as her nails dug in.

"You are *not* a fuckup, Axel Finnegan."

I started to shake my head, but both her hands came to my face, cupping my jaw and holding me fast.

"You are *not* a fuckup."

The words struck me hard, settled somewhere deep inside me, somewhere...that had me making a joke because it was too fucking deep, too fucking vulnerable. "Okay, maybe I'm just a fuck-*her*."

She snorted and surprised the shit out of me by slanting her mouth across mine and kissing the absolute shit out of me.

There was tongue and teeth and lips and suction, and my dick went hard and my lungs seized and my hands cupped that glorious ass of hers and—

She broke the kiss, lips swollen, breaths coming in rapid inhales and exhales. "You are a good fuck-*her*," she agreed, mouth twitching. But her eyes were serious when she added, "but not a fuck*up*. Okay?"

Was I supposed to believe her, just like that?

Apparently so because she stopped talking and then leaned forward and kissed me again. And with her lips on mine, her hands coming to my shoulders, her tongue slipping into my mouth, tangling with mine; with her body close and her scent all around me; with the need for her filling me in a way that had become normal for me with this woman, I believed it.

In that moment, I believed it might actually be the truth.

In that moment, I believed in her.

In...us.

Twenty-Eight

Bailey

We'd made out like teenagers.

Behind a dumpster.

Okay, so maybe that part was less teenager and more a bit icky, but I hadn't had the words to heal the hurt inside Axel. I'd just...wanted to make him feel something that wasn't the hurt written into his eyes, the stark lines surrounding his mouth.

He wouldn't have listened, not really, if I kept reassuring him.

I didn't know enough about what had happened, about the process for drafting a player, about the old wound that had sat unhealed and festering for the last seven years to be able to rid him of that burden.

Because he knew about my old wound.

Or part of it, anyway.

And even though some of the weight had been shed, the edges just beginning to heal, the rest of it wouldn't just disappear with a conversation.

It would take time and action.

So, all I could do was show him what it felt like for me to have lost some of that bulk, to show him all the things he made me feel.

To stop being so fucking afraid and to just...*do.*

And, truthfully, it wasn't a trial to kiss Axel, to have his hands on me, his body close. It *was* a fucking trial to have to *stop* kissing and touching him in order to go back to dealing with straw bales and twinkly lights and candy corn, but alas, he'd come to his senses with a rough curse (and this man growling, "*Fuck!*" with his hands clenching on my ass had made me want to forget about making out like teenagers and start fucking like grownups).

Unfortunately, he'd gently propped me to my feet and found his own, and when he'd smoothed back the messy strands of my ponytail, I'd nearly melted on the spot.

Hell, when he'd laced our fingers together, I'd stumbled.

He'd caught me against his side, and truthfully, I'd stumble many times over if it meant that he'd hold me like this.

Even if it meant that Billie Rose's expression went calculating when we walked by her (and her copious rolls of ribbon she was sifting through to choose just the perfect one to wrap around each of the many street signs and light poles lining Main Street) on the way back to my truck.

Somehow the bales hadn't been unloaded, and I was impressed by Billie Rose's self-control to have left the task unfinished (and unchecked on her spreadsheet) while I sorted myself out.

But she had.

Same as she exhibited that impressive self-control by not cornering me immediately for details.

Axel slowly released me then reached for a bale, but I caught his arm, halted him, the words welling up in my throat, floating off my tongue. "Not a fuckup."

Emotion in blue eyes, hot and heady and vulnerable and... squeezing my heart tight.

His palm came to my cheek, his lips brushed my forehead.

His exhale was shaky.

Then he straightened and mischief crept in, wrapping itself around the tenderness. "I think I liked you better when you were busting my balls."

I grinned. "Liar."

Another kiss to my forehead. "Yeah," he murmured. "You're right. I liked you better when I was handcuffed to your porch."

I turned away.

He caught my arm. "I'm kidding, buttercup."

"I know." I ignored all good sense—and the gossips watching—rose on tiptoe and pressed my lips to his. "I was going to find Billie Rose and another set of handcuffs."

I might not be able to make my baggage—or his—disappear with a few kind words, a single conversation.

But I could make something spectacular happen.

I could make this man laugh.

And it was like the world had suddenly come back into full color.

"That's not quite straight."

I narrowed my eyes at Axel over my shoulder. "Seriously?"

We were behind schedule.

My dumpster meltdown—and okay, probably our dumpster make-out session—had put us behind Billie's spreadsheet schedule. We'd been working double time at hanging the lights that would help illuminate the festivities in the park.

And we had only...oh, eight million more trees to go.

Exaggerate?

Me?

Nah.

But if this man critiqued my light hanging ability *one more time*, I was going to...something—

Oh!

I was going to get those handcuffs and...restrain him in my bed—

No. That wasn't right.

On the porch, so he'd get splinters up his backside while I had my wild way with him.

Better, minus the last part.

Because that wouldn't be a punishment for him.

Cocky much?

Cocky...time.

Heh.

"No," he said. "That loop isn't hanging the same length as the other."

His voice was a little closer, and I knew I was losing it because I was mentally waxing poetic about *cocky* time and my thighs were trembling and I really couldn't give two fucks about the lights and—

The ladder creaked, shook slightly.

"Here," he murmured, lips brushing my ear, body coming very close behind me, arms gripping the sides of the ladder. His front pressed to my back, and cocky time came right back into the front of my mind.

Mainly because his cock was hard and pressing into my ass and...I wanted him.

"Problem?" he asked, voice silky smooth, his hips flexing, making me shiver.

Punishment.

I needed a punishment.

I'd put him in the barn, hitched to the wall on the wrong side of Picard's behind and let him deal with all those cow patties.

Nodding, I slid up a rung, reached out to fix the "uneven" loop.

"Steady," he said when I wobbled slightly.

"Really?" I muttered, glancing at him...and then down toward his hands that had covered my breasts.

"You were going to fall." He tried for innocent.

"And this is the proper hero's way to save the damsel from crashing to the ground?"

"First"—his hands massaged my breasts—"no one would ever call me a hero."

"I seem"—my voice caught when his thumb slid over one nipple and then the other, hips arching back—"to remember you saving me from another ladder."

"Hmm." He pressed a kiss to my nape, slowly released my breasts. "It seems to me that I need to protect you from ladders."

"I—"

His hands went to my hips, a groan slid from my lips.

Then I was on the ground, slightly wavering from the sudden

change in altitude, my next reply lost somewhere in the vicinity of that ladder.

He reached up, fixed the strand, then climbed back down and moved the ladder over to the next tree. I moved, realized he'd taken advantage of our brief moment of being blocked by a tree trunk to come up behind me.

The stink.

Now my nipples were hard and aching, my pussy wet and needy. "What's second?" I asked, tilting my head to the side to watch his ass flex against the tight denim encasing it.

Damn, that was a nice view.

He glanced over his shoulder, smirking when I jerked my gaze up to meet his. "Second, I can't stay on the ground, staring at your ass for much longer."

"Oh?" I asked, bending to grab another strand of lights and undoing a length of it, giving him another glimpse of my butt—which happened to be encased in some tight denim of its own.

His soft groan felt like a physical caress between my thighs.

"Third," he rasped. "I'm hungry and we're behind schedule."

I handed up another length of lights. "There's a table of food over there"—I nodded to the far side of the park, where we'd already hung lights through the trees—"I can grab you something—"

"I plan on eating you for lunch, buttercup."

Oh.

Oh.

I wanted that, too, as I watched him on that ladder stretching his arms overhead as he strung the lights through the branches and mentally calculated the now four million remaining trees.

He was suddenly on his feet in front of me, towering over me, a movement that was so abrupt I startled, jerked back.

"Sorry," he murmured, starting to reach for me, stopping just before touching. "Is this—too much?"

My throat tightened, heart pounding, that knot of my past heavy in my stomach.

"No," I whispered. "I've worked hard to get past what Colt did. I—" I forced myself to hold his gaze when I said the next because it wasn't shameful, because I'd worked hard to get where I was, because I was going to *keep* working, "I've seen a therapist for the last couple of years. Even when I could barely afford food and the ranch's mortgage, I made sure that I saw Jennifer once a week. It's... I don't think I could have gotten here without her."

His hand drifting forward, cupping my jaw. "You would have," he said, fingers drifting back, sliding through the ends of my ponytail. "But I'm glad you got help."

"It might help—"

Another kiss to my forehead. "A man who's luckier than a shitton of other kids I passed by on my way here?" He straightened. "Thank you," he whispered. "For—"

A shriek.

We both jumped, and as we did so, I saw Billie Rose barreling our way. "Uh-oh," I muttered.

Axel's hand rested lightly on my back. "Brace for impact," he muttered.

It was so absurd that I laughed out loud...just as Billie Rose reached us.

My aunt slid to a stop, her head tilting to the side, considering.

His arm was pretty much around me. I'd been ogling his ass all of a minute before. We'd made out behind a fucking dumpster.

There was nothing to consider.

I was one of the Finnegan Floozies.

Which...had me laughing again, Axel's eyes coming to mine. "What?" he murmured.

"I'll tell you later," I murmured back.

Billie Rose's brows lifted. "Care to fill me in on the joke?"

"Nope," I said, popping the P. "We've got lights to hang."

"And a pussy to eat."

The words were so soft and silken.

I rose on my tiptoe, mouth just barely able to reach his earlobe. "I'm going to lick your dick like it's my favorite ice cream cone."

He froze then turned to face me, heat in his eyes and mischief in his expression. "Okay," he rumbled, "now you're going to make me find a dumpster."

I giggled.

He tugged the end of my ponytail.

I turned back to Billie Rose—

Or started to, anyway.

Because the ladder and lights were gone, and a gaggle of high school-aged boys had taken our task over a respectful six trees over.

"You two!" Billie Rose bellowed. "Lunch."

She tossed a pointed look in my direction, but I wasn't able to focus on it before an arm slipped around my waist, tugging me back against a big, strong chest, a hard cock against my ass, a rasping voice in my ear. "I'm fucking starving."

Twenty-Nine

Axel

I shoved the door open so hard that it collided with the wall, denting the sheetrock, and I didn't give one fuck.

Not when Bailey launched herself into my arms the moment my key was clear of the lock. Not when I was doing my best to get those clothes off her, and the fucking tight jeans I'd been admiring all day were a pain in the ass to draw down that ass, those plump thighs.

Not when she was yanking at my clothing.

And look, I wanted to be naked, too.

But I had a pussy to lick, a woman to make come.

And a limited amount of time for "lunch" before we had to get back to it.

Dropping to my knees, I yanked at the laces of one boot, managed to wrestle it off, and chucked it over my shoulder. Then I went to work on the other, repeating the process and cursing the entire time.

Bailey reached for my shoulders, tried to tug me up, but I'd finally gotten the second boot off, was lifting her up enough to tear off her jeans.

They dropped soundlessly to the floor as I moved for her panties.

"There's my pretty pussy," I crooned, and didn't bother to set her feet down, just lifted her, tossing her legs over my shoulders and moving so that her back was against the wall. Then I did what I've been dreaming about since I'd had her.

I got my mouth on her.

Dipped my tongue through wet folds, finding that spot just to the left of her clit that made her cry out and arch against me, her fingers gripping my hair tight.

Then I set about finding *all* her spots.

Wet dripping down my chin, inner muscles clenching around my tongue. Her cries in my ears, her thighs squeezing me so intensely that I worried for a second I might not be able to breathe.

The worry faded because my name was rolling off her tongue.

Because her breath was hitching.

Because as much as I was tongue-fucking her, she was fucking my mouth.

Fucking, incredible woman.

"Axel," she hissed, arching back, her head bumping into one of the generic photos I had hanging on the wall.

It fell off its hook, crashed to the ground, probably breaking, but I didn't bother looking. Not when the tempo of her hips had changed, had sped, had roughened as she ground against my face.

She was close and I couldn't give fuck-all about the frame.

Then she was coming, and I still couldn't give fuck-all about the frame.

I just spun us, crashing into my coatrack, nearly knocking over the narrow table where I dumped my mail and keys. I needed a flat surface and I needed it now. The couch was closest, and I set her on the edge, helping her rip off my shirt, toeing off my shoes, shoving down my pants before I remembered the condom and had to dig out my wallet to snag the plastic square.

Her hands were on my chest, nails skating over my nipples, dragging down and wrapping around my cock.

Hard and sure strokes that did absolutely nothing for my control.

"Kiss me," she demanded, dragging my head down to hers.

Our mouths came together in a long, drawing kiss, tongues tangling, lips and bodies pressed tight.

Nothing better than my naked body against hers.

Except one thing.

I broke the kiss, sliding my mouth down her throat, worshiping the curve of her shoulder, the fragile collarbone, the hard buds of her nipples, the soft underside of each breast.

I wanted to taste every inch of her, to worship every centimeter.

But she had different ideas.

A shove had me sprawling back on the couch cushions, and then she was clambering on top of me, sinking down on my cock, her head falling back, her breasts jiggling as she worked her pussy on me.

"Fuck," she hissed.

I grunted, reaching for her hips, coaxing her forward.

She was tight and hot and the fucking view of her tits hanging down, so near my mouth that I had to lean up, to suck a nipple deep, had all my intentions of savoring disappearing.

Fast and hard.

Fast and deep.

Fast and...fast.

Luckily, she was right there with me, grinding on my dick, fingers digging into my shoulders, pussy clenching around me.

I snaked a hand between us, rubbed her clit, felt her pussy convulse even harder, even faster.

And thank fuck for that.

I needed her to come.

I needed to fuck *her*.

I needed—

"Axel!" she gasped, those contractions rhythmic and rapid, strong enough to nearly send me sailing.

But I held on, waiting for her to slow before I reversed our positions, before I pressed her back into the cushions, stroked hard and deep and—

"Fuck," I growled, way too soon.

I couldn't help it.

Stopping my orgasm would be like stepping in front of a train and expecting it to just halt on a dime. It was impossible with her milking me, with her tugging me close, her legs wrapping around my hips, her chants of "Yes, fuck. Yes. Keep going. Like that, don't stop. Don't—"

I groaned, my orgasm exploding at the base of my spine as her pussy gripped me even tighter, milking me.

A moan, her body relaxing, eyes sliding closed, legs falling from around my waist.

I slumped forward, barely able to get my elbows beneath me so that I didn't crush her, my heart thumping in my chest, sweat sheening my body, lungs and limbs burning in equal measure.

"Fuck," she whispered a moment, a minute, an eternity later.

"I know," I muttered. "I can't feel my legs."

Her hands slid through my hair, lightly traced my tattoo on my rib cage. I tensed, just slightly before I forced myself to relax. Yeah, I had the ink, but I didn't like to think about it, about what it represented—

And she fucking had the radar for that.

"Why the lines?" she asked.

I had a choice.

I could tell her the rest of it, sit in the past, let it shade this moment. Or I could shove it back down, know that she knew enough, knew more than anyone else besides my mother.

We'd both been rubbed raw that day.

I wanted to enjoy her.

Enjoy the peace of us being together before I had to glue candy on picture frames and dress up as a fortune teller.

I wanted...this moment.

"Another time, okay?" I said, smoothing back her hair.

Brown eyes searching mine for several long seconds. Then a nod, her hand moving away from the ink, down to my ass and squeezing tight. "Fuck," she breathed, "hockey players have the best asses."

I grinned, bent, and nipped her bottom lip, slipping my hand between the cushion and *her* ass. "I was thinking the same thing about ranchers."

Laughter on her face.

Joy in her eyes.

Then mischief.

"Should I tell you what else I was thinking?"

My dick twitched.

Her mouth curved.

And then she leaned up, her mouth coming to my ear, her words hot puffs of damp air as she told me.

And then because she'd told me I had to take her into the kitchen, bend her over until her breasts were flush against the pale gray marble of the island...

And then I had to fuck her until her legs collapsed.

Luckily, hers gave out before mine.

Thirty

Bailey

"Ow," I hissed, blowing on my poor, abused finger.

Hot glue guns were deadly dangerous.

"You know," Dessie said. "If you stopped staring at a certain hockey player with a big cock, you'd be less likely to burn yourself."

She had a point.

I still glared at her. "We weren't going to talk about that, remember? Plus"—I glanced around—"there are children about."

"Unfortunately, not any of them close enough at this moment to save you from this conversation."

I scowled because my glance had told me that, too.

It was just...I *was* distracted.

Because of my big hockey player with a giant dick.

Because he was being...cute?

More smoothing of my hair and kissing my forehead and holding my hand until we'd needed to go our separate ways to our respective stations. I'd painted faces for hours, and he'd brought me drinks and a plate for dinner when my station was slammed and I couldn't get away to take a break without turning away a line of adorable kiddos. Then I'd watched between bites when things had calmed down as he'd giggled with little kids when he'd taken his turn on the picture frame station, his big hands having no problem with the glue gun.

No burns on his fingers.

Probably because he wasn't remembering what it felt like to have his strong, hard body wrapped around me as he'd pounded deep and—

A candy corn beaned off my forehead.

I glared at Dessie again.

She smirked...then confiscated my glue gun.

"No crafting while under the influence of Axel Finnegan."

Rolling my eyes, I began sorting candy. But I didn't turn away from Axel.

Because I was considering returning the favor of providing food and sustenance.

Axel—a.k.a. the Fantastic Finnegano—was telling fortunes. In costume. With a hokey accent and a painted-on (okay, *I'd* painted it on) mustache.

And the line was out of control.

I could hear an occasional prediction and they had me cracking up.

But...I also kind of wanted to be close to him, even if just for a few minutes. A drug addict getting my fix. Dangerous and maybe stupid, but...he was...well, he wasn't Colt and I liked him and—

A hand on my arm.

I turned to Dessie. "He watches you, you know?"

"Because he's a fucking creeper."

Dessie smirked. "Because he's as into you as you're into him."

Okay, so maybe that was the truth. Maybe I needed to talk about Axel and me and pop the bubble that had surrounded us today, dissuade the hope cocooning me in safe, cotton wool.

But...I wanted this day.

I wanted *my* Harvest Festival.

The good memory to hold on to.

The joy of simple pleasures and liking someone who made my heart skip a beat.

So, I didn't walk down the obvious conversational path that Dessie was trying to lead me down. Instead, I said, "I like him. It's probably stupid and will implode"—oh, God, I hoped not—"but... I do, Des. I do like him, and I haven't had this in a long time. I know his reputation. I know *him.* So...let me have this, okay?"

Desiree studied my face, her lips pressing flat. "Okay," she said softly.

Then, miracle of miracles, let the subject drop as we worked to make extra frames.

Another round of cake boogying would be finished soon, and we'd have more pictures to print and cut and stuff into the frames, more kids who would want to put their own frame together, more busy work to fill the cool, fall evening with the twinkling stars overhead.

So now was the perfect time to bring him food.

Couldn't have my hockey player withering away now, could I?

I dropped the sorted candy and prepped frames in front of Dessie, nudged my friend's shoulder, and said, "I'll be back."

"Spring that man and go do something fun."

I waggled my brows. "Like a cake boogie?"

Dessie's expression went serious then softened, and she snagged my wrist. "It's good to have you back, Bay." A squeeze. "Just saying."

My heart thumped hard. "You too, Dessie."

A nod. Then her tone went brusque. "Go before I'm overwhelmed with little terrors who try to eat the stale candy."

I grinned but left her anyway, winding my way over to the food table, buying him a plate of food (and then a second because he was a giant hockey player and I wanted him to have enough energy for later). Then I snagged two beers, a couple bottles of water, and made my way back to the Fantastic Finnegano's tent.

The kids had cleared out.

The hockey players hadn't.

A gaggle of them had clustered in the entrance of the tent, their laughter booming.

I side-stepped a mountain-sized blond and, yeah, my heart skipped a beat when Axel glanced up and his gaze focused on me. His smile was a cozy blanket and the warmth in his eyes...well, it meant a lot.

"Who's this?" the mountain-sized man said.

"Back off, Joel," Axel snapped. "She's—"

I set the plates on the table, the beers and waters. Then I turned to the mountain, to *Joel*, apparently—and what a stupid name *that* was—and narrowed my eyes. "You here for a fortune?"

His mouth turned up at the corner. "You gonna give me one, sweetheart?" He reached forward like he was going to touch me.

I snagged his wrist, put just enough tension on the pressure point on the inside of it to halt his movement. "Yes, a broken wrist is in your future if you think about touching me."

"Should I point out that *you're* touching me?"

I released him. "There. Happy?"

"No," he said, stepping a little closer, eyes warming, voice dropping. "I *like* it when you touch me." A tilt of his head. "Want to get out of here, baby? I've got really big...fingers." The last was said as though he were imparting state secrets.

My lips twitched.

Laughter bubbled up in my chest, my throat, and, what the hell, I let it rip. Then let it continue flowing when his expression went completely befuddled. I laughed so hard I had to brace myself on my knees, that I couldn't catch my breath, that I barely felt Axel's hand on my back.

That I barely processed that it was his hand.

That it didn't make me panic.

Because my body knew his now.

Because his fingers had dipped under the hem of my shirt, the roughened tips brushing lightly over my skin.

"Brutal, buttercup."

I straightened, turned into his body, his arms coming around me. "God, I thought your lines were bad."

A snort had me glancing over my shoulder.

One of the guys—black hair, thick beard, chocolate brown eyes, all-around stunning—was smirking behind Joel.

The other was staring at his feet, but I saw his shoulders were shaking.

Axel tugged my ponytail, glanced up at his teammates. "Beat it," he ordered.

Joel huffed, but his mouth was still tipped up at the edges. "Rude."

"I mean, I'm not the one talking about fingers."

Joel chuckled. "Not you." He pointed one of those large digits in my direction. "Your smack talk is on point. You"—he jabbed it at Axel—"are an ungrateful teammate. We're all just here to show our support."

I squeezed Axel's wrist when he tensed. "Oh, you guys want to support the town. Oh my God!" I stepped out of his grip, clasped my hands to my chest. "That's so sweet."

Joel paled. "I—no— That's okay."

I giggled. "Oh now, don't be shy!" I moved toward the entrance and the fates were kind because my aunt happened to be passing by. "Billie Rose!"

She spun, brows together.

I waved. "Come over here."

For a moment, it seemed like she didn't want to approach, but then her face cleared, and she smiled, walking toward me.

"Hey, honey," she said, pressing a kiss to my cheek.

I grabbed Joel's wrist when he tried to slither away, and damn, the man was strong. But I'd wrestled cattle nearly my entire life. I could hold one hockey player in place, long enough for him to fall into Billie's snare, anyway.

"These *three*," I emphasized the last when the other two players tried to slink to the side, "were just telling me how they're quite desperate to show their support." My aunt began to smile. "I know that they're happy to jump in wherever, especially since it's getting late, and we always need more help at this time of night."

Considering.

Billie Rose's expression was considering.

No, *plotting*. Calculating. Like in a Pinky and the Brain, gonna take over the world type of way.

She smiled.

It was *awesome*.

"Fuck," one of the men behind me muttered.

I smothered a giggle. Just said, "Can you find these three some way to help?"

"Oh, I sure can, baby girl." She kissed my cheek again, waved at Axel, and said, "Close the flap on this tent and it's dinner break time for you." Then she turned to the trio of men and her voice was authoritative when she clipped out, "You, three, with me."

Joel shot me a glare over his shoulder.

I just finger waved. "Have fun and thanks for your...support."

A chuckle in my ear, fingers dipping into the cleft of my ass. "You know he's going to take a run at me the next time we're on the ice together."

I shrugged. "You can handle him."

"But can I handle you?" he murmured, nipping at the top of my ear.

"That's a nope." I reached out and snagged the edges of the tent, tugging them closed, then drew him over to the table. "Okay, Fantastic Finnegano, you need to eat dinner before the next rush."

"Hmm," he said, sitting on the edge and drawing me in between his legs. "I thought we'd already talked about what kind of food I'm craving."

"Well, *I* need you to have energy to satisfy that craving," I pointed out. "Otherwise, you're useless to me."

Without another word, he picked up the plate and began eating.

I giggled.

He offered me a bite of the pulled pork, and even though I wasn't really hungry, it was Dusty's pulled pork, so I ate it. "I like it when you do that."

"Do what?"

"Smile and laugh and relax against me." He popped another bite into my mouth. "Look happy and relaxed with a loser like me."

My heart clenched tight, and I ran my fingers through the bristles of his beard. "I thought we talked about this already."

"About what?"

I slanted him a look. "Don't play dumb."

"Then stop being so fucking sexy."

"Eat your food."

"Will you let me eat *you* later if I do?"

I rolled my eyes, even as a pulse of need slid between my thighs. "Didn't you already do that?"

He bent, pressed his nose to my throat, and inhaled deeply. "Yeah. So?"

"So that's the big, dark secret for the big, bad hockey player? You're obsessed with oral sex?"

"Is that a problem?"

"For me or you?" I teased.

Fingers in my ponytail, male laughter in my ears. "For you. Fuck knows it's not a problem for me."

"Hmm." I took the fork from him, started feeding him bites. If I had a night ahead of me with a sexy man who was planning to spend it between my thighs, then I'd better feed him.

And I was doing it purely for selfish purposes.

Not because I liked doing it, or because it felt intimate and I wanted more of these quiet, familiar moments, our bodies touching, our breaths intermingling, our hands brushing and stroking and—

The plate was torn out of my hands, plunked onto the table, rattling the crystal ball.

Hell, who was I kidding, I was *so* doing it because I liked all of that.

Almost as much as I liked him sliding a hand into my hair, tugging my head back, and kissing me senseless.

Heat, too much considering we were in public with only a couple of tent flaps between us and discovery.

Except, Billie Rose had told us to close them.

I knew that no one would disturb us.

I could get on my knees and—

A groan. "What are you thinking about?"

"Blowing you."

He choked.

I grinned.

"Trouble."

"So says the man who tore through my town."

"So says the woman who tore through my ego."

My grin was back, but all I did was say, "Happy to be of service."

His hand was bracketing my hip, long fingers digging into the top of my ass, drawing me flush against him so that I could feel his cock. It was like granite. It made my mouth water more than that pulled pork. But when he nuzzled the underside of my jaw, nipped lightly at the spot where it met my throat then inhaled deeply, he rasped out, "Apples," settling right in the vicinity of my heart, my grin faded.

"Are we doing this?" I asked softly.

I was scared and not. I was excited and hopeful and needy and weirded out and—I was, for the first time in a long time—looking forward to what the future would bring.

A future that wasn't just the ranch and the cattle, fences and horses and shag carpeting.

A future that involved this man.

His blue eyes, his words, his actions didn't prevaricate.

He didn't play coy, didn't pretend to not understand exactly what I was saying.

He just stroked back the wayward, uncooperative hairs that were escaping my ponytail and kissed my forehead, saying simply, "Yes, we're doing this."

Thirty-One

Axel

We were naked in Bailey's bed so we could be near the ranch and the animals that would need care in the morning.

We because I wasn't going to lounge in bed while she worked her ass off in the morning. *We* because I had ideas about that work-bench in the barn and the fence near the empty stall, and the hay bales, and the walls with the old photos and tools and horse tack.

We because...I had *lots* of ideas.

I'd used some of them that evening, which was why she was naked and passed out, her arm around my waist, her soft, slow breaths puffing against my shoulder.

I was naked and staring out the dark window.

So quiet. So many shadows and secrets.

But it was peaceful rather than scary. I was with Bailey. *With* her in a way that wasn't dating.

It was more.

Maybe not my girlfriend, not yet. Not when I'd just barely convinced her to take a chance on me, when I'd just barely convinced myself. But it was more than dating, more than a simple meal with a side of fucking afterward.

She was...*more.*

Just quite simply *more*.

And I owed her a fucking date.

I owed her candles and flowers and worshiping her body slowly, incrementally, beautifully, after the fourth date.

I owed her some time in her fucking living room that had been pulled apart because of a leak, helping her put it back together, even if she assured me that the contractors were showing up to fix the mess in a couple of days' time.

I owed—

My cell rang.

Her brows drew together, breath hitching, and I reached for the nightstand, wanting to shut off the call before it woke her.

But when I saw that it was Coach, my brows drew together, and I quickly swiped at the screen, lifted my cell to my ear, and slid out from between the sheets. "Hello?" I said quietly, moving into the hall and closing the door.

"Finnegan, did you see the game tonight?"

For a second, I was confused because we hadn't played.

Then I realized...the Gold had.

"Rogers got tagged with a cheap hit tonight and went into the boards hard," Coach said. "Broke his tibia and fibula. He's in surgery."

My heart began to pound.

"But he's out at least three months. Maybe longer."

I inhaled. "Oh?" I croaked.

"They want you in San Francisco in the morning." A beat. "I'd suggest you pack a big bag. If you play this right..."

He kept talking, letting me know the team had offered transport and already set me up with a room in a hotel, that practice was at 1:00 the following afternoon, that I needed to be at the arena before that to meet with someone from the back office to go over details, that someone was going to reach out in the next couple of days with more information about amending my contract for a long stay in the league.

Me.

A long stay in the league.

My chest went tight. My lungs refused to expand. My pulse

pounded through my veins, and my throat had gone so freaking taut that I couldn't force out any sort of reply.

"You could make a go of this, Finnegan," Coach said. "Don't fuck it up, yeah?"

I cleared my throat. "Yeah," I managed. "Thanks—"

But I was talking to dead air.

Slowly, I lowered my phone to my side.

"Axel?" A gentle touch, slightly calloused fingers on my side. "Who was on the phone?"

"Coach," I rasped.

Her fingers tightened. "Is everything okay?"

"They want me in San Francisco in the morning."

Her brows lifted. "That's a good thing, right?"

I nodded. "I—" A breath. "Rogers, the normal center on the third line, broke his leg tonight. He's in surgery and will be out at least three months."

"Shit," she whispered.

"Yeah." My hand slid up her back, holding her to me like she was my lovey, and I needed the stuffed toy for comfort. And hadn't I just spent the last months realizing that I *did* need it, that I needed this woman in my life?

"But it's a good thing, right?" Her head jerked. "I mean, bad for him, but good for you, right? This will mean more time on the Gold, right?"

"Bad for him because it was a dirty play that led to him getting hurt." I swallowed hard. "Good for me so long as I don't fuck it up."

She went still. "Axel."

Clearing my throat, I lightly nudged her back. "Ignore me. You need to get back to bed, and I need to get packed and I, fuck, *I*"—I made a face—"need to text the tornado that is your aunt that I won't be able to take my shifts at the festival tomorrow."

Her hands came to my cheeks, and she turned my head toward hers. I hadn't even realized that I was staring down the hall, not looking at her, not *seeing* her.

Already, a curl of panic was coiled in my belly.

Threatening to expand, to fuck everything up.

I slid out of her hold, wanting, needing to go, to lock this down, to—

"Don't."

A sharp clipped-out word that had me blinking.

Those hands came to my face again. "Your mom didn't fuck the player who hurt Rogers."

"What the fuck, Bailey?"

"Don't," she said again, just as clipped out, gripping my biceps tight. "Your mom didn't do this. No one but *you*—" She poked me in the chest. "You did this. You got here. *You*— "

"And the fucker who hit Rogers."

Another poke. "Do people get hurt playing hockey?"

I knew where she was going with this. I knew what she was going to try and prove.

But none of that was going to make the coil of panic in my stomach disappear.

"Buttercup," I began.

"No," she snapped, stepping close, wrapping her arms around me, her body flush to mine, her voice low and intense and sliding over me, sinking in through my skin, settling onto my soul. "You're not going to do this when we've finally figured our shit out. You aren't going to be an asshole and push me away. You are going to fuck me and you're going to give us both enough orgasms to hold me over for a while because you're going to be there, on that fucking team, and you're going to be there a while."

Her mouth pressed to mine, one fierce kiss that sent my heart skittering and my cock hardening. "Then you're going to go back to your place and pack your shit for a good long stay with the Gold because you're fucking incredible and you're going to *be* incredible, and if you're not, if you make me drive my ass down to San Francisco to kick *yours,* then we're going to have a problem."

The coil loosened.

Amusement slid like jelly through my veins, warming me, slowing my pulse, making my movements languid and slow and steady.

"You're going to kick my ass, buttercup?"

A flash of a smile, as though she sensed my panic cooling, my humor growing. "Damn right I am." Her hand slid into my hair. "Even if I have to bring down my shotgun and my saw."

I barked out a laugh.

She kissed me again, long and slow and deep. "You're going to be great," she whispered when she'd pulled back enough to suck in a breath. "So *fucking* great."

"Or you'll saw off my dick?" I said lightly.

"Fuck no, I need that," she quipped.

More laughter bursting out of my throat, that panic disappearing.

This woman.

Leaning down, I swept her up into my arms.

She squeaked. "What are you doing?"

"Orgasms."

Her teeth pressed into her bottom lip; her eyes went hot. But there was no sass, no fire, no arguments.

She just reached between us, wrapped her hand around my aching cock, and said, "Enough to tide us over."

I grinned. "Damn right, buttercup."

Thirty-Two

Bailey

"You know," I said into the phone. "Tonight was the first time I watched a hockey game from beginning to end."

A soft huff of amusement. "I'm almost scared to ask what you thought."

He sounded tired.

Unsurprising, since he'd worked his ass off. Even as a hockey newbie, I'd been able to see that.

But this was his first game—or well, not the first, but this was the first since...whatever we were, the first since he'd told me about his mom, his implosion, his insecurities.

So, I was going to make fucking certain that he went to bed with a smile on his pretty, albeit somewhat annoying face.

The man had been texting me regularly since he'd left the day before.

Mostly dirty memes and GIFs that were designed to make me smile, but along with the occasional—*At the hotel. At the rink. Back at the hotel.*—they'd made me...miss him.

"What's with that face, buttercup?"

I blinked, returned my focus to the screen and video call that was showing that pretty and slightly annoying man. "What face?"

"The face that says you miss me."

He rolled over, the crisp, white sheet sliding down his bare chest, the chest I'd kissed my way across less than forty-eight hours before. He smirked, tugged it lower still, showing me *all* the goods that had gotten me in trouble with missing him in the first place.

Terrible man.

"I don't miss you," I said, adding when he sniffed, "I just miss your cock."

He snorted, but the man had never missed an opportunity to talk, touch, or bring attention to his penis, so it didn't surprise me when he reached down, wrapped one big hand around his cock and stroked.

I choked, on my own spit, I'd be the first to admit.

But that man stroking his own cock, the taut skin moving over the hard jut of his erection, the tip glistening with precum had need tearing through me, setting fire to my veins. I was wet. I could feel my desire gathering at the tops of my thighs, my nipples beading against the fabric of my sleep shirt.

"Whatcha got under that big ugly shirt, buttercup?"

Ugly? Yes, I was wearing an oversized blue cotton shirt with a huge print of Wish Bear on the front. But she was adorable, and he had no right—*no right!*—to insult the fluffball of adorableness.

"Wish Bear isn't ugly," I snapped.

A sexy grin, that hand still stroking, making it very difficult for me to concentrate on what had gotten my feathers ruffled in the first place. "That shirt is."

"You're an ass."

"I fucking *love* it when you get all growly with me."

More heat. More dampness coating the tops of my thighs. More...need for this man who was nearly four hours away.

"You're sick."

"You like it."

A shake of my head. "No, I don't."

Now his grin was absolutely unrepentant. "Put your fingers between your thighs, buttercup. They come up dry, and I know you're telling the truth."

"You're—"

"An asshole, I know. Tell me again." He stroked faster, his groan rumbling through my phone's speaker. It might as well have been against my skin for how my body reacted.

Burning up.

Trembling.

Fighting the urge to rip off my "ugly" shirt and put my fingers between my thighs, to show him he was right. That I was turned on and wanted him here and—

Fuck it.

He seemed to make it his mission to shock me.

I needed to give him a taste of his own medicine.

So, I propped the phone up next to me, reached for the hem of my shirt, and whipped it over my head.

Showing him what I was wearing under it.

Which was...nothing.

"Fuck," he groaned, his muscles straining as he jerked his cock.

"I want you to stroke yourself," I ordered, rubbing my hands along my chest, squeezing my breasts, brushing my thumbs over my nipples, pretending they were his hands, his fingers.

His hand worked.

Sweat began to glisten on his skin.

"I want you to pretend it's my hand wrapped around your cock, that I'm there with you, that when you come, it's on my breasts."

"*Fuck,*" he hissed, the head of his cock turning an angry red, moisture beading, making slick sounds.

Or maybe that was from me, from my hands, my fingers between my thighs.

"Spread your legs, buttercup," he rasped. "I want to see you, want to see those slick folds." I sat up, rearranging the pillows, shifting the phone so he could see between my legs and spread my thighs. Wide.

Not shy.

Not scared.

I'd learned to own this part of me.

This man had given me nothing but pleasure and confidence. He felt as deeply as I did.

He was...the most dangerous person I had ever met in my life.

And the safest.

Because he made me feel safe.

But he didn't let me sit in that feeling, curl into it, sink into the peaceful oblivion. He pushed me to grab for more, to *take* more.

"Rub your clit," he ordered. "*No*, not like that." A growl. "Rub it like I'm there. Rub it like how I would. Hard, buttercup. No fucking mercy. Rub your clit like I'm demanding you come on my fingers, my tongue."

I shuddered.

Then I rubbed harder.

And—oh God—that was good.

"Don't stop, buttercup. Keep going but push a finger inside. Hard."

I did what I was told, sliding my middle finger inside my pussy, curling it forward, hitting my clit from the inside and out. "It's not enough," I whispered, hips jerking.

"Then give yourself more."

Another finger.

And then another, until I could pretend it was his hands on my clit, his fingers inside me, his lips and teeth and tongue sending me up that mountainside.

"Fuck," I whispered.

"Don't stop."

"*Fuck*," I whispered.

"Don't *fucking* stop, buttercup."

My head flopped back against the headboard, gaze catching on his through the phone, holding scorching blue eyes for a moment before my gaze drifted down his body.

Pecs.

Abs.

Cock.

All glistening.

All begging for my attention.

All driving me closer to that edge.

Pleasure wound itself tight in my belly, the ends of that strong spiral twisting taut until one side sparked, caught, and went alight. Like a lit fuse, it ignited, burning rapidly.

"Axel, baby," I begged.

"Don't fucking stop. Don't—"

"I'm gonna come."

"Do it."

His expression was feral, all the muscles of his arms, his torso, his neck standing out sharply in relief.

"I'm gonna—"

"*Do it.*"

I shattered, my back arching, hips bucking, moan escaping from between my clenched teeth. By some small miracle, I managed to keep my eyes open, and I was rewarded with the glorious sight of Axel falling over the edge too.

Jaw clenching.

Curse words tangling with my name as his hand worked, as... white jets of cum shot out of his cock, coating his belly, making my mouth water and wish I had it on my body, my tongue, my taste buds.

A swell of exhaustion chased the wave of pleasure.

Drawing my lids down as I tried to catch my breath.

"Fuck," he rumbled, recovering a lot quicker than I had—because professional athlete and all that. "I wish I was there."

My mouth tipped up, and I couldn't resist teasing him, couldn't resist giving him that sass he said he liked. "I'm glad you're not."

A groan, his hand clenching something—oh, a T-shirt—rubbing roughly at his belly. "So fucking mean," he growled. "Is that any way to treat the man who just made you come?"

"Is this the point in the conversation where I remind you that I took matters into my own hands?"

"Is *this* the point where I tell you I really fucking miss you, and not just your body?"

My breath caught. "Axel," I whispered.

"Buttercup," he murmured, and the warmth in that filled my veins with helium, so much until I felt like I could float. He tossed the soiled shirt aside, tugged the sheet up to his waist, and following suit, I used a tissue to clean up then snagged my shirt, pulled it over my head.

"How was the rest of the festival?"

"The kids had a blast," I said. "I'm still not a huge fan of plastic gourds and candy corn, but I did get a slice of delicious chocolate cake today, so it wasn't a total loss. Though I do still have to get through the parade tomorrow and all of the breakdown." My lips twitched. "I *am*, however, a big fan of a certain mystic with a painted-on mustache."

He groaned.

"Is that sound of displeasure because you're sad you don't get to see the parade?"

"No," he muttered. "It's sad for two reasons—one, I'm now officially on the team diet plan, so that means no chocolate cake for me on any day but a Cheat Day, and two, the guys have learned of my moonlighting in the fortune-telling booth."

My lips twitched higher, but I managed to keep my voice neutral when I asked, "Is that a bad thing?"

"Well, considering my nickname is now Balls, yeah, it's not ideal."

I giggled. "How'd they get to Balls from the Fantastic Finnegano?"

"Fortune Teller to Crystal Ball to Ball to Balls." A grunt. "Because apparently Ball doesn't roll off the tongue quite as well as *Balls.*"

I giggled again.

"God, I love it when you laugh."

God, I love *you*.

I almost blurted that out, barely caught it on the edge of my tongue. My heart began pounding—too much, too soon, just...too *much.* But I forced my voice to be light. "Even if it's at your expense?"

A shrug. "There are worse things when it comes to the woman who makes me jerk myself off on FaceTime."

"Well, gold star for me then, huh?"

"When it results in orgasms, fuck yeah." His laughter joined with mine then he yawned, rubbed a hand over his face.

"I should let you get some sleep."

He nodded. "Heading out on a road trip tomorrow."

"I know." Then to his raised brows, "I've now made a study of the Gold's schedule. It's in my calendar, and I've even upgraded my streaming service, so I get the games."

I'd done that even though it would take a little longer to get out of the black, but then today I'd sold Picard to a petting zoo in the next town over for a decent sum. He'd get loved on every day. I'd earned some extra cash.

And maybe even some sandwich money.

"I'll give you some money for that next time I see you."

"Axel," I said firmly. "I don't want your money, so don't offer to give it to me and ruin both our good moods."

"Bailey."

"I miss you more than wanting to argue."

He stilled. "Buttercup."

"Exactly." I curled up on my side, cuddled up under the blankets. "Now take the win, rest up, and focus on hockey."

"No ladders."

"Had to get one last order in, huh?"

"Well, I can't let you be the only one who's good at them." A beat. "Promise?"

My heart squeezed, affection for this man filling every single one of my cells. "Promise," I whispered.

And then, Axel Finnegan, former nuisance and world-class asshole, gave me the gift of a gentle smile and soft words.

The best part?

I knew he'd saved those just for me.

Thirty-Three

Axel

A tap on my shoulder from Calle, one of the offensive coaches, had me glancing up at the former National team player. She'd blown out her knee, taken up coaching, and was killing it.

"Next up," she said, just as the whistle blew to stop the play on the ice.

We were on the penalty kill, down a man because Coop was in the box for a trip, and I wasn't normally on the PK squad.

But I wasn't going to argue.

Not when we were down one goal, another could put the nail in the coffin for this game, and we couldn't afford to just give up two points in a long season where every single point made a difference. More wins meant more points, meant a better playoff position.

Home ice advantage.

Better seeding.

And...I was thinking to the future, about what we could do as a team, instead of worrying about living up to the promise of now.

Bailey would give me that gold star.

Bailey...

I missed her.

Ridiculous right? I'd spent twenty-five years without her, and all of a few days with her, if I wasn't counting the nightly phone calls and regular texts, and I felt like I was missing part of myself.

The ice, the game...that felt right.

Not being in the same town to share it with her?

That blew.

But I knew she was watching. Every game. Every night.

Her commentary was hilarious because of her limited hockey knowledge—hating their third jerseys, calling the puck a ball, asking when halftime was—but...even though she wasn't here, even though I had that missing piece sitting heavy in my chest, I didn't feel alone.

And I wasn't going to stop.

Not now.

No fucking way.

Plus, I'd picked her up a present and was going to give it to her two days from now. We had two days off after the next game, and I was spending them in River's Bend.

With Bailey.

Tonight?

I was going to make her proud.

Determined, I jumped over the boards, lined up, and took the face-off, winning it back to Logan who chipped it up off the glass.

Then it was a race down the ice—first a conservative one (because I didn't want to get caught up and leave my teammates down *two* players), then it became a balls-out one when I realized that I had a very real chance at getting to the puck before the other team's defenseman.

My heart pumped, my lungs burned, my quads were on fucking fire.

But I didn't feel any of that.

Urgency.

That was the chief feeling.

I needed to get to that fucking puck.

The defenseman bumped me, and not expecting the fucker to have caught up enough to make contact after I'd already passed him, I nearly ate shit.

But I recovered quickly, kept skating.

Ten feet from the puck.

Five.

Two.

One.

I got it on the blade of my stick, just barely corralling it as my opponent slammed me hard into the boards.

I'd been expecting *that,* though, so I rolled with the check, exhaling so my breath wasn't lost, so that I could keep the oxygen coming, my body moving. A kick brought the puck in front of me, and I got my stick on it again, freeing up a little bit of space.

Giving me enough time for me to glance up at the clock, to see that the penalty only had three seconds left.

Another crushing hit, slamming me into the boards.

But my mind was already five steps ahead.

I needed to protect the puck.

For three.

Two.

One.

Then a burst of effort, of movement that broke the hold the defenseman had on me, that shoved me past the other one who'd come in to double-team me. I saw a flash of black, another, knew that Blue had followed me into the offensive zone, just like I knew that Coop was streaking in behind him, his penalty having ended and our man disadvantage coming to an end, allowing him to jump back on the ice and join the play.

I gained a foot, knew I had a moment—and only a moment—to look, to get my bearings, to get the puck to my teammate.

A flick of my wrists.

A pass from the corner to the front of the net, floating past Blue, jumping over his stick.

But that was okay...

Because Coop was there.

A shove had the defenseman off my ass. Then I was moving to the net, to the far side, sneaking up behind the goalie.

Coop faked a shot, passed it to Blue.

Who'd seen my cut, my positioning, and passed the puck over.

Five feet, four, three, two—

I wound up.

Swung down.

My shot…hit the goalie in the pads as he read the play and slid over, blocking the puck.

But the goalie was moving too fast, and the rebound didn't make it to safety, didn't fly out into the corner or out of the zone. It dropped…right into the center of the crease, the small cylinder of vulcanized rubber bouncing.

Right *fucking* there.

I lunged forward, jabbed at the puck.

Sticks slashed down around me, hands shoved, mouths formed curse words, but I got my blade on that puck, and I hit it fucking *hard*.

Hard enough that it slid forward, shooting forward, drifting toward the goal line.

Over the goal line.

I saw it in the net.

And then I was shoved forward.

Harder than that puck.

I fell forward, eating ice, tasting blood, dodging the skates suddenly surrounding me as my teammates came to my defense, doling their own pushes and shoving, chirping, and cursing.

But I couldn't give one fuck.

Because…the puck was in the net.

The score was tied.

I was earning my keep, my place.

I was thinking about these men—and Brit—as my teammates.

Progress.

Fucking finally.

I was checking my phone in the locker room after the game.

But I didn't get a chance to open the texts that were waiting for me from Bailey before Brit sat down next to me, lips curving at the edges. "I see you flushed the bullshit."

Setting my phone down, I gazed at her innocently. "I don't know what you're talking about."

"Bullshit...*Balls.*"

I grunted.

God, that fucking nickname.

"What do they call you? Smiles?" I asked, considering her biggest sponsorship was for a popular toothpaste brand and her grin was well-known, having graced many a magazine cover and billboard.

"No," she said.

"Grinny Weasley?"

She snorted. "Now, if Mandy got a hold of that one." A nudge of my shoulder to hers. "You're doing good, kid."

Stupid that the sentiment meant so much.

But I didn't have time to process that, not when my phone buzzed. Brit snagged it from beside my hip before I could react—fucking quick ass glove hand—and glanced at the screen.

"Who's Buttercup?"

Fucking *hell.*

I snatched it from her, narrowed my eyes.

"Another problem you solved because of Auntie Brit." She smiled beatifically. "So, when do I get to meet her?"

I scowled. "Never," I muttered.

She was completely unfazed. "You know the crew would accept her."

That I didn't have any doubt of, not now that I'd spent a full week with the team, saw how tight they were, how much like a family they functioned—and not the fucked up one I'd grown up with, but an actual family that loved and cared about each other.

"I know," I said, shoving the phone under my leg—on the far side for good measure and safekeeping from Brit's reach. "But... we're new, and she lives in River's Bend."

Brit winced. "The long-distance thing sucks, but River's Bend isn't that far, you know."

"I know," I said. "I guess the bigger thing is that I only just got her to agree to see me. I don't want to push too much too fast."

"Wow."

I frowned. "What?"

"Just surprised, I guess. A big, tough, alpha hockey player admitting that he needs to take things slow and steady? Color me surprised." A toss of her blond ponytail, a flash of that million-dollar smile. "Apparently, River's Bend makes them insightful and sensitive."

Heaven help me if the guys caught wind of *that.*

"I'm not from River's Bend."

"You did a good job of making a spot for yourself," she said, voice quiet. "And not just as a shit-stirrer."

I grunted again. "A certain goalie helped kick my ass in gear."

Now I got the full Brit smile. "Flatterer."

"Wants this conversation over-er."

She punched me in the arm. "No broody assholes, puh-lease. Especially, since I came over to do you a favor."

That sounded...ominous.

People didn't do favors, not for me, not without strings anyway.

Except...people did.

People on this team. People in River's Bend.

I pushed that realization down, focused on Brit.

"I have an apartment not far from the arena. It doesn't make the commute to the practice facility all that great, but it's close enough and convenient for home games, and best of all it's empty, furnished, and free, since Lucas and Rome"—two rookies who'd been signed right after training camp at the beginning of the season—"moved out."

"I—" My words faltered because I didn't really understand.

She plunked a set of keys into my hand. "Hotel life gets old real quick. The apartment is yours for as long as you need it."

"I haven't signed the contract yet."

"Word is it'll be ready for you when we land in San Francisco."

"I—my agent—" He hadn't said anything to me. In fact, I'd been trying to get in touch with him from the moment I'd been called up and had gotten nothing but radio silence.

One of the reasons I hadn't signed yet.

Not the only one, considering they hadn't asked me to sit down and actually put pen to paper yet.

But...maybe that was because my agent was a fuckup?

Shit.

My temples began to ache, and I resisted the urge to rub them. Another thing to deal with when all I wanted was to get home to Bailey.

"Another word of advice?"

I blinked up at her.

She handed me a card. "Call Prestige, bump your shitty agent, and get Olivia to represent you. She's a BAMF and a total shark and is used to negotiating with the back office. She'll get you the deal you need."

"I—" I fumbled for a few more moments, scrambled to find the right thing to say.

How did this woman know?

Brit stood, clapped me on the shoulder. "And maybe call her tonight."

My brows dragged together.

A shrug from the goalie. "I might have already told her that you were interested in new representation. No offense, but Manny Douglas is shit."

I sucked in a breath.

Shook my head.

The power of Brit.

"Are you related to a woman named Billie Rose?" I asked as she started to walk away.

Consternation on a pretty face. "No, why?"

"I think you'd better do a 23andMe, just to be sure."

A flick of that ponytail, another smile. "Sounds like I'd like her."

"It'd either be love or a battle to the death."

Laughter. Another clap of my shoulder. "I like you, Balls. You're good people."

I started to reach for my cell, stopped when she called, "Oh, Balls?"

Rolling my eyes, I glanced up. "You'll manage the distance," she said softly. "She somehow managed to get through all of your walls, wound her way through the barbed wire around your heart. You'll figure out a couple hour drive." A nod that was nothing if not encouraging. "I know you will."

And then she strode away, leaving me to my text messages.

With a set of keys in my hand.

A business card in the other.

But, most important, with hope that I'd finally sorted out my shit.

Thirty-Four

Bailey

I was finishing up the touches on my dinner sandwich—this week's selection was salami, cheddar, with a fancy Dijon mustard that made me feel especially bougie. Of course, the bread was the cheapest variety I could find to pay for that fancy mustard.

The farm...was a money pit.

Gramps's old truck had needed new tires.

Another pipe in the "remodeled" section of the house (and, yes, that was air quotes because I had serious doubts about how complete the remodel had been) had a leak. I was thinking it was more like a lipstick-on-a-pig situation rather than actually going in and updating the things that needed updating.

New pipes to replace the eighty-year-old ones? Nah, that would be too smart. They hadn't actually replaced them all. Instead, they'd done a poor patch job, and now that poor patch job was responsible for me having to tear the carpet out of another bedroom. It was ugly, but still.

New wiring because the updates my grandparents installed in the seventies might be a fire danger? Of course not.

But fancy carpet and tile and wallpaper?

Oh, absolutely.

Now a large portion of that wallpaper was in the trash, along with the sheetrock it had been adhered to.

And I'd spent the rest of Picard's money on pipes.

And fancy Dijon mustard was going by the wayside once this bottle was done.

Because wiring.

And circling back to money pit.

Sigh.

For now, I'd turned off the breakers in the remodeled section, had made sure the water was off in that part of the house.

I'd had a few electricians and plumbers out to give bids, and now the fancy Dijon mustard fund was going toward pipes and wiring.

Fun times.

But I'd make it through.

I always did.

Plus, now that I was splurging on fancy streaming services, I had plenty of things to watch while I stuck to my sandwich diet.

Go me.

I took my plate into the family room, still sans carpet and couch, but I'd commandeered Gramps' old recliner from the barn.

It smelled like horse and faintly like Gramps. His cologne, the spice and sandalwood mix that I would never forget. Sitting in it felt like he was giving me a hug, so even though I'd had to toss that old, ugly couch of Gran's and the memories that came with it, I'd found this.

I was reaching for the remote when I heard tires crunching on the gravel outside, saw the flash of headlights across my driveway.

Considering how far outside town I was, I didn't get a lot of casual visitors.

I was catching up with Dessie tomorrow, a promised full report at her place, and I had no doubt that Billie Rose would tag along for the reporting. Frankly, it was a miracle that I'd gotten nearly a ten-day reprieve from the conversation, and I had to chalk that up to Billie Rose wrapping up the Harvest Festival and prepping for the Holiday Parade.

More parades.

More snotty-nosed kids and picture frames and twinkly lights.

I smiled.

Maybe I could convince Axel to take another turn at the Fantastic Finnegano. I found that I had a particular fondness for the fortune teller tent.

I set my plate aside when the headlights flashed through my living room windows, telling me that this wasn't a turnaround, but rather a car parking in my driveway.

"Damn," I muttered, not feeling particularly social, but also knowing that if it was a neighbor who needed assistance, I wouldn't be eating my sammy any time soon.

A push to my feet, a pause to grab my shotgun—because a woman who lived alone in the middle of nowhere couldn't be too careful—and moved to the front door, reaching the hall just as the bell rang.

Keeping my gun at my side, but ready all the same, I opened the door a crack.

And felt my heart go *whoosh*.

Axel was on my porch—fully clothed, sadly. He had a bag over one shoulder, another in his hand, and was wearing a suit that was slightly wrinkled but still hugged his body in all the right places. Powerful thighs. Broad shoulders. Biceps a woman could (and I had) cling to. His eyes warmed when he saw me, danced with mirth when his gaze flicked down.

"Do you have handcuffs?" he asked.

His voice was...a warm blanket wrapping around me.

"What?"

Grinning, he pushed the door open, nudging me back, his bags hitting the floor. My shotgun was plucked out of my hands and settled into the rack I had mounted on the wall.

Then his arms were around me and my face was in his chest and...home.

I was standing in my house, and it felt like I'd finally come home.

"Hi, buttercup," he murmured, running his hand over my hair, wrapping his other arm tightly around me. "Miss me?"

"Just your dick," I returned.

Then felt his chuckle in my soul. "I missed you," he murmured.

"Meh," I said. "I'm the pain in the ass who orders you around and threatened to shoot you."

Another chuckle. "I told you I'm open to anything in the bedroom." A nip to the top of my ear. "Or out of it."

I choked.

He laughed, swept me up into his arms and marched into the living room, steps faltering when he took in the space. "What the fuck, buttercup?"

He knew about the leaks, the carpet, the missing sheetrock.

I'd also told him I was taking care of things. Which I was.

It was just sometimes on a ranch like mine, other things took priority, and then...there was the whole money thing.

Still, all I said was, "I have it under control."

"You *have* no carpet." A beat. "Or furniture."

"Gramps's chair is good enough for the moment. Plus, I'm not going to fix the trimmings until the base is settled." His gaze flicked to mine. "I have bids for plumbing and electrical, since the first leaked again and the second is a fire hazard." I pushed lightly at his shoulders, indicating that he should put me down.

Which he understood, apparently, because he walked over to Gramps's recliner, set me down.

Gently.

Always gently—except in bed, of course.

Then he gave me a little bit of rough. Which I liked.

"I didn't know you were coming up," I said softly, reaching for his hand and trying to tug him down into the chair next to me. He came close but didn't sit. "When do you need to go back?"

"Tomorrow night."

My belly went squiggly. "Yay," I whispered.

His fingers smoothed back my hair and he kissed my forehead. "Sorry, it's not longer."

"You and your dick are here," I said lightly. "That's enough."

Heat creeping into the edges of his eyes, warming that icy blue to a temperate river to heated springs. He started to answer, and I braced myself for whatever filthy thing he'd say that would set my clit buzzing, nipples hardening, but before he replied, he turned, and I saw his gaze hit my plate perched on the crate I was using as a coffee table.

A breath that had his broad shoulders rising and falling, his frustration a palpable presence in the room.

I went for a change in subject.

It seemed most prudent. "So, how are you feeling with everything? You're looking good on the ice. That...deke—I think they call it—was on the top ten plays of the week."

"It's 9:30," he said, completely ignoring my attempts at conversation change.

"Uh, yeah? Are you tired from the drive? Do you want to go to bed?"

Yes, please.

I'd really prefer *that* topic change.

A muscle in his jaw flexing. He nodded at the plate. "Is that dinner or a bedtime snack?"

I pulled my hand back, tucked it into my lap. "Dinner," I admitted.

A sigh. "Fencing?"

"That had me working late?"

He nodded.

"No." I swallowed. "Um, I—a broken water line."

Another sigh.

Now, I shrugged. "The cows need water."

"So, you did what?" The question was quiet, his face suddenly impenetrable.

"It was only a ten-foot trench I needed to dig and run a new line on." I grinned, not sure why he was all growly when I damned well wasn't going to stop taking care of the ranch, of myself, but not wanting to bicker about it when we had all of a day together. "The mud was the worst part, but I bet you would have loved it. All that muck and wet clothing, the only thing I was missing was someone to wrestle with."

He grunted. "Ten feet," he muttered, eyes sparking.

And I lost a thread of patience. "Look," I said, "you have your job, this is mine. I can handle everything the ranch throws at me, and I have for years. And, a word of warning, I'm not going to tolerate you getting all growly and protective when I'm just trying to do my job." I dropped my hand onto his shoulder. "Most importantly, I'm doing fine. This is all normal maintenance and putting out fires and just day-to-day for me. I promise." A beat. "And how you're acting right now makes me feel like you don't think I can do it. Even though I know I can because the only reason the ranch is here right now and not some tract of homes because the bank foreclosed is because of me."

Fingers on my cheek, stroking gently. "You're right." He tugged at the end of my ponytail. "I'm sorry, buttercup."

"Thank you," I said, and I meant it. I was doing my best to support him, support his job, even though we were new. I needed the same from him...and I needed the apology when he overstepped, I needed him to see me, see what I was doing.

A kiss to my forehead before he plunked the plate in my lap. "Eat."

It was more order and grunt than request, but both made my heart roll over in the best way possible. Because he was taking care of me, but in a way that wasn't overstepping, or at least didn't insult my ability to take care of the ranch.

Myself on the other hand.

Well...he wouldn't be the first person to point that out. "Did you eat?"

He nodded. "I've got my approved meal plan food in my bag. I'll just put it in the fridge."

"Okay," I said as I picked up the sandwich, but before I took a bite I saw his face, saw the *concern* on his face. "Axel, honey, it's all good."

Half of his mouth tipped up. "Yeah."

Then he moved back out into the hall, asking me what else was up as he headed into the kitchen.

"Not much, I mean, Gramps's truck decided to be a bastard, but I managed to get it up and running before I put my limited plumbing skills to work on the trough. Just call me Jill of All Trades."

He came back in, carrying the bag he'd had in his hand on the porch.

"Of course, considering it came with a side of mud wrestling, it reminded me that I definitely need a professional to take care of the house. Otherwise"—I smiled, took another bite, and spoke around all that yummy Dijon— "it would take me a decade to finish the house."

The vibe I was getting from him was oddly intense, but he didn't comment, just sank down onto the arm of the chair and watched me eat the sandwich.

When I was done, he took the plate, asked, "Still hungry?"

I shook my head.

The plate went to the crate.

But still, he didn't say anything.

And now I was getting a *weird* vibe.

"What is it?" I asked when he didn't say anything, just stared out the windows, hand stroking through my hair.

"I have something for you."

"Okaaay," I murmured when he didn't say anything further.

After a long moment, he added, "It feels big."

I inhaled, let it out slowly. "Do you—I mean—we don't have to do it today if it feels like it's too much."

He shifted off the arm of the chair, big palms resting on my thighs. "I want to fuck you senseless because that feels familiar and safe and something I know how to do." My throat went tight. "But...I want something different with you. I want...*more.*"

"Axel," I whispered.

"So, I want to give you something, but I'm sort of freaking out that it's too much too soon, especially since I haven't even gotten to take you out on a date yet, and we've been...I don't know, a couple, together, my girlfriend, *more*. Fuck"—he shoved a hand through his hair—"now I sound like a goddamned idiot."

"No," I said, sliding forward and wrapping my arms around his shoulders. "You're not an idiot. I...we're not doing this in any way that's normal. But...you know parts of me that no one else does, and that doesn't scare me. *You* don't scare me, Axel Finnegan. Not any longer. Not since I've seen that big heart of yours." I ran my thumb along his jaw, the bristles brushing over my skin.

"Big...heart?" He'd relaxed, expression gentling, but his eyes were filled with that Finnegan mischief.

I rolled my eyes as I sat back and extended a hand. "Pretty puh-lease!"

Thirty-Five

Axel

Why was I so fucking nervous?

Because she was important.

Because she was more.

Because—

I focused on the task at hand. "Right," I said, reaching into my pocket. "There are actually two presents, and if you don't like them, it's no big deal, I can—"

Her hand came to my free one, squeezed lightly.

"I'm sure I'll love them." Her lips turned up into a crooked smile. "So long as it's not an engagement ring—"

I pulled out the small box I'd shoved in my pocket.

The small *ring-sized* box.

She made a choking sound.

I plunked the box into her hand.

"I—" She visibly recoiled, and suddenly I fought back my laughter. "Axel, I'm sorry, but I don't want to get married again."

Considering what her ex-husband had done, I didn't blame her.

"Open it."

Her throat worked and her hands shook as she tugged open the box. "Oh," she breathed, so much relief in those two letters that I lost my hold on the laughter.

She glared up at me. "Not funny."

I tugged her into my arms, the tension gripping my insides breaking. She didn't want to marry me, and that was cool, that was actually refreshing. We were what we were then, in that moment. We were new and learning and...it was just us. "No marriage, buttercup. Just us, and...all your secrets."

I gave her my best evil villain laughter.

She swatted at my shoulder, but when I pulled out the necklace I'd spotted in the store's window, the one that had made me think of her, that I'd *had* to stop and buy for her, she gasped quietly.

"That's—"

"You gave away your secret when you mentioned Picard."

Her bottom lip trembled as she ran a finger over the charm. It was a silly thing, a cow in a traditional red shirt, something that I was only beginning to know about because I'd begun streaming the show in my downtime.

"You weren't supposed to pick up on that," she said softly.

"Well, I might not have if I hadn't heard you call that horse Data."

She groaned, but her lips were curving. "It's really cute," she whispered.

"I know," I whispered back.

Her hand came to my jaw, and her eyes were wet when she said, "Thank you."

"It was nothing."

"No." Her eyes were wet. "It's not nothing to me."

"Okay, buttercup," I murmured, wrapping my arms around her. "Okay." And then I held her, just held this woman who'd somehow become important to me, who was fierce and brusque and soft and sweet, a fucking juxtaposition that made me want to find out every single secret, everything that made her laugh or smile, everything that made her sad, made her cry. I wanted vengeance on her ex. I wanted to hunt down anyone who had hurt her. I wanted... every single piece of my life tied to hers.

After a few minutes, her sniffing stopped, and she pulled back slightly.

"Just what you wanted, right? A crying woman at ten o'clock at night after driving for four hours?"

Amusement in my belly.

Laughter in the air.

"Should I give you the other present?"

"I don't think I'll be able to handle it. Not unless you want a watering pot in your arms."

"Meh." I leaned back and over, grabbed the box, and plunked it into her lap. "Full disclosure. This wasn't all me."

A frown.

"Brit helped me arrange it. Well, no"—I shook my head—"Brit *arranged* it."

"Brit, goalie Brit?"

I nodded. "She wanted me to formally issue an invite to the Gold family."

"I—"

"She's *my* Billie Rose."

Bailey pushed back her hair. "Oh, Lord."

"Yeah."

She shook the box lightly. "Now I'm scared to open this."

"It's not going to jump out at you."

"You said you didn't arrange it, so how can you be sure?"

I shifted, scooping her up so that she was in my lap and my ass was in the recliner. "Because I know what's inside."

"Oh."

"Yeah." I tugged her ponytail. "*Oh.*"

She tore off the black ribbon (that I hadn't tied on) then the gold paper (that I *had* used to wrap the box).

Then opened the top.

She started, breath sliding out on a hiss. "*Axel.*"

My jersey. Or, well, a game-weight Gold jersey with my name on the back. Slowly, she pulled it out of the box, her touch reverent, almost as much as mine had been the first time I'd ever seen my name on a Gold jersey. It was big and important and...it fucking meant everything.

My name there.

Her getting the weight of it.

She clambered out of my lap and tugged it over her head, and I laughed when I saw how it engulfed her, hanging off her hands, dropping nearly to her knees. “You’re kind of small, buttercup.”

“Well, not everyone can be a behemoth like you.”

“True.”

She cocked her head to the side, a jaunty smile on her face. “You’re imagining me in this without anything underneath it, aren’t you?”

“I’m *always* imagining you naked,” I said.

But imagining her naked with the exception of my jersey skating over her thighs, my name on her back, her body wet and aching and ready beneath that material and just for me...yeah that was fucking *good.*

She reached for her waist, and in a flash, her leggings were on the floor.

A glance showed me her underwear was tangled in the black material, but even as I was processing that, her arms were moving inside the jersey, and there was a flash of skin, a flash of mouth-watering curves.

Her shirt landed at my feet.

Then her bra.

Then I caught a glimpse of a peach-shaped ass, wet, glistening folds as she bent, slid off one sock and then the other.

Growling, I jumped to my feet, snatched her to me.

She squeaked, the socks dropping from her hand to the floor.

“Fucking teasing,” I said, picking her up and tossing her over my shoulder.

“You like it.”

My hand sliding up her thigh, cupping that ass for a moment before I dipped my fingers into her slick pussy. Wet. So fucking *wet.* I brought my fingers to my mouth, sucked them deep, apples and woman on my tongue.

“Axel—” she gasped.

“Too much?” I asked.

“Not enough.”

A tart reply that earned her a smack on her gorgeous ass.

“Too much?” I asked again.

"No, baby," she said, turning her head, nipping at my jaw. "I want you to give me everything you've got."

It was a fucking miracle there was any blood left in my legs, enough in my brain to carry her to her bedroom when all I wanted to do was drop her to her feet and fuck her right there on the hallway floor.

But I had enough—just barely—to make it to her bed.

And it turned out that I had enough to give her everything I had.

I'd turned off her alarm and stumbled my way through chores, luckily having heard her describe her mornings enough to hold the animals over for at least a few hours.

She needed her rest.

She was on her own too much.

She needed someone to take a little of the pressure off her shoulders. I didn't completely understand where that protective urge came from, especially when I'd spent my life protecting myself and avoiding contact with anyone who might require more than I could give them.

Which was sex, orgasms, nothing more.

But I wasn't that with Bailey.

And I was going to be away a lot. I'd signed a contract, one that converted mine from the Rush into one that would keep me on the Gold.

For three years.

It was entry level. One way. It meant I was going to be on the roster, and I was going to stay there.

So, I couldn't be here all the time.

Which was why I was turning off alarms and making coffee... and studying the contents of her fridge.

And looking at the bills piled on the countertop.

And staring at the bids for new plumbing and electric for the house.

And...hating that I hadn't realized exactly how much she was struggling. I'd brought her a necklace and a jersey, and she'd sold her fucking cow to pay for a streaming service so she could watch me play hockey.

She'd dug a ten-foot trench, wrestled with pipes in the mud.

Hurt her back.

Fallen from a ladder.

By herself.

She didn't ask for help.

Wouldn't. I might not know every single thing about her yet, but I knew that she wouldn't.

So, I was brewing coffee and doing what I could.

And if I took some pictures with my phone of those bills, if I scheduled a grocery delivery because her fridge and pantry were mostly empty (more so than should be for any person, even if it was just for one person in this house) then so be it.

I couldn't be here every day.

I *could* find a way to make sure she was protected even if I wasn't.

"What are you doing?"

I spun around, casually shoving my phone and nodding to the bowl I'd begun prepping on the counter. "Bemoaning my breakfast."

Her hair was a mess, eyes half-mast, lips swollen, throat scuffed from my beard.

She was wearing my jersey.

She was the most beautiful woman I had ever seen.

I poured her a cup of coffee, offered her some of my overnight oats (she refused, sticking with the black brew), and when we went down to the barn (after she'd put on pants and shoes) and her face softened when she saw my clumsy efforts at completing her morning routine, I knew...

She wasn't just my now.

She was my future.

And it was my job to make sure she was protected.

Thirty-Six

Bailey

I frowned at the truck in my driveway.

It wasn't Axel's little sedan and anyway, my hockey player —yup, *my* hockey player was currently on a plane, heading for Seattle.

But the white work truck looked familiar.

So did the man who was coming out of my house.

"Jerry?" I asked, bringing Gramps's truck to a stop and manually (because it didn't have automatic *anything*) rolling down a window. "What are you doing here?"

The man, black hair, beer belly, and a typically genial smile, slid to a halt.

By a pile of pipes.

Um.

What?

I'd gotten a quote from Jerry, but I wasn't going to go with him, not when his bid was the most expensive. He did good work, but, frankly, I wouldn't be able to afford him and also do the electrical.

Hell, truthfully, I couldn't afford either.

But I'd planned on dipping into the savings I'd managed to

squirrel away, and I could go back to PB&Js, and I could maybe even pick up some evening shifts at Monroe's.

I'd get to hang with Dessie *and* practice my beer pulling techniques.

All I'd ever wanted.

Yay!

And yes, that was sarcasm talking.

"Um," Jerry said, drawing me back to the conversation at hand. "I'm fixing the pipes."

I blinked.

Then bit back my curse. "Is there a reason you're fixing the pipes when I haven't actually *hired* you to do the job?"

Now it was his turn to blink.

"I got the check, Bailey, and the request to start as soon as possible." He cleared his throat, shoved his hands into his pocket. "I had a cancelation this morning, so I figured I'd get a jump on it while you were out in the field."

My temple was starting to pound. "But was I the one to make the call, Jer?"

That had him freezing.

"It wasn't me, yeah?"

If there was ever an *Oh shit* moment to cross someone's face, Jerry's was the quintessential one. "But I cashed the check already. I used it for the down payment on Jennifer's room and board."

My other temple began to pound.

Jennifer was his daughter who'd gotten into a kickass school after being waitlisted in the fall. I knew, because this was River's Bend, that she was starting in January, and apparently, she was starting because of the proceeds from this job. Proceeds that could have only come from one person.

"Do you want me to stop?" he asked.

"No, Jer. Thanks."

Relief in his eyes before he nodded and hurried back to the pipes and then headed back into the house. I opened my mouth, almost called him back, and then realized it was on me.

River's Bend was safe.

Really safe.

This far out from town with so few visitors?

Even safer.

Thus, I rarely locked my doors—when I wasn't trying to keep naked troublemakers out, that was.

Apparently, I needed to make a habit of that if Axel was going to start doing things like this.

I grumbled as I pulled out my cell, typed a message to Axel, knowing that he was unlikely to get it since he was in the air, but as I turned back to the house, to the pile of pipes and the plumber who was fixing up the ranch house, my heart wasn't annoyed.

It was...touched.

"Oh, Axel," I murmured, "what am I going to do about you?"

Not run. Not avoid.

I was going to live.

I was going to embrace what might be.

I was going to take care of a certain hockey player who had spent years pretending he didn't care about anyone but himself.

Because he deserved it, needed it...and I needed to give it to him.

All of that was true, and my heart might be soft for him.

But I still cursed that certain, troublesome hockey player when I saw another van pull up.

A&E Electric emblazoned on its side.

"I ought to flay you alive, Axel Finnegan," I snapped, later that evening.

Much later because Axel had just gotten off the team bus, after he'd gotten off the team plane, after they'd taken on Seattle and won again that evening.

A six-game streak since Axel had been pulled up.

He was looking good.

On the ice, I thought, based on my limited experience. But mostly off it. Granted we hadn't spent loads of time together, but we'd spent enough now for me to read his moods, to understand when he was rattled and nervous.

And he was...settled.

Confident.

Secure.

Part of that was from the contract.

He'd made it, and while I knew that he probably was thinking about Rogers' injury and how it impacted his rise, I wasn't seeing it impact him as much. I could pick up nerves, especially if we talked before the games, but when we talked after each match up, I could see a difference. Day by day, I was watching his confidence grow.

That didn't mean I was going to put up with his bullshit, though.

"Because I'm sexy and you miss my cock?" he asked, and though we were on audio only as he drove back to the hotel room—a room he'd not so subtly left a key for me to use if "I happen to be in town" before he'd left two days before—I knew that he was smirking at me. Unfortunately, he *was* sexy, and I definitely missed his cock, almost as much as I missed the way he wrapped himself around me when we went to sleep.

But that was beside the point.

"I'm not a charity case, Finnegan," I growled.

"I know that, *Donovan.*"

"So, what the hell are you doing paying for repairs on my house?"

"Is this about the carpet?"

I blinked. "What carpet?"

A muttered curse. "Right," he said quickly. "It's about the pipes and wires and shit."

My sigh rattled through the speakers of my phone, echoing in my ear. "Axel, please tell me that you didn't buy me new carpet."

A beat then, "She'll be there tomorrow. You pick out the kind you want and the furniture you need—"

"I don't *need*—"

"And if you don't pick it out or try to cheap out or put her off, then I have given Desiree strict instructions to work with Margaret to pick out what she thinks you'd like and need."

My teeth clicked together. "You've given *Dessie* strict instructions?"

"Yup."

"To work with Margaret Butcher."

The only interior designer in River's Bend, and also the only Margaret I knew.

"Yup."

"For *my* house."

"Yup."

"Okay, I've said it once, you arrogant, pushy bastard, but I'll say it again, I am *not* a charity case!"

Yes, I was yelling.

No, it wasn't my finest moment.

But seriously? What in the fuck-all did this man think he was doing?

"No," he snapped, and the sharp tone made me blink, made me realize exactly how gently he'd been treating me since that day on Main Street, since he'd found me behind the dumpster. "No," he said again, taking a breath and evening out his voice. "You're not a charity case, buttercup. But you are *my* woman, and I can't be on the road or four hours away in San Francisco worrying that your fucking house is going to catch on fire, or the pipes are going to burst and ruin something that's more important to you than ugly-ass carpet." He sighed, and I knew he was shoving a hand through his hair, frustration mussing the strands. "I can't worry about you and play one hundred percent, because you're important to me, because I need to know that you're good." A breath. "I can't focus on work here when my heart is there and doesn't have food in her fridge."

Well, I guess that meant that Billie Rose wasn't the one who'd stocked my fridge.

Which was what I was focusing on because him saying that I was his heart?

Oh, mama.

That meant a lot.

That meant...*everything*.

"Baby," I whispered.

"I know it's too much," he said. "I know you like doing things on your own. But...I need to do this for you, I *want* to do it. So, will you let me?"

My pulse was galloping through my veins, sending my blood zooming through my limbs, making my head spin, my tongue feel swollen, my throat tight. Could I let him?

Every cell in my body was screaming no.

I couldn't trust him.

I *couldn't*.

But...

Couldn't I?

"I'll pay you back," I managed to force out.

"In orgasms," he countered so quickly, so dryly that the tension in my body faded, that amusement took its place.

And I laughed.

I was leaping forward into oblivion, into a dark, unlit abyss that I didn't know how to navigate, creating ties between us, putting myself in his debt, and...

I was laughing.

"In *money*," I countered.

"Sure," he said easily.

Too easily.

"You're never going to cash my checks, are you?"

"Fuck no."

I groaned, plunked my head back onto my pillow. "What the hell am I going to do with you, Axel Finnegan?"

Love him.

I was going to love him.

That was what was at the bottom of the abyss.

And...somehow, I couldn't find my fear, my barbed wire, my concrete to shore up my defenses and keep him at a distance.

"Orgasms. Blow jobs. Your sexy pussy on my face as you ride yourself to an orgasm."

"I'm sensing a theme here," I said dryly.

"Well, that's what happens when my woman is hot as fuck and I can't stop dreaming about making her come."

I bit back a groan as heat blossomed in my body.

Luckily, though, he went on, easing up on the talk that was making me horny and without my man to soothe the ache. "Add in the occasional sandwich and hockey commentary where you talk about halftime and how our jerseys are the prettiest."

"That was *one* time!"

But I didn't miss the fact that he'd said *our jerseys.*

Didn't miss that he was settling in further.

He chuckled then asked softly, "We good, buttercup?"

I sighed. "We're good, baby."

"Good, honey. Now go to bed."

A yawn delayed my reply. "Are you almost back to the hotel?"

"Pulling into the garage."

"Okay," I whispered. "You make sure you sleep soon, too."

"I will."

My finger moved to the end button, pausing when he asked, "Promise me one thing?"

"Yeah?"

"No floral."

And that was how the man made me fall asleep with a laugh on my tongue and a smile on my lips.

Thirty-Seven

Axel

"You don't have much stuff," Brit said, letting me into the apartment.

I had a key, but it had felt weird to let myself in when I knew she was inside, doing a last-minute check of the place.

Her eyes hit the backpack I'd brought with me upon leaving my hotel room, and I wasn't imagining the hint of disapproval in those hazel depths.

"I have to make one more trip," I admitted. Truthfully, I'd left most of my shit back in the hotel. Partly because I was hesitant to move into the apartment, to be in debt to Brit, to accept something so big from a woman I was just starting to know, but just as I'd come to terms with the fact that I *was* going to accept something this big from a woman I was just starting to know, housekeeping had begun knocking on my door. Normally, they'd just come back when I was out, but the woman today was determined to come in and get started, and had all but barged her way in.

New to the job, I supposed.

But who was I to stop her from finishing her work, especially when I was leaving anyway?

Still, her coming in to clean meant I'd ended up rushing

around, dodging her as I tried to shove enough in a bag to make it seem like I wasn't taking Brit's favor for granted while she worked.

Eventually, though, I'd had enough to fill my backpack and had slipped out into the hall, leaving her to it.

Or probably, more accurately, getting out of her way.

Though, she'd pretty much been done by then, leaving the cart in my open doorway as she'd fussed with something on the cart outside the door.

Oh well, all I could do was make sure to leave a good tip for them when I checked out. For now, I was dealing with Brit's slightly disappointed expression as her gaze went from the bag hanging over my shoulder and slid back up to my face.

"Did you think it would be full of tampons and unicorn pillows?" she asked archly.

"I'll have you know unicorns are my favorite animal." A shrug as I set my backpack on the counter. "Plus, tampons are excellent for nose bleeds."

"So, what? You weren't sure if it was going to be a shithole, Balls?"

"No, Brit," I said, guilt slicing through me. "That's not—"

A punch to my shoulder. "Breathe, Axel. I'm fucking with you. I get it," she said. "It's hard to shed all the bullshit and natural to be cautious. Especially because we're like fantasyland with the way we stick together. I'm just glad you're here, one bag or ten." She passed me a clicker and her voice went no nonsense. "Now, this is for the garage. There are two parking spots"—a grin—"so your girl can come visit."

"And so you can get your gossip fodder?"

That grin went unrepentant. "Damned right."

"She's busy and works a lot."

"Good."

I frowned.

"That means she won't be hung up on fancy Axel Finnegan and his fancy hockey skills." A finger to her bottom lip, tapping once, twice. "Maybe Fancy would be a better name for you. God knows that you showed off those *fancy* hands last night."

"Concrete hands, you mean."

She giggled.

"Also, Concrete isn't a good nickname either."

"Better than Balls," she pointed out.

There was that.

"Well," she said, hopping up onto a plain gray barstool and resting her hands on the white marble countertop, "I should probably leave you to take that trip back to your hotel room, let you have a chance to move in."

"Why do I sense a *but* coming?"

Her million-dollar smile. "Because there is one."

And right on cue, there was a knock at the door.

"Apartment tradition," she said, hopping down and moving to pull open the wooden panel. "You get to host the first Cheat Day."

As I processed that, the door was tugged wide, and the guys began pouring in, bags of food and beer and the odd cheerfully-wrapped box in hand.

Less Cheat Day.

More housewarming.

In a borrowed apartment, with the utilities set up and rent that was minimal (because I'd refused to accept free, and Brit and I had come to a compromise) and—

I was one of them.

I *belonged*.

Because I contributed and worked hard and—the truth settled deep inside me—because I'd done it.

On my own merits, but not alone.

Brit had helped and Billie Rose and Bailey and—

I wasn't in a vacuum.

I couldn't do it solely by myself.

But I could *earn* my way.

I could make the most of this chance, this life, this—

I accepted a beer that Coop shoved in my hand, laughed at a joke Brit told.

I could make the most of this team who could become my family.

Thirty-Eight

Bailey

"This is crazy," I whispered as I navigated the winding San Franciscan roads. "Really fucking crazy, Bailey."

It was late.

Middle of the night late, like it was closer to morning than night late. But I'd been *kept* late because Desiree was fucking *into* home decorating and she and Margaret hadn't let me leave until I'd looked through every fucking stitch of fabric and carpet and flooring option.

Three days of that.

Three days of decorating discussions in between taking care of the ranch and dodging the workers in my house and—

I'd been ready to scream.

Luckily, Billie Rose, with all her first-rate gossip skills and her nose for knowing when a River's Bend resident needed help, had come in that evening and sprung me.

She was going to be on ranch duty for the next twenty-four hours.

Which meant...I was going to my first hockey game.

Ever.

Well, I hoped I was.

The Gold were playing tomorrow night, and I was hoping that

I could buy a ticket, or maybe my hockey playing man had the hookup and could secure me one, or—

However it happened, I was going to get into the Gold Mine and watch Axel play.

Eek.

But first, I was going to use that key he'd left for me.

I was going to surprise him.

I was going to give him copious orgasms and then we were going to sleep together, and I wouldn't have to get up early to feed the animals and—

"There," I whispered, spotting the hotel and shifting over a lane.

Of course, since this was San Francisco and none of the streets made sense and traffic was ridiculous, even in the middle of the night, I ended up circling the block twice before I managed to maneuver Gramps's old truck into the parking garage and cram it into a stall.

But I'd made it.

And now...nerves.

I had never done anything like this. *Never.*

Not once in my life had I dropped everything to come and surprise a man in his hotel.

Not once since Colt had I even been open to putting myself out there to a man.

For a man.

And yet, here I was.

The churning in my gut was so intense that I nearly backed my way out of that stall, turned away, and made the drive home.

But...I couldn't.

I was done letting my past rule my present.

"Exactly," I muttered, grabbing my backpack and slinging it over my shoulder. A breath. Shoring up my spine.

Then opening my door.

Was it with shaking hands? Yeah.

Was I doing it anyway? Damn right I was.

I locked up, moved to the lobby, and headed straight for the elevators.

Up.

Stopping on Axel's floor.

Searching the signs, finding the right direction to turn, and then...I was there. Outside his door.

To knock or not to knock.

To breathe or hyperventilate.

To run screaming away through this hallway or to...run screaming through this hallway.

To...use the key on the lock and push open the door.

The lights were mostly off—but then again, it was late. So, I carefully set my backpack down, moved quietly down the hall, and headed for the bed.

Five feet.

Four. Three.

Two—

The light flicked on.

I blinked.

Blinked again.

Because what the fuck?

The covers flew back, and I spun away, thinking for a minute that I was in the wrong hotel room, horrified that I'd broken in and seen—

That.

A woman.

A woman I *recognized.*

What the fuck?

What. The. Fuck?

It was the girl who'd spilled beer on me, who'd complained that Axel never went out anymore and...she was naked.

And skinny and pretty and *naked.*

And pissed.

"What the fuck?" she snapped, snatching the comforter off the bed, and holding it to her body—a body that was much nicer than mine, it had to be noted.

"Shit," I said. Wrong room. I had the wrong room. "I-I'm so s-sorry," I stuttered, slamming my eyes closed for a moment before I realized I needed to get the fuck out. I turned and…I saw Axel's jacket hanging over the back of the chair.

Axel's bag on the floor.

Axel's shoes in the corner of the room.

Axel's cologne on the dresser near the TV.

Stabbing.

He was stabbing me. He wasn't even there, and he was sinking the knife into my flesh.

"Where is he?" I asked.

"He needed…nourishment," said the woman.

Nourishment?

Like…he needed to regain his strength after a long night of activity?

No. He wouldn't do that. He wouldn't. There had to be an explanation for this. Like she was crazy and had broken into his room. But the door hadn't looked like it had been tampered with, or at least it wasn't kicked in, the lock not working. I'd needed to use the key.

So…maybe this wasn't Axel's room and she'd stolen…almost everything he'd brought down from River's Bend?

Or—

I turned back, opened my mouth to say…something.

She beat me to it. "I think my favorite part of Axel"—a laugh—"besides his cock, of course"—another laugh and it pierced right through me—"is that tattoo. *Whew.*" She fanned herself. "The way it wraps around his ribs, how it dips down and nearly touches that scar just above his hip…*fucking* chef's kiss."

That was…very specific.

That was…making it very difficult for me to think that she wasn't in Axel's room because she'd gone full psycho ninja, but rather because he'd invited her.

"Tell me," she said. "Have you ever tried to take him deep, but he was so big that you choked?"

I had.

Because he was.

But I'd been working up to it, had all but been making it my fucking life's work to be able to take that big cock deep.

"Why are you here?" I asked.

"He *brought* me here."

"No," I whispered. "He wouldn't do that."

"Because he's with you?" she asked and there was that laugh again—piercing, knife-like, *painful.* "Oh, honey, Axel doesn't do monogamy. Hell, he rarely does one woman at a time." A smirk. "Unless, that woman is enough for him."

Thunk.

That wasn't right.

Yet...I was here.

This wasn't happening.

This wasn't—

I needed to go, to get the fuck out of this room. I needed to get away from this woman who was adding to the stab wounds, who was slowly, incrementally bleeding me dry so that I could breathe and think and reason this out—

I needed to *go.*

A breath.

I whipped away from the woman, from the scene that was fucking with my head, that was cutting me deeper by the second.

"Where are you going?" she trilled. "Stick around and maybe both of us can play."

I was going to be sick.

In that room, with that condescending woman looking on and talking about threesomes with the man that I had been in love with.

Swallowing hard, trying to keep the bile down even as it burned up the back of my throat, even as my stomach churned and roiled anew. Sweaty palms, shaking legs, but I managed to move to my backpack, to wrap my fingers around one of the straps.

I started to pick it up, but I was too off my game, too shaky and barely holding on and—

My fingers spasmed and my bag dropped to the floor, the contents scattering.

I fell to my knees, started grabbing my shit, shoving it back in, even as she laughed at me, as she kept talking.

But all I could hear at this point was buzzing, her words no longer distinguishable. My pulse was pounding in my ears, the steady thrumming making it impossible for me to process anything.

Especially while I was scrabbling for my lip balm and my phone charger and my tiny bottles of travel shampoo and body wash and conditioner.

Nails biting into my shoulder. "Look, bitch, I'm talking to—"

I had to go.

I *needed* to go.

One more stretch had me snatching the last of my things, had me breaking free of her grip, and then I was on my feet, shoving her back. Spinning for the door, yanking at the handle.

I pushed into the hall, ran for the elevator.

No.

Stairs.

I couldn't wait for the fucking elevator.

So, I shoved through the metal door, rushed into the stairwell, pounded down the stairs until I reached the parking garage. Tears were burning in my eyes, were *escaping*, dripping down my face, but I knew, *knew*, I had to first get to Gramps's truck.

Out of the parking lot.

Away from that room, from this hotel.

I needed to get someplace safe.

Thirty-Nine

Axel

A siren blared outside my windows, startling me.

Totally unused to the sounds of the city after having spent so much time in River's Bend.

Groaning, I stretched, snagged my cell, and glanced at the time.

Too fucking early.

Too fucking early even to call Bailey.

We'd only exchanged a few texts in the previous days, mostly her cursing me for putting her through HGTV Bootcamp and me snarking about an orgasm count that kept growing.

But I had the day off and was planning to drive up to River's Bend to see the progress, see if I could coax a favor out of Billie Rose to watch the ranch the next time I had two days off in a row.

I wanted to bring Bailey down to the city, wanted her to see the apartment, and depending on how long Billie Rose was willing to grant, to bring her to the rink...and—heaven help me—introduce her to the team.

Brit was going to be thrilled.

I was fucking terrified...and ready.

That too.

The conflicting emotions meant that it was unlikely I was going to go back to sleep.

Last night had gone on later than I'd planned, the guys busting out board games—and look, *I* was competitive about all things, but the Gold squad took *Ticket to Ride* to a whole new level.

There were set matchups and brackets and playoffs and—

Everyone had stayed late to watch Coop, Blue, Logan, and Rome battle it out for first place.

Which had, surprisingly, gone to Rome.

Apparently, that meant he had to host the next board game throwdown.

Fine by me.

I'd gotten my ass handed to me in the game. I needed to study up, to practice, to come back ready to take those fuckers—cough, I mean my *teammates*—down.

The siren went again.

Sighing, I pushed out of bed. I needed to get my city ears back if I wanted to sleep in. But since I was awake, I might as well get the rest of my shit from the hotel before heading up to River's Bend. Check out, drop my shit, sneak up for a taste of my woman that would need to tide me over for another week.

A quick shower—and a quick thanks for Brit, whose nosy ass had invaded my apartment and brought me fresh linens.

Then I was heading out of the apartment building, getting in my car, driving across town.

I parked in the underground lot of the hotel, frowning when I thought I saw Bailey's truck, but she'd specifically told me yesterday that Margaret was bringing her to the flooring store to make her final selections.

So, another old truck.

But the sight of it made me smile, made me miss her.

Maybe I could call her on the way back out, she'd be up by then, could yell at me about the home décor choices, and I could hear the way her voice went soft when I told her I was coming up to see her.

Sliding my card on the reader, I moved into the lobby, waited for the elevator to open, and got on.

Thirty seconds later, I was stepping into the hall, swiping my keycard for a second time, this time on the door for my room.

I pushed in—

And then didn't process what in the fuck-all I was seeing.

What. I. Was. *Seeing.*

Lights on.

The bed a mess.

A phone in the hall. I stopped at that, actually backed up into the hall, making sure that I had the right room, because, well, it was fucking early, and it was easily possible that I wasn't operating on all cylinders.

But the placard to the left of the door told me I was in the right place.

So, I moved back inside, and the first thing I did was stoop down and pick up the phone. It wasn't mine, obviously, and when I saw the case, my gut clenched. But it wasn't until I hit the button on the side, saw the picture of Picard on the screen, that my nape went ice cold.

Bailey's.

It was *Bailey's.*

I should be excited—the truck, the phone, the evidence that Bailey was here in San Francisco. But...something about the lights being on, the lack of a greeting, the way my belongings were spread around, as though someone had gone through them.

Bailey wouldn't have gone through my stuff.

She wouldn't be asleep with the lights on, her phone on the floor, the room a mess.

She—

"Hi, baby."

Not her voice.

Not Bailey's.

I looked up and saw a naked woman, and that naked woman wasn't Bailey.

But I *had* seen her before.

She was...the housekeeper. The one who'd all but demanded her way into my room.

Yes, she was that woman.

But also...

I saw the tattoo above her breast, the glint of glitter on her skin, and another memory floated up in my mind. She wasn't just a housekeeper. She was from River's Bend. I hadn't recognized her yesterday because she'd changed her hair, because I didn't spend a lot of time looking at her face, not when she spent the majority of her time with her tits nearly hanging out. But naked, she was familiar enough, and I remembered her love of the sparkling stuff, remembered that it was in some sort of lotion that she wore, and the glitter always clung to the guys' skin after they fucked her. And most of the guys had fucked her.

Though I hadn't.

Yeah, I'd fucked pretty much everyone willing to have me over the years I'd been in town, but I'd never fucked *her*.

There was something desperate about...Candice? Cassidy? No, *Candi*. With the traditional "i" and a fucking creepy-ass expression on her face.

But I'd fucked her friend, and I'd done it at Joel's place.

On his couch while Joel had taken Candi to his bedroom.

And when I'd finished, when I was getting dressed to leave—because that was what I did then, fuck, come, go—she had been standing in the doorway. Naked.

Watching us.

Watching *me*.

Like she'd been ready to join in.

I'd been drunk enough to brush it off, and hell, I'd been with enough people over the years to not give a fuck that someone might have seen me having sex.

"What the fuck are you doing?" I asked, shoving her back when she came close.

She stumbled, lips parting on a gasp, tears immediately forming in her eyes.

Fucking tears.

Dammit.

I didn't have time for this.

"I'm here for you," she said, those tears slipping over, immediately turning her mascara into raccoon eyes.

I stepped close, didn't miss the way her eyes lit up. But all I did was stick my face in hers and demand, "What did you do to her?"

Candi's tears dried in an instant—because they were on command. "To whom?"

"To Bailey, you fucking bitch."

Her lips pressed flat.

I resisted the urge to throttle her. "Did you hurt her? Did you hurt, Bailey?"

Candi's chin lifted. "I just told her the truth."

Don't touch her. Don't touch the bitch because then I might kill her. "What truth?"

"That you're not happy with her." Her hand came out, and I stepped back. "That you'll only ever be with me."

"You've lost your fucking mind."

I reached in my pocket for my cell.

Should I call security? The police? Who would sort out the shit-show in my room sooner? I was backing toward the door, considering just that, when her face screwed up, something scary sliding across it.

Fuck the call.

Fuck retrieving my shit.

I'd buy new stuff.

If she'd put this poison into Bailey's mind, I needed to find her as quickly as I could, stop her before she ran off and did something stupid.

I reached for the handle, yanked the door open.

"I love you, Axel. Don't go—"

Her voice was close enough to make me spin back around, and I barely had time to brace before Candi launched herself at me.

"Oof," I grunted, pushed Candi back when she tried to latch her mouth to mine.

A moan when our lips brushed, a groan when I shoved her, not so gently away. "Get dressed," I snapped, and when Candi didn't move, I wrestled open the door, thrust her into the hall.

Then slammed it shut.

Took two minutes to grab Candi's shit.

The look on her face as I chucked it out into the hall told me that my first call was going to be to the police.

The woman had lost her fucking mind.

But first, Bailey.

I needed to get to her, make sure she knew that nothing had happened. Even if that meant navigating the crazy in the hall.

Except, the moment I reached for the door, Bailey's phone began ringing.

Billie Rose.

Fuck.

I swiped, answered the call. "Hey, Billie Rose. I need your help—"

"Axel," she said, cutting me off completely. "We have a problem."

Forty

Bailey

It took until I was nearly home for my tears to dry, my breathing to calm, for me to carefully consider all the thoughts spiraling through my head.

We hadn't made any promises.

We hadn't exchanged any vows.

We'd barely spent any time together.

I was...expecting too much. We hadn't agreed to be monogamous, and it wasn't like he'd asked me there and then I'd caught him with his dick in another woman.

I'd gone down to surprise him.

But I'd been the one who'd ended up surprised, wounded, hurt, broken, no...*shattered*.

He was finally getting to live out his dream.

I was just...old, beaten down baggage.

Holding him back.

Each thought had me shrinking into myself, the big, open world I'd begun tiptoeing into closing down, walls slamming into me, making it difficult for me to breathe, to think, to *drive.*

I pulled over, rested my head on the steering wheel.

And then I screamed.

So fucking loud that I nearly jumped out of my own skin, and *I* was the one making the godawful noise.

"No!" I yelled. "Just fucking *no!*"

This wasn't right.

This wasn't *him,* wasn't what Axel and I had.

It just...wasn't.

"So what?" I whispered, catching my own reflection in the rearview. "What are you going to do about it?"

Call him.

That was the first step.

But when I reached into my backpack and tried to grab my cell, it wasn't inside. "What?" I yanked the zipper fully open, dumped everything onto my seat. Lip balm, underwear, a change of clothes, my tiny shampoo and conditioner bottles. My phone charger. My hairbrush.

His jersey.

That one hurt.

I breathed through it, kept searching.

But no cell phone.

"Fuck," I whispered. "Fucking hell." I looked around, like the rolling hills outside River's Bend would give me my answers.

And they did, I supposed.

I was less than thirty minutes from home.

I'd start there, track down Billie Rose, and then I'd call Axel.

I'd figure out what was going on.

I wouldn't panic and run and shut him out. Not without talking to him first.

"Right," I whispered, taking another breath, trying to calm myself as I shoved my shit back into my bag, as I calmly checked over my shoulder and then pulled onto the road. "One step at a time."

I could do this.

I could be calm and sure and logical with my actions.

So, I drove through the winding roads until I reached the turnoff for the ranch. Then I bumped my way down the gravel driveway, relief pulsing through me when I saw Billie's little SUV was in the driveway.

I'd use her phone.

I'd call Axel.

It would be okay.

No matter what happened, I would be okay.

Blond curls entered my periphery as I pulled to a stop, just barely visible over the top of Billie's car. They moved my way quickly, but I didn't suspect anything was amiss.

Billie Rose did *everything* quickly.

I snagged my backpack, forced myself to be calm as I hopped out of Gramps's truck. "Billie, hey, I need to—"

In a millisecond, she was in my face. "Get in your truck," she whispered. "Get in your truck and get out of here."

"What?"

She began shoving me back, reaching for the door handle.

"Get in and drive to my place—"

"My baby!"

The voice was nails on a chalkboard.

The voice was...my mother's.

Gasping, I looked around Billie Rose and saw my mother, looking tan and thin and clad in designer hippie clothes. Looking the same as the last time I'd seen her when she'd dumped the problem of the ranch in my lap.

She extended her arms. "Come and give your mommy a big hug. I've missed you so much, baby!"

That was a blatant lie.

It always was.

But my gaze had drifted beyond her.

To my father.

He nodded in my direction but didn't pretend he'd missed me.

There wasn't any love lost between us, hadn't ever been. Mostly because our relationship was transactional, and one-sided, and he'd never had time for me except when I could do something for him.

"Shit," I muttered.

Billie Rose gave me another shove. "Honey, I need you to go. Right now. Straight to my house and—"

My dad shifted, and I saw there was a third person with them.

That third person made me understand why Billie Rose was so determined to get me back into the truck.

That third person was a man.

One I'd thought I known.

One I'd thought I'd loved.

My heart dropped to my feet and panic gripped every single cell in my body when Colt stepped out from behind my parents.

Part 2

Filthy Puckboy

Prologue

Bailey

I'd dreamed of a two-towered bridge painted in International Orange.

I'd dreamed of fog crawling along the hill-filled city, creeping around skyscrapers, dancing over the rooftops of the Painted Ladies.

I'd dreamed of walking along twisting streets crowded with cars and of buying crabs fresh off the boat, steamed right there on the street corner, and made ready to eat with bare hands, delicious dunked in melted butter, napkins optional.

I'd dreamed of strong arms wrapped around me as we watched the sea lions bark on their platforms that floated alongside the pier, of sharing sourdough with a crust so thick that chewing it made my jaw hurt.

I'd dreamed of divvying up an ice cream sundae as big as my head, of music blaring out of club speakers, vibrating through our bodies melded together on the dance floor.

I'd dreamed of holding hands while riding the Ferris wheel in the park, my insides leaping and dipping as we rounded that big, *big* circle.

And more than anything, I'd dreamed of a sexy smile. *His* smile widening in surprise of me being there, of that surprise turning to excitement and joy and *heat*, his calloused hands trailing over my naked skin, of kisses and a hard cock and a night lost to lovemaking.

I'd dreamed of a man who could look at me and love me for me.

Of a man who looked at me and knew that I was enough.

A woman with small dreams and a quiet life.

A woman with heavy baggage and a prickly exterior.

A woman who was a little dinged and dented and...still enough.

But...dreams didn't come true.

God, I knew that.

I'd lived that enough in my twenty-five years to understand that my dreams didn't matter. Because every time I thought that my life was going to be different, that I was going to glide toward an ending that was happy and warm and everything my fantasies were made of, those dreams turned to nightmares.

One thread tugged and it all unraveled.

One wrong move and it all shattered.

One stuttered heartbeat and...I was broken.

One

Bailey

Her nails dug into my arms tight enough to hurt.

She smelled like roses.

The familiar perfume was gentle and sweet.

But it didn't fit my mother.

Oh, her outside persona was all that was soft and womanly, with the feathers and fringe and loose, but perfectly draped clothing, the curls in her hair, the pale pink sparkles on her eyelids, the peach blush on her cheeks. But inside...*inside* she was a selfish snake who would go to any length to get what she wanted.

My mother should be in sky-high heels, a tight skirt, an equally fitted crisp white button-down, with red lipstick shining in the late afternoon sun. Heavy brows, fake lashes, tasteful and understated jewelry, hair slicked back into a fancy bun.

A shark in a businesswoman's clothing.

Instead...the woman standing in front of me was...what she was...

Awful.

And somehow, all of her femininity made it worse.

"My baby!"

It was loud and shrill, and I winced, pulling back, but that only made the nails dig in deeper. "Mom," I began, trying to pull back.

"I missed you so much!"

It was still loud and shrill...and it was a tactic to manipulate.

To distract me from the person, the *man* behind her.

Which I knew because those nails dug in, hard enough to leave deep indents on my skin, to send pain flaming through my arms, exactly like she used to do when I made her unhappy when I was a child and we were in public or with my grandparents, and she couldn't just smack the shit out of me like she did if we were alone.

Blond curls appeared in my periphery.

Billie Rose.

My aunt, who was closer in age to a sister, began to come near again.

And just as quickly the talons dropped away, my mother's face —and her fake smile—coming into view as she pulled back. Then she swung a hand in the direction of the house and my stomach began to churn. "The remodel is gorgeous!"

"The remodel." My voice was dead.

Because I already knew where this was going.

"Yes, honey." She laughed. "And I know you don't mind, but I moved your stuff into the guest room." A wink, like she was playing over-involved mother.

As if that had *ever* happened.

Under-involved was more like it.

Or only involved if it suited her or she got something from it.

Still, I braced, because I could already feel in my bones the next thing she was going to say. I already *knew* it.

"You and Colt can share," she stage-whispered.

I inhaled sharply.

So fiercely that I choked on the dust my truck had kicked up from the gravel and dirt road, and my throat spasmed in my effort to not bend over coughing.

I couldn't take my eyes off Colt.

It wasn't safe.

I stared at the man who'd left me with three broken ribs, a black eye, and running barefoot through the rain-filled night. A man I'd trusted with my heart and soul. A man I'd thought was my savior, my hope, my steady.

He wasn't.

He'd become...my nightmare.

But as I stared at him, I felt phantom fingers winding into my hair, gripping tight, yanking my head back. Felt those fingers clenched into fists colliding with my ribs, my stomach, my face. I could still feel the cold rain soaking into my clothes, my skin, chilling me, but not as much as the change the unraveling of my hope had rent on me.

That was when the numbness began to sink into my skin.

And...

I supposed I expected to feel real fear, coming face to face with my abuser.

He'd hurt me and left me with bruises and cuts and wounds that were far more than skin-deep. He'd lacerated my organs and soul and personality.

And...I didn't want to be that person again.

But...this day had been...

A lot.

Too much. My mind and senses were overwhelmed. I'd reached my limit before I'd even driven onto this scene.

So what I was feeling right at that moment was decidedly *numb*.

"You need to leave," I began—

Right as a car tore down the driveway, screeching to a halt behind me, kicking up more dust and sending my mom coughing, Billie Rose's expression turning into relief, and Colt skittering back, as though the dusty air might touch him and heaven forbid, he be contaminated by anything with the ranch.

That had been one of the final straws of our relationship—or maybe *the* final straw, if I was truly thinking about it, if I was actually putting the pieces of that demise together in my mind.

Gramps had asked me if I might be interested in moving closer, if I might help him and one day take over the ranch, and Colt...

Well, he hadn't liked that.

A car door slammed behind me, and I spun, heart squeezing hard when I saw Axel striding over to me. Relief, hurt, and worry rippled through me.

I'd driven four hours to get away from him, to run from the

hurt that finding a naked woman in his hotel room had inflicted on me. I'd driven for four hours, sitting in the hurt, basking in it, wrapping it tightly around me...until it had turned to worry and I'd realized he wouldn't do that, realized I'd made a terrible mistake in running when I should have paused and just talked to him.

But by then I'd realized I'd lost my phone somewhere along the way.

I couldn't call him, couldn't talk things out.

But now...he was here.

And...his expression was a mix of too many emotions for me to decipher.

Then I didn't have a chance to because he was coming close, gripping my arms, but not how my mother had, not digging in, not hurting, not bruising and leaving marks.

"Buttercup—"

The morning came back.

The excited drive down. Knocking on his hotel room door.

The naked woman inside—

The lonely, heavy drive back.

And now this scene in my driveway, my parents, Colt, Billie Rose, and Axel...*Axel.*

Bad boy hockey player with the soft heart beneath. Former AHLer and now current San Francisco Gold starting forward. He'd made it to the big leagues. His hard work had paid off, finally, and even now, even after I'd driven home, spending almost four hours convincing myself that he might want to move on and it was better to let him go, I knew I couldn't. Mostly because after I'd realized I'd made a mistake, had reacted without thinking, I'd *then* spent the rest of the drive reminding myself that letting him go was a stupid thought because we'd pretty much crocodile death-rolled ourselves away from forming a relationship, but had still fallen and done it deep and...

He knew more about me than *anyone,* and I trusted him, and he was pretty much the best man I'd ever met and...

I didn't want him to let go, didn't want to be the one to disconnect.

Not without at least talking to him first.

I-I couldn't do that.

So that was why I covered his hands with mine and whispered, "Colt's here."

His fingers convulsed, but still not tight enough to cause pain. "The fucker who hurt you?"

"Yeah," I whispered.

He knew about Colt, but he didn't know *everything* about Colt, and I knew we had a lot to unpack there, too. But...later. Because I'd driven eight hours that day and half of them had been spent crying (or yelling) and the other half had been filled with hope and joy and *all* my dreams. I just didn't have much more emotion in me.

His eyes flicked over my shoulder then he bent closer. "And your parents?"

"Yeah," I whispered again.

"Fuck," he whispered back.

We had a lot to unpack there, too, but he knew enough to understand it wasn't a happy reunion.

Hell, we had a lot to unpack *everywhere*—from the naked woman in his hotel room to the shitstorm that was my past being here right in this moment.

But right then, all I wanted to do was step closer, to feel his arms wrap around me, to soak in his warmth and strength and—

Fuck it. I was going to do just that.

Forget the disaster waiting behind me.

Forget the turmoil that had prompted me to drive four hours with tears streaming down my face.

Forget everything but the way this man made me feel.

I was going to focus on that.

I needed Axel's arms around me, and that was that. Stepping forward, I said, "Axel, I—"

"Baby—"

Axel's arms had begun to wrap around me, instinctively giving me that closeness I craved, that I needed, but it wasn't his velvet rasp giving me the endearment.

It was Colt's gruff, cold voice.

Two

Axel

"Baby—"

My head shot up.

The fucker was staring at us unhappily, like I was encroaching on his territory by holding Bailey. He'd relinquished any claim the moment he'd hurt her, when he'd left her with trauma that had her flinching from my touch in the middle of the street, running from me when I would never *ever* lay a hand on her in anger, never intentionally hurt her.

But this man had.

And just that quickly, with only one thought, my anger was a dangerous thing.

Welling up like a storm gathering strength off the coast, getting ready to move slowly on shore, getting ready to wreak devastation in its path.

The fucker deserved a fist in the jaw, deserved *to have every bone in his body broken*.

But Bailey needed me more at that moment.

"No," I snapped when *Colt*—and what a stupid ass name the man had—came closer.

Bailey jerked in my arms when I spoke, but I just held on to her tighter. We weren't doing this. That fucker wasn't getting any closer to the woman I fucking *loved*, wasn't going to hurt her again. Not *ever* again.

"No," I repeated, sliding her to my side, tucking her close. "Stop *fucking* moving," I growled when it looked like her ex was going to reach forward and snatch her away from me.

Not that he would succeed in that.

But I didn't even want him breathing her air, let alone within five feet of her.

I was big. I was broad. I could take a hit and a punch or a puck to the fucking balls and keep on going. I could kill him, and wouldn't hesitate if Bailey's life was in danger.

This fucker knew it.

Because he stopped, though his expression made it clear he wasn't happy that I was still touching Bailey.

There was possession in the other man's expression, and plenty of it.

And *I* knew it, could identify it easily.

Because I felt the same way about this woman.

I *needed* to possess her, mark her, to make her mine in every single sense of the word.

The only difference was that I wouldn't hurt her.

Except, I could see the swelling around her eyes, the way the ends of her lashes were clinging together. She'd been crying. Because of me. Because of fucking *Candi* in my hotel room. Because Bailey had been there, too and she'd seen something that had sent her flying home...flying away from me. Away from me and into this fucking mess.

Away from me and onto a collision course with her ex.

Christ.

And her parents.

Fucking losers from what I knew, neglecting her, dragging her all over the Bay Area, running this place into the ground and then flitting off, leaving her to pick up the pieces.

Now the pieces had been picked up, had been fitted back into place.

And shocker of shockers, they'd "randomly" shown up.

"Who's this?"

A silken, feminine voice from the woman who looked like Bailey, but wrong. Too many feathers. Too much fringe. A hint of cleavage in a way that I knew was deliberate, would be wielded as a weapon at the first opportunity. I'd seen that predatory look on many women's faces.

"Axel," I said, not bothering to extend my hand.

I was an asshole.

That was my default position with most everyone.

River's Bend had somehow managed to get under my skin, Bailey even more deeply, so maybe I wasn't quite as much of a jerk with these people as I was with the rest of humanity, but I wasn't going to waste any of my limited niceness on this woman, on these fuckers.

"Baby—"

My gaze jerked to the side, to *Colt, who'd decided for some asinine reason, to speak again.*

God. What a fucking stupid name.

What a fucking stupid man if he thought that I was going to let him get any closer to Bailey.

"You moved my stuff into the guest room." Bailey's words were faltering at first, shaking before they steadied. She wasn't looking at Colt, hadn't acknowledged him in any way. Instead, her gaze was glued to her mother's. "You moved my stuff into the guest room so that I could stay with *him—*"

Now they were shaking again.

But not from fear.

From fury.

"You moved my stuff from *my* room," she snapped. "From the room I worked my *ass* off to save so this entire place didn't end up as some fucking development—"

"Language, Bailey."

A sharp whip of sound.

But not from her mother.

From the *fucker* with the stupid name.

From *Colt.*

And the effect it had on Bailey was instantaneous...and I

fucking hated it. She jumped, burrowing against me, fingers tightening and they buried themselves in the fabric of my shirt.

I was going to kill this fucker.

But nearly as quickly as she'd tightened her grip, she released a breath, and I felt her forcing herself to calm, to steady, to straighten and pull slightly away from me.

The last, I hated.

I *got* it, understood why she did it, and I was fucking proud of her when she lifted her chin and whispered, "I will fucking talk however the *fuck* I want."

My fingers tightened on her waist.

"Now," she said, voice growing stronger. "I want you to leave." A beat. "*All* of you."

Her mother's face went from soft and sweet to sharp in an instant, and I knew, *knew* that my previous thoughts about her being predatory weren't unfounded. The woman might be the most dangerous person here.

Though the father hadn't spoken.

He might not be a *total* fucking useless sack of shit, standing there, doing nothing to protect his daughter, and surprise me...by being even more of a threat than the two assholes in front of us. But...life goals and all that.

Because at the moment, he had about as much use as one of Bailey's cows.

Less, I supposed, since we couldn't sell him for profit.

"Honey..." Bailey's mother began.

I turned away from her and the load of bullshit she was about to start spinning, gently cupping Bailey's jaw and tilted her head up so that her eyes hit mine. "Buttercup."

A shudder through her frame.

"I'm okay."

"I know." I ran my fingers gently over her skin, over the red around her eyes, gently across the damp lashes, separating them. "It'll be okay."

A tendril of fear in her chocolate brown eyes. "This is—"

"Breathe," I said when she broke off. "I'm here. We'll handle it together."

Another shudder, but this one wasn't from fear. It was relief, and fuck if that didn't settle into my heart.

I ran my thumb over her bottom lip. "Breathe, honey."

Honey because I wasn't ever going to call her baby again.

Because that motherfucker and the icy cold endearment that prickled along my skin, that disquieted my soul, wasn't going to be in our relationship. Not in a small way. Not in a big one. Not in *any* fucking way.

Her lips parted. Her breath slid out.

And then she inhaled. Exhaled.

Once that was steady, I tucked her close again, turned to the trio of assholes, "She asked you to leave."

"My stuff—" her mother began.

"Right here," Billie Rose said cheerfully, bursting in a little breathlessly, as though she'd been running around. And maybe she had, considering that she dropping a turquoise bag onto the gravel just in front of Bailey's mother's feet. Several more soon joined the others—though they weren't suede, just a mix of plastic-sided suitcases and a couple of plain duffles. "Don't worry if I forgot something," Billie added sunnily. "I'm happy to drop it by where you're staying." A beat, all warmth having left her tone. "Which is, hopefully, not in River's Bend."

I had the feeling that even if they tried to stay at the B&B in town or the hotel that bordered River's Bend but was technically the next town over, they would find all the rooms had been filled up.

Thus was the power of Billie Rose.

The mayor of River's Bend had her fingers in everything.

Couldn't stop these fuckers from showing up on Bailey's doorstep though.

Couldn't stop *Colt* from hurting her.

Couldn't stop—

"My bag!" It was a screech as Bailey's mother lurched forward and picked up the suede tote from the ground, clutching it to her chest like it was a baby who had just bonked her head. She began frantically dusting it off, trying to remove every last speck of dirt. "How dare—"

“She asked you to leave,” I said.

“And I’ve already called Frank. That’s the sheriff,” Billie Rose added in a stage whisper. “In case you’ve forgotten.”

Bailey’s mother hissed out an annoyed breath.

“Also, since I know that none of your names are on the deed or the mortgage”—another annoyed breath—“I don’t think he’ll take kindly to you three trespassing…”

She trailed off.

The silence stretched.

And stretched.

Until Billie Rose glanced behind them, eyes narrowing as she presumably focused on some spot in the distance. “Ah, yes, I see that he’s coming right now.”

Thankfully, that was the impetus to get the fuckers moving.

The bags made it into their rental car.

The people—Colt with another glare at me—climbing into the driver’s seat.

A fact I noted.

A fact I really didn’t like.

But then the doors were closed, and they were skidding out of the driveway, kicking up rocks and dirt and dust.

I turned to Bailey, opened my mouth,

And didn’t get one word out before Billie Rose snagged her arm and dragged Bailey away from me.

Three

Bailey

Billie Rose's grip was tight too.

But it didn't hurt either.

I sucked in a breath, released it slowly as the truth of that hit home.

And if anything, it settled me further, allowed the tightness gripping my lungs to loosen.

"What happened?" Billie asked once we were five feet away from Axel.

As though that would stop him from listening. He wasn't a good guy—okay, so he was the *best* guy—but he didn't have pesky things like...morals.

At least when it came to eavesdropping about things that concerned me.

He...was protective.

He was mine.

And if the shit that had just gone down in my life had gone down in front of me in *his,* then I'd be playing starfish, clinging to a rock nearby and doing everything to make sure he was okay.

Bad analogy.

Still the truth.

Which was why I glanced over my shoulder and caught his gaze.

His eyes were gentle, though his face was still set in hardened lines that were so sharp they threatened to cut. I wanted to shrug off my aunt's hold, wanted to walk right back into his embrace, to wrap my arms around him and make that hard and sharp go away. But then Billie Rose tugged at my arm, and I pulled my stare from the pretty, pretty man behind me and focused.

"Are you okay?" Billie asked.

I laughed.

Because I was pretty much as far from okay as I could be.

"You mean because I drove four hours to surprise my boyfriend, only to knock on his hotel room door and have it opened by a naked woman who said he'd brought her there?" I laughed, and yeah, it was slightly hysterical. "But she was gracious and offered to let me stay around because he prefers fucking two chicks at once, so at least I've got that going for me."

I heard a growl, saw the lines of his face grow even harder.

I softened my tone. "And maybe I could have discounted it outright because she was giving all sorts of crazy, stalker woman vibes, but then she described my boyfriend's tattoo and the scar just above his right hip and—"

That growl grew louder, and I felt Axel move closer.

"And then after driving almost four hours back home thinking I'd made a huge, huge mistake in letting that man into my life and not recognizing until I was nearly home that I hadn't actually talked to him and that I probably should..." I sighed and Billie's face gentled. "But it was then that I realized I'd left my cell in the hotel room with the naked woman so I couldn't actually call him." I shook my head. "But *then* I drove right onto a scene where my estranged parents had moved my belongings into my guest room so I could share with my ex who beat the shit out of me, leaving me with broken ribs, a concussion, and shredded feet."

Billie's hand convulsed, her face no longer anywhere near gentle.

"*What?*" Axel's voice rose. "I'm going to *kill* that motherfucker."

Right.

I needed to prioritize here.

Tugging free of my aunt, I spun back to face him.

Yup. All sharp lines and fury having burned away any glimmer of soft.

"It's okay—" I began.

"*It's not fucking okay.*"

A burst of sound, guttural and fierce and sounding as though it had been torn from him.

"I meant," I said, walking toward him, my heart squeezing tight when his arms immediately opened and he welcomed my body against his, "*I'm* okay. What he did wasn't and never will be, but... *I'm* okay and I-I don't want to go back there, okay? I just want to be here with you and—"

Naked woman in his hotel room.

He must have seen that thought—or maybe the insecurity—flit through my mind, because immediately his face softened, and he cupped my cheek. "We need to talk," he whispered.

"I know," I whispered.

"Buttercup—"

Rocks crunched behind us, and I turned to see Frank pulling into the driveway, his cruiser's lights off, but his speed urgent enough that I knew Billie Rose had lit a fire under his ass to get out here.

"For the record, even with all my fuckups, you didn't once threaten to call the sheriff on me," Axel said lightly, and I knew he'd both tempered his anger and set aside the soft.

At least for the moment.

Snark was back.

The arrogant, filthy puckboy who had a wall up between himself and the rest of the world was back.

That sent a curl of fear through my belly.

Then his thumb trailed over the inside of my wrist, a featherlight touch that told me...enough.

That the wall might come up around others, but that the wall didn't exist, not for me.

I took a breath, released it slowly, my eyes drifting to the dust cloud in the distance, the speck that was Colt and my parents' car growing smaller with each passing moment.

Billie Rose chuckled softly, and I glanced over in time to see her pat his arm. "I didn't need to pull out the big guns, honey bun," she said, grinning at Axel and then at me. It was a bit frayed at the edges, but it was there. Progress. Another pat to his arm. "You're harmless."

Somehow, despite everything, amusement bubbled in my chest at the notion of anyone calling the six-foot-plus, over two hundred pounds of muscled hockey player harmless, and the fact that I could feel *anything* except horror and anger and fear and fury was a fucking miracle.

But thus was the power of Billie Rose.

She backed up, turned toward Frank, who was now getting out of his cruiser. "Stop right there, Franklin Horst."

Frank stopped, eyes widening. "Um, what?"

"Back to the high school with you," she said. "The football fans won't police themselves."

"I—" He lifted a hand, gestured toward us, himself. "But you—"

"Back in the cruiser, Horst," Billie Rose ordered.

Another gesture. "I—"

"Shoo."

Frank's hand fell to his side. Then he shook his head, once, twice. *Then* he turned and walked back to his car, pulling the door open, getting in, and backing out of the driveway as quickly as he'd pulled in.

"Right," Billie Rose said, nodding sharply.

Axel stiffened next to me, and I braced.

"I've got things to do to prepare for the Winter Festival." She dragged the handle of her purse up her shoulder, clapped her hands together. "My spreadsheet is sorely out of date and..."

She didn't bother to finish the sentence.

Just turned and walked away from us.

And then her car joined the cruiser on the road, trailing dust and turning into a barely visible speck.

I glanced up at Axel.

He stared down at me.

I opened my mouth—

"There's a Winter Festival?"

Four

Axel

She was fucking beautiful in the fading sunlight.

Even more so when she smiled.

"Yeah," she whispered. "There's a Winter Festival and a Spring Festival. And Summer and one for Valentine's Day called Spread the Love, and a Bunny Hop, and—"

"Buttercup?"

She'd been ticking them off on her fingers, but at the nickname she stopped, looking back up at me. "Yeah—"

I didn't stop to think, didn't wait to consider.

We needed to talk. We needed to talk about so many things.

But the woman I loved was in my arms.

And I needed to taste her.

So, I did.

Just bent my neck and let my lips hit hers.

She melted, and I nearly did too as *right* surged through every cell in my body. Her lips were the softest thing I'd ever felt, and she smelled like an apple orchard, floral and fruity. Her body fit against mine, just fit in a way that was so *right* that it deserved poetry or some shit, but it was romantic shit that I never fully managed to grasp or verbalize and so I just had to settle for slipping my tongue between her lips and kissing the shit out of her.

Hands palming her curves.

Tongues tangling.

Mouths battling for dominance.

But she always let me win, and that had my cock going hard in an instant, remembering *all* the ways she'd let me win...even when she'd ended up on top.

But—

I tore my mouth from hers.

"Candi and I didn't—"

Her lips were swollen, eyes half-mast. But my words had the heat fading from those pretty chocolate brown irises, her expression going somber. "I know."

My brows dragged together. "Then why—"

"Did I leave?" she asked.

I nodded. That seemed to be the obvious question.

A half-smile curved her mouth. "It took me approximately three and a half hours to realize that I might have misinterpreted what went down with Candi. Like I mentioned before, she was... very specific about parts of your body and the things you did and..." A sigh. "I was hurt and ran...and by the time I realized that I needed to call you and get some answers, I was closer to home than San Francisco." She shrugged, her eyes asking for forgiveness. "And then I didn't have my phone. I'm sorry, honey. Sorry I scared you. I should have stopped and thought and—"

I touched her cheek. "Right. First." I dug into my pocket, pulled out her cell, and handed it to her.

"Thanks," she whispered, pocketing it.

"I showed up at the hotel room and I found it, along with—" I broke off, unsure how to phrase all that had gone down with Candi.

"A gorgeous naked woman with more than slightly crazy eyes?"

Of course she'd sum it up perfectly.

"Yeah," I whispered. "*That.*"

Teeth pressing into her bottom lip, her eyes locked on mine. "What happened?"

"You know Brit offered me her old apartment."

She nodded.

"I went over last night to check it out and bring some of my stuff. Then Brit and the guys showed up and we ended up having an impromptu game night, so I slept there." Her hair, that gorgeous silky brown hair that shone like the fucking sun, was in her eyes so I pushed it back, tucked a strand behind her ear. "Then in the morning I went back to change and grab the rest of my shit because I was going to come up and surprise you and—"

"Candi was there."

"Yeah. With an *i.*"

She froze.

And then she did the most wonderful thing ever. She *laughed.* "With an *i?*"

My lips twitched. "Yeah."

"Yikes." Another laugh, but this one was accompanied by warmth dancing through her eyes, amusement gilding her smile. "It's worse than I thought."

"Yeah." I tucked another strand of hair behind her ear. "Worse."

She went sober again and I watched the insecurity creeping back into her expression. Fuck. I hated that *I* was the cause of that hurt. That the pain in her eyes was because *I'd* caused it. "What did she say to you?"

White teeth into a plump bottom lip. "She was...very descriptive about you...and um...your tattoo."

I stilled.

"And..." A sigh. "Your scar. She was *very* detailed when talking about your scar."

Fuck.

Fuck.

I inhaled, released it slowly.

"I know that you...um...were with a lot of women before me." Her lips tipped up and her smile wasn't anything close to real, her stare tempered with pain. "Hell, I know I wasn't the town manwhore, but I was with enough people to know that I can't fault you for the same. It was before me"—she paused, eyes glinting with enough hesitation that I nodded, even though it fucking stung—"it was before me," she repeated.

"It was before you," I said, giving her the words because I *had* to, because she needed to know.

She needed *to know.*

She nodded again, the edges of her eyes warming.

"And I wasn't with her. Not *ever.*"

"Axel—"

"Not *ever*, buttercup," I said again. "I was with her friend. We finished and—" I winced, because, fuck, I was an asshole. But I pushed on and gave her the rest. "I looked up and Candi was standing there, watching me—" I broke off, shuddering.

Her fingers tightened on my chest, the warm growing, being joined with empathy. "Being creepy as fuck?" she whispered.

"Yeah." I took a breath and released it. "So that's how she would know about my scar, about my tattoo. She was watching, and apparently doing it for a while. But I swear I didn't—not with her—not—"

"I know."

Now her tone was steady, full of conviction, and finally, finally, I relaxed. "Yeah?"

A nod. "Yeah, honey."

My breath slid out of me, slow and steady. "Then want to tell me why we're still standing out here when we're finally together?"

"I—"

She froze and then her hand came to my jaw, rested there lightly, fingers stroking gently through my beard.

I shivered.

Fuck, I loved it when she did that.

It set my nerves on fire.

Then she smiled, fingers pressing in, the tips hitting my skin and sending need billowing through me. My cock was still hard from the kiss, from her body against mine, but when she smiled like that, smiled at me in a way that told me I was very likely going to *win* very soon, I was a haze of need and desire, one spark away from imploding.

"I don't know why we're still standing out here," she murmured, grabbing my hand and lacing our fingers together, dragging me toward the house.

Toward the porch Billie Rose had handcuffed me to.

Twice.

Because I'd needed to get my head straight and she'd somehow known that no one but Bailey was going to help me get my head out of my ass.

And it had worked.

"Shit," Bailey whispered, halting on the top step.

Tension immediately coiling in my belly. "What?" I asked, drawing her close.

"The animals. I need to get them ready for the night—"

She started to spin, started to turn for the barn, but my phone buzzed in my pocket and when I pulled it out as I followed her, glancing at the screen, my lips curved up. I drew her to a stop. "Buttercup."

"Data needs—"

I held up my cell. "Two guesses who?"

Bailey frowned.

I turned the screen so that she could read the text…

From Billie Rose.

Animals are taken care of. Now take care of my girl.

"Christ," Bailey muttered, shaking her head.

"Thus is the power of Billie Rose?"

Her mouth turned up. "Something I literally say to myself every single day."

I smoothed my free hand down her spine. "You still want to check on them anyway?"

Teeth into her bottom lip, a tinge of embarrassment in her pretty brown eyes. "Yeah," she whispered, dropping her gaze from mine.

"Buttercup."

She tugged at her hand, my fingers still laced through hers. I held fast.

"*Buttercup.*" A little firmer.

Her eyes hit mine again.

"You give Data his sugar cubes, I'll check the water buckets."

Data was her *Star Trek*-named horse who had a penchant for the little white squares. The water buckets were obvious and went along with checking the feeders and stalls. Something I never would have understood two months ago.

Something I knew now.

Something I was *happy* to know, happy to do.

Because knowing it, *doing* it, meant that I got to watch Bailey's eyes warm again, got to feel her lips brush my cheek in thanks, watch her ass, her hips sway when she strode away from me.

It meant that I was taking care of the woman I loved.

It meant...everything.

Five

Bailey

He had hay in his hair and smelled like horse.

I thought that—perhaps—the combination was the best aphrodisiac on the planet.

Big, broody, sexy hockey player talking sweet to my horses, shoveling out a few stalls without complaint. Or prompting for that matter—just seeing that there was a mess that shouldn't wait until morning and cleaning it. See? An aphrodisiac.

Maybe it said something weird about me, the fact that the man got me wet just by wielding a shovel.

But...I was wet. I was horny.

I wanted to be in my bed with my man and—

Fingers along my jaw.

The smell of horse a little stronger as his body came close.

I'd been watching Data settle in for the night, mostly because I'd spent the better portion of our time in the barn staring at Axel's ass.

Hockey players had the *best* asses.

Let that be noted for the record.

Maybe it was all their time on the stationary bike or bending their knees on the ice or the squats...or just a combination of all three.

Hockey players equaled nice asses.

And Axel's was *the best.*

Probably because he was *my* hockey player and that was *my* ass and I'd readily argue with anyone about both of those facts.

Plus, his was lush and round and bitable and—

His chest pressed to my back.

Big.

All of him.

One hand dropped onto the top of the stall door next to my chest, dangerously close to my breasts, so close, in fact, that I could feel the heat from it soaking through my clothes, its proximity hardening the bud of my nipple, making the flesh tingle.

Or maybe I just had Axel detectors in my titties.

Which had me giggling.

Unfortunately, right before his mouth touched the hinge of my jaw. That was one of the spots—*the* spots—that never failed to make me shiver, to have me arching back, my softness instinctively seeking out his hard, my thighs clenching, wetness gathering, and—

"What?" he asked against my skin.

"What?" Yeah, it was a breathless question. But his body was close, his lips closer, and like one of Pavlov's dogs, the bell had been rung and I was ready.

I was *ready.*

"Why'd you giggle, buttercup?"

Oh, right.

Well, that was embarrassing. I was thinking about my boobs—referring to them as titties, no less—and Axel and Pavlov and—

I spun in his arms, rose on tiptoe, intent on his mouth—

Hands on my waist, spinning me back around, his body coming close, pressing me into the stall door. Splinters on one side, a hard body on the other.

"Spill, honey." An order.

And, though I knew I shouldn't like it, that my body shouldn't be growing all tingly, the dampness soaking through my panties, gathering at the tops of my thighs, I liked every part of those two words. The slight growl, how his face dipped a little closer so I could feel the demand on my nape, his hands dropping onto the stall door again, caging me in completely this time.

Body close.

Axel close.

His tongue flicked out, hit skin, and a soft (and yes, breathy) moan slid from my lips. "Tell me." Another demand. Another rush of hot, damp air on the back of my neck.

And my throat unlocked, the words burst out. "My boobs are Axel Finnegan detectors. They get all tingly when you're nearby."

He froze.

I refused to be embarrassed, lifting my chin, arching my ass back so that it rubbed along the hard length of him (even though I was secretly dying inside because I'd just admitted to my titties being my tall, dark, and talented hockey player detector).

Then I was facing him again, and the heat in his bright blue eyes was a scorching summer sky, the threat of fire right there on the horizon.

One spark and everything around us would go up in flames.

My arms dropped to my sides, brushing against something soft, and I glanced down, then up, and realized that I'd missed the blanket that had been draped over the wooden wall of the stall. Right behind where my body was pressed. Not a blanket I'd put there. I wouldn't have. Data would probably eat it and then I'd be dealing with a sick horse. But it didn't surprise me that it had "magically" appeared when Axel came close, that he'd managed to position my body exactly against it.

His was a quiet kind of care (minus the *stubborn* care that came with all but forcing me to accept his help with the remodel inside).

But it was the little things like this that had eventually crumbled the walls around my heart.

That had me falling for this man and doing it deeply.

The reminder reinforced the realization I'd come to on the drive, even before he'd given me the full explanation about *Candi*.

He wasn't the kind of man who'd hurt me in that way.

He was brutally honest and had a wide self-protective streak... which usually manifested in asshole.

But once a person was allowed inside his heart there was only loyalty, only protection, only—

Love.

Then he grabbed my hand, pressed it to his granite hard erection, and I wasn't thinking about love.

Only *heat.*

"You think this thing isn't hard for you *all* the time?"

It was a rasp, his fingers flexing on mine. Not that I needed any encouragement to wrap my hand tighter around him, to feel every long, thick inch of his cock. Even without his hand tightening, I was already gripping him through his sweats, thankful that the material let me feel everything. The rock-hard length, the scalding jut, the pulsing erection. All beneath *my* hand. All for *me.*

I didn't stop with squeezing him through his pants.

I dove my hand beneath the waistband of his sweats, sliding it beneath his underwear, getting my fingers on that hard length.

I wanted my mouth on him.

I wanted to drop to my knees.

I wanted him to hit the back of my throat, to swallow the hot spurts of his cum as he fell apart.

I wanted—

His hand grasped mine, wrapping his fingers around my wrist, drawing me off him, spinning me, and dropping my palm onto the top of the railing. Then the other.

"You want it, don't you?" A velvet scrape on my nape, a dripping heat over my breasts, clinging to the hardened buds of my nipples, drizzled over my stomach, sliding between my thighs. "You want me to fuck you right here, don't you?"

Oh God, I wanted that.

So badly.

Before I could get the words out, he was on his knees. He was dragging down my pants. He was tugging my hips back.

"Christ," he muttered, palming my ass. Big, rough hands massaging. A finger dragging between my cheeks, pressing lightly against the puckered bud.

I gasped, arching back, instinctively seeking more, moaning when he gripped the top of my thong, tugged it up slightly, dragging the emerald lace through my slick folds, putting pressure both on my clit and on the sensitive flesh between my cheeks.

I needed—

A nip had me gasping again, a sting blooming on my ass before it was gently soothed by his lips and tongue.

"You want it," he murmured silkily, hand gliding over my skin, his finger tracing the line of lace. "Fuck yeah, honey, you want it."

I did.

I wanted it so badly that I was shaking.

He slid my panties down my hips, trailed his fingers back up the inside of my thighs, and then—

His tongue dipped in.

Six

Axel

I was a fucking freak.

I loved that her cheeks—both sets—had flushed when I talked about fucking her right there in the barn where anyone might come upon us. Loved that I could feel how she grew even more wet when I told her I *knew* she wanted me to fuck her right there and then.

I loved her. Period.

Not that I'd told her.

It was too soon, and after this shitshow of a day, with my tongue in her pussy, it definitely wasn't the right time.

But I'd make the time and do it soon.

And I'd make the gesture grand and worthy of her.

But, for now, I wanted to corrupt Bailey.

I wanted to fuck her with my fingers and then with my tongue and then with my cock right there with her hands clinging to the top of the stall, and then with hay prickling my back as she rode me hard, and then on that old, worn workbench that housed the saws that had brought us together…or apart and *then* together.

But first, my tongue.

I flicked it through her folds.

And even though I kept one ear on her moans, on the sexy as

shit little gasps she made as she ground against my mouth and teeth and tongue, my other one was on our surroundings.

I would hear the gravel first if anyone drove or walked up the driveway.

I didn't mind playing with her, enticing her with the thought of being caught.

But she wouldn't actually want anyone to see her like this, see her vulnerable.

And I wouldn't let it happen.

And that she wasn't looking around, wasn't worried about being caught, that she was trusting me with her body open like this, lost to her pleasure...it meant more to me than perhaps anything else ever had.

I wouldn't fuck it up.

But first, I needed to fuck her.

A tug of her hips had her angled better for my mouth, and I didn't go slow or gentle or easy. It was one of my favorite activities and I dove right in, showing no mercy, sucking at her clit, tonguing her labia, slipping it inside, deep enough that my face was buried in between her cheeks, that her liquid heat was all over me—on my lips and in my beard and on my jaw and in my nose. I wanted to swim in it, to swim in her. I loved the way she smelled...everywhere. I loved when she was in my every pore. I loved when she was soaked and dripping down my chin.

But she needed to come.

Because, already, my control was fracturing.

Just weeks without her and my need was almost overwhelming.

But...Bailey first.

Always, I would put Bailey first.

Another jerk back and then I was crawling between her legs, using my shoulders to spread them wide, spinning so that I could latch onto her clit, so that I could suck deeply.

She jolted. "*Axel.*"

Fuck, yes.

I gripped her ass, a hand on each cheek, drew her more firmly against my face, sucking hard and fast, even as more shudders wracked her frame.

Her body was talking to mine, but I didn't know that she was close because she was shaking and her pussy was convulsing around my fingers. I knew it because of how her voice broke, how my name sounded as it tumbled off her tongue over and over again. I knew it in the press of her hips, in how she ground her pussy against my face.

I knew it like I was coming myself.

And it was nearly as good.

The way her pussy grew even more slick, how tightly she clenched my fingers, her knees shaking, her head dropping back.

Her groan filling the air.

And finally, finally, her body going limp against me.

I caught her in my lap, let her rest her head against my chest, my dick still fucking aching, but not in any hurry to assuage the ache.

Because she was close. Because only I got to see her like this.

Because *I'd* made her feel good.

Because—

She moved in a rapid flash of movement that was almost too quick for me to track, and by the time I did, she was pushing me onto my back, hay prickling my skin through the fabric of my tee, her shaking fingers yanking my pants down before she clambered on top of me, slid down...

And fuck yeah, that was good.

The tight, wet clasp of her.

My cock buried deep inside.

I didn't give a fuck about the dissolution of my plans to make her come again, this time with my mouth on her tits and my fingers inside her. I didn't give a fuck that I'd been content to wait and here we were going fast again.

I didn't give a fuck—

That she was moving.

Okay, I gave *many* fucks about the last. Mostly because the way she felt was...

Everything.

"Axel," she whispered, arching back, hands hitting my thighs, lifting up and driving down. I couldn't decide where to look—watching my cock press deep into her, watching her face lit up with pleasure. And then I wasn't thinking about any of that. I wasn't even thinking about fucking her, or that it was really her fucking me, or just the fact that being inside her was better than winning a game, better than scoring that match-winning goal. I was thinking—

No.

No more thinking.

Doing.

Only doing.

I reached for the hem of her shirt and leaned up, yanking it over her head, exposing her breasts clad in dark green lace. So different from her typical function over fashion.

Not that I gave a fuck.

I could appreciate the effort, the glimpse it gave me. But I just wanted her naked. I wanted my mouth on her breasts, wanted to feel her hard nipples on my tongue.

So, I took a mental snapshot, and then I pounced.

Sucking one nipple hard, palming the other breast, bringing one hand to her ass and driving up as I yanked her down onto me. Sweat began to bead on my forehead, began to drip down my back. My abs were already on fire.

But I didn't give a fuck.

And I certainly didn't stop.

Not when my name was already rolling off her tongue and filling the air, not when she was clenching me tight inside, not when every time I pulled on her nipple, her pussy convulsed around me.

Not when I was so fucking close to coming that I knew I had to get her there and do it fast and—

I slid my hand in, gripping her ass, dipping down into the cleft between those sweet cheeks. She was soaking there, too, and my finger slid over that taut pucker, slid *into* that tighter clasp of her body.

Her rhythm faltered.

Her head shot up.

"What—"

I pressed in a little further.

Her eyes widened and I nearly stopped, nearly pulled back, but then her head dropped back, a moan tumbled out of her mouth, and her pussy went so tight around me that I saw stars.

"Axel," she groaned, that rhythm totally lost, her movements frantic and out of control and—

I was out of control too.

Feasting on her tits, thrusting my finger into her as I jerked her up and down my cock, my orgasm barreling down onto me.

No chance of slowing.

No chance of waiting.

Nothing but hitting the gas, jamming the pedal into the floor, speeding toward oblivion—

And crashing over the precipice.

"Fuck," I groaned, and then I was coming, my cock growing even harder as she milked me, as her nails dug in, as she met me thrust for thrust for thrust, our bodies seeking each other in a way that wasn't finessed or controlled but was still fucking perfect as pleasure threatened to incinerate me, to reduce me to nothing but ashes.

And I was more than happy to become dust.

Seven

Bailey

Girl was going to be sore tomorrow.

That girl was me.

I was going to be sore.

Newsflash, I was a total dork.

But…I don't think I'd ever ridden a cock so hard, taken a man so deep…and that didn't even begin to take into account the finger.

Oh God, that finger.

Somehow my poor, overworked pussy convulsed, remembering the different kind of pleasure Axel's touch had wrought in me, the strange mix of pleasure and pain and needing *more*. Feeling full and also empty. Wanting another finger there. Wanting a toy there. Wanting—

His cock there.

I shivered again.

And that seemed to rouse him, his finger still inside me and flexing lightly before it gently slid free of my body. But he didn't go far, just rested his palm on my ass, his fingers between my cheeks. Did I shift slightly, body searching for him again? Yeah.

But was I *always* addicted to Axel and his body and how effectively he played mine? Definitely yes.

Was I going to fuck him again and soon? Also yes.

Just...when I felt like I had control of my limbs again.

Meanwhile, I'd collapsed against his chest, was listening to his heart pound against my ear, loving the way his arms held me so tightly.

Good enough.

This right here was good enough.

A breath that brought Axel into my nose, into my pores, into every inch of my body.

And, yeah, that was enough.

I relaxed against him.

My eyes slid closed.

The smell of something delicious had my stomach rumbling, and I frowned, stretching and remembering all of my soreness, a tiny groan slipping from between my lips.

A soft hand brushing back my hair.

A gentle kiss to my temple.

Who in the world had ever thought that Axel Finnegan could be gentle?

Except, he'd helped me when I tweaked my back. He'd caught me when I fell from a ladder, had gently picked glass from my body so it wouldn't cut me. He'd made sure I'd gotten home when I'd had a few too many beers (that being *two* total, which was one too many). He'd seen the state of my house and helped. Not given some bullshit "call me if you need anything." Instead, he'd stepped up, had done *something*.

So yeah, even though the man could crush someone on the ice, could be an asshole in real life, I knew he could be gentle.

Because he was gentle with *me*.

"Barn fucking a bad idea?" he asked, tucking a strand of hair behind my ear.

My mouth tipped up, eyes peeling open and taking in my sexy hockey player. His hair was a mess, and his shirt had been full of hay, so he'd taken it off—then hadn't bothered to put a new one on (oh the humanity and my eyes, my poor eyes)—and I...wanted to jump his bones, wanted to collapse in bed together and talk about nothing and everything.

I wanted him.

With me.

Always.

But he'd be leaving in the morning.

Sigh.

"I don't think us fucking is *ever* a bad idea," I said, forcing my tone to be light.

Hot blue eyes. A wicked grin. "Now, that might be the smartest thing you've ever said."

I growled, managed to rouse my limp limbs, and poked him lightly in the chest. "Jerk."

"Sexy, smart." A kiss to the tip of my nose. "*Mine.*"

"Hmph." But I didn't argue, and maybe considering that my ex who'd claimed me as his had been in my driveway just a couple of hours before, warning me of all the risks that came from men and their penchant for claiming, I should have rebuffed the statement.

But...

Axel wasn't Colt.

And as much as I should be leery of men and relationships...I'd carried Colt's shit for too long. And, frankly, I'd been to too many therapy sessions, had worked too hard to get my life and mind and heart together after Colt to go backward now.

There was a time I couldn't even think his name, couldn't imagine letting the good man in this room into my life.

I wasn't going back there.

Wasn't going back to isolating myself and living in the shadows.

Life was good, and I was going to embrace it.

'Cause, God knew, shit was about to get fucked if my parents had shown up on my doorstep.

Right.

Didn't want to think about them or Colt. Not when Axel was here and had to leave in the morning and I didn't know when I'd see him next.

"How'd I get to bed?" I asked as Axel bent away from me and

set the plates he had balanced on his free arm on the nightstand. I remembered enjoying my personal Axel pillow, but that was it.

"You were out," he said by way of explanation, turning back and sliding in so that our bodies faced each other, our hips touching, his big, broad palm resting between my legs and reminding me all over again that I didn't want food.

I wanted him.

But I wanted *all* of him.

So while I didn't close my legs—that would both reveal too much *and* trap his hand against me (thus undoing any of my progress in wanting to know more of his big, juicy brain instead of his big...juicy—*ew*—hard—*yeah, that was better*—cock)—and while I was hyperaware (*hyper!*) of its proximity to all the parts of me he was very good at rousing to liquid attention, I forced myself to focus on him, on us, on our conversation.

I lifted my brows. "And me being out means what?"

"It means you're little and I'm strong." His smile was cocky now. "So, I carried you in."

"You do know that I have two feet, right?" I nodded toward the body parts in question. "And those feet are attached to legs that could have walked myself into the house."

"You were *out*." Axel didn't seem bothered by my tart tone. In fact, he seemed to be fighting a smile. "And since you weren't using those feet or those legs, I used my *two*"—the emphasis on *two* would have driven me crazy a few months ago, it was so condescending, but since I knew him, and since I was dishing out the sass just as heartily, his tone had me biting back a smile instead—"arms to carry you up into bed and set about rousing you by showing off my culinary delights."

I cocked my head to the side. "Set about?"

A shrug, though his cheeks took on the barest hint of pink.

"Culinary delights?"

Another shrug, more pink. "I might be dating a woman who is a Trekkie, but I also know she likes certain books."

Delight—of the non-culinary variety—bubbled up inside me. "And?"

"And maybe those books are..."

I grinned, clapped my hands together. "Amazing? Hot? Make you want to get me in a big, puffy dress so that you can take advantage of me in a carriage or pin me to an alley wall, flip up my skirts, and—"

"Right," he growled.

I blinked.

But didn't get the chance to actually get any words out, not when he was moving.

One jerk had the blankets yanked down, revealing my naked body.

The next movement had him on top of me, his lips stopping just a hairsbreadth away from mine.

"What about your culinary delights?" I asked, and was it breathless?

Yes.

I had Axel Finnegan pinning me to the bed, his blue eyes full of storm clouds and lightning, and I was very much looking forward to being caught up in the maelstrom, so *of course* my question was breathless.

He snagged my wrist in another of those quick movements, bringing it to his mouth, tongue flicking out and tasting the tiny tattoo I had there. "I want to know what this means," he said in his velvet rasp.

"I—"

Before my answer could fully form, he lifted my arm higher, over my head, wrapping my fingers around the cool metal bar that ran along the bottom of my headboard.

"But later."

He lifted my other arm, encouraged those fingers to wrap around the bar, too.

"Wh—?"

"First"—he snagged something from the plate on the nightstand—"my culinary delights."

My lungs were struggling from the onslaught of his body, from the ache in my breasts, fully on display with my hands gripping that metal bar, my nipples all but begging for his mouth, but when I caught sight of what was in the little bowl he dipped his fingers into, I glanced into those thundercloud eyes, into the flurry of lightning sparking through his irises. I was holding a metal bar in the middle of a giant storm, all but calling for the cloud's electricity to coalesce onto me...

And I smiled.

Bring on the storm.

EIGHT

AXEL

"I hate that you have to go," she whispered, arms tight around my waist, face buried in my chest.

Right against my heart.

That beat for her.

Only for her.

Something that never should have happened, considering all the walls I built, reinforced with concrete, with barbed wire, encircled with a giant ass moat that was filled with toxic waste-laced water and crocodiles that had mutated into freakish beasts.

Maybe I was watching too much *Star Trek* and it was mixing oddly with those historical romance novels I'd become secretly addicted to.

Women.

They seriously fucked a man up.

Except, even as I was thinking it, my heart smiled.

Yup. I wasn't even going to kick my own ass for thinking that bit of trite nonsense. It was the fucking truth.

This woman.

This woman fucked me up in the best possible way.

But I still had to go.

I had practice that afternoon and a long drive to make before that.

"I know, buttercup."

Her head tilted back, soft brown eyes hitting mine. "We didn't get to talk much."

No. We hadn't. Between the barn and then her nap and my *culinary delights,* we hadn't had energy for much talking when we'd finally collapsed.

After a shower.

After changing the sticky sheets.

Because my *culinary delights* mostly extended to breakfast.

A nip to the hinge of her jaw. "Keep the syrup warm for me."

Her lips tipped up. "I think I have a Costco trip in my future to make sure we don't run out."

I kissed them. "The vat I ordered is coming on two-day shipping."

Now she grinned. And that was better. I didn't like leaving her, but I liked leaving her even less when she was sad, and even *more* less with her parents and asshole ex potentially in town and ready to unleash trouble.

I knew Billie Rose would rally the town to keep an eye out.

But I knew that I was going to take further precautions.

I had to.

I couldn't be fucking states or a country away and not know she was safe. I couldn't do my job with worry sitting heavy on my shoulders.

I already hated that she wasn't in San Francisco, waiting for me to get back from a road trip or watching in the team box with the other WAGs.

"You'll be careful?" I asked.

Her palm came to my cheek, and I felt the gentle touch like it was a brand on my skin. "I'll be careful," she promised.

Turning my head, I kissed the inside of her wrist, kissed the tattoo there. "We talked enough for me to know what *this* means."

Now her cheeks flushed.

Because I'd learned something about her.

Learned that the apple on her wrist wasn't an homage to Data's second favorite treat, but it was an homage to her dream.

She wanted to teach high school English.

I couldn't imagine why.

Teenagers were assholes and getting them to read serious books rather than consuming thirty-second TikTok videos seemed to be a lesson in futility. But then again, she'd gotten a dumbass hockey player to watch *Star Trek* and read historical romance novels, so Bailey could probably get those high schoolers to do anything.

"It's silly," she'd whispered. "I mean, I didn't even get my credentials and now I have the ranch—"

"It's not," I'd whispered back. "It's not silly to dream."

And when she'd looked into my eyes, I knew that she saw.

Knew that she saw how much she'd impacted *my* dream. Knew that she understood I was demanding that she not give up on hers.

And for once, she didn't give me shit about demanding.

She'd just laid her head back down on my chest, wrapped her arm around my middle, and my heart had smiled again.

"Don't give up, okay?" I whispered now, pressing another kiss to the mark.

"I still have at least a year before the ranch will be out of the financial hell-hole my parents left it in, and that's not including anything that might happen with them showing up." She dropped her head to my chest. "I'm trying not to worry about how fucked up this is going to get—"

Fingers on her jaw, tilting her head back so that she would look at me. "Buttercup."

"Horses and cows are easier than people," she muttered.

"You won't hear me arguing with you about that."

Her nose wrinkled. "At least you get to shoot pucks at them."

Fuck, she was cute.

I bent and kissed those little lines creasing her adorable upturned nose. "True." A kiss to her forehead. "Next time I'm in River's Bend, I'll pull some strings and get you a couple of hockey players to practice shooting pucks at."

She laughed.

I had to taste it, taste her smile.

So I did, and it filled a part of me that I hadn't even known was empty, not until Bailey had come into my life.

When we'd broke apart, chests heaving, her hand found my jaw again. "I love that you make me laugh."

I love...

Those two words slid through me, weighty and intense and fucking perfect.

Minus the fact that they hadn't ended with *you.*

But after the shitshow of yesterday, I'd take making her laugh any day of the week, any *moment* of the fucking day.

"I love—"

Her breath caught, and I pressed her hand to my face, imprinting her touch on my skin, so I could carry it with me while we were apart.

"I love," I said again, "that I can do that for you."

A glimmer of disappointment in her chocolate brown eyes before it was dutifully tucked away.

Because it was too soon.

Because we had too much going on.

She deserved better. More. *Everything.*

I smothered my impatience.

Slow. So I didn't fuck this up.

Because I wanted to keep her forever.

"We're going to be okay," I said.

Because I *wouldn't* fuck this up.

The disappointment was gone, and then she was pasting on a smile I knew was as much for her benefit as it was for mine. "I know."

Determination and a spine of steel.

Part of why I loved her. But only part because there wasn't anything I didn't love about her—not her stubborn pride, not the way she was terrible at accepting help and exceptional at giving it, not the way she cared for her animals and the people in her life who'd made it past that treacherous stubborn pride.

I could go on.

But I was just prolonging the pain.

I had to leave.

She knew it, too. "Go," she whispered, and kissed me. "I'm going to ride Data. Something," she added, dropping back onto her heels, face gentle and warm, and I knew *that* was what I was going to be dreaming of tonight, the way she was looking at me in that moment. "I get to do because my hot, hockey-playing boyfriend got up early and mucked stalls for me."

"Buttercup—"

She reached behind me, tugged open the driver's side door. "Go, honey."

I inhaled, fought down my protest, and got in the car.

Not before I stole another kiss, though. One hot and *warm* (yes, there was a difference between hot and warm—one was for my dick, the other for my heart) and long enough to tide us both over.

"See you soon," she whispered, her fingers clinging to mine.

I nodded, forcing myself to peel my hand away. "Text me when you're back from your ride with Data."

She inclined her head.

And then I didn't have any other reason to delay, or couldn't think of any, anyway.

So, I pulled the Band-Aid, making it easier on both of us, closing my door, starting the engine, reversing slowly out of the driveway so as not to disrupt the gravel.

And then I drove away from the woman I loved.

And I hated every fucking minute of it.

When I hit the highway and cell coverage wasn't spotty, I called Joel.

My former teammate was a real ballbuster and general pain in the ass.

But he was big and scary and could handle himself.

He was also a dog who'd made it most of his life's duty to score as much pussy as possible. Pucks and pussy. That had been our motto.

Before Bailey had pulled a shotgun on me.

Before Billie Rose had helped me sort my shit with a pair (two?) of handcuffs.

Before I'd realized that so much of what was stopping me from achieving what I wanted was in my own fucking head.

Joel was still living that motto, albeit without tearing up the town.

Which I approved of.

Once I'd allowed myself, I'd found that River's Bend was pretty dope.

Or maybe it was the woman living on the outskirts of it.

Or—

"Hello?" Joel's voice was groggy.

No doubt because the guys had played last night and then celebrated their win (or loss) with booze and chicks.

"Hey, it's me."

"Axel?" A grunt, fumbling in the background. "Christ, do you know what time it is?"

"Yeah. I'm sorry to..." A feminine protest in the background that had me biting back laughter. Fuck. Some things didn't change. "*Interrupt*, but I need a favor."

A beat of quiet.

But then there was the sound of material sliding against material, of footsteps on hardwood floor, of a door closing.

"What's up, man?" Joel rasped.

"It's about Bailey..." And then I spent the next couple of minutes explaining about her ex and what I knew—which wasn't nearly everything, not all that had he'd done to Bailey, but even just explaining the bare bones that I *did* know along with what had happened the day before had my blood boiling all over again.

Joel cursed several times during my explanation.

I knew he would.

As much pussy as he chased, as much as he liked to let it rip and tie one on, he had three sisters and if any of their husbands had treated them like Colt had treated Bailey...

They'd be six feet under.

"I'm not there," I finished. "I mean even when the team is playing at home, I'm still not nearly close enough. I know Billie Rose and the rest of the town will look after her, but..."

"You're not there," he finished for me.

"Yeah," I whispered.

A breath, but then Joel's voice was fierce. "I'll—*we'll* be there when we can. Keep an eye out. Make sure that fucking harpy of a mayor doesn't slack in her duty of keeping an eye out, too."

Even though the last made me smile because I knew from first-hand experience how much of a handful Billie Rose could be (though I'd say less harpy and more of a confident, definitely scary Cupid), I didn't laugh.

Because this might have been the most serious conversation Joel and I had ever had.

And that made me sad.

How much I'd been holding back from my teammates.

How much I'd missed out on because I'd been so good at isolating myself.

I wouldn't make that same mistake with my new teammates—Brit and the rest of the Gold crew wouldn't let that happen even if I tried—but I wouldn't have the chance to go back and have a do-over with these guys.

I'd just corrupted them and led them astray and then went onto the Big Show.

Not entirely fair to me, I knew.

They were adults and made their own choices, and once I'd gotten my shit together, I'd encouraged them to do the same.

But it wasn't enough.

"Thanks, man," I said, and I knew my tone revealed too fucking much.

But, for once, Joel didn't dive into the weakness and give me shit. Instead, he just grunted back and said, "No thanks needed. Now I'm awake at a godawful hour and have a hot, naked chick in my bed. I'm going back to do what I'm best at."

I snorted. "Giving orgasms?"

"No." A beat. "Playing fucking Twister."

I blinked.

"Get it?" A chuckle. "Playing *Fucking* Twister."

Ah. There was the Joel I knew. Lame jokes, dirty mind, and all booming laughter through my car's speakers.

"God, I hope she wins," I muttered.

"Oh, she will," he countered.

Before I could quip back, he disconnected.

Probably for the best.

"*Fucking* Twister."

Laughing, I shook my head.

Mostly because I was jealous.

And maybe because a new activity for Bailey and me had just been scratched onto my mental To Do List.

To *Do.*

I grinned.

Fuck, one conversation with Joel and I was turning into a child.

But I still drove with a smile on my face for the rest of the way back to San Francisco.

To. *Do.*

Heh.

Nine

Bailey

The rolling hills were one of my favorite parts.

But most especially this time of year.

It was cool, mist clinging to the grass, glimmering from the sun rising in the east, turning them into tiny crystal-like statues. Like something my grandmother would have collected if they really *were* crystal and sparkly and something she could have picked up from River's Marketplace, the same store downtown that carried everything from sweatshirts to tubes that could be inflated and rode down the river to tiny crystal statues.

Statues that definitely would be collecting dust on my shelves.

I much preferred to admire them like this.

With the breeze in my hair and through those long blades of grass, sending both waving.

I could control only one of those—the former—and spent a minute tying it back, letting Data have her head, have a bit of freedom.

Not that I was ever tight on the reins.

Not with Data.

We'd been riding together for long enough that we didn't need that communication.

We were one.

And I needed the bit of freedom myself, to not have to be in charge, to be able to pause and enjoy the quiet...and reflect.

The last twenty-four hours had been...

Insanity.

A fucking roller coaster.

Christ.

My parents. *Colt.*

Colt, I had no fucking clue what he wanted. He hadn't contested the divorce, hadn't sought me out after that night in the rain, when he'd left me with broken ribs and a swollen jaw and split lip and black eyes and a mild concussion.

He'd just...pushed me to my breaking point then had discarded me like trash.

So, him being there, him being with my *parents,* was a fucking mystery.

My parents' motivations, on the other hand, were obvious.

They were out of money. Again.

The ranch was doing well, and it was—cue jazz hands—freshly renovated. Of course, my mom would want to spend time in a house that had a suite she'd designed, and the remainder of the house was almost on par with that luxury she desired.

No more floral on floral on floral couch.

No more old shag carpeting that grabbed every crumb.

Sleek wood floors. New tile in the bathrooms. New cabinets *and* appliances in the kitchen. New furniture. New carpet. New electrical and plumbing. Paid for by Axel. All selected by me and Dessie and Margaret, who was River's Bend's only interior designer.

Gramps's house was no longer the explosion of the eighties and before.

It was *mine* now.

And my mom wanted her talons in it.

I needed to talk to my lawyer, find out if my parents had any right to the house. I'd gotten a loan, bought their portion of the property outright. Billie Rose didn't even have a share of the property itself. She got a small cut of the profits, but that was the extent of my aunt's legal ties to Russet Ranch.

But my parents shouldn't have any say, any claim. They shouldn't be *here.*

Someone might think that my dad would give a fuck about the ranch.

It was technically his legacy, after all—though Gramps had only left him a third (something I'd found out when I'd begun desperate proceeding to buy their share so Russet Ranch didn't go under and was sold to developers).

But I'd never been able to figure out *what* my father actually cared about. He just...existed on the outskirts of my life, living his own, and so unattached that he made my mother look like Mom of the Year.

He certainly didn't give a fuck about the legacy—he'd hated bringing me up to the ranch during the summers, had left that to my mother or made Gran or Gramps or Billie's parents pick me up. He didn't give a fuck about his parents—I'd never seen him visit, not once. He didn't give a shit about me—he'd never been bothered to check a homework assignment, to go to a school activity. Hell, he hadn't been bothered to get me to school at *all.*

I suppose I should be happy that at least my mother pretended sometimes.

She'd driven me to school when I was too little to walk myself.

She'd cooked me dinner before I figured out how to pour myself a bowl of cereal and not dump it all over the floor, and...I'm sure there had to have been a few other things, even if they didn't spring immediately to mind.

The point was, I'd survived to adulthood.

And while I'd done it mostly eating cereal, or consuming the remnants of my friends' lunches at school, and learning how to wash my own clothes in kindergarten...

I was here.

And I'd had Gran and Gramps.

I had Data and Billie Rose and maybe I'd had to sell my pet cow, Picard, to a petting zoo so I could afford the premium streaming package to watch my boyfriend play hockey.

But I had a boyfriend who played hockey.

And he was nice and sexy and had a big cock.

And he got up early with me so that all my big chores were done and I could take Data out.

And maybe he was a fucking miracle.

Or maybe he was just *Axel*.

I smiled, sitting in this quiet moment with the waving grass and sun peeking up over the hills.

Pausing so that I could soak it in, hold it close, lock it up safe.

Because I had the feeling that this peace that Axel had given me, the small slice of happy and contentment that he'd managed to carve out for me wasn't going to continue for long.

"And I'll have the Caesar salad with dressing on the side and extra—"

"Cracked black pepper, Parmesan, and none of the stemmy leaves," Bonnie finished, gaze flicking up to mine, her pale brown eyes twinkling as she took our lunch order. A secondary perk of the hot boyfriend with the big dick who got up early and helped with chores was that I had enough time to actually socialize every once in a while. Which, I supposed, could be good or bad. But today it was good. I loved Billie and was happy to take her to lunch for all her help with my house. "I've known you for almost thirty years, Rosie girl. I've got your salad order memorized. *And* your ice water with lemons and not *too much* ice covered," she added, writing a note on her pad.

"I just like what I like," Billie murmured, and strangely, she looked a little insecure.

Which was an odd look on my typically assured aunt's face.

"Of course you do," Bonnie said, patting Billie's hand, whose expression quickly cleared and returned to its normal commanding presence, making me almost think that I'd imagined it.

I *must* have imagined it.

Because then she said, in normal Billie Rose fashion, "I know you've got it covered, but I'm still going to ask for rolls hot from the oven and extra butter."

Bonnie laughed, tucked her pen behind her ear. "Of course you are, honey bun."

A wink at me. "The special for you, booboo?"

I nodded, passed over my menu. "Sounds good. Thanks, Bonnie."

"Anytime, girls."

She turned away, moved over to the large window so she could call their order to Deke, who was on that day, and I was watching her, laughing at the sass she tossed the chef (who also happened to be her husband), when Billie Rose asked, "What's the special?"

I turned back, shrugged. "I don't know."

Billie gaped at me.

Literally gaped.

But she recovered quickly, as was her power. "You *don't* know."

I sat back, smothered a laugh. "Nope."

"But—but—" Her lips pressed together, fell open again. "But how can you just order and not *know?* What if you don't like it—What if—"

I let her sputter for a few more moments and then took pity on her, covering her hand with my own, squeezing it lightly. "Deke doesn't make anything I don't like to eat." A shrug. "Plus, there isn't much that I don't like to eat, anyway, and everything Deke makes..."

"You like," Billie finished, as though she were giving the answer to the most baffling question in the universe.

Now I chuckled. "Yup."

"I—"

Bonnie saved me from further explanation and Billie from having her head explode because of it by bringing our drinks—water with lemons and not too much ice for my aunt and a Diet Coke for me.

See?

She knew her shit and would take care of me.

I smiled sweetly at Billie Rose before sipping from my glass.

And then I took pity on her.

"Tell me where we're at with the Winter Festival."

A pained look. Because she wanted to gab about her plans. I

knew she did, knew how much she loved putting on the festivals. But she was worried about me and trying to be a good friend and aunt. "We should talk about your parents and Colt." A beat. "And Axel."

We *should*.

But I didn't want to (and yeah, I said that in my head like a whining toddler).

"Later," I promised. "Right now, I want to hear if the City Council approved the ice rink."

Billie's eyes flared with excitement.

And then the excitement went verbal.

I heard about the ice rink (approved of course) and the carriage rides and the brand-spanking-new lights and decoration contest (using donated potted pines that would be planted when springtime came around, making the whole contest competitive and eco-friendly, and Billie Rose to an absolute T).

I heard about hot cocoa stabds (and permission to sell a spiked variety for those twenty-one and older).

I heard how she commandeered more Rush skaters to volunteer their time as ice attendants.

I heard about all the small details that made Billie Rose the perfect mayor for River's Bend—the care, the love, the enthusiasm, they all swept me along.

Until I was volunteering for more than I should.

Until I was going to be all-in on the festival, rather than voluntold.

Until I knew that so much had changed inside me because I never *ever* would have been able to open myself up to her, to the town, to the event—too many painful memories, too much of a reminder of what I'd missed.

And I knew that change had begun with Axel.

No. With Billie Rose.

Because she'd handcuffed Axel to my porch.

Ah.

The sweet, *sweet* stories of love and inner growth...and shotguns and handcuffs and crocodile death-rolling my way into a relationship that I would one day tell the grandkids.

But I was thinking about grandkids...

And not running screaming, like my hair was on fire, from the diner.

See? Progress.

I was making it.

I was making a *lot* of it.

So maybe my intuition on the hill was wrong, maybe this would be perfect and happily-ever-after.

Maybe the peace would hold.

And if it didn't maybe I'd be able to easily navigate my way through it, considering all that inner growth.

Maybe.

I smiled, ate my food when Bonnie brought it.

And for the record, Deke's Reuben was incredible.

Ten

Axel

"Yeah, yeah, yeah, *yeah!*" Coop yelled for the puck, but I'd already seen him breaking for the net, watched him slide in and lift his stick in preparation for the one-timer.

My stick was already moving, almost before my mind was.

The puck sailed toward Coop, hovering a few inches above the ice before dropping down right where I'd wanted it—

A couple of feet in front of him, so my teammate could pick it up and keep moving without breaking stride or losing speed.

Ben, one of the newer guys on the roster, whistled.

Oddly, he was sporting a black eye, and though I didn't ask, I knew it had something to do with the fact that he'd been caught in Josh's sister's bed.

Normally, I would have thought that would implode the locker room.

And, not gonna lie, there was plenty of tension there, but no one was putting fists through walls, no one was excluding Ben, no one was cornering anyone in the showers or the hall or an empty corner of the training suite and beating him to shit.

Oh, Josh's face still turned murderous every time he looked at his teammate...

But Ben was doing a good job of laying low, and the guys—*all* of them, including Josh—were letting him.

No cheap shots on the ice.

No blacklisting from group hangouts.

Just dirty looks and the occasional blip of tension in the locker room.

Yeah, these guys were too fucking healthy.

And I loved it.

I hadn't been this happy, work-wise, ever. I hadn't been this happy *hockey*-wise probably from the moment I stopped playing just for fun and started playing competitively.

It was...the dream.

The *dream*.

"Hell of a pass," Ben muttered, thwacking me in the shins with his stick.

A mere love tap, that was all.

Grinning, I tapped him back as we watched Coop finish the rest of the drill, the two "opponents" working on their coverage as he danced with the puck in the corner.

Fucker had a featherlight touch with the biscuit, and he was fast as hell.

And he just kept getting better with age.

I was jealous as fuck, but I was also taking note of every single pointer I could.

Coop had years on me—both in age and in the league—but he'd overcome injury and mental blocks and was one of the best players in the league.

So, I'd be stupid to *not* soak up every single thing I could.

"He's got good hands," I muttered and, look at me go, being all modest and shit.

Grinning, seeing right through me, Ben tapped my shins again and skated off, lining up to take his turn.

"Give me another of those pretty passes, Balls!" Ben yelled.

A man helps out with *one* Harvest Festival, tells a couple of pretend fortunes using a fake crystal ball...and is saddled with the nickname *Balls* for the rest of his life.

The man was me.

My nickname was Balls.

Sigh.

But I'd take the ribbing.

Because it meant that I was one of them.

I snagged a couple of pucks, lined up to be ready for Ben when he started the drill. On the whistle, he took off, and I waited... waited...waited then—

Pass.

Right then.

It was the right *time.*

Ben slid through the first defenseman, snagged the puck on the bounce and—

I winced when Josh squeezed Ben out on the boards, their bodies and the subsequent collision making the glass rattle.

It wasn't a game-grade hit.

But it was a reminder that Josh still wasn't all that happy with the fact that he'd found Ben naked in bed with his sister.

Ben just took the hit—luckily rolling with it and not escalating. Probably because he had a younger sister himself and knew what it was like to be protective. Also, probably, because Josh might be pissed, be a big brother in every cell of his body, but he was a good captain, and he wouldn't jeopardize the team.

Not when his sister made it clear she was an adult who made her own decisions.

One of which was that sleeping with Ben had been consensual and—

"Whatcha thinking about, rook?" Brit asked, coming up behind me.

I turned to the goalie, her helmet propped back on her head, her wide smile on full display. "That Ben is lucky Josh isn't a loose cannon."

She grinned, that smile growing somehow wider. "Definitely lucky."

"Though the black eye..."

"Probably the least of his concerns," she said, "considering how they were discovered. Joshie can throw a mean ass right hook. I've seen it from the crease more than a few times." A laugh. "Just another reason that I'm glad goalies aren't out here fighting." She buffed her nails on her shoulder.

"Just saying, goalies *do* fight."

She let her hand fall to her side, shoving it into her glove before nodding sharply so that her helmet dropped into place. A practiced motion that spoke of years of playing. "Just saying"—she rolled her shoulders—"*this* goalie doesn't fight."

"Just watches the Neanderthals duke it out and then sneakily cup checks any asshole who skates through your crease."

A flash of straight, white teeth. "It's *my* crease."

I laughed.

She gave my shin guards a tap. "Keep it up, Balls. You're doing good."

"Thanks, Brit," I murmured.

The whistle trilled again, and she moved in to take her turn on the drill, swapping spots with our backup goalie, Harrison.

Coach Calle kept me on the passing station, and I dished pucks out to Rome, Lucas, Will, and Kaydon before Coop swapped out with me. I did my time grinding it out on the boards, managed to do a couple of good moves and get a decent shot on net—

Which Brit cursed me out for, since she really had to scrabble to save it.

Though she did the cursing with a smile, and I was grinning as the f-bombs rained down. Because it was good, it meant *I* was doing good.

Something I wouldn't have been able to do if not for Bailey, if not for Brit, if not for Billie Rose.

B-named angels.

Which was a thought I knew I was *never* going to let out of my head.

If any of those three caught wind of it, the shit-giving was going to be unbearable.

But it was the truth.

And fuck, I missed *my* B-named angel. I missed *my* Bailey.

A half day away from her and I was a mopey asshole.

Probably why I missed the puck flying at my head. "Look alive, Balls!"

I didn't look alive. I was thinking about the intervening B-named women in my life, and was knee-deep (mind-deep?) in my ever-growing list of sexual fantasies I wanted to act out with the woman I loved—was fucking her on skates doable? How about on her horse?

I was thinking about *all* of that.

So, I didn't see Brit launch the puck.

Didn't see it lofting through the air toward me.

Didn't see it until it was nearly at my head, and by then it was too late to dodge.

It beaned me right in the visor—and let me thank the hockey gods for whoever had decided they were now mandatory on every player's helmet. But I didn't thank them for anything else, not when I jerked in surprise, leaned too far back on my skates and promptly went ass over tea kettle.

My ass hurt like hell.

My mind spun with the sudden turn of events.

Then Brit was in front of me, concern on her face...except it was concern mixed with amusement. So much amusement that she was having a hard time holding back her laughter.

"I—"

"Oh, shit," Brit said, bending over and resting her hands on her knees. "Fuck, I didn't think you would fall like that and—" A giggle escaped. "I mean, you went *down.*"

Kayden swatted her, but he was biting back a smile.

As were Coop and Rome.

"My ass," I moaned, rolling to my side. "Good God, *my ass.*"

Brit's head jerked up, her eyes going wide. "Oh shit, are you hurt? Like really hurt?"

"My pride? My ego? My *ass?*" I quipped.

She choked.

"Yeah, maybe," I finished.

And...she lost any hold on her laughter, busting up until she was collapsing beside me on the ice, her body shaking with it, her smile and amusement infectious.

And I couldn't hold out.

I lost it, too.

"Maybe we shouldn't call you *Balls*," Logan said, extending a hand once Brit and I had gotten ourselves under control again.

I grabbed it, hauled myself up, ignoring my aching ass (and it *fucking* hurt since there was barely any padding in that area…mostly because professional hockey players didn't usually land square on their asses…because they could do things like, well, *skate*).

"Maybe his name should be B&A," Coop called once I'd gotten vertical, Brit beside me, ice clinging to the ends of her ponytail.

I glanced over.

Coop's eyes were dancing.

And, honestly, the rest of the guys were either laughing, amused, or smiling.

Christ. I braced as I turned back to Brit, mouthed, "B&A?"

She lifted her brows, shook her head in answer.

Coop clarified for me. "Balls and Ass."

My groan bubbled up in my throat, and out of the corner of my eye, I saw Brit start shaking with mirth.

The guys busted up, their laughter ringing across the ice, filling in spots inside me that I hadn't even begun to know were empty.

And, fuck it all, I started laughing, too.

Eleven

Bailey

The Gold were playing, and I was watching it on my new TV, sitting on my new couch, next to my aunt and Dessie.

My bare toes were buried in the plush carpet.

(Beneath which was the extra thick pad that Margaret had insisted upon…and I wasn't hating, especially since it felt like I was walking on clouds anytime I made my way across this room).

"I think I'm actually getting the hang of this whole hockey thing," I said, finally able to follow the puck on the screen without having to search for it.

"Yeah?" Billie Rose murmured. "Wanna tell me what that whistle was for?"

The ref had called the play on the ice to a stop…and I had no clue why.

"Um…" I began, trying to discern the gestures and not making heads or tails of them.

"High-sticking," Dessie said, eyes glued to the screen. "Four minutes because your hot hockey player is bleeding."

"What?" I gasped, jerking up and watching the camera pan to Axel.

There was a woman in a black polo, Gold logo embroidered above the breast pocket, holding a piece of gauze to his nose.

And yup, that was blood.

A lot of it.

"Is it normal for a nose to bleed that much?" I asked, heart pounding so hard it felt like it was in my throat.

"If it gets smacked with a stick," Dessie said dryly, "then I would think so. I think it caught his lip too." A beat. "Though, for the record, since we're watching it happen on live TV, I think we can say it can bleed that much. It's not like they're CGIing things out there."

I threw a pillow at her. "Asshole."

"You love me." She grinned, threw it back. "Also, look at my friend," she said all too innocently, all too sweetly. "She's all concerned for her pretty, hockey boyfriend's face."

"Dessie," I warned, glaring at her before turning back to the screen and watching Axel mop up his nose and mouth.

The trainer said something, gestured to the hall, and the camera cut away.

Probably because they'd reached the max of how much blood could be shown on national television.

But I wanted the camera to pan back.

I wanted to see him, make sure he was okay.

And, Christ, it was just a bloody nose. Why was I so worried?

Because I was here and he was there and I was hopelessly, pathetically in love with that man.

Ugh.

I was turning into one of those sappy, lovestruck women.

"I need another beer," I muttered, pushing to my feet and heading for the kitchen.

"Me, too," Dessie said.

"More wine for me," Billie Rose said, lifting her glass.

"What, am I your waiter?" I snapped.

"Chilled, please, honey," Billie Rose replied, not cowed by my tone in the least. Hell, the order didn't even leave her voice.

Sighing, I plucked the wine glass from her hand and took it into the kitchen, grabbing the bottle of white from a local winery that Billie had stashed in the fridge. Then two beers. Then a plastic container of salsa. A bag of chips and a container of caramel corn from the pantry (now fully stocked since Axel had groceries delivered to me every Sunday afternoon).

I was balancing everything and moving back into the family room, all while trying to pretend that my gaze didn't keep going to the TV, searching for Axel.

Still, hopelessly, pathetically in love with that man.

Ugh.

Not that I'd expected my feelings to change in the five minutes I was away from the space, not that I wanted them to.

I just...was falling in deeper and deeper and deeper and—

That was scary.

I was scared.

And—the pieces in my mind clicked into place—that was okay.

Big feelings. Big changes. Big—

I glanced back to the screen, saw that Axel was back on the bench, dried blood caked around his nostrils, a bruise already forming on either side of his nose, a cut on his lip. His eyes met the camera, and it seemed like he was staring right at me, then I knew he was *looking* at me when he mouthed, "I'm good, buttercup."

I sucked in a breath, turned away from the TV, eyes stinging.

My gaze caught on Billie Rose's, and I didn't miss the approval in my aunt's eyes. Nor did I miss the pride that took up nearly as much space.

She'd started this, after all.

No surprise that she'd be proud of herself.

She should be, I supposed.

She played me and Axel both like puppets, guiding us right to each other, putting her matchmaking skills to work, and then stepping back at the right time so that Axel and I could sort out our own shit.

"Billie," I began.

But there was a knock at the door.

Frowning, I turned toward the hall, not able to see much since the curtain was drawn. Though the lights were on, illuminating the porch—I wasn't going to be too careful with Colt around—I couldn't see anything more than a few shadows through that swathe of fabric.

My gut clenched.

But then I relaxed.

If it was my parents, my mother, her shrill voice would be coming through the glass.

And if it was Colt...

My intestines tangled again, fear having turned into thorns that were stabbing my veins. I shoved it all down, took a breath.

If it was Colt, my shotgun was nearby.

"I'll get it," Billie Rose murmured, taking the popcorn and chips from me, setting them all on the table.

"No," I whispered, setting the two beers down and handing Billie her glass, plunking the salsa next to the chips. "I've got it."

Heart in my throat.

Pulse beating painfully in my veins.

Fingers grazing the shotgun mounted on the wall right near the door as my other hand reached for the handle, turning it and...

Not Colt.

Not my parents.

A big, broad hockey player.

One of the shadows shifted.

No. Make that *two* big, broad hockey players.

Neither of which being the one I actually wanted to have somehow teleported himself from his game to be standing on these wooden planks.

Shaking myself, I managed only, "Umm..."

I thought I'd reached my limit of big, broad hockey players showing up on my porch.

But apparently there were two more in my future.

"Hey, babycakes," the bigger one with blond hair and green eyes said. If I was remembering right, his name was Joel and he'd been Axel's second in command, though lately he'd seemed to have laid off...well, the *laying* of every single female in town.

Another man was next to him, also clearly a hockey player based on his build and the Rush-branded hoodie he was wearing, though his name didn't come readily to mind.

I'd never really watched hockey before getting with Axel, and that meant if the players weren't gossiped about around town, then I didn't really know them.

It was the big one and the bigger one and...*this* one.

Joel clapped me on the shoulder. "I'm sure you're disappointed that we're not naked—"

A sniff from behind me.

I glanced back and saw Billie Rose had come into the hallway and was standing behind me (of course she had). Dessie was just a few paces behind her, leaning against the wall, ankles crossed, curiosity on her face...as opposed to the fury on Billie's.

"You shouldn't be here," she snapped, moving so that she was next to me.

"The big man asked me to keep an eye out for her so that's what we're here to do."

I felt my eyes go wide. "What?"

The other man stepped forward slightly, extended his hand toward me. "Hi, Bailey. I'm Ryan. I don't think we've officially met."

I shook my head. "No, I don't think so either," I said softly. Ryan hadn't hung out with the other Rush guys, not that I'd seen anyway. Not...that I'd been in town, hanging in the bars to say that with one hundred percent confidence.

"Axel asked if we could check in on you every once in a while, since he's so far away."

A simple explanation.

And yet, *my* reaction to that was anything but simple.

That fear of falling fast and hard and deep dissipated. The love I felt grew, swelling like a balloon hooked up to a helium tank, getting bigger and bigger and *bigger.* Until I threatened to burst. He was looking after me in the only way he knew how. He was looking out for me by asking other people for help—which wasn't an easy thing for him to do. I *knew* that. And...truthfully, threaded through all of that was a tiny sliver of annoyance.

Just a little one.

He was meddling again.

He was taking care of me when I could take care of myself.

He was...

Loving me the only way he knew how.

So, I sucked in a breath, ignored the dirty look that Billie Rose was shooting Joel's way, and embraced Axel's love, no matter what form it came in.

"You guys want a beer?"

Twelve

Axel

"Finnegan?"

I stopped in the hall, my messenger bag tossed over my shoulder, and glanced up in the direction of the slightly accented voice.

Pascal…I didn't actually know his last name.

Just…Pascal.

Like Madonna or Lizzo or Cher.

I forced myself to not smile at the thought. Mostly because that was going to split open the cut on my lip, and despite me considering myself a tough-ass hockey player, my little booboo on my bottom lip hurt, throbbing to my heartbeat.

Also, I didn't smile because I didn't think Pascal would appreciate the comparison to pop superstars.

But what did I know?

He might have a secret pop addiction and be out singing karaoke, finding his inner diva every time he disappeared into the shadows.

"Axel?" he asked, and I yanked myself out of my head.

Right. Less thoughts of pop divas and more focus on what the man was saying.

Pascal was the head of security for the Gold, and despite him having the impressive sneaking ability to appear and disappear seemingly out of thin air, at that exact moment, he was merely leaning against the wall, a duffle in his hand, no sneaking on display.

He tossed the bag to me. "The rest of your stuff."

I caught it. "Thanks, man."

"We checked out the hotel's camera feeds." A shake of his head. "She left after you did and didn't come back. No sign of her since that day, and a fake name on her application."

Damn.

I'd been hoping they could track down enough about her so that I could get a restraining order or at least a last name.

But no one seemed to know her.

Candi—yup, with an *i*—had spent lots of time in barrooms with my former teammates on the Rush—had spent a lot of time in *bed*rooms with them too. But no one knew her last name, and even Billie Rose didn't know exactly who she was, which was a surprise in itself.

She knew everyone from her town.

Which meant...Candi wasn't from River's Bend.

"We'll find her," Pascal said, clamping a hand onto my shoulder. "She won't get into any team facilities or events, I'll make sure of that. And I have some men checking leads in River's Bend."

Shock rippled through me. "I mean...that's really cool of you, but that's not really under the purview of the head of security of the Gold, right?" I shrugged. "I mean, so long as she doesn't come to my apartment or the rink or the arena...then the team doesn't really..."

"Care?"

Fuck.

Right, that sounded...dickish.

"No, it's not that—"

"You've got people you care about back home," Pascal said by way of explanation...which wasn't really an explanation, but it at least explained why he was looking into Candi and River's Bend. "I'll make sure they're safe so you can focus on things here."

"No offense, but..." I trailed off before I began to sound *dickish* again.

"Why do *I* care?" Pascal's lips tipped up just slightly at the edges.

Fuck.

More dickish.

I cleared my throat. "I—"

Pascal smirked. "I'm just fucking with you." Then he sobered. "I know what it's like to..." A pause that spoke of more than words. It spoke of pain and loss and—

Fuck if my long dead—and only recently reawakened heart—didn't twitch.

I hated the trap of feelings.

Or I had.

Before I fell in love.

But I hated that the trap of feelings opened me up to this situation, my heart going out to the other man.

Because I didn't know what to say.

I never did.

I hadn't grown up with empathy or sympathy or any -pathy.

My existence had always been...carve out every bit I could, hold tight like a dog protecting a bone, forget about everyone else.

Not in hockey.

Not at first.

But it had become that. Eventually, it had become that.

About me, about my misery, about wringing my time on the ice for every drop of pleasure it could produce.

About wringing that pleasure out of life and fuck everyone else's feelings.

Because *I* got what I needed.

Until handcuffs and pretty brown eyes and splinters in my ass. Until Brit and the players on the Gold had taken me under their wings. Until I'd realized all of what I was missing out on by living my life just for myself.

But that change didn't give me the right words to say to this man.

There *weren't* any *right* words for the kind of pain trapped in Pascal's dark brown eyes.

"...to be worried," Pascal finished quietly.

Firmly.

Putting a period on that part of the conversation before I had the chance to say *anything* of value.

"We'll find out her last name," he said. "And then I recommend filing a restraining order." A casual shrug of his shoulder. "Probably, won't dissuade her from approaching, but it will give you a paper trail in case things kick up again."

"Yeah," I said, my voice quiet. "That makes sense." I swallowed hard, scrambled for some words, for any fucking useful words. "Thank...uh...you for...um...putting the time in. I appreciate it."

Pascal glanced up at me, studied me closely.

Then he just squeezed my shoulder again...and disappeared.

I didn't know how the man did it, but one second he was there, and the next he was gone, and then I was staring at an empty hall like an idiot.

"Right," I whispered, knowing that I wouldn't discover Pascal's disappearing secret, not that day, probably not ever.

Shrugging, I continued out of the arena.

The night air hit my skin, cool and a little damp from the fog clinging to the sky, and I found myself sucking in a breath, soaking it in, something I never would have been able to do just months ago.

So maybe I didn't have all the right words.

Maybe I wouldn't *ever* have them.

But I'd also never been the kind of man to stand in the cool night air and *appreciate* it, to pause and even *notice* it.

So maybe I didn't have those words and maybe I'd spent my lifetime being a selfish asshole.

Maybe I wouldn't ever be perfect.

Maybe I wouldn't ever be good enough for Bailey.

But I was going to damn well try.

I inhaled that cool air, rolled my shoulders, and headed to my car.

Just as I gripped the driver's side handle, my cell rang.

Digging it out, I swiped and lifted it to my ear, listening to who was on the other end for just a couple of heartbeats before my lips turned up and warmth filled my belly as surely as the cool air clung to my skin.

This was the call I'd been waiting for.

Fucking *finally.*

Thirteen

Bailey

The sun was just drifting over the hills to the east as I walked through my house.

Coffee was brewing, set to start on a timer before my alarm went off, thanks to the fancy new coffeemaker that Axel had bought for me.

It smelled glorious, helped clear the last of the cobwebs.

One would think after waking up this early for years—first during the summers with Gran and Gramps, and then after I'd taken on the ranch on my own, clawing it out of the financial black hole my parents had left it in—that I would be used to the early hour.

But every morning, I woke with crusty eyes and a foggy mind, and nothing cleared it until my first cup.

So, I headed straight for the kitchen, filled my mug.

Black, since I'd gotten used to it when I hadn't had the money to buy sugar and cream. Plus, the concentrated brew meant that the caffeine hit my bloodstream sooner and cleared all that fog out.

I blew on my cup until it was cool enough to drink and sucked down my elixir of life then quickly filled a travel mug so I could take it with me while I completed my morning chores. I was never hungry this early in the morning, so I didn't bother making anything, just grabbed my lined flannel jacket from the hooks by the front door and reached for the handle.

I couldn't lie and say that my heart didn't skip a beat every time I stepped out onto my porch, half expecting, half *wanting* there to be a hot, naked hockey player on the worn wooden planks.

Alas, that morning, it was empty of all naked, sexy hockey men.

It was empty of *everyone.*

Which was a good thing.

I didn't want to walk out and find my parents on the porch, or worse, Colt.

That had a shudder sliding down my spine, the cold morning sending me shivering, despite the belly full of coffee, despite my well-made flannel that could keep me warm even in the middle of winter—which, yeah, wasn't all *that* cold, since my Golden State blood was thin, but it didn't keep me warm.

Not that morning.

Probably not for a while yet.

Because...Colt.

He'd been on the farm.

He'd been in my house.

In my *house.* Maybe in my room.

Maybe touching my things.

I'd changed the sheets, bleached them, ran them twice through the water on the hottest cycle my washer could dish out.

And, even knowing it was in my head, I'd still thought that I'd caught a whiff of Colt's scent on them.

Impossible.

But...

"Enough," I whispered. Being stuck in the past was not what I needed this morning. Focus on the ranch, on my chores, on moving forward one foot at a time.

That was how I survived.

Plus, I'd woken up to a text message and a selfie from Axel, teasingly asking if I would still love him even with the fat lip and bruised nose.

I'd replied, even though he wouldn't see it until later, considering how late he normally fell asleep after games.

Sometimes, if I had a ton of shit to do on the ranch and had to get up early—or, well, had to get up for an earlier start than normal—he was just settling down from the adrenaline of the game and heading off to sleep.

We'd chat then as I was getting my coffee, as I walked across this empty porch, mug in hand.

Today, though, he didn't reply as I locked my front door—something I was doing every single time I left, even if it was just to go into the barn—and I was glad that he was sleeping, was getting some rest.

He was working hard.

I *wanted* him to rest.

Who was I?

Wanting to take care of a man when I promised that I would never trust my heart to one again.

But...my heart was safe with Axel.

I knew it.

I loved him, and at some point, I'd find the courage to tell him.

Soon.

Definitely soon.

Except...I didn't know if I'd really get there, if I'd be able to tell someone that again, to be *that* vulnerable and open and—

Actions were easier.

I could show him my love, show him without really putting myself out there.

"Coward," I muttered.

Sighing, I clomped down the stairs, walked along the path, and opened the door to the barn. Right now, I only had three horses inside—Data, and two others that were being boarded. Something I did to get extra money, and while I liked seeing the animals, it was something I was looking forward to stopping once I didn't need to scrimp and save and dig myself out of the hole my parents had dumped the ranch into.

I loved the horses.

I just wanted...less poop to clean up.

Grinning, I flicked on the lights, moved to Data's stall, and reached over to pet my baby's nose, feeling the soft huffs of her breath on my face.

She blew harder when I didn't immediately give her the apple I had in my pocket.

Something she knew I always had.

Thanks to Axel.

Which was another tick in his column, in the column of why I knew my heart was safe.

Because he noticed that I gave Data apples (and the occasional sugar cube because my horse was spoiled) and so there was always a supply of apples in my fridge and an airtight container of sugar cubes in the tack room.

Data huffed again, and I grinned, patting her nose one more time before stepping back and turning for the cutting board and knife I kept on a shelf nearby. "I need to slice this up, little miss," I said lightly. "As you well know." I plunked the apple down, lifted the knife, and...then nearly sliced my fucking finger off when a soft *"Moooo!"* radiated through the space.

Whirling, the knife dropping to the floor, I glanced at Data.

Who still had her head hanging over her stall door but hadn't suddenly gained the ability to make cow speak.

"Moooo!"

I jumped, thankfully without a sharp pointy thing in my hand this time.

"Moooo!"

"What the—?" I whirled from Data's stall trying to figure out—

"Moooo!"

There. The noise was coming from the far end of the barn, the stall that I always kept any orphaned or rejected cows in to get them big enough to rejoin the herd. It wasn't often, but occasionally a mama cow would give birth out of season and wouldn't take care of her calf and because I was...a soft touch, usually I stepped in.

Just like I'd stepped with—

"Moooo!"

"Picard," I whispered, seeing his adorable little head poking through a gap in the slats. My mouth fell open. "Picard?" I asked louder.

"Moooo!"

"What—I—" Then my feet were carrying me across the barn, and I was yanking at the stall door and—

There he was.

His gorgeous cow (calf? *steer?*) eyes on me and swear to fuck, it was almost like he was smiling at me, like he was happy to see me.

I'd sold him to the local petting zoo to pay for some expenses (namely, a cable package that meant I could see every game Axel played in), but hell if I hadn't shed a tear when I'd dropped Picard off. Yes, he was going to a good place with nice owners and kids who'd shower him with attention.

But Picard was *mine*.

I'd bottle-fed him for days, making sure he'd lived when it had been touch and go.

And—not that I'd admitted it to anyone—but I'd really missed him.

A *lot*.

"Oh, buddy," I whispered, skidding to a halt in front of the stall, dust and straw kicking up in all directions as I scrabbled with the door and yanked it open.

Then promptly found myself back on my ass, Picard clomping forward, dropping his head on my shoulder, and hell if he hadn't gotten bigger.

That was what animals did, I supposed.

Grow up.

I scratched behind his ears and tried not to be bowled over by his weight, laughing when he pressed his wet nose to my throat, mooing softly in my ear.

My cell rang, and I managed to drag it out of my pocket.

Axel.

Of course it was him.

I swiped, put it up to my ear.

"Hey, buttercup."

My heart knew it was safe.
Emotion danced in my veins.
Bubbled up in my throat.
And the words just rolled right off my tongue.
“I love you.”

Fourteen

Axel

I was in bed with the blankets around my waist, counting the minutes after I'd gotten her text trying to guesstimate how long it would take her to get to the barn, to see what I'd managed to set up last night.

Thanks to Billie Rose.

And an obscene donation to the petting zoo that Bailey had sold the cow to.

They'd better put my name on a plaque somewhere.

Smirking, I hit her name in my contacts, listened as it rang through.

"Hey, buttercup," I said when she answered.

"I love you."

Shock ricocheted through me, stronger than a check from that fucker on the Breakers. Conner something. Smith.

That was right.

Smitty, his teammates called him.

That fucker could hit like a Mack truck.

But he had nothing on those words.

They flew through the airwaves, collided with my eardrums, and—

I dropped my cell.

Then I heard them in my mind again, her soft and gentle voice telling me she loved me. She *loved* me.

And suddenly I was a flurry of motion, scrambling for my cell, trying to grab it again, trying to find it in the blankets which had somehow seemed to multiply into a fucking dumpster's worth of fabric. I could hear Bailey's voice faintly coming through the speakers.

Fuck.

She'd just given me something big, and for all she knew, I was disavowing it by not answering, by cutting off the call.

I was an idiot.

I had a voice. I could hear hers, so clearly she'd be able to hear mine. I just needed...to fucking *use* it.

"Bailey—Bailey, I'm here," I said, still scrambling. *Fuck. Where was my phone?* "I'm here and I love you, too and—" A glimpse of black, the edge of my phone case. I snatched it and— "Bailey? Bailey? Did you hear me? I love you, too. I love you so much."

Finally, I got the cell up to my ear.

And was greeted by laughter.

Ah. Romance.

"Really, buttercup?" It was a snapped-out question. It was totally not the right tone for this moment.

More laughter.

"Oh God," she gasped, the air crackling through the speakers, hitting my ears. "This is too perfect. We started with splinters in your ass and a saw near your femoral, and now I'm making you scramble by declaring my love for you."

I growled. "I didn't scramble."

"Oh, so that noise I was hearing was you just lying in bed relaxing?"

"You're a pain in my ass."

"I'm *your* pain in the ass."

I growled again but didn't answer. Because it was true.

She was mine. *Mine.*

"One you love, too," she added softly.

My lungs went a little tight with that, all the emotion in my veins going taut as I warred with the need to protect myself, to lock everything down and hold it tight, to get my slice and keep it for me, me, *me.*

But...I loved her.

So, I didn't argue, just whispered, "Buttercup."

She laughed softly. "We're a pair, aren't we?"

I clenched my cell, pressed it harder to my ear. "Yeah," I whispered. "We are."

"So scared of love and attachment that Billie Rose had to get involved."

That had me relaxing, my laughter joining hers. "Fucking Billie Rose," I grumbled.

A pause then, "Worth all her interference though, huh?"

I thought of Bailey's aunt, the mayor of River's Bend, and the fact that she'd been there for Bailey time and again, had stepped up again, just the night before to help me smuggle Picard home, and I smiled. "Definitely worth it, buttercup."

My voice had gentled in a way it never would have before.

Because I loved this woman.

"I'm guessing you found him?"

"Him?" A beat of amusement before she changed the call to video, showing me a feed of her...and the cow I'd bought from the petting zoo that had practically crawled into her lap. "Oh, you mean Picard?" She rubbed the cow's neck, tone going babyish. "Aren't you just the sweetest little boy," she crooned. "You're the best boy. The best cow-boy ever."

"Cow-boy?" I teased.

Her eyes hit mine through the video. "Really?"

"I mean, I'm not the one who's going all gaga over a cow-boy." God, I missed her. If she was there with me, I could have pulled her into my arms, could have held her as I teased her, kissed away her annoyance.

Could have kissed something else.

"He's a steer," she said icily, propping the cell on the stall door and wrapping her arms around him.

"Named Picard."

"And you're not even here for me to smack away your teasing."

"Is that *smacking* in the way I hope?"

She frowned. "What—"

I waggled my brows.

Her face went slack. "Really?" she asked dryly.

I grinned. "Don't tell me you haven't been thinking about me touching that ass, me squeezing and smacking and *taking* it."

Her lips parted, pink on her cheeks. "Damn you, Finnegan."

"What?" I asked innocently.

"You're turning me on in front of my—"

"*Moooo!*"

"—cow-son," she finished.

And now I was laughing again, and she was too, and then her face was going serious. "Axel?"

"Yeah, honey?"

"You really did this for me?" The question was a little damp and that hit me. Hard.

"What?" I asked lightly. "Paid to get your cow-boy-son back or because now I owe Billie Rose a favor for helping me smuggle Picard in?"

"I love you," she whispered. "You know that, right?"

"I know that. And"—it was different saying it when I could see her face, her eyes, her soft, soft expression—"you know I love you, too."

A long pause.

"Terrifying saying that aloud, isn't it?" she whispered.

I sucked in a breath. "Buttercup."

"But you know how I know it's right?"

I shook my head.

"Because of—"

"*Moooo!*"

She stilled.

Then burst out laughing.

"Because of moos," she said once she'd gotten control of herself, "and carpet in my house, food in my fridge, text messages I wake up to"—her lips turned up—"even sad-eyed selfies with swollen lips I want to kiss. I'm terrified, scared out of my fucking mind to love you, but I also know there's no other choice. You're mine."

Fuck if my eyes didn't sting as those words settled deep.

"I wish I was there," I murmured.

"For ass play?"

That was so far from what I'd expected that I felt my mouth drop open, felt it flop like a fish for a few moments.

Then I remembered that I was Axel Finnegan.

Bailey might make me feel like I could be someone else, someone else down to my very core, but I still was me.

And that meant I had bravado. I had snark.

I smirked at her.

"I'm looking forward to seeing that ass the next time I'm home." A beat. "To taking that ass."

Her lips parted, that pink coming back.

"I seem to remember you saying you could resist my smolder," I teased.

A smile, and I knew she was probably remembering the same thing I had. Being in that barn, our bodies close, the attraction tugging us together even as we were desperate to stay apart. I expected sass in return, expected her to be sharp back.

But instead, I got soft.

I got Bailey.

And it reminded me why she owned me.

"I could never resist you, Axel Finnegan," she murmured. "Now go to bed," she ordered. "I have chores to do."

"Okay, buttercup," I said, scooting down in bed, fatigue wrapping loosely around my ankles, ready to tug me into oblivion. "Whatever you say."

"What if I say that I want you to take my ass, too?"

My eyes shot wide.

Sleep was forgotten.

She smirked.

"Sweet dreams, honey."

"Wait—"

She hung up.

And I...

Well, sleep was a long time coming...mostly because my fingers wrapped around my cock and I stroked hard and fast...and dreamed about seeing that smirk in person.

And that ass.

Fifteen

Bailey

Well, I'd said it.

I hadn't meant to.

And...

He'd said it back.

I pressed a hand to my heart.

It still thudded against my ribs, my palms were still slick, and my legs...sweet baby Jesus, they trembled when I went to stand.

Like I'd just reached the end of the biggest adrenaline letdown. Ever. And it had left me nearly unable to stand.

"*Moooo!*"

Picard bumped me, and he was so big that he nearly knocked me over.

"*Neigh.*"

I grinned. Clearly, Data wasn't happy about the delay in her morning apple. "Coming, baby," I called, and sucked in a breath, tucking my romantic heart down, *way* down. Then I left Picard's stall door open since he would follow me around like a little puppy.

Not so little anymore.

But he still did follow me around.

First to the shelf.

Where I finally cut up Data's apple and then made a pit stop for a sugar cube since she'd been so patient through my phone call and Picard love fest.

She huffed indignantly, but accepted my offering, and then I moved around the barn, refilling water and feed buckets, putting my pair of boarders out into separate paddocks since they couldn't be trusted to get along.

Shoveling, raking, sweeping—the part of this job that kept me most in shape.

Then I tucked Picard back into his stall, knowing he would be ready for some food and rest and would be content while I went out on Data to check on the fences and the herd.

Data danced a bit when I settled her saddle on top of her, cinching it tight, but it wasn't because she was unhappy. She was impatient, ready to have her head, ready to go galloping through the foothills, and okay, maybe a *little* unhappy that her run had been delayed by Picard.

I slipped her another sugar cube.

She huffed in approval.

Then I finished with the reins, led her out, and mounted up, and I...rode.

Fuck, it was the best feeling outside of an orgasm.

It was almost the same, the pleasure and joy, the oblivion and how it pulled me from my head. The way it exploded from my middle and filled every part of my body.

It should be part of the job.

It was something I did for hours, almost every day.

But...it wasn't pedestrian. *Never* did riding Data feel pedestrian.

This was...freedom.

The thud of Data's hooves, the wind against my skin, through my hair, the hiss of the grass waving in the air, the chirps of birds, the *moos* in the distance. A quiet place, and yet full of so much noise that I never failed to notice something different.

Though, that morning, it was a stretch of fence down.

That wasn't different, I supposed.

The fencing was old and I'd gotten around to replacing a lot of it, but the elements were rough, and I'd often had to scrape together the materials. Which meant that they didn't last as long as they should or as long as I wanted.

This stretch I'd done right around the time I'd taken over the ranch.

And now the half-rotted posts had given away.

Sighing, I made a mental note of its location, moved on to survey any further problems, and made sure the water troughs were clean and full.

Then Data and I were heading in, my fun done, the real work ahead.

The other horses—Sam and Frodo—needed their rides. Hay had to be brought out on the UTV, since there wasn't enough grass left at this point in the year for the entire herd to graze and get enough nutrients from it.

I wanted them fat and happy before I sold them off.

First, I used the UTV—and the hay on its back—to tempt a few heifers who'd decided to go rogue on me through the broken stretch of fence. Then I sorted the downed posts, restrung the barbed wire between them and made sure there would be no further runaways, at least through *that* section of fencing.

Then I dropped the rest of the hay in a few separate spots and headed back in to take care of Sam and Frodo.

Unfortunately, I wasn't alone on the ranch.

There was a car in the driveway, and I knew who it belonged to.

And as I drove in, I debated just driving by and moving straight to town. Except that would leave my ex too fucking close to Data, to Picard, and Christ almighty, I couldn't have that.

And...I wasn't that woman anymore.

I was stronger, had been forged in steel and fire.

And I...wasn't alone.

Slowing before I reached the driveway, I typed out a text to Billie Rose, letting her know that Colt was there.

And...then I blew out a breath and drove the rest of the way.

Colt opened the door.

The fear was...overwhelming, intense, but I breathed through it, or at least I pulled up my big girl panties and decided that I was going to *brazen* my way through it.

I stopped the UTV outside of the barn, not wanting to be closed in if he got close.

And he would probably get close.

He moved toward me, eyes cold in that way I'd always thought were warm. But I knew now that the warmth was actually a façade.

Beneath was a coiled rattled snake with venom-tipped fangs.

"That's close enough," I said when he'd begun to move around the UTV.

He didn't stop. *Of course* he didn't.

He rounded the hood and closed the distance between us.

My fingers closed around the cold metal barrel, just as he said, "Baby."

I lifted the shotgun out of the rack on the back of the UTV, turned—

And pointed it to the center of Colt's chest.

"That's. Close. *Enough,*" I growled.

Amusement in his dark brown eyes, cold and barbed and sharp enough to wound. "Baby," he said again, the condescension so heavy that it nearly knocked me to my feet.

I locked my knees, lifted my chin. "I said—"

He jerked forward, the movement so fast that my eyes couldn't track it.

But my body did.

My body was familiar with those sharp, jerking movements of his, and it had a deep-buried instinct to protect itself from this man.

So even before he could touch me with that brutal, horrible hand, I was already scrambling back, already putting distance between us.

And my finger was already...

Closing around the trigger.

Sixteen

Axel

"So," Olivia said, "what are we going to do with that pretty boy face of yours?"

My agent was pretty.

My agent was *gorgeous*, actually.

My agent was a shark, recommended by Brit, who wore six-inch heels and bright red lipstick and...a suit that showed off every inch of her baby belly.

I slouched back in the visitors' chair, stared at her, the wide wooden expanse between us. "I like to think of it as a pretty *manly* face."

Her lips tipped up. "Po-tay-to. Po-tah-toe." Then she reached for some papers, passed them over, tone going businesslike. "It's always good to plan for a career after hockey. Hopefully, you'll have a long time in the league"—a smile—"but hockey is a dangerous sport, so I like to plan for other eventualities."

That seemed logical.

That seemed responsible.

Planning for a life after hockey.

Except—

"Planning isn't really something I do a lot of."

Now, her smile widened. "That's why I do the job *I* do, and you do the job *you* do."

"Brit was right."

"That I'm a badass?" Olivia quipped, buffing her knuckles on her shoulder. "Damn right."

I folded my hands over my middle. "No, though that's true also. She was right that you guys are the best." And that my previous agent had been shit.

Though, I was working on my diplomacy skills.

So, I just thought the last and left the rest to her imagination.

"Yeah, well," she said. "I don't know if you'll be saying the same for me when I've got you modeling underwear."

I shrugged. "I'm down with modeling underwear."

"I—" Her eyes went wide. "What?"

"I've spent more than my fair share of time being naked." Another shrug. "Actually wearing clothes—even underwear—would be a nice change of pace."

Now *she* sat back, smiling again. "I think you're going to be my favorite client. All the rest of them"—she waved a hand—"get so shy about showing off their moneymakers."

Money.

Right.

That was another good point.

Money I could use to help Bailey with the ranch. Money I could use to get her some help, give her some freedom so that she could get her teaching credentials, do something that wasn't ranching, wasn't her dream.

"How much can I make modeling?" I asked.

"Depends," she said, nodding toward the papers.

I scrolled through the stack, reading through the summary she'd Post-It-Noted to the front of each contract. That was...

That was a lot of money.

Even the ones with less money still offered more money than I'd seen since I signed my Gold contract...and there were *a lot* of them. I could...I could do a lot with this money.

"Okay," I said, glancing up.

"Okay?"

"I'll do them. All or whichever ones you think are best." I set the papers on the desk, leaned back in the chair.

"All?"

"I'm down. I don't have kids or a wife. I've got a girlfriend who's four hours away and a loaner apartment. I want her here. I want roots. So, I'll do what you advise, and I'll bank that shit so that when I'm done on the rink, I can give my woman a good life."

She lifted one black brow. "I thought you said she was just a girlfriend."

Yeah, girlfriend didn't really encompass everything.

Didn't encompass *anything* about how I felt.

"I meant that she's my forever."

For a second, Olivia's brash, tough exterior faded, her expression going gentle. "I know something about forever." She pointed to her belly. "Which is why the first contract I'll ask you to take is the most selfish one—and the one with the smallest paycheck."

Frowning, I just lifted my brows and waited.

"Cole"—her husband and a former NHL player—"has a charity. It brings city kids to the outdoors—kayaking, horseback riding, camping, s'mores, anything they might not have when they're stuck in a place with lots of tall buildings and limited green space. They need someone to model their merch, but they can't afford any big names, and Cole will do a lot for the camp, but he won't do that."

"Okay," I agreed.

Her brows lifted. "Just like that?"

"It helps us both—" And shit, was I seriously, without a single second thought, willing to do something for someone without it solely benefitting me and just me?

I paused.

Breathed.

Yeah. I fucking was.

Miracles happened, I supposed.

Or maybe I was just growing up.

"My woman has a cattle ranch up in the Sierra foothills," I said. "It's a lot for her to manage." I shrugged. "I want to help her."

"A bigger contract would make more sense then," Olivia countered.

"Probably," I agreed. "But I've also seen her face when she comes back from a ride. There's something magical out there for her."

Olivia blinked.

"And the kids deserve to find that too," I finished, feeling a bit dopey, but glad I got the words out anyway.

Olivia paused, studying me closely. "I thought you were supposed to be an asshole."

Laughter bubbled through me. "Oh, I am."

She began flipping through papers, pulled open a drawer, closed it. Opened another.

"What are you doing?" I asked after a moment, frowning.

"Looking for your assholeness."

Said without the slightest bit of hesitation.

Fuck she was funny.

Kind of like another woman I knew.

"Is it next to your lipstick?"

Her head shot up, her mouth, painted that bright red, twisted up. "There it is."

"My assholeness?"

"Yup."

I laughed again. Then shook my head and focused, even though part of me felt like I could banter with her all day. "I'll do the merch," I said. "And then the rest of them."

Her eyes gleamed and she reclined in her chair, back to business. "I think I'm going to love working with you. A perfectly moldable block of clay."

"I can't decide if that's an insult or a compliment."

Her head tilted from side to side. "Maybe a little of both?"

"Fuck," I said, laughing. "Give it to me straight, why don't you?"

"Always," she said and her tone was serious enough that I felt that word like a vow.

So I made the same back with a nod.

"If your woman wants to come out to the ranch," she offered, "I'm sure Cole would love to talk shop."

Now *that* got me excited. Bailey would love that. "Let's make it happen."

"See?" A beatific smile. "You like me."

I grinned and then because I was me, I added, "My bank account likes you."

"Asshole." A smirk. "But mine likes you for the same reason."

"I—"

My cell rang, and normally I wouldn't have answered it, but it was Bailey's ringtone. "Sorry," I told Olivia. "I need to take—"

"Take it." She stood. "I'll give you some privacy." She started to move toward the door, hand going to the knob, ready to close it behind her as I answered the call.

"Buttercup—"

"Oh fuck, Axel," she said. "Oh fuck, I— Oh fuck, oh fuck, oh *fuck!*"

Seventeen

Bailey

My finger closed around the trigger.

Colt smirked, bending close until the barrel pressed right against the center of his chest.

My finger tightened.

"Back up."

It wasn't strong. It was breathless, bordering on begging.

And he knew it.

He knew he could do that to me again.

Could hurt me and I couldn't stop him and—

My finger rested on that small piece of curved metal.

"Baby," he said in that frozen silken tone. "I came all this way to see you."

Fingers wrapped in my hair, yanking so that my scalp burned, chunks being ripped free.

Fists connecting with my ribs, a boot with my side.

Rain pelting down on my body, my clothes soaked through and chilling me to the bone. My hair plastered to my skull, my scalp burning from the frigid downpour, from the pain this man had borne on me.

The memories cleared.

I breathed.

"I want you to go," I said, stronger now.

But still not strong enough.

He leaned in, pushed against the barrel, and I had to brace myself so that I didn't fall back. "But if I went, if I stayed away..." He ran a finger over the cylinder of metal. "Then I wouldn't get what I want."

The smooth metallic trigger was still cool beneath my finger. "You won't get anything from me, not ever again," I vowed.

His arm came up like a shot, hand streaking toward my cheek.

I flinched, but when he touched me, my finger didn't tighten, it didn't do anything but stay there on that trigger, resting limp against the crescent-shaped metal.

Cold crept up my toes, gripped my ankles, anchored me in place when I should have run. *Run.*

Back in the UTV.

Back away from this man.

I managed a half step in retreat.

"Aren't you going to ask?" he asked, the words a dagger's point.

"Wh-what?"

"Aren't you going to ask what I want?" he asked silkily.

Dangerously.

No. I wasn't. I couldn't. Not after all of this time. After all the work I'd done to get better, to forget, to move on and not be this frightened cowering woman. I *couldn't—*

Finally, there was steel in me.

Steel that had my knees going steady, steel that forged my spine into a stiff, metal spike.

Steel that ordered him to "Back up."

Colt cocked his head to the side. "Don't you remember?" he whispered. "Don't you remember how much I enjoyed sucking the fight out of you?"

That steel went cold, threatened to shatter, threatened to send me to the gravel.

But I lifted my chin, held on. "I remember," I said. "But that was then."

His mouth turned up. "If you give me what I want then I won't have to hurt you *now*."

My finger tightened.

"Back. Up."

A smirk. "You won't shoot me."

"I will," I gritted out. "I'll kill you if you touch me again."

He was close in an instant, fingers grazing my cheek.

Almost gently.

But he was Colt, so they were a threat and ultimately not gentle, not really. They were a soft promise of violence.

I just didn't understand why he was here, why he was here *now*.

A noise sounded behind me, but I didn't dare look, didn't do anything except caress the metal trigger.

"Back. Up."

The noise grew.

I knew it was soft. I knew that unless someone had spent summers on this ranch, had spent several lonely years since, the quiet cocooning all around them, they wouldn't recognize it.

Knew that Colt wouldn't understand what it meant.

But I did.

The shotgun still pointed at his chest, I took another step back.

"I want this ranch, baby," he said, leaning toward me. "I want the land and the cattle and that sweet little setup of that house."

No.

That wasn't going to happen.

Not ever.

"I don't give a fuck what you want," I said and it was strong now, a fierce snap of words. "That's not happening. Now go or I'll call—"

"Who?" he sneered. "I don't see your man around." He threw a hand out in the direction of the barn then the house. "And you're certainly not going to shoot me."

Axel wasn't around.

And wouldn't be around much. Not until the season was over.

But still...I wasn't alone.

Remembering that was why I had kept the picture—the

wedding picture of me and Colt. Why I had left it exactly where Gramps had first placed it years ago, why I hadn't torn it to shreds and thrown it away when I'd moved in. It was for *this* moment, when the memories were swirling, the *fear* had sunk itself deep. *This* was why I held tight to the reminder of what life could be like, what *I* could be like under the wrong circumstances.

Not alone.

Not any longer.

Not that woman.

Not ever again.

"I don't need a man around. I have myself. I have my friends. And yes, I have Axel. But more than that, even when I'm by myself, I am"—my eyes flicked to the side as the sound of gravel crunching seemed to finally reach him—"*not* alone."

His eyes narrowed. "I'm not going to stop until I get what I want."

"You'll never get what you want from me," I whispered.

Sparks of fury in his gaze, a muscle in his jaw flexing, and then, quick as a snake, he cocked his fist back.

He was going to hit me.

Hard.

With that tight fist.

And I didn't think.

I didn't *think.*

My finger just tightened around the trigger, tightened and tightened and *tightened* until...

The shotgun went off.

I screamed.

Or maybe that was Colt.

Or maybe it was just all in my head.

But as I tried to process that, the gun was snatched out of my hands, and I was yanked back and—

"Steady now," the male voice said. "I have you."

And then my eyes were opening, and I was staring at a broad back.

At *Joel's* broad back.

And I started trembling.

"Easy," he said, and the arm that had wrapped around my middle tensed, pressing me into his back. "I'm here—"

"You could have killed me, you fucking madwoman!"

Colt.

I burrowed into Joel, and he gave me one more squeeze before dropping his arm.

"You invited onto this property?"

It was a rumbled question, and a deadly one.

"I—how dare—"

"He wasn't," I whispered. "I asked him to go, again and *again*."

Joel went even more tense, even more still. Even more deadly. "She asked you to go?"

Another dangerous query.

"She doesn't know what she wants," Colt snapped.

"But she *did* want to be hit?" Joel asked coldy, telling me that he'd seen Colt wind up, that he wasn't mad at me for taking the shot.

That his anger at my ex was an icicle perched on the ceiling, ready to fall.

To pierce.

To kill.

"No," I said, my shock having worn off. "I didn't want to be hurt. To be *hit*." I slid slightly to the side, moved so that I could see Colt, see that he was unharmed.

Mostly.

A series of holes had been left in the ground, rocks and dirt dispersed by the blast. They must have ricocheted up because there was blood dripping down his legs from the ricochet of the bird shot.

But he was otherwise unhurt.

I hadn't killed him.

I'd wanted to—*wanted* to so fucking badly.

But at the last minute, I'd aimed at the ground anyway.

And now I realized that my legs stung as well.

"I didn't want to be hurt," I said again, leaning against Joel, taking strength from him when I hardly knew him, except that Axel had sent him and if Axel had been here he would have let me do the same—

"I didn't want to be hurt *then,* and I didn't want to be hurt now." I straightened slightly. "I want you to go, to get the fuck out of my life." I swallowed hard. "I want you to get out and never come back."

Colt's eyes flashed and he took a step toward us. "You don't get to—"

Joel moved.

One second he was next to me.

The next he had Colt's shirt in his grip and was shoving my ex back, step by step by *step*.

Until they were at his car.

Until Joel had him pressed up against the middle and then said something that had Colt going pale, his fingers scrabbling for the handle, yanking open the door, and wrestling himself from Joel's hold.

Or maybe Joel let him go.

I didn't know.

I only watched as Colt slammed the door, tore out of the driveway, rocks skittering in all directions.

And then Joel was back in front of me, hands on my shoulders. "Bailey—"

We both turned to the sound of another car coming down the drive, and I saw that it was Billie Rose's.

The next moment she was skidding to a halt.

But before she got out of her car, Joel reached into the UTV and handed me my cell. "Call Axel. I'll handle that harpy."

Probably, I should be insulted for my aunt's honor.

Except I was shaking.

Trembling so hard that I had a tough time holding my phone.

"Call him," he repeated, squeezing my fingers around my cell. "He'll make it better."

I sucked in a breath.

But he was gone, moving toward Billie Rose, stopping her when she would have run toward me.

And...finally.

I got my fingers to move.

To dial.

Eighteen

Axel

"You can't keep doing this," she whispered.

The moment I'd gotten the phone call, I'd driven like a bat out of hell.

Making the four-hour drive in just over three hours.

Too fucking long.

Too many things that could have gone wrong, too easily.

But I was here now.

Holding Bailey, in her bed, and trying to figure out how in the fuck to get away with murder.

That bastard had come to the ranch, had gotten in Bailey's face, could have so easily hurt her if Joel hadn't already been on his way to the ranch. If Billie Rose hadn't gotten Bailey's text and, because she wasn't close, had called Joel, finding out where he was and telling him to hurry.

Lucky.

So fucking lucky.

"How are your legs?" I whispered, smoothing my hand down her thigh.

She was wearing sweatpants, so I couldn't get a look at the bandages I'd painstakingly placed that afternoon. Small cuts on her shins, her ankles.

"I told you they're fine."

"Buttercup."

"Look," she said, sitting up. Her tone was stern, though there was soft in her eyes. "I…appreciate that you want to protect me, but—"

"You're *fine?*"

That phone call had been…

"Joel forced me to call you then." She shook her head. "I shouldn't have. Not right then."

That…

Stung.

Fucking hell, it stung.

"I love you," I said. "I should have been here and—"

She cursed and pulled out of my grip, pushed out of bed. "And I love you, too. And I don't want to be a fucking distraction, a fucking *burden*. Maybe…" She pushed her hair out of her face. "Maybe we should stop seeing each other."

The sound that rose in my throat was animalistic.

A raw, inhuman sound of pain.

"Just until after the season is over," she added quickly. "This has all moved so fast, and it's a lot, and you're in San Francisco. You're trying to live out your dream, honey. I-I can't be the reason you don't get—"

I was moving before I realized my feet had carried me across the room.

"Why do you think I'm where I am?" I snapped, throwing out a hand, hating that she winced at the abrupt movement, hating that her *ex* had made it so *that* was her reaction when I got a little heated. I took a breath, gentled my voice, slowed my movements despite the blood pumping through my body, demanding that I end this conversation with her here and now before it…before it damaged something between us. "If it weren't for you, if it weren't for what we found together, what we've *shared* together, I'd still be here in town, fucking and drinking and sitting in my misery."

She didn't respond, just looked away, was quiet for a long time.

Then she turned back and her mouth opened and I knew, *knew* that she was going to spew some fucking bullshit. "What we have isn't—"

I pressed a finger to her lips. "Don't," I whispered or begged or—

"Don't what?" she asked against my skin.

"Don't take what we have and ruin it."

Her eyes slid closed. Her body went still.

And slowly, oh so slowly, I wrapped my arms around her and held her against me.

My heart was a fucking drum in my chest, my body demanded that I carry her back into bed, that I fuck her until she was limp and satiated, until she wouldn't dream of leaving me.

But...I wanted more with Bailey.

I wanted forever.

When she remained silent, I didn't relax. We seemed to be on a precipice, and one word from her, one sentiment that this didn't mean as much to her as it did to me, would send me over the edge, tumbling down to the gully below, sharp rocks ready to impale me, heavy ones overhead ready to break off, fall, and crush me.

Eventually, though, she nodded, dropping her head to my chest, her body slumping against mine. "I'm used to taking care of myself."

"I know."

"I was scared today. Really scared." A pause, long and taut and *painful*. "I hate that he still scares me."

"He hurt you. Even the simplest of animals avoid pain."

"He *took* me..." A sigh. "He took me away from myself, turned me into someone I didn't recognize. And he did it today, too. At least for a little bit." Her voice dropped to a whisper. "I don't want to go back there. I don't want to be that woman."

"I know."

Her head tilted back, eyes on mine. "No blanket assurances that I won't ever be that woman again?"

I cupped her cheek. God, I wish I could. I *wanted* to. But I wouldn't lie to her.

I couldn't.

"I don't think anyone can make them. Not with one hundred percent certainty anyway."

Teeth pressing to her bottom lip, but then she sighed again, and then eventually...she nodded. "No," she agreed. "No one can."

"But I believe in the woman who stood up to me, who stood up to *him*. I know she has an inner strength that I envy, that I *respect*, and because of that, I have faith that she'll never go back. Because she—" I smoothed my knuckles over her cheek. "Because *you've* come far, buttercup. And I don't think you'll allow yourself to do anything but to keep inching forward."

"Axel," she whispered, her head dropping forward again, resting against my chest.

"Buttercup."

She shuddered.

"I'm sorry," she whispered.

"I know. And I love that you would try to protect me, but—"

A sigh. "We're not like that." She lifted her head, met my gaze, and her mouth turned up. "We're just two broken people who found each other."

My lips twitched, but I drew her closer, pressed my body to hers. "I know something that *isn't* broken."

"Yeah?"

I nipped the tip of her nose. "Yeah."

"What might that be?"

"Besides my cock desperate for your ass?"

She laughed. "Such sweet, romantic words."

"One of these days, I'll tempt you into it."

Her hand slid down my chest, flitted under the hem of my T-shirt. She rose on tiptoe, mouth finding my earlobe, sucking lightly. "For the record, you won't have to do much to tempt me into it."

Grinning, I smoothed my hand over the ass in question. "Yeah?"

A kiss to my jaw. "I've enjoyed everything you've ever done to me." To my cheek. "I don't suspect you'll ever do anything I don't like."

I wouldn't.

I'd make it my mission to give her only pleasure. Never pain. She'd had too much pain in her life already.

"I wouldn't."

"I know that." Conviction in each word that settled deep in my heart.

"Yeah?" I asked again.

She tsked. "Don't get rid of my filthy puckboy, not *now*."

"Why not *now?*"

A kiss to my jaw. "Because I like him." A kiss to the corner of my mouth. "I like you." A beat. "*All* of you."

"Yeah?"

She grinned, and her fingers dipped under the waistband of my pants. "Yeah, honey."

Nineteen

Bailey

Axel had left around nine the night before, needing to get back into town so he was fresh for the game today.

I'd waited up until I'd gotten his text that he'd arrived at his apartment

And now I'd wandered into my kitchen only to find a note.

There should be a delivery on your porch by the time you wake up.
-A
P.S. He's safe. But call me if you need confirmation.

"He's?" I muttered.

But the note didn't bring me any further answers, and neither did my phone.

No illuminating text messages.

No additional post-scripts on the back of the note.

Frowning, I screwed the top on my to-go carafe, grabbed my flannel, and headed to the door, my boots clomping on the floor.

Joel couldn't possibly be out there.

He'd had to get on the bus to an away game yesterday afternoon, and he and his fellow Rush players wouldn't be back for several days.

And Axel was, obviously back in San Francisco.

I turned the handle, cracked open the door, and—

Gasped.

"Oh my God," I squealed, moving forward to the crate, to the adorable ball of fluff—gray and white with black spots and—

"Oh my God," I squealed again.

And two different colored eyes—one a light brown, one a pale blue.

"An Australian Shepherd," a lightly accented voice said from the shadows.

I jumped, squealing for a third time, though this time it didn't have anything to do with puppies and their adorableness. It had to do with a strange man on my porch, one who seemed to magically appear out of the shadows.

"Pascal," he said. "Head of security for the Gold."

I frowned. "Long way from home, Pascal." Then I lifted my cell and called Axel. I hated to wake him, but...was the delivery the dog, the man, or both?

"Buttercup," Axel answered on the first ring.

"The man or the dog?"

"Both," he responded without hesitation. "Pascal owns a security firm in addition to his work with the Gold. He was in town looking into Candi for me. He's going to take over from Joel to keep an eye on the ranch until he can get someone to stay there with you."

"What?"

"Just until we sort out your parents and Colt," he added in a hurry. "Or the season's over and I can stay there."

"The season? Axel? I can't ask—"

"You didn't ask," he said, still hurrying.

How much did live-in security cost?

More than I could afford, certainly.

"It's too much money—"

"Nothing is too much to make sure you're safe."

Fuck. That had my heart going all squirmy.

"I'm doing this, honey."

I sucked in a breath.

"You're not that woman from the picture anymore, not the woman from your nightmares."

I released that breath.

"You're not alone, buttercup," he said softly. "Which means that you have me, you have friends. You just need to accept the help."

"You've done so much for me already. I can't—"

"It'll give me peace of mind so I can play better," he countered.

I sighed, clenched the phone tightly. "You already used that line on me."

A pause. "I don't recall that conversation," he teased.

I snorted, pressed the cell to my ear, keeping it in place by lifting my shoulder as I bent to scoop up the puppy. "*Right.*"

"Nope." A pop on the p. "Don't recall it at all."

"I accepted the house stuff," I pointed out.

"So, you'll accept this, too?" A hopeful question.

I sighed, stroked my hand down the puppy's back, feeling my fingers sink into the soft fur. "*Axel.*"

"Please, buttercup?" he asked, sounding truly pathetic, though laughter bubbled up in me when he added, "Just saying, if we were on a video call right now, I would be giving you sad puppy eyes."

"Which is the perfect segue for the ball of fluff currently giving *me* sad puppy eyes?"

"You like him?"

I already *loved* him. "He's adorable."

"Australian Shepherds are working dogs—*herding* dogs," Axel said. "He can help you on the ranch, and they're protective as well."

"Fuck," I whispered as his words flowed through me, made my heart skip a beat.

"What?" he asked softly.

"Why are you doing this to me?"

To his credit, he didn't need to ask me if I was being serious. He knew I was, but he knew also exactly what I meant.

And how *I* knew this?

Because his response was, "Loving you?"

"Yeah," I whispered. "Exactly that."

"File a police report, okay?"

"I already did that yesterday. Frank is going to fast-track a restraining order."

"Good, honey."

The puppy glanced up and yawned and I had to bite back a giggle. Then I couldn't hold back my laughter when he put his paws on my shoulders and licked my chin. "Yeah. It is good."

Axel.

The pup.

Joel and Pascal, who was standing, his back against the railing, eyes on me, face placid, but not impatient, not cold.

He was dangerous.

Anyone could see that with a single glance at the man.

But he wasn't dangerous to *me*.

He wasn't like Colt.

I felt that in my bones.

Because of that, I glanced back down at the pup just as Axel spoke again. "What are you going to name him? Spock?" A beat. "Or Wish Bear?"

"God, I hate that you know all my secrets," I grumbled.

"Not *all* of them."

I sucked in a breath. "No," I agreed.

"But I will."

The air hissed out of my lungs. I took another breath, released it slowly, and admitted the truth, "Yes." A beat. "But only because I know you'll share all your secrets, too."

"Yeah, buttercup. I will."

I laughed softly.

"What?" he asked.

"I want to tell you that I love you, but I can't abide by the fact that I'm turning into a sappy asshole."

"You're not an asshole. That's my job, remember?"

"Yeah," I said, thinking of our rocky start, "I remember."

"Ouch, honey." But I knew he was in his bed, knew he was smiling, knew he loved me, knew he loved when I sassed him. "Spock, yeah?" he said. "To continue the theme."

My heart. My *heart.*

It couldn't survive Axel Finnegan.

But still, I said, "Yeah honey, I think you're right." A breath, shaking off the sap. "Now, go back to bed. I've got chores to do and apparently, a puppy to train."

"There are supplies in the barn. A crate and beds and food."

Of course he'd thought of that, even before I'd managed to put together that I would need to take a trip into town for supplies.

I couldn't survive Axel Finnegan.

I couldn't.

But it'd be the best sort of death.

"Now, I really do have to tell you that I love you," I said.

I could hear the smile in his voice. "Lay it on me, buttercup."

I opened my mouth, the words bubbled up in my throat, and—

Grinning, I hung up the phone.

Spock barked in approval.

My cell buzzed just before I pocketed it.

I'm gonna smack that ass.

I typed out my reply.

God, I hope so.

Then my phone was in my pocket and Pascal helpfully brought the crate inside the house. I locked up, looked down at Spock, and said, "I guess we should start our day, huh?"

Another little bark, followed by an earnest lick across my chin.

And hell if I didn't fall in love all over again.

Twenty

Axel

"I ought to smack *your* ass for pulling that shit with the alarm," she said two days later.

I leaned back on the bed, bending one arm and shoving it behind my head. "I'm down."

Her face froze for a second, surprise sliding through her expression, and I would have thought our video call had a bad connection if not for her shaking her head in the next heartbeat, mouth turning up at the edges.

"Christ, I want to fuck that mouth," I muttered.

Her mouth turned up further. "You've done that before."

"I want to do it again."

A shrug. "I'm down."

Groaning, I tossed my arm over my eyes. "Why must you torture me so?"

The audio went a little staticky, and I lifted my arm, stared through the phone and sweet Christ, why were we hours apart?

"God, I love your tits."

She grinned now, hands coming up, cupping her breasts, fingers drifting over her nipples.

"Squeeze them harder," I ordered, unable to stop myself.

"Bossy."

"Harder, honey."

Her hands tightened around the globes even as she gave me an order of her own. "Get naked."

I tossed back the blanket. "Already am."

Her laughter turned to a moan when I propped my cell on the nightstand, when I reached down and wrapped my fingers around my dick, stroking hard, knowing that I was pathetically close already. But then again everything about this woman did it for me.

Silky brown hair.

Curves for days. Wide eyes. Tan skin. Lips that begged for my cock to slip between them, begged for mine to be pressed to hers, tongue delving in.

And speaking of tongues delving...

Her pussy was a six-course Michelin-star meal.

And her ass...well, I'd discussed her ass already.

"Fingers between your thighs," I ordered. "Now."

"I'm not even naked yet." She did some phone-propping of her own, showed me that she was wearing a godawful pair of Care Bear pajama pants.

"Well, Christ, woman. Get naked."

"Why?" she asked innocently. "Is there some reason you might want me to take my clothes off?"

I had a hundred reasons.

A thousand.

But I couldn't verbalize any of them.

Instead, all I could manage was another command. "Open your nightstand drawer."

She stilled, hands on the waistband of those pajamas.

"Open the drawer."

A long, slow blink. And then she rolled, tugged open the drawer, and I knew she saw it when her entire body went motionless.

"Naughty man."

"*Smart* man," I said. Then, "It's charged." A beat. "Put it in."

Her lips parted. Her eyes went molten.

And then she was naked.

And *then* she was putting it in, slipping the toy through folds I could see were dripping, the blunt tip disappearing inside her.

"That part goes over your clit," I rasped.

"I know how sex toys work," she said tartly.

"Do you?" I asked, hating to minimize the video of her, but having to as I opened the app. "Press the button on top."

She pressed it.

And her toy popped up on my phone.

Fuck yeah.

"What—?"

I'd thought about this a lot. I had a plan, though fuck if I could remember it. Instead, I pulled up the portion of the app that let me create my own rhythm. Create my own rhythm that would go to her phone, that would connect to the toy...and it would vibrate in the pattern I wanted.

The pattern I'd learned.

A pattern that had her gasping.

"What—?" she breathed.

I grinned.

And it was a fuck of a long way from my fingers stroking through her wet pussy.

But it was me, it was her, it was the best I could fucking do with the distance between us.

So I stroked the phone screen. I kept up with the pattern. I brought her to the brink...and then over it, my cock aching as she cried out my name.

It was bearable because it was my name on her tongue.

It was perfect because it was my name on her tongue.

It was—

She lifted her head. "Wrap your fingers around yourself."

"Buttercup. This wasn't—"

"And stroke hard until you come." She propped herself up on one elbow. "Pretend you're coming on me, on these—" She cupped her breasts again.

I could argue.

I could be chivalrous, make this only about her.

But...that wasn't me.

That wasn't her *and me.*

So I gripped my dick, stroked...and when I fell over the edge, my rough groan was only her name, over and over again.

I crossed my arms and waited, ass on the boards, feet on the bench.

"Too good for us, pretty boy?" Joel called as he skated by.

"Yup," I called back, but I was already hopping down, already moving toward him as he walked off the ice, his helmet pushed up, sweat dripping down his temples.

Bailey was at a planning meeting for the Winter Festival with Billie Rose.

I had the night off from hockey, though I'd need to leave early tomorrow to be back at the arena for a game—a game I was hoping that Bailey would join me at. So I was catching up with the guys and then, later, Bailey and I would meet up at Monroe's.

I couldn't wait to cuddle up with her at the bar, to steal sips of her beer and press my body to hers.

But, for now, I was watching the guys fuck around on the ice, wishing I could be out there.

My gear was in San Francisco.

Plus, it wouldn't do for me to get hurt practicing with a team that wasn't mine any longer.

I met up with Joel in the hall, and he was serious. For once.

"Your girl okay?" he asked, leaning against the wall and crossing one big skate over the other.

"Yeah," I said. "Thanks for looking after her until I could get her security sorted."

A nod. "That guy doing right by her?"

"Pascal is a professional."

"Fucker had scary eyes." He straightened slightly. "Though, just saying"—his mouth tipped up—"your girl has scary eyes, too."

"Asshole."

Joel grinned, pushed off the wall. "Of course, I think that mostly came from the fact that she was serious about wielding a shotgun."

"That she is."

Joel sobered. "That ex of hers is trouble."

"Yeah. We're working on tracking him down," I said. "Between him and Candi, I'm going to be paying Pascal for the next century."

Joel grunted and looked so serious that I gave him the rest.

"Pascal has a man with her at all times and installed an alarm system at her place. She's got a panic button to carry with her that goes straight to the police department and Pascal's office. Plus"—I smiled—"she's got her shotguns and clearly knows how to use them."

Joel held up his fist to bump. "Damn right she does."

I bumped it back. "Not sure that's something to celebrate when she's used them to threaten my balls more than once."

Joel smirked and lifted his fist again.

This time I didn't bump it.

But I did begrudgingly accept the punch on the shoulder.

"I'm gonna shower," Joel said. "And then we're going to light this town up!"

I punched him back. "In a very respectful, responsible way, correct?"

"Responsible?" Joel shrugged.

I shot him a look.

"Fine. Fine," he said both hands up in surrender. "But only because I don't want to hear it from Billie Rose if we start trouble again. Plus, we're finally out of the dog house and welcome at both bars in town again."

I grinned. "Progress."

"Respectful, though?" he asked, tapping a finger to his lips. "Don't you think that's asking a lot?"

"Fucker."

A smirk. "Damn right."

I rolled my eyes. "Ass."

"That too."

Sighing, I let my head drop back, stared up at the ceiling. "Why do I fucking bother?"

"Respectful," Joel said, surprising me. "Of the women and

property only." A punch to my shoulder and fuck that hurt. Why the hell did Joel have to be so strong?

"As for you..." he added, clapping me on the side of the head and moving down the hall.

Jesus.

"*You,* however...I am gonna bust your balls at every *single* opportunity."

Twenty-One

Bailey

"And," Billie Rose said, typing on her laptop, "that is the last of my list."

"Thank fuck," Dessie muttered, grabbing her beer and finishing it off. "I've got to help Roger"—the owner of Monroe's—"behind the bar. Don't"—she pointed a finger at me—"let her sign me up for anything else."

I saluted.

Dessie grinned, started to say something back, but was cut off by the front door opening, boisterous laughter filling the air.

And my heart stopped.

"Aw." Dessie yanked at my ponytail. Not hard enough to truly hurt, but also not a light tug. "You're sooooo in loooove. Did you kiss his boo-boo from the other night, too? I know you were worried about *your man.*"

Sweet Christ. *This* was why I didn't have friends.

Heat at my back.

"She kissed me a *lot* of places," Axel said silkily, fingers trailing down my nape.

Billie Rose wrinkled her nose. "That's my niece you're talking about."

"That's my *woman* I'm talking about." I glanced up in time for him to stare down at me, to *wink* down at me. "And don't yank her hair," he told Dessie. "I like it on her head." He looked up at Billie Rose. "Especially since I like it dragging across my naked body."

There was a gagging sound and I turned to see that Joel had closed the distance between us.

"Give a guy a break," he muttered. "Not all of us are getting laid."

Billie Rose snorted. "Sure, Lothario."

Joel's eyes flashed. "What, harpy? I know it's been a few days for me, but how long has it been for you? So long that you only got dust up there?"

"Joel," Axel warned.

"I'll have you know—" Billie began, finger pointed in Joel's direction.

"Billie," *I* warned.

"Beer." Dessie plunked a pitcher on the table, having somehow made it to the bar and back while Billie Rose and Joel sparred. A stack of cups hit the table next. "Drink. And order some food so you don't get fucked up in my bar and start trouble."

"I resent that comment," Axel said lightly.

She tossed him a look. "The people of River's Bend have long memories."

Axel smirked. "Menus, bar wench." A clap of his hands. "Now."

Dessie poked him. "You're incorrigible, Axel Finnegan."

He grinned. "And I'm cute, too."

She grinned back. "Don't forget that you only got your boo-boo kisser because of me."

Billie Rose gasped. "Excuse me?"

Dessie plunked her hands on her hips. "I told him where to find her *and* got him to take her home when she was sloshed after *two beers.*"

The look she shot me had me reaching for a glass, filling it.

Reminding me.

I was going to have my two beers, get pleasantly drunk, and then get pleasantly *fucked* by my man.

"I was the one who hand—" My aunt clamped her mouth together.

Axel shot Billie Rose a look. "Was the rest of that statement going to be —*cuffed?*"

"Why would you ask that?" Billie Rose asked innocently.

An innocence that no one near or at the table believed.

"I should thank you, I suppose," Axel said. "Because of those handcuffs—"

"And *I'm* done with this conversation." I slid out of my chair, my body brushing against Axel's as I shifted past him and moved into the booth, forcing Billie Rose to scoot in further. "My *man*"—I narrowed my eyes at Axel then at my aunt and Dessie in turn—"is here. Our dog is at home, probably trying to figure out how to escape his crate and destroy my new carpet. On the plus side, though, our work is done for the moment, and I've got a mind for some bar food."

Joel moved to the other side, along with a few other Rush players. I only knew one of their names since I'd met him on my porch —Ryan. Axel scooted in next to me, shoving me along the polished wood until I was pressed up against Billie.

And then he kept pushing.

Until Billie Rose and I were *both* sliding.

Until we were both sliding and the Rush players, including Ryan, abandoned the other side and were scooting into the booth behind Axel, filling in the circle-shaped booth.

And I didn't miss that somehow—and yes, that was me doing air quotes—in the shuffle, *somehow* Joel ended up next to Billie Rose.

I dropped my gaze to my hands, trying to bite back my smile.

"Jesus fucking Christ," Billie Rose muttered. "Just give me a second and I'll put my things away and—"

She was pushed up against Joel.

Who was busy glaring at Axel.

Billie Rose jerked.

"Cool it, harpy," Joel said, wrapping his fingers around her arm. A wicked smile on his face. "Unless you're going to crawl that sweet ass of yours into my lap."

Billie Rose's face went pink.

She glared at me. At Axel.

"Don't you dare touch me," she snapped.

"Just saying"—Joel's voice was golden silk, floating in the air—"*you* pressed yourself to *me*."

"Children," I warned.

My aunt glared.

But Joel seemed to relax, leaning back against the booth, throwing his arm over the top of it and manspreading...directly into Billie Rose's space. Then his eyes came to mine and there was none of the bravado. Not any longer. Only that gentle warmth he'd given me after I'd called Axel, that he'd given me after the call when he'd led me onto my porch, then into my living room, tucking a blanket around me and watching crappy TV with me as we waited for Axel to make the drive up.

A big softie under all that asshole.

Just like Axel.

What was it with these Rush men?

"I'm good," I told him. "Colt hasn't been back, and neither have my parents," I added when Billie Rose's gaze came to mine. "Axel's taking care of me."

My man pressed a kiss to the top of my head. "And she's fighting me every single step of the way."

"As one does."

It was a bit of a lie.

I was.

And...I wasn't.

It would be all too easy to fall into the trap of letting him take care of me.

Of forgetting myself and just *letting* him.

Become me. Telling me what I wanted, what I needed, *who* I was.

Which he understood. Because he just kissed me on the top of my head again, but didn't press any further, didn't tease me about that anymore.

"I went down to the planning department today," Billie said.

"What?" I asked, focusing fully on her.

She tucked her laptop into her messenger bag and then shoved the bag between her and Joel. "I think the developer Colt"—I smothered the chill that came through me at his name—"mentioned is Garret Smothers."

"Why does that name sound familiar?" Joel asked.

"Because he built that monstrosity of house you call yours," Billie Rose told him.

A shrug before he picked up the pitcher and poured himself a beer. "Real estate is a good investment."

"Not sure that real estate built on either side of a former firebreak is a smart investment, but I know he certainly made the houses *look* pretty."

Joel puffed up.

"What do you mean?" I asked before they could continue snapping at each other.

"Colt is his real estate agent."

I frowned.

"Colt has brokered properties for Garret all the way from Sacramento up to Tahoe. And Garret has wanted in on land in River's Bend for years."

"And Colt saw his way into River's Bend through me."

"Or through your parents," Billie Rose said. "They owned the property when you two were married, right?"

Yeah, they had owned it.

Until I'd bought them out with every last bit of savings I had, every bit of inheritance I'd received from Gramps and Gran, my retirement I'd cashed out early, money I'd borrowed from the bank based on paystubs for a job I quit to work the ranch.

My parents had cashed out their third.

Then they'd gone, to flit around, to ignore me, to live their lives for themselves.

As they'd always done.

I was an afterthought, *if* I was a thought at all.

"I would never sell the ranch," I whispered. "Not ever."

Axel went still next to me.

"I won't leave it. I won't. I *won't*."

Billie squeezed my hand.

But Axel didn't react. He was a statue next to me.

I glanced up, stared deeply, but couldn't discern what message was in his bright blue eyes.

What was *hidden* behind those blue eyes.

Then he looked away and I lost them altogether.

His arm was around me; his thigh was pressed to mine. His scent was in my nose, his warmth surrounding me, his body was *right* next to me.

But he wasn't here.

And I had the distinct notion that I'd just lost Axel Finnegan.

Twenty-Two

Axel

The arena was loud.

The ice was running fast.

But I was only focused on one fan in the stands.

Twelve rows back, just above the glass, though the netting that stretched from the top of the clear plexiglass to the rafters overhead would keep her safe from any stray pucks.

Because I was the type of man who thought about that now.

Worried about it.

Two weeks since that asshat had confronted her, and two weeks since she'd fired the shotgun that had left her with a scar on her shin.

And a glimpse of shadows in her eyes.

The memories gripping tight.

But between the alarm system and Pascal's man and Joel occasionally checking up on her and me going up whenever I could, she'd been safe, and slowly, the claws of her memories seemed to be easing.

The national anthem finished, and I rolled out my shoulders, got ready to focus on the game, on impressing my woman who was in the Gold Mine for the first time.

It was loud.

Then again, the fans had a lot to cheer about.

Three Cup wins since the team had been formed just over a decade and a half before.

A constant competitor in the playoffs.

They'd done everything right (after they'd begun very, very wrong).

So now they had camaraderie. No drama. No bad press. A fixture in the local community.

They were loved and successful and had die-hard fans.

All of that was why the Gold's home arena was known as one of the loudest stadiums in the league. And tonight the crowd was living up to that image. *Tonight,* they were cheering so loudly that it seemed to shake the rafters.

But the moment the puck dropped, the moment the game began, I didn't hear any of that.

I was a man possessed.

My woman was in the stands. My team was playing our rivals.

There would be big plays, big hits, and then, later, Bailey and I would fuck like rabbits and—

The player I was changing for sprinted to the bench, and I snapped into focus, jumping over the boards, landing on the ice and immediately springing into motion. The puck was heading toward our zone, the opposing team closing in on Brit, and I wasn't going to let Brit get scored on, not on my watch.

Certainly not with Bailey in the stands.

I sprinted into our zone, beelining straight for the player with the puck while Josh took the better angle and cut off the opportunity for the pass.

My breath hissed out as I shoved my shoulder into the other player's, our bodies crashing together, our sticks clashing. We battled for the puck, and I earned stinging palms and a slash across the hands for my trouble, but I had the jump on him. I guided us into the boards, using strength and hips and ass and arms and shoulders and stick. And then as my breath hissed out again, the impact from the boards driving through my body, I used my feet.

To kick the puck over to Kayden.

He was moving with speed already, shooting toward me, and I held my breath as...he picked up the puck.

Yes!

Shoving off the fucker I'd been dealing with, I joined him in the rush, skating after him, accidentally—okay, on purpose—colliding with a Kings player who was jumping on the ice, getting in his way so that Kayden had a good chance at it.

He made excellent use of it as I pushed off my opponent, using the motion to slow me and shoot me forward.

Ha.

Fucker.

And then I was skating again, moving into the zone.

Kayden closed in on their goalie, shot, and...

Missed.

But I was there. And the puck was in the slot, and I could...*just* get my stick on it.

Not to shoot. Just enough to tap it to Rome who was streaking in.

Rome who buried it into the back of the net.

Hell *fucking* yeah!

I shot toward Rome at the same time Kayden did, the three of us crashing into the boards, rattling them, and while we were bumping fists, while we were exchanging "Fuck yeahs," my gaze drifted up. To Bailey.

Who was grinning like a loon and bouncing around in her Gold jersey.

I knew it had my name on the back.

Mine. *Mine.*

Damn, I was turning into a possessive fucker.

And I was living for every second of it.

She caught my gaze, waved, and winked.

And that felt...even better than assisting on this goal, even better than all the wins, all the success. It was better than *all* of it.

She was better than all of it.

Kayden punched my shoulder one more time, and I tore my gaze from Bailey's, from that wink and smile and all that mine, mine, *mine.*

I turned back, ready to focus on the game.

But as I did so, as I rotated around, spinning on the ice, ready to move to the bench, I caught a glimpse of blond.

Bleach blond.

Blinking, I started to turn back, to search the stands, the fans for that hair. It was distinctive. It was fake and bright and *blond.*

But then Kayden bumped into me as he started skating for the bench and I lost sight of it.

And when I glanced back, when I spared a moment to *look* even though I needed to get back to the bench so the game could keep moving, I didn't see any blond.

Just a sea of faces.

Dark hair, red hair, even some blue and green and purple hair. A variety of skin colors, light to dark and in between.

But no blond. Not a single strand of hair that light.

Not in the section in front of me, not in *Bailey's* section.

"Fuck," I whispered, still searching.

"Let's move it, boys," the ref yelled, and I knew he was talking to me, wanting me to get my ass into gear, knew that if I stayed long enough to search through every row, every section, every aisle to assure myself that the glimpse of blond wasn't Candi, and I risk a penalty for delay of game.

So, I forced myself to turn away, to skate to the bench.

But inside...fucking hell, *inside,* I was replaying that glimpse.

Replaying it over and over again.

Replaying it until I convinced myself that I hadn't seen it in the first place.

Twenty-Three

Bailey

I showed my pass and they let me onto the elevator.

No lie, my hands were shaking.

I was about to go up to the family suite, to meet the rest of the team's wives and girlfriends and kids—or at least the ones at that night's game.

And it was because of the woman next to me.

Deep brown hair the color of dark chocolate, pale caramel eyes. A Gold T-shirt and simple black sweats.

And mischief written into each line of her face.

She'd come down to my seat during the final commercial break, introduced herself as Mandy, and invited me to meet her at the elevators after the game was over so I could "Meet everyone."

A fact that brought terror to my veins.

Mostly because she was...exuberant.

Even now the elevator car rose, she was practically vibrating next to me.

"You all right?"

"Uh-huh." She tossed a smile my way. "I just like getting in on the ground floor of these things."

"These things?"

"New relationships, making sure two people who are perfect for each other get their heads out of their asses so they can have their happy ending—"

"But Axel and I already love each other."

Mandy's face fell. "You do?"

"We do."

Such disappointment on her face, so much that I nearly laughed out loud. "Unfortunately, we've already figured out that we want to be together." A beat when she sighed and her shoulders slumped. "We've got other problems though."

A light in Mandy's eyes. "Problems?"

This time I *did* laugh.

"I have an asshole ex, freeloading parents. He has a woman obsessed with him and a selfish mother. We have four hours between us, and my career and responsibilities mean that I can't just move down here and his job keeps him best case, those four hours away, and worst case on the road for eight months out of the year."

It wasn't until I listed all of that out that I felt the weight of those obstacles, those problems.

"Let's start with the asshole ex."

My lips tipped up. "That's where Axel started, too."

Mandy's eyes warmed, but she didn't get to say anything because the elevator doors slid open and then we were stepping off the elevator and she was guiding me to the right, through a door, and...

Into chaos.

"And then you squish this together—"

My eyes went wide as I stared at the slime sliding through the little boy's fingers and dripping down onto his pants.

"Oh no," I said, reaching for the container and a pile of napkins.

"It's okay." He dropped his hand, scooping up the slime and leaving a trail of goo in its wake.

"Uh—"

A hand on my shoulder, one of the few men in the room. He

had an adorable little girl propped on one hip and a gentle smile on his face.

He was also one of the prettiest men I'd seen in my entire life.

And I thought that, perhaps, all of that gorgeousness came from inside.

He was blissfully happy, and it showed.

"This one," he told me, snagging the napkins and making a good effort to clean up the slime, though there definitely were dredges left, bits that wouldn't come out. Not ever. "This one loves art, so his parents make sure to dress him in clothes that can get dirty." He smiled at me. "Especially on Art Night."

The door to the family suite opened and the little boy glanced up. "Daddy!" he yelled. "Look!"

And tore off straight for the tall, suited man striding into the room.

Who scooped him up and hugged him tight and there wasn't one—*one*—bit of hesitation for the slime in proximity to the clearly expensive suit.

No harsh rebukes.

No setting him away.

Just a hug between a father and a son and—

I turned away, my eyes burning, and quickly began consolidating the slime mess. I was jealous of a child...and sad for myself.

Very, very sad.

"I'm Stefan."

I glanced back up. "Bailey."

He grinned. "I know."

And then I processed his name, a name that even I—as a non-sports fan before dating Axel—knew. "Stefan?" I asked. "As in Stefan Barie?"

That smile widened. "I prefer Brit Plantain's husband."

The former captain of the Gold. The one who had turned the team from a league joke into a dynasty.

"Mama!"

My head jerked up, and then the toddler perched on Stefan's hip wriggled down, running across the room and clinging to her mother's legs.

"Nice to meet you," I said when it seemed like he was going to move away.

He squeezed my shoulder again. "It gets easier."

I blinked, brows dragging together.

His voice dropped. "That emptiness inside you. It shrinks and shrinks until one day..." A breath. "One day it's just gone altogether." His fingers tightened, and then he released my shoulder and moved across the room.

Slinging an arm around Brit's waist, kissing her cheek, ruffling their daughter's hair.

"It's her last season, you know."

I turned to see Mandy standing beside me again, her eyes looking misty. "I'm going to miss her."

"You've been friends for a long time?"

A nod. "Since the moment she first walked into this arena."

"That sounds wonderful," I whispered.

"She's the reason the team is like this"—a nod toward Brit, who'd picked up the boy covered in slime and blew a raspberry on his neck—"she's the reason we're a family."

"I—"

"She taught us—empty or full or in between. She taught us how to make a family. How to be loyal and how to tie us together so tightly we wouldn't break. Not ever." Mandy blew out a breath. "It's a business. Of course it is. But it's also more. We're that family, that community, and you're part of that, too."

That sounded sappy as hell.

Too fucking sappy for my cynical heart.

I'd been a part of a family.

And their sole purpose, seemingly, had been to fuck me over time and time again.

But the part of me that loved Axel...that part of me wanted this to be true, wanted to be part of their big, happy family.

"You're not convinced," Mandy murmured.

"I—well—" I glanced up, saw Mandy's knowing gaze. "No offense, it's just..."

"Just what?" she asked when I trailed off and didn't finish.

"It's just—" A shake of my head. "That's not what I had growing up, and it's not like I'm really part of anything—"

"Bailey."

I opened my mouth, closed it.

"You'll—" She stopped. Then patted me on the arm as the door opened again and Axel walked in. My heart, oh God, my heart squeezed so hard that it felt like I would pass out.

I loved that man.

So *fucking* much.

And talk about sappy as hell.

"Give it time, honey," Mandy said, squeezing my arm again. "Just promise yourself that much, okay?"

My brows drew together. "I—"

Axel was getting close. I felt it in the tremor down my spine, the warmth in my belly.

Mandy nudged me forward.

"Go, honey," she whispered.

And then Axel's arms were around me, his lips were on my throat, and his mouth was at my ear, velvet rasp trailing along my skin. "Ready to go home, buttercup?"

Twenty-Four

Axel

"This is nice," she murmured, toeing off her shoes and leaving them on the rack by the front door before walking slowly through the kitchen. "Really nice."

"I know," I said, closing and locking the door, slipping behind her and wrapping my arms around her waist. "Probably the nicest place I've ever lived in."

I *had* to touch her.

I needed to touch her.

It was urge and calling and obsession.

She spun toward me. "Aside from my freshly remodeled house that you bankrolled, you mean?"

I smiled, tugging a strand of her hair, thankful all over again that Billie Rose had been willing to babysit both the ranch and Spock for a few days, despite the fact that the latter was proving to have a preference for his great aunt's heels. "Aside from that."

Fingers on my cheek, against my jaw. God, I loved it when she touched me like that. "Your place," I murmured. "Well, it feels like home. More than this apartment, as nice as it is. More than anywhere else I've ever spent time living in."

"Axel," she breathed.

"I mean that fancy carpet is like walking on a cloud."

She rolled her eyes, but she was smiling.

That was my favorite thing ever.

Her smiling.

"I mean it," I said.

Her smile gentled. "I know." A beat. "Which is why I'm gonna clean out a couple of drawers for you, clear some space in the closet." A kiss to my cheek. "You, sir, have just gotten the ticket out of Duffle Bag Life."

I chuckled.

"And tonight was..." She shook her head. "I've never been to a professional sports game. Not the Giants or Warriors or anything, and I've only seen you play on TV. And *God*." Her voice took on a breathless quality that had my cock twitching. "The crowd. The noise. The *speed*. You guys look fast, but until I actually was there, in the stands..."

Fucking beautiful.

She was fucking beautiful.

And she was talking about me.

Now that was the ego boost I probably didn't need, but the one I really liked anyway. "And what else?"

She swatted me. But she gave it to me anyway. "You were beautiful." A flash of white teeth. "And brutal. And *big*. You're *my* big, broody hockey player. But you're not even that big, not compared to some of the other guys."

I wrapped my fingers around her waist, drew her into the bedroom. "Ouch."

She blinked.

"Size matters, buttercup."

Another blink then she was giggling. "Does it really all come down to size then?"

"Of course it does."

She slipped her wrist free of my grip, turned and wrapped her arms around my middle. "You're big." Her lips turned up. "The *biggest.*"

Laughter bubbling in my chest. "Tell me more."

A tendril of heat in her eyes. "Really?"

"Tell me more about how watching your big, *big* man skate and check and *win* turns you on. Tell me more about what my big, hard body does to you, what it makes you feel. What it makes you *want.*"

She rose on tiptoe, and I bent automatically, so that her lips could reach my ear.

"It makes me want you all the time. Every second, every moment of the day."

I inhaled sharply when she nipped at my earlobe.

She dropped onto her heels, took my hand, and dragged it across her belly, fingers interlaced as she unbuttoned her jeans.

"It makes me go wet the moment I hear your voice, feel the heat of your body."

A shove and her jeans hit the hardwood floor.

"I've gone through so many pairs of underwear, drained the batteries of my vibrator more times than I could count, and—*here*—with you, fuck if it's a struggle to not melt into a puddle every moment you're near. Now"—she kissed my jaw—"have I stroked your ego enough?"

"My ego, yes. My cock, no."

Laughter in the air, something that was better than her giggles, her smiles. Something that roused the need, the possessive man inside me.

Claim. *Mine.*

Knock her over the head, drag her back to bed.

Her hand drew mine between her legs, to the scrap of fabric covering her pussy.

Soaked through.

She hadn't been lying.

Then again, she never did.

"Speaking of stroking," she murmured...spreading her thighs.

I might not be the brightest guy. I might not have gone to college, gotten a fancy degree. But I knew how to stroke a pussy.

With my fingers. With my tongue.

She gasped when I pushed her back, when I tumbled her onto the mattress, squatting at the edge and tugging her panties down her legs. But when she reached for the hem of her jersey, I stopped her. "Gonna fuck you in that, honey."

Pink on her cheeks.

Desire in her eyes.

Underwear...on the floor.

And I stroked.

With my fingers. With my tongue.

Tart and sweet. My woman on my taste buds. My name on her lips. I wanted to be inside her, wanted the tight heat of her surrounding me, clasping around me. But first, I wanted her to fall apart. On my fingers. On my tongue.

I sucked hard on her clit, and she gripped my hair.

I knew she was close, had been between her legs enough to read every movement, to know that she was going to come.

So, I spread some of her slick, wet heat down, back between the cleft of her ass, drifting over the tight rosebud, pressing lightly.

A gasp.

Her hips jerking against my face.

My name in the air.

I pressed harder, my finger slid in...

And she went crazy, bucking against me, pushing herself down onto my finger, clamping down on me front and back. I wanted my cock there. I *needed* it there.

But...

Not yet.

And then she was coming.

And then I was flipping her over, jerking her up onto her knees, sliding into her from behind.

She was still in the jersey, the hem of it rucking up and exposing that ass I was desperate to be inside. My name was emblazoned across her shoulders, and I was enough of a possessive male to fucking *love* seeing that.

My number.

My name.

Mine.

A flex of my hips and I was inside her tight wet heat, and fuck, *nothing* felt better than that. Than her.

Not being on the ice, playing in front of an arena full of fans. Not scoring a game-winning goal. Not even making her smile and laugh and giggle.

Though those were close.

But this...Bailey trusting me with her body, me bringing her pleasure...

The best fucking moments of my life.

I gripped her hips, ground deep.

"Axel," she groaned, back arching, pushing her body against mine, shoving herself against my cock, and loving every fucking second of it.

Fuck.

I was going to come.

I was going to come without her and—

She gasped.

I knew that hitch of her breath, knew that it meant she was close, that she was going to come, that I just needed to hold on a little longer.

Her pussy convulsed—

I lost it.

I thrust hard and fast and was barely aware that she was with me, that she was tumbling over the edge.

But I was aware enough, just that bare sliver of consciousness—thank fuck, because *I* didn't come first, my woman came first—to keep going, to make sure her orgasm was long and sweet and completely finished before I collapsed, dragging us both to our sides on the bed, my lungs moving like bellows, sweat dripping down my back.

"I'm guessing"—she sucked in a breath—"you like the jersey?"

I groaned.

"What?"

I heaved myself up, flipped her over so she was facing me. "Now I have to fuck you again."

She smoothed her hand down my chest. "Another orgasm might kill me."

"But what a way to die." I waggled my brows. "I'm game to give it a try."

She giggled. "Another time." Then she yawned and cuddled closer. "Right now, I'm tired."

"Okay, buttercup."

I held her, stroking my hand through her hair, along her back, cupping her ass, letting my eyes drift closed, just for a moment.

Then I forced my body away from hers, went into the bathroom and cleaned up, coming back with a cloth, sorting her out despite her protests, and tucking her into bed. I got rid of the cloth, pulled on a pair of underwear, and crawled in next to her, loving the drowsy way she automatically curled into me.

As I held her close, I thought of how I'd planned to approach my offer, to explain about the modeling contracts and spokesperson offers, about Cole's charity, and Olivia's invitation for us to visit.

But I'd just had an orgasm that practically melted my brain.

So none of the explanations came out.

Instead, I just blurted, "Want to visit a different ranch with me?"

Twenty-Five

Bailey

This horse wasn't Data.

She was beautiful, with a deep chestnut coat and a sweet disposition.

But we didn't have the same mind meld that Data and I did, didn't have the same responsiveness, the same way of predicting what the other was going to do, almost before either of us did.

"What do you think?"

I turned and looked at the hockey player on the horse next to me, his blond hair gleaming in the sunshine.

He dwarfed his horse, was one of those players who made Axel seem small.

But he'd rode his mare like he'd been born in the saddle, and as a woman who'd spent a fair amount of time on horseback, I could appreciate the smooth, easy way that he moved.

"Your man gonna be jealous?"

I blinked, tore my gaze from Cole and his horse.

"Of me appreciating your horsemanship?"

A small grin. "Is that what you're appreciating?"

I eyed him up and down. "How is Axel the small hockey player?"

Cole's grin grew. "Sport's changing. Less about crushing people into the boards and more about skill and speed and finesse. That's why pretty boy"—he nodded to where Axel stood in the distance, a photographer next to him, snapping pictures of the camp's merchandise he was modeling—"is doing well. Decent sized, good foundations, great speed. Even *if* he's old for a rookie."

"And cheap for a model."

A shrug, his eyes dancing with mirth. "It's for the children."

Laughing, I kicked my horse, riding it up to the viewpoint Cole was taking me to while Axel's agent—and Cole's wife—Olivia, and Axel went about their business.

I was dating a model.

That was...hilarious.

But it was also amazing.

Because he was so much more than that. He made me happy. He was thoughtful and not the arrogant asshole I'd first thought he was. Yeah, he was a filthy puckboy, but I liked all those filthy things he did to me. How he touched me and treated me and—

I liked how he was with me.

"He's a good guy."

I blinked, realized I was daydreaming and missing the gorgeous view of the Pacific Ocean in front of me, beach visible in the distance, frothy white caps forming zigzagging lines over the tops of the waves as far as the eye could see.

Beautiful.

Prime real estate.

And Cole hadn't turned it into boring track houses, ruining the landscape all while making a hefty profit.

He was doing something good with it.

"I watched him." A beat. "You know. Watched him for years and wondered why in the fuck he was tanking his career." He paused, and I thought the answer, *knew* the answer.

His mother. What she'd done, supposedly in his name. *For* him.

Even though it was all for everything *she* wanted.

But I didn't speak it out loud.

Cole's expression was approving, and I turned back to the scene below, the scene we'd ridden from because Axel wasn't allowed to ride at the moment, not during the season. Wasn't allowed to do something physical like horseback riding that might result in an injury.

So he was back to being a pretty boy. I grinned, watched as Axel scooped up one of the kids he had been modeling with for the last couple of hours, plunked him on his shoulders and said something that made him laugh.

"He's a good man," Cole said softly.

"Yes, he is."

"I'm glad he's where he should be."

"Modeling for pennies on the dollar with that pretty boy face?"

Cole chuckled. "Damn right. Why do you think I married my shark of an agent?"

"She got you underwear modeling contracts?"

That was Axel's next job, posing in his skivvies.

More laughter. "No underwear. Not for me." A nod. "That one, though, I think he's game."

"Just because he's more comfortable naked than clothed?"

His lips twitched. "I may have heard about the handcuffs."

"My aunt is..." I shrugged. "Well, she has ideas and those ideas..."

"Sometimes result in handcuffs?"

Now I was chuckling. "You're terrible." A beat. "You're doing wonderful things at this ranch. But you're a terrible, terrible man."

His eyes still danced with humor. "Why does that please me?"

More laughter and then I watched Olivia turn toward where we'd paused, her gaze unerringly finding us. She waved.

Cole lifted his hand in answer.

"She can't ride in those heels?" I asked lightly.

A glance in my direction. "You'd be surprised."

I smiled. "You can go back," I murmured. "I'm gonna ride just a little longer."

Cole glanced at me. "If you keep going, the trail will loop and bring you back to camp in about an hour."

I nodded as he turned his horse around and disappeared down the trail.

It wasn't until I'd ridden for almost forty minutes before I realized that I'd been had.

The pergola was alight. There was a blanket on the ground, a couple of baskets, and a small outdoor heater.

And a hockey player.

Wearing a hoodie emblazoned with the ranch's name.

About an hour, my ass.

It'd be a hell of a lot longer than that after I showed Axel my gratitude for—

"Would it be a cliché out of one of your books if I helped you down so our bodies can brush together?"

"Yes." But I reached out to him anyway, shivering when his hands came to my waist and he lifted me off, slowly letting me slide along his body so that every inch of me brushed against every inch of him.

A perfect scene out of a historical romance book—minus the poofy dress.

But still yummy.

"Cliché," he murmured. "But a good one."

I arched against him, felt the length of his cock. "A *big* one."

His smile was a flash of white and then he was reaching behind me for the reins, tying them off on a hook before moving us to the gazebo.

"You don't need to woo me," I whispered.

"I do," he whispered back. "Forever and always."

I sucked in a breath. "You're not supposed to worm your way further into my heart, you know that, right?"

He kissed me.

And then I wasn't thinking about breathing, sucking in, letting it out, or anything in between.

"Plus," he said when we broke apart, casually, as though his chest wasn't heaving, same as mine. "I owe you a first date."

I grinned. "I think we're past that by now, don't you?"

He cupped my cheek. "Never." Then he drew me to the blanket, pulled me into the crux of his arms, long legs bent on either side of me. "Now. I know it only takes you two beers to get sloshed and start taking off your clothes, so"—he kissed the side of my neck, reached forward, and plucked out a bottle—"how many glasses of wine does it take to accomplish the same?"

I turned in the circle of his hold, watched as he poured for us, and smiled. "Let's find out, shall we?"

It had taken us much longer than an hour to get back to camp.

Mostly because we were lying on our backs under the gazebo, bellies full of wine and cheese and the homemade bread that I could have lived on for a long time.

For the next ten years at least.

For the rest of my life.

Now we were staring up at the night sky and I was pleasantly drunk and...

"What about the ranch?" he asked me. "When it's paid off. What will you do then?"

I sighed, watching Orion glimmer in the dark reaches of space. "I'll go back to school. Live that dream of teaching annoying high schoolers."

His arm flexed behind my head. "You'd be a good teacher."

"I wouldn't make them read all that dry as hell 'classic' literature. I..." I smiled, remembering Mr. Lee, one of my favorite teachers at the many schools I attended over the years. "I'd be the cool teacher. The fun one."

"I know you would."

"Because I'm so fun?" I asked dryly. I'd done nothing but work for years, and that hadn't made me particularly happy or a joy to be around.

"You *are* fun." A kiss. "But I think you'd be good, mostly because you care."

That meant...*God.* That meant a lot. Even in my fuzzy, sloshy brain. "Honey," I began.

"I mean it, buttercup."

I knew that.

Which was why it meant so much.

"Honey—"

"I love you," he said. "You're obligated to accept my compliments."

"Axel—"

He bopped me on my nose. "Just accept the compliment."

Irritated—over accepting compliments (and yes, I understood exactly how asinine that was)—I pushed up on my elbow, rolled toward him. "I'm *trying* to take it. If you would just shut up and listen to me—"

He grinned, tweaked my nose. "I know, buttercup." Then his face went serious. "You know I'd pay for it, pay off the mortgage on the ranch, pay for you to go to school, pay for you to move down here or even pay for someone to manage the ranch if that's what you wanted."

And with that offer...

That was the moment I fell in love with Axel all over again.

TWENTY-SIX

AXEL

Her face went gentle in that way it often did for me.

That way I felt right in my heart.

The way that made me want to have her give it to me over and over again.

I lightly tweaked her nose and meant every word as I told her, "You know I'd pay for it, pay off the mortgage on the ranch, pay for you to go school, pay for you to move down here or even pay for someone to manage the ranch if that's what you wanted."

"Honey," she whispered after a long moment. "No."

"I—"

"*No.* Listen." She clambered on top of me, straddling my waist, and resting her hands on my chest. "This isn't something that you can convince me to accept. It isn't a compliment. It isn't you maneuvering around me so that I'll accept some repairs on my house." She stroked her fingers along my jaw. "This isn't something I'll *ever* accept. Gramps and Gran. They worked hard for that land. It's been in my family since the Great Depression, and I've done what I've done to keep it for us, for *them.*"

"I wouldn't expect anything back," I told her. "It would stay in your name, in your family's name."

"I know you wouldn't." A beat. "Because I know you. But it

isn't for my sake or my grandparents' that I wouldn't accept that. I wouldn't accept it because of *you.*"

That...stung.

"I—"

"*Listen,*" she said again. "Your mother always needed something from you, always wanted it and demanded it, and I can't be like her—"

That whipped through me even more violently, even more sharply.

That *burned.*

"You're not her, not in the least." I gripped her arms, wanting to shake her because that notion was so *fucking wrong*. "Not *ever.* You couldn't ever be like her. Just—"

"Honey," she whispered. "Please. Just *listen.*"

I wanted to continue denying it, to rebuke every single bit of bullshit that was currently sliding out of her mouth, to reproach it for the vitriol it was.

But...she'd asked me to listen.

So, I shut up and did so.

"Sweetheart," she said, more gently than she had ever spoken to me. I loved the sass, loved when she snarked back at me, when she was fire and spine and steel. But the soft, the gentle, the way it was just for me, *only* for me...

That burned in a way that was all that much more acutely painful.

That stole my breath and made it hard for me to focus on her words rather than kissing her, *fucking* her under these stars until both of us sank into oblivion.

"You can't pay for my school, my home, my life. You can't because not only do I need to understand that I can take care of myself, but you need to as well. You need to know that I'm okay on my own."

"God, Bailey," I said, sliding my hand up and cupping her cheek. "You're the most capable person I know."

"You need to know," she said again, "that *I'm okay on my own.*"

I inhaled. "Bailey."

"I'm in this. I love you. Not for what you can give me," she whispered, "but because I would be okay on my own without you, without your help, and despite the fact that I *don't* need you, I *choose* to be with you."

I inhaled sharply.

Deeply.

That struck...deep.

"Buttercup."

"I choose *you*. Not some sexy, up-and-coming hockey player who's a pain in my ass."

"I—" A shake of my head. "What?"

"I choose *you*. Not a meal ticket or a man who can do something for me. But you. *Axel Finnegan*. The man I love. The man who loves me back." She wrapped her fingers around my wrist, held my palm to her cheek. "Not for *any* other reason aside from the fact that you own my heart."

My eyes stung. "Fuck, Bailey."

"Do you understand?"

I understood, every *inch* of me understood. I nodded. "I understand."

"So, you'll promise—no maneuvering around me and doing things like going to my bank and paying the mortgage behind my back?"

I scowled.

"Finnegan," she warned. "Promise me you'll let me handle that on my own."

I didn't want to. But I understood, what she needed. What *I* needed. I blew out a frustrated breath. "I promise."

She softened. "Thank you."

"Anything," I whispered. "Anything for you."

Laughter...turning wicked, taking the seriousness out of the moment as she asked, "Anything?"

I slid my hand into her hair, doubled down. "Anything."

"Good," she murmured. "Because I want to teach you to ride."

Frowning, I started to sit up, but she pressed me back down. "You know I can't—"

A nip to my jaw, my throat. "I want to teach you to ride *me*."

Now *wicked* turned my laughter rich and husky. "That"—I flipped us—"I don't need any lessons in."

A raised brow. "Oh?"

I reached for the button of her jeans, smirked. "Oh yeah, buttercup."

"Do you ever think you would move?" I asked.

Her eyes shot to mine, a glimmer of hurt in the chocolate depths.

"I'm not saying to get rid of the ranch," I said quickly, knowing how that came off after all we'd just talked about. "I get how important it is to you." I tugged her closer, held her tighter. "I just...when you manage to pay off the debt, are able to hire someone to manage everything...would you live somewhere else?"

She paused.

For a long time.

Then, "I don't know."

That stung, hurt deeply, even though it shouldn't have. We loved each other, yes. We were together. I wanted her forever.

But we were new.

She wasn't just going to uproot her life, not after she'd fought so hard to cling tightly to it.

I just...kind of wanted her answer to be like, *"Yeah. I want to live with you. Wherever that might take you. Even if you're traded. Even if you move halfway around the world, I'll be with you."*

"Would you?" she asked.

"I'm used to living wherever," I said. "I don't care where I end up. So long as that's with the people—the *person*—I love."

She inhaled. "Speaking of that."

Now *I* inhaled. "Yeah?"

"I was kind of hoping that you would stay."

I frowned.

I mean...I did stay. Every time I was up in River's Bend, I stayed at her place.

"You know, 'cause the long-distance stuff sucks," she said. "So, I was thinking that like...maybe in the off-season you could stay, you know, with me, and then make the ranch your home during the rest of the time—when the hockey schedule allows it...to— and I—"

Funnily enough, her nervousness relaxed me.

It meant she cared enough about me, about us, to be nervous.

And that allowed me to find my way back to me. My annoying, cocky alter ego. The one that she pretended to hate, that she loved despite the fact that it exasperated her, the one that brought out her sass and fire.

Which *I* loved.

"You asking me to move in with you, sugar?"

"I—that's what I—" She froze, her face a mask of disgust. "*Sugar?*"

I grinned, nipped the tip of her nose. "Yeah. Goes well with buttercup, don't you think?"

"Uh, no—"

"No? Okay, well then, it goes well with *honey." I waggled my brows. "Or syrup?"*

A groan, though her eyes flashed with heat, hopefully at the memory of my culinary delights. "You're the worst, Axel Finnegan."

"And by the worst, you mean the best?"

I felt the look she shot me in my cock, as though her fingers had wrapped around it. No. Her mouth, her tongue. "The. Worst."

I shifted closer, trailed my fingers down her spine. "Can I negotiate for more dresser space?"

She swatted me, but now her lips were curving. "Seriously. The. *Worst.*"

A kiss to her jaw. "Hanging room in the closet?"

"The—"

I flipped her over, pinning her between my legs, cupping the side of the throat. "You gave me two drawers, buttercup."

Teeth pressing into her bottom lip. "Yeah."

"You gave me your heart," I said simply.

A roll of her eyes. "I told you I loved you. It's not like I served the organ up on a platter."

"You gave me *you.*"

Her body softened. "I…well…yeah," she whispered.

"Then, as long as I'm with you, I'm home."

That had her lips parting, her eyes warming.

"Yeah," she agreed.

"And have two drawers."

Bailey let her head flop back onto the ground with a groan. "The. Freaking. *Worst.*"

But then she kissed me.

And if that was the *freaking worst,* then I would happily take it every day for the rest of my life.

Especially when she straightened, smirked down at me, and said…

"Okay, I'll give you a third."

Twenty-Seven

Bailey

I'd spent three days with Axel.

In. A. Row.

It was the most since he'd gotten the call-up.

And it had been filled with bickering and fucking and watching him play and lying out beneath the stars...and more fucking and more bickering.

And it had been the best three days ever.

Now, I had to say goodbye and go back to my lonely life without my boyfriend's big cock, and—

Boohoo.

Poor me.

Grinning, I turned off the highway and began weaving through town, eager to get home and see my pooch and my horse and my steer, even as I was mentally crafting the saucy text I was going to send.

Maybe something about how he was going to have to *earn* his three drawers.

Perfect.

That would be perfect.

Couldn't make it *too* easy on him. When we sparred verbally—or otherwise—and he got all growly and turned on...

Chef's kiss.

That would be perfection.

And then I would have a week's worth of saucy to send his way, a week's worth of pent-up Axel Finnegan...and how so sad I would be to have to deal with the fallout from that pent-up week apart, from the mood he'd be in when he came up next Tuesday.

Oh, the humanity.

My cheeks were hurting because I was smiling so widely, but I didn't even care how much of a dork I was.

I was happy.

I was dating a sexy model hockey player with a big dick and a bigger heart.

I was *happy.*

I'd spent too much of my life being miserable to worry about being a dork when I was finally happy.

In fact, I hit the button to roll down my window.

Stuck my head out, felt the wind on my face. "I'm happy!" I yelled into the air. "I'm happy!!"

A dork.

But a happy one.

At least until I turned into my driveway and saw...

It.

There was a real estate sign on my driveway.

Right there, staked into the ground.

Like it belonged there.

Like I'd asked for it.

Like I *wanted* it.

For Sale.

Smothers Holdings.

I'd parked. I'd stopped and parked, staring at the abomination in my driveway, knowing instantly it was Colt, that he'd done this.

That he'd think I would just roll over and die and *accept* this.

That *motherfucker.*

I got back in Gramps's truck, mentally pulling in further,

parking next to the barn, like I did every time I came home.

But then...

Something came over me.

Maybe something as cliché as a cold rage. Maybe something simpler, hotter, burning through me. Maybe something—

My foot hit the gas.

The sign made a satisfying *crunch* as it succumbed to the heavy iron rust bucket that was Gramps's truck.

I reversed.

Heard that crunch again.

And I smiled.

I was still smiling when I pulled up to the offices of Smothers Holdings, Spock in the passenger's seat, happy for the ride. Admittedly, I was less happy and my smile had become more of a grimace in the hour-plus drive to Sacramento.

But my lips were parted. My teeth were showing.

I was smiling.

I was holding on to my happy.

By pure dint.

Screeching into a stall, I shoved out of Gramps's truck. "Stay, Spock," I ordered, cracking the window for him, thankful it wasn't hot. I slammed the door and reached into the bed of my truck, grabbing the largest remaining chunk of the real estate sign. Then I was in through the sliding glass doors.

A receptionist at the half-moon-shaped desk glanced up at me. "Can I..."

"Colt. Where is he?"

"I—I'm sorry. Mr.—"

"Where is he?" I asked on a hiss.

"I—"

Fuck it.

I moved past the desk to the directory posted on the wall. It didn't take long to find him. Not too many assholes named Colt in this world.

And then I was striding down the hall, carrying the sign behind me, barreling toward his office...

Only to find it empty.

That was...disappointing. Infuriating.

Laughter.

Not mine. I hadn't completely lost my mind—not yet, anyway. It was...*his.*

Spinning in a circle, I saw the receptionist had come my way, but I wasn't going to get bogged down in her bullshit, so I moved further, walking away from her.

Spotting him.

Through the window of a conference room.

Perfect.

I shoved through the door, enjoying the shock on the three men's faces when the strange woman with a broken sign burst in—strange to all but one of them, anyway.

I dropped that sign on the wide conference table, smirking when they jumped.

"Baby," Colt began.

It settled frost between my shoulder blades.

"Who're they?" I asked.

Colt's eyes narrowed, taking on a dangerous glint.

"I'm Garret Smothers," the taller of the three said. I should have figured, just based on the expensive suit alone.

I turned to the other man. "And you?"

"*Bailey.*"

A snapped-out rebuke.

One that used to have me rocketing to attention, have me cowering and treading carefully so that he wouldn't lose it, wouldn't step over that edge.

Careful. Careful.

Don't crush any of those shells.

"John Wilkens."

"Owner"—I nodded at Garret—"lackey"—to Colt—"and...?"

"Co-owner," John said.

"Ah."

A pause, long and drawn out. Then Garret spoke. "And you

are?"

"His ex-wife."

The pause was longer this time, more drawn out.

"Want to know why we divorced?"

"Bailey—"

"He beat the shit out of me." Taut air, Colt jerking, taking a step toward me. But I held my ground. "Not once," I pressed on. "*Many* times. But the worst time, the final straw for me was when he broke my ribs and gave me a concussion, when he hit me so hard, so many times that I thought I was going to die in our house." A breath. "So, I ran out, barefoot, not giving a damn that it was raining, that my feet were sliced to shit by the time I got safely away. All I wanted was to get away from *him.*"

"A typical ex-wife," Colt sneered. "Spewing vitriol and—"

"Lies?"

It brought me great satisfaction to cut him off.

"I have pictures," I said softly. "Billie Rose made me take them, even though I wouldn't press charges back then. She made sure I had proof." I turned to John and Garret. "Would you like to see them? Like to see what your employee did to me?"

Colt lurched toward me, fist raised. "You—"

But I wasn't afraid. "There it is." I nodded at his fist, at his expression. "There's the man who hurt me. But," I said, glancing over at John, at Garret, "you probably don't give a shit about him, about me. I do think that you give a fuck about a man illegally listing properties."

Two pairs of brows rose.

"Your parents—"

"Don't own Russet Ranch," I snapped at Colt. "*My* name is on the title. *I* am the one who pays the mortgage. *I* am the one who will decide to sell"—I leaned forward—"and *newsflash,* asshole. I will never agree to sell my home. *Never.*"

I turned back to Garret. "Now I know you've had run-ins with Billie Rose. I know what it's like to have her not be happy with you, the trouble she can bring for you." I narrowed my eyes. "I'd advise you to stop fucking with me, with my land, with the people of River's Bend."

"Now, little girl, I'm not much for hurting women." Garret's gaze pinned me in place. "But I don't take to threats kindly."

"It's not a threat."

I pointed at the sign.

"That is a sign of you overstepping. That is a sign of *him*"—I pointed at Colt—"overstepping in River's Bend. That is the truth. That is *fact*. And if you *really* want to build, want to be part of the future of our town, then don't pressure people. Don't push. Wait for them to sell and then buy your land, build your houses."

Garret rocked back.

"That's not a threat. That's free...*advice*."

I thought I saw a smile on Garret's face, but then Colt was grabbing my arm, jerking me to face him, and—

Suddenly he was six feet away from me, pinned to the wall, and...

Pascal had an arm pressed to his throat.

"You will *not* touch her."

"I—"

Pascal pressed harder, hissing, "You will *not* touch her because if you do, I will *destroy* your life. And *that's* a threat. And *that's* advice—advice I really hope you won't follow because, fuck, what I would *give* to have the opportunity to destroy you piece by piece by *piece*. Now," he said even more intensely, "if you think that I'm going to leave her open for you to take some kind of fucked up revenge, to come back and hurt her as punishment, then think again. I will be *watching*. I will be *waiting* for you to come, to make a mistake, and I will love fucking tearing you apart."

The silence that stretched was quiet, was long, was almost smothering.

And all the while, Colt was turning purple.

I supposed I should be frightened of Pascal, of how he could move, of what he could do. He was effortlessly subduing the man who'd beaten me half to death and not struggling in the least.

He could...he could wreck me.

I just knew that he wouldn't.

Garret broke the silence. "I'll make sure the listing for your property is removed."

"Thank you."

More silence.

Then, "Now, if you don't mind, we have a meeting to finish."

I glanced from Pascal and Colt to Garret and John...

And suddenly I was tired.

So, I just nodded, left the sign where it was, and went out to Gramps's truck.

Not surprised when Pascal met me there, gentle hand on my shoulder, eyes searching my face.

A smile curved his mouth.

"You're going to be okay, Bailey Donovan," he murmured.

I looked at the splinters in the bed of my truck, looked inside *myself*, and I knew he was right.

"Yeah," I whispered.

"Go," he ordered softly. "It's getting late."

"Okay. And...thanks—"

"No thanks necessary."

"I know." I covered his hand with my own. "But thank you all the same."

His face gentled. "We'll keep an eye on you, just to make sure he doesn't decide to do something about that bruised ego."

"Now you're just asking for more gratitude."

A soft groan. "I'm going now."

"Pascal?"

He turned back. "Yeah?"

"Thank you. I mean it. For everything."

"Always." A beat, his lips turning up at the edges. "And remind me to never get on your wrong side."

"Just saying, that's down the barrel of my shotgun."

A grin. "Noted."

And then...

He was gone.

Melting into the shadows. Disappearing from sight.

Gone.

But I knew he was still watching over me as Spock and I drove home.

Twenty-Eight

Axel

It wasn't until a week later that I got the full story of what had happened between Colt and Bailey.

Bailey had given me a bit.

Pascal filled in some more.

But it hadn't been *all* of it.

Not until Bailey had laid it out to me that night, lying on the couch, Spock curled up beside us as we watched a stupid movie on TV, belly full of beer and junk food.

Properly plying me so that I'd take it okay.

No surprise, I didn't.

I hadn't.

How could I?

She'd driven right to her ex, to the ex who had hurt her.

Pascal said she'd been amazing.

Bailey said *he'd* been amazing.

And I...I hadn't been there.

Rage had boiled through me, along with guilt, with disappointment. I *hadn't* been there.

"This is some of that *you have to see that I can take care of myself* bullshit, isn't it?" I'd grumbled.

Which had her cracking up.

Which had her body moving against mine in all the right ways.

Which had led to me moving against her in the *all* the right ways.

Now, she was in the bath and I was unpacking my stuff...into three drawers, thank me very much. But as I went through my duffle, shoving sweats and extra underwear into my drawer, my fingers caught on a folder.

Frowning, I pulled it out, flipped through the pages.

And realized what an idiot I was.

Weeks ago, I'd had someone write up a valuation for the ranch, wanting to know what it was worth, how much was left on the mortgage. How I could help Bailey dig out of her hole.

But then I'd made that annoying—albeit both logical and touching—promise.

To let her make her own way.

And this was worthless.

I'd still thought to show her, just so she knew, had all the information, but after Colt and the For Sale sign and that drive down to Sacramento...

Well, it could all wait.

I shoved the papers in the back of the drawer.

Later I'd show her and she could marvel at how much the land had increased in value, how much equity she now had.

Today, tonight, right *now*, she needed the issue of anything happening to the ranch that didn't involve horses, fencing, cows, and hay to be shoved away, to be forgotten.

I shoved in my final pair of jeans and shut the drawer.

Then I turned for the bathroom and smiled.

She was taking a bath.

I'd see if she wanted a companion.

And then I wouldn't take no for an answer.

Lucky for me, I found that Bailey was always up for a bath buddy.

"You know you've just bought yourself hot cocoa duty at the Winter Festival," Billie Rose said, sitting down next to me and sipping deeply from the mug of hot chocolate I'd made her.

"I think I'm busy that night."

Billie glanced over at me, blond curls bobbing.

"You're not."

Unfortunately, she probably knew my schedule better than I knew it.

So I didn't argue.

"It feels weird to be on this porch with you and not be naked or handcuffed."

She just sipped innocently, eyes in the distance where Bailey had disappeared, riding Data, Spock at their side. "For the record, you were too drunk to remember being naked or handcuffed with me on this porch."

I chuckled. "You know, I never did ask you why you did that."

"Didn't you?"

I just shot her a glare.

"You already know that you like to get naked when you get drunk"—she slanted a look my way—"something you and Bailey have in common."

My glare didn't shift. "And the handcuffs?"

"I had to make sure you didn't wander off." A shrug. "There are dangerous creatures around—rattlesnakes, mountain lions. Hell, we even get the occasional black bear that has wandered out of Tahoe and down through the basin. I wanted you for Bailey, not to be out meandering naked and getting yourself killed."

Woman had a point.

"Did you consider that it was closer and easier to take me to my apartment?"

She took another sip from the mug. "I consider everything."

"Including Joel?"

The mug hit the step next to me with a soft *clink.*

"Joel is an ass."

I nodded. "He sure is. Though he's a *good* ass."

"Is there such a thing as a *good ass?*"

"Yes," I said simply.

She rolled her eyes, picked up her mug. "And anyway, Joel has no bearing on anything. I'm just glad that he's stopped tearing his way through my town." A beat. "Though, you have something to do with that."

I lifted my brows at her. "Though, I could say that *you* had more to do with that."

Billie didn't reply to that, just sipped her hot cocoa and sat silently next to me.

"I never did thank you." A breath, and I forced my tone to be light. "For the handcuffing and the nakedness. *Both* times."

"You're welcome for the handcuffing." She sipped again. "Though not for the nakedness, as we've established that was all you."

"One of my many talents."

"I'm not joking about the hot cocoa for the Winter Festival, you know."

I reclined against the porch pillar. "I know. I'll send you the recipe so that you can have the proper supplies on hand."

She drained her glass, placed it next to her. "If you need extra practice, I'm here as an official taste tester."

"Taking one for the team?"

"Taking one for my hips." She tapped the top of her cup. "And speaking of which...please, sir, my hips would like another."

I laughed, picked up her mug, and stood. "Only one refill per customer. Both for you." A beat. "*And* your hips." A flash of white teeth, her chuckle filling the air. "Plus, Bailey would have us both on the wrong end of her shotgun if we didn't save her any."

"True." I moved to the door. "Though, just saying, Axel..."

I paused, glanced back.

"If you make another batch..."

I lifted my brows.

"It'll give you more practice for the Winter Festival *and* make sure we have enough for Bailey to have seconds"—her smile widened—"or *thirds*, if the batch happens to be big enough."

Sighing, I shook my head.

"Good thing Bailey now has a really big pot."

"And lots of chocolate?" Billie asked hopefully.

"And enough chocolate to fill that really big pot."

Billie Rose grinned.

And I followed the unspoken command.

More hot chocolate, hockey wench, I imagined her order.

So, I was smiling as I moved back into the kitchen and made more hot cocoa.

More for me. For Bailey. And one more for Billie Rose.

And her hips.

Twenty-Nine

Bailey

I was an elf.

Not a sexy elf.

No short green skirt, striped green and white tights.

Just pointed ears, a jaunty hat, and a whole lot of ugly moss and scarlet-colored sweater. With embroidery.

And my man was looking like a snack in a simple polo under a tight black jacket with the Gold logo emblazoned over his heart.

Color me surprised that he had a hot chocolate recipe at all.

And extra surprised that it was fucking delicious.

So delicious that his line was longer than mine.

Though that was probably because he was there and Joel and Ryan had been signed up to help, so there was a trio of hockey yumminess offering cheap chocolate goodness to the masses.

Instead of an unsexy elf with stale candy canes.

Okay, fine.

They probably weren't stale. Billie Rose wouldn't let that happen.

But a woman had to have her excuses.

"I want to see Santa!"

I turned away from my yummy neighbors and glanced down at the little girl. Now *she* looked like a cute elf, complete with the proper outfit—red shoes, green sweater dress, those striped tights I really was going to have to buy for next year.

"Come on," I told her. "You can go right to the front of the line."

Tiny brows pulling together. "There is no line."

Small details.

And too smart for my good.

I unhooked the velvet rope (see? Billie Rose was on point about those details) and ushered her toward the big, red-suited man.

"Make sure you have your list ready!"

The little girl ran forward.

I manned the camera, got the obligatory pictures, and set about printing them out, trying to pretend that I hadn't noticed Billie Rose glaring at Joel from the homemade snow station. We didn't get snow where we were, other than the odd twenty-year storm with an inch or two of snow that didn't really stick. Hail was more likely, though it still didn't stay long on the ground or come all that frequently.

In the distance, there was a small ice rink, and I could see that some of the other Rush players had been roped in to give lessons.

There were lots of happy kids swarming around their legs.

And lots of happy women gathering close, staking their claims, trying to get their hot hockey man for a night or a month or a lifetime.

I was one of those women now, I thought with a small smirk.

Hooked my star to my hot hockey guy.

Grinning, I printed the picture of my cute elf girl and Santa then stuck it in one of the precut cardboard holders that had been ordered for this event. Some foam stickers, a candy cane (not stale) joined it in the bag that I passed over once she'd finished talking to Santa.

By then, my stall was seeing some action, and the next hour of my life was a flurry of ushering kids forward, printing pictures, passing out stickers and candy canes and the occasional hug.

My feet hurt.

My *newly* pointed ears hurt.

My brain hurt.

A hand on my nape, lips at the base of that pointed ear, a warm body shuffling me off to a shadowed alley. "The line—"

"You're on break."

I glanced back, saw that I indeed had been relieved by Dessie, who winked at me and waved me off.

A nudge forward, sending us further away from the bustle of the festival, tucking us into a shadowed alcove, his front to my back, his arms around me. His tongue flicked out, traced the shell of my ear beneath the prosthetic. "These are hot."

I shivered.

"And I'm gonna fuck you in them tonight."

I bit back a moan, started to straighten, but his hands came to my hips, holding me in place.

"That sweater is ugly as sin though." A nip to my earlobe. "I'm going to get that off you and burn it."

"It is *not* ugly."

That was a lie.

My sweater was ugly as sin.

He bent so that his chin rested on my shoulder. "Are these supposed to be candy canes?"

Palms sliding up my sides, stopping just beneath my breasts.

I tilted my head back, nipped at his jaw. "My candy canes aren't ugly."

"Hmm." His fingers drifted, slightly brushing the underside of my breasts, where the curve of the candy canes dipped down. "This sweater is."

I pinched the back of his hand. "Enough about the sweater."

"I'm only stating the truth."

I spun in the circle of his arms, glared at him. "See if I show you *my* candy canes later."

"Just saying, I've spent a lot of time between your thighs, and I haven't seen evidence of any candy canes." A kiss to the tip of my nose. "Though maybe I should buy you some red and white striped lingerie, make you my own personal candy cane, and lick every inch of you."

That was so cheesy.

But fuck if it didn't send a shiver through me.

Sigh.

This man had me so wrapped around his pinky finger it was pathetic.

"If I *had* a candy cane," I said begrudgingly. "I wouldn't let you see it now that you called my sweater ugly."

A nip to the side of my throat. "I bet I could convince you to show me."

"I—"

"What?" He flicked his tongue out. "You think I'm lying?"

He could probably convince me to do anything.

But I couldn't admit that.

"I think that you don't *think* you're lying," I prevaricated.

"Oh now, buttercup." Teeth on my throat, my jaw. "Them's fightin' words."

His hand dipped down, the roughened fingertips brushing against my skin. Oh yeah. I liked the fighting words, liked what they brought me.

How they felt drifting against my clit.

"How are you going to fight me?" I asked breathlessly.

He stepped forward, pressing me against the wall, hand sliding lower, dipping through my wetness.

Yup.

I was wet.

Sigh.

"Hold this for me."

The cup was plunked in my hand and my heart squeezed hard at that glimpse of his huge soft center beneath all my big broody hockey player. Taking care of me.

Bringing me hot cocoa.

Loving me.

I grabbed onto the cup and then his hand was smoothing back along my belly, this one drifting up instead of down, dipping beneath my bra, massaging my breast, dragging across my nipple.

I bit back a moan—

"Bailey."

I stiffened, but didn't get a chance to move before his hands were out from beneath my clothes and I was tucked securely behind him, his big body in front of me, between me...

And I peeked my head around.

Fucking hell.

Axel stood between me and...my mother.

Thirty

Axel

What. The. Fuck?

I was trying to get my girl off into the shadows, to sneak a kiss, a touch, a—

Okay, a quick orgasm for her. A chance to cop a feel for me.

But now her mother—*her mother*—was standing there and—

Seriously.

"What. The. Fuck?" I muttered. "Go away."

"I need to see my *baby!*"

Now her voice was rising, and it was shrill. That awful type of screech that had my eardrums aching in protest.

"I want to see my baby. I need to see her and—"

She *was* shrill.

So I went for calm, strived for calm, held it by the tips of my fingers. Barely.

"This is not the way. If Bailey wants to talk to you, she'll reach out."

Tears in eyes that looked like Bailey's, in a face that looked like the woman I loved...except wrong. "*If* she wants to see me? If my own daughter wants to see me?" A tear slid down her cheek. "My *own* daughter!"

Sweet Christ.

She was exhausting and manipulative and I knew that it was pure show, not only because of what Bailey had told me about her.

But because she reminded me of my own mother.

Which, admittedly, wasn't the best place for my mind to go. Not when I wanted to be calm and in control and steady for Bailey.

"You need to go," I gritted out.

"I will not—"

"Just to clarify, I *know* she doesn't want to see you." I gestured down the street. "So, fuck right off out of her life."

Just that quick, the tears and shrill were gone.

"How do you *know?*" she snapped. "She hasn't sent me away now, has she?"

"I want you to go," Bailey said, calm and steady and…*all Bailey.*

Bailey's mother sputtered. "Wh-what?"

"How could you possibly think that I would want you in my life?" she asked. "After *everything*. After my childhood and the chaos, the selfishness of you and Dad." She paused. "Who's where, by the way?"

"What?"

"Where's Dad?" Bailey asked.

Her mother stiffened.

"Yeah," Bailey said softly. "He's not here. He's *never* around—not when I needed him, probably not when you needed him, either. He might as well be a traffic cone, standing useless and off to the side."

Eyes flashing, Bailey's mother sucked in a breath. "Your father isn't the point. I sacrificed everything for you and—"

Bailey chuckled.

"My life was about—"

"You," Bailey finished. "It was about *you.*" A breath. "Because you've never given me something without strings. Not once."

"I carried you in my *belly*—"

"I'll amend my statement. You've never done anything for me beyond keeping me alive." Bailey stepped up to my side, wrapped her arm around my waist, and leaned close. "And that's more than some people get, so, lucky me, right?"

"I—"

She cut her mother off. "But I wasn't lucky. I was stuck with you, with Dad, with that chaos and drama and sneaking off in the middle of the night, moving before someone could come after us for overdue rent, always being forced to leave things behind, never able to trust that the connections I was making were going to be for a few days or weeks or months, if the time was going to be so short that it was pointless to get attached—"

Her voice broke and I laced our fingers together, held tight to her hand.

I wanted to step in.

Wanted to sweep her away.

But...she needed to do this, needed to do it for herself...

And...

She needed to do it for me as well.

Because seeing her like this, understanding this part of her—the strength in the face of pain, the courage to keep pushing—and the pride I felt for her...

Well, for a moment, it even eclipsed the love I had for her.

Just for a few seconds.

Because then the love was swelling up, sucked back like water along the ocean floor, resembling a beach before a tsunami and then the wave was slamming forward, crashing into me, eclipsing every emotion in me.

Except love.

Then it was just *love*.

"You did that," Bailey whispered. "You hurt me over and over again. But I could have forgiven you then if not for how you acted when I came to you about Colt." Her voice raised. "You encouraged me to go back to him. After he beat me. *Me.* Your daughter." She shook her head. "*That* was the moment I knew that you wouldn't love me or maybe *can't* love me, maybe you can't love anyone but yourself. Because if you did, if you actually cared about me...how could you send me back?"

I squeezed her hand, trying to temper my fury, mindful of my strength, not wanting to hurt her, not ever.

Because she'd been hurt too much already.

"You did all of that and then you *still* went behind my back and tried to sell the ranch. The *ranch!* Dad grew up there." She tossed up her free hand. "For all intents and purposes, I grew up there, too. For *all intents and purposes*, it's the only home *I've ever* known. And you tried to sell it. To have my abusive ex-husband sell it." She dropped her hand, let it land at her side, her voice dropping alongside it. "And if the fucked-up scheme had worked, who would get the money? You and Dad? Colt?" She laughed. "Because I know it wouldn't be me. It would *never* be me."

"Baby."

This time it wasn't shrill.

But it was manufactured all the same.

Pathetic. Destroyed. Fake tears out of Bailey's mother's eyes.

"Baby, I would never—"

"You would. You have. You would again," Bailey said. "In a heartbeat."

"I—"

Her voice was all sharp edges, all pain. "I paid you for that land." A beat. "Three years ago. I paid you." Bailey sighed. "So where did the money go?"

"I—"

"Here's the thing, *Mom*," Bailey said over her, not giving her the chance to answer, and her next words explained why. "I don't care where the money went. I don't care about Colt any longer. I don't care that you and Dad are out of money or got fucked over by some get rich quick venture again. I *don't* care."

More tears. More pathetic in her mother's voice. "You would say that to me? Your—"

"I'm going to stop you right there," I finally interjected.

Mostly because the moment that Bailey had uttered that last *I don't care*, she'd slumped against me and begun shaking.

And she'd shown her strength.

She'd proved how tough and brave she could be.

But I was done letting her carry this alone. I was down with her proving to herself that she could handle her own shit, but I wasn't cool with her shouldering this by herself. I was here. I was hers. We held hands and muddled through the shit times so that we could enjoy the good ones.

I slipped my fingers free of hers and wrapped my arm around her, tucking her close, holding her tight.

Then I turned back to her mother.

"Bailey is *mine* and I will go to any length to protect her."

A toss of her head. "That's good—"

"Let me clarify," I said. "I will protect her from you. From her shit of an ex and her useless traffic cone of a father. I will protect her from anyone who would hurt her or fuck her over or accidentally step on her goddamn pinky toe."

Flashing eyes, a venomous glare. "You—"

"She is mine," I snapped, "and I don't take kindly to people trying to fuck with what is mine." I stepped forward, bent so that my face was level with hers. "You got your money for the ranch. You got your time tonight, you had your chance to be a part of her life for twenty-five fucking years." I jabbed a finger in her direction. "But *you* fucked that up. So" —I leaned a little closer— "I am *telling* you that we're done here. *Done*. And the next time that you show your face, I *will* get the police involved."

Bailey's mom sucked in a deep breath, shoulders lifting, lungs expanding.

I held her gaze, willing her to see the intensity of my determination, and waited, ready to deal with the explosion when that air she'd sucked in was let loose.

But instead...

She surprised me, spinning on her heel and disappearing into the crowd without another word.

Bailey released a shaky breath.

"Well done, buttercup."

Her head jerked away from where her mother had disappeared, and she glanced up at me.

And then she was in my arms, her mouth on mine. I heard a crinkle, felt warm liquid gush down my side, and spared a moment of prayer for her hot cocoa (and for the fact it was no longer burning hot, but rather *warm* chocolate as it soaked into my clothes).

"Oh shit," she said, jerking back. "I'm sor—"

I just lowered my head, kissed away her apology. “It’s nothing, buttercup. Nothing at all.”

“I—”

“*Nothing.*”

A breath, nostrils flaring, and then she slumped against me. “Okay.” Her arms came around my middle. Her forehead rested on my chest. “*Okay.*”

I smoothed a hand down her back, down along that ugly as sin sweater. “Think Billie Rose will let us off early since I need to change now?”

She lifted her head, grinned up at me. “I think Billie Rose probably has a whole wardrobe at the ready, just for this eventuality.”

I laughed. “*I* think...” I kissed her nose, because it was cute and *there* and *cute.* “You’re right.”

A smile, finally a real one that settled my protective instincts, calmed the urge I was feeling to go after her mother and tear her to shreds.

Alas, I didn’t want to go to jail.

I wanted to be right here with the woman I loved.

Though, preferably, without the side of wet shirt and pants.

She kissed my pec through the fabric. “Damn right I am.” She started to straighten. “Let’s find you something dry to wear.”

Fingers on her cheek, sliding down, resting on the side of her throat, stilling her when she would have moved away. “Promise me that if she shows up again, you’ll call the sheriff and file a report, try for a restraining order?”

“We collecting those fuckers?” she quipped.

I brushed my thumb over her pulse point. “Fuckers referring to people or the paperwork?”

A flash of white. “Either. Both.”

I smiled back. “Hopefully, if we collect enough of the latter, then we can avoid the former?”

Her eyes gentled, palm smoothing over my cheek. “Still no sign of Candi?”

I shook my head. “We have the fake name, and they’re scouring social media for any profiles. But right now, there’s nothing that Pascal can find.”

"Shit," she whispered.

"You let me handle it, okay?"

One brow lifted. "Because you're a big macho male?"

I brushed my finger over it. "Because...there's nothing more either of us can do and Pascal is already working his magic, so there's nothing to do but worry." I covered her hand with my own. "And you've got enough to worry about."

A frown. "We're supposed to—"

"Worry about pointless shit neither of us can fix at this moment?"

"Yeah. *That.*" She narrowed her eyes at me. "I'm supposed to worry and care about you."

When had I had that?

Never.

And fuck, my heart. It couldn't take this, couldn't take her, the love, her care.

"So," I said, "just to clarify, this is us agreeing that we both get to worry about pointless shit neither of us can fix?"

A brush of her lips over mine, allowing me to taste her smile. "Damn right it is."

"Collecting restraining orders like candy. Worrying for no reason." I tucked her close to my side and turned us back to the festival, waving a hand in front of us as though I were a magician about to reveal my best trick. "What's next for us?"

Now she smiled and it was warm...but it wasn't soft. It was full of that tsunami of love I felt, that maelstrom in my belly, the one ripping me from shore and propelling me right toward it again, faster than my eyes could process.

"Everything," she vowed. "What's next for us is *everything.*"

She was right.

In that moment, I just...

Didn't understand all that *everything* encompassed.

Thirty-One

Bailey

"I feel like we should be bringing more than just some alcohol."

I held up the twelve-pack of craft beer I'd picked up for the annual Gold holiday party—Axel was carrying two others—and was regretting not stopping at Costco.

Those pumpkin pies were delicious and huge.

A couple of them could fill up some hockey players' bellies, right?

Add in a few cans of whipped cream and call me Martha Stewart.

Axel leaned in and kissed me on the temple. "I was given strict instructions as what to bring." He gave me a lazy grin. "Apparently, without carefully detailed commands, the potluck ends up being one main course, beer, and a shit-ton of pies."

I nearly missed the step leading up onto the wide craftsman-style porch.

Carefully detailed instructions.

Right.

So maybe I wasn't anywhere in the realm of Martha.

Alas.

Oh well, I'd survive.

Hopefully with plenty of pie in my belly and an aunt who was willing to watch my mischievous dog at some point again in the near future.

Just before we'd parked, I'd gotten a text.

It was just a photograph of another chewed-up pair of heels.

Spock despised footwear that hurt women—at least, that was what I was trying to convince Billie Rose of.

She wasn't exactly impressed.

And I made a mental note to buy her a gift card as a thank you...and to replace the heels.

Grinning, I got it together and moved up the steps next to Axel, opening the door for him when we both spotted the sign taped in its center announcing to *Come Right In*.

We did.

Went right in, and stepped *right*...into chaos.

Kids were running in all directions. The conversations were a wall of noise. The people...oh God, there were a lot of them.

Holy bejeezus, there were a *lot* of people.

And none of whom I recognized.

The urge to run was strong with this one—*this one* meaning me.

But Axel didn't falter, just shifted the twelve-packs he was carrying so he had two in one hand, wrapped his other arm around me, and waded into the fold.

Tugging me along behind him.

Eeek.

People greeted him as we made our way through and they were friendly enough when he introduced me that the cacophony of sights and sounds—*and smells*, I realized—began to have less impact on my mind. I began to be able to focus more, to listen and smile and pick out which of the people were the hockey players and which were staff and which were...

Like me.

Girlfriends.

Wives.

A stutter in my heart. Maybe someday.

Eeek, indeed.

"And this is Bailey," Axel said, thankfully drawing me out of my eeeking.

I waved. “Nice to meet you, Coop,” I murmured, and then when they began talking shop, I took a moment to look for some place to set the beer down.

Which Axel noticed, of course.

And apparently Coop noticed as well.

As Axel said, “We’re going to find some place to go put these—”

Coop plucked the twelve-pack out of my hands. “I’ll show you guys where the coolers are.”

The protest that I could carry it was on the tip of my tongue.

But I was waylaid by—

“Bailey!”

Startled, I glanced down, saw the little boy from the family suite a couple of weeks ago, the one who had been having the time of his life with slime.

Today, thankfully for the state of my one nice pair of jeans, he was slime-free.

“Aiden!” I said back, bending and offering up my palm for a high five. “How’s the slime making?”

He pressed his lips together, nose wrinkling.

Uh-oh.

“I got it on the carpet and Mom got mad,” he grumbled.

Carpet and slime seemed like the worse combination of worlds.

“Were you supposed to take it on the carpet?”

His nose wrinkled further. “No.”

“What happened?”

He was full-on scowl now. “I had to scrape the slime off with a butter knife.”

I smothered my smile. “That sounds like a lot of work.”

“It was.” All that was missing from his pout were his crossed arms.

Curious, I asked, “Are you going to bring the slime on the carpet again?”

Now those arms crossed to complete the affect, and he sighed. “No,” he muttered.

“Well then, it sounds like your mom did good parenting.”

A sigh and more muttering. "Yeah."

That pout didn't fade, and call me a softy, but I couldn't take it. "Maybe you could show me how to make slime sometime?" He perked up. "I've never done it before."

"Really? Never *ever?*"

"Never *ever,*" I told him solemnly.

His eyes went wide, lips parting and...

Then he screamed.

"Mom!"

I jumped, nearly fell back on my ass.

A slender blonde with a little girl propped on her hip spun, as though her superpower was somehow being able to know exactly when her kids were calling out their version of "*Mom!*"

"Bailey has never made slime." A beat. "Never *ever.*"

Her face softened as she walked over to us. "No?"

"Uh-uh."

"Well"—she tapped her chin with one manicured finger—"I guess we'll have to have another slime making day and invite Bailey."

A fist pump, no pout in sight. "Yes!"

Then he was gone, his yell of "Maddy! We're going to make *slime!*" echoing through the party.

She smiled down at me, extending her hand and helping me up.

Not that I needed it.

But the gesture was kind and warmed me in places that had long been cold.

"Thanks," I said once I was standing.

"I'm Anna."

"Bailey," I said unnecessarily.

Her blue eyes sparkled with humor. "I know." A smile. "Though not just from my son."

"Team gossip?"

"Team gossip," she affirmed. "You're as pretty as they said."

My brows drew together. I was wearing my nice jeans and a Christmas sweater that was decidedly *not* ugly—mostly because it was a deep green that I thought went with my skin tone well and that was only mostly *because* I hadn't bought it (I had Billie Rose to thank for that). Anna was...beautiful. Like one of those angel statues.

She was a woman who belonged with these men.

Sleek and slender and blond.

And wearing a black dress and heels I could never *ever*—here I smiled, sucking back the comparisons, knowing they would only drive me crazy—pull off.

"That dress is beautiful," I told her honestly.

Another smile. "Thanks." Then her expression went knowing. "Overwhelmed?"

"With this crowd?" I asked lightly.

Her eyes danced. "I think this crowd overwhelms more often than not." She leaned in, lifted a brow. "Want a pro tip?"

"Absolutely."

She widened her eyes. "Don't show fear."

Those were not the comforting words I'd expected to hear.

Anna's solemn lasted for approximately two-point-two more seconds. Then she bent over, laughter rocking her frame. "I'm just fucking with you," she managed to gasp out after a moment. "Oh God, your face." More laughter before she got it together, and I found myself chuckling alongside her, not minding being the punchline of this particular joke.

It didn't feel like she was ridiculing me.

It was...like we were all part of the joke and so it was okay to laugh about it. Laugh about this wild life and the crowd of hot hockey players and the slime-obsessed kids.

It was like...I didn't have to pass some sort of test to be welcomed in, didn't need to survive a hazing ritual. I was enough without having to make my way through the *Legends of the Hidden Temple* course, avoiding temple guards as I scrambled to collect the Life Pendants and—

I was losing my mind.

Just a little bit.

Mostly because...this was...

Nice.

So *nice* that my laughter faded, and my eyes stung.

And...

Anna slung an arm around my shoulders, turned me in the direction of the huge island that was dominating the packed kitchen. "Come on. Let's get something to eat."

"It's pie," I whispered approximately two minutes later, having made my way through the clusters of people (all of whom smiled and nodded or exchanged a brief greeting with me as we walked).

I was staring at the big island.

And...there was only pie.

Anna grinned.

But it was Brit who gave me the explanation. "It's tradition. Pie for dinner. Real food for dessert." She chuckled at my expression. "Comes from the first time we tried to do this. Most of the guys were single, didn't know how to bring anything but beer and chips and pies." Her smile was huge and had been plastered on many a billboard advertising a popular toothpaste brand.

My lips twitched. "So, pies for dinner?"

A shrug. "It stuck. Plus, it's Cheat Day." She reached for a knife. "So we get to go wild. And"—that smile again—"you get to go wild along with us."

"Shit," I whispered when my eyes burned, just a little bit.

"What?" she whispered back.

"You guys are too good to be true."

"No," she said gently. "We're nosy and annoying, and you'll probably be pulling your hair out before long."

"Family," I said.

"Family," she agreed. And then she grabbed a plate, slung a piece of pumpkin pie on it, and held it out to me. "But the good news?"

I nodded as I took the plate.

"New family eats first."

My lips twitched. That *was* good news. Especially considering the crowd.

A fork was tucked next to my slice of pie, and then she turned to the room, announced over the din. "All right, peeps! Soup's on!"

Thirty-Two

Axel

I was in a sugar coma.

I thought I'd eaten the equivalent of one turkey breast, a dollop of mashed potatoes, and about six pieces of pie.

And Bailey was curled up next to me, watching the final showdown in *Ticket to Ride.*

"They're ruthless," she whispered, her eyes glittering with amusement when they hit mine.

"You're just saying that because you were knocked out in the first round."

"Like I said"—a grin—"they're ruthless."

"Or cheaters."

A poke to my chest. "You're just saying *that* because you got knocked out in the third round."

"No!" Mandy cried, clutching her hands to her chest and falling back on the rug.

Coop jumped up. "Fuck yeah!" Then he immediately clamped a hand over his mouth. "I mean...uh...woohoo!"

Mandy glared at him.

"You, ma'am, are just glaring because I won," he countered. "The kids have heard worse, and anyway"—he glanced over his shoulder as though double-checking his statement before he said it —"they're all watching the movie outside."

Bailey chuckled, and I took her hand, hauled her to her feet, and led her into the front room, leaving Coop and Mandy to finish up their trash talk...and clean up the board.

The winner's spoils.

Putting all the pieces back.

Grinning, I took a detour beneath the mistletoe then we found a spot on the couch. It was covered in the remnants of wrapping paper from the kids' present opening earlier that evening, and there were crumbs and empty wine glasses and mostly eaten pieces of pie all around.

I made a mental note to clear some of them so the mess wouldn't be too terrible for Brit and Stefan.

"I didn't get it," Bailey whispered. "When you talked about how they were, I thought it was total bullshit, some PR nonsense they fed the public with carefully crafted Instagram posts. But it's real. All of it." She glanced up at me. "Even the way they welcomed me. They truly *welcomed* me."

"Yeah, I know." I tucked her hair behind her ear. "No joke, it wigged me out the first time I experienced it."

She sighed, leaned into me, her hand resting on my thigh, and by the way her fingers drifted upward, tracing nonsensical patterns along the inside of my thigh, I knew she was one eggnog away from stripping down.

I should get her home.

But sitting here with the noise around us yet cocooned in our own little slice of peace, was perfection.

So, though I captured her hand, stilling the movements, I didn't get off the couch.

I just sat there with the lights of the Christmas tree glimmering around us, and I knew that I'd never had a better holiday.

Never.

A lot of it was because of this team.

Even more was because of this woman.

But the last of it, that bit had come from me.

I'd helped create this.

And that realization had a jagged piece deep in my belly filing itself smooth. That serrated spike had been buried so deep that I hadn't realized it was there still, jabbing at me. I'd thought them all long gone, all long smoothed out.

They weren't apparently.

But that one was gone now.

I breathed long and slow and deep, holding Bailey tighter when she sighed, her eyes closing as she leaned even more heavily against me.

Because she'd known.

She had understood there were still edges to me, still spikes wounding me, even though they were buried.

Entombed so deeply that I didn't know they existed.

She'd known.

And now, because of her, another had disappeared.

I glanced down to ask her if she wanted to go.

What came out instead, was "I love you."

I tucked her into the corner of the couch, covered her with a blanket.

And then I set about cleaning up some plates.

"Here."

I glanced from *Home Alone* down to the package she'd tossed on my bare chest.

We were on our second watch through because Bailey hadn't seen it, and we'd gotten naked halfway through the film, missing a lot of the antics, and since it was the best Christmas movie of all Christmas movies, I had declared Bailey needed to see it from start to finish without missing any of the good stuff in between.

So, we'd started it over.

I didn't mind.

Not when it meant she cuddled close.

Not when it meant we were taking advantage of one of my last days off before I had to drive back down to San Francisco to get ready for a road trip and series of tight home and home games that would take me away from my woman for nearly two weeks.

"What's this?"

Christmas was tomorrow. We had that.

Then on Boxing Day (we had to throw a bone to our Canadian brethren), I'd drive home in the afternoon, sleep in my bed, and get my ass up early to catch the team flight.

I still couldn't believe I wasn't going to park my ass on a bus, spend hours crammed in with my teammates while driving to San Diego or Stockton or San Jose.

But I wasn't living while holding my breath, thinking that I was going to have it all ripped away from me in an instant.

I was *living.*

For now. For the future.

But none of that changed the fact that my woman had just tossed me a cheerfully wrapped package, even though it wasn't Christmas.

It wasn't time for presents yet.

And that fact had me frowning at Bailey and sitting up, capturing the package before it slid off my chest. "What are you doing, buttercup?"

A defiant look. "I'm starting a tradition."

"With presents?" I asked. "That's for tomorrow."

A shrug, a bit of pink hitting her cheeks. But her chin came up, and she gave me that tart I loved so much. "It's *my* tradition. I can do what I want."

"Or we could wait"—I glanced at my phone—"thirty-two more minutes and it would technically be Christmas...where this tradition fits."

Now she sighed. "Why am I in love with a man who's such a pain in the ass?"

"Do you really want me to answer that?"

"Is it going to involve some innuendo about you fucking my ass?"

"Do you want me to answer *that?*"

Bailey dropped her head back, eyes on the ceiling. "Why?"

I wrapped an arm around her waist, dragged her on top of me. "You love me."

A glare in my direction—her pouty lips and wrinkled nose so fucking cute that I had to kiss her.

So I did.

And then, when we were both breathing heavy, I released her. "Should I open my present?"

"Like I've been trying to get you to do for the last ten minutes?"

"Don't make me kiss you again."

Her eyes narrowed. "Just open the present, or *I'm* going to."

I snatched it back when she reached for it. "Don't think so. It's *mine.*"

A huff.

But when I drew us both up on the bed, propped us against the headboard, she didn't complain. She didn't say much of anything, actually. I slanted a careful look her way, taking stock of her expression, the emotions in her eyes.

She was...nervous, I realized.

"Is this the moment that I should tell you the wrapping paper is ugly as sin?"

A hand on my chest, propping herself up—all the better to glare down at me.

But she knew me, knew my game.

Knew I was trying to irritate her, to get her out of her own head, and because I liked the sass, because that sass she threw my way meant that she wasn't closing down on me, wasn't locking me out of her heart, her head.

Which was why she cupped my jaw, brushed her lips over mine. "Stop worrying about me—and *my* worrying—and just open the fucking present."

I shut up.

I stopped pushing and poking and prodding (and worrying)...

And I opened the *fucking present.*

But I wasn't prepared for what was inside.

"So, you don't have to pretend that wind blew open the door," she said, referencing the first time I'd been in this house, the first time I'd gotten a glimpse of who Bailey was beneath her hard shell.

Soft and sweet and loving.

Mine.

Mine to keep, to protect, to...reveal myself to.

To give her every bit of myself.

I grabbed the key to her house, held it close to my pounding heart, feeling like the sappiest motherfucker on the planet.

But this meant *everything.*

"I'm so getting *four* drawers."

She opened her mouth, ready to give more sass...

So I kissed her.

For so long that we had to start the movie over for a third time.

Thirty-Three

Bailey

I abhorred roses.

Except when Axel gave them to me.

Yup.

I was an ooey gooey puddle of slime because my boyfriend had bought me a bouquet of crimson roses...

And crimson lingerie.

And a toy.

I grinned.

I'd enjoyed that toy a whole hell of a lot before we'd gotten dressed again (and funny story, I was wearing that crimson lingerie beneath my dress...a dress that Anna had helped me pick out).

Axel and I were on a date.

A real date.

Dinner. A show. Walking around the city in an obscenely short dress and heels that I was teetering in, just a little bit.

Holding hands.

Tucked close to his side.

Of course, we'd fucked like rabbits in the hotel room *before* we'd gotten dressed up and gone out to dinner.

Out of order.

But I'd needed a shower after the long drive down—thankful

that, though still into major mischief at seemingly every opportunity—Spock had lost his taste for Billie Rose's heels.

She was much more willing to watch him when she wasn't losing her footwear.

So, I'd made the drive, gotten the shower...

And Axel had needed to join me beneath the hot stream of water.

Needed.

Yup.

Now we were tucked into a shadowy corner booth, eating steaks and crab legs and chocolate cake that was sinfully rich.

And Axel's big, hot palm was drifting higher and higher up my bare thigh, finger occasionally brushing along the lace covering me.

Lace that was growing damper by the moment.

Which he knew—or felt, I supposed—considering the smirk he was wearing on that pretty, pretty face.

Just as I was getting ready to say let's forget the show and go back to the hotel for round two, I heard, "Ex-excuse me?"

We were tucked in our shadowy booth.

In a fancy restaurant.

On Valentine's Day.

But there was a teenage boy in front of us, shifting from side to side. "I'm sorry to interrupt—"

Axel slid his hand out from my dress.

"But I just wanted to see—"

An older woman came up beside him, and it only took a glance to glimpse the family resemblance between them.

"Carter," she hissed. "I told you that you could absolutely *not* come over here and bother—"

The teenager—the kid, *really*—looked ready to die a thousand deaths, right then and there, but before I could open my mouth and save him, Axel had squeezed my thigh and was up and out of the booth, extending his hand (thankfully *not* the one that had been under my dress mere moments before).

"Carter?"

The kid nodded energetically. "And you're Axel Finnegan," he breathed.

Axel smiled. "Yeah. You play?"

Another energetic nod. "Yeah. I want to be in the NHL one day."

"Keep working hard, yeah?" Axel encouraged.

"Yeah," the kid breathed, nodding vigorously.

"Want a picture?" Axel asked after a few moments where the kid just stared and seemed to forget why he'd come over.

Kid was turning into a bobblehead.

I smothered a grin, extended my hand, offering, "I'll take it if you give me your phone."

The kid's cell was in my hand an instant later and then Axel had slung his arm around Carter's shoulders, and I was taking a couple shots.

I glanced around the phone, caught his mom's eyes. "Want to get in on this one?"

Pink on her cheeks as she started to shake her head. "I—"

My smile was gentle. "It's okay," I told her. "Really."

She stepped in.

I snapped a few more shots.

Then I handed the phone back and spent the next couple of minutes chatting with Carter's mom, who spent the first half of those minutes apologizing for interrupting and then the second half of those minutes thanking me for giving Carter this time.

"It's nothing," I said. "I promise."

"Really, man?" I heard Carter exclaim. "You don't have to—"

Axel ruffled his hair. "Friday. Go to the Will Call window and tickets will be waiting for you."

The kid's smile was *huge.* "Whoa, that's awesome. Thank you."

"We should go," Carter's mom said, tugging at her son's arm. "Leave you two to your dinner."

"It's—"

But then they were gone.

I slid back into the booth. Axel slid into the other side, his body coming flush with mine.

"Was that..." I glanced around, dropped my voice. "Was that your first public recognition?"

His eyes were wide. "Yeah. I mean, *here* it was. River's Bend doesn't count because everyone knows everyone else already. But here...in the city? Yes," he whispered. "That was the first time."

"How'd it feel?"

He stilled then whispered, "I don't...actually I don't really know."

I grinned, poked his shoulder. "It felt *awesome!*" I bumped his arm with my own. "You can admit that much."

A breath, his eyes focusing. "Okay, it felt *awesome.*"

"Good." I leaned closer, nibbled at my bottom lip. "Axel?"

"Yeah?"

"I think you owe me a celebratory kiss."

Heat in his eyes. "Yeah?"

I nodded, playing at being a bobblehead myself. "Yeah."

His palm on my cheek, thumb drifting across my bottom lip, pressing down slightly. "Yeah," he murmured.

And then he kissed me.

Long and hard and with too much tongue for a restaurant... even *if* we were in a shadowy booth.

Eventually, though, we had to pull back, if only to pay our bill and leave, since our show was starting soon.

We walked to the front door, and I shivered when he helped me into my coat, sliding my hair free before he straightened the collar then bent to press a kiss to my nape.

I turned, touched his jaw. "Thanks, honey."

A half smile that sent a bolt of heat through me. I'd seen that smile when he was between my legs, smirking up at me because he'd made me come *again.*

"I love you," I whispered.

"I know."

Groaning, I let my head fall back. "You can't be quoting the wrong *Star* to me."

"*Trek*, *Wars*, what's the difference?"

I pretended to sputter, knowing he was just trying to irritate me. Because then he would kiss me and try to make that irritation go away (which also usually worked...both the trying to irritate *and* the disappearing of that irritation).

But I also knew him well enough to understand that he was playing.

With me.

Teasing.

Me.

Loving.

Me.

"Them's fighting words," I said playfully as we stepped out onto the street, a cold gust of wind driving me into his arms—or at least, that was what I was telling myself.

Truthfully, he was the opposite dipole of my magnet.

When we were close, I wanted to be plastered to him.

Luckily, he didn't seem to mind.

Not at that moment—when he curled his arms around me, plastering me against his body. Not ever—his arm always coming around me or his hand taking mine or his body close enough that I could feel the heat of his.

"I like your fight."

"I know," I quipped.

His mouth tipped up.

And despite his poking of the bear, despite the cold air and the holiday and our tickets to the show, I wanted to sit in what had just happened inside. "You had a fan come up to you," I whispered. "Recognize *you.* Want to be *you.*"

"It wasn't—"

I stopped him before he could demure further, rising on tiptoe and pressing a finger to his lips. "It was about you. *You.*" I cupped his cheek. "And you deserve it, honey," I told him earnestly. "I am *so fucking* proud of you."

"Buttercup—"

"You," I repeated. "I am proud of *you.*"

He inhaled sharply.

And I took advantage, pressing my lips to his, accepting the hard kiss he gave me in return, feeling all the emotion he was pouring into it, into me, into *us.*

"You," I said again when he released me.

His eyes were a little glassy, but he just smoothed his thumb over my lip, spun me so my side was tucked into his, and wrapped his arm around me.

Keeping me close.

Loving me.

I smiled, rested my head on his arm, content to just walk beside him.

Content until we turned a corner and I caught a flash of blond, of something familiar...*someone* familiar.

"You good?"

I didn't realize I'd stopped, not until Axel cupped my cheek, tilted my head up.

"I'm fine. I just—"

I glanced back.

Just a crowd.

Not one familiar face.

Shaking myself, I smiled up at the man I loved. "Let's get this show over with." My smile turned wicked. "So, we can go back to the hotel, and I can give you *my* show."

Thirty-Four

Axel

"We've got a hit on Facebook," Pascal told me. "Her full name is Candice Walters."

Candice Walters.

That sounded respectable.

It didn't sound like a buxom blonde with a penchant for glitter who'd spied on me while I fucked a woman and then later had broken into my hotel room and tried to separate me and Bailey.

I didn't know her.

And she'd somehow fashioned in her mind that we should be together.

Which was crazy and dangerous and had *hurt* Bailey.

So, Pascal getting a hit on Candi's real name, him getting me one step closer to being able to keep a record of that crazy, to file a restraining order that would hopefully stop her from wanting to come around me was a good thing.

"Won't be long now," Pascal said. "And if the restraining order doesn't deter any future interactions...I'll have a word with her."

I didn't know what that word was, nor what it might be.

I only knew that it would be scary.

I only knew that it would certainly convince her to keep her distance if she ignored the restraining order.

"Thanks." I leaned back against the wall of his office, the space surprisingly messy—including his single visitor's chair, which was full of papers and files. Forcing my gaze from that, I held his stare. "I mean that, and I want to pay—"

"No thanks needed," he said. "And you gave me a deposit so I could pay my guys. We go over that, I'll let you know."

"I—"

"You gonna argue with me about keeping your woman safe, son?"

"You need to be compensated—"

"I have plenty of money. But a good job, good people—" A pause that said...well, more than Pascal usually ever said. "I'm good." His eyes sliced through me. "And I'll let you know when I'm not."

No lie, that sent a little shiver of fear down my spine.

Because...Pascal was scary.

But luckily for me, all that scary was currently being used for my good.

"Okay."

"Okay."

I might have thought that was a dismissal, except for the fact that Pascal had asked me to meet him in his office after practice to discuss two things.

Candi was one.

The other—

Pascal picked up a folder, opened it. "I just got word from my guy up in River's Bend. Colt hasn't been seen around town at all since Bailey and him had their *chat*"—which was a nice euphemism for Bailey's sign wielding, along with Pascal's threatening (both of which I would have paid to have seen)—"and word has it that he's moved up to Eureka since he's no longer working for Garret Smothers. Trying to start his own real estate company."

The inflection on trying told me that it hadn't been successful and that it probably wouldn't be.

But there was distance between my woman and that man.

And I couldn't give two fucks about the bastard, so long as he kept well away.

"I'll keep regular tabs on him, but—for now—with Colt gone and Candi nearly run to ground, it's probably safe to pull my guy off Bailey in River's Bend."

I didn't like that.

It was logical.

Pascal was the expert in this situation.

But my woman...

I didn't like the term *probably* safe.

Pascal's mouth curved as he closed the file and set it on a teetering stack. "We'll keep him there for another week."

"You don't have to."

"Another week." And *that* was a dismissal. So, I didn't protest, just nodded, gave him another "Thanks" that I knew he was going to ignore since gratitude made him uncomfortable, and hit the hallway.

"Axel."

I turned and I couldn't help the nerves that immediately began swirling in my belly. Authority did that to a person who cared, and the man standing in the hall ten feet behind me was the ultimate authority for the Gold.

Pierre Barie.

Stefan's father.

Brit's father-in-law.

And the boss of all my bosses because he owned the Gold and the Rush.

So, yeah, even though I'd been playing well and producing, and the scoresheet had my name on it more often than not (and not just because I was spending all my time sitting in the penalty box), the nerves still hit me, hard and fast and *intense*.

"Mr. Barie."

"Pierre."

Yeah, that wasn't going to happen, though I nodded in agreement, not about to argue with the boss of all my bosses.

The silence stretched.

And all the while my stomach churned as I waited.

The last time I'd seen this man, he'd hijacked my workout from hell—*hell* because I'd been putting myself through the wringer, trying to avoid Bailey, and more importantly trying to avoid what I *felt* about Bailey.

The last time I'd seen this man, he'd told me I'd had potential, had fire for the game, for my career, for my future...and I'd pissed it all away.

The last time I'd seen this man, he'd made it clear that he saw I could find that fire again.

And I had.

But was it not enough?

So even if I wanted to speak, wanted to find the words, I knew I couldn't open my mouth.

I might vomit on his shoes. Hell, my throat was so dry, my tongue felt so swollen that I didn't think it could actually help me form words.

Thankfully, he didn't need me to.

After that long, intense moment of quiet, he broke the silence.

"You found it."

Three words, but they freed my throat, shrank my tongue. "I found *her*."

Twinkling blue eyes. "You found her, and she led you back to it."

I'd worked my ass off to get here. I *still* worked as hard as I could, tried to take advantage of every opportunity and advantage and bit of help, training, and coaching that came my way.

But there was absolutely not one fucking bit of doubt in my mind that if not for Bailey, I wouldn't be here.

"Yes," I agreed.

Solemn blue eyes, studying me like he could see into the depths of my very soul. Maybe he could. Maybe that was his fucking superpower, or maybe the fact that I loved Bailey with every single part of my being was just so fucking obvious to every other person on the planet that it wasn't hard to see.

To know what was driving me.

To understand it wasn't because Bailey wanted me to be successful in the league, wasn't that she wanted to date a professional hockey player, wanted to be with someone who made a lot of money or was on TV and the occasional billboard (and slightly more than occasional online ad) selling underwear.

I was here, now, because Bailey had made me *see.*

That I wasn't my past, even though the mistakes riddling it were vast, were awful, made me more than a bit of an asshole.

That I wasn't my mother, who made my mistakes, my multitude of fuckups seem like they were equivalent to winning a Nobel Prize.

That I wasn't defined by what I did on the ice, or even what I did when I was off it.

I was...a culmination of all those things.

But more importantly, more impactful than that entire list of all the things I wasn't, she saw that it was who I was inside that defined me.

Not the asshole who was afraid to let anyone get close, lest I get hurt.

But the man inside, who craved someone I could call mine, craved a place in a family that was healthy and loving, even if that family wasn't related by blood.

Me.

What I needed.

Who I was beneath the shield.

Me.

And that man, stripped of barriers and shields and protective asshole insulation, was enough.

Just me.

Pierre patted me on the shoulder.

"Welcome back."

Thirty-Five

Bailey

It was my third hockey game. Ever.

And it was like I was a newbie all over again.

Not that the two previous games I'd gone to made me an expert, but it was a completely new experience rooting for the *away* team.

And doing it while watching *playoff* hockey.

I wasn't sitting in the Gold Mine.

I wasn't surrounded by fans rooting for *my* players.

In fact, I was a shining gold gem in a sea of teal, easily picked off by the ocean of San Jose fans. I'd better watch out and keep my shouts of encouragement to myself, otherwise the foam board shark teeth cut-out a pair of teenage girls were wielding behind my head might come for me.

The lights dimmed and the players darted out onto the ice, skating a couple of laps, rolling their shoulders, lining up for the anthem.

It was loud—cheers filling the older arena.

But—I smirked to myself—not as loud as the Gold Mine.

That noise had my ears hurting, the screams having me consider earplugs. These were...meh. Good.

Just not as good as *my* boys.

Though, of course, I may be biased.

Okay, I *was* biased, especially as I watched Axel complete his laps and take his place on the bench. He was the prettiest and most talented hockey player of all time. *Right*. Now I actually let my smirk free as they all took their positions. He was *my* big, broody hockey player and *I* thought he was the best ever.

Mentally, I shrugged.

Perspective.

I had *one* of them.

And the fact that I got to go home and fuck him? That I got to go home and *love* him?

Small details.

Best. *Ever*.

Grinning, I stood as the lights overhead grew bright and saw the carpet rolled out near the boards, a teal-jersey-wearing singer already holding the microphone and waiting for her cue to belt out the anthem.

The music went.

She sang.

The crowd cheered, adding a few good-natured "You suck!" calls during the second verse...as one did (though I didn't love when Finnegan got his turn).

But then the anthem was over.

The crowd was sitting.

And the puck had been dropped.

It was intense, even more than the game I'd made it to a few weeks back. I'd wanted to come to more—and had watched nearly every game Axel played in, at least on TV—but the schedule was tough, and Axel preferred that if I drove down, we actually spent time together. Not just a few stolen hours in the evening before I had to go home, or he needed to go to practice. But *actual* time together that didn't have thousands of people, ice, and glass between us.

So, we took advantage of his days off.

But this was probably going to be the last game I could make it to for a while.

The cows were almost ready to go to market.

Not just for me, but for all my neighbors. The next few weeks would be a flurry of work for me up at the various ranches in River's Bend and, if Axel and the Gold managed to keep winning, their work wouldn't stop either.

This was crunch time for both of us.

But Axel and the guys needed to just focus on one game at a time.

I crossed my fingers, heart in my throat, and tried to breathe. This was only game one in the series. There was still lots of time for the matchup to go either way, so there were plenty of opportunities, even if they did lose tonight, for the guys to win four games and move on. But the stakes were higher, and my body knew that, was pumping me full of nerves and adrenaline.

If that was happening to *me*, I could hardly fathom what the actual players were going through.

Give me manure and repairing fencing every single day.

"Ooh!" the crowd said, and I winced at the hit Coop took along the boards.

The *boom* from the contact was loud enough to reach my ears even over the noise and I held my breath as Coop got up, the boards still shaking, the glass rocking back and forth in a way that seemed like it was going to fall out from the metal holders on both sides. But get up Coop did, hardly missing a step as he sprinted up the ice, joining in the play.

And seriously, *give me cow shit* any day of the week.

I groaned when San Jose scored.

Cheered when the Gold got one back.

Clenched my hands together when Brit took on and shut down a breakaway.

Cheered again when Axel's line scored (and he made a beautiful pass—see? My hockey knowledge was improving).

And then clutched my hands back together as the game went back and forth, good scoring opportunities to be had on both ends of the ice.

The final buzzer went off, and the teams circled up near their benches, players patting each other on the backs before heading back to their respective locker rooms.

I finally breathed...then cheered my freaking head off.

Because the Gold had won, two to one.

Axel glanced up at me, smiled that special smile, the one that was just for me.

My heart squeezed as I smiled back and watched him disappear into the bowels of the arena. I didn't bother standing, didn't worry about winding my way through the departing crowd. I stayed seated, waiting in my seat for a while, knowing it would take a bit for the fans to disperse out the exits, to get in their cars and drive home. Just like it would take a while for Axel to finish what he needed to after the game—media requests, cooldown, shower.

He'd meet me when that was all done.

And it sometimes took a while.

Not that I minded.

I was content to be here, to give him something back when he'd given me so much.

I waited until the rows around me were empty then made my way up the stairs and into the concourse, pit stopping in the now uncrowded bathroom before making my way to my own exit.

He'd take the bus back to the Gold's practice facility and pick up his car.

I'd be in his bed by then.

Naked.

And I really wouldn't be sad with the way he woke me up.

I was speaking from personal experience...of his tongue and fingers and cock.

Heh.

My smile hurt my cheeks as I exited the arena and headed to my own vehicle, unlocking the doors and starting to get in when I saw the scrap of paper on my windshield.

I snagged it, frowned when all that was written on it was *Bitch.*

Well, I supposed I *had* parked pretty close to the line on the passenger side.

Either that or the Gold license plate holder that Axel had given me a few weeks back hadn't been appreciated after they'd beat the home team that night.

Shrugging, I balled the note, shoved it into the cubby in the driver's side door then hefted myself up into Gramps's truck.

I drove to Axel's apartment.

I got naked.

And...he woke me up in the most glorious way ever.

I went back to River's Bend the following morning, Spock and Billie Rose greeting me in the driveway with kisses—both on my cheeks, one albeit much more wet.

I sorted the ranch and my chores.

Axel and the Gold got back to work.

And as the days wore on and my knee-deep adventure in cattle, manure, and getting calves and heifers and steers ready for market began, the Gold *kept* winning.

The first round—four games to three.

The second—four to one.

The third—four to three.

And finally, they sailed into the fourth and final round, the Cup within grasp. The series was brutal, the teams tied two games to two.

And that...

That was when everything fell apart.

Thirty-Six

Axel

I'd gotten used to the pressure.

Kind of.

It was...not exactly bearable.

But I was tolerating it well enough.

Or had been.

After tonight though? My body was tired. I was sore from head to toe, and ibuprofen, massages, and ice baths were my best friends of late.

But I didn't have any major injuries.

Rome was playing with a broken thumb, Coop had a sprained back, Ethan was sporting a bruise the size of a locomotive on his ribs. Blue had a stress fracture in his ankle, Ben had stitches on his arm from an errant skate blade. Brit had tweaked her groin.

Logan, Kayden, Josh, and the rest of the team were in my camp —healthy, but tired, sore, and trying to focus on the goal within our grasp.

The Cup was close.

We needed to win two more.

Because we'd lost tonight, and for the first time in the playoffs, we were down in a series.

Now we were in a sudden death situation—win or it was all

over, and we had to do it on the road, away from our support system, our normal routines, our families.

Christ.

This sucked.

I was tired, so damned tired.

I wanted to be done.

I wanted—

A bump on my shoulder had me glancing up, looking into Brit's milk chocolate eyes. She'd played well tonight, but had left the game early.

"How's the groin?"

A shrug. "Everything hurts at this point in the season," she said. "But we'll survive."

"Yeah."

Another nudge. "You played good tonight," she said. "One of the few of us who did."

"You—"

She handed me a towel. "I'm giving you a compliment."

I wiped the sweat from my face, grunting softly in answer.

"Thanks, Brit, you played great, too," she said in a rough—and terrible—approximation of my voice. "We couldn't do it without you." Still in a rough voice. "We couldn't do *anything* without you."

I chuckled despite myself. "It's funny because it's true," I told her.

She tossed me one of her award-winning smiles. "I know."

I slung the towel around my neck. I needed to summon up my energy, to get in the shower, get home, get some rest.

All the gets.

Bailey might still be up if I hurried up and got my shit together.

But I didn't move.

I felt...off.

Wrong.

"You know," Brit said. "I've had a lot of coaches in my life."

I slanted a look her way, lifted my brows.

We'd *all* had a lot of coaches by the time we made it to the Big

Show. Dozens of them, at least. Maybe more than that if I considered them all from the time I first began playing.

"Yeah," I prompted when she didn't go on.

"But I had one that really stood out."

I waited.

Prompted her with "Yeah" again when she didn't fill in the rest of the blanks for me.

"He was an asshole most of the time, old, crotchety as fuck, and had gotten his PhD in screaming."

That sounded familiar.

"Occasionally, though, he gave us a gem to hold on to, something that made me not hate his guts, at least for a few moments."

"Are you about to impart to me one of those gems?"

"Ding. Ding. Ding." She tapped her nose. "Got it in one."

"And that gem is?"

"Flush it away."

She'd given me that advice once, way at the beginning of the season, when I was just squeaking out an occasional game in the big leagues.

And I'd flushed the bullshit way.

"I remember that."

A lifted brow. "You sure about that?"

"I think I'd remember hockey advice packaged as a toilet analogy."

She grinned. "Okay, that's fair. But that's not the entirety of the gem I wanted to share."

Heaven help me.

"Hit me," I ordered.

"Flush it away." I nearly groaned. "Or sit in the pile of shit forever."

"How poetic," I muttered.

She laughed. "That was Coach. A poet, right down in his cold, dead heart." A beat. "But he was right about it. We either sit in our own misery, sit in our own shit, or we flush it down the drain." That *poetry* was accompanied by a jaunty bend of her finger, mimicking the flushing of a toilet, and hell if I didn't laugh.

Which earned me another bump.

"Take a breath, flush it down, regroup." She stood. "Trust the process and refocus for the next game. We'll get them."

"How do you know?"

A pat to her sweat-clad legs. "I feel it in these old bones."

Snorting, the idea of her, a woman in her thirties, calling herself old—especially one who played as well as she did, even if retirement was in her future—was absurd.

But her grin told me she knew it was absurd.

So did her pat on my knee. "Flush it down, and put these young bones to work. Keep doing what you're doing and..."

"Flush the bad stuff down."

"Yes!" A beat. "But, also, no." She crouched a little so that we were eye to eye, her standing, me sitting. "We got this, yeah?" Her eyes went to mine, held for a long moment, and then she repeated, "Yeah?"

Her belief slid through me, curled around my mind, my heart, my *belly*.

And I knew we had it too.

"Yeah," I agreed.

"That's fucking *right*." A punch to my shoulder before she straightened, turned away, though not before tossing over her shoulder. "But for fuck's sake, *Balls,* take a goddamned shower. You stink."

Then she was gone.

And so used to the nickname—rendered from my Harvest Festival crystal ball fortune-telling self—I ignored it.

I didn't ignore her advice, though.

Just stood up, stripped down, and got my ass into the shower.

After, smelling much cleaner (and theoretically now up to Brit's smell standards), I went back to my locker and started getting dressed.

Underwear. Socks. Pants. Shirt. Shoes.

Except as I shoved my foot into my shoe, something crinkled.

Which was...weird as fuck.

I toed it off, reached my hand in, and tugged out the small piece of paper. It was a crumbled label for...a type of lotion?

Weird.

But the guys used weird shit all the time.

Even—I took one more glance at the label before crumpling it up and tossing it in the trash—lotion with glitter in it.

Probably something that found its way from one of the guys' kiddos or wives.

Likely it had been bandied around the room while I'd been giving interviews or had been balled up and launched at someone's head, starting shit...or ending it...or just blowing off some steam pre- or post-game.

Either way, that glitter lotion bullshit was now in the trash.

And my feet were in my shoes, minus the crinkling.

I shrugged into my jacket, slid on my belt, pocketed my cell and wallet, noting on the former that Bailey had ordered me to text her, no matter how late.

I sighed.

Flush the B.S. away.

Refocus and regroup.

I tugged out my cell, sat back down on the bench.

The room was empty, and it was late. Bailey had to get up early. I shouldn't bother her, shouldn't keep her up any later. But I still unlocked my phone and hit her contact anyway. I told myself that it was to put her at ease earlier than if I waited to call until I got to my car or until I made it home. That calling her *now* was better for her.

But it was better for me.

Because I knew of no easier way to get my head sorted, to flush it all down, than to talk to my woman.

The phone rang.

Bailey picked up before it rang a second time. "Hey, honey," she said gently.

And...I was right.

That soft *honey* had the shit flushed right down.

Not even five seconds and she got my head straight.

Thirty-Seven

Bailey

Hot coffee. Cold air.

A pupper at my side.

Cattle to be sorted.

But the trucks would be here soon, and my calves would be loaded first, then the extra heifers and steers that I couldn't afford to feed any longer would make it on the next truck. Both would still bring a good profit, especially since all of our neighboring ranches had pooled our resources and herds so that we saved on transport costs, shared expenses, and got a better deal at the auction.

This year we were trying for two trips to market.

Our normal late spring and one in December to take advantage of the increasing frequency of off-season calves and the changing California weather—shorter winter, warmer months.

Go us.

Marketing extraordinaries who were hustling-hustling (and yes, I sang that in my head every time I thought about it).

We weren't big ranches, but together we brought a decent haul, and if we were smart, that haul meant we were all set for the year. A second auction would just be icing on the cake...and hopefully my ticket to paying off the last of the second mortgage and go toward tuition for my credentials and hiring someone to take over the brunt of the ranch duties so I could actually attend classes.

I told Axel I'd find a way.

I had.

I was just lucky that my neighbors were on board and willing to take advice from a woman who was relatively new to the business.

Though, Tommy and Hank and Eli knew me, had known my grandparents, and I'd earned their respect these last years, earned the right to propose something, earned the right to try something new, earned the right to run the ranch like Gramps might have.

But just right then, I was sitting on my porch, thinking about cows and Axel and my life.

So different from what I'd planned.

And I was still happy.

Smiling, I sipped my coffee, feeling settled in a way I had never expected. Part of that came from handling my own shit—airing out shit with my mom, confronting Colt, sorting out my finances so that I had a full fridge and didn't have to subsist solely on sandwiches and hard work, planning for the future. But the rest of it came from having a person in my life who treated me like an equal.

I didn't have to agree with everything Axel said, didn't have to walk on tiptoe or hide parts of myself or be hurt.

We were equals.

And...he had turned to me when he needed me, wanting to hash out the tough game from a couple of nights ago, needing me to help him get his head sorted.

That had—

Well, there had been a lot of moments with Axel that I could pinpoint where I might have fallen in love with him if I hadn't already been in deep, hadn't already passed over my heart to him.

I just...

Didn't expect them to keep coming, to keep falling in love with him deeper and deeper.

It was more than I expected, more than I'd ever hoped for.

I was happy. I was settled. I was standing on my porch wanting him to be there, but knowing that us being apart was okay, too.

Look at me, being all sappy at a quarter to five in the morning.

Grinning, I brought my mug back inside, Spock trailing me as I took my mug to the sink, setting it inside, and heard the sound of the trucks approaching, smiling when I thought that perhaps the anticipation, the adrenaline already flowing, the way my body went into an instant ready mode might be a little like what Axel experienced before he jumped on the ice.

I'd have to ask him.

But later.

Because gravel was crunching.

My neighbors were rolling in. We had cattle we needed to sort and get on a truck.

It was my version of game time

It was go time.

The water was still running brown.

I was standing in the shower, letting the water flow over me, trying to summon the energy to reach for the loofa and add some soap to the party.

So far, that battle hadn't been won.

I was just under the warm stream of water, letting it soothe my sore, overworked muscles and congratulating myself on a day that had gone well.

It was done. The trucks were loaded. The calves and culled heifers and bulls were all off to auction.

We could breathe.

For a few moments anyway.

Smiling, I snatched the loofa, loaded it with soap, and set about cleaning myself of the layers of dirt.

It took a while, but in the end, I was clean and smelling like my normal apple-scented self.

I managed the energy to shampoo and condition my hair then sat in the hot water for just a few more minutes because it felt so freaking good.

Then I dried off and slapped some moisturizer on my face and moved into the bedroom.

Pajamas.

Text Axel to let him know I was done.

Then sleep...for a thousand years. Or until tomorrow, when I vegged out, did the bare minimum around the ranch, and then cuddled up on my couch with copious amounts of snacks to watch Axel kick some hockey ass.

Grinning, I scratched Spock's ears then turned to the dresser, started to tug open my drawer, intent on my pajamas, but stopped, my fingers on the handle. I didn't want to wear my boring tank and shorts. I wanted to wear something that belonged to my man.

I said that to myself as though it were a new thought.

But really, I'd been having this little battle—pretending like I should wear my clothes then stopping and opening up Axel's drawer, tugging out one of his shirts and wearing it instead—for weeks now.

Long enough that I'd started to deplete his supply of tees.

Well—I mentally shrugged—I guess tomorrow would be laundry day.

My lips twitched. If could lift my arms that was.

So maybe the next day.

Laughing to myself, I tugged open the drawer, snagged a tee, one of the few that were left in the back.

But as I was tugging it out, it caught on something.

Frowning, I bent closer, yanked a little harder, saw the edge of a...folder?

Which was weird, but I was tugging hard now, until I was a little worried about ripping the shirt, but whether it was autopilot or just fatigue seeping into my mind and making it hard for me to shift tasks, I didn't know. All I understood was that it was like my body had taken over my brain and I couldn't stop, couldn't let the shirt go, close the drawer, and put on my own pajamas.

Instead, I'd started pulling and I couldn't let it go, not until it was free.

I wanted the shirt.

I needed it.

And...I had it.

The shirt suddenly came free, and I'd been pulling so hard that I stumbled back a few feet, nearly fell right onto my ass.

But the tee wasn't the only thing that suddenly came free.

The folder did too.

And papers flew...everywhere.

"Fuck," I whispered, tugging the shirt over my head before squatting down, intent on gathering up the papers, putting them back in the folder. I'd explain to Axel. I'd apologize. I'd—

I froze.

Because during my fretting, I'd already snagged most of the papers, was stacking them up, but then I actually saw what they were.

Saw that they were a real estate valuation.

Of my ranch.

In my house. My dresser. *My* drawer.

No. They were in *Axel's* drawer.

Axel had a real estate evaluation in his drawer.

After everything—after I'd shared how important the ranch was to me, to my grandparents, to my future, after the bullshit with Colt, after these *months* together, giving him everything I was, everything I hope to be—he had a valuation for selling *my* ranch in one of the drawers I'd given him.

I'd given *him.*

Hurt was a blistering firestorm through me, burning my insides, my throat, the backs of my eyes.

But I didn't cry.

Couldn't cry.

I just let that hurt burn through me, scald me, and set fire to all the pain seeing those papers created.

I was too tired, too weak, and then thankfully, too...numb to cry.

So, I curled up in my bed.

Spock curled up next to me.

And I slept.

Thirty-Eight

Axel

I hadn't heard from Bailey the night before, but I tried not to worry.

She'd warned me the day would be long and that she might not have the time to talk at the end of it.

I'd figured she'd text me though.

We always texted before we went to bed, even if it was a quick, *I'm home. I'm thinking of you. Night*, kind of thing.

But last night.

Nothing.

And I hadn't wanted to text her, hadn't wanted to risk waking her up if she was sleeping.

She worked too hard as it was.

I was in a hotel room, alone, and clearly the one of us with more time on our hands, at least for the moment.

So, I was watching TV, trying not to worry, and killing time before we took the bus to the arena.

And finally, *finally*, she FaceTimed me.

"Thank God," I whispered, shutting off the TV, and answering the call.

The video came through and I'd already been smiling, but one glance of her face had my smile fading.

"What is it?" I asked quickly. "Are you okay?"

The silence, the pause...they both killed me.

Then she held up a paper. "Why is there a real estate valuation hidden in the back of your drawer?"

My gut clenched.

Hard, fast, tight.

Painful knots that stole my words at exactly the wrong time. What I should have been doing was explaining immediately that I had it done way before we'd had a conversation about her needing to figure out her finances and the ranch on her own. What I should have told her was that I'd had it done before we'd had our conversation about how important the ranch was to her in terms of her grandparents and her family heritage (her parents excluded).

But all I could do was swallow hard, clear my throat, and die slowly, painfully inside while the words slowly, painfully died in the back of my throat before they could make it to my tongue.

"I can't believe you did this to me," she whispered, and the quiet, shaking words sliced through me.

A thousand slices.

A hundred punches to my gut.

"You really have nothing to say to me?" she whispered.

And that, finally, shook off the fog, loosened my throat. "Bailey." Except, that was as far as I got, was as far as I managed before my words stoppered up, before I stood there like a useless pile of crap.

She paused, waited for me to talk, to say more than her name.

I didn't.

I couldn't.

Then she shook her head, sighed, and the look flashing across her face...

I'd hurt her. I wasn't doing anything about it, wasn't fixing it. I wasn't any better than her ex, her parents. I wasn't—

Going to do *this*.

"Wait," I blurted when I saw her finger moving to the bottom of the screen, knowing she was going to end the call. "Just. Please. Let me explain."

Her hand dropped back to her side, but she didn't say anything, didn't reply.

Just waited.

Like I'd asked.

I inhaled, released it slowly. "I had that done months ago. Right after I found out about the second mortgage."

She didn't respond.

"I—then we had that conversation at Cole's ranch, you talked to me about what Russet Ranch meant to you, and I knew the report wouldn't matter. I just put it out of my mind, didn't pursue it." I shook my head as my phone buzzed, telling me it was almost time to head down for the bus. "But I didn't cancel it. I'd already paid the real estate agent for her time, and I figured even though you weren't going to sell, it would be good information for you to have, to know how much it's worth now."

"So why didn't you show it to me?"

"Because I got it back shortly after all the shit went down with Colt trying to list your place. I wasn't going to talk about it with you then—"

"Why?"

The sharp question had me freezing again, my throat struggling to allow words through.

"I didn't want you to think I was pushing you to sell, especially after you'd dealt with Colt." I cleared my throat. "And because I'd forgotten I even asked for it until it was delivered, and then since I was heading out on the road, I just threw it into the bag I was packing. It was a big one, 'cause I had to fill up the drawers you'd given me." I tried for a smile, but her face didn't change.

She just lifted a hand, rubbed her forehead. "I don't know why you hid it."

I'd come home, grabbed the bag, gotten into my car, and immediately headed up to Bailey.

I hadn't been thinking about the valuation.

I hadn't been thinking about anything except getting to Bailey.

"I wasn't thinking," I admitted. "I just made a pit stop to grab the duffle and went up to see you."

"But you hid it in the back of the drawer."

"I didn't hide it."

She dropped her hand, lifted her brows.

"I was unpacking and I came across it and you'd had a shit week and I wasn't going to bring up a sore subject about something that didn't matter."

"Axel," she sighed.

"And because I didn't want you to think that I was trying to pressure you to sell."

She was quiet, for a long, long time.

"Buttercup?"

A breath, and then she rubbed her forehead again. "I need to think about this."

"Bailey, honey—"

"We're supposed to be partners. You're supposed to be my equal, to share stuff, not to hide it and—"

"Trust me," I said, and my phone buzzed again with the reminder that I needed to get downstairs, to catch the bus to the arena. "Please just...*trust* me. Look at the dates. Look and read the report—"

"I read every word."

"Buttercup."

"I *read every word*."

She sighed and though her voice was soft, the pain in it cut right through me. "I have...I've trusted you, trusted you with everything I ever was and ever hope to be and I trusted you with *me*. I trusted you to do the same, to share the same, not to keep things from me because you need to protect me, because you don't think I can handle—"

"Bailey, that's not it at all," I protested. "You're one of the strongest people I know. You're my partner. Please don't doubt that for a moment."

"This—" A shake of her head. "I need time."

"Please, honey. Please just—"

There was a knock at my door.

I glanced up.

"This is—"

"Time to go, motherfucker!" Logan yelled through the door.

She sighed. "This is shit timing," she whispered. "I'm sorry. You have a game you need to focus on. An important one. I shouldn't have done this now, not when you're playing for the fucking *Stanley Cup.*"

"You're more important," I said.

And meant it.

She was, and there would never be a moment in my life when I doubted it.

"Honey," she whispered.

"Wakie wakie, Balls!" Logan yelled. "Time to get pumped!"

I ignored him. "Bailey—"

"This is your dream, Axel." A breath that rattled through the speakers. "This"—she held up the papers—"can wait. It can all wait. Focus on the game. We'll talk tomorrow."

This was my nightmare.

I didn't want to talk to her tomorrow.

I wanted to erase the hurt from her eyes. Right then.

"You're right," I said. "You're right that I should have just told you. I'm so sorry. I—"

One more knock.

"Go," she whispered.

"Buttercup."

"I'm fine. *We're* fine. I'm sorry, too." But she didn't sound fine. She didn't look fine. I didn't *feel* fine. "This isn't the time. We'll talk tomorrow."

"We should talk now."

"Axel. Go, honey. We'll talk tomorrow."

Not one edge of soft in her tone. Not one opening that I could see in her face.

Just hurt.

"I love you," I whispered.

"Tomorrow," she whispered back.

And then she hung up.

Thirty-Nine

Bailey

I sighed as I reined Data in.

It was just me, Picard, and Spock on the ranch (and two hundred head of cattle). My boarding horses had been gone for the last week with their owners on a long trip out of state and wouldn't be back for a couple more weeks.

So today, it was just me and my animals and the ranch.

Just me, in my life, and not struggling for a change.

Not financially.

Not stuck in an abusive relationship.

Not dragged down by my family.

I had friends, was building my own family, and I'd picked the worst time ever to throw a wrench into my life, to do my level best to implode it.

Why had I confronted Axel earlier that morning?

I should have just waited until he was in town and we were together to bring it up.

I should have waited until the series was over.

I sighed.

I had shit timing.

Mostly because I knew that me thinking I should have waited to confront him meant that I was thinking I should have done exactly what he *had* done.

I wanted to protect him. *Should* have protected him.

And it wouldn't have been lying to him or thinking that he couldn't handle the tough stuff in our lives. It wouldn't have been thinking he wasn't my equal.

It would have been choosing the right time to talk to him.

Instead of going zero to a hundred, not thinking of the consequences, and barreling through.

Fucking our relationship up, dumping shit on him when he was on the other side of the country and unreachable and playing one of the biggest games of his career.

And I'd barreled. I'd fucked up. I hadn't thought or loved or protected.

I was his girlfriend. I should be thinking of ways to make his life easier, just like he did for me all the fucking *time.*

"Shit," I muttered.

God. I was such an idiot.

And I couldn't call him. He wouldn't have his phone. The players weren't allowed to have them this close to game time.

I still tugged my cell out of the saddle bag and sent him a text anyway.

Because I was an idiot. Because I wanted him to know that, to know I was sorry.

Because he'd told me he loved me, and *I'd* told *him* that I would talk to him tomorrow.

The last time I'd done something this stupid, had run off without thinking, it had bought me a four-hour tear-filled drive with my parents and ex waiting for me at the end of it.

This time...

I might have really fucked up Axel's headspace.

And that might mean that I'd really fucked up his game, his team, his career...the close family he was building.

"Fuck," I whispered, wanting him to text back, to see my message and feel better about the fight, hoping he wouldn't hold my idiocy against me, even though I knew he couldn't see my text, wouldn't for a while, knew that he wouldn't be able to respond.

So, I was riding around the ranch on Data, Spock at my side, and sitting in my misery.

But now I was back at the barn.

I was at the house with all its reminders.

I was watching my adorable—and still mischievous—pup, watching the puppy *Axel* had given to me run circles around Data, yipping as he chased bugs, stuffing his nose into the gaps of the fencing to check out Picard, who mooed back in greeting.

And their antics made me feel a little better.

I'd find a way to make it right.

And Axel would be okay. He was a professional, just one piece in a tapestry of other professionals. He'd put me out of his mind.

He'd focus.

He'd play some hockey and tomorrow we'd talk and—

It would all be okay.

It wasn't okay.

He was a mess.

Christ.

Nothing was working.

Passes were off, shots were blocked or went wide. He'd even fallen in the middle of the ice, when no one was even near him.

But more than that, I could see it in his eyes.

See that he wasn't there.

I'd done that.

Fuck.

And I was trapped on the other side of the country, fucking hamstringed from being able to help him, and I couldn't do jack shit but watch him struggle, watch him hurt, watch his game play get worse and worse and *worse* as the period went on.

And it wasn't just affecting him.

It was affecting the entire team.

My fault. My fault. My—

Fucking hell. *Fucking*—

My gaze caught on my cell, sitting on the coffee table, the screen black. Billie Rose had called earlier, asking if I wanted to go into town, but I had put her off, claiming fatigue for yesterday. Thankfully, she'd bought my excuse and had left me to my own devices, aka misery.

I wished I could talk to Axel, could apologize.

Could make it right so that he could start kicking some hockey ass.

But I couldn't hop on a plane and get there in time, couldn't get in my car and drive to the arena, couldn't do anything but watch my boyfriend fall apart on national television.

"Fuck," I whispered, picking up my phone, scrolling through.

As though me looking through my messages might actually make a bit of difference, might change something.

But there was nothing.

Just my text from that afternoon. Axel's from the day before.

And a long chain from a few days before with several of the women from the Gold, trying to organize a girl's night that worked with everyone's schedules—Brit, Anna, Calle, Mandy—

Wait.

Mandy.

Brit was on the ice.

Anna was home with her and Blue's kiddos.

Calle was on the bench, coaching the team my actions were threatening to implode.

But Mandy...Mandy was a trainer. She was behind the scenes, was certainly watching the game, helping anyone who needed it. But she might have her cell.

She might be able to help me get a message to Axel.

She might be able to help me get Axel's head straight, to help me get the team back on track.

She might not pick up.

She—

"Fuck it."

I selected her contact, hit the button, and listened as the call rang through. Listened as it rang once, twice, three times. Then rang a fourth, sending my heart sinking. But even then, I planned my voicemail, was already drafting my follow-up text that I would send right after I hung up, when I heard, "Hello?"

For a second, I almost thought that it was my imagination, that I was hearing things in my mind.

Then I heard, "Bailey, hello? Are you okay?"

And I snapped up, sitting ramrod stiff. "Mandy."

She'd picked up.

She needed me to talk.

I needed to do it soon and—

"Bailey."

Sharper now. Calling me to focus.

"Mandy," I whispered. "Oh my God. I fucked up. I really, really fucked everything up."

"Breathe, honey. Tell me what's wrong."

So much.

So many stupid things.

"I need your help."

"I'm here."

She was, I knew she was.

So, I took a breath...and I told her everything.

And then Mandy and I came up with a plan.

Forty

Axel

I fumbled the pass and immediately was picked, my opponent snagging the puck, taking off for our zone, for Brit.

Creating another scoring opportunity.

We were already down two and didn't need to be digging out of an even bigger hole.

But if I didn't get my ass back, that was a real possibility.

I scrambled, fought to keep my edge, and then started skating back, closing in on the player, putting enough pressure on that Brit made the save, kicking the rebound out into the corner.

From there it was a fight to get it clear of our zone, to just survive the pressure from the other team long enough for us to get to the bench, to let someone else come on the ice and hopefully do something better than the shit I was shoveling out.

My lungs squeezed, air rushing out when I was checked into the boards.

Nothing I didn't deserve.

It was shit. The game was shit. *I* was shit.

But I managed to get the puck over the fucking blue line.

Then I hauled my ass to the bench.

I couldn't make eye contact with Calle, couldn't let myself see what was probably going to be disappointment in her eyes.

So, I just kept my gaze on my hands.

Get it together, Finnegan.

I was fucking trying. We were all out there. We were all scrabbling. We were all doing...well, not our best since we were fucking up left and right.

We were trying.

It just...wasn't good enough.

Not even close.

Don't think like that. Don't focus on the shit. Flush it down. Flush it away.

I was trying to flush. I was trying to let it all be washed down the drain.

But the goddamned drain was clogged. I needed a fucking plunger. I needed—

To get back on the ice.

So, I fucking got out there. I did it, and I kept stinking it up, kept fucking up. No matter how much flushing, how much I tried to compartmentalize my brain. No matter how much I tried to. Nothing helped.

But by some fucking miracle of miracles, we managed to hold them off to just that two goal lead.

No one, least of all me, was feeling good about it.

"Fucking hell," I muttered, tossing the water bottle back into the holder then standing, following the guys off the bench and down the hall, still trying to keep my gaze off Calle's, off Coach's. Definitely away from the cameras so on the off chance that they were on me, were streaming back home to our fans, to Bailey. Or, just as bad, onto the Jumbotron. I didn't want anyone here to see my despair.

We were going to lose this game.

I knew it.

My season was going to be over.

We weren't going to get Brit another Cup before she retired.

We were just going to lose, go home, and—

Someone grabbed my hand.

Blinking, I looked up, saw Mandy.

"Do I—" I started to ask if she needed me to step into the modified training suite they'd set up for the duration of the series.

But the look on her face had me shutting up.

I'd never understood the idiom of *ice in my veins.* Not until that moment. In that moment, when I saw Mandy's expression, I *knew* it. I *felt* it.

"What's the matter?" I rasped.

She tugged me into a room.

"What?"

She shoved a paper into my hands.

"*Mandy*, what's the matter?" I asked. "Is Bailey okay? Is—"

Her hands came to my shoulders, and she squeezed tightly enough that I froze, that any words in my mind fled.

"Read it," she ordered.

And then she was gone.

Then the door had closed behind her, the *click* of the latch sliding into the strike plate gunshot loud in the silent room.

It was loud enough to make me jump.

To crinkle the paper.

Read it.

It was just plain white computer paper, folded in half.

Heart pounding, I opened it up—

And then read the words scrawled on the inside.

Forty-One

Bailey

Mandy had helped me write the note.

She'd promised to get it to him as soon as possible.

I was glued to the television screen, watching the guys walk off the ice, and then trying to not pull my hair out as the commentators spent the next fifteen minutes talking about how the Gold were basically getting their asses handed to them.

Over and over.

Talking shit about my guys—and gal.

Were they playing their best? Fuck no.

But were they out of this?

Hopefully not.

Hopefully, not with the note.

Hopefully, it would help and not make things worse.

Hopefully, I wasn't so overconfident or delusional thinking it would settle Axel enough that he could work a miracle.

Because it was *all* I could do.

So, as they talked about my family being out of this, out of the series, out of the running for the Cup, I was shoveling cookies and popcorn into my mouth, and I was drinking a beer and I was hoping against hope that something might change.

Because I wasn't sure if I could forgive myself if I was the cause—

Which wasn't fair to me.

They were big boys. They were professionals.

They were tired and had injuries and were maybe ready for the season to be done.

Yes, they should be able to put it all aside and *play.*

But it was a long, tough road.

And I'd made it tougher. On Axel. On the rest of them because they were a team and each piece in the team mattered.

Sighing, I stood up, shaking my arms, rolling my shoulders.

I needed to stop spinning on this roller coaster.

I needed to breathe and just take the outcome as it was.

I'd fucked up. I tried to fix it.

"Right, Bailey," I whispered. "You fucked up. You owned it. You tried to fix it." I let that sit for a minute, until I could almost believe it was true. "You *tried* to fix it. That's all you can do."

The commercials cut out and the game was back on, the players skating out on the ice, circling around, and lining up for the face-off, the rest loading up both benches, even as the commentators kept yapping about the slim chances the Gold had.

I plunked back onto the couch, clutched a pillow to my chest with one arm, my other going around Spock, fingers dipping into the soft black and white fur.

And I was breathing like I'd been sprinting around there on the ice, trying to keep up with those big behemoths of hockey players.

Both teams got settled. The goalies dealt with their creases, scraping their skates across them in the way they preferred, bunching snow up, shoving it in the goal, spreading it around the blue half circle. Then the doors were closed and the refs were in position and—

The puck was dropped.

It took exactly two seconds for me to see that there was a different team out on the ice.

There was a fire under the ass of every Gold player that hadn't been there last game, last period.

Hope blossomed anew.

My breathing steadied, or maybe I didn't breathe—didn't breathe as Josh scored about five minutes in, didn't breathe as Coop tapped one in a few minutes later, didn't breathe as Axel shoved the puck home with just thirty seconds left in the period.

Which, look, I got was actually impossible.

But it felt that way, felt like I hadn't moved an inch, hadn't breathed, hadn't blinked.

And anyway, that wasn't the point.

They were ahead, and—

I gasped.

Axel's face was on TV and as if he knew the camera was on him, he stared deep into the lens, as though he were looking at *me.*

Buttercup, he mouthed.

And every cell in my body relaxed.

He'd gotten the note.

He was telling me it was okay.

I *breathed.* For the first time in a period, I actually *breathed.*

And then I watched my man kill it on the ice.

They'd won.

I was bursting with excitement.

Because they'd *won!*

The game was more even in the third period, but the Gold had scored once more and Brit had made some really good saves that had helped keep them on top of the scoreboard.

And then the final buzzer had sounded, and it was like they'd already won the Cup.

They'd battled back.

They'd won decidedly.

They were back in the series.

I inhaled, eyes prickling, and began clearing the remnants of my snacks, doing my dishes, getting all my things ready for the morning.

The chores never stopped.

But that was okay.

Because I'd made it right—or I hoped so anyway.

I probably wouldn't be able to fully relax, not until I heard from him, not until we talked and—

Right.

Enough spinning.

I shoved my cell into my pocket and grabbed my jacket, shrugging into it as I stepped out onto the porch, Spock scooting out the opening and trailing behind me as I sat down on the porch steps and stared out into the late evening sky.

There was just a bit of light still present on the horizon, but the rest of the space overhead was navy, was twinkling with stars, draped with clouds.

I started to pull out my phone, but a noise drew my gaze to the road, and I watched as a sedan slowed.

The interior light was on.

I couldn't see the driver, just a silhouette.

A woman.

But just as I thought they might pull into my driveway, the car sped up, zipping down the road and disappearing around the corner.

Weird.

But maybe the woman had been lost. It was easy to get twisted up around here, to lose your way, especially when night had fallen.

Spock cuddled closer, and I leaned against the porch pillar, stroking my hand through his fur.

Not relaxed, necessarily, but content to wait for Axel to call, content to sit out here and just be for a few minutes after the stress I'd made out of my day.

A deep breath, releasing all that tension.

My eyes slid closed, and I just sat there in the quiet.

Spock whined.

"It'll be okay, bud," I murmured, scratching his ears.

I inhaled again, let it out.

And just sat.

Until...I caught a whiff of something in the air during one of my inhales.

It was...smoke?

My lids flew open, and I sucked in another breath, a deep one this time, and what hit my nostrils had me shooting to my feet, pulling in more air, trying to pinpoint the location, to smell for certain, to *know* for certain.

My gaze searching as I darted out toward the barn, spinning both ways, looking, *looking*—

And seeing…

An orange glow on the horizon.

Smoke in the air.

That orange glow.

A dry spring and—

Fire.

There was a fire on the hills.

And it was coming for the ranch.

Forty-Two

Axel

The win tonight was...

Incredible.

It felt like we'd already won it all, that we'd crossed our biggest hurdle, could go home, and just cruise into the Cup.

I'd gotten it together.

We'd *all* gotten it together, had decided that we weren't ready for the season to be done.

So...we'd pushed on.

Scored some goals, got them on their back feet, and we'd won the *fucking game*.

Now we were giving the requisite interviews and I was hoping that Bailey had seen my homage into the camera, knew that I wasn't upset with her, not in the least.

It was okay.

And that she'd been worried enough to find a way to apologize to me mid-game, to let me know that she loved me, that we'd be okay...

That meant a lot.

It meant everything.

Love wasn't perfect, wasn't a smooth road without any bumps.

There were potholes and divergences and rumble strips and peeling paint.

But she'd tried to make it right, even despite the circumstances. Because she was worried that I was in my head and not playing well because of something she'd done.

She was right, of course.

I wasn't playing well.

And I'd been stuck in my own head.

But I was beating myself up, wasn't mad at her, not in the least.

I was desperate to get this shit over with, to get to a place where I could call her. Hell, I was desperate to call in a few favors and get her to San Francisco so she'd be in the stands when we won it all.

For the moment, though, I'd settle for a few quiet moments and a phone call.

Finally, the questions were done and the media gone, and I hit the showers, speeding through so I could get dressed, maybe find my way out to a quiet corner for that call.

But when I came out, rubbing a towel through my hair, the room had gone quiet.

Tense.

And my skin prickled, my stomach twisting, instincts instantly on full alert.

What the hell had happened?

I glanced around the room, but eyes didn't meet mine—gazes on their phones or their hands or their feet or...

Anywhere but mine.

Except Brit's.

She was sitting next to my spot.

Her cell was in her hand.

But her eyes, her eyes came to mine, held, and that ice settled into my veins all over again.

Only this time, I didn't think there was going to be a note

On numb ass legs, I walked over to her, sinking down onto the bench next to her, body still dripping with water, towel barely covering anything at all, and not giving one fuck that someone might walk in and see my balls.

Because the moment my ass hit the bench, Brit handed me her phone.

For a second, my eyes didn't register what I was seeing.

What I was reading.

Then it all hit at once.

I turned up the volume, listening to the local reporter talking about the fire that was burning up in the Sierra foothills.

For a moment, I hoped.

For a moment, I thought that because I'd finally dealt with my shit, gotten my life together, that for once, for *fucking* once, the universe wouldn't throw my life into a blender and hit the switch when I was happy.

That for once, I'd be able to *stay* happy.

Then I heard what had made everyone go so sober, so quiet.

"...the fire burned so hot and fast. It's being fueled by strong winds and unseasonably hot weather. CalFire and local departments are on scene, but the state of many of River's Bend's residents and buildings is unknown at this point. Evacuation orders have been issued for the entire county as the fire..."

I pulled out my phone.

I dialed Bailey.

The call wouldn't connect.

I texted, saw that she'd reached out earlier.

But that was before the game.

My text went through.

But there wasn't a reply.

And my calls, on the odd time they did connect, went straight to voicemail.

"The system is probably overwhelmed," Brit said softly.

"Yeah," I agreed.

But my stomach was in knots. I'd been down this road, had known better than to think I'd be able to have my happy ending.

Not *my* happy ending.

Not *my* life.

I was destined to have a glimpse of it, to have it just for a little bit...and then to lose it.

And I knew that wasn't just more bullshit, wasn't more

spiraling in my fucked-up mind, because when Brit connected her phone to a local news station that was covering the fire, we all saw the banner at the bottom of the screen as the reporter talked—

River's Bend is on fire.

And I knew it wasn't a bullshit news story, trying to make something out of nothing.

Because I texted, I called, doing both over and over again.

And Bailey didn't answer *any* of them.

Not *one* time.

Instead, I got silence. I got calls that didn't connect. I got voicemail.

I got...worry.

And increasingly dire news reports.

Part 3

So Pucking Over It

Prologue

Axel

Smoke and ash.

Heat radiating up off the asphalt.

Abandoned cars stuck, literally *stuck* to the road, tires melted, metal rims coated with ash and oxides, windows shattered, exteriors reduced to rusted steel frames.

Car after car after *car*.

But no trucks. No trailers.

No sign of the woman I loved.

Embers still coated the air, choking me worse than the panic that had gripped me from the moment I'd seen the news reports, that continued to claw and twist and shred my insides as more and more time went on without hearing from her.

Hot air singeing my throat, burning my skin.

Had she felt this?

Had she felt a hundred times worse as the flames had closed in?

Heat licking ever nearer, the roar of the fire and wind giving way to this quiet, this eerie, mournful silence.

This...*death*.

I stared out at the hills, once covered with long, slender stalks of grass that whispered in the breeze. Those hills were now black and smoking, something out of a shitty Hollywood dystopian movie.

Except, this was real life.

Except, the woman I loved had been right in the middle of this.

Except...the woman I loved hadn't been heard or seen from since.

And my heart, the one that had shed all the chains and armor keeping itself safe, the vulnerable organ that had opened and accepted my woman, had loved her with everything I was, had hoped, had pleaded with the fates, with the universe that this would be the first time in my fucking life that I actually got to keep the good in it.

Instead, the universe had sent us a big *fuck you.*

It had sent flames closing in on this town.

Fire tornados spinning through the superheated air.

Houses reduced to nothing but chimneys and concrete foundations.

Street signs melted.

Parks and trees turned to ash.

And my woman...was gone.

Gone.

All while the rest of the world continued to spin onward.

One

Axel

Hockey was life.

Hockey was everything I had, all I'd *ever* had.

It was something I'd loved and hated, almost in equal measure over the years—hating the grind, the travel, the way the long seasons could close in on me, hating the commitment it took, the gym time, the off-ice training, the volunteer work and meetings and watching tape, hating that it wasn't easy, that the hours weren't regular.

But the love always came back around to smother the hate.

Love of the cool rink air prickling over my skin, sinking down through my jersey, finding the gaps in my pads. Love for the cheers of the crowd, the high when I connected a really good pass with a teammate, when I scored or crushed one of the motherfuckers on the other team into the boards and most especially when that fucker deserved it.

Though, I was equal opportunity.

Take the hits, dish them out, so long as I didn't mar this pretty face.

Bailey liked it.

Bailey—

I closed my eyes, dropping onto the side of the bed in the cheap ass motel. It was the only place I'd been able to get a room, the only place within fifty miles of River's Bend, California that had space for me.

The rest were under evacuation as the firefighters continued to get the fire under control or were filled with evacuees.

I knew because I'd gone to every single one in search of Bailey.

I knew because I'd gone to every single shelter between here and River's Bend.

Phones weren't working this close to the fire, and I hadn't seen one glimpse of Bailey's big truck, of Bailey's curvy body that I'd worshipped every inch of. I hadn't heard her voice or her laugh or watched her smile that special smile she saved just for me, her brown eyes warming to liquid chocolate.

But I'd found a place to stay.

I'd get a few hours of sleep, would get back on the road, searching.

Not stopping until I found her.

Not stopping until the hope inside me was incinerated, reduced to ashes like the trees and houses out there.

Not stopping until there was nothing left inside me.

Because my heart hadn't actually beat until I'd met Bailey. I hadn't truly lived, not until I'd been lucky enough to love her.

So, hockey didn't matter.

I didn't give a fuck that final game in the series was two days away from now.

It was a dream that existed in another life altogether.

Because Bailey was my dream now.

And I just had to hold tight to the tiny bundle of hope still flickering with life in my heart, had to carefully shield it, to keep it alive.

Because without it, the man I was—Axel Finnegan, professional hockey player, reformed fuck-up with a heart that couldn't be cracked open…

Well, he would cease to exist.

And I was terrified to see what sort of monster I would turn into.

. . .

My eyes were gritty when I woke to my alarm two hours later.

The smell of smoke clung to the air, to my clothes, my skin, my hair.

But I was awake and dawn was approaching, and I needed to get moving. I pulled out the printout of the map—Brit's idea before she'd driven me to the airport directly from the game, not blinking an eye when I'd said I needed to leave immediately.

None of them had.

Pierre, the owner of the Gold and Rush hockey teams, had offered his private plane, had it fueled and ready to take off by the time I made it to the airport.

And Brit had promised to hold down the fort, no matter if I made it back for the game, and on that front not *one* member of the coaching staff, of the support staff, not *one* teammate had made a comment, other than to offer their help.

Because they knew that family was the most important thing.

And Bailey was mine.

So I looked at the map, at the printout that Dani had run into the locker room and stowed in my bag as I'd gotten dressed—brought thanks to that idea of Brit's—and picked the next section I was going to start with.

I'd covered the western route into River's Bend in the few hours remaining of the day before, thinking it had been the easiest path out of town, considering where the ranch was located.

But I hadn't been able to get through to the ranch, not with all the abandoned cars, the smoke and ash and utter destruction.

River's Bend was destroyed.

I'd seen that much.

The beautiful downtown with the historic buildings that were supposed to be the backdrop to the Summer Festival in just two weeks' time were gone. Monroe's, where I'd finally made my move, finally given in to the draw between Bailey and myself was also gone. As was the park where I'd snuck kisses. The apartment building that I'd sublet.

Gone.

All of it.

Gone.

I worried about Bailey. I worried about her horse, Data, her cow, Picard, her dog, Spock, knowing she wouldn't leave the pets she loved behind. I worried about her cattle, the herd that was her livelihood, and the poor animals were probably scattered and scared and maybe dead. I worried about Billie Rose and Dessie, the women I had to thank for my heart belonging to Bailey. I worried about my former teammates, whose season was over, but those that had property in town would have been in River's Bend when the fire broke out.

I worried. *Period.*

It sat heavy on my soul, was a knot of barbed wire in my gut, making it difficult for me to think, to focus.

Especially, as more time went on without a word from Bailey, without contact.

All while the fire burned on.

But...I couldn't focus on that.

It would paralyze me. It would make it impossible for me to focus on finding the woman I loved.

So, I shoved the worry down, smothered it until it was buried deeply in the back of my mind.

I could allow the nightmares to come later.

Mind settled, I folded the map, set it next to my cell. Then I took a quick shower to get the ash off, to rid myself of the smoky scent that was seemingly embedded into my cells.

Ten minutes later, I was grabbing my shit and going back out to my car.

And I was driving toward the rising sun, the midnight navy of the early morning sky glowing with a narrow swathe of orange above the hills in the distance.

I searched.

I scoured every inch south of River's Bend for any sign of a big, old truck, of shining brown hair and the woman I loved.

But I still didn't find Bailey.

Two

Bailey

I didn't know where I was.

Didn't know what time it was, not with the smoke so heavy in the air, so heavy that I could barely breathe.

Everything burned—my exposed skin had been scalded and blistered from the flames, my lungs were on fire with every breath. I'd tied a spare sweatshirt around my face, trying to prevent further inhalation, but it hadn't—*didn't*—do much. Not with the smoke still choking me, stinging my eyes, the unnatural heat in the air suffocating me.

There were so many unknowns—was I moving the wrong way or the right one? Toward the fire or away? Would I find water soon? I *had* to find water soon.

I'd been searching for a stream, for any water source for a while now as I made my way down the narrow trail that had been my savior, but I hadn't yet had any luck. Partly, because it was hard to see. Hell, I couldn't tell if it was day or night or somewhere in between.

So, it was impossible to know if the orange glow was from the sun shining through the smoke, or if it was even more flames in the distance.

And it was silent.

A deadly sort of quiet that was absent of the sound of insects, of birds and critters. No cars. No other people.

Just me in the smoke-filled hills.

The only peace I could find in my current surroundings was the fact that it *was* quiet.

The roaring of the flames, louder than I could have ever imagined, weren't bearing down on me any longer.

Not like they had when I'd been trapped on the road south of town, blocked off from the other routes, trying to get out through any possible means.

Somehow, I'd managed to get us all to safety—me, Picard, Data, and Spock—but it had nearly killed me. Literally. I'd barely managed to get Picard and Data harnessed and out of the trailer, the wildness of the flames spooking them, making them not want to leave the false safety of their rolling enclosure. I'd barely been able to get them out of the trailer and then to stop them from running into the chaos of the road, the flames, before the wildfire had closed in near enough to blister the skin of my hands and bared arms, to singe my hair.

Not to mention, leading a horse, a cow, and a dog (and myself) through a smoke-filled, flame-lined road and into the surrounding hills and doing it while we were all freaked the *fuck* out (including myself) had been a goddamned miracle.

I didn't want to risk riding Data, not when we didn't have water and it was taking so much effort to keep them calm.

I might get thrown and that could be a death sentence, especially if I was injured.

And I might need Data's strength later.

For now, though, we were okay. I was moving downhill, hoping that was taking me away from the fire, hoping the flames would keep moving in a direction that wasn't toward me.

I couldn't outrun it.

I had to get away from it.

I had to—

The wind picked up, rustling through the trees surrounding us. Their branches and trunks were untouched, at least for the moment. But the rush of air drifting through the ends of my hair, over my skin was hot and other worldly and—

Spock whined.

"It's okay," I said, keeping my voice soft, even though I was the only one here, even though there wasn't another soul nearby to tell me to be quiet.

I scratched his head, thankful that he was a good listener, that he'd stayed right at my side through this insanity—though, if I could tell him to go, to get to safety, I would in a heartbeat.

He whined again, and I straightened. "I know," I whispered. "We need to keep moving."

So I kept walking, kept picking my way down the trail, kept helping Data and Picard navigate the rocky and oftentimes steep path, kept Spock close.

Calm voice.

Calm body.

Calm movements.

But none of us were buying it.

The air was too stagnant, too still. The smoke wasn't lessening. It was...growing thicker, heavier, pushing on us.

Or maybe, it was that my lungs weren't working as well?

Maybe the heaviness growing in my feet wasn't because fatigue had reached up to grab me tightly, to tug at my ankles and legs, to make my footsteps grow unsteady.

Maybe it was because my body was shutting down, with my mind not far behind it.

How many hours had I been walking?

How long had I been running?

A *long* time, I thought.

Or it could be that there wasn't enough oxygen in the air, that I *couldn't breathe. I couldn't breathe.* I was being smothered. I—

Spock whined again and I jerked, managed to snap myself out of my panic.

"Calm, Bay," I murmured, giving myself the same gentle tone my pets were getting, forcing myself to focus on the words, even though they were a lie when I added, "You've been in worse scrapes than this.

You'll be fine." A breath that sent me coughing so hard that I bent in half, the force of the wheezing taking my hands to my knees. "You'll be fine," I rasped out again when I'd managed to stop hacking.

I paused to tie the sweatshirt I'd secured around my face a little tighter, folding it again, trying for another layer between my nose and mouth and the smoke.

"Fine," I whispered again.

Except, even as that word crossed my lips, I hit a loose patch of rocks and my feet slid out from under me.

I managed—just barely—to have the forethought to release the ropes on Data and Picard's halters, so as not to take them down with me.

But that was all I could do as I collided hard with the ground, began to slide down the steep hill.

Spock barked, and Data whinnied in surprise.

But I couldn't get any words out, not when my already damaged lungs couldn't draw in enough air, not when rocks and dirt were scraping my back, shredding the skin of my bare arms.

Eventually, I slid to a stop, pain intruding on every single one of my nerves.

"Fuck," I whispered, just lying there for a minute, trying to get my breath back, trying to summon the energy to get up.

Rocks skittering.

Spock appearing at my side, gently licking my face.

"Hi, buddy." I managed to lift my arm, to scratch his ears. "I'm okay."

Nothing about this was okay, least of all my bruised and battered body.

But I had to keep telling myself that, had to keep moving.

Blood trickled down my nose, and I realized I'd lost my makeshift mask somewhere along the fall. I couldn't see it as I looked up at the hill I'd slipped down, so there was nothing to be done about it. The path was steep, and I didn't have time to waste looking for a sweatshirt that was hardly helping. I just had to hope I could get Picard and Data down it.

Swallowing hard, I began inching my way up, beyond thankful when Data started taking careful steps toward me.

"Come on, baby," I coaxed, helping her over a particularly slippery portion of the trail.

Finally, though, we both made it to the bottom.

"Good girl," I murmured, rubbing the spot between her eyes. "Wait here, okay?"

She huffed and I turned back to the hill, summoned the energy to make my way back up to Picard who was stomping nervously at the top.

"Come on, honey," I said, grabbing his rope halter and trying to draw him forward.

He dug in his hoofs.

"We gotta go, baby." More stern now.

A soft, protesting *moo.*

Grunting, I tugged harder. "*Come. On.*" Another tug, but then I heard something that I made ice cold daggers dig into my spine.

I froze, horror collecting in my belly as the telltale rumble grew.

What I heard was death.

And it was coming for me.

Again.

Three

Axel

The hours were passing me by—too fucking fast.

Each mile closer back to River's Bend brought landscape that looked increasingly more and more like it belonged in a post-apocalyptic novel.

Blackened tree trunks, barren branches, smoking ground.

Brown and orange-hued air.

Twisted rebar and bare foundations were all that remained of every house I could see.

The hotel the visiting teams would stay in when they drove up to play the Rush had been reduced to a pile of blackened beams, floors having collapsed and gone topsy-turvy, leaving it to look like a fucked-up house of cards.

I drove over the bridge that led toward River's Bend, ignoring the lights from the sheriff's cruisers that were blocking the route into town up ahead.

I was getting in.

I was getting to the ranch.

Because Bailey hadn't been at any of the hospitals, not at any of the police stations or fire departments or churches or school gymnasiums. She wasn't in any of the shelters.

So she was here.

And I was going to find her.

The bridge thrummed with its familiar vibration as I drove over the steel and concrete. The river was extremely low after a dry winter and spring, mostly exposed gravel and riverbed at this point in the year. That dry weather was most certainly why everything had gone up like so much tinder.

The banks that were normally covered with thick green oaks—save for a narrow trail on River's Bend's side of the waterway that people used to access the water—were now unrecognizable. Normally, during the summer and on weekends, there were kids splashing and skipping rocks and generally just making a ruckus, their adults supervising, or for the few early souls who were up with the sun (which didn't include me—anytime I'd seen fisherman it had been when I was heading to bed, not getting out of it), standing in the waist-deep water fishing for rainbow trout.

But all of that was gone now.

An empty river due to the drought.

The trees surrounding it all but sticks of tinder. The ground blackened and devoid of vegetation. The trail and its wooden handrail reduced to ashes.

Devastation.

That was the only word I could think of.

Absolute and total devastation.

It was clear the fire had jumped from one bank to the other, its embers carried on the wind and igniting both of the dry, tree-filled sides, those strong gusts of off-shore air growing the flames into the out-of-control complex blaze that was still burning west of town.

But not here.

Everything *here* had already burned.

So, I didn't stop driving across the bridge, didn't stop at the police cars, just began to swerve around them.

Except, then Frank, the sheriff, was standing there.

Exhaustion was written into the lines of his face, his uniform wrinkled and soot covered.

And he was at the front of my car, hands on the hood, and leaving no space for me to get by.

Unless I wanted to run him over.

Which was a thought that crossed my mind, I couldn't lie.

But while I was an asshole, I wasn't one who would commit vehicular homicide.

Plus, I was an asshole who might need Frank's assistance. Crushing him beneath my car probably wouldn't endear me to him, least of all get him to help me.

I threw the transmission into park but left the engine running as I pushed out the driver's side.

"I can't let you pass, Axel," he said before both of my feet hit the asphalt.

I shook my head. "I need to get to Bailey."

Something crossed Frank's face that had my gut twisting, that barbed wire gouging through my middle, leaving me flayed open and bleeding.

"What?" I rasped.

Frank rubbed a weary hand over his face. "The fire—" He dropped his hand, eyes lifting to mine, but only for a second before he was staring out over my shoulder.

"What the fuck, Frank?" I snapped, taking a jerking step toward him. "Just tell me."

"It started on her property," Frank said softly. "The whole fire did. And it spread fucking fast. So fast," he added, still quiet, so fucking quiet I had to strain to hear his words, "that we couldn't get help out there in time. Everything on Russet Ranch is gone—the house, the barn, the cattle, maybe there are a few head that managed to get away. But her other animals? No sign of them. And Bailey—"

My pulse had begun pounding so loudly in my ears that I couldn't hear the rest of what he was saying.

Everyone on Russet Ranch is gone.

Bailey—

Bailey was...what?

She couldn't be gone.

She couldn't be.

But Frank was still talking, and some distant part of my brain was processing that the sheriff had been out there, that he'd born witness, had seen the entire collection of ranches was gone.

That they'd already found more than one burned body.

Fuck.

Fuck.

It had to be a mistake. The flicker of hope was still alive and well in my chest.

She *had* to be okay.

I just needed to find her.

"I'm sorry, Axel," Frank choked out. "I just don't see how she could have survived that."

Those words came in crystal clear through the buzzing in my ears, my mind, slicing through the fog that I'd managed to cling to.

And it tore the fight right out of me.

My legs buckled and I barely felt the pain as my knees cracked against the asphalt. Skin broke, blood was a hot rush soaking into my jeans.

I felt a hand land on my shoulder, the rest of Frank's words fading away again.

Gone.

Gone.

My body was free of physical pain, too far gone to feel it. But that was only because the internal agony was too much, too overwhelming, too suffocating. The barbed wire grew and knotted, slicing my insides into ribbons, leaving me bleeding, the fluid choking me, filling my lungs, making it so I couldn't—

"It'll be okay, son."

How would it be okay?

I wanted to rail at him, to get back in my car and run over the man who was trying to smother the flickering bit of hope, who *was* smothering it. I wanted to toss him over the bridge, to punch and kick and slam him into the roadway until he didn't resemble a man, until he was a pile of flesh, resembling the useless piece of shit he was.

Fair? No.

But my person—*my person*—was out there and she w-was—

"We'll figure it out," Frank said and I wasn't so far gone as to miss the regret in his voice, the emotion turning it thick and rasping.

But I didn't care.

Because figure *what* out?

How to bring the woman I loved back from the dead?

How to fill in the hole in my heart, my soul, my life?

How—

I staggered to my feet, the physical pain finally slicing through the haze in my mind, sending the bone deep ache into my knees, up through my legs.

But it was still nothing compared to the pain *inside*.

"I need to get through," I said, trying to shove past him. I needed to see, needed to get to the ranch and—

The hand returned to my shoulder. "I can't let you through, son. I can't."

Fuck it.

I was going to run Frank over.

Yanking out of his hold, I spun back to my car then reached for the handle on the driver's side door.

But a flicker on the far bank caught my focus.

A flash of white.

The hand returned. "Axel—"

I shook it off, pointed to the opposite bank of the river. "What's that?"

"Axel—"

"*Frank*," I said. "*What's* that?"

Frank shut up, moved to my side. "What—?" I pointed again and he leaned forward, as though that would help him see better. "What *is* that?"

I didn't know, but I was already hopping over the end of the bridge where it met the bank on this side of the river and running down the hill, sprinting for the water, moving across it and—

The speck of white was moving down the bank, growing larger, coming into focus.

Then I was finally close enough to see it for what it was.

Picard.

Four

Bailey

One second, I was tugging on Picard's harness and the next, I was sliding down that hill a second time, knocked there by my pet steer.

He hadn't meant it, I knew.

He was panicked by the roar of the flames that were too fucking close again.

But him panicking and trying to get away, to abruptly move down that hill because the fire sounded like it was moving in behind us again meant that he'd stumbled over me as I fell, as I slid through rocks and leaves and pine needles and dirt.

Worse was that when Picard started running forward and down, he didn't miss *me*.

I cursed, covering my head, curling up trying not to get trampled.

One of his hooves—carrying his three hundred and something pounds of steer—stepped on my thigh.

White hot pain seared through my leg. It was lightning down through my toes, electricity shooting up to my hip, my spine, my shoulders and neck. Blood soaked into my back, making my T-shirt stick to my skin, and my arms and palms were scraped to shit, but I still tried to get up, still tried to move.

I *had* to keep moving.

Groaning, I managed to roll over, to get onto my hands and knees.

Except, I couldn't push to my feet. The leg that Picard had stepped on wasn't working right—maybe a bone was broken or perhaps the nerves just were shot from the sudden impact. I didn't know.

All I *did* know?

I needed to get the fuck out of there.

The fire...it was too damned close.

Spock whined when I began crawling, staying at my side, nudging my jaw with his cold nose.

It was no longer wet, which concerned me, especially considering how thirsty I was, but I couldn't do anything about it, not at that moment anyway.

Right then, I needed to keep moving forward.

So that was what I did.

"Picard!" I called when he didn't stop, but he disappeared ahead of us, lost from view in the brush, too panicked to heed my cries.

It hurt my heart, fucking hurt like *hell* to let him go. But I had to. The rumble was growing behind me, and I had Spock and Data and myself, for that matter, to worry about. "Move, Bay," I whispered. "Just keep moving."

So I did, clicking my tongue and thankful that Data trusted me enough that she started following me.

I knew I should ride her, but that would mean making it all the way up onto her back, and I didn't think that was possible for me at this point. Maybe if I found a rock I could climb on top of or an edge of the trail I could heave myself up onto, it might be possible to crawl onto her back, but here, *now*, it wasn't happening.

I barely had the strength to keep going.

But I did, rocks digging into my palms, slicing through my skin, and between my hands and my legs and my back, I worried I was bleeding so much that I didn't think it was possible for my body to lose any more blood, worried that I'd lost so much I was going to pass out and the flames were going to come for me.

Were going to get me.

"No," I whispered. I wouldn't let it.

Except, each foot I gained got harder, that constant drain of blood making my body grow weaker.

I embraced that fucking fish from *Finding Nemo*, except instead of swimming, it was crawling.

Just keep crawling.

Just keep crawling.

I did.

Somehow, I did just that. Continued moving, clicking my tongue, coaxing Data forward occasionally, but she and Spock weren't leaving my side and that fact made my eyes prickle with tears that couldn't actually form.

I was too dehydrated.

So the tears didn't come, but I continued moving down that steep trail, continuing hauling myself forward, and Spock and Data were right beside me.

Spock nudged me, that cool, dry nose hitting a sore spot—and truthfully there weren't really any spots on my body that weren't sore—but it still hurt, causing me to hiss out a breath, but when he nudged me again, I blinked, realized that I'd somehow stopped, even despite all of my *Just keep crawling.*

I was too weak.

I needed to rest, just for a little while.

But Spock kept nudging me and kept nudging me, even though I tried to bat him away.

That was when I realized the noise had grown, the flames were closer.

A bark. A sharp nudge.

I opened my eyes and there was a rock. A rock that I could clamber on top of. A rock that would get me high enough that if I could just get to the *fucking* top of it.

Spock barked again.

"Okay, okay," I whispered. "Yes, I know."

I pushed up onto my good leg, dug my hands into a crevice of the huge granite boulder and heaved.

My other leg got beneath me, held long enough that I managed to make it halfway up.

Cursing, grunting, groaning, *begging*, I did all of that.

But eventually I made it to the flat top of the rock.

Spock barked, encouraging me as I sank onto my bottom. "Yeah, boy. I know," I said again. "Come here, Data."

My horse, my friend, my best girl, shifted so that she was right next to the boulder.

A breath, sucking in my strength, holding tight to it.

Then I shifted enough to drop my bad leg over her back, to push with my good one, to...

I pushed too hard, nearly flew over to the other side.

"Fuck," I hissed, managing to grip Data's mane, to stop myself from toppling to the ground. I was lightheaded, my lungs on fire, my entire body one raw, exposed nerve.

But I was on Data's back.

Crackling was in the air, branches and tree trunks catching fire. The temperature increased, causing sweat to drip down my spine, my chest, burning and stinging all along the salty tracks.

The smoke was coming back, clogging my nose and mouth and lungs.

We *had* to go.

I clicked my tongue.

Data started moving.

I focused on keeping my seat, on making sure that Spock was staying next to us.

And then all my focus turned to staying conscious.

And...I didn't succeed.

Five

Axel

I ran toward the white and brown cow. Bull. Steer. Whatever the fuck the non-milk producing, ball-less variety of cattle was supposed to be called. Bailey had corrected me more than once, but to me he was a cow.

Brown and white with four legs and a tail and big, cow eyes and hooves.

A *cow*.

Who was sprinting down the hill now, hooves sliding, big body moving fast.

Fuck.

Too fast.

He was going to slip and fall and break something, and I didn't know cows or steers or whatever well at all, but I didn't think him breaking a leg was going to end well.

My feet splashed through the water, skidding on the slippery rocks, but I'd grown up on skates, so I moved with the skid, slid across the slick stones and then I was on the other side of the water, up onto the rocky bank and then moving across the sandy shore.

Crashing in my ears, rocks skittering down toward me, and then Picard was there, covered in soot and ash, small burns all his sides, blood streaked across his face to create a ghoulish mask.

He was wearing his halter, a rope dangling from its end.

"Hey, buddy," I said gently, reaching out and taking the end of the rope, pulling it, slowing him down, harder now because he had to weigh a good three or four hundred pounds and he was scared, but I did manage to turn him before we both ended up in the water, though he was still dragging me forward.

And then Frank was there beside me, helping me haul Picard to a halt.

"Easy, buddy," I said again and, finally, Picard stopped fighting me, stopped lurching against the harness. He froze, sides heaving, snot and blood and drool coming out of his mouth and nose. But he was there and he was okay.

So Bailey must—

I dropped the length of rope I'd grabbed on to. "Get him up the other side." I turned for the hill Picard had sprinted down.

"What are you doing?" Frank asked.

"Bailey might be up there."

Frank grabbed my arm. "You can't—"

"He's harnessed," I snapped. "That means Bailey got out. Got out," I said sharply, talking over him when he opened his mouth to reply, "soon enough to get him harnessed and off the ranch."

Frank's brows dragged together, but thankfully, he shut up.

"I'm going," I said. "She's got to be close."

The vee between the sheriff's brows deepened and unfortunately, he began talking again. "Axel, that's not—"

I ran out of patience.

"Get him up the bank. At least save *hi*—" I snapped my teeth together, not willing, not able to have this conversation. "Go," I ordered.

And then I was done talking.

I was sprinting up the hill, feet sliding on the loose earth, hands gripping the burned branches to haul myself up the extra slippery parts.

Lungs burning from smoke, from exertion. Legs shaking but not giving out.

Then I was in amongst the charred trees, eyes searching for a glimpse of shining brown hair, ears listening hard for any sound of movement.

Nothing.

All quiet.

Not even the whisper of the wind.

My heart sank, but I kept moving, kept making my way up the trail, up through the trees, until I'd reached the precipice...and saw nothing but...

Nothing.

Trees turned to cinder.

The hillsides bare.

My disappointment was acute, biting and sharp and leaving me bleeding out on the remains of the forest floor.

But still I looked, still I searched, that flicker of hope in my heart, my belly guttering, fading, threatening to go out. Somehow, I managed to keep it aflame, mostly because I kept walking, kept moving forward, kept *looking*.

Picard had come down the bank, had come from this direction.

The ranch wasn't all that close, at least ten miles north, but that wasn't a straight path. The hills followed the curves of the river, and the fire had burned along both sides at various stretches. For Picard to be *here*, to be here now...it meant he'd—*they'd*—taken a circuitous path from the ranch.

They'd taken a circuitous path.

I inhaled, that flicker blooming anew.

Then I started walking again.

Down through the trees, the loose dirt kicked up by my shoes, creating a cloud of dust that choked almost as much as the smoke. It was thick. That was why I couldn't see her.

That was why she wasn't immediately visible—the visibility sucked. How could I see her through it?

So I just needed to keep moving, to keep searching.

Up the next hill, beyond the parking lot for the river trail. Then I was climbing my way through patches of random green trees, completely unburned, completely untouched by the devastation. Patches that gave me hope, that fed the flicker in my belly.

If these weren't destroyed then they—

Then she was okay.

Then she was *okay.*

I inhaled, the air tighter here, not as much oxygen available for my lungs, for my mind. The doubts creeping in all over again, wondering how in the fuck she could survive in this, how she could have survived *any* of this.

"Fuck," I whispered, fingers digging into a tree trunk that was still hot from being burned. "*Fuck.*"

I should go back, should make sure the Picard—

A rustle.

It had been so quiet, so silent. No noise except for the sound of my footsteps, the rasp of my breathing, the pounding of my pulse in my ears.

Except for that rustle.

I froze listening harder.

Hearing it again.

"Bailey!" I shouted.

It was just torn out of me, so loud, so abrupt that I shocked the shit out of myself, nearly tripped as I started running.

"Bailey!" I yelled again, not surprised this time.

Determined.

A bark.

A *bark.*

That hope growing, bursting outward.

"Spock!" I shouted, speeding forward, tripping and landing hard on my knees again, the cuts from the bridge stinging, but I just pushed up to my feet again, just started running again, just—

A flash of dirty fur, white parts dyed gray and brown from the smoke and dust.

A yip of excitement.

A dog crashing into me, nearly taking me off my feet again. I scooped him up, held his wriggling body close. His tongue hit my cheek and it was dry, so dry that I knew he needed help.

But he lived his life glued to Bailey's side. I knew he wouldn't leave her.

And just as I had that thought, as I *knew* that she had to be close, I looked up and saw chestnut fur.

It was grayed out. It was muted and stained.

But it was chestnut-colored.

It was *Data's*.

I inhaled sharply, coughing on the ash, and setting Spock down and then I was moving again, sprinting now.

Because I could see there was a harness similar to Picard's over Data's nose. No saddle, no stirrups down her naked side.

No...Bailey.

I cursed, knees threatening to give way again.

But I had to see, had to get closer.

And when I did, when I got to Data, stroked her nose and watched her panic-filled eyes settle slightly, I saw I was right.

No saddle.

No Bailey.

No—

Spock barked again, bumping my legs as he ran back in the direction from where he and Data had just come, drawing my gaze after him.

My mouth parted to call him back.

Then he barked again.

And every cell in my body went ramrod still.

Brown hair coated with dirt and ash.

A glimpse of exposed skin that I'd kissed my way across, that had felt like silk beneath my lips, smelled like apples and horses and hay.

I'd told her once that she smelled like shit, so fucking scared of what was in my heart and head, so fucking scared of feeling like *this* —like I'd lost her, like I was clinging to hope that she was still breathing—that I'd done every fucking *thing* to keep her from getting close.

She'd gotten in anyway.

And now...she was going to destroy me.

Bracing myself, I approached the unmoving body of the woman I loved.

Six

Bailey

My eyelids hurt.

Everything hurt.

But the part that stood out the most was the fact that my eyelids hurt so much I couldn't even stand to open them.

And I was trying to open them because I'd figured out that I wasn't in that burned forest, that the flames weren't coming for me.

My skin was burning. My lungs ached. My leg—there was a deep, radiating sort of bone-deep pain. But my eyelids. *God*. They hurt so fucking much and all I wanted to do was to open them, to see where I was.

"Wake up, buttercup. Pl-please just wake up."

The voice was fuzzy, slow to penetrate.

But then it did, and my lids flew open. It *hurt*...but not as much as seeing the look on Axel's face.

The area beneath his eyes was bruised with dark circles. His skin was deathly pale. But it was the agony etched into his expression as his stare left my body and drifted up to stare at the wall over my head that eclipsed any of the pain currently present in my body.

"Axel," I whispered.

Too quiet.

My voice gone.

But I tried to clear my throat, to get it to be loud enough for him to hear me, needing him to know I was here, I was okay.

"Axel," I whispered again.

His head snapped back toward me, eyes going wide, pain replaced with shock and, for now, that was enough.

"Hi," I whispered.

He collapsed.

That was the only way I could think to describe what happened to his body—it was as though all of the inner struts, the support structure that was keeping him together just totally collapsed. His body folded forward, going limp, his head dropping to my belly, his arms wrapping around my middle, squeezing, but doing it gently.

So, so gently.

And then his back began to shake, his tears soaking through the blanket, through the hospital gown I was wearing.

Which was the first time that I realized I was in a hospital.

I was safe.

Though, I supposed, I had known that I was out of harm's way the moment I'd heard Axel's voice.

He was my safe space. He was my lodestone, my guiding star in a midnight sky.

So, I just lifted a hand, smoothed it down his shaking back, ignoring the slight tug of the IV in my hand, and waited for him to finish.

When he did, when he lifted his head and I caught sight of those reddened eyes, the pain radiated right through my veins, more intense than the flames bearing down on me. "Picard—" I began, voice cracking.

"He's okay," Axel murmured, gently smoothing back my hair. "He's the reason I found you. Data and Spock, too. They're all fine. Olivia and Cole picked them up, had their vet check them out, and then took them to their ranch. They can stay there as long as we need."

Relief was a cool drink of water after the hours of everything being so hot and dry and *parched.* I knew that Axel's agent and her former hockey playing, now charity ranch owning husband would take care of them. Just like I knew—

I laced our fingers together, held his gaze. "I knew you'd find me."

My certainty seemed to shoot like electricity through him, through his expression, down through his body, taking it statue still, turning it rigid. Then everything seemed to relax in him and he brushed my hair back again, telling me about Picard flying down the riverbank, hearing Spock, spotting Data, and then finding me, seemingly having finally fallen from Data's back.

How I'd managed to stay atop her to make my way through the miles between where Picard had spooked and run off and where Axel had found me, was a miracle in and of itself. I couldn't be certain precisely how many miles that was, but I did know that it was more than a few.

I'd been thoroughly lost in those woods.

And Data and Spock had gotten me out—and Picard, even though he'd run off, had helped with the rescue just as much.

Axel touched my cheek. "I love you."

Those words were electricity through *me.*

And all that had happened was pushed away for the moment. Because then I *remembered* what had happened before the fire. What I'd done. What—

"The game," I blurted. "I'm so sorry I did that—"

A shake of his head, his thumb gently rubbing over my skin. "It doesn't matter."

It *did* matter. It mattered to me a whole hell of a lot.

I was a fuck-up. I—

Guilt seeped into my skin, into my bones.

I'd hurt him and—

"Oh, my God!" I shot up—or partway, anyway—because my sudden jerk up to sitting sent waves of pain ricocheting through my body. Monitors began beeping, my heart rate increasing, but I couldn't focus on that, couldn't focus on anything except trying to get my breath back, on trying to not let the wave of black pain take me under again. "Fuck," I hissed, dropping back to the hospital bed...and aggravating all of those hurts all over again.

God. That *hurt.*

"Bruised ribs," Axel murmured, gently stroking my forehead.

"Broken leg, second degree burns on your arms, contusions and bruising and cuts on your back, several of which required stitches. They also treated you for severe smoke inhalation."

I wanted to tell him not to touch me, to back the fuck up and let me breathe.

It was hard enough to suck in air, even with the oxygen mask strapped to my face, and the agony coursing through my body made every nerve so fucking raw that I could barely think.

But the careful recitation had reached my brain, even through the haze of pain.

And it tempered my...well, it tempered my temper.

So I stayed still on the bed, breathed, let him touch me, waited until the hurt faded to a more reasonable level before I opened my eyes again.

"The game. When is the final game?" I asked the question I'd been working up to before I'd set off a whole cascade of pain through my body.

For a second, he wasn't computing what I was asking, but then it seemed as though he did because his body stilled and he started shaking his head, eyes drifting away from mine. "I'm going to get the nurse, let her know that you're awake, see if she can give you something for the pain."

He stood up, chair skidding back.

"Axel."

Rounded the end of my bed.

"*Axel.*"

He stopped.

Wouldn't look at me.

"I'll get the nurse," he said again, starting forward.

My gut clenched, the monitors going crazy again, my heart racing again. Then I pulled out the big guns. "Don't leave me."

That stopped him.

But it didn't bring him closer, didn't unlock his face, didn't bring him to my side.

"Axel, honey, please," I said, lifting my hand.

Finally, he came back, taking my hand in his. "You're hurting," he murmured.

"So are you," I whispered.

A breath.

"Did you miss it?" I asked. Because of me? Did he miss game seven, miss his chance to win a Cup because of me? Remorse and guilt tangling through me, sinking barbs into my belly. And sinking them deeper when a worse notion entered my mind.

Had they lost?

Because of me? Because of the fire? Because Axel was here, had been in River's Bend searching for me? Had they lost because I'd needed him, but they'd needed him too?

"Calm down, buttercup," he murmured. "Just breathe."

"It's my fault."

A shake of his head. "No, honey. It's not your fault. The game is tomorrow."

My eyes went to the clock, saw it was almost midnight. "You need to go," I said. "You need to go *right now.*"

Seven

Axel

She had lost her ever loving mind if she thought I was going to leave her.

Wasn't going to fucking happen.

Not for hockey.

Not for anything.

I'd nearly lost her. I was playing Superglue with her for the rest of her fucking life.

"You *need* to go," she repeated.

"I'm not leaving you." I didn't say anything else. I didn't need to. It was as simple as that.

Argument in her eyes, frustration in her frame. And pain. Too much pain. I needed to get the nurse, needed to get her some more meds.

Maybe they'd make her drowsy enough that she'd lose that argument, would close her eyes and rest. Now that I knew she'd wake up, that she was okay, every part of me wanted to demand that she rest, that she recover and heal.

But surprisingly, the argument faded from her expression, from her pretty brown eyes. Instead, she relaxed further into her pillow and turned her head toward me. "Where are we?" I asked.

"Sacramento," he said, "The trauma team brought you here."

She nodded.

I took her hand again, found myself saying, probably stupidly, "The team is fine. They don't need me."

Her eyes flared, lips pressing flat beneath the oxygen mask. "They *need* you."

They didn't.

They'd won Cups before. They could do it now.

And that wasn't me being all self-deprecating. It was fact. The San Francisco Gold were a force in the league, and they knew how to battle back—case in point the game two days before where they'd been down, where they'd faced elimination and the series being over without winning it all.

They'd regrouped, made a comeback.

Of course, a lot of that had to do with the woman in this bed, for her managing to get a message to me that had gotten my head straight. And yeah, I'd helped with that comeback, had pulled my weight. But we were a team. It was more than just me on the roster. And maybe it made me an asshole, but someone else could step up and shoulder that burden.

Bailey was more important.

Than *anything.*

Even winning it all.

"Axel, you need to go."

My eyes narrowed. "I'm not leaving you," I growled. "So just get that fucking idea out of your mind."

"The game tomorrow isn't a normal one," she said. "It's important. It's a once in a lifetime game. It's a dream—*your* dream—and you know it."

I *did* know it.

I'd wanted to hoist the Cup from the moment I'd first seen my heroes doing in on TV as a kid. That I'd played in the finals at all was a fucking momentous occasion, that we were one game away from winning it all was even bigger.

Plenty of players never got that opportunity.

That *I'd* made it was something special. I—a fuck-up who'd nearly dive-bombed my own career and made it to where I was by sheer dumb luck (and yes, the part of me that was growing and maturing knew that it had also been via hard work)—*done* it.

And I might never get another chance.

So, I wasn't taking missing that game lightly.

But I needed to be here, be with the woman I loved. No fucking *game* was more important than what I had with her.

"It is a dream," I admitted, "but it pales in the face of the dream of you."

She inhaled sharply, and then again when she winced from the sharpness of her previous breath.

"You should rest," I told her.

Her skin was still so pale. Her body broken. Her eyelids growing heavy, even after the small amount of time that she'd been awake.

"Billie Rose?" she asked instead of letting them slid closed, instead of allowing herself to drift off.

"She's okay. I saw her in one of the shelters, along with Dessie and most of the town. Because of you," I added, smoothing my knuckles along her cheek. "Billie got your call and activated the town's emergency system. Joel and Ryan and the rest of the guys helped evacuate almost everyone since they were all downtown together watching the game."

That was the only reason the casualties were so low when the destruction was so vast.

Many had left cars behind, packing the biggest ones full of residents—people only returning to their homes for pets, for kids.

All of it had meant less cars on the road, less traffic.

Because when they'd heard from Bailey, seen how quickly the fire had been moving, Billie Rose—mayor of River's Bend and Bailey's aunt (who was somehow only two years older because, well...small towns)—had used her militant planning skills for good. I should have known she'd been prepared, she was positively obsessed with planning and preparation.

Having done so for an emergency was right in her wheelhouse.

Bailey's warning, Billie Rose's preparation, the residents' knowledge of the plan and willingness to follow it all meant that the casualties had been minimal.

And all from Bailey's end of town.

Which was why I was here, holding her hand, not leaving her after she'd nearly left this fucking planet, after she'd nearly left *me*.

I knew there would be time for her to find out that all of her neighbors had died, that her herd might be completely lost...there would be plenty of time for loss later. Right now, I was going to focus on the fact that she was still here.

She nodded, lids growing heavy. "I'm glad."

"Rest now, buttercup," I murmured. "I'll get the nurse and come right back."

Another nod, this one punctuated by a yawn. "Okay."

Her eyes closed.

I rose, pressed a kiss to her forehead, stood up again, and this time wasn't pulled back to her beside—or at least, not before I managed to get the nurses attention and let her know that she'd woken up and was hurt.

I stepped out into the hall when asked, barely able to hear Bailey's sleepy voice as she answered the questions the nurse—and then the doctor, when she slipped into the room— asked. But her voice was there, and it soothed the razor's edge of need slicing at me to go to her, to hold her hand and touch her and convince myself that she was safe and alive and *here.*

The doctor and nurse were in there for long enough for my nerves to prickle, and by the time they let me back in, my heart was beating hard enough for my knees to shake as I moved over to her.

She was awake. Barely.

But the oxygen mask was gone, the lines of strain that had been etched into her face were fading.

"They give you some pain meds?" I asked.

"Yeah, honey," she said, lifting her hand.

I tugged the chair close to her bedside again, took her hand, lacing my fingers through hers. "Good." Bending, I kissed her knuckles. "You should rest now."

I would just sit here and watch her.

Creepy, yes.

But also, I needed to remind myself that she was alive and safe, to keep reminding myself. To—

She tugged lightly and I shifted my gaze from our interlaced hands up to her face. "Lay next to me?" she asked.

"No—"

"If you won't go," she said softly, her tone cutting right through me, "then at least hold me." Another tug when I looked away, drawing my eyes to hers again. "Let me have this," she whispered. "Let me know that you're resting too. Let me take care of you so that I can rest easy."

I glanced toward the far side of the room, nodded. "I can sleep on the cot."

I didn't want to jostle her leg, to hurt her, to—

"With me," she whispered and I opened my mouth to argue further, but then she said, "Please, honey."

And denial was an impossibility.

Denying her *anything* wasn't in my DNA.

So, I carefully helped her shift enough so that I could crawl in on her uninjured side. Then, just as carefully, I took her in my arms.

Her breathing evened out.

Sleep took her under.

And then I was slipping down right beside her.

Eight

Bailey

He wasn't going to go.

He wasn't.

He could be a stubborn asshole when he really put his mind to it.

And his mind was set. S.E.T. Set.

But I hadn't survived a wildfire—hadn't survived what I'd just survived only to be responsible for imploding Axel's dream.

So, I just had to prove to him that I could be sneakier.

My groundwork had been laid hours before, when the doctor had come in to examine me. It continued now, with him resting beside me, resting up for the game of his life.

It would continue into the morning.

The doctor was coming back at the end of her shift, would be checking on my vitals, making sure my lungs were strong enough to be...

Discharged.

My leg would be a pain in the ass. My ribs even more so.

Even now with the morphine in my system, the edge of all my injuries was razor sharp just beyond my focus, a hazy throb.

Tolerable.

But there.

Maybe less tolerable when the morphine wore off.

But I would manage. I always did.

And anyway, I could manage it for this.

I *would* manage it for Axel.

Next step of that?

Sleeping enough so that I would have the strength to fight him when he heard about my plan.

"Absolutely fucking *not!*"

Okay, so I might need more than strength to fight Axel on this.

I might need handcuffs and several big, broody hockey players and maybe a security specialist.

Luckily, I had several men who fit those categories on hand, having called them while Axel slept deeply. They were standing out in the hall—all except Joel, who was standing in the doorway, his face pointed in my direction, brows lifted in question.

I nodded and he came into the room.

"Axel, man," he muttered. "Take a breath."

"She is *not* leaving this fucking hospital bed," Axel snapped, shoving a hand through his hair. "She almost died an-and—" Breaking off, he pressed both of his fists to his eyes, spinning away from me, his back as stiff as a board.

Joel moved over to him, leaning close, talking quietly.

The doctor squeezed my shoulder lightly. "I'll get the paperwork going, and make sure that referral for the respiratory specialist is on it. Any difficulty breathing, you don't mess around. You go to the ED."

I nodded. "I will."

Another squeeze and then she pushed in the keyboard tray connected to the computer that she'd been logging everything and slipped out of the room.

Axel still had his back to me, Joel at his side. Ryan slipped inside the room when the doctor left, nodding at me and moving over to the pair.

I hoped they'd get through where I couldn't.

I inhaled, released it slowly.

It didn't feel normal, my lungs were going to take a while to heal, but it didn't feel like it had when I'd been in the trees, in the smoke, in the ash. They weren't tight, didn't make me feel like I was suffocating, like I couldn't pull in enough air. The burns on my arms hurt, my leg was a constant ache. Unfortunately, I knew from past experience that my ribs were going to give me trouble for a good long while, and my back felt beyond tender, like even the sheet pressing into it was too much sensation.

But I was alive.

I was okay.

I was getting the fuck out of here.

"Fuck, man," Axel snapped. "It doesn't matter how many different ways you say it, you're not going to convince me that it's a good idea for her to leave that bed." He spun, his gorgeous face a harsh contrast of lines and furrows, of twitching muscles and a beard growing out of control. "You're not leaving that"—he jabbed a finger in my direction"—*bed.*"

I loved this man.

I understood that he must have been out of his mind with worry.

But I was a grown woman. I'd been taking care of myself for a long, long time. Hell, if I was really thinking up about my fucked-up past and my childhood, the truth was that I'd been taking care of myself for almost my entire life. Add in a dash of my abusive ex, Colt—who'd broken me down, who'd controlled me, who'd hit and kicked and punched me—and I wasn't going to roll over and let someone make decisions for me.

Yes, I loved him.

Yes, I could grant him some patience, dish out plenty of understanding.

But that patience and understand wasn't unending.

And—spoiler alert—I was getting to the end of it.

Very quickly.

Taking a breath before I could snap back at him, I gripped tight to my restraint, said quietly, "Don't tell me what I can or can't do."

His blue eyes were filled with sparks of anger, with sparks of fire, with sparks that sent a chill down my spine because it took me right back to those moments on the ranch—scrambling to reach Billie Rose and Dessie, to reach Tommy and Hank and Eli as I hooked up my trailer, as I struggled to get Picard and Data harnessed, to get Spock in the truck and to get on the road.

My pulse sped on the monitor, the rapid *beep-beeping* drawing Axel's focus, drawing *everyone's* focus.

Another breath.

Deliberate breathing.

Focused inhales and exhales.

The beeping slowed.

I held his gaze. "I'm going to that game, honey."

His mouth opened—

Billie Rose strode into the room. She looked at Axel, at me, probably understanding all that was going down in that one glimpse, taking that single reading of the room, even though her clothes were dirty and soot-stained and wrinkled. She had ash on her cheeks, dark circles beneath her eyes, and looked like she hadn't rested since the fire had broken out.

She probably *hadn't*.

And now she was here. Safe.

A bit of tension—tension I hadn't even realized that I'd been holding on to—slid from me.

My aunt was one of the few people I could trust wholeheartedly, and she was okay.

My eyes burned and not from fucking smoke for once.

I glanced at my hand—now free of the IV, thanks to a helpful nurse—and concentrated on not losing my shit.

Later, I could freak the fuck out, could process all the fear and grief that was swirling in my mind.

Right now—*today, tonight*—I needed to hold on to my strength.

For Axel.

"Why's big, hot, and hockey glowering?" she asked chipperly.

"I'm being discharged," I told her.

Billie smiled. "That's a good thing."

"She thinks she's going to Game Seven tonight," Axel gritted out.

My aunt's gaze had swung toward Axel at his announcement. Now it swung back to connect with mine, her brows lifting in silent query.

I dragged mine together, making a silent point.

I *was going* to the fucking game...and more importantly, *Axel* was going.

A flex of her brows. Was I sure?

Mine drawing together even more tightly. Yes, I was fucking *sure.*

A slight nod and then she was turning back to Axel. "So," she said in her typical Billie Rose Voice (determined, authoritative, not to be trifled with), "are you taking her? Or am I?"

Fury on his face.

A muscle twitching in his cheek.

But it was my aunt speaking. It was Billie Rose and she had that magical ability to get everything to work out, to get everyone to behave.

To get my stubborn man to give in, even when it was in regard to something as important to him as my safety.

Because after a long silence—taut and furious—Axel gritted out, "*I'm* fucking taking her."

I smiled.

He softened, crossing over to me, taking my hand.

But as he leaned down, brushed his lips over mine, murmured, "You so owe me," I caught a glimpse behind him.

A glimpse of Joel.

And he was looking...pensive. No, not *pensive.* His expression was gentle, almost that same sort of soft that Axel's had when he was looking at me.

But Joel's gaze wasn't pointed at my hospital bed.

It was fixed on Billie Rose.

Nine

Axel

My focus was fucked.

I felt like I had to tell Coach that.

I owed it to the team. They should scratch me, bench me, get someone else who was more focused, more motivated.

My whole heart was several floors up, in the Family Suite, sitting on the couch, her leg propped up with pillows.

I'd gotten her settled upstairs, Mandy—the head athletic trainer for the team—having taken over from Billie Rose, who'd needed to get back to River's Bend, back to her town, her people.

The fire was still burning, still out of control, still consuming acres of land and houses by the second.

A fucking monster.

A *complex*, not just a fire.

But none of the neighboring towns were faring as bad as River's Bend had. The firefighters had time to dig in, to set up fire lines, to protect them.

Sighing, I tried to push that from my head, but it was pounding and I was exhausted.

Two more reasons to tell Coach I couldn't play.

Along with the fact that I'd barely slept. And my body was beat up. Plus, my legs—hell, I wasn't sure if they could hold me.

"She's okay."

I glanced up, not realizing that I'd just been sitting there while everyone else was getting dressed, just sitting there staring at my hands, *sitting* there being completely useless.

Mandy, the team's head trainer and the person who was supposed to be looking after my woman, was crouched in front of me.

Fuck.

My body immediately tensed with concern. "Bailey—"

"Is with Stefan and Mia and Charlie." A smile. "And the rest of the crew. They're not going to let her so much as lift a finger." She held up her cell. "And they know to call me if there's any issue, big or small. Not just Bailey," she added at was no doubt the obvious protest welling up on my face. "*All* of them," she told me. "And I'll be checking on her." She passed over some smelling salts. "Sniff. Breathe. Clear your mind. I've got her."

"I should—"

"Be down here, doing your job," Mandy said. "Just like she ordered *me* to do. Make her proud," she whispered. "Don't make her carry the weight of this game—whatever the outcome—on her shoulders."

I stilled.

And for the first time I understood exactly why Bailey was pushing this.

My legs *were* shit. I *was* exhausted—both from the long ass season and the events of the last couple of days.

But I'd worked my ass off for this.

Win or lose, it didn't compare to Bailey, to what I felt for her.

I would give my chance to hoist that Cup up in an instant and have absolutely no regrets.

But *she'd* have them, and now I had a choice—allow those regrets to settle on her shoulders, to fester, to make her carry something else, something she damned well shouldn't have to. Or to make a different choice.

It was *no* choice.

I couldn't do that to her.

I *wouldn't.*

I gripped the smelling salts.

I inhaled and immediately felt my mind grow clear, getting that sharp jolt of alertness so many of my teammates avowed that the salts gave them. Supposedly, they expanded the blood vessels, allowed a person to draw in more oxygen. That said, I still wasn't sure if it was something that actually worked.

But, in that moment, I didn't care.

Between Mandy's words and the smelling salts I was finally thinking clearly.

I was finally ready.

"We got her," Mandy said softly. "And we've got you, okay?"

My heart—the formerly ice-cold, almost completely dead organ, at least until Bailey had entered my life—convulsed. Feelings. Too many of them, and each one of them was too fucking big.

But I wouldn't go back. I was too selfish to give them up—any of them—the feelings, the people, the love in my sappy fucking heart.

"Okay," I whispered.

Mandy squeezed my knee, stood, and left the room.

And that was when I finally processed my teammates' mood—they were all deliberately getting dressed, all completely focused on prepping for the game. I could see that in the way they moved, in the lack of chatter and jokes and back talk.

But that wasn't *us*.

Yeah, we played hockey, and did it intensely, because it was our fucking job.

But we weren't this quiet, tense locker room, everyone afraid to speak, to disturb the hushed atmosphere that had descended.

We were laughter and shit-giving.

We were tossing sock balls across the room, and then busting the other type of balls when someone didn't dodge fast enough.

We were leaving it all on the ice but coming back to *family* in the room.

I knew the hushed air, the quiet that had descended, was because they were thinking about me—and no, that wasn't ego talking. They were worried. They were focused. They wanted to bring this game home for me, for Bailey, for the community that was rooting for us and had now lost everything.

The stakes were high, about as high as they could be for us.

This wasn't life or death. We weren't firefighters out in the wilderness trying to save houses and lives and pets.

But it meant something.

Meant something *more* after everything that had happened.

Which was why I knew that I needed to pack away the fear, the tumult, and get my shit together. Which was *why*—and maybe to someone who hadn't spent the last months wouldn't understand why I did what I did next, but...hell, life didn't make sense sometimes, *hockey* didn't make sense sometimes. Pucks bounced off unseen chunks of ice, sending passes askew, causing a goal because it ricocheted off a skate or an ass or the butt end of a stick.

All of which was why I took the sock that was sitting on the bench next to me, rolled it into a ball—something I had lots of practice with, considering that my nickname—Balls—had unfortunately stuck.

Originating because of my excellent Harvest Festival fortune telling, a la the Fantastic Finnegano—and if *that*—me caressing a crystal ball, me wearing fucking *guy*liner as part of my costume—didn't illustrate *exactly* how much I would do for Bailey and Billie Rose and River's Bend as a whole then I didn't know what would.

But right then I was taking advantage of the fact that the name Balls had stuck to put my...

I paused, knowing that my next thought was bad. *Really* bad.

I finished it anyway.

Because today I was about finishing things, finishing *this* thing, getting that motherfucking Cup.

So right then, I was going to take advantage of my nickname Balls and put my *balls* to use.

Heh.

"Brit?"

More than a little distracted, she glanced in my direction, but her focus wasn't on me, not really. "Yeah?"

I let the ball fly.

It sailed across the room, and truthfully, I expected her to catch it. Her reflexes were incredible, snagging hundred mile per hour shots out of midair, so a sock ball should be easy pickings.

But she didn't catch it.

The sock ball flew right through the air...

And beaned her directly in the middle of her forehead.

If I'd been my normal self, I think I might have fallen over because I'd be laughing too hard. As it was, I was too shocked to react.

I felt my eyes go wide.

Will, sitting beside me, turned to face me, expression an exhibit of shock.

Rome, on my other side, was less shocked. He started busting up laughing, nearly falling off the bench in the process.

And that was enough.

The laughter encompassed the room, ringing off the walls, a pin into a balloon of tension, suddenly releasing it...and leaving them...*them.*

Brit launched the sock back at me. I dodged. The shit-giving commenced. The laughter continued. The focus stayed, right on the edge, but it was that loose, Gold focus.

I got dressed.

I laughed.

I breathed.

I thanked fuck that we were in this position, in this *place,* in this moment.

Geared up, Brit crossed to me, thwapping me on the side of the head. "Balls?"

I waited for the payback, or maybe, for another, harder *thwack.* "Yeah?"

"Let's fucking go, yeah?"

My pulse began to speed up, and I nodded. "Let's fucking go."

Ten

Bailey

This was maybe one of the dumbest things I'd ever done.

But I was still glad I was doing it.

Even as the pain was creeping in past the painkillers, my leg a solid thrum of hurt, I wasn't going to give in.

I wasn't going to miss this.

"If you were mine, I'd paddle your ass."

Startled, I blinked up at Stefan. He was so gentle, so easy-going that the words coming out of *his* mouth surprised me. Though, I supposed they were tempered by the twinkle in his eyes. "I think that Brit would paddle *your* ass if she heard you say that."

"Damn right, she would." A flash of a smile. "But I like to keep my wife on her toes." A beat of quiet. "Otherwise, she's hell on wheels."

That made *me* want to smile. "I think she's hell on wheels, no matter how much you try to keep her on her toes."

He touched my cheek, eyes soft. "Yeah, she is." Then he held up the pain medicine bottle. "But I'd still make her take the pills her doctor prescribed."

"They make me sleepy," I protested. My plan was to try to make it through the game, to take it toward the end, so that I didn't miss anything.

"They also make you not hurt," he said. "And since I promised Mandy to take care of you and *she* promised Axel that we would *both* take care of you, I'm"—he shook the bottle, the pills rattling in the plastic container—"keeping you to your schedule."

I bit my lip.

"I'll keep you awake," he said, mouth turning up at the corners. "*If* our guys are playing so well and the game is so much of a blowout that you're dozing off." He winked. "Otherwise, I think this will be a live wire of a matchup and you'll be riding the adrenaline high late into the night."

A sigh. Then I stuck my hand out for the bottle. "Fine," I grumbled. "Give me the drugs."

He opened the lid, which was nice of him (then again, that was Stefan Barie, former captain and current hubby of the illustrious Brit Plantain), and handed me the container. I dutifully took my pills, which truthfully, hurt more than a little bit going down my poor, abused throat. Then I passed the bottle back. He screwed the lid back on, studied me closely. "They'll take this game," he said softly. "If only because Axel knows exactly what—" His eyes focused on me, intense and warm and...suddenly my pain wasn't as bad, and whether it was because Stefan was just so freaking nice or a placebo effect from me immediately taking the pills, I didn't know. All I *did* know was that when Stefan looked at me like that, when he gently squeezed my hand, when he said, "He—*they* know exactly what they're playing for," I felt better.

I felt good.

I felt like the world might end up okay.

"Good," he said, seemingly reading those thoughts as they drifted across my face. "Good."

I didn't like hockey.

I didn't *like* it.

In fact, I was deciding that I despised the sport, despising what it did to my man, to my friends, to the family I was slowly becoming part of.

It was brutal.

It was fast. *Too* fucking fast.

I was watching the game on the big screen TVs mounted to the wall of the Family Suite, knowing that while I might make it down the hall and to the luxury box where I could watch the game from a spot perched high above the rink, I wouldn't last long there. It was too cramped, too full of people, and I was too nervous, too on edge, too ready to jump with every crack of the stick on the ice, to wince with every brutal hit, to gnaw my nails down to their nubs.

At least here I had a sort of privacy.

Sort of because there were lots of people in this set of rooms.

But they were also jumping with every play and missed pass and shot on goal. They were wincing and biting their nails with each hit and good scoring chance on Brit. Basically, they were as riveted to the TVs as I was, and because I was taking up an entire couch—and the littles had been warned to keep their distance because of my leg (and burns and stitches)—I pretty much had a slice of the room to myself.

And Stefan.

But I was only somewhat aware of him.

Because I was spending the majority of my time hating this sport.

The Gold had gone up on the scoreboard quickly, Coop scoring a goal that even my non-hockey appreciative brain knew had been all sorts of pretty. But then, less than a minute later, the game had been tied up, the puck sailing in on an impossibly fast shot that I hadn't even *seen*.

It had taken me two replays to see it sail into the tiny sliver of space between Brit's head and shoulder.

Now it had been almost three full periods and the score was still tied one to one, and I was...

Hell.

I was freaking the fuck out.

Stefan was right.

I didn't need to worry in the least about the pain medicine putting me to sleep. I was so freaking alert, so attuned to every play, big or small, on the ice that I didn't think I'd be able to sleep ever again.

The pillow I'd crammed behind my head was making my neck ache, my leg was a constant thrum, my burns alternated between itching and hurting, but my mind was only distantly processing that because every bit of focus was on how much I *hated* hockey.

Mostly because I was watching the man I loved, the people I liked fight and bleed and *try* so freaking hard.

And I couldn't do anything to help them.

Ugh.

I hated it.

I hated hockey.

Yes, I knew I'd said that. But it bared repeating.

"I feel exactly the same."

Blinking, I glanced up at Stefan. He was resting a hip against the back of the couch I was laying on. He'd been alternating between that position and pacing, though he'd spent most of his time pacing.

"What?" I asked.

"I hate being up here," the former captain of the team playing several stories below muttered. "It never gets easier, the ache never goes away." He sighed, shoved a hand through his hair. "I know I had my time, and I don't regret retiring, but *fuck* do I hate being up here while they're battling down there."

I had never played a minute of hockey in my life. I hadn't watched it before Axel, hadn't known any of the rules.

But I knew something of aching to do what I loved.

I knew something of aching, of *wanting* something so bad, but that not mattering. Because my wants didn't factor into the universe's plan, didn't factor into my life. Of course, me wanting to be a teacher was nothing like the longing Stefan must be feeling watching some of his former teammates, watching his wife out there.

And not being able to help.

Especially in a game this big.

One of the Gold defensemen lost an edge and went sliding, losing their skate's grip on the ice, taking themselves out of the play, and in an instant, there was an odd man rush heading straight for Brit.

Stefan's wife didn't flounder, didn't hesitate, just challenged the players like the boss she was, making them force a pass across...

That Josh managed to get a stick on and deflect into the corner.

A second later, the game was rushing the other direction, and the Gold got a shot on net.

"So how do you handle it?" I asked once the goalie had frozen the puck and the game went to commercial break. "How do you handle being up here when they're down there?"

Stefan's smile was small. "You learn how to handle the agony." A beat. "And then you learn how to handle theirs when it doesn't work out."

Eleven

Axel

I'd never played in a game that had gone this far into double overtime.

The network was getting their money's worth, that was for damned sure.

But meanwhile, we were all dying on the ice, this slow war of attrition eating away at us piece by piece.

Exhaustion weighing down my legs.

Hands growing heavier by the moment.

This was the type of game where the series-deciding, the *Cup*-deciding goal wasn't going to be a pretty one, wasn't going to be a fluttering puck sailing across the ice and onto a teammate's stick who made a masterful deke and then chipped it into the top corner of the net.

Nope.

At this point in the game, it was going to bounce off someone's ass, squeak between the goalie's pads and the ice, barely cross that red goal line, or ricochet off a stick or skate or *several* sticks and skates.

Yup, it definitely was going to be an ugly ass goal.

And it was going to be heartbreaking for one of the teams.

But this game was going to end eventually.

Or at least, *that* was what I was telling myself.

Sweat was stinging my eyes. My feet were numb in my skates, which was an improvement on the cramping, aching pain from the previous ten minutes. My stick somehow had invisible weights attached to it, the negligible burden it had been for me to carry previously getting heavier by the shift. Hell, the puck had turned to iron, so much harder to move, sticking to the ice, requiring extra focus I didn't have available when I was mentally and physically exhausted.

"Yup. Yup!"

I glanced up, saw Josh breaking up the ice, somehow moving like he wasn't tired, like it didn't matter that we'd almost played two full games, one right after the other. Will was on with him, the two having created some excellent chemistry and chances in recent games, and this time was no exception. Will threaded the needle, sending the puck up to Josh's stick. Josh carried the puck into the zone, crossing over the blue line, closing in on the net and—

The crowd groaned.

I winced in solidarity.

Because fucking *ouch*.

Josh slammed into the ice, head bouncing off the hard surface, the puck squirting out from beneath him. The opposing team picked it up, started sprinting the other direction, and...

Fuck.

Josh wasn't moving.

But the officials wouldn't blow the whistle, not when the other team had possession of the puck and had a chance to score.

Not in game seven of the finals.

Not in double overtime of that game seven.

My fingers tightened on my stick as the players—four to our two—closed in on Brit.

I sucked in a breath and my lungs seized.

Fuck.

The puck slid from one side of the ice to the other.

Brit followed, keeping her angles, keeping her focus, trusting her defense to take the biggest threat while she tracked the puck, continued moving, never being caught flat-footed...

At least until her skate caught on something—a divot in the ice, a piece of tape, or maybe nothing, maybe she was just as tired as we were and she made a mistake.

Her feet slid out from beneath her.

She landed on the ice in an awkward heap, hard enough it must have stolen the air from her lungs, but even as the crowd gasped, as *I* gasped, she was recovering. Moving. Sliding.

But she was too slow and the other team was too close.

Half of the net was open.

Fuck.

My teeth clinked together, jaw aching from the force. My lungs weren't working and neither were my ears.

Time slowed down.

They were well over our blue line now.

The pass sailed back to the other side of the ice, splitting our defense.

Now they'd closed in on the top of the circles. One of their players dropped the puck back and—

"Go."

Blood was dripping down Josh's face, and his eyes were wild, but he'd somehow made it to the bench.

"Go!" he said again.

I blinked.

Processed.

And then I was over the bench, skate blades hitting the ice, sprinting for our zone.

Coach hadn't told me to go—or maybe she had.

All I knew was that I was the closest and I'd reacted the fastest and suddenly I was on the ice. And heading for our zone.

But I didn't get there in time.

Brit was still on her side, scrambling to get her edges under her, to find her skates.

The four players for the other team had become five, and our forwards were hustling back to help our defense, but they still trail behind.

Five on two.

Brit made it to her knees.

The other team reached the hash marks.

A pass to the wide-open back door.

A pass that would allow the opposing player positioned there to just tap the puck home.

Fucking hell.

I couldn't get there in time.

None of us could.

All I could do was haul ass toward our zone, hope and pray to the hockey gods that I might make it in time to do *something*.

I wouldn't.

I *wouldn't* make it.

But luckily...I didn't need to.

The puck fluttered to that back door, landed on that players stick. He shot—

And Brit threw a leg encased in a broad, rectangular pad out.

It was that broad, rectangular pad that was our saving grace.

The puck hit the edge of that leather protective covering.

I sucked in a breath and everyone on the ice seemed to freeze, to hold their breath...

As the puck rolled just wide of the net.

It hit the boards with a soft *clink* that I swore I could hear, and maybe I did, maybe the entire arena had fallen silent, leaning forward on the edges of their seats, watching, waiting for that puck to go in the net.

And when it didn't...

The collective inhale was loud enough to hurt my ears.

Then Brit was on her feet.

Then Logan was at the boards, scooping up the puck, glancing up—

Electricity all along my spine.

I'd only gotten on the ice when Josh had made it to the boards.

I hadn't made much progress back-checking when Brit had somehow made that save.

Which meant I was behind all of their players.

Something that Logan saw.

Our eyes connected. That electricity fizzled. I started hauling ass.

Because I knew it was coming.

Logan fired the puck off the boards.

Turning as I scooped it up, feeling the sting of the impact with my stick blade in my palms. It was a good thing, jarring me to pinpoint focus. One that had me putting every bit of strength I still had left in me into my legs, into my hands.

Keep moving. Keep that puck on my stick blade.

Put distance between myself and their players.

Move. *Move.*

I *did* move.

Over the red line at center ice. Across their blue line.

Down over the tops of the circles.

To the hash marks at the midpoints of those circles, right into the slot that led to the front of the net.

I don't know how I knew what the goalie was going to do—maybe it was instinct, maybe it was knowledge buried somewhere in my mind from watching all that tape the video coaches had prepared for us.

Maybe it was just...luck.

But, regardless, I knew the goalie was going to try for a poke check.

He choked up on his stick. I swerved hard to the right, my skate blades digging into the ice with a sharp grinding sound.

I trusted them, trusted the equipment guys to have set me up for success, trusted my coaches to have drilled into me the knowledge and muscle memory I was using, trusted myself to know my limits.

The goalie's stick shot out.

The puck came with me...but only for a moment.

Because then I slid it beneath the outstretched stick and along the goalie's other side.

Toward the net.

Twelve

Bailey

He was skating so fast that he shot past the net, colliding with the boards, and landing in a heap that had me wincing.

That had to hurt.

But then I was looking away from him.

Because *where* was the puck?

Stefan was the first to process it, probably since he'd been down there many times before. He could just *see* better.

"It's in!" he shouted.

And I winced again—both from the shout and also because I jerked upright.

Because Stefan was right.

The puck *was* in the net.

Holy shit.

The puck was in the net.

A fact that everyone in the room, in the boxes, in the arena, on the ice, on those player benches down below at rink level seemed to realize all at once.

The. Puck. Was. *In*. The. Net.

I felt my mouth drop open as I glanced up at Stefan. He was smiling widely, gaze pointed on the screen.

I turned back to the TVs just in time to see the Gold sprint off the bench and mob Axel, taking him down to the ice under a dog pile of black and gold clad teammates. Smiles and fist-bumps and hugs and skates in the air and—

Axel emerging from the pile, his face stark, his eyes wide and surprised.

As though it hadn't hit him yet.

And then Brit moved up beside him—her helmet having joined the plethora of other equipment on the ice in a yard sale of epic proportions—and slung her arm around his shoulders, leaning close and saying something into his ear.

It was impossible to hear what she said, the crowd's cheers echoing even through the walls to where I was. It was impossible to read her lips, not with the chaos on the ice.

But whatever it was she said had that surprised look fading, had a smile spreading out on his face, a smile that was so fucking beautiful I immediately felt my eyes well with tears.

He must not have known or processed that he'd scored.

My beautiful, wounded, strong hockey player had scored the game-winning goal. During game seven. In double overtime. After the game had very nearly gone the absolute opposite way.

"They did it," I whispered.

Stefan gently touched my shoulder. "They did."

His eyes were glassy too, but I only caught a glimpse of those watery blue irises before he bent down and scooped up Roxie, hugging her tight. "Mama!" she shouted, pointing a chubby arm toward the TV.

"Yeah, baby," he said. "Mama did it." A glance up at me. "Everyone did it."

I bit my lip, nodding, and then turned back to the TV, watching the celebration, so fucking thrilled for them that I could barely take in the scene, could barely comprehend them shaking the other team's hands, barely saw the carpet being rolled out, the big silver cup being brought out to the ice.

The cheers grew louder, reverberating through the walls and humming in my belly, my heart.

My soul.

They'd done it.

And Axel was here for it.

Swear to Christ, my heart couldn't take it. This moment was too perfect, was too wonderful. But I didn't look away.

I just watched as Josh, a bandage around his head, red seeping through, moving stiffly, but upright, his smile huge, his hands reaching for the Cup. He lifted it from the podium, skated a small circle on the ice, and then...

Passed it to Axel.

Whose expression was one of shock, of awe, of reverence.

The crowd roared.

He skated...

And I felt it again in my veins, in my heart, in my soul.

His loop completed, I watched as he passed it to Brit, whose brown eyes were luminescent, her patented smile on full display.

Fucking beautiful.

Her. Him.

All of it.

"Want to take a walk down to ice level?" Stefan asked as Brit passed the Cup to Coop. "Or a hobble, rather?" he asked lightly, one half of his mouth turning up.

Right.

I had the big, dumb cast on, couldn't maneuver how I wanted, but I wasn't hurting right then. I wasn't feeling anything. I was running on happiness and adrenaline and whatever fucking pixie dust the fact that my boyfriend having just won the Stanley Cup created. I wasn't in pain. I—

Wanted to be in Axel's arms.

Was desperate to tell him how proud I was of him.

"Yeah," I told Stefan. "I'm ready for a hobble."

Grinning, he got my crutches for me, and I shoved them under my armpits, managed to get myself upright, to get my feet under me. I wanted to move quickly, but crutches were hard as fuck, and I was surviving on fumes, even if the adrenaline had temporarily banked my pain. Slow and steady was going to be my way forward.

It had helped me survive.

So I wouldn't discount it.

And that night it meant that I made slow, careful progress across the room. I made it into the elevator. I made it down to ice level.

I made it to the hallway that led to the ice.

Though, not on it, not like many of the families and kids and wives and girlfriends who were joining in on the celebration.

"Want me to help you?" Stefan had asked, Roxie on one hip, the little girl leaning so far forward it was a miracle he was able to hold her in place.

"No," I told him. "I don't think Axel would be happy if I took the crutches onto the ice."

And I wouldn't do anything to ruin this moment for him.

Plus, I'd survived a forest fire. I had a broken femur, burns and healing lungs and stitches. My mobility was limited to this slow hobbling around on crutches. I wasn't about to go out onto the ice and break my head and ass by trying to up my game and bring that slow hobbling onto a slippery surface.

I'd had enough pain for a good long while.

Stefan touched my cheek. "Probably not. I'll check in with you in a bit."

"Go," I ordered. "Be with your wife. Hug her tight for me for that save."

He grinned, and then he and Roxie were walking out onto the ice.

The fans noticed, the volume increasing as they caught sight of him, their love for the former captain still intense.

Brit moved to them and my ears rang as they embraced, my eyes stung.

It was the perfect end to her career—a hell of a game, winning it all, going out on top, and being able to skate right into her husband and daughter's arms, to have her daughter pulling her close and smacking a sloppy toddler kiss to her mouth.

Love. Family.

Perfect.

My eyes went beyond stinging.

They were leaking, dripping down my cheeks. Fuck, if six

months ago I would have been able to predict that I would be here, feeling this way...I would have laughed myself silly.

I never *ever* could have imagined feeling this open, this in love, this *happy*.

Because the person *I* loved was here, had been part of all this amazingness.

Was—

A calloused thumb brushing the skin beneath my eyes. "Who do I have to kill for these tears?" Axel asked softly, towering over me in his skates, his skin flushed, his hair sweaty and mussed from his helmet.

And still, he was the most beautiful man I'd ever seen.

I smiled up at him. "The man who scored the game-winning goal."

His cheeks went a little more pink. "It was nothing."

I leaned into him, reaching up, the crutches slipping free and falling to the black skate mats. But he had me, it was never a thought that he wouldn't. Reaching up, way up, I cupped his cheeks. "I am so *freaking* proud of you."

A shake of his head. "I—"

"You," I whispered. "I am so proud of *you*, honey."

His arms banded tightly around me and he buried his face in my hair.

Then his shoulders began to shake.

And I knew my big, broody hockey player had lost it.

Thirteen

Axel

My heart was pumping.

The crowd was cheering.

The ice was full of people.

But the woman I loved was in my arms, and she had helped me accomplish something amazing.

So, yeah, admittedly, I lost it for a moment.

These last couple of days had been a lot, and having Bailey in my arms, hearing her say she was proud of me…

Hell, it fucked with my tough hockey player image, but I couldn't deny that my eyes were full of tears—and that maybe a few of them escaped. And truthfully, I couldn't give a fuck if the cameras caught that.

Because Bailey was my heart.

Her hands went to my hair, holding me to her.

And I just sat in this moment, soaked in the way it felt when she held me, breathed through the fact that I'd just been part of a team to win a Cup, that we'd won because of a goal *I'd* scored.

It was the stuff of lying in bed as a kid, lying on a bare mattress, my one blanket tucked over me, staring at the stained ceiling overhead and fantasizing to drown out my reality—to drown out my mom, who was fucking some guy in the other room or drunk and pounding on my door, pissed because I hadn't done something (on the odd times she remembered I was there at all) or yelling at whoever she was fucking because she was drunk or because she was pissed that he hadn't brought her enough booze.

I'd dreamed then.

Wished then.

But never really accepted that it could actually happened.

And today it had.

"Fuck, buttercup," I whispered.

Her fingers dug into my jersey, into my shoulder pads where the bottom part wrapped around the back of my ribcage.

I felt the slight bite of her nails, knew she felt just as flayed open as I did. "Yes," she whispered. "*That.*"

I chuckled and leaned back enough to see her face. "You hurting?"

"In the best way," she whispered, rubbing the space on her chest, beneath which sat that beautiful heart.

Fuck, she was so fucking sweet. Bending, I slanted my mouth over hers, dipping my tongue into her mouth and kissing her way too deep and way too long considering there were people and cameras all around.

And case in point—

The cheers grew loud enough that I lifted my head, saw that we were on the jumbotron.

Her cheeks were pink, but she just glanced at the camera and waved...to more cheers.

"You're amazing," I said when she looked back to me.

Her inhale was shaky. "I love you." Our eyes locked and time stretched between us—just us, just our love and our lives and being thankful we were right here in this moment. But eventually, we managed to tear our gazes apart, to look back out at the ice. "You should go back out there," she murmured, leaning her head against my arm.

"Come with me."

"I know I'm stubborn and like to do everything on my own," she said, turning her head and pressing a kiss to my biceps—or at least where my biceps would be if my jersey and my shoulder and elbow pads hadn't been in the way. "But even I don't think I can manage the ice on my crutches."

"Who says you need your crutches?" I asked lightly.

The little vee that appeared between her brows made me want to kiss her all over again. "Um, the *doctor* says I need my crutches, and for that matter so do yo—*ah!*"

I swept her up, careful to support her leg, making sure to not bump it on anyone or on any of the equipment or on boards or... well, just making sure to not ram her broken leg into something. Luckily, when I got out onto the ice there was more room, even though it was crawling with family members and back-office staff and players and—

I carefully set her down, waiting until she was steady on her good foot, still taking a good portion of her weight so that I could make sure that she was safe, wasn't going to slip and fall.

"Axel," she breathed, almost too soft for me to hear over the din.

"I know, buttercup," I whispered.

And then we just stood there at center ice, staring up at the stands, at the crowd, watching my teammates take their turn with the Cup, and I knew she felt much of what I felt, knew she was as awed as I was.

It was in her eyes, her expression, in the way that she leaned up and kissed my jaw.

A miracle.

A dream.

A future I was never going to let go.

Because she was in my arms.

It was just after dawn and I hadn't slept a wink.

We'd stayed at the rink too long, had spent way too much time with the guys in the locker room, had done too many fucking interviews.

But eventually, I'd managed to get away, to convince Bailey that we'd stayed long enough.

The team would be getting together later today. The party would continue.

My woman had needed her bed.

She hadn't said a word about being tired or wanting to go—of course she hadn't, of course she *wouldn't*. But I'd watched her lids droop and the fatigue write itself into the lines of her face.

Stubborn, though.

She'd refused to leave several times over and because the celebration and press and staff were all around, everyone wanting to be part of this moment, we'd stayed.

Until I'd looked over and seen her propped in the corner of the locker room, back against the wall, leg propped up on the bench, Roxie curled up in her lap. They were both fast asleep, and though I'd paused to take a picture, because—fuck—who wouldn't want to document all of that beauty, after I'd managed to signal to Stefan.

We'd tag-teamed our women to the car—minus Brit, who'd stayed behind to finish speaking to all of the media and the few lucky fans who'd been allowed behind the scenes.

Bailey had protested when I'd carried her through the halls, but she was exhausted and plus, Stefan, had found her crutches and was carrying both them and Roxie, so Bailey hadn't been able to stubborn herself outside on them.

She'd fallen asleep in the car.

I'd gotten her up to the apartment, tucked into bed, thankful that Stefan had given me the bottle of pain medicine before he'd left with Roxie, because I'd managed to rouse her enough to take them. Then I'd gone back to the car, retrieved her crutches and settled into bed beside her.

Pitch black night had given way to the early morning, navy creeping into reds and oranges and yellows as the sun began to rise in the east.

And still I didn't sleep.

Not because I wasn't tired.

I was exhausted, so tired it was pulling at my bones, sinking my body heavy into the mattress, tendrils winding their hooks into the edges of my mind, drawing me down.

But I couldn't sleep.

Not a surprise.

I was replaying the game. And then I was going over the last few days. And then I was thinking about how everything could have easily turned out so, so differently, and just wanting to close my eyes, to let sleep drag me under.

But it was like I was waiting for something.

Or maybe part of me was worried that the moment I *did* fall asleep, I'd wake up and realize this had all been a dream.

I'd wake up and I'd be right back in that nightmare.

I'd wake up and—

My phone rang.

That wasn't unusual. It had been going off for hours, pinging with texts, buzzing with calls, voicemails stacking up.

But when I glanced at the screen, my spine froze solid.

Because I knew that even though I had stayed awake...

The nightmare was going to yank me under anyway.

Fourteen

Bailey

For a minute, I didn't know where I was.

The ranch. The hospital bed. No...

In Axel's apartment. In his bedroom. In his arms.

I started to roll toward him, but he dropped his hand onto my hip, holding me steady. "Easy, buttercup," he murmured, stopping me from rolling over onto my broken leg.

Smart man, he was.

He shifted, coming over me, his hand braced by my head, his eyes coming to mine.

God, he was pretty.

And mine.

"Hi, honey," I murmured, reaching up, stroking my fingers through the thick brown beard coating his jaw.

"Hi," he murmured back.

"Stanley Cup Champion," I whispered, my lips turning up into a grin I could feel was taking over my whole face.

His eyes were full of emotion. "Because of you."

I shook my head.

"I never would have made it this far," he said softly. "Not without you."

"Dammit!" I hissed, feeling the burn in the corners of my eyes. This *man*.

"What?" he asked, lips tipping up again before he bent and brushed them over my forehead. "Because I'm going to make you cry?"

"Yes." A huff. "I'm not a crier. I'm a tough cowgirl who kicks ass on my ranch, but you—" Except, my words caught up with me and now my eyes stung for a whole other reason.

My ranch was gone.

I knew it.

I *felt* it.

The fire had moved too quickly, had burned too fast, swooping down the hills toward the barn, toward the house.

God, Gramps and Gran's place.

My place.

The pictures, the horseshoe over the door, the wine barrel pots filled with cheerful flowers.

Gone.

"Hey," he said softly, covering my hand with his own, lacing our fingers together. "It's okay."

It wasn't.

Not really.

The incandescent joy of the night before had been punctured by reality, had been burned to ashes by the hot licking flames that left blisters on my arms and my lungs weak and my hair singed.

"It's gone," I whispered.

His face gave me the answer I already knew, but *fuck* it still hurt so freaking much.

"Tommy, Hank, and Eli?" I asked, mind racing away from that pain. "Are their places—?" But I didn't finish the question, because the look that entered his eyes when I said their names sent a dagger directly into my heart.

"No," I whispered, tears escaping in earnest now. "*No.*"

I had to be reading Axel wrong.

Maybe their *ranches* were gone, but it couldn't be what I was seeing in Axel's eyes, couldn't be the truth that was roaring through me about those flames that had moved so quickly, burned so hotly.

"*No,*" I said again when Axel's face didn't clear, when that heavy, *sad* look didn't leave his eyes. "*No!*"

"Honey," he whispered.

And that was enough. It sliced through me, had the truth settling on me with all the force of an atom bomb.

The tears didn't just burn my eyes, didn't just singe my cheeks, they hitched through my body in wracking, painful sobs, rending my heart, my bones, my *soul*. Axel shifted to my side, tugged my body against his, arms holding me tight. I felt him distantly, because I couldn't be there, couldn't be truly present in my body, not in that moment.

I was thinking of Tommy and Hank and Eli, thinking about how they'd taken me under their wings, how they'd helped me fight to keep Gramps' ranch going. I was thinking of the pride in their eyes when they'd agreed to my plan for extra income. I was thinking of them showing up with hay and fixing my tractor and answering all of the questions that had been generated from a young, naive girl taking over a failing ranch.

And now they were gone.

"How?" I eventually managed to whisper.

A long pause. Then Axel smoothed his knuckles over my cheek, said softly, "Frank said the fire just moved too fast. They couldn't get out, even with your warning."

Fuck.

Fuck.

Another sob wracking my body, and then he was holding me again. Not telling me to stop. Not telling me it would be okay. Just wrapping me in his arms and pressing me close, my ear to his chest, his heartbeat steady beneath his rib cage.

That pulsing, even rhythm eventually settled me.

"I'm sorry," he said long minutes later, his fingers sliding through my hair.

"I know," I whispered. "But *I'm* the one who's sorry. I ruined your post-Cup—"

His fingers tightened slightly and he tilted my head up, eyes locking onto mine. "Don't you dare apologize."

"But I—"

"Don't," he repeated, tucking my head back into his throat, his fingers going to my hair again, drifting through the ends. "Just don't, buttercup."

So, I didn't.

I didn't make further apologies and I didn't harp on the fact that I was crying on the morning after he'd achieved something huge, bringing the mood down, even if it was an accident and things were raw and I hadn't meant to turn into a sobbing woman in his arms.

Because everything was so fucking heavy and I needed someone to help me shoulder the burden, at least for a little bit.

I was homeless. I'd lost everything. People I loved were gone. My home and town were destroyed. My body was broken.

So, I just stayed in those arms.

Just let him hold me.

Just listened to his heartbeat in my ear.

It was steady, so steady, and that steady was the single thing grounding me to this world.

For now, that was enough.

He'd driven through the smoke-filled roads, drawing us closer to River's Bend.

But that wasn't our destination.

Not at first, anyway.

The fire was fifty percent contained, though the firefighters had managed to keep it from engulfing any more towns as they encircled the blaze. It would probably be weeks before it was fully out, before the smoke fully cleared, but they'd begun allowing people back into town to see what remained.

Many of River's Bend's residents were still in the shelter, still staying at hotels and motels along the highway, miles from town, miles from whatever remained of their homes.

I needed to see them.

Needed to see Dessie and Ryan, Billie Rose and Joel. Needed to see my friends. Needed to make sure they were okay.

Axel had said the only casualties were on the ranches on my side of town.

But I *needed* to see the people I loved.

So, I'd crammed myself into his car, endured the uncomfortable drive, and convinced Axel to first take me to the shelter and then up to River's Bend.

Now, as the smoke got thicker along both sides of the road, clawing its way between the trees, my nerves were prickling uncomfortably.

My throat was tight.

My skin stung in memory.

My fingers formed tight, tight fists.

"We can go back," Axel murmured, reaching over and carefully loosening my hold, lacing our fingers together. "Do this another day."

Was the smell of smoke triggering me?

Were my lungs already feeling tight?

Yup. And yup.

But I needed to do this, to see them, see my friends, needed to know that th-they'd survived and were okay when the others weren't.

I tightened my grip on his hand. "No," I whispered. "I need to do this."

A nod. No further arguments.

Just holding my hand, taking us through the smoke-filled road, and turning into a parking lot.

It was for a neighboring town's high school, I realized, my eyes just able to make out the concrete sign, the letters etched into the surface.

He parked in the ash-covered lot, pressed a kiss to the back of my hand.

Then he released me and was out through his door, rounding the hood, and opening mine. "Ready?"

A soft question.

My big broody hockey player all soft and gentle, but only for me.

I nodded, let him pull me up and out of my seat, holding on to the top of the car until he retrieved my crutches from the back seat.

Under my armpits.

Hobbling my way inside...

What I didn't realize was that I would be hobbling my way into hell.

Fifteen

Axel

I felt the shock go through Bailey and moved a little closer to her, wishing that I could hold her hand, that I could hold *her*.

Because I knew exactly what she was feeling.

This was hell on earth.

Dogs barking in wire crates, blankets tossed over the top in a valiant hope that they might quiet, might find some peace amid all this chaos. Kids sat on cots, their eyes wide and shocked, all of them too quiet, staring off into space like they were living their own personal nightmare.

And they were.

Their town as they knew it was gone.

So they were in a nightmare. Living it, surrounded by it.

I thought of the phone call I'd received in the early hours of that morning while Bailey slept in my arms.

Knew that I understood something of living in a personal nightmare.

How life could swivel from one extreme to the other in just a few days was unfathomable, *untenable*.

But this wasn't about me, not right now.

This was about Bailey and Billie Rose, who I could see organizing supplies in the far corner of the room. This was about Joel beside her, shifting boxes. This was about Dessie, laying out food on the folding tables set up along one side of the gym.

This was about the people of River's Bend.

This was about finding ways to help them.

"Billie is over there," I said, leaning in to whisper in Bailey's ear and pointing toward her aunt. "Can you make it over there, buttercup? Or do you want me to go get her?"

A shuddering breath. "I can make it."

No surprise there, I thought, smothering a smile.

This wasn't the place for smiles, even though I was beyond glad to see a glimpse of my woman in amongst all this awfulness.

We picked our way over to Billie Rose, pausing when Bailey needed to give her ribs, her body a break.

A few people spoke to her, to me, checking in on her injuries, offering quiet congratulations for the game, but I felt very far removed from the victory of the night before. There were no winners here—everyone in this gymnasium had lost something or someone.

"You need to take a break."

Not me ordering Bailey to rest, though it sounded very much like something that would come out of my mouth.

Instead, it was from Joel, who looked like he'd been pulled backward through a hedge.

"I'm fine."

That was a statement that sounded like it could have come from Bailey, demonstrating all that stubborn.

But then again Bailey and Billie Rose *were* related, so it wasn't a surprise that stubborn ran in their DNA.

It also wasn't a surprise that Joel was giving orders.

My former teammate and I had similarities aside from hockey—being annoying and bossy with a tinge of asshole, at least according to Bailey. Joel was nicer than me, though. Although not with Billie Rose. With Bailey's aunt...well, buttons were pushed.

Regularly.

And she returned the favor.

Oil and water. Enemies united solely for a common cause but prepared to stab each other in the back at the first opportunity.

Hell, I'd heard Joel refer to Billie Rose as *harpy* more than a few times.

But there was no *harpy* in sight, not on his tongue, not in his eyes. Just concern and orders to rest and—

Bailey glanced up at me, lifted her brows, the first lick of mischief I'd seen on her face since finding her in that forest making my breath catch.

God, she was gorgeous.

God, she was *mine.*

Joel snagged Billie's arm. "I said you need—"

A jerk, Billie Rose stepping back. "And *I* said I'm *fine*. I need to sort these supplies and get them over to the other shelter." She yanked a box out of the stack and did it so abruptly that she nearly toppled backward. *Would* have toppled backward if not for Joel catching her.

Bailey looked up at me again, her brows still raised, that mischief glowing bright, and this time, I couldn't smother my smile.

Because I was thinking the same thing that my woman clearly was.

Sparks. Irritation. Bickering. Trying very hard to stay away from each other.

And it had ended up with us in love, with me absolutely devoted to this woman who held my heart, knowing we had ties between us that would never be broken.

"You're about to collapse," Joel snapped, so focused on Billie that he hadn't noticed our approach. Or maybe he had and he didn't care, his worry and attention solely for the blond firecracker who took planning and preparation and love for her town to a critical level. "The black circles beneath your eyes have their own fucking black circles. You need to lay down for an hour and then can get back to it. You won't do anyone any good if you burn out, sweetheart."

Billie finally released the box, setting it down with a *thump*. "I'm not your *sweetheart,*" she snapped, jabbing a finger into his chest.

Joel snagged her wrist. "Okay, *sweetheart*, so I'll go back to harpy."

She tugged, nostrils flaring, gritting out, "Let me go."

Joel didn't.

I could practically see the smoke coming out of her ears, but curiosity had gripped me and I found that I couldn't bring myself to interrupt. Not when I wanted to see how this played out.

"Ugh!" she growled, pairing the animalistic sound with a stomp of her foot, looking ready to close the nearly two feet of distance between herself and Joel and clock him over the head...probably with that box.

It was heavy, but she was motivated.

And *I* was thoroughly entertained.

Bailey, apparently, thought it was prudent to intervene. "Billie," she murmured.

Her aunt jumped about three feet in the air.

I smoothed a hand down Bailey's back, stopping probably too close to that lush ass of hers, considering we were in public. "I was enjoying the show, buttercup," I murmured in her ear.

An arch look in my direction. "Behave."

"You first," I grumbled and nipped the dangling lobe.

Another arch look, but relief slid through me when she leaned back against my body, letting me have some of her weight. I knew from experience that crutches were a pain to use, not to mention, seriously hard work, especially given the span of her injuries.

"See?" she muttered. "Behaving. Now you."

"Never," I teased, pressing my lips to the spot behind her ear, the one that always made her shiver. "And you don't want me to."

She rewarded my insolence with a kiss to my jaw, made easier because I'd bent down to her ear, hadn't been able to resist being as close as possible to her, even with the difference in our heights. "That's true, honey," she murmured and she gave me more of her weight. I soaked in this bit of light, this bit of humor on her face because I knew, *knew* that it was going to get tougher from here. Knew that the light would be blocked out by the dark clouds of reality soon enough.

Another kiss to my jaw, then she returned her attention back to her aunt, just as Billie Rose and Joel managed to stop focusing on each other and spun to face us.

To Joel's credit, Billie *did* look exhausted—lines around her mouth, her eyes, those dark circles certainly prominent. Her face was pale and streaked with ash, same as her hair.

She needed a shower and a bed for a good ten hours.

But Billie Rose was a force, and I wasn't going to be the one who could force her there.

Bailey might succeed.

Or Joel, I thought, biting back the smirk.

Billie moved toward us, gently cupping Bailey's cheeks. "You look good, honey," she said, moving in and carefully hugging her niece (yes, they were almost the same age; yes, that was weird; also yes, thinking about Bailey being Billie's niece was weird, even though it was true). "I'm glad to see you up and around. I thought after last night you'd be sleeping the day away."

"Axel's been making me rest and take my medicine. Funny how that works and makes me feel better," Bailey said dryly.

Billie Rose's piercing blue eyes hit mine, approval and gratitude in those depths.

I didn't need the latter—Bailey was my heart and I'd give everything of mine to take care of her. The former, I couldn't lie, the former felt good.

I hadn't had a lot of approval in my life.

My fault, yes.

But also not something I'd grown up with.

Which was a line of thinking I didn't want to go down, not after that morning, and—

No.

I sliced straight through that thought, cutting it off in its tracks.

Later, I'd worry about phone calls and the bullshit I grew up with and all the things that made up my nightmares.

Right now, we needed to deal with the problem at hand.

Sixteen

Bailey

"You get your aunt to rest," Axel murmured in my ear, his hot breath making me shiver. "I'll take Joel."

My brows dragged together, not sure why he'd need to take Joel.

But then I took a closer look at the man who'd stepped in, protecting me from my abusive, asshole ex when he didn't have to put his neck on the line, not for me, a relative stranger. That closer look showed me enough.

Because the big, broody hockey player who was hovering by my aunt was equally as exhausted.

He was complaining about her dark circles?

Well, his were big, broody hockey player sized. And paired with enough lines of fatigue drawn into his face to form a roadmap, stubble that was long and scraggly, even for a big, broody hockey player, and I understood precisely why Axel was going to take him.

Glancing up at *my* big, broody hockey player, I nodded in agreement then crutched forward to Billie. "Show me around," I demanded. "I need to do something to help."

"You should rest—"

I lifted my brows. "Is this where I say I'm rubber and you're glue?"

A frown, her blond curls bouncing.

I just held her eyes, waited.

Until she huffed, those curls bouncing again, and then she spun on her heel. "Fine. You can help over here."

Since over *here* was closer to several empty cots, these in a more isolated corner of the gym, I nodded and followed her.

When I'd made it to her, she was dragging several boxes over so they were within arm's reach of those cots. I glanced back, saw Joel start to me toward us, his expression thunderous, but Axel stepped in front of him, and I watched, waiting to see what would happen.

Terse words.

That thunderous look darkening.

But eventually, Joel spun on his heel and stormed away.

Letting out a silent breath, I turned my attention back to Billie Rose and wondered if I would need to tackle my aunt to get her to chill the fuck out for an hour or two to get her to stop sorting through boxes that didn't need sorting, just because she had to find something to keep her busy.

So she didn't think.

So she wouldn't be sucked down into the sad.

Because I knew my aunt.

She would be the rock, the tough one, the person who everyone turned to, and she wouldn't allow herself to be sad, to feel, to sit and cry and grieve for what they'd lost.

She'd hide behind that wall of capability.

Until people stopped trying to help her.

But today, I was there.

Today, I was *going* to help her.

No arguments.

Now I just needed to figure out how to get her to lie down for a few minutes without tackling her to the cot, because I was damn sure if I *did* tackle her in an effort to get her to rest, that she wouldn't hesitate to launch me off her and onto the floor in order to keep on with her busying.

And that launching would hurt.

And I'd had enough things hurting for a while.

For a *damned* long while.

"We need to sort these," Billie said. "To split them up into smaller sets." She dropped another box onto the one she'd set in front of the cot. "Pair them together with"—turning, she scooped up a third box—"these and put them all"—another box landed uncomfortably close to my toes...the ones on the broken leg—"in here." She clapped her hands together, started to turn away. "Good? *Good.*"

She began to walk back toward the original stack of boxes.

"Um, Billie?"

My aunt froze, her shoulders hitching up so tightly that they were practically at her ears. "Yeah?"

"Can you help me sit down so I can do this?" I asked, nodding at my leg and the crutches when she spun to face me. "I can't—" I tilted my head toward the cot. "I can't sit all that easily."

A pause.

Her impatience almost palpable.

But Billie Rose was also a caretaker, and I knew that she couldn't—and thus *wouldn't*—leave me to struggle down to sitting by myself.

She made me wait a good long time for her help, though.

Eyes narrowed, lips pressed flat, jaw clenched.

A sigh.

Then she was back at my side, wrapping her fingers around an uninjured part of my arm, easing the crutches away and helping me onto my ass.

Ouch.

I hissed out a breath.

"Shoot," she said loosening her grip. "Are you okay? Did I hurt you?"

It *all* hurt, including Billie's hold on her arm, but it wasn't anything my aunt was doing. It was just...because I'd been trapped in a wildfire and was dealing with burns and stitches and a broken leg and bruised ribs. *Everything* hurt.

"I'm fine," I said. "Just..." I released a breath, the pain subsiding. "Sit here and let me lean against you."

"You should be in bed." But Billie dutifully sank down next to me.

"I've spent all my energy fighting with Axel about going to the game, about coming here today." I dropped my head on her shoulder, sighed. "I don't have any energy left to fight with you."

"Yeah, tell me about wasting energy fighting," Billie Rose muttered.

I smothered my smile. "Joel's superpower does seem to be pissing you off."

A snort.

"You know, *I* know something about fighting with a big, broody hockey player."

Billie tugged my hair.

"Ow!" I rubbed a hand to my stinging scalp. *That* had been the one part of me that hadn't hurt.

"Behave," she grumbled, tucking me back against her. "Joel is an ass."

"A good-looking ass who can't keep his eyes off you," I pointed out.

She threatened to pull my hair again. "Hilarious."

"I'm not joking."

A sigh. "I'm not having this conversation with you."

There was a finality to her tone that had me backing off. But because I was me and she was my aunt and one of my closest friends, I let it go (with just one more comment). "Also, just saying, hockey players have the best asses."

She turned to glare at me, but my comment had her shaking a head, lips turning up at the edges. "You think you're hilarious."

"I think that I'm glad you're okay."

Her throat bobbed, eyes going glassy. "Me too, honey." A beat. "God, Bay, you scared the crap out of me."

"*I* scared the crap out of *me*."

"When we found your trailer on the road..."

Fear in my belly, in my throat, remembering the flames closing in, the road blocked ahead, the desperate scramble to get Picard and Data out of the trailer.

I inhaled. "I know," I whispered. "It was...I was really scared, Bil."

My aunt slipped an arm around me, held me close. "I know, honey. I'm sorry that happened."

"Tom, Hank, and Eli—" My voice broke, cutting off my words.

"You heard," she whispered.

"I—" My throat was tight. "I heard."

"I'm sorry."

"*I'm* sorry," I said. "If I'd seen the fire sooner, had gotten the warning out before—"

I gasped when Billie spun to face me, hand coming to my jaw, glare fixing me in place. "You have nothing to apologize for. *Nothing*." She shook my face lightly. "Your call is why the only deaths were because the fire moved so fast by the ranches. *You're* the reason we were able to use the evacuation plan, why we were able to get everyone out."

I started to shake my head. I'd made a call. That was it.

Billie and the rest of them had gotten everyone safe.

"Look around you, Bay." Billie swung out an arm. "This is because of you."

I inhaled, knowing I could keep arguing, but that wasn't getting Billie to rest. That was keeping her up, triggering her dog-to-a-bone mentality.

So I covered her hand with my own, agreed, "Yes." Though, not able to completely let it go, I added, "But it's also because of us."

Seventeen

Axel

I glanced over, watching Bailey sitting with Billie Rose, the pair lost in a serious conversation.

I didn't think it was about Joel being an annoying bastard.

But I wouldn't put it past them either.

"She needs to rest," Joel—speak of the devil (or annoying bastard)—muttered. "She's been up for two straight days."

"You'd only know that," I pointed out, "if you'd been up with her for those two days."

A shrug. "I'm used to going without sleep. You know we are."

Late nights. Aborted sleep. Schedules that were fucked six ways to Sunday. Yeah, Joel and I knew plenty about surviving on minimal rest, and that wasn't even during a fucking emergency.

But we could only maintain that for so long.

"She'll be more likely to rest when if you do it yourself. You know it's true," I added when he opened his mouth to protest.

"No," he muttered, "she'll probably take the opportunity to stay up for another twelve hours."

"Bailey's got her."

I nodded toward the two of them sitting on the cot, still talking, though Billie's eyelids were looking droopier by the second.

Give my woman a few more minutes and the mayor of River's Bend was going to be sprawled out on that cot, dead asleep.

"Right," Joel muttered. "So help me move these boxes."

I didn't argue. Joel was a stubborn asshole, and I wouldn't get through his thick, dumb head with a straight on attack.

So, I helped with the boxes.

I stacked them where he directed—which was actually in several different spots—and opened the ones he ordered me to open. Then I was distributing the supplies inside to the correct locations—food to the kitchen and tables set out for people to grab what they needed, clothes hung up on the proper racks, organized by size, underwear and socks similarly sorted and in boxes down below, water and other drinks in coolers, first aid supplies to the nurses' station with simpler things like bandages and antibiotic cream in small baskets just outside the door.

Trying to be thoughtful about balancing the people who were staying here having access to what they needed and making certain that all of the proper materials were with the people who needed them to help whoever might seek them out.

Once we'd finished with the boxes, I managed to shove a plate of food into Joel's hand—thanks to Dessie and her being aware of him burning the candle at both ends.

We moved over to the bleachers, half-unfolded to leave lots of space open for the cots, and climbed to the top, taking a bird's eye view of the space and leaning against the wall, pieces of the huge mural of the mountain lion—this school's mascot—visible above the worn wood.

It had been a long time since I'd been in a school gymnasium, but it felt similar to those high school years.

The buzz of conversation.

The squeak of shoes on the hardwood.

The emotions that were filling up the space.

Of course, there wasn't any excitement, just disappointment and frustration and sadness, like their team had lost the biggest game of the year.

Not a surprise given the circumstances.

I'd taken a plate too, even though Bailey and I had eaten on the way up. Not because I was hungry, but because I didn't think Joel would stop and sit down with me unless I was stuffing my face too.

And, hell, I was happy to be off the team diet plan for a few months.

Costco muffins the size of my head sounded like a damned good plan.

I peeled the wrapper of the chocolate muffin with chocolate chips, was about to take a huge bite when Joel's head suddenly shot up and he seemed to actually see *me* for the first time since I'd come in. "Fuck, man," he said, his plate forgotten on his lap. "You won the Cup."

My lips twitched. "Yeah, we did."

We, not *I* because I couldn't have done it without it the rest of my team. Because, while my contribution might have come at the right moment, I definitely couldn't say that it was any more important than the save Brit had made a half-minute before, than the hit Logan had laid out in game three, than the consistency Blue and Coop and Will and Rome had brought throughout the entire season.

Now that I'd gotten my head out of my ass, I'd finally figured out what a team could be like.

Something I could have had years before if not for said head in ass.

"How's it feel?"

I sighed, setting my muffin onto my plate, not doing Joel the disservice of giving him a canned answer. This was my former teammate. This was a man who'd had my back more times than I could ever count, who'd had Bailey's back.

He deserved consideration and a thoughtful answer.

And, truthfully, I hadn't really thought about how it felt.

Other than *good.*

Ha.

That was real deep and reflective, and maybe six months ago, the notion of me being deep and reflective would have been the most hilarious joke I'd ever heard. Today, it wasn't. Today, I was different. I'd grown.

Look at me go!

Snorting inwardly, I met Joel's green eyes, saw that some of the tension that had been present in them from the moment Bailey and I had walked into the gym had faded. Or, well, since Bailey had crutched and I'd walked in behind her, enjoying the view of her ass that I fucking dreamed about (or, rather, dreamed about fucking) in the leggings that were tight enough to caress her curves.

They'd been a bitch to get over her cast, but the view I'd enjoyed while trailing her had made that struggle well worth it.

I was a sick bastard.

Luckily, my woman loved it.

Joel shifted next to me, and right, I was supposed to be answering him, not playing inner monologue.

"It feels..." I shoved a chunk of the muffin in my mouth, chewed as I pondered that question. "I guess it still feels surreal and strange and not *real*, you know?" I said once I'd swallowed.

Joel nodded, gaze drifting out onto the floor, toward a certain pair of women, sitting on a certain set of cots, though the one with blond curls was currently sprawled on one of the fold-out beds. "You had quite a span of experiences this year," he murmured, seemingly tearing his eyes away, bringing them back to mine, though, I couldn't help but note them sliding back to the cots just a few heartbeats later.

But, focus on Billie Rose or not, Joel spoke the truth.

I'd had quite a run of it over the last months.

Almost washing out of the AHL and making a name for myself as solely a troublemaker, to NHL roster spot fill-in, to getting a permanent contract on a team that was a contender for the playoffs, to winning the Cup by putting in the game-winning goal.

Big things.

Once-in-a-lifetime *huge* things.

But not one of those things was as important as Bailey.

Not even the family I'd become part of with the Gold.

And yeah, did that make me a sappy fuck? Both because I was all in on the family talk and because I was thinking my buttercup was the heart of my heart, that my soul sang for just one her, for that wonderful fucking woman and no one else on this planet? Yes. I was sappy. I was in love. I wasn't scared to think about it.

Not any longer.

I saw it for the gift it was.

"Maybe it'll sink in at some point," I told Joel. "But right now —especially with all of this"—I waved my hand at the gym, at the people, the cots, at the fact that we were in this shelter in the first place—"it hasn't quite settled that deep."

"I feel that."

I shoved another bite into my mouth, chewed and swallowed. "I almost lost her," I whispered into the silence that had fallen between us. "And I would have lost everything. None of it would have meant *anything.* The win. The goal. The Cup. It would have all been just...*nothing.*"

Silence.

But then he dropped his hand onto my knee, squeezed tightly. "She's your person."

"Yeah," I agreed.

The quiet fell again.

Then I couldn't resist saying, "And I'm starting to think that Billie Rose is—"

"Don't," he snapped.

"She's smart, driven, and local," I pointed out.

"*Don't,*" he repeated.

"And you're protective over her, and she pushes your buttons. Plus, she has a great ass and—"

He shoved me. "Cut it out, fuckhead."

"—and," I repeated, ignoring him, "there are sparks for days, man." A beat. "So much so that you can't keep your eyes off her, even when she's sleeping."

Joel tore said eyes away from the cots in the corner of the room, glaring at me.

I grinned, shoved the rest of my muffin into my mouth.

"Just saying."

Did it sound like *jush shayling?* Yes.

Did I give a fuck?

No.

Especially, if it meant that it would help Joel find his person.

EIGHTEEN

BAILEY

We'd left Joel sleeping on the cot next to Billie Rose, blankets tucked up around both of their chins, boxes sorted, the shelter as stocked and organized as possible.

For the moment anyway.

The winds were dying down, and the smoke was beginning to clear—or at least, not being pushed toward River's Bend.

So more people would be leaving the shelters.

Some going home—a precious few whose homes were safe and utilities would soon be restored to. Some moving onto hotels or apartments or friends or family—places they could stay until they were able to rebuild. Some would be staying in the shelter for a bit longer, having no place to move on to. And some...some would be leaving and never returning to town.

The fear too great.

The devastation too close to home.

That hurt my heart in the worst way.

But I was tabling that hurt for the moment. There would be time to wrap it around me later, to let it bring out my tears. Deep in the night, when the world was quiet and my mind didn't want to settle.

Now, I was struggling to keep my breathing even, my pulse steady.

Because fear was sitting heavy in my belly, clawing deeply and dragging it talons through my soul.

Heat and smoke.

Terror and knowing I was going to die.

Losing—

Axel's fingers lacing with mine, holding tight, steadying me without a word.

The talons loosened and I glanced up at him, saw that he'd stopped on the bridge outside of town, not driving across it.

Waiting.

Until I was ready.

Fuck, I loved this man.

Looking away from his eyes that saw right through my shield, my mask I was trying to keep in place. If I could just pretend that I would be okay, then I would *be* okay.

But that hadn't ever been true.

That was what had landed me in a relationship that had nearly destroyed me.

Hiding from the truth, brutal and fearful and painful. Pretending, masking what was really inside my heart.

I wasn't that woman anymore.

Because of the man next to me. Because of *me.*

So, I owed both of us the truth.

Fuck the masks.

Let me be *me.*

I held his fingers tighter, swallowed hard against the knot in my throat and whispered, "I'm scared."

His fingers grasped mine, holding just as tight, keeping me grounded into this moment and not the past. "I'm scared, too."

Whoa.

That surprised me.

Because...well, I don't know why it surprised me.

He'd been here, searching for me, surely panicked. God knew, *I* would have been freaking the fuck out if a fire had burned through his town while I'd been away, not able to contact him, just watching the news grow more and more grim with every special report.

"So we do it together?" I asked, lifting our interlaced hands and pressing them to my chest, to the spot over where my heart pounded hard against my ribcage.

"Do we do things any other way?"

That had my lips twitching. "No," I said. "Not anymore anyway."

Fingers brushing my hair off my forehead. "That's the correct answer."

"Well," I mock-grumbled. "You don't have to be all cocky about it."

A lifted brow. A smirk that I loved. "Yeah, buttercup. I *do* have to be all *cocky* about it."

I snorted. "That was bad, even for you."

Laughter, beautiful, *Axel* laughter rang through the car.

That was my man. That was the man I loved.

"Ah, my Bailey and her sweet, *sweet* love words," he said dryly.

I sniffed. "I seem to remember you telling me that I smelled like shit once upon a time."

He waggled his brows, grinning over at me. "What I *didn't* tell you was that I actually love the smell of horse shit."

"*Bull* shit."

Now we were both laughing at this ridiculous conversation—which, face it, didn't feel the least bit good on my ribs—but *we were laughing* and it had cleared away the fear, freed up my lungs.

I could do this.

I could cross this bridge.

I could see what was on the other side and handle whatever may come.

Axel sensed that resolution in me, the laughter fading away, his hand still tight in mine. "Ready?"

I nodded.

He put the car into drive and took us over the bridge.

It was gone.

The barn. Reduced to jagged, blackened chunks. One wall still standing, the others collapsed on each other, the roof in pieces and jumbled like dominos. Data had been born in that barn. I'd bottle-fed Picard in the far stall. Cut apples and used Gramps' tools and stashed sugar cubes in my pockets. Axel had caught me when I'd fallen from the ladder, shielded me from the shards of glass when the large fluorescent lightbulb had shattered over his back.

And everything else was gone, too.

The fences I'd battled to keep in place for years. Charred and collapsed.

My herd. Out there somewhere—scared and lost or worse, dead.

The paddocks devoid of grass, of life.

But I hadn't brought myself to be able to turn to the house, to see what remained.

I needed to, but—

I kept my focus on the fields, the scorched hillsides, the broken barn and the downed fences and the paddocks that wouldn't be suited for riding for a good long while.

A warm hand on my nape.

No words. Just silent support at my side, my back.

I leaned back against Axel and slowly allowed my head to turn.

The impact took my breath away.

Gone.

There was *nothing* left except the chimney and the concrete foundation—not the porch where Axel and I had met thanks to Billie's interference, not the kitchen and family room where we'd made so many memories, not the hall and the long, narrow table of Gran's, the pictures from my childhood stacked five deep. Blackened gravel lead up to...

Nothing.

One second, I was on my feet—or one foot and one cast.

The next, my legs were giving way.

Crutches hitting the ground, my body wavering, my mind blinking out.

But then, strong, warm arms were around me, holding me up,

holding me so tightly that my ribs protested. I needed it, though. Needed that bite of physical pain in order to ground me from the emotional pain.

The loss.

"Damn," I whispered, tears dripping down my cheeks.

"I'm sorry, buttercup."

"I know." Still whispering.

But *fuck*. It was *all* gone.

And I stood there, staring at the charred remains of something that had made me so freaking happy, and also so sad and so frustrated and so hopeless and like I was drowning...and none of that mattered in that moment.

Because it was gone.

I didn't know if I was grieving the loss or crying in relief, but I did know that the guilt was real.

Russet Ranch had been in my family for generations.

And now it was gone under my watch.

After I'd fought so hard to keep it, after I'd resented that fight so intensely. After I'd *loved* it so much.

The tall grass and soft moos.

The whisper of the wind and the blazing heat of the summer sun.

Gone.

All of it gone.

I stood there, leaning against the one thing that remained.

Axel.

And he was holding me tight, holding me together.

Not rushing me, letting me look my fill, needing to commit it all to memory.

Until I'd had enough.

"Can we go?" I whispered.

He nodded, but instead of bending and handing me my crutches, he carefully scooped me up and carried me to the car, tucking me inside, buckling the belt over my middle.

Then the door was closed and he disappeared.

I stared off at the hills, at the otherworldly damage, assuming he'd gone back for my crutches. Not realizing that he'd been gone for longer than that.

Not until the door behind me opened, the smell of smoke intruding.

My crutches hit the back seat.

The door closed.

He rounded the hood, climbed in through the driver's side, and then gently set something in my lap.

Surprised, my gaze drifted down, shocked by the heavy weight.

My heart squeezed tight.

It was the horseshoe Gramps and I had hung over the front door, all those years before.

Nineteen

Axel

She'd fallen asleep less than an hour into the drive back to my apartment, and I couldn't deny that I was relieved.

She needed rest.

And I...needed the quiet, needed the break, needed the rest, too.

Bailey had fallen apart, understandably, had needed me to be her rock. I wasn't holding that against her, wouldn't ever hold it against her.

But I was riddled with fault lines.

One more impact was going to break me into pieces.

I couldn't let it.

She *needed* me.

But the lines kept appearing, kept spreading, kept threatening to shatter me.

Her house destroyed. The barn. The fields burned and the gravel scorched and...

Fuck.

How close I'd come to losing her—

A breath, my fingers clenching on the steering wheel, my vision growing just a little blurry. For a few hours, I'd managed to think about hockey, to be in the moment of winning, but bookended on either side of that almost unreal dream were the nightmares.

The hours on the plane.

The time spent searching for her.

The smoke and heat and devastation left behind.

The people in the shelter.

The ranch—or what was left of it.

The...call that morning.

I released a shaky breath, allowed myself to glance over at her, to watch her resting peacefully, just for a moment.

Then I focused on the road ahead.

I couldn't take care of her and be broken at the same time.

So...

I needed to find a way to fill in those cracks.

I needed...to find a way to be enough for her.

I was worried that—

I wouldn't.

That I wouldn't find a way.

That I wouldn't be enough to make those nightmares in her mind and heart fade away.

"Are you okay?" Bailey asked.

I blinked, jerking my head away from the gathering of my teammates. It had started as a game night at my place to celebrate the win (though later, after the kids went to sleep, I was sure the guys would get back to partying in a more adult way). But for now, my teammates and Scarlett, along with the team's former publicist and Scar's mentor, Rebecca—were posting on social media and coordinating donations while live-streaming a *Ticket to Ride* marathon.

But people weren't just donating money online. They were also bringing supplies in person.

Because of Rebecca and Scarlett and their PR mojo. They'd sent out a few tweets, had gotten sound bites from me, from Bailey, from Billie Rose and they'd gone viral. Rebecca had coordinated getting volunteers to the Gold Mine to load container trucks she'd also somehow managed to gather. Scarlett was on the horn, finding out the biggest need for those donations and somehow also organizing local housing for those displaced by the fire.

California's landscape was designed to burn.

Hell, one species of the state tree, the Giant Sequoia, couldn't grow without fire—the seeds trapped in its tiny cones until flames dried them out enough for them to crack open. Only then would those seeds hit the forest floor, have a chance at growing into the huge California Redwoods.

Was this a useless piece of information?

Maybe.

But had I stayed up way too late researching fire and fire danger and California's climate and where it was safest for Bailey to live?

Yes.

I had.

And had basically learned that there was nowhere safe.

"Axel?"

I rubbed my forehead, stared down at the woman I loved. "Yeah, buttercup?"

Her hand rested on mine, fingers digging into the ache, massaging lightly, as though her touch might make it go away. Another day maybe it would. Today...it was just a reminder of the agony crawling through my mind, creating the dissonance that had me firmly in its grip. "I think you need to go lie down," she murmured.

No.

I needed to stay awake.

Needed to make sure that this all went okay, that Bailey was okay.

If I slept and something happened and—

"Honey." Her hand slid down, rested on my shoulder. "You're exhausted."

I'd driven up to River's Bend and back down that morning and afternoon, we'd spent time in the shelter, at her ranch. I'd played late into the night the previous evening, had spent a frantic day and night and day searching for her, worrying about her, thinking I was going to lose her.

So, yeah, I was exhausted.

But I could look after the woman I loved.

I *needed* to look after the woman I loved.

I—

Her hand slid down to rest on my chest, over my heart. It was pounding, thumping against my ribs. "Axel, honey, you—"

I shook my head, yanked myself firmly out of my mind. "I'm fine, buttercup." I glanced at the clock, registered the time, realized I'd fucked up. Again. "Let me get your meds. You need to have your next dose." Late. It was late.

I had one fucking job.

She needed the medicine on time, needed the antibiotics to make sure she healed.

Bailey dropped her hand from my chest, reached for her crutches. "Oh. Right. I forgot. I'll get 'em."

My feet were under me before she could get up. "Stay there. I'll grab them." Then I was moving into the kitchen, bypassing the crew on the couches, the board with colorful train tracks laid out in front of them, and going to the stack of discharge papers, the bottles of antibiotics and pain medicine. Opening them, shaking out the proper dose, filling a cup of water for her.

I needed to take better care of her.

I'd almost lost her.

I'd *almost* lost her.

Pulse thudding in my ears, I dropped my hands onto the counter, squeezed my eyes tightly closed.

"You need to give yourself some grace."

My lids flew open, and I straightened, not letting my eyes go to Brit's. I hadn't heard her move up next to me, but I knew she would see too much if I *did* look at her.

"Axel."

Her hand covered mine on the counter, holding it tightly.

I could feel the pressure, but it wasn't warm, wasn't totally connecting.

Maybe that might have worried me on a normal day.

But life hadn't been all that normal of late.

"I'm fine," I said, slipping my hand free, turning toward the loaf of bread. Bailey needed to eat something with the pain meds, otherwise it might upset her stomach.

Two slices of bread in the toaster.

Butter out of the fridge. Cinnamon and sugar—her go to—out of the cabinet.

Knife. Plate.

Brit still leaning against the counter.

My eyes still determinedly kept away.

"Don't shut her out."

I blinked and this time my gaze slid to Brit's, unable to keep it away, and what I saw punched me right in the gut.

Pain. Hers.

Pain from past experience.

Pain from a woman who was so tough and self-assured and confident that it almost seemed like she *couldn't* be hurt.

"Brit," I murmured.

Her mouth tipped up, that pain fading, her normal unflappable self making a reappearance. "That hurts us," she whispered. "Not being able to help the men we love sort out their heads."

My hand shot out, gripped hers. "You and Stefan—"

"We're fine." She smiled. "But last year..." A shake of her head. "He was dealing with some stuff, and him not talking to me, shutting me out made me feel like shit."

I hated that she'd felt that way but was glad it was an old hurt, that she and Stefan were past it.

"You guys want to take care of us, protect us. But shutting us out of what's in your heart and head isn't that."

I inhaled.

Bailey didn't want to know what was in my head.

Hell, right now it wasn't *safe* for her to know what was in it.

It wasn't protection or care or—

The toast popped up.

Brit turned her hand over, gripped mine when I started to pull away. "Are you hearing me?"

I was...but, for once, her advice didn't apply to my life.

I wasn't going to tell her that, though.

I just nodded. "I'm hearing you." I tugged my hand free, buttered the bread. A glance up. "I'm hearing you," I repeated more firmly when she didn't move away.

Hearing, yes.

Just not going to listen.

Brit knew a lot, had advised me plenty over the last months.

I trusted her judgment.

Just not in this.

Bailey didn't need to know this.

Not now.

Maybe not ever.

Twenty

Bailey

He wasn't touching her.

He wasn't sleeping.

Or if he *was* sleeping, it was barely more than an hour or two at a time.

He was doing a good job of faking it, and I'd been in so much pain, so tired from everything that it had taken me a solid week to realize how far gone he was.

Now the pain was better—my ribs were feeling better, the stitches had come out, the bruises had faded.

My leg barely hurt—the cast more of an irritation and the actual break wasn't bothering me. Though, the crutches weren't more of an irritation. They were *definitely* one.

Mostly because my armpits were angry anytime I was using them.

But considering I'd barely had to get out of bed, or off the couch, they were far from as bad as they could have been.

Because Axel had hardly let me use the toilet, let alone going anywhere where I might be tired out. Not without a fight anyway.

And I'd fought.

I was me, so *of course* I had.

In the last two weeks, we'd been back up to River's Bend several times, helping at the shelter, but the last time we'd been there it had almost been empty. With the fire contained and slowly burning—and being put—out, people had either been able to go home or had been moved into more permanent temporary housing.

An oxymoron. But people couldn't live permanently in a large, open gymnasium.

They needed their own space and privacy and a little bit of normalcy returning.

The Gold had helped with that—mainly Rebecca and Scarlett, the team's publicist. They'd managed to keep the fire in the news, to coordinate donations, to link available housing with people in need.

Because it wasn't just River's Bend—though it had the biggest need in the aftermath of this fire—other small towns had been damaged, their residents needing help.

People were getting it.

Not Axel though.

He was still off.

And I was trying to be understanding, trying to be patient, but swear to Christ, the man was shutting me out tighter than a vault at a high security secret government organization. I was attempting to give him that time, knowing that it had been traumatic for the both of us.

But he wasn't talking to me, wasn't touching me, except in a distant medical way, as though constantly assessing my injuries. He was barely looking at me, and he certainly didn't appear to notice that I was getting better.

Hell, half the time I felt like he wasn't even *seeing* me.

It was like he was still back out in the woods, in the town, searching desperately for me.

What did I do with that?

What *could* I do with that?

Other than to just be here and be patient and try to get better, to show him I was here and safe. But as the days went on and he turned into more of a zombie, every night I went to sleep with him still and awake beside me and in the morning, I woke up with him still and awake and not touching me.

I wanted him to touch me.

I wanted him to unfreeze.

I just...had no idea how to make that happen, and everyone had more than enough on their plates—you know, with rebuilding a town and finding people places to live and coordinating supply drops and all.

Meanwhile, I was stuck here, wanting to help but not able to do much.

And the only thing I could potentially help—namely sorting Axel's head out—I was failing miserably at.

His phone rang, and he looked at the screen, swiped as though he was supremely hesitant—and maybe he was. I'd gotten my replacement cell just a few days before, and it had been ringing off the hook with media requests.

He was certainly being hit up even more frequently—though Olivia, his agent, was fielding most of the offers.

Now, though, he listened for a moment, body going statue stiff, then hung up on the caller.

Tapping a few buttons, presumably blocking the call.

Considering I'd gotten more than a few of *those* types of callers too, I understood the need to block them.

We were living in strange, strange times.

I sighed.

"What?" He'd pushed to his feet, hustled into the bedroom before I'd even fully processed that I'd made a noise at all. I'd told him I was going to rest, but really, I'd been thinking, trying and failing to come up with a way to break through.

Impossible when he was both distant and so close I couldn't wind up to punch through.

"Nothing, honey," I said.

He stopped in the doorway.

A few days ago, he'd stopped a few feet from the bed.

Before that it had been the edge of the bed.

Before *that* he'd been in bed with me.

A slow retraction. A slow walling over.

I was trying not to take it personally.

Trying not to wonder if that he was having second thoughts about us.

"What?" he asked again, still from the doorway.

My gaze drifted to the window, to the tall buildings outside it, to the fog and the busy city beyond the glass. I wanted to be out there.

But also, I wanted to be out amongst the tall grass, riding on Data's back, feeling the cool, fresh air on my face, the sun tightening the skin on my cheeks. I wanted to be back a few weeks, to what Axel and I were then. Not what were now, this weird in between, like both of us were afraid to take a breath.

"Buttercup, *what?*"

And suddenly, the in between we'd been existing in constricted tightly around me, making my lungs feel like I was back in those smokey woods, making me feel like I couldn't breathe.

Two weeks of this.

Two weeks of this slowly getting worse.

It was too much like what I'd had with Colt, good being slowly poisoned until it was untenable, until it was something I couldn't handle, until it smothered and sucked my life out of me and turned me into someone I didn't recognize.

Axel wasn't Colt.

Not even close.

Colt was a fucking monster, and Axel was good down to his core.

But I still wasn't going to let us, let our relationship and love and connection die by inches.

"What?" I asked, turning to face him, seeing that he'd taken another step toward me.

Which pissed me off.

Because there were still at least ten more between us.

We weren't supposed to be separate. We were supposed to be together. I'd fought to stay alive, fought to get to him. Just like he'd fought to find me, fought to make sure I stayed alive.

"*What?*" I asked again. "You're seriously asking me that?"

He blinked.

"Who was on the phone?"

His teeth clicked together.

"What aren't you telling me?"

Because there was something eating at him and maybe it was all the calls—but then again, the solution to that was easy and started and ended with turning the damned thing off—but though the nasty phone calls weren't entirely pleasant—I could attest to that—I didn't think that was the right explanation.

Things were foggy from exhaustion and pain pills, but I thought he'd been off before then.

He'd been off from the moment we'd gone up to the ranch?

From the morning after the game?

I rubbed my forehead.

I didn't know precisely. But he'd been different from that day forward.

"Are you hurting?" he asked, turning toward the kitchen. "I can get your—"

"*Stop.*"

His expression went wounded.

Probably because I was snapping at him. Okay, that wasn't exactly true. I was pretty much yelling at him. Which made me an asshole, I knew. Especially after all he'd done for me.

"You're hurting," he said.

A step away from me.

And fucking hell. But, dammit, I was done with this.

Done.

"Stop *right* there."

Something about my tone clearly got through because he stopped, slowly spun back to face me. "Buttercup."

"*What* is going on in your head?"

His face clouded over.

"No," I said. "Axel. Honey. You *need* to tell me what's going on in your head."

"I'm fine."

I laughed and, yeah, it was more than a little brittle. "*That's* what you're going with?"

He frowned, brows dragged together into a tight vee. "What are you talking about?"

"You're not sleeping." I threw up a hand, palm out, cutting off the protest before it passed his lips. "You're hardly eating. You jump when I breathe or sigh or wince or move. But somehow, you're doing all that without actually touching to me or talking to me or *looking* at me."

"In fairness"—he crossed his arms, leaned back against the doorframe—"I've touched you plenty."

"To help me shower or get into the car or bed or get dressed. All of which I appreciate," I added. "My recovery would have been a lot harder without you."

"So what's the problem?"

His body language was telling me to back off, to not press this.

But I wasn't that woman anymore.

I'd let this slide for two weeks. I couldn't let the gulf between us continue to grow.

"The problem is you're not *yourself*," I whispered. "Ever since we went up to River's Bend you haven't been the Axel I know."

"I've been—"

"Please don't make a quick excuse," I said, hurt blooming in my chest, bleeding over into my tone. "Please just stop and think and *talk* to me."

His shoulders rose and fell on a breath. He pushed up off the doorframe, took a step farther into the bedroom, took a step toward me.

I braced, ready to hear whatever it was he was going to tell me.

But I didn't *get* to hear it.

Because he spun on his heel and left the room.

"Ax—"

The front door opened.

Closed.

Twenty-One

Axel

I leaned back against the closed front door, my phone's case creaking in one hand, my keys clutched tight enough to hurt my palm in the other.

My heart was pounding, sweat dripping down my spine, my lungs working desperately to modulate my breathing.

I couldn't.

I *couldn't.*

"Fuck," I whispered, eyes sliding closed, trying to smother the panic. "*Fuck.*"

A thump from inside the apartment, the sound of Bailey crutching her way toward me following a few seconds later.

That had me pushing off the door, my eyes snapping open.

Had me heading for the stairs, bypassing the elevator because I couldn't wait for it, couldn't risk Bailey catching up.

I needed to go.

I needed space.

I needed to *breathe.*

Yanking open the door that led to the stairwell, I released a sigh of relief when I found it empty. Then I was moving down the stairs, boots pounding on the treads.

Down. Down. Down.

Bursting out into the parking garage, moving out through the ugly concrete space.

Then onto the street.

I got a few looks, but it was San Francisco. Weird shit happened all the time, so my bursting out of the garage didn't garner more than couple of sideways glances before people were going about their business.

Lucky for me, considering the news coverage that had been trailing the team of late.

The last thing I wanted to was to have to put on a happy face for a fan...and the last thing I *would* do was ruin someone else's night by being an asshole.

That was the old Axel.

I was...

Enough.

Inhaling sharply, I turned off the busier street and down one that was quieter, darker, that fit my mood...just as my phone buzzed.

I love you.

Three words from the woman who held my heart and was tearing it to shreds at the same time.

"Think, Axel," I muttered, drawing to a stop, resting my fists against the graffitied wall. "*Think.*"

The news had turned me into a hero.

Those same forces would love to tear me down.

One word would set the bloodhounds down the trail and then I'd be in pieces. Something I could survive—I'd done it before. But the hounds wouldn't stop with just me. They'd go after the team and Bailey and—

I couldn't let them do that.

I couldn't let *her* do it.

So I had to find a way to stop her, even if—

I love you. YOU, Axel. I don't know what's going on in your mind, but I'm here to listen.

I turned my cell away, not wanting to see those words on the screen.

I *couldn't* see them.

But when my cell buzzed again, I flipped it over again, read the message from Bailey anyway.

And I'm not going to run from whatever demons are chasing you.

"Fuck," I whispered then slammed my fists against the wall. "*Think.*"

Bailey didn't text again, and though I was disappointed, I wasn't surprised. I hadn't replied to her, hadn't acknowledged the words that meant too much. I'd left her when she was injured and—

"Think," I whispered again, shoving my cell back into my pocket, cutting the useless spiraling off. I had to shut it down, shut it all down. To focus on the problem at hand. To come up with a solution that wouldn't ruin everything and slice away the only bit of happiness I'd ever truly allowed myself.

I started walking again, mind turning over the problem.

Studying it from every angle I could think of.

And not finding a solution that would protect her, protect them, not without exposing every single vulnerability that I'd long buried.

Because if I gave in to the threat, it would never stop.

She would never stop.

I should have stayed away longer.

I knew the risk of going back to the apartment.

But it hadn't been a conscious decision to go back, not really.

My feet had just...led me up to the apartment.

In through the door, closing and locking it behind me.

Boots off.

Cell on the counter. Jacket on the hook.

And my eyes hitting Bailey's, who was sitting on the couch, waiting for me.

There was a plate in front of her, the remnants of a sandwich on its plain gray surface. An open bottle of beer sitting on a coaster next to it, something I would have gotten on her about, if not for the fact that she'd been refusing to take the pain medicine for near on a week now.

But, pain medicine or not, she'd still had to make herself dinner, and that couldn't have been easy with the crutches, with the unwieldy cast, with the ribs she said weren't bothering her but still made her wince when she moved too quickly or twisted to the side.

Guilt.

Fuck, it was a dagger-wielding bitch, stabbing me over and over and *over* again.

My gaze dropped from the warm chocolate of hers, dragged over the gray-tinted hardwood floor, searching the pattern of woodgrain that would distract me from the repeated impact of that remorse.

Fucking this up.

Fucking *all* of this up.

"I'm good at flying off the handle, rushing forward and not thinking things through." Her voice was gentle, and that was somehow more abrasive, more painful than if she'd been yelling again. *That* I'd deserved. The gentle...it felt like a kick to the teeth.

Not for me.

Not with what I might lay at her feet.

"But *you're* good at closing everyone out and getting lost in your pain," she murmured. "Only"—a breath, as though she were bracing herself—"It's not hiding behind alcohol and sex this time."

My gaze flew up to hers.

"Instead, you're hiding behind taking care of me."

I sucked in a breath.

"And"—still gentle—"I'm happy to be that shield."

My lungs compressed silently, the air sliding out in a rapid silent shot. "But only if you let me inside *yours*."

Now my lungs compressed for another reason, one completely different and stifling.

I *couldn't* let her in.

That was fucking laughable.

"Buttercup."

She held up a palm. "Not an ultimatum. Just...something I need you to think about and take seriously."

I froze. "I love you."

Her smile was small...and a little sad. "I know." A whisper. "Which is why it's *not* an ultimatum."

But the unspoken threat beneath that statement was clear.

It could easily become one.

And it would be my fault.

My fault.

I could ruin the best thing in my life so, so easily.

That sent the dagger-wielding regret bitch stabbing away again, but even though each wound left me bleeding even more heavily, I didn't see how I could dump this on Bailey's lap. Not when I hadn't even been able to wrap my own head around it, hadn't come up with a plan, a way to make things better, hadn't figured out how to protect her.

So, I dealt with something else she'd brought up.

"You said I hadn't touched you."

Her chin came up slightly, the slightest bit of defensiveness in her posture, as though she expected him to deny that statement. "You haven't," she said. "Not like how a man should touch his woman."

I got the distinction. Because I'd touched her. Of course, I had. But it had all been helping her—into the shower, getting dressed, steadying her when she wobbled. It was care, just not for her heart and soul.

Because *my* heart and soul hadn't been able to take it.

Not since the call.

Not since *seeing* how close I had come to losing her, knowing that the call might result in that anyway.

So no, I hadn't touched her as I should.

Not since my head had gotten well and totally fucked up.

"Not since we got back from the ranch that first time." Her voice shook just the slightest bit, making me feel like an even bigger asshole.

Congrats, Axel.

Asshole to the world.

Asshole to the woman you love.

"You haven't touched me, honey, and I don't know how to make it feel like you can, how to break through."

More voice shaking.

More dagger stabs.

More regret welding itself to my cells.

I had to give her something.

I had to at least give her part of the truth.

So, I did.

I walked across the room, knelt at her feet and *gave*.

"I haven't touched you because I need you so badly that I'm afraid I'll hurt you."

Twenty-Two

Bailey

I inhaled sharply enough to have my still healing ribs protesting.

I haven't touched you because I need you so badly that I'm afraid I'll hurt you.

This man.

What he did to me.

What *I* was doing to him.

Fuck.

His eyes were haunted. His jaw taut. His hands clenched into fists that were resting on my thighs. It was those fists that undid me. That unfroze me.

That had me giving in to what my body and heart needed.

Leaning forward, I wrapped my arms around Axel's wide shoulders and hauled him against me, my lips finding his.

For one second, they were unmoving against mine.

Then he was in motion, and the man I loved, the man who'd been able to handle my body like it was a puck on his stick, easy to manipulate, to make it do what he wanted, to push it over the line and in the goal, was back.

He was excellent at getting me over the line.

So good that he often left me as a puddle of goo who could barely lift an arm.

But I didn't want to be goo, didn't want to be pleasured within an inch of my life.

Okay, I *did* want that.

But I needed to be right here with him more.

Something that was made immeasurably more difficult after he'd snapped out of his shock and his tongue slipped between my lips, tangling with mine. The man could *kiss*. The man knew exactly when to go fast and when to slow things down...*way* down until my brain went fuzzy and my body went molten and...

Oh yeah, I was ready for him to sweep me up into his arms, ready for me to carry him to the bedroom and lay me on top of the comforter.

I was ready for my shirt to disappear—*poof, look at it go*—over my head.

I was ready for him to come over the top of me, for him to give me some of his weight. Not too much, because he was Axel and he was aware of my body, of what still hurt, what was still healing.

But, oh man, did I like the feel of his body gently nudging my thighs apart, his torso pressing to mine. His lips, his teeth, his tongue dragging over my skin.

Goosebumps on my flesh.

Heat in my belly, drifting lower.

Just like his mouth.

I wasn't wearing a bra, had lost that the moment I'd traded in my daytime sweats for my nighttime sweats (that being a plain black cotton pair he'd loaned me that I could get over my cast and still tie around my waist for a patterned pair that Brit had bought me with adorable abominable snowmen that had wide legs and an elastic waist). Being braless was a perk in most instances, but it was especially one in that moment because it meant that Axel was free to slide his lips over my collarbones, down over the tops of my breasts.

A flick of his tongue between them, the days old growth of his beard tickling my skin, causing my nipples to bead tightly.

I arched up, instinctively seeking his mouth, desperate for the slight rasp of his tongue, for the suction of his lips.

He didn't disappoint, didn't make me wait.

Just sucked one taut bud and did it hard and deep.

I gasped, his name tumbling off my tongue, my free leg wrapping around his waist, pelvis arching, hips seeking purchase. I needed hard. I needed *in.* It had been too long without Axel stretching me wide, without his thick cock pressing home, without his body making mine sing.

Teeth on my skin, a rough palm on my ribcage, dragging up, cupping one breast as he went and worked my other one with his mouth.

I'd lost control.

I was slowly turning into a pile of goo.

Which wasn't what I wanted, wasn't what he needed, but every time I tried to focus, to remember what it *was* that I wanted (because what he was doing was really, really nice), to recall what he needed, Axel worked his magic.

Goo.

That puck being drawn closer and closer to the goal line.

Which was the moment that my mind wrenched to full attention.

"No!" I said, pushing his head back, his mouth pulling on my nipple for one extra tug before he released me.

And blinked, eyes out of focus, red tinting the edges of his cheeks. "Did I hurt you?" he rasped.

No.

He'd been pleasuring me into goo.

He'd been giving, but not taking, not accepting *my* care.

"No, honey," I murmured. "You didn't hurt me."

"Then—"

"I want you," I said, cupping his jaw. "But I also want you with me. This"—I tapped his chest, just above his heart—"and this"—his temple—"need to be with me, too."

Axel was stiff above me, his fingers clenched into fists again.

But worse, his blue eyes were filled with hurt.

"I'm with you," he said. "I'd never think of anyone but you while we—"

Fuck.

That wasn't what I'd meant.

I mean, okay, it kind of *was* what I'd meant. I just...needed to make sure he wasn't trying to distract me with sex, wasn't using it to keep me at a distance.

Wasn't leaving me the object to be pleasured and cared for while he himself was able to keep his distance because he was in control.

"I know."

His eyes didn't clear.

"Honey, *I know.* I just..." A breath. "I need you to go a little slower, to let me touch you, too, okay? It's been a while for us and I-I—"

His face softened. "I'm rushing you."

"Being wanted by my sexy hockey player isn't a bad thing." I leaned up, pressed a kiss to his cheek. "I just...be here *with* me, yeah? Don't take over."

Give me a little.

Don't wall me off and make this just about getting off.

Don't keep your distance and make me feel like this doesn't mean as much to you as it does to me.

Us.

I needed for this time together to bring us back to *us.*

His knuckles brushed over my cheek, the ghost of a cocky smile on his mouth. And, fuck, that smile was such an *Axel Smile* that relief rushed through me.

Maybe this was truly all that was the matter.

Maybe he *was* scared of hurting me, scared of going too fast and wanting me too much (and didn't that feel good?). Maybe it was...

Simple.

Maybe the answer was just something simple.

We let each other back in this way. We find our way back to us.

"I know it hasn't been *that* long since I've been inside you, buttercup. Have you forgotten?"

Ho, mama.

"Forgotten what?" I asked softly.

His fingers trailing over my sternum, down my belly, drifting beneath the waistband of my sweats.

"Forgotten how good it feels when I take over." A nip to my jaw. "Forgotten that you *like* it when I take over."

I did like it.

I liked it very, very much.

But...*focus woman!*

Which was why I summoned my strength and pushed him. Rolling to my side, taking him with me until our bodies were facing each other. I knew he'd let me press him back, that he was too heavy for me to shift him if he didn't want to go. I still took advantage of the shift in our positions, sliding down, glad there was no footboard on the bed because the damned cast was unwieldy.

I managed to get down the mattress, to get *me* down the mattress.

Until my nose was pressed just above the waistband of his jeans.

My lips twitched in what I presumed was a very Axel-like smile.

Because *this* was exactly where I was desperate to be.

Twenty-Three

Axel

Her fingers were...

Oh sweet baby Jesus.

They were brushing the top of my cock.

"Bailey—"

Flick.

The button on my jeans popped open.

Her fingers became her palm *and* fingers slipping beneath my underwear, wrapping around my dick, squeezing tightly enough that I saw fucking black.

I wanted to flip us over and stroke into her until we both found oblivion.

I wanted to take over, to make sure that we were both lost in pleasure, to not think about everything that had gone wrong and everything I was holding back.

I wanted—

Her mouth joined her hand and then I wasn't thinking about what I wanted to do or desperate to take over.

I was in taut, wet heat. There was suction. There was tongue moving along my shaft, flicking over my head, over the sensitive spot right near the tip.

Tight.

Slick.

Then she did something with her hands and tongue and...*oh fucking hell*. My cock bobbed against the back of her throat and...

Shit.

She swallowed me down, her lips brushing against my pelvis, her mouth stretched wide, her eyes a little damp as though she'd taken me too deep.

But she didn't stop.

And yeah, I guess I was still that asshole, because I didn't stop her.

Because I let her inch forward, her nose bumping against me, my cock down her throat.

And just that quickly I was three strokes—maybe less—away from exploding.

"*Bailey*."

"Mmm."

Oh *fuck*. That was...making it seem like it would take less than three strokes to make me come. I was...

Milliseconds away from it.

"Buttercup, you need—"

She gripped me tighter.

My eyes rolled back. My hips arched up, taking me deeper. She coughed, and I felt like the biggest dickhead on the planet, even more so when tears slid out from the corners of her eyes, but she didn't stop.

And neither did I.

My balls tightened.

Pleasure coiled at the base of my spine and...

I came.

Another cough, but when I would have pulled back, she swallowed me down, swallowed the hot jets of my release, wringing me dry.

One second, I was safe and sheltered and *separate*.

And the next, I was safe and sheltered and held by the woman who loved me.

A long, slow withdrawal, her tongue darting out to the corners of that pink, swollen mouth. Someone had tied concrete blocks to my wrists, to my ankles, my head, I was so weak and limp with pleasure.

My cock, though, wasn't limp.

It was somehow still hard, still bobbing like a radar detector to the woman who owned it.

Bailey had wriggled up so that our faces were equal and drew a long, slow hand along my chest, my stomach. "Normally, I'd climb on top and take care of you all submissive with pleasure," she murmured, her lips turned up at the edges, the flushed and puffy flesh making me want to slip my cock between them again. "But," she whispered, one finger trailing over the sensitive head of my dick, "I don't think I can manage that with the cast."

The chains holding the concrete blocks to me snapped, and the heavy weights flew away.

Then my hands were beneath her, shifting her on the bed, making sure her head hit the pillows and not the hard wooden frame.

Her sweats were tossed over the side of the mattress a second later, after making certain to carefully draw them down over her cast.

Then she was gloriously naked.

Mouth swollen, breasts pinkened from the rough bristles of my beard.

More assholeness because I should have cared, should have shaved so as not to mark up her pretty, pretty skin.

But...

I liked her marked up.

I liked her *mine*.

Then I was crawling between her legs, pressing her uninjured leg out to the side, making room for my shoulders, my mouth.

I was going to make this pussy mine, too.

A long, rough flick of my tongue, slicking up from her entrance to circle the bundle of nerves of her clit. Her slick folds were sensitive and I made sure to use my knowledge of her body, of all of special spots that made her melt for me.

Just for me.

Only for me.

Because she was *mine.*

No quarter on that fact, even if the truth of what I was keeping from her might tear us apart.

She was mine.

And I wasn't letting her go.

That lack of quarter meant that I showed no mercy on her pussy, on her body. My tongue working against her, making her writhe and cry out my name, making her mine, branding her soul.

Mine. Mine. Mine.

She'd burst through the barriers I'd tried to erect, brought out the man who needed someone to be his. There was no going back, not when she'd owned my heart from the moment she'd tipped back her cowboy hat and pointed a shotgun at me.

A finger through that slick heat, pressing in.

"No," she murmured, head thrashing on the pillow. "I want *you* inside me."

No quarter here either, not as her pussy clamped tightly around the digit, sending that pattern of convulsions straight to my cock.

Mine. Mine. Mine.

But I'd see her fall apart first, see her shatter so I could pick up the pieces.

Like she'd done for me.

Leaning up, I dragged the rough stubble of my beard over her labia, latched my lips around her clit, sucked hard.

"Axel!"

Yeah, the asshole in me liked the way my name sounded as she screamed it.

I was the man who loved her, not willing to accept any other sign of her need, of her pleasure, of her desire for me.

I kept sucking, kept stroking that finger in and out.

Added another despite my cock throbbing, angry at being denied all that tight, wet heat.

Luckily, it didn't need to be denied for long.

Because then she was coming on my lips, my tongue, my fingers.

I slipped from her clenching pussy, came up her body, and thrust inside, capturing her gasp on my tongue.

I tasted myself on her, knew she could probably taste the same, and it only served to drive me closer to the edge. I stroked into her, slow and steady at first, drawing out the pleasure of her orgasm, then faster when she wrapped her good leg around me, arched her hips so that I slipped deeper.

A jolt through my belly, my cock, signaling that my control was fucking bullshit, that I was one second away from forgetting everything—every healing wound and bone and bruise—and just pounding into her.

Something she knew apparently.

Because she tore her mouth from mine, gaze pinning me in place.

"Everything, honey," she murmured, palm coming to my cheek. "I'll always want every part of you."

I shuddered.

Her lips parted, eyes going heavy-lidded, pussy tightening around me.

But still she repeated, "Everything."

And it was that *everything* that finally shattered me.

"Now, honey," she whispered, maybe minutes, maybe an eternity, later, our breaths still coming quickly, her sexy body covered in a fine sheen of sweat from the orgasm I'd led us both to those minutes, or maybe that eternity ago. "Now," she said again, "you need to tell me what's going on in that head of yours."

I had a choice.

It was clear as day now, obvious in this moment, after what we'd just shared.

I could keep building walls, keep trying to protect her, keep finding ways to keep her out.

But she wasn't leaving.

And...I was hurting her. Hurting the woman I loved by making her continue to have to shove through those barriers.

I worried—which was why I'd held this all so close—that this truth would hurt her.

But now I had to make a choice.
Did *I* hurt her?
Or did my past?
I stared into her gorgeous brown eyes.
And I knew that this would be a case of both.

Twenty-Four

Bailey

The look in his eyes told me two things.

One, he was finally going to share what had been tearing him up these last couple of weeks.

Two, it was going to flay me to the bone.

For a moment, panic gripped me tightly enough to steal my breath, to send my pulse skittering, a cold sweat gathering between my shoulder blades. But then I managed to fill myself with steel, with focus.

I loved this man with every cell in my body, every fiber in my being, every breath that carried oxygen to my blood and brain and all the other pertinent parts.

I would take whatever burden he was shouldering, and I *wouldn't* collapse beneath the weight.

We'd been through too much, had come too far.

Lungs screaming from the lack of oxygen, I didn't let them fill quickly, didn't allow him to see what the look in his eyes did to me, the sheer terror in my belly. Instead, I released my hold on them slowly, carefully, breathing gently as I'd done in the days after I'd left the hospital, easing my aching ribs back to full use.

They were still sore, didn't like that I'd been holding my breath, but they weren't anything like the agony in those first few days.

But the slow, steady breath allowed the oxygen to hit my system, helped me to breathe more easily, to ease away the panic and even out my pulse. The sweat would dry into the comforter, into my skin, both of which were already covered in their fair share of dirty from the events of the previous thirty minutes.

From *our* little bit of dirty that had unlocked my man.

Finally.

I inhaled again, released it just as slowly.

Then I nodded, sat up, and pulled the blanket that had been folded neatly and spread out along the bottom of the mattress and was now rucked up into a ball of fabric, over my lap. "I'm ready."

He shifted a few pillows behind me, tucking them so that I would be comfortable—always looking after me, always protecting me. Then he straightened and his fingers brushed over my cheek as his lids slid closed. A heartbeat later, they were opening again and instead of agony in the piercing blue depths, there was resignation and determination and caution.

"Hold on," he whispered, and then he was shifting off the bed, moving to one of the nightstands, upon which he'd carefully propped Gramps's horseshoe against the lamp. He opened to the top drawer, reaching inside and pulling out a large manila envelope.

He handed it to me.

"The morning after we won the Cup, I got a phone call from my mother."

I braced.

"She threatened to expose me to the new management on the team, to the media if I didn't pay her off."

My rage was a taut, coiled beast, ready to lash out at the piece of shit that was Axel's mother. God, she'd already done so much harm to him, and now she was going to do more, going to make it so that his life was even harder.

For money?

The envelope made a crinkling sound in my hands, but I forced myself to find my control before I crushed it. I didn't know what it was, didn't know how it fit in to the pieces Axel was sharing, but I wouldn't destroy it.

Not yet, anyway.

Carefully, I set it on my casted thigh, one hand going to my hip, clenching the knitted material of the throw, the other finding his. "The team—"

"Would stand by me," he whispered. "I know that." His chin dropped to his chest, and he inhaled, let it out slowly. Then his head came up again. "But how can I ask them to?"

I squeezed his fingers. "Because you would do that same."

His eyes on mine, silence heavy and taut.

I waited for him to say something to dispute that fact, prepared to argue because he and I both knew that it would be a lie and I was ready to take him to the proverbial mat if he tried to pass that bullshit over on me.

I knew him.

Knew him.

Once he had made a place for someone in his heart, once he'd let someone in, there were no outs. And if someone was lucky enough to have his love and respect and loyalty, no sane person would ever want to. Could he be abrasive and a bit prickly? Yes. Had I thought him more than a bit of an asshole before I'd truly understood what was beneath that jerky shield? Absolutely. But it *was* a shield. And he'd been protecting himself.

And I knew more than a little bit about protecting myself by being a porcupine.

I'd made a life out of it until Billie Rose had intervened.

The thought of naked Axel and handcuffs and my fury at finding him on a porch that no longer existed made me both want to smile and cry at the same time.

I held both back.

He needed something else from me in this moment.

He needed steady and calm.

And braced.

"Yes," he whispered. "I would protect them with everything I could." A beat. "Which is why I was trying to handle this on my own."

He might have been able to—he was capable of so much—if not for the fact that I knew him, that we were living together, that I could feel his hurt like it was my own. Because we *were* together, he couldn't just shove everything down and wall me off.

I would know—*knew.*

So I wouldn't let him.

"I didn't want my mom to taint what I'd done, what we have." He glanced away from me, out the window, out to the bright lights of the city. "But she did anyway."

My lips parted, ready to dispute that, to argue that she would only have power if he gave it to her.

But that wasn't true, was it?

Sometimes the people in our lives exerted their power, their influence, without effort, those pathways built through childhood or adulthood or through friendship or love so ingrained that it was impossible to shut them out.

It was like trying to stop a big rig with just a simple plastic barrier gate.

They were so powerful, so big, so *heavy* that they would barrel right through.

Unless there was enough steel and concrete to bring the huge weight to a halt.

I understood that because I'd built walls that Axel had just waltzed around, had found an unlocked door in that huge expanse of steel and concrete and rebar and just strolled through. I also understood because, sometimes, no matter how thick the wall, it wouldn't be strong enough.

That pathway would still exist.

Like it did for my parents.

Even though I'd finally stood up to them, finally erected strong enough barriers so they couldn't hurt me any longer, we were still connected in ways that maybe couldn't be undone.

No contact didn't mean no power.

(Of course, with my ex, no contact meant no *fucking* contact and luckily, Colt had gotten the memo to leave me the fuck alone).

As for my parents, I hated them and yet part of me still loved them, still wanted them to wake up and be different.

And even though Axel's mom hadn't been much of one, had spent most of his childhood drunk and fucking her way through his friend's dads, through his coaches, through the scouts and people who might help him achieve his goal of making it to the NHL, that love and yearning of a child for a parent didn't ever really go away.

I knew because I'd lived that.

No stability, bounced from place to place, not knowing when the ties of my friendships might be erased, when I'd have to leave behind a prized possession because we had to leave quickly to avoid the police or an irate landlord. Not wanting to connect with teachers, to make a huge effort to be a student they'd remember.

Because who knew how long I would be there?

But I still ached with a desire to have a family like the one Billie Rose had.

Supportive parents who loved her, a stable house, friends at school, in town.

It was why my time in River's Bend with Gramps and Gran had meant so much.

But Axel hadn't had that.

Though, maybe, he'd found something *like* it with hockey.

Perhaps, that was why he'd worked so hard to find ways to play, even without the support of his mom.

Later, I'd ask him.

Now, I needed to deal with the agony creeping back into his expression.

Releasing the fisted bit of blanket, I leaned forward and rested my hand on his chest, rested it over that big, beautiful, *wounded* heart.

"What did she do, honey?"

He lungs shuddered, but he just caught my hand and brought it to the envelope.

Twenty-Five

Axel

"Read it," I managed to rasp out, my heart in my throat, stifling any further words that wanted to escape, blocking out the explanation that I wanted to give her.

The *warning.*

Her fingers shook as she reached for the envelope, turning it over and opening the flap.

Mine had shaken in very much the same way when I'd received it, received the final bit of proof that had shown beyond any doubt that my mother wasn't lying.

Not about this, anyway.

The sheaf of papers sliding out was a mere whisper of sound.

But it was also somehow more, almost gunshot loud in the quiet that had fallen between us. Now, my breaths increased in speed, in volume, joining the noise in a grating report that prickled down my spine.

I couldn't manage to slow them, though, not when Bailey had dropped her gaze to the papers.

I watched her eyes move across the page, her brows drawing together, probably trying to make sense of the first paper in the stack.

It was a medical report.

It *was* a DNA report, generated from a sample Pascal had surreptitiously collected for me and my own saliva.

But because it had come straight from a lab, it was filled with a lot of scientific mumbo jumbo.

She reached the bottom, that frown still in place, but then she was flipping to the next page, and I knew, *knew* that if she hadn't been certain of what she'd been reading on the first piece of paper that the second would make it crystal clear.

Because it was a picture.

Of a boy.

Who had my eyes.

Who was mine based on that DNA report.

Her gasp punched through the numb that was threatening to settle over me, striking my heart with the force of a bullet. This time the papers crinkled as she flipped back to the first page, gaze flying over the words. Her mouth dropped open.

Another flip. Back to the picture.

Then to the remaining pages in the packet.

Pascal's team had done a thorough job. There was a birth certificate that listed me as the father, more pictures of him, of *my son* at school, with his mother at the park, her financial records, even a photograph of him at his birthday party.

Five.

He was five.

He was mine.

And he didn't know me. I was as absent as my own father had been. My throat went tight all over again, the guilt tearing me up, slicing me to ribbons.

"I'd gone home," I whispered, staring at the stitching of the comforter. "I'd gone home after I'd been bumped down into the minors. My mom wanted money, and I was miserable, wanted to punish myself for trusting her, for trusting myself. I-I—don't really remember much of that weekend. I gave her the money but vowed it would be the last time I went home, the last time I funded her bullshit. Then I spend the rest of the weekend being *exactly* like her —drinking myself into oblivion and having sex."

With Veronica.

I knew her name now, though hadn't then.

Hadn't cared to.

Not when I was just looking for oblivion, when I was barely conscious.

"She went to my mom, apparently," I said. "Thought that she could get into contact with me. It didn't take long for her to know that was a dead end. My mom only sucks people dry." I drew in a breath that felt like hot pokers jabbing into my lungs, my next words barely a whisper. "My mom never told me, not when I called to check in on her, not when I slipped up and sent her money a few times after. She just filed it away, stored it to be used against me at the most opportune moment."

Like after becoming national news because of the fire and the game-winning goal for the Cup.

That was a prime blackmail opportunity.

That was the proof that killed the final spark of hope I'd stupidly held on to that she might change, might be different.

Fucked up.

Beyond idiotic.

But I'd officially learned my lesson now.

"What did"—Bailey flipped through the pages—"Veronica say when you talked to her?"

I swallowed, looked away again.

"Axel?" Bailey asked for a moment.

"I—" I clenched my jaw, released it. "I haven't talked to her."

"Then how—" Bailey broke off. "Pascal got this for you."

I nodded.

"I wonder why she didn't reach out to you through the team," Bailey murmured. "When your mom didn't help her."

That was a question I had as well, one that sent a sick feeling swirling through my belly. Had my mother threatened her? Or had she just decided that a fuck-up like me shouldn't be in our son's life? "I don't know."

"So..." My eyes slid back to Bailey's. "What are you going to do?"

That was another question I had.

One that I didn't know the answer to.

How could I move into their lives? How could I disrupt everything they'd built together? How could I insert myself, pretending to be a parent when I'd barely gotten my own life together?

But how could I not?

How could I miss out on any more time with my son?

How could I risk making him think that he wasn't worthy of a father or was unwanted or—any of the other things that *I'd* felt growing up?

I couldn't.

I had to reach out to them, to make contact.

I just...didn't know how.

"We'll figure it out," Bailey murmured, shifting on the bed, coming close, wrapping her arms around me. Her scent filled my nose. Her body pressed to mine, thawing out the ice that had gripped my veins. Then she leaned back enough to cup my cheeks. "Yeah?"

"I don't want him to think—" My voice broke, vision going glassy.

But Bailey didn't hold it against me.

She just held *me.*

"He won't," she whispered.

I rested my forehead on her shoulder, let her hold me, knowing that *this* was what Brit had talked about those weeks ago, knowing that it if I'd listened to her sooner and just talked to Bailey, the agony that had gripped my insides for these last couple of weeks wouldn't have been there.

But...I was an idiot.

But...luckily the woman who loved me knew that and knew when to push me, knew how not to be pushed *away* from my idiocy.

So, I stayed there, my head on her shoulder, her arms holding me tight, the maelstrom in my gut somewhat soothed. Because of her. Our relationship one that was going to get stronger despite my efforts at going it alone. Because of her. My heart was hers.

Because of who she was inside.

She was the one person on this planet who I could be vulnerable with, the one person who would never hold it against me.

Which was why I vowed that I wouldn't let the same dumb instincts put distance between us.

"You know," she said softly. "I'm usually the one who's a dumbass and doesn't talk things through."

That startled a laugh out of me and I found I could lift my head, that the weight on my shoulders wasn't quite so heavy.

Because of her.

Her thumb brushed over my smile. "You know it's true."

She was the woman who owned me, but she wasn't perfect. She'd been hurt too, and that meant she'd sometimes retreated, sometimes acted without thinking.

Human.

Bailey was human.

And maybe...I guess I was too.

Yes, that sounded stupid, even in my own head, but I was having a revelation here, okay? I was realizing that...I could be an idiot, too, and she would still love me.

So maybe...my son could still love me, even though I hadn't been there.

Hope in my heart, small sparks that grew to something larger.

Because I was going to try.

Bailey's fingers brushed my cheek. "I don't want to wipe this look off your face"—she ran her thumb over my lips again, beneath each eye, as though memorizing my expression—"but I know your mom didn't connect you guys *then*." Her hand dropped to my shoulder, probably because I felt my face harden, knew the look she'd liked had disappeared. She kept talking though, and with one question, the ice was back in my veins.

"How does your mom factor into this now?"

Twenty-Six

Bailey

"Moo! *Moo!*"

I grinned at Roxie, who was excitedly petting Picard as Brit held her daughter in her arms, having the distinct thought that this very scenario was likely going to be Picard's future—at least for the foreseeable amount of time.

I'd made it up to Olivia and Cole's ranch.

Visits from kids yelling *Moo!* were sure to be happening on the regular, especially with summer around the corner and Cole's camps fully booked for the next three months.

Picard would love it.

Data would, too.

Though there was still no riding in *my* future, a fact that my horse was definitely not happy about and had made clear to me with her various huffs and puffs when I'd visited her in the pasture. She was a bit too wild for the kids to ride, but Cole had managed to take her out without breaking his neck, so she was getting some exercise at least.

Not that it mattered to Data.

She'd been huffy and standoffish even though she'd been my first stop and I'd brought apples and sugar cubes.

Thankfully, the key to her heart was her stomach, so my oldest baby had forgiven me my absence. Though my oldest baby probably wouldn't forgive me when my youngest baby, Spock, came home with Axel and me. I'd need to buy an apple orchard in order to bribe my way back into her good graces.

Oldest baby. Youngest baby.

All those thoughts of *baby* had me inhaling, knowing that I wouldn't be able to think of that word for a good long while without that noun being tangled up with everything that Axel had told me two nights before.

Yesterday, we'd stayed in bed.

He'd fucked me practically raw—in the best way, if raw could be described as something good. Which it probably couldn't. But anyway, he'd worked his sexual magic and eventually I'd had to cut him off to give us both some time to recover. What I needed was a soak in a long, warm bath, but since that wasn't going to happen with this unwieldy fucking cast, I'd settled for a garbage-bag-wrapped shower and reveling in the fact that I was deliciously sore and every muscle had been turned to jelly, my pussy convulsing at regular intervals, reminding me of how good it had been fucked.

Woe is me.

My life was so hard.

A pussy that was fucked well.

A man who loved me.

Snort.

Anyway, I was still here, still on this planet, which was something that made me feel guilty when I thought about it, when I thought of my neighbors and how their lives had been cut short, but I knew that was survivor's guilt talking, so I was trying to acknowledge the feeling and not shove it down. I was trying to talk about it when I could, to not give it power over me. The guilt was still there, though, and I thought it probably always would.

Was my life complicated? Yes.

With plenty of hurdles and road bumps, especially given the bit of information that Axel had finally shared the night before last? Definitely.

It was also fucking beautiful (with plenty of *fucking).*

Heh.

"Now *that's* a look."

The softly accented voice had me jumping—Pascal, even as I'd gotten to know him a little bit over the last months—was still very, *very* sneaky.

And—not that I could tell based on his placid expression—but I thought that he got a kick out of scaring the shit out of me every time he materialized out of the shadows.

I narrowed my eyes at him, communicating what I thought of his amusement at my expense.

His mouth curved, just slightly.

Something I would have missed if I hadn't been studying him so closely.

But I *was* studying him, wondering about the secrets of this man, knowing I wasn't the person who'd ever get to the heart of them. And still wondering about them anyway.

Ah, well.

The mystery of Pascal would probably never end.

"What look?" I asked instead of pondering that further.

A thumb brushing over my cheek, surprising the shit out of me. His finger was calloused, skin golden, eyes unfathomable. "I'm glad you're okay."

"I—"

"Bay Bay!"

I jumped and turned at Roxie's shrill—albeit adorable—little voice. She was just old enough to start being able to communicate, to put names to faces, but still not old enough to say all of them correctly.

Her name for me might be minus the *-ley,* but I *loved* being called Bay Bay by the gorgeous little nugget, so it wasn't any skin off my nose.

"Roxie Rox," I called back, glancing back over my shoulder to see that Pascal had fucking disappeared again.

Seriously, I needed to put a bell on him.

"Bay!" More urgent now, so I stopped my search for Pascal, knowing he'd reappear when he wanted to, considering that Axel had asked him to meet us at the ranch so that we could sit down with Olivia and Pascal and come up with a strategy for dealing with Axel's mom.

Who was blackmailing Axel.

Threatening to share something that wasn't bad—no, it wasn't great either. But babies were born every day, and sometimes parenthood was complicated. The fact would ding his public image, and he might lose some sponsorships, especially considering that the offers were coming fast and furious after his game-winning (and game-saving during the previous matchup) play for the Cup. He was fast becoming the face for the Gold, so losing sponsorships would definitely affect his bottom line.

That was the least of his concerns, though Olivia had reminded him that it needed to be one, especially if he wanted to have a plan to take care of his family—which now included a son—in the future.

He'd conceded that point.

But he'd still been more worried about what this bit of news might do to the team and to Cole's ranch, considering that the first sponsorship job he'd taken had been to help fundraise for the programs here.

Far beneath that concern was his need to preserve his income.

And, did I mention that my big, broody hockey player had a huge heart?

Yes.

One that was mine and I was going to do everything to protect.

Which had meant that I'd called in the big guns—Brit and Stefan (who both knew plenty about bad press and how to deal with it), PR Rebecca and her husband and former player for the team, Kevin (both of whom were wicked smart and media savvy), current publicist and Rebecca's protégée, Scarlet and her hubby, and one of the most consistent and popular players on the team, Kayden.

And the biggest risk of all.

I'd sourced the number of Pierre Barie—Stefan's father and the owner of both the Rush and the Gold.

He was en route, and Axel probably wouldn't be happy (especially after he'd snapped at me...and then kissed me breathless when he'd seen the group gathered in the ranch's meeting when we'd first shown up). He didn't get it.

I did.

They did.

Or maybe it was that he just still didn't believe it, believe that his family would have his back.

Well, I was going to *make* him believe it, my stubborn, beautiful, sexy, big, broody hockey player.

And luckily, the rest of the group here was happy to prove it, too.

Pierre had told me he could give us an hour, and I'd jumped at that fact, knowing that an hour with the successful businessman and entrepreneur was worth its weight in gold.

No pun intended.

Heh.

Roxie practically lurched into my arms then and when I scooped her up and held her close and she smoothed her hand over my cheek, patted my smile, grinning back at me, I had to think that Pascal had been right.

My happiness, the happy that was now embedded in my soul, was obvious to the rest of the world.

Maybe once that was something I would have hidden, would have protected.

Now I wanted the rest of the world to know it.

Axel Finnegan was a great man—one who made me deliriously happy.

And he'd still make me happy, even if his mother succeeded in trying to destroy him.

Twenty-Seven

Axel

I was dying inside.

Slowly, incrementally dying.

Or maybe I was being reborn.

Maybe I was fucking delirious and trying to write shitty ass poetry in my mind that couldn't process all of the people having taken their time out of their vacation or their workday or stepped away from their families.

For me.

To help me deal with my fucked-up mother.

And not *one* of the people in this group, all of whom I respected beyond measure, had looked at me with disapproval or had exchanged thinly veiled insults because of my predicament.

They'd taken the problem in stride.

They'd been angry on my behalf.

And now they were all sitting around this big conference table and thinking of the best way to deal with this.

Because my mother was...

Well, I'd said it before and I'd say it again.

She was fucked-up.

She was blackmailing me not with the fact that I have a son, but also with the scout story and also with embarrassing information about me, not the least of which was a recording of the final call I'd had with her.

When my head had been messed up from everything I was feeling about Bailey.

It made me sound pathetic, though there wasn't anything truly bad in the recording.

But added to the parade of women I'd fucked, the damage I'd done to the bars and properties in River's Bend, garnering the initial ill-will of the townspeople, the son I hadn't accepted—never mind that I hadn't known about him because of her, but I knew that she was going to spin my absentee parenting to the nth degree.

Which was ridiculous considering she'd gotten the fucking gold medal in shitty parenting.

Still, all of those things together weren't looking good.

Add in the pedestal I was on right now because of hockey and my tracking down Bailey and Olivia was concerned.

Very, very concerned.

It would be very easy to knock me down.

I wasn't perfect—God, I fucking knew that. But I also understood that sometimes people loved nothing more than to tear someone who was on top to shreds.

And, for all intents and purposes, I was on top right now.

A hero who'd found his woman, despite all odds, then had made a stamp on the sports world.

It was something out of a movie.

But it was something that would make the shit my mom wanted to use against me—both truth and fiction—spread like wildfire.

Didn't matter.

I was going to own all of this. I wouldn't lie about my past, and I wouldn't put Veronica through the ringer. She had been through enough.

Alex—my *son*—had, too.

It also didn't pass me by that his name was close to mine (though minus a side of stupid, since Axel was a stupid name for a kid, but Alex was perfectly normal), but I didn't know if it was a coincidence or because Veronica hoped that we might someday connect.

I hoped for the latter.

I braced for the former.

Just like I braced for the shitshow that my mom was going to unleash.

"You guys don't have—" I began after they'd outlined how they were going to handle the fallout.

Brit waved a hand at me, cutting me off in that way she had. It was what had made her a force in the locker room. It was something I was going to miss—not the cutting off, that was annoying, even though I loved her like a sister, but rather it was going to be hard to not have the atmosphere she'd brought to the space.

She'd fostered the guys, me, built us up, left us with ties that were strong as hell.

But I was going to miss *her*.

"We're doing what we have to in order to protect our family," Brit said, eyes drifting to the plate glass window that gave a viewpoint into the play area the next room over.

It was full of Gold kids, another facet of my family.

One that was going to go out and make s'mores and visit the animals some more after we were done with this meeting.

That was the only reason guilt wasn't eating me alive for Bailey having dragged everyone up here.

Olivia and Cole loved hosting people here. The kids had loved visiting the animals and, in particular, had loved mooing at Picard. Spock had been beyond excited to see us, and I hadn't realized how much I'd missed the fuzzball until he'd bounded over, licked my hand, and then permanently stationed himself at Bailey's side.

Helping me look after my woman.

Just like the rest of the mammals in this room.

A thought that almost had me laughing—because I didn't think the perfectly dressed with four-inch heels and a power suit that put Olivia's to shame, Rebecca, would appreciate being referred to as a mere mammal—but I didn't get that far.

Because Rebecca jumped into the conversation. "I didn't get

this team—no offense," she added with a glance toward Scarlett, her mini-PR-badass who'd taken over the publicist mantle.

"None taken," Scar said with a smile.

"Good." A no-nonsense nod. "Because I didn't get this team to this place of social media superiority to allow some shitty alcoholic mother to ruin it, to ruin one of *my* players," she said tartly, not holding back. But then again Rebecca *didn't* hold back.

There was a reason the mini-PR-badass Scarlett was doing so well.

Trained at the feet of the master, she was bound to have picked up more than a few tricks.

Pierre nodded—and God, when Pierre *fucking* Barie had walked into the meeting room a half hour before, I'd alternately wanted to throttle the woman I loved and run for the fucking hills.

This was embarrassing.

This was everything I'd worked to overcome.

But...I was finally understanding that this was also family. Okay, maybe I'd already known that and the issue had been that I'd expected the family I'd become a part of to shunt me off. That was what usually happened—or had been my experience in the past. Plus, this wasn't a little problem. This was something that could easily turn toxic.

They'd be within their rights to tell me to fuck right off with my drama.

Except, they weren't.

So maybe I could finally learn to trust in this family we'd built. Trust it wouldn't just be there for the good times.

It would also be there for the fuckups.

All of which meant that I hadn't throttled Bailey.

I clutched her hand, kissed her temple, whispered to her exactly how much her going to bat for me meant.

It was *everything*.

"I agree," Pierre said and I saw the same sort of icy blue steel that Stefan had manifested on the ice when he'd still be playing. This was not someone to be fucked with, business acumen and power aside. Pierre was as determined as one of my teammates—and twice as scary. "No one fucks with my players." He sat back, sighed when he checked his watch, no doubt having somewhere more important to be. But he didn't get up, didn't leave. Instead, he steepled his fingers and said, "But that aside, this needs to be handled with precision."

Nods all around the table. Bailey's fingers clenching around mine.

"So let's all go over the plan for me, step by careful, precise step."

A blip of silence.

And then Rebecca flipped back to the front page of the pad of paper she'd been jotting notes on, Scarlett doing the same beside her.

They exchanged glances, nodded again.

Then Rebecca began to talk.

And as I heard the plan again, this time from start to finish, this time with all the roles everyone needed to play, all the moving parts, all the time and effort that my family was going to put in, I felt my throat get tight.

Thankfully, I didn't need to speak, just had to incline my head in agreement for my part.

But I knew that my family saw what it meant.

And instead of exploiting the weakness...

What I got was support.

Twenty-Eight

Bailey

I was nervous, so nervous that I was having a hard time operating my crutches, so I had no clue as to how Axel appeared so relaxed.

But then again, he'd been relaxed from the moment we'd reached the midpoint of the meeting of minds up at Cole's and Olivia's ranch.

Sanguine.

Comfortable in his own skin.

Even as we were meeting his son.

His. Son.

Rebecca had arranged this—a quiet call to Veronica, an out of the way meeting—and now we were walking (crutching) down the hallway of a luxury hotel several hours south of the city, toward a set of rooms on the top floor.

The presidential suite.

It should be ridiculous to be in a room like that.

But they'd wanted the space to have privacy and this could be framed as a business meeting if word got out before the rest of the plan was unleashed.

They'd factored a lot of variables in, but the single most important one was that Axel's mother wouldn't know the storm was bearing down on her.

I, for one, couldn't wait until those hurricane force winds tore her to shreds.

But, then again, I was protective of my man.

"Slow down, buttercup," he murmured, gripping my arm, holding me steady when the rubberized edge of my crutch threatened to catch on the carpeting.

I hated these crutches.

They were Satan's...Satan's...Satan's dildo, fucking my armpits raw (and that was in a bad raw way, not the delicious Axel way).

But I'd be on them for at least another month.

Freaking cow, steer, fucking middle child of mine for stomping on and breaking the largest bone in my body.

I was lucky, according to the orthopedist, that the fracture hadn't gone all the way through.

That could have killed me.

I told him to add it to the list, behind the flames and smoke inhalation.

He hadn't thought my pithy comment was very funny and neither had Axel. But, alas, I was me and pithy was all I could be.

All of which was to say that I was hardly ever pithy and I'd been damned proud of myself for my quip and...

None of these thoughts were distracting me from the fact that I was about to come face to face with a woman that Axel had made a baby with. A baby she'd named Alex. A baby who she'd made Axel, whose mother had apparently filled her head with such vitriol and nonsense—and maybe threats—that she'd not breathed a word about the child to anyone in Axel's circle.

Not for the entire five years of his existence.

So yeah, I was nervous, really *freaking* nervous.

For a multitude of reasons, not including that fact that we were all of a few minutes away from meeting him and his mother.

"We'll handle it," Axel murmured, not releasing my arm, and making me slow my pace down the hall. Ensuring that I wasn't going to eat shit on the carpet, which *was* luxurious, but also which was something that I didn't want to eat shit on.

That would hurt.

And there were cameras in the hall. Pascal was manning them, making sure the footage didn't leak, but I knew that he'd fucking laugh his ass off if I *did* eat shit.

After making sure I was okay first.

After—

"Relax, buttercup," Axel murmured. "I can practically feel the whirlwind in your mind." He rubbed his temple, smothering a wince, and guilt assuaged me anew. I was making this harder on him, making him comfort me when he needed to focus on the task in front of him.

"Sorry," I whispered.

"Hey," he whispered back, tugging me to a halt and capturing my face between his palms when I would have focused on that plush, albeit ugly, carpeting. "Look at me."

I didn't want to.

But I didn't have any power *not* to.

"*We'll* handle it," he said again, giving my words from a few days before back to me.

They meant...everything and nothing.

Because we were together and *could* handle it. But also, what if it *wasn't* okay? What if he decided that he should be with Veronica—

That thought finally registered in my belly.

And I knew I had to give it to him, knew that was what was prickling my nerves to uncomfortable proportions.

"I'm worried that you'll want to make a family with them," I said, so softly, it barely reached my own ears. "I'm worried that you'll need me to step back and I don't want to stand in the way of—"

His arms wrapped around me so quickly and so tightly that I lost all the air in my lungs.

But he didn't let go, didn't ease up.

Just kept holding me so tightly that it was difficult to breathe.

I was shaking, I realized. From a fear I hadn't truly accepted could take hold but had shoved down because it wasn't the time to think about it when he was telling me what he'd learned, when we were all getting together to solve the mess his mother was laying out on him. But that fear had been there, and it wasn't until it had crossed my mind, my lips that I'd truly understood what I'd buried.

This wasn't the time—*oh* how it wasn't the time.

But Axel didn't get mad at me for dropping this bomb on him.

He just...held me.

And slowly, I managed to breathe, to rest against him, to get that fear to ease enough for my pulse to stop pounding, for my mind to clear.

"I'm sorry," I whispered. "I know this isn't the right—"

"There is no right or wrong between us, buttercup." His palm slid up, cupped my cheek. "There's just you and me and *us*. That won't change, no matter how big our family grows."

Because love wasn't finite. And neither was family.

Brit had shown me that.

So had Billie Rose.

"I know," I whispered.

His face went gentle, and he brushed his lips over mine. Laughing slightly as he pulled away. "It actually makes me feel a little better that you're nervous. You've been holding so much together, superwoman." He tugged a strand of my hair. "I was starting to get a complex."

That startled a laugh out of *me*. "Takes a super person to know one," I teased. "Mr. Crosses Fire Lines to Find His Woman, and oh, no big deal, then becomes Mr. Scores the Game-Winning Goal."

He snorted. "You would have found your way out without me. I just...sped up the process."

Maybe.

But also, probably not.

Thankfully, that wasn't something we needed to focus on right then.

Not when we were five feet away from a door that, when opened, was going to forever change the course of our lives.

Eeek.

That was terrifying to think about.

Another tug of my hair. "Breathe."

"You and your commands," I muttered.

"You like it when I give you commands."

"In bed," I countered.

A wicked smile that was so hot, so tempting, so much like *my* Axel that it took my breath away. "Yeah." A nip to my bottom lip. "So, I'll give you some tonight."

I shouldn't be turned on in this instance.

I still was.

But I found that I didn't care, *couldn't* care.

Not with Axel by my side.

"Ready?" he asked.

I nodded, took my hand off my crutch for a brief moment to give him a two-fingered salute. "Yes, sir."

Another nip on my bottom lip, this one turning into a full-blown kiss—one that left me breathless and wondering if I should just accept the inevitable and lower myself onto the plush, ugly carpet beneath my feet and spread my legs for him. "More of that later tonight," he murmured.

"The yes sir?" I asked. "Or the fingering?"

He'd started to move past me, hand lifting to knock.

My questions had him choking on air, surprised eyes hitting mine.

I waggled my brows.

And he gave me the most wonderful thing ever.

His laughter.

It was warm and robust and filled my heart and soul and ears...

Just as the door he'd been about to knock on swung open.

Twenty-Nine

Axel

I expected to feel something different.

To feel *something*.

But all I had was an odd sort of numbness when I looked at the woman who'd given birth to a kid who belonged to me—or at least to a kid who possessed half of my DNA.

Veronica's eyes gentled when she looked at me, and then she stepped back and into the room, holding the door wide as I allowed Bailey to go in ahead of me. I caught the heavy panel when she released it once Bailey was clear, letting it close without slamming.

Then I flicked the lock.

I'd spent enough time in hotel rooms to make that instinct.

My gaze moved around the room, searching for Alex and not finding him, even as disappointment grew in my belly. He wasn't here. She'd decided not to bring him. Which I got, considering that my mother had turned her away, had painted me in the same broad strokes of someone who wouldn't look after her, wouldn't look after Alex.

But...I was disappointed.

Something Bailey must have sensed because she paused next to me, shifting so her shoulder brushed mine.

Telling me she was there, would be there, no matter the outcome.

"He's in the bedroom."

Blinking, I glanced away from the empty couch, that dismay slipping into confusion as I looked back at Veronica.

"Alex is having some quiet time," she whispered. "It was a bit of a drive."

My throat worked.

"Sorry about the drive," Bailey murmured. "I'm sure it's not easy to travel with a young kiddo, especially that far."

Veronica smiled and I remembered her now. Remembered why I'd been drawn to her, the drunken haze fading just enough for me to recall the quiet brunette, nursing a glass of wine and reading on her phone. Pretty, but extremely shy. I'd taken it as a challenge to get her to loosen up.

And had left her raising a kid on her own for the last five years.

Cool.

Go me.

"Did you guys want to sit down?" She inclined her head to the couch, gentle and soft and warm.

She should be pissed at me.

Why wasn't she pissed at me?

Thankfully, Bailey was much less of a statue than I was. She nodded and moved across the room so she could take a seat on the couch, asking Veronica about the drive up from the LA area as she went.

That was where my mom lived now, had lived ever since I'd gone pro.

In a house she'd bought with *my* money.

Rage churned through me and I wanted to pick up the coffee table, to launch it at the plate glass window. But I was also aware that rage was a useless emotion right now. There was nothing that I could do to change what had happened and coffee-table-launching wasn't the most dad-like thing to be doing.

It would probably send Veronica packing, and then I'd miss out on—

"I heard about the fire," Veronica said softly. "Did you lose your house?"

Bailey inhaled softly, pain etched into her face. "Unfortunately, yes."

"I'm so sorry," she said, reaching over and squeezing Bailey's hand. "I—can you rebuild?"

Another inhale. "I have insurance," Bailey said softly. "But I'm not sure I can rebuild all that was lost. It was a family property," she added when Veronica's brows pulled together. "A lot of the outbuildings and fencing were lost, along with our house. The history—" A shake of her head. "I know I'll rebuild something, but I'm not sure what form it'll be."

"Too soon to make those decisions." It was a statement, but also kind of a question.

Bailey nodded in answer.

Silence fell, the soft chitchat dissolving and both Veronica and Bailey looking at their hands, probably searching for something to say, considering I wasn't contributing, that I was standing there like a big, dumb rock and—

"What does he for quiet time?" I blurted.

Not gently.

Not quietly.

I'd like to think it was warmly, but I wasn't sure it was that either, not when the volume was wrong and—

"He likes to watch a movie on the iPad." Her gaze flicked to mine and then away. "He doesn't get electronics for hours and hours a day, I promise. Just a bit on days like this when we both need a break."

"We all need a break sometimes," Bailey said into the silence that fell again, uncomfortable and taut and—

I stopped thinking of all the things that I was desperate to know about Alex, about all of the explanations that I owed Veronica. That was getting me nowhere except stuck in the fucked-up place that was my head and it wasn't helping anyone.

Level with her.

Right.

I moved to the coffee table, and sat on it, facing both women.

Bailey's leg shifted, pressing to mine, silent, steady support for me as I looked Veronica straight in the eye and said, "I'm sorry."

Veronica's gaze dropped to her hands, but not before her eyes went a little misty. "I-it's okay. We were young and—"

I reached forward, took her hands. "I'm sorry," I said again. "My mother...she didn't tell me that you—"

"I know."

That had me straightening in surprise.

Her head popped up. "Or I know *now*. I...I was young and hurt and you..." A breath. "You'd made me feel special. So when your mom told me I was just like dozens of other girls, that I'd never get close to you again...I was hurt."

"Veronica—"

Her throat worked again, but her chin came up. "I was stupid, too. I thought I'd go to your house, that you'd tell me it would all be okay and we'd get married and..." A shake of her head. "I thought that you were my ticket out of my stupid, boring life. Your mom made it clear that she wouldn't let it happen and...I hadn't found my spine yet." Her eyes flicked to the closed bedroom door. "I hadn't found it for him yet. I should have talked to *you*, should have done anything except what I did, which was move away from town and claw out an existence for us on my own. I could have given him so much more, could have been a better mother, worked less—"

She shook her head, that silence falling again.

I squeezed her hands. "I should have been there for you. I—"

"So when Rebecca called and wanted to arrange this meeting," she said over me, as though the explanation had begun to come and she couldn't stop it, not now. "I pressed her to answer some questions before I agreed to this. Because I was absolutely furious that you'd reach out *now*." A shaky breath. "I don't need you now. I *needed* you then."

I flinched.

Bailey reached out and grabbed my knee, holding me steady when I might have gotten up, might have paced away.

Might have missed the rest of what Veronica was saying.

"But then Rebecca explained that you'd just found out about Alex." Veronica pressed her lips together, was quiet for several more moments, searching, carefully putting the words together, her tone almost gentle when she said, "And I realized that you might actually have been the man I'd glimpsed that night."

"I wasn't," I told her quickly.

She sat back slightly, tugged on her hands.

I didn't release them, couldn't until she understood. "I wasn't that man, wasn't the man to step up and be father of the year. I was..." I sighed. "I wasn't in the right frame of mind to be the man you both needed, even if I *want* to think that I would have stepped up for you both once I'd found out about the pregnancy, would have been there for you every moment." I cleared my throat, my tone more than a little raspy with emotion. "The truth is that I was fucked up for a long time—" My eyes flicked to Bailey's, held for a few heartbeats, before I managed to press on. "Even now I...I'm not sure I can be what he needs, what you need." A breath, hope welling in my heart. "But I at least would like to be able to try."

"Not exactly a ringing endorsement of yourself," Veronica said, her tone cool.

I nodded, released a breath. "I won't lie to you. Not after all I've missed."

Her lips pressed flat again, but this time it was almost as if she was trying to smother a deep-seated and heavy emotion.

Considering I was doing the same, I didn't comment on it.

I just held her hands, her gaze, willing her to understand, hoping that we might find some way out of this. "I don't want him to grow up like I did," I told her. "I don't want him to think his dad didn't want him, to be desperate and searching for approval in other places, hurting when he doesn't find it. I don't want him to have this *hole*"—I released one hand, slammed it to my chest, beneath which, my heart was pounding—"inside him that can never be filled because he's always thinking that the reason I wasn't there was because he wasn't good enough."

Bailey released a shuddering breath, her fingers clamped to my thigh, and I realized that she was crying, silent tears leaking out of the corners of her lashes.

Veronica, too, was emotional, her eyes damp, her throat bobbing.

"He deserves to be loved, and I promise you that I will do my best to make sure that he *never* feels the lack of me, of my absence, not ever again."

Silence.

Long and fraught with tension.

And Veronica not looking at me.

Thirty

Bailey

I willed Veronica to accept Axel's explanation, to be as moved by it as I was.

I knew how much it cost him to say what he'd just said, to admit what he'd admitted, to expose the wounds he carried deep inside.

But Veronica didn't reply.

Just sat there next to me in a silence that grew increasingly more tense.

Until I was about to burst out of my skin and throttle her until she understood.

Violent, yes. But also...she *had* to understand.

I kept my hand on Axel's thigh, the other gripping the handle of one of my crutches, tightening as the silence went on.

"Fuck," Veronica said.

I blinked, gaze jerking up to her face.

She turned her hands over in Axel's, shifting so that she was holding him instead of the other way around.

"Fuck," she said again, a barely audible whisper. "I want to be mad at you. I *want* to hate you."

My lungs inflated so quickly that my mostly healed ribs ached.

"But..."

Axel's expression killed me.

"But I know something of what it's like to have a mother whose sole purpose it is to fuck with your life, with your head, with your heart."

I exhaled.

"So," she said softly. "I'm sorry I went away, sorry that I didn't find you after your mom threatened me. I'm sorry that I didn't find my spine until recently." She swallowed and her chin came up. "I'll accept your apology for not being here, and we'll both be mad at the proper people—your mother for acting like she did, mine for breaking me down so completely, I couldn't see past my own face."

"Just that easy?" Axel asked.

Veronica's mouth turned up. "I have the feeling that none of this will be easy. But I'm going to try." A blip of quiet. "Just like I know you are as well. And together"—now she looked at me too, and I nodded, wanting her to know that I was right there with her on the fucked-up parents and also with the this-being-something-we-would-do-together part—"we'll make Alex know that he's always loved, always wanted, always a part of a family that will look out for him."

"Yes," I said softly. "You're part of us now. You're not alone."

Maybe I shouldn't have stepped in, shouldn't have spoken in this scenario that was far from being centered around me.

But I needed Veronica to know that I was with her.

That Alex was innocent and had a place in our lives, in *my* life.

I wouldn't ever make him feel unwanted, not after having been subjected to a lifetime of that very same thing.

"Thank you," she whispered, releasing one of Axel's hands and gripping my own. "I know this was probably not in your plan."

My lips turned up. "Neither was having a big, broody, hockey player for a boyfriend," I said, trying to lighten the mood. "But I dealt with him and all *that*"—a smile in his direction—"I can definitely get along with you, with Alex. Because you matter. *Both* of you," I added softly, seeing that emotion tear through her expression again. "You're family and soon you'll see that with us, with the Gold that means there's no getting out. You're stuck with us. Pucks in, no outs."

Veronica's laughter was a bit watery, but her voice was steady when she said, "We've been alone for a while. Getting stuck with you guys sounds just about perfect."

Great, now my smile was watery. "Good."

Axel squeezed her hand then covered the back of mine where it was still resting on his leg.

The silence fell, but only for a few moments this time, because then they were discussing all the things that Alex liked—all of which were things that I was becoming intimately family with thanks to the gaggle of Gold kiddos. Minecraft. Legos. The occasional graphic novel. Watching people play video games on YouTube. Watching people unbox things on YouTube. Watching... YouTube. He was also into horses (win for me) and was currently watching *Black Beauty*.

I told her about Data and Picard and Spock (and their hand in saving me from the fire, which she demanded that I tell Alex, because he would *die*—her words, not mine).

She shared that they'd watched some Gold hockey and that he knew he was going to meet someone today, but that he didn't know it was his dad.

"I didn't want to get his hopes up," she murmured. "Just in case things didn't"—her teeth found her bottom lip for a beat before she released it—"go well between us."

"I understand," Axel murmured.

And I knew he did, knew that Veronica realized that as well when he asked a bunch of other questions—favorite color and food (blue and cheese pizza), what sports he liked to play (soccer and baseball), if he liked certain music or songs (anything pop-related because that was all Veronica listened to), if they'd gone on vacation at all and what was their favorite (Disney and the Grand Canyon).

"Though only for about two minutes," Veronica said, her eyes bright with her memories. "Then he was like, *Is this it?* And *I* was like, *Is this it?* And that *was* it. Just a giant hole in the ground...so we ended up going back to my car, turning on the audiobook of *The Lion, The Witch, and The Wardrobe* and drove to the Petrified Forest. He liked that much better." Her lips turned up. "He pretended to be a dinosaur all day so he'd be as old as the trees."

I laughed. "Sounds like he's smart."

"*So* smart."

Axel's fingers squeezed mine. "Must have gotten that from his mom," he said softly.

Veronica inhaled, opened her mouth to reply.

But then the bedroom door opened and a tiny head poked out. "Mom?"

Between one instant and the next, my stomach tied itself into knots, and I knew Axel felt the same when his hand tightened convulsively around mine, hard enough that a bolt of pain shot up my arm. But I barely felt it because then Veronica said, "Come here, honey."

A moment of hesitation.

Then the door opened farther.

And Alex walked out, headphones still covering his ears, the cord dangling at his side and plugged into the tablet he carried. "Yeah, Mom?"

"I want you to meet Axel and Bailey."

Axel was a statue again.

And I was no better.

But then Alex was rounding the table, moving to sit by his mom on the couch, curling into her lap. "Hi," he said shyly.

Veronica wrapped her arms around her son and I watched her shoulders rise and fall on a deep, slow breath. "Axel is your dad, honey."

I braced.

Hell, I wasn't sure I even breathed.

I knew that Axel didn't as we waited to see what Alex would say, how he would respond. Would there be tears? Questions? Anger?

How would a five-year-old react to meeting his father for the first time?

In the end, it wasn't in any way that I would have ever predicted.

Alex glanced from his mom to Axel to me, was quiet for a couple of seconds. Then he shrugged, said, "Okay," and asked Veronica if it was time for dinner.

I shot my gaze to Axel's, worried that he'd be disappointed in the response, but his expression was filled with so much love that I immediately wanted to throw away my birth control and have a dozen babies with him.

He had *so* much love to give.

"Would it be okay if we all eat together?" he asked softly.

Alex turned back to Axel, tilted his head to the side, studying his father closely. "What are we going to eat?"

Luckily, we'd been primed with key intel, and Axel used the insider knowledge to say, "Pizza?"

A bit of suspicion drawing Alex's brows together. "What kind?"

"Cheese," Axel said. "Because that's the best kind, of course."

Alex's brows relaxed and then he nodded sagely. "It is the best."

Veronica squeezed him gently. "What do you say, honey? Should we eat with Axel and Bailey?"

A tilt of his head, consider. "Okay," he declared a moment later, sounding like the most regal of kings. "We can eat together."

I smothered a laugh, saw Veronica do the same.

And I knew that things wouldn't be perfect, but they'd be okay.

Because we'd figure it out together.

And because I was always going to have a cheese pizza on speed dial.

Thirty-One

Axel

"What does a dad do?" Alex asked the following day.

We'd eaten pizza, had watched *Black Beauty* from start to finish (and I'd gotten to see Bailey sniff away tears because my horse crazy woman loved the movie and especially the ending). But then Alex had been getting a little cranky—not a surprise after the long drive and having to meet two strange people, one of whom was his dad.

So, Bailey and I had gone back down the hall, to the room that Rebecca had reserved for us.

We'd made it *maybe* another thirty minutes before we'd both passed out and slept all the way until about an hour before.

Then we'd showered, met Veronica and Alex for breakfast (and I'd learned that pancakes were also one of his favorite foods).

Now we were at the park.

And Alex and I were making quick work of this jungle gym.

Who knew I could still climb like I was five years old?

I sat down on one side of the double slide, giving myself time to come up with an answer to his question as he clambered down next to me.

"What do you want your dad to do?" I asked, stalling.

I didn't know what a dad did.

I hadn't had one.

I...wasn't sure I knew how to be one.

I was going to damned well try, but...questions like this threw me.

Alex didn't immediately answer me, but I was learning he wasn't the kind of kid to rush into anything. He was calm and thoughtful, as was his reply when it came a few moments later. "Play with me," he said, pushing off and shooting down the slide.

Chuckling, I followed him, legs creaking a bit as I found my feet, because the slides were set low to the ground, *way* low, and I was tall, so not landing on my ass in the tanbark meant that I had to do some quick maneuvering. Alex didn't rush off until I'd stood up, but once I'd made it up, he led the way to a green pole that led to the second story of the play structure, though luckily, this one was surrounded in a spiraling outer pole that I could climb.

"And eat pizza with me," Alex said as he made his way up. "And pancakes," he added once I began to follow him.

"So we've got that part covered," I said, climbing after him, making sure he was steady, that he wouldn't fall.

A nod as he stretched a foot out, spanning the distance and making me hold my breath.

He made it onto the black platform.

I relaxed, focused on my own climb.

"What else?" I asked.

Brows furrowing, he considered my question.

"He would come to my soccer games."

"I can do that."

"And watch YouTube with me."

I nodded. "That, too."

But now he paused, teeth worrying his bottom lip, eyes drifting away. "Live with Mom and me."

I nearly ate shit off that twisting pole, but luckily, I managed to snag the handhold and pull myself onto the platform next to him. "I live with Bailey, bud. Because she and I love each other."

A pause. "And you and Mom don't?"

"We love *you*."

A frown between his brows. "Oh."

"Your mom and I are friends"—they were starting to become them, anyway, and I was determined to make that the truth—"and Bailey and your mom are friends," I added. "So that makes it really cool for you. You have three adults who love you."

Quiet.

So quiet for long enough that my insides churned.

"Like Cassie."

I blinked, not understanding the reference. "Is she a YouTuber?" I asked, having already had my lack of knowledge of popular YouTubers exposed several times that morning.

Alex laughed. Hard. "No, Dad." More laughter. "She's my friend at school."

I was still recovering from the fact that he'd called me *Dad,* so it took me a minute to process the second half of his statement. "Cassie has three people who love her?"

Sweet Jesus, don't let this be me opening up a discussion about a thruple.

"Four," Alex said, matter of factly, shaking his head, and for a moment, I was distracted, thinking I'd seen someone watching us from between the shadows in the distance. But when I glanced back toward the trunks, there was no one there.

Weird.

I shrugged.

It was probably another parent watching over their kiddo. Either that or I was slightly delirious. Alex was awesome, but exhausting.

"Four?" I asked, refocusing on my son.

"Yup." A jerky nod. "Her mom and dad divorced and they both got another person they married, too, so Cassie has two moms and two dads."

"Oh, that's cool," I said, relieved to not have corrupted my child during our first serious conversation.

"Yup." The p at the end popped before he started for the slides again. "I thought of something else dads do," he said as he plunked down on the molded plastic.

"What's that?" I asked, sitting down next to him.

"They give great hugs."

Aw, fuck.

This kid was going to be the death of me.

"How do I rate on the hug scale?" I asked.

A shrug. "Fine," he said with brutal *kid* honesty, "but I know you'll get better with practice."

Truer words, I knew, had never been spoken.

"We'll be down next week," I said softly, not wanting to wake Alex, who'd passed out in the back seat.

They'd had breakfast and playground time. Lunch and spending some time hiking in the forest. Then they'd grabbed dinner—not cheese pizza this time, but it *was* mac n cheese, so his son had been satisfied.

On the way back to the hotel, the busy day had caught up with Alex and he'd fallen asleep, slumped back against the headrest of his booster seat.

Bailey had waited with a sleeping Alex while he and Veronica went back up to the room, the latter making quick work of packing up and checking to be sure they hadn't left anything behind since she'd decided to take advantage of Alex's sleeping and start the drive down to SoCal that evening.

I didn't like the idea of her on the road through the night, but I got it.

They'd both sleep better in their own beds.

And if they left now, it would be just a bit after one in the morning by the time they made it.

"He'll be excited," she said, zipping the top of her purse.

"And I'll practice my Dad Hugs," I said lightly. "Since I clearly need more practice."

"I'd die of embarrassment," she said with a smile before bending to check under the bed and finding a small stuffed toy. "Except, one of my favorite things about my boy is that I always know where I stand with him."

I grinned, leaning back against the wall, gaze dropping to their suitcase, packed and ready at my feet, waiting as she ran through her mental checklist.

"Though"—the sudden seriousness of her tone had me looking up, studying her face—"I can't really say that he's *my* boy anymore, can I?"

"What?"

"He's ours." A shaky breath that had me pushing off the wall. "Ignore me," she whispered, pushing back her hair. "I'm just...it's been an emotional few days."

Because I'd come in and imploded it. Again.

I moved to her, tugging her into my arms, knowing Bailey wouldn't begrudge me giving Veronica the hug she so clearly needed. There was something soft and vulnerable about Veronica that called to the protective streak he'd buried, called to the same one that Bailey had in her.

Three people brought together via childhood trauma.

Cool.

But it was also three people who'd been brought together by a little boy who already owned a chunk of my heart.

I smoothed my hand down her hair. "It's okay to be emotional. I was...well, I still am a bit of a wreck. I just...part of me is always surprised when my mom does something to fuck me over. I know I shouldn't be. I just..." I sighed.

"Expect things to be different," Veronica finished.

"Yeah," I agreed. "But more than that, I hate that she affected you and Alex. I—you guys—we all—" My throat got tight. "I'm just really sorry that you had to do it on your own for the last five years." I released her, crouched a little to meet her eyes, hating that they were damp. "I promise that you both won't be alone again."

Her exhale was shaky, her smile equally brittle, but she squeezed my shoulder and gave me honestly. "It'll take me time to trust in that."

I knew that.

I understood it.

I still fucking hated it.

"We'll be down next week."

Her hand dropped to her side, fingers clenching into a fist, but she nodded. "Okay."

It would take time to build a friendship with this woman who'd been hurt because of me, time and practice to be the father that Alex deserved.

Once I wouldn't have believed I could get there.

Now...I knew differently. I *knew* I would.

So, I just nodded, grabbed their suitcase, and led Veronica to the door, the elevator, the car. "Things might get a little hot for a while once Rebecca starts with everything," I said as we walked.

Everything being the plan we'd come up with at Cole and Olivia's place.

To own my past.

To make sure my mother never interfered in my life again.

"I know," Veronica said softly, holding the car door steady as Bailey used it to haul herself out of the seat. *Haul* because my stubborn, independent woman wouldn't accept any help when she could do it herself—of course, she wouldn't. Once she was steady on her feet, Veronica passed Bailey her crutches. "Rebecca told me the plan and gave me her number." V glanced between Bailey and I. "I have both of yours, too. I'll call you if there are any issues."

Quiet words. Quiet with a dash of forlorn and I wanted to say something that would make this all okay.

But no words would do that.

It would just take...*time.*

Yeah, I was really going to hate that word.

Bailey's fingers brushed mine and I leaned closer, wrapping an arm around her shoulders, telling myself I was steadying her when really, she'd been *my* steady in this.

Veronica smiled, but it was laced with more than a bit of pain and regret. "Next week," she said.

I nodded.

Bailey reached forward and squeezed her hand, suddenly earnest when she said, "I can stay up here." A glance up at me. "Give you guys some family time."

That pain and regret erased themselves from Veronica's face in an instant and she moved close to Bailey before I could get between them, her expression thunderous. "Don't you *ever* say that." She clasped Bailey's cheeks in her palms. "Not *ever*. Alex needs more people in his life who love him, and I know that you'll be one of them. So, that makes us family in every way that matters." Her hands shook slightly. "*Every* way."

"Okay," Bailey whispered.

"I'm sad because I was an idiot who made my baby miss out on this, on *both* of you." A flick of her gaze to mine, telling me that was the truth, but also that there might be something else there, something buried I wasn't yet privy to.

Time.

Yup. Fucking hated that word.

Slender arms wrapping around Bailey's shoulders, a hug that lasted longer than it probably should, considering that these two women had just met.

When they both pulled back, it was with damp eyes.

And I knew that, yeah, it was going to take time to get fully there.

But I also knew that we *would* get there.

That the family we were building was going to kick ass.

Thirty-Two

Bailey

There were reporters outside our apartment.

Well, not in the hall, but they were on the street, several stories below, the late afternoon sunlight glinting off camera lenses when I dared to move the curtain a fraction of an inch to peek out.

A gaggle of middle-aged men in dumpy clothes who could yell my name in a way that sent a chill down my spine.

I didn't like it.

I liked it even less that I still had a week to go on my crutches and that I wasn't fast enough on them to get away from the photographers whose cameras made loud whirring and clicking sounds when they shot a million frames per second or the reporters who loved to shove microphones or cell phones with their recording apps on and at the ready under my nose. The reporters, both male and female, were better dressed than the paparazzi and cameramen, but they were equally annoying.

I'd known what I was getting into, though.

Rebecca and Scarlett had made every step of the plan we were implementing very clear.

And, truthfully, it had all been okay.

There'd been a bit of a kerfuffle when the story first broke, but

Axel had settled that with a nationally aired interview and several videos on TikTok. He'd given his side of the story, and though not all of the press coming at him had been positive, it had been manageable, and most of the people he'd interacted with or who'd been commenting on his videos had appreciated the honest way he'd owned his shit.

It had helped that the media had then gotten pictures of him having a tea party with Alex and his best friend from school, Cassie. The little girl was adorable, but then again, so were Alex *and* Axel, especially when he'd dutifully worn the tiara Cassie had plunked on his head while he'd sipped from a tiny mug that was absolutely dwarfed in his big, broad hand.

The photographs had been a violation, taken by a neighbor over the fence between Veronica's back yard and their own.

But they'd also shown the softer side of Axel.

And Alex, for that matter, whose favorite activities skewed fairly far away from tea parties and tiaras.

He and Axel had indulged Cassie, though.

The photos had indulged the public.

But what had really turned the tide was Billie Rose and the others taking his back. River's Bend had been in the news plenty, what with the city attorney filing a lawsuit against several insurance companies who were trying to screw over its residents, even though they had fire insurance and had paid their premiums, because evidence had been brought to light that the cause of the fire had been arson.

Arson.

A person had been responsible for starting the flames.

That was...unfathomable and infuriating and—

It made me sad.

People had died. Others had lost everything.

Because some idiot—who hadn't been caught yet—had been playing with matches.

And then the insurance companies weren't even going to follow through on their expectations?

Yeah, that wasn't a good look for the well-to-do and profit-hungry companies, so it was no surprise that public opinion was highly negative on that fact. However, I knew from personal experience that Billie was a dog to the bone. She'd made certain that River's Bend had stayed relevant as the paperwork was filed and was still keeping the town in the headlines as the rebuilding slowly got underway. I thought it was highly likely the companies would pay out or settle the suit and that residents would get their money.

My aunt was a badass.

Meanwhile, I was stuck hobbling around on crutches by day and packing supply kits by night, adding in the occasional visit up to River's Bend and down to Alex when Axel could take me to either place.

Axel, too, had been busy.

With the interview requests and several commercials and ad campaigns. With Alex and his soccer games and building a slow but strong bond with his son. And with River's Bend. He'd spent a lot of time helping Joel and Ryan and the rest of his former teammates get settled in their temporary housing.

The Rush had lost everything too.

The rink. Their homes. Their equipment.

While Axel had helped with the move, I'd been stuck at City Hall, one of the few buildings downtown that had been spared the flames, and had coordinated.

No surprise, it wasn't my favorite activity.

I preferred to be out there, getting my hands dirty, not looking at Excel spreadsheets and making phone calls to beg for supplies.

But I'd done it.

Because the people of River's Bend were my family just as much as the Gold were.

They needed help, and because of my infernal cast and slowly healing body, that was the only way I could assist.

So, I had.

Photographs of Axel working out there—lucky man, getting *his* hands dirty—had also been front and center of many a news story. And that final image, of a man helping out former teammates, working hand in hand with the people who supposedly hated him (if those spinning the tales of his destructive attitude in the media could be believed) had been the final piece of the puzzle.

Then the stories had been less about Axel and women getting their fifteen minutes of fame by sharing stories of his drunken antics, and more about his mother and how awful she'd been in that role.

Old coaches had come forward and shared how she'd sexually assaulted them. Old teammates had given very similar—and uncomfortable—stories.

A former teacher had recalled a time she'd come to a parent-teacher conference drunk, needing to have the cops called on her so that she didn't force Axel into the car with her.

An ex-girlfriend from high school had pulled up old Facebook messages that showed the vitriol that his mother had launched at her for "daring to take her son away."

Her neighbors related the nightmare of living next door to Clarice Finnegan, even as some intrepid reporter discovered that Axel had paid for her house.

All of which had been all part of Rebecca and Scarlett's plan.

Discrediting the trash that was Axel's mom, making the public despise her as much as I did, as we all did. Luckily, *that* hadn't been hard, just like it hadn't been hard, either, to meet Axel's only demand: that they not lie.

Lying hadn't been necessary.

Clarice had spent a lifetime making enemies.

Now they were coming out of the woodwork like it was termite swarming season.

But her regular appearance on the gossip sites and on TikTok as people shared more and more instances of her assholeness weren't the reasons why the paparazzi were on the street out front of the apartment building.

Nope.

That came from the news today.

Something we *hadn't* predicted. Something that hadn't been part of Rebecca's and Scarlett's plan. I supposed none of us were dastardly enough to have thought of it—or maybe, we hadn't believed it would actually happen.

But it had.

Clarice Finnegan had been arrested today and had been taken

on a very public perp walk from her front door to the police car and then from that car into the station, media crowded all around on both instances.

And the charges had been released or ferreted out.

Sexual assault.

Extortion.

Drunk and disorderly.

Trespassing.

I wasn't sure if any—or all—would stick, but, man, had it been *satisfying* to see her led out in handcuffs on national television.

I hadn't met the woman—and hopefully would never have to—but it had still brought a smile to my face.

The only unfortunate part?

Because we hadn't known about the charges, hadn't know the arrest was coming, we weren't prepared.

Alex and Axel were out and presumably didn't know that Clarice had been hauled off in handcuffs. They'd gone to Pier 39 and the Exploratorium, hitting the touristy sights even though there was a risk of being stopped with everything that had hit the media. But this was Alex's first visit to the city, so Axel had wanted to do it right.

And things had been relatively calm before the news broke.

Now, though, I was feeling more than a little on edge.

I wasn't alone.

Veronica, having decided to let Axel have time alone with Alex, was curled up on the couch, a glass of wine in her hand, her book forgotten in lieu of the television. We'd planned on some girl time, something I knew was a rarity for her because she'd been doing the heavy lifting when it came to parenting, but the news about Axel's mother had derailed that.

She'd grown increasingly more tense as the minutes went by, as the news continued to play in the background.

And now V wasn't the picture of glee or relaxation.

She was the visage of nerves.

"Right," I said, knowing that it was time to shut off the TV and focus on something else. "Let's—"

She spun toward me, eyes wide, panic clear as day on her face. "Do you think my baby will be all right?"

"Of course he will," I said, frowning. "Axel will—"

"But what if those men who're outside surround them and he gets scared?" She bit her lip. "He's not used to being without me and—"

"I texted, Axel," I said gently. "When I saw the news, I gave him a heads up. I'm sure they're both—"

She jumped up.

Spock, who'd been sitting next to her, followed suit, whining softly.

And, yeah, gentle wasn't penetrating in the least bit.

Now she was heading for the shoe rack, yanking down the gray sneakers she'd set there a couple of hours before.

"V—"

"I need to get to my baby. I need to get to him *right now.*"

Mind prickling because this reaction wasn't the Veronica I knew (though, in fairness, I didn't know her all that well since it had only been a couple of weeks), I debated what to do.

But then that debate ended.

Because Veronica reached for the door and yanked it open.

Thirty-Three

Axel

My phone buzzed with another text, drawing my focus from where I'd been staring into the crowd, thinking I'd caught a glimpse of a distinctive blond I hadn't seen in months, and back to my son. I'd been messaged often enough over the last couple of hours to make me want to launch the damned thing over the railing, so I didn't give it more than a cursory look before shoving it back into my pocket.

No one was dying or in the hospital. Nothing was on fire.

Bailey had texted an hour before, telling me everything was fine.

That was reassurance enough. Everyone else could wait.

I was with my son.

I wanted this time.

Uninterrupted.

But I checked it because Bailey was at home and she was still healing. Not to mention she and Veronica were alone, having some girl time, and while Bailey hadn't given *any* indication that she was uncomfortable spending time with my baby mama—had, in fact, made a huge effort to include Veronica in *everything*—I couldn't help but worry that the shine was going to wear off that relationship at some point.

Bailey was mine.

Veronica wasn't. Hadn't ever been.

But did some small part of her think things might change now that I was back in their lives? Was some small part of *me* wondering if she'd tried to sabotage my relationship?

Possibly.

Was I fully aware this made me a cocky asshole?

Yes.

Didn't mean I stopped worrying, though. Didn't mean I stopped looking for any sign that things weren't okay in paradise.

Didn't mean—

"Look, Dad!"

Fuck, my kid undid me when he called me that. I…hadn't thought I'd get there with him. Not this soon. But he had the same gentle, sweet nature that Veronica did.

Not a surprise, I supposed, shoving my phone back in my pocket.

She'd been the only parent in his life.

Biting back the guilt, the regret in missing out on so much, I focused on my son who was currently strapped to some heavy-duty elastic thing with a trampoline below him and a leather belt around his little hips. He was jumping, the elastic bringing him higher than he normally would have been able to leap, and when my gaze came back to his, he shouted again, "Look!"

And then he did a back flip.

He was strapped in. He couldn't fall and the bouncy trampoline and stretchy ropes clearly gave him the ability to complete the flip.

I was still beyond fucking proud to see him do that.

Kind. Empathetic. Open.

And just a dash of daredevil.

He was an easy kid to love.

"Nice, bud!" I called, knowing my smile was huge and probably a bit dopey. But I had a kid and he called me *Dad* and did backflips while strapped into stretchy things. Life was pretty fucking great. Especially, with Bailey in it, with Veronica in it, with Billie Rose and Brit and the guys. Even better now that the media attention had died down (today aside, because I'd noticed more than a few cell phones surreptitiously taking photos in the last hour, no doubt fueled by the fact that we were in tourist-heavy areas).

My life was good.

I was happy.

The people who mattered to me were happy, too.

My cell buzzed again, and since it was just a text from Brit, I slid it back into my pocket. I was going to have a shit-ton of messages to return tonight, but right now was just Alex and Axel time, and yes, I was referring to myself in third person, and no, I didn't care.

But then my cell vibrated. *Again.*

"Christ," I muttered, yanking it out, seeing that Bailey was calling. My annoyance faded, even though I still wasn't pleased at the interruption. "Hey, buttercup."

"We have a situation," she said quietly.

"What's that noise in the background?" I said, my stomach immediately clenching.

"I need you to switch to FaceTime and I need you to put the camera on Alex. Can you do that?"

"I—why?"

"Axel."

Warning in her voice had me stifling the rest of my questions. I pulled the phone from my ear, pointed it at Alex who was still bouncing on the trampoline, the elastic bands pulling him higher, and hit the button to turn it into a video call.

Veronica's face immediately came on the screen, panic written in her eyes in a way that I hadn't seen before.

"Where is—" She cut herself off, face gentling as she presumably saw Alex bouncing.

Her relieved breath was loud through the speakers.

"Dad, look!" Alex called again. And then he did another back flip.

Veronica gasped, and I watched in complete and total confusion as she started crying. Big tears leaking out of the corners of her eyes, her skin pale, her hand shaking as she lifted it, pressed it to her mouth.

Then I was watching her sink down to the ground, her forehead pressed to her knees.

And Bailey was holding the phone again.

"Buttercup," he said softly. "What the fuck?"

"The paparazzi are stationed outside the apartment because of your mom's arrest." Her voice dropped. "Veronica got a little panicked about you guys being caught out in a crush."

A little.

Yeah, that was far from *a little.*

But there were more pressing topics to address.

Mainly, "My mother was arrested?"

Bailey's brows dragged together. "Did you *not* read my text?"

"I only looked at the preview," I said with a wince. "I saw *Everything is fine* and—" Another wince. "I didn't read the rest of it."

She huffed out a breath that was half annoyed and half amused. "*Helpful*, honey."

"Sorry, buttercup. In fairness"—my eyes cut to where Alex was still jumping on the trampoline, back-flipping like a champion now—"I didn't want to miss out on time with him."

Her expression went soft. "I know. But be forewarned, you might need to head back soon before the press figures out where you are."

"We'll head back to the car as soon as I get him his sourdough-shaped turtle."

A grin. "Softie."

I was. There was no doubt about that.

"He saw it through the window and since it wasn't a giant bag of candy or chocolate I thought—"

Bailey smiled. "I think it's a good thing, honey. Get him his treat and then"—she glanced over her shoulder and I saw that Veronica was still curled up into herself—"come home."

I nodded, saw that Alex was being lowered down, his feet now flat on the trampoline. "I need to go."

"Tell him awesome job on his backflips, yeah?"

Another nod.

Then she signed off.

Leaving me to retrieve Alex, to tell him that his mom and Bailey had seen those awesome backflips. Leaving me to get him that sourdough-shaped turtle.

Leaving me to try to focus on my son as the news she'd given me bounced around my head.

My mother arrested.

How had that happened?

I resisted the urge to shake my head, forced myself to focus on the convoluted tale that Alex was telling me about some fight that had broken out at school over who had the best sharpened pencil.

"And then Cassie held up her pencil and—"

That sounded more than a little bit dangerous, but I didn't comment on that, just listened, just tried not to focus on my mother, on *Alex's* mother, worry knotting itself in my belly.

Veronica had been *wrecked*.

I needed to find out why.

But first we had bread to buy, a car to return to, and...

Media to avoid.

Thirty-Four

Bailey

I turned back to Veronica, wondering how to approach the other woman.

She'd stopped crying, but the quiet that now filled her set my teeth on edge.

There was something wrong.

Something was very, *very* wrong.

I pocketed my cell. "They're going to head back," I said quietly.

A nod was the only sign that she heard me, her head still pressed up to her knees which were clutched to her chest, her arms wrapped tightly around her legs, fingers interlaced, knuckles standing out in sharp relief.

Now what?

I didn't know Veronica all that well, but this certainly wasn't what I was planning for our first foray into a Girl's Night In, and I wasn't all that sure she *wanted* my interference, wanted me to hobble my way over to her, to clumsily make my way down onto my ass next to her, Spock joining me and wriggling his soft, furry body in between us.

Because I couldn't leave her like that.

Despite my clumsy movements and cast that I was so fucking ready to get rid of, it wasn't even funny.

Something else that wasn't funny?

Whatever was happening to Veronica right now.

But I didn't push her, just sat there next to her, hoping that she would unfreeze if just given a little more time.

When she didn't after my ass started going numb, I realized that I was going to have to break the silence. Except, how to do that? Gently, like Veronica herself? Brashly, like the route Axel probably would have gone, shocking her out of her quiet (most likely by pissing her off until she broke)? Or...honestly, with the same kind of straight shooting that I appreciated?

I chose option three.

"Well, clearly something is wrong," I announced.

Veronica went somehow *more* still.

Then she looked up at me.

Thank fuck.

Though, her incredulous expression *did* make my lips curve, something that was probably inappropriate given that she'd been sobbing minutes before. Thankfully, though, she smiled in return, scrubbing a hand over her cheeks, and so I couldn't fault my tactics.

"Yes," she said with a half-hearted laugh, with a shake of her head. "Something is wrong."

I waited for her to expand on that statement.

When she didn't, I asked, "Well...um...want to clue me in on what that is?"

Her gaze went a little unfocused. "I was going to talk to you guys about it tonight." Her throat worked and I winced in solidarity to the painful swallow I bore witness to. "After Alex was asleep."

That didn't sound good.

And yeah, thank you, Captain Obvious.

I inhaled, exhaled. The apartment was only one bedroom, but we had a pullout sofa that Alex and Veronica had been staying on.

Not perfect, but considering we were just beginning the process of looking for a house near the city and the ranch would take a while to be rebuilt (and considering I still wasn't sure what form that rebuild would end up as—a big house? A barn? Something completely different because trying to recreate Gramps's and Gran's place might be too cripplingly painful?).

We had options.

But we'd decided to make those options with Alex and Veronica in mind.

That thought freshly drifting across my brain, I said, "We can wait until he is, if you want."

Her throat worked in that painful swallow again and her fingers threaded into Spock's fur, stroking him when he wiggled closer.

"No," she whispered. "I—I need to tell someone. I just..." A shake of her head. "I found out yesterday before we drove up, and I didn't really have time to process."

Process what? I wanted to ask.

Patience.

Thankfully, I didn't require a lot of it.

Because then she laid it out in a blunt sort of honesty I definitely appreciated...

Even as her words tore me to shreds.

She'd pulled herself together in record time, I thought. No evidence of the tears that had reignited and dripped down her cheeks as she'd told me what she'd learned before they'd made the drive up to Axel's apartment.

And the more I'd learned, the more I'd respected her.

How she'd held herself together for Alex...

Veronica might be gentle and sweet, but there was no doubt that there was a huge well of inner strength that she was able to draw from.

But she'd been drawing from that well for too long, and it was growing dry.

I watched as she smoothed her hand down Alex's back, the little boy having already eaten the turtle's head and two legs, along with some cheese and cold cuts and an apple. Not the healthiest or most gourmet of dinners but considering he hadn't wanted to partake in the Thai food I'd ordered after finding out it was Veronica's favorite, I thought it was a win. Protein, fruit, carbs, dairy. It hit most of the necessary food groups.

And considering I'd parted with one half of my favorite Crumbl cookie—and considering it was only rotated onto the menu at very infrequent intervals, that was akin to me sharing a once-in-a-lifetime treasure.

But...I loved the kid and he'd given me puppy dog eyes and what his mom had told me...

Well, he was going to need that cookie.

For now, though, I was killing some time reading in the bedroom—and by reading, I was basically scanning the same page over and over again, trying to make sense of the words...and not making any progress of it.

Axel, for his part, was practically vibrating as he reclined next to me.

He'd read Alex a chapter from a book I'd found in a local store, chronicling the trials and tribulations of a young horse finding his way in the world. And though it did something to me to watch him read to his son (and made my ovaries squeeze in a way they really never had before), I was as on edge as he was.

I'd intercepted him before he could pull Veronica aside, something he hadn't liked in the least.

But he'd listened to me, had banked his impatience and made it through dinner, through the movie (a rewatch of *Black Beauty* which had sung to my horse-crazy heart), through bath time and a round of *Sorry* and a chapter of that horsey book.

Soon, his patience would run out.

Though, I knew he'd wait until Alex was asleep, even if it *was* eating at him.

I set my book down, giving up on the page I clearly wasn't going to be able to process, and reached for his hand, lacing our fingers together.

"You know."

Two words, not accusatory, but his hand was holding mine tightly, his gaze locked with mine, trying to ferret out what I wasn't telling him. Not hurting me. Not trying to intimidate. Just... knowing that I knew and looking for hints of what it might be.

"Yeah," I said.

"And it's not good."

Now *I* was the one who was swallowing painfully, knowing that this was going to hurt Axel, going to hurt Alex, going to hurt Veronica.

"No," I murmured. "It's not good."

His fingers convulsed, lungs inflating, shoulders lifting and then falling, lungs deflating on the deep breath he took. "Okay."

This man that I loved had been through too damned much.

I hated that he was going to have to shoulder even more.

"We'll handle it together." My eyes drifting from his to Veronica, who'd stood up from the couch, who was crossing to the kitchen and sitting on one of the stools.

He pressed a kiss to the back of my hand, to my knuckles, and then he was reaching underneath me, scooping me up, carrying me across the apartment and settling me on a stool. Saving me from my crutches.

He didn't step away once I was steady, his front pressing to my back, one hand on the counter, the other on my hip.

Using *me* to steady him.

Trusting me.

And *that* was how I knew we'd be okay.

Even after Veronica told him her news.

Thirty-Five

Axel

A little over a month later, I carried the last box into the guest house and looked around, pleased that we'd gotten this together so quickly.

The guest house was all flat, all one story.

Something that Veronica was going to need in the coming months.

That thought send the rage soaring through me all over again, a familiar wave that had been burning through me at regular intervals.

Because Veronica was sick.

She'd had a pain in her ribs, a persistent ache that she'd attributed to a strained muscle or getting older.

But when it hadn't gone away after several months, she'd gone in to see her doctor.

Who'd dismissed her complaints, prescribed her some painkillers, and told her when those ran out, to switch to ibuprofen.

V was a busy mom, had moved on, dealt with the pain for several more months. Until it had gotten so bad that the ibuprofen hadn't touched it and neither had the stronger medication that she hadn't bothered to take before.

That was six weeks ago.

That was when she'd gone to a different doctor.

That was when they'd found the cancer, news shared over the fucking phone with her before she'd made a six-hour drive up to the apartment I'd rented from Brit.

The thought of her sitting on that news, of her damp eyes as she'd told me she hadn't wanted to ruin my first full weekend with Alex in San Francisco had pretty much destroyed me. I loved her—in a way that was completely different from the way I loved Bailey, in a way that probably made me a fucking softie instead of, as Bailey liked to say, a big, broody hockey player, because I'd only known her a short amount of time and I loved her like a sister. But I also loved her in a way that was filled with respect and admiration and no little amount of guilt and regret. She'd given me Alex. She'd given *Alex* a good life. She'd been warm and vulnerable and open to letting me and Bailey both join in on Alex's life.

There was plenty to love about her.

"That's the last one," Bailey murmured, her arms full of several grocery bags as she moved to the fridge, finishing the stock up.

There were two bedrooms in the guest suite.

One for Veronica and one for Alex.

There was also a bedroom for Alex in the house and space for Veronica, as well, just in case she needed to be closer.

For now, I'd wanted to give her space.

Or, well, that had been Bailey's idea—to modify our house search to include space for both of them, to find the best doctors for the particular kind of cancer Veronica had been diagnosed with.

Kidney cancer that had metastasized to her lungs.

That rage flowed again, digging my fingers into the box, making me want to launch it across the room.

Noting that, I sucked in a breath, released it slowly, tucking that rage away—channeling it for future use on the ice. October couldn't come soon enough, and I'd sure as shit be burning through the anger during any ice time I could rustle up in the meantime.

Luckily, I had connections.

I carried the box into Veronica's bedroom, setting the box of sweaters in the closet.

She wouldn't need them for a few months, but she *would* need them, especially with the San Francisco fog drifting south of the big city and gathering in the hills where I'd bought this house. The evenings could get chilly in fall and winter, even in temperate California.

When I came out of the bedroom, Bailey was done with the fridge and shoving the canvas bags that had held the groceries into one another, stashing them in the cabinet next to the refrigerator.

She must have heard me come in because she straightened, took one look at me, and then she was crossing the space, wrapping her arms around me, making me thank fucking God that I had her in my life.

"Hey," she murmured, when I held her tight and didn't let her go for a long time.

"I'm fine."

A snort. Her not buying my bullshit.

Not ever.

Which was a good thing.

I don't know how I would have made it through all of this without her.

I wouldn't have. Bar none.

"I love you," I rasped.

"Those are some intense eyes, honey," she whispered, leaning back enough to bring her hands to my face. "And an intense declaration of your feelings."

"You've done—"

Her grip on my face tightened. "No more of that. You've thanked me a hundred times already. We love each other. We get our shit done together. I don't need your undying gratitude, honey. I just need you to keep loving me." Her mouth kicked up. "Okay, so maybe I also need your cock and fingers and tongue and all the ways they make me come, but"—her palm rested over my heart—"you have to breathe, to live right now. We're doing what we can for them both. We're going to keep doing that."

We were. I knew that.

Bailey had found the doctors and got Veronica in for treatment.

I'd found this house.

We were making them both a home. We were doing it together.

But...it wasn't easy for me to accept help, not even from the woman who owned me.

Something she knew because her mouth kicked up again. "Easy to say," she told me softly, raising up on tiptoe and brushing her lips over mine. "Hard to do. Especially for stubborn assholes like us."

"You're not an asshole."

Another brush of her lips, her hand skating down, drifting toward the waistband of my jeans. "Stop looking for an argument and come out front with me so we can doublecheck the moving truck and send them off. Alex and Veronica aren't coming in for a few hours, and I want to fuck you in our new house."

I inhaled.

Yeah, I wanted to fuck her in our house. Yeah, I wanted to use her body to forget.

We'd had precious little time for that between Alex and Veronica's illness and the season and the fire and her injuries and subsequent lengthy recovery—

Way too many fucking things getting between me and sinking into her lush, wet body.

So I let her dip her fingers beneath the waistband of my jeans, dance them across the already hardening ridge of my erection. I allowed her to indulge—and yeah, yeah, my life was *so* hard with my woman's hand wrapping around my cock—as I took her other hand, pressed my lips to the inside of her wrist, trailing them up along her inside of her elbow, knowing that was a spot that never *ever* failed to make her shiver.

Then, because we were indulging, I kissed her.

No brush of our lips.

But a melding of our mouths that took the rage inside me and transformed it into need that blistered along the insides of my veins, that threatened to make my knees weak, that had me drawing her flush to her body.

"Hey, we need to—"

I jerked my mouth away from Bailey's at the sound of the

mover's voice trailing in through the open door, cock aching, mind fuzzy, rage trickling back in.

At being interrupted.

The mover cleared his throat, eyes deliberately not on me, not on Bailey.

Yeah, that was probably because I had my hand on her ass and the other one under her shirt and cupping her breast.

Bailey touched my jaw and I glanced down, saw that her eyes were dancing with amusement.

"You clear the truck"—her lips tipped up, and she squeezed my dick again, making me have to smother a groan, the fucking minx—"I'll meet you in the bedroom."

Proud of herself for the teasing, she slipped out of my hold, strutted—yes, *strutted*—to the door.

A flash of a brown ponytail.

A glimpse of that gorgeous, denim-clad ass I was desperate to be inside of.

The mover cleared his throat. "I..."

Right.

I needed to get rid of him.

And then I was going to fuck the woman I loved until she felt me inside her with every breath, every step, every heartbeat.

Poor, *poor* me.

Thirty-Six

Bailey

I shivered, thinking of the look that Axel had shot me when I'd brushed my pelvis against his, the heat in his eyes threatening to turn my bones to jelly.

He was going to fuck me senseless...and I was here for it.

Lips twitching, I kicked off my shoes, not caring they ended up thumping against the wall, landing haphazardly on the wooden floor of our bedroom.

We'd moved our stuff over the previous week—not that Axel and I had a lot of furniture.

Mine had turned to ash, minus the horseshoe that Axel had saved for me.

Though, I supposed that couldn't be considered furniture. A knickknack. A keepsake. The one item that had survived the fire.

Axel'd had it framed, and that frame was currently living on my nightstand.

It always sent a pulse of joy to my heart and a pulse of pain.

But, even with the pain, I was so happy I had it, so touched—

I heard the rev of the moving truck's engine, and realized I was staring off into space, not taking advantage of this moment to prep the surprise I'd cooked up for Axel.

Well, it was for me too, something that would hopefully end with me having many, many orgasms.

I'd bought *supplies*.

"Why are you grinning?" he asked, making me jump as I'd bent over, intending to yank off my jeans.

Dammit. I'd daydreamed too long.

"Stay right there," I ordered. "I need to grab"—his hands came to my hips from behind, pelvis pressing to my ass, the hard jut of his erection almost exactly where I wanted it (minus the clothes between us)—"*hey!*" I snapped, trying to kick off my pants. "I need to grab—"

His palm slid up, under my bra, cupping my breast and plucking at my nipple.

Suddenly, I wasn't thinking about my *supplies*.

Because, oh God, his big, warm hand felt *divine*.

He rolled my nipple between thumb and forefinger, sending bolts of pleasure down my torso, coiling in my belly, gathering between my thighs. Then my bra and shirt disappeared and—

"Axel—"

"Hush," he murmured, pushing me forward—

And, oh look at that, I fell right onto the bed.

Hands skating down my spine, the backs of my legs, pausing to tug my jeans off my ankles.

They landed almost silently on the floor, but I wasn't paying attention to where they ended up, not when his hands were sliding back up, cupping my cheeks, massaging the sensitive globes.

"Fuck, this *ass*," he groaned, leaning forward and nipping one cheek, making me arch up and press that ass against his mouth.

His tongue flicked out, dragging over my skin, making me shiver as he used teeth and lips and, yes, that tongue to trace patterns, to kiss his way along my skin, my curves. His beard was the best type of abrasion, raising goose bumps on my arms, on my legs, pebbling my nipples, tightening them into stiff buds that rubbed against the comforter and made me gasp.

But I gasped again when he shoved my legs apart, his shoulders spreading me wide.

One long, slow flick of his tongue from my clit to the taut rosebud between the cleft of my cheeks.

"Honey—"

Fingers gripping my ass. "Hush," he ordered again.

And then his tongue...well, the things he did with it should have been illegal, one hand holding me still, keeping me against his mouth, the other slipping beneath me, teasing my breasts, sliding down to circle my clit.

Wet.

I was so *fucking* wet.

Then the tip of his tongue slid in.

I moaned, his name on my lips, my hips grinding back against him.

But he didn't stop, didn't show me any mercy.

My plan, my supplies, my thoughts of distracting him with pleasure, with enjoying our bodies, finding something pleasurable amongst all the things weighing us down had completely flown out of my mind.

I was a creature reduced to sensation, working myself against his tongue, his fingers.

Then I found myself up on my hands and knees, his big fingers inside me, my orgasm so, so close.

His tongue going deeper. His fingers thrusting faster.

And then my orgasm wasn't close.

It was barreling down on me, tearing through me, filling every single inch of me with pleasure, and swear to fuck, I blacked out for a moment.

I came to, still on my hands and knees, my body singing as his cock stroked through the wet folds of my pussy.

It was then that I remembered my supplies.

Sliding forward, even though I wanted nothing more than to arch my hips, to slot the head of his thick cock at my entrance and push back, to bring him inside me, to buck against him as he fucked me good and deep.

But...there were things I wanted to do, things we'd been talking about for months, things he'd been teasing me toward since almost the first time we were together.

Things he was preparing me for.

Just like he'd been doing with his tongue tonight.

"Buttercup," he growled.

I glanced over my shoulder at him, watching his eyes drift up from my ass, my pussy, up to my breasts—or at least the side of one, a view he'd told me more than once that he enjoyed.

And today, tonight, I felt the heat of his stare traveling through my breast, my nipple, pleasure coiling, taunting me, calling me to move back to him, to spread my legs and prepare to be fucked. Shivering with need, I crawled to my nightstand, reached for the drawer and pulled out my *supplies*.

Heat had been warring with a scowl on his face, but when he saw what I'd retrieved that heat went molten.

He crawled up next to me, sliding a hand all along my side, up and down and *in*. "You trying to tell me something, buttercup?"

"I think I already told you."

His hand didn't stop that slow and easy trek. "You sure?"

I leaned in, nipped the underside of his jaw, the bristles of his beard teasing my skin. "I brought the lube and toys, didn't I?"

Those hot eyes stayed glued on mine as his nostrils flared.

Then he gave me a smile that I felt deep inside me, stroking through me, just like his fingers and tongue had. "You did at that, buttercup."

I opened my mouth to reply but didn't manage to get any words out.

Because Axel had turned into a whirlwind.

His mouth hit mine for a scorching kiss that stole all the air in my lungs, then it was moving over my body—along my throat, my breasts, my belly, *lower*. Using my supplies to take slick folds and make them even more wet, his finger drawing through that dampness, dragging it back, pressing it in.

One finger.

Two.

Three.

All while his tongue and lips worked me. All while his free hand roved over my body, teasing my breasts, rolling my nipples, dragging down to circle my clit.

When he used the toy I'd bought, I found I couldn't breathe, couldn't think, could hardly concentrate on sensation as pleasure flowed through me, whipped me into a frenzy, sent my mind to haze, my body to a trembling mass that needed...

Oh God, it *needed*.

As though he'd heard me, and hell, maybe I'd said it aloud, maybe I'd begged him, maybe I'd gasped out to "Please! Get *inside* me," he slipped the toy free and reached for the lube, rubbing it over the hard length of his erection, turning the crown of him slick and shiny, even as the fingers of his other hand slipped back inside me and flexed, stretching me, preparing me, driving me wild.

"Buttercup?" he asked.

I managed to tear my eyes open, saw him poised between my legs.

"Yes," I said, assuring him again that I was there with him.

His fingers slid out, wrapped around his cock, and his pressed gently against that tight, *tight* rosebud nestled deep in the cleft of my ass.

I gasped at the slight burn, at the stretch, gasped as the muscles gave way and he was suddenly partway in.

He stopped. "Bailey."

"*No*," I moaned.

But then I realized what that sounded like because he started to pull out, saying, "It's okay—"

"*No!*" I moaned again, eyes finding his. "It's good." I shifted hesitantly against him, wanting him deeper, needing him fully inside. "I need more. I need *you.*"

His jaw going tense, eyes flaring with heat.

And then he was pressing in deeper, that burn expanding, leaving me feeling so fucking full that I could barely think, especially when he slid two fingers inside my pussy, his thumb coming up to rub my clit.

I moaned.

"Fuck, honey," he groaned, stilling when he was fully in, my pussy clenching around his fingers, my hips shifting. Needing him to move.

"Move, please," I begging, arching against him. "Fuck. Please, just fuck me."

He did—with cock and fingers, with lips and teeth and tongue.

And—

My pussy convulsed.

He grew bigger inside me, his strokes losing their steady, controlled rhythm as he teetered toward the edge.

But that was okay, because I was the balance beam of pleasure myself—one touch, one breath, one stroke away from falling off.

His lips closed over my nipple, sucked just a bit too hard.

And that bit of pleasure-pain sent me falling.

Distantly, as bliss flowed through every inch of me, I heard his rough grunt, my name tumbling off his tongue, the strokes going hard and haphazard and *wild*.

I held on to him as we both came down to Earth, with arms and legs and *heart*, this wicked man who made me trust him with every part of me.

Who'd never abused that trust.

Who'd showed me so much more than I ever could have imagined.

My lips curved as my brain slowly cleared, as I came to sprawled across his chest, his hands gentle as he held me.

I giggled.

He tensed, hand stilling.

"You okay?" he asked carefully.

I pressed up enough to see his face, my smile growing. "I can't wait for you to corrupt me some more."

He gave me his most sinful smile, the one that never failed to make me melt. "Who would have thought I'd corrupt the woman who pointed a shotgun at me and ordered me off her porch?"

I giggled again, buried my face in his throat, knowing that I'd have many more years of his corruption ahead. "Well," I said, pressing my lips to his skin, my fingers trailing through the silk of his hair. "It *did* start with handcuffs."

His laughter after so many weeks of tension and darkness was the best gift he'd ever given me.

Aside from the orgasms, that was.

Thirty-Seven

Axel

We were both limp and dozing when the doorbell rang.

Eyes wide, we looked at each other, pushed off the bed and hustled for our clothes strewn around the room.

Or at least, I was.

Bailey had snagged her robe, was shrugging into it, knotting the tie around her waist.

I paused, my jeans unbuttoned and hanging on my waist. "Umm..."

"Not it." She grinned. "I'm due for a nice hot bath."

Her eyes.

Fuck, the naughtiness in them, the unspoken "Yeah, you made me dirty," had my cock twitching, my fingers itching to get her dirty again, to corrupt her some more.

I'd taken a step toward her.

Only the doorbell rang again.

Groaning, I ran to the bathroom and rushed through washing up, skidding to a halt back in front of her a few moments later, giving in to the urge to kiss her until my lungs burned.

We broke apart and I brushed my knuckles over her cheek.

"Be down in a bit," she murmured.

I squeezed her ass. "See that you do."

"Be down in a while," she replied, sassing me without hesitation.

I loved it. I loved *her.*

"*Terror.*"

A nip to my bottom lip. "Damn right." Then she turned for the bathroom.

I swatted her ass before she managed to make it out of reach—the one I just about killed myself fucking not long before, every single one of my fantasies nowhere near comparable the way she'd felt, how she'd lit up for me, the smirk she'd given me when she'd come on my fingers and cock.

I couldn't wait to do it again, wanted to follow her right into the bathroom and coax her into another round.

But...

The door.

She blew me a kiss, disappeared into the bathroom.

Growling, I tugged my shirt over my head and then I hustled down the stairs.

But any bit of irritation left my body when I opened it and Alex threw himself into my arms, shouting, "Dad!"

Because the rest of my family was here.

And, later, after Bailey emerged from the bath, damp curls of hair clinging to cheeks that were flushed pink from the heat, joining in on the board game in progress without missing a beat, her body leaning against mine, her hand on my thigh and her laughter in the air, I was settled in a way I'd never anticipated.

The love of a good woman.

Friends who were better than blood.

My son, who brought utter fucking joy to my heart, and his mom, who was wonderful in her own right.

This was all right.

Because *all* of my family was here.

The next couple of weeks were filled with plenty of good.

It was awesome having Alex there, and the more that I got to know my son, the more I liked him. He had a big heart, rarely lost his temper, showed kindness to everyone, and had so much energy that we'd started going on daily hikes.

Easy because the house backed up to green space.

Great because it gave us time to get to know each other and drain that energy that never seemed to wane.

Terrible because the kid was turning into a marathoner—running up the trail, keeping just to the edge of my sight. Sprinting back down to me, taking my hand and dragging me along even as he chatted my ear off somehow without getting out of breath. Then he'd get impatient with my slow and steady pace (me, as a professional hockey player, trying to not let my son show me up because the kid had *energy*) and run off to do it all again.

We'd found him a soccer team.

He'd been folded right into the Gold crew, right into the gaggle of kiddos who were always around the team, had regular playdates, had gone to the summer camp the team put on.

Friends and sports and other activities—and plenty of time at the Dairy.

He'd discovered his love of soft serve and running under the strings of lights hanging in the large oak trees.

See? Boundless energy?

But all of that good had been tempered with bad.

Veronica had begun treatment, and though she'd been fine for the first couple of weeks, those treatments were now taking their toll on her.

She was pale, sleeping a lot, and no matter how many hikes Alex and I went on, it wasn't going to make it any easier for our son.

Case in point, the call I'd just gotten.

The reason I was heading to the rink to pick him up from summer camp.

He'd punched someone.

My kind son with the big heart had punched one of the other campers.

I should have kept him home today. I'd debated the action just that morning, knowing that he'd heard Veronica being sick for much of the night, that we couldn't hide how terrible she was feeling from him, not when they were so close.

But we'd—V, Bailey, and I—had a quick chat about it that morning, had decided that normalcy was better.

Now, I knew that was the wrong call.

Sighing, I turned off the ignition and opened my door, trying to be all mature and shit, knowing that I wasn't going to always make the right parenting decision, that I was going to fuck up.

But shit, this didn't feel good.

"Neither does he, asshole," I muttered, slamming the door and heading to the ring of tree trunks where I could see Alex and a counselor sitting.

My son's swollen and reddened eyes killed me.

The counselor tilted his head, and I followed him a little distance away, got the briefing of what had gone down, and felt my own rage well up, felt the need to punch the little shit of a kid myself. Unfortunately, I had to be a grownup.

Nodding when the counselor informed me the other kid wouldn't be welcome back because he refused to apologize, even after Alex had shown genuine remorse for his outburst. And considering what the little shit had said, I appreciated the teens and young adults running the camp taking a stand for my son, and knowing what he was going through, showing support rather than holding to hard lines of discipline.

Not that violence was ever the right answer.

But verbal abuse could be just as bad.

"Alex is welcome back tomorrow," the young man said, "so long as he keeps his hands to himself."

I nodded. "Thanks. I'll talk to him, see what he wants to do."

The counselor disappeared back around the side of the building where I could hear young voices yelling and screaming and generally having a great time.

Now I had to figure out how to handle this.

Once that thought would have paralyzed me. I was young, hadn't had a dad, hadn't really had a mom, how would *I* make the right choice? But I wasn't alone...I'd had good coaches, I'd watched my teammates, internalized their parenting choices, banking it to use later, to use in times like these.

Not that they were perfect.

But I'd learned from them.

And I'd built the beginnings of a bond with my son. He trusted me. Of course, we'd mostly just had fun times so who knew if I'd make the right call here—

"And you're stalling, dumbass," I muttered, inhaling and exhaling in a way that settled my nerves.

I was stalling.

Time to stop that shit.

Shoring myself up, I moved over to Alex and sat on the log next to him.

He didn't make me wait for it, didn't make me *work* for it, just turned to me with those red, swollen eyes and said, "I'm a bad person."

A knife to my heart.

"No, buddy," I told him quickly. "You're not bad. You made a mistake."

His bottom lip quivered, but he didn't say anything, just looked away from me, shoulders hunching more.

And, hell, I went with my instincts and scooped him up, drawing him into my lap, wrapping him tight in my arms. "You were wrong to punch him," I said, hating that his little body grew even more stiff at my words. "But you already know that, yeah?"

A tense moment of silence.

Then a very, *very* slight nod. "Yeah," he whispered.

"You can come back to camp tomorrow," I told him. "As long as you keep your hands to yourself." His stiff body didn't relax. "Barker won't be allowed back."

Shock had Alex's head shooting up, eyes wide.

"They know what he said." I cupped the back of his head, his hair silk on my palm. "So I get the urge," I told him, allowing my mouth to quirk up, just slightly, thinking that he needed a little light after being forced to face a fact that we'd all been trying to protect him from. "But even with the provocation, you can't go around punching people."

"You do it on the ice," he pointed out.

Smart kid. Too fucking smart for his own good.

"True, but even on the ice we get punished."

Alex considered that, nodded. "I want to come back tomorrow," he said. "They're making tie-dye shirts and they said I could make one for Mom."

Kind. Sweet. A growing spine of steel.

Alex was going to be a good, good man one day.

Now, he was young, a kid who was learning and making mistakes and fuck—

"I love you," I said fiercely, hugging him close.

He wrapped his arms around my middle, squeezed me tight. "I don't want Mom to die."

That was what the little shit of the kid had said, what had triggered my kind, caring son (with the spine of steel) into getting physical.

Shattering a barrier we'd been trying to keep in place.

One he had probably already been smart enough to see behind.

One that had probably hurt anyway, because we'd all been trying to focus on that not being a possibility.

But it was.

The cancer was serious.

The treatment was too.

Veronica had a long road ahead of her.

And that road might not lead to living a full and healthy life and—

Alex sniffed.

Fuck, I hated this for V, for Alex, for all they might lose.

But I couldn't lie to him, couldn't pretend that it *wasn't* a possibility, wouldn't insult his intelligence by pretending his worry wasn't a reality.

We could lose her.

So, all I said was, "I know. I don't want to lose her either."

And then I held him while he cried, those tears soaking through my shirt, and when he was able to stop, when he looked up at me again, I threaded my fingers through his hair, kissed the top of his head, reminded him, "She's going to fight for us, bud. Let's make sure to do the same for her." Though, his intent nod had me tacking on, "Minus punching."

Alex's mouth curved and then he was giggling, those giggles turning to shrieks when I stood up, taking him with me, tossing him over my shoulder and jogging to my car.

And because we were already on the right side of town, we hit the Dairy.

Because hugs and jokes, crying and being held, I'd learned how important all of those could be to feeling better. And because of the Gold, because of Bailey, I'd also learned in-depth about the healing properties of soft serve.

Especially, when it was mixed with cookie crumbs and peanut butter and lots and lots of chocolate syrup.

THIRTY-EIGHT

BAILEY

The wind was weaving through the short grass, giving me that soft *shush* of sound that I had missed so *fucking* much.

It wasn't what it once had been, the noise quiet instead of ringing through my ears.

But it was a touch of peace, a sign of regrowth.

The town was coming back.

And so was the ranch.

I inhaled, happy to find that for the first time since I'd come back to town, there was not one whisper of smoke and ash and destruction on the air.

Just...home.

Though, now, I could comfortably say that I had *several* homes—the ranch, the house Axel and I were living in with V and Alex, the sun and wind and sky, and Axel.

He was my home, too.

Though, it was funny. Because V and Alex had become such a big part of my home too, even though it was all so new, I couldn't imagine life without them.

"I'm not surprised that you've bonded with them so tightly already."

I blinked at my aunt, her blond curls shining bright in the early afternoon sunshine. It was blazing hot, and I was sweating. I knew that soon enough we were going to head back for the air-conditioned interior of the car, that we'd head to downtown and buy a meal at one of the newly reopened restaurants—supporting another facet of my family, of my home. But for now, I was enjoying watching Veronica sitting on a blanket, soaking in the heat when she'd spent so much time feeling cold since her treatments had begun. I was enjoying watching Alex run around the field.

Axel was talking to the contractor I'd hired, the pair of us having already walked through the stakes and flags and bright pinkish-orange tape that had been strung, denoting the two houses we were going to build, the barn that was going to come up.

My herd was in the hills, greatly reduced in number in a way that had brought tears to my eyes, but it was also bigger than before because I'd taken on the remaining head of cattle from my neighbors. Not up here as often as I would like, I'd had the fences rebuilt and was paying some local teens to check the fencing and put out hay.

They were healthy and well-fed and okay for the moment, and with the remnants of Tom, Hank, and Eli's herds the expense wasn't cheap.

But...their memories were alive in that way. And for the moment, I couldn't part with them.

"What do you mean?" I asked, focusing on her, on the comment she'd made. "It's not exactly a well-kept secret that I'm not great at letting people in."

Billie snorted. "The issue was never letting people *in*." A nudge of my shoulder. "It was the hurt they caused once they *were* in."

My aunt had always had a gift at seeing right through me.

It was annoying at the best of times, heart-rending at others.

But together it struck true and deep, and I narrowed my eyes at her. "That's just mean."

It was too close to the freaking truth, too close to bringing up memories of the people who'd hurt me—the people who'd hurt me over and over. No. Not people. They were supposed to have been my family, two by blood, one by marriage, and they'd instead they'd left me wounded.

Thank God they weren't in my life any longer.

"It's the truth," she said.

And it was.

I'd spent plenty of time looking back and locking myself in my own head, burying the needs of my heart.

I didn't do that anymore.

Not since a certain interfering aunt had made it her mission to make that task impossible.

"Annoying," I muttered, since I couldn't deny that she *was* speaking the truth.

"Stubborn."

"Takes one to know one," I grumbled, sticking my tongue out at her.

A begrudging sigh. "Unfortunately you speak the truth."

"Is it a truth that I should be speaking to *Joel* about?" Did I draw out his name? Hell, yeah, I did. My aunt was hell on wheels, and Joel wasn't much better. They'd spent more time than not sniping at each other—and it was a well-known fact that Joel's nickname for Billie was harpy.

Not that I would necessarily say it was well *deserved*, but then again...it wasn't out of the realm of possibility.

"Annoying," *she* muttered, taking a page out of my book. "And for my nosy niece, we called a truce right about the time the town burned down. Not that I've seen much of him since we were able to move out of the shelter."

The edgy statement was more than a little prickly and it sent a note of understanding down my spine.

Hmm.

But, as I'd said, my aunt was hell on wheels, and she wasn't easily distracted.

Not even by a certain annoying hockey player who liked to push her buttons and call her a harpy.

Her palm rested on my cheek for a moment, sliding down to cup my jaw. "Back to the people who *matter*—"

"Ah."

She frowned.

"Apparently delusion is a family trait."

Billie Rose went still for a long moment.

Then she glared at me. "You always *have* been a pain in my ass." She brought her other hand up, holding both sides of my face and freezing me in place with piercing blue eyes. "What I'm trying to say is that they're vulnerable. You spent too much time feeling the same growing up to let anyone in your vicinity feel the same, especially when they're innocent."

I sucked in a breath.

"Even if that innocent is an unexpected child and baby mama."

My breath slid out on a hiss, a kernel of outrage in my heart. I didn't like the insinuation. Not at all. It was something that had been made too often during the time we'd spent getting our fifteen minutes of fame. Veronica was only one-half of what had happened. Axel bore responsibility too. And Clarice, well, that bitch owned more than her fair share of blame.

Especially since she'd been released from jail pending those charges and had spent the majority of her time denigrating Axel and Veronica (and me! Go me!) on social media. Though, Colt had been kind enough to give an interview as well.

Flattering, it hadn't been.

But he was my ex for a reason and I'd had my say with him.

So, we'd all ignored the blip in coverage that came from him getting his few minutes of fame off of Axel's...then I had determinedly changed the channel.

I'd done the same when my parents made the rounds.

Because, clearly, they hadn't wanted to miss an opportunity to rake in funds.

Luckily, neither they or Colt had gained much traction and ignoring them had been relatively easy.

Too bad we couldn't lock them up and throw away the key.

Alas, at least for Clarice, while she was annoying, she wasn't a violent criminal, so we had to deal with her having her freedom, as temporary as it may be.

"Alex and Veronica are great," I said, focusing on the positive.

"Yeah, they are." Billie tossed me arch look. "But the reason you're not threatened is because you know what it's like to be innocent and vulnerable and would never willingly subject anyone to the same fate."

"I'm not a saint."

"No," Billie said with a smile. "Though, it is easier to be open to said son and baby mama when your man looks at you like *that.*"

Her gaze slid to the side, mine following and immediately all of the air seized in my lungs.

Because my man was heading my way and the look on his face...

Ho. Mama.

Heat curled in my stomach, moisture gathering between my thighs, dampening my panties.

Something he knew, based on the way his lips turned up into a smirk. Our sex life...was *fire*. It had been great before, but now that my injuries were healed and my cast was off and we were spending so much time together because it was the off-season (something that would be ending soon, since he had to start training and getting back into ice-ready shape in the coming weeks), our sex life had transformed from heat and soaking up orgasms (not a bad thing) to intimacy and explorations and, yes, plenty of orgasms.

Hence, the smirk.

Hence me creaming my panties.

"Buttercup," he murmured, pulling me back against his chest.

"Did you get your manly time in with the contractor?" I teased.

I'd thought the run-through was more than thorough, but Axel had so many questions and kept the contractor here for so long, that I'd ended up calling Billie and she'd come out to kill some time while catching up before dinner.

He kissed the top of my head. "Have to make sure my family"—a nip to the top of my ear—"my *woman* is looked after."

"You do that already," I murmured, turning in the circle of his arms, throwing mine around his neck. I kissed him because he was mine and I could and he was here and—

"Geez," Billie grumbled. "Don't you get enough of that?"

"Never," I said against his lips.

A sound of disgust.

Then one of outrage.

Which—geez herself—I thought *that* was taking things a little far. I was just kissing my man.

Then I heard gravel crunching behind me, turned to see Joel's truck pulling into the driveway.

Ah. That was the cause of my aunt's outrage.

I glanced up at Axel, lifting my brows.

He just leaned close, lips finding my ear, his words hot and damp on my skin. "Payback for the handcuffs."

I burst out laughing...

Just as Joel strolled up.

Thirty-Nine

Axel

"I oughtta smack you for putting me in the harpy's crosshairs again," Joel grumbled, winding up, ready for the puck I slid to him.

I passed.

He shot.

The crack of the stick on the ice ringing in my ears, ringing through the rink.

It was quiet, late in the evening, after all the games and practices and summer camps had wrapped up. Now, it was just me and Joel and Ryan on the empty sheet of ice. We'd even traded a signed puck with the ice attendant and had managed to get the ice cleaned of extra snow, the thin layer of water smoothed over the surface thanks to the Zamboni.

Now we had our skates and gloves (and helmets because, as Bailey had reminded all of us when she'd dropped us at the rink, we each only had one brain, and just because we decided not to use it sometimes, it was still something we should probably preserve) on and were fucking around, my woman's tart teasing still in my ears, still tucked close to my heart. God, I loved it when she sassed me.

I couldn't wait to smack her ass in punishment because of it.

Knowing I was grinning and not giving a fuck because my woman was fucking awesome, I just passed Joel another puck.

He shot.

It hit the top corner of the net.

I lined up another pass, prepared to send it over.

"I don't know," I said. "I think you've got something"—I slid the puck across—"going with the hot mayor."

Joel was mid-shot when my words reached him and his follow-through went wonky.

The puck missed the net by a fucking mile.

Grinning for a whole other reason now, I knew Joel well enough to easily duck the glove he chucked at my head. It hit Ryan, though, who stuffed it full of some snow that we'd managed to chew up on the ice from our fucking around.

Joel was too busy glaring at me to notice Ryan's antics.

But I saw him working out of the corner of my eyes.

And decided to give him more time to work some magic.

"Those curls," I said. "They taunt a man to tug on them, to see what they'd look like when they're straight…to see *where* they'd reach when she's naked." I smirked. "Maybe down to those breast—"

This time I didn't duck fast enough to avoid the glove.

Mostly because Joel might be a giant, but when he wanted to move quickly…he could.

Case in point, my teasing being cut off by eating the worn leather of his glove. "Bailey's gonna chop off your dick if she hears you talking about another woman's breasts," he said with a glower.

"She's related to Bailey." I shrugged. "I can appreciate the assets that come from shared DNA without getting in trouble."

Joel glared. "You're so full of shit."

"Yeah." I grinned. "I am."

And with perfect timing, Ryan pounced, dumping the glove full of snow right over the top of Joel's head.

Now, Joel was used to hockey players, used to the shit-giving that we dished out on a regular basis, but he was on edge from my teasing, on edge from whatever was brewing between him and Billie

Rose, and he had a temper—slow-growing and not easy to ignite, but once it did, it fucking *erupted.*

Like it did in that moment as the snow was sliding down his face.

He growled and shot forward, taking me to the ice, then whipping around and taking Ryan down to the cold, hard surface in a movement that was so fast I could barely track it.

Then he was back, shoving my face into the ice, spinning and doing the same with Ryan.

I found my feet, danced away, laughter in my chest that was bubbling up and escaping so intensely that I bent at the waist, hands on my knees, and then I couldn't stand, couldn't keep those feet I'd found. I collapsed back down to the ice, the cool seeping into me.

Luckily, Joel's temper burned out quickly.

Probably because Ryan was laughing his ass off too, the noise our amusement was making even louder than our shots had been.

Joel balled up some snow, launched it at me. "Fucker," he grumbled and tossed it.

The cold, wet stuff exploded on my chest, soaking into my T-shirt.

It didn't bother me.

I was here with my friends, who'd stayed over at my house the night before. Veronica had finished her first round of treatment and even though she was still weak and had lost her hair, the doctors were feeling positive.

Dodging another snowball, I started to get to my feet again. At least I could get out of throwing distance.

But as I started to skate away, my gaze was drawn to movement near the glass windows leading out to the lobby of the rink. A flash of color, of blond. I blinked, looked closer, but it was gone. The games and practices and public skate times had concluded for the day, but workers were still around. Probably one of them wondering when the idiots (that being me and Joel and Ryan) were going to get off the ice sheets.

I started to turn back but realized my distraction had proved a critical error.

The fuckers—also known as my friends—had snuck up on me.

"Fuck!"

Half-melted snow ended up down my T-shirt, trapped between the fabric and my skin and making me jump like a fucking rabbit across the ice as I tried to get it out.

Which, of course, had the effect of turning Joel and Ryan into goddamned hyenas, cackling as they sprawled out on the cold surface.

"Assholes," I muttered, standing there.

Then deciding to pay them back, I backed up a few steps, took off and skated toward them full bore, stopping an inch from Joel's side and—I smiled with pride—showering them with snow. "Fuck—*ah!*"

Hell, my ass was going to be covered in bruises the next day, I knew.

That knowledge didn't stop my fall to the ice (head protected by the helmet, though, thankfully) and I ended up sprawled next to my friends, next to my former teammates.

All of us were out of breath, soaking wet, and still laughing like the idiots we were.

And I didn't care.

Because these assholes were part of my family too.

"I think that we were actually supposed to do more than shoot a couple of pucks and roll around on the ice," Ryan said once we'd sort of regained control of ourselves—or weren't laughing our assess off anyway.

"Meh," Joel said. "I needed to blow off some steam."

I scooted out of arm's reach. "Because you can't stop thinking about Billie Rose's breasts."

Joel's head swiveled toward me. Then back to Ryan. "I'm going to kill him."

Ryan stood up, brushed off his hands. "I'll hold him down for you."

And then we were off again.

Being idiots.

But fuck, it was fun.

. . .

Later, still soaked to the bone because we hadn't bothered to bring a change of clothes when we'd just planned on "fucking around with a few pucks," we let ourselves quietly into the house, having decided to take a Lyft back, since it was late and I didn't want to disturb Bailey.

Speaking of which, my woman smiled up at me, her legs curled up beneath her on her chair, her book laid out over its arm.

She lifted a finger, pressed it to her lips and I saw that Veronica was sleeping on the couch.

Pale and thin, a silk scarf wrapped around her hair.

There was a blanket tucked up beneath her chin and the lights were dimmed.

Bailey rose in the fluid, graceful way that made her so beautiful to watch on horseback, crossing to us as we quietly stashed our shit in the mud room. "I was going to see if you could carry her to her bed. But"—her gaze drifted down his torso, no doubt taking in his soaked shirt—"I see that you've"—spinning on her feet, seemingly looking at his former teammates—"all been getting into trouble."

"I'll go change and bring her over, buttercup." I wrapped an arm around her middle, drew her back against me, knowing that I was getting her wet and not caring.

Because then *she'd* have to change.

Just call me an evil genius.

Bailey narrowed her eyes at me, communicating that she saw right through me.

"I'll take her," Ryan said. "My shirt's mostly dry."

"Thanks, Ry," Bailey murmured, ass rubbing lightly against my hips. "Alex is in his room in the guest house, so do you mind carrying her out there?"

A shake of his head. "I'll do it now."

There was something about his...well, it wasn't eagerness exactly and I was probably overthinking this interaction, considering that Ryan was a much nicer guy than I was. Still, this didn't sit right with me. Veronica was vulnerable and—

Bailey rubbed against me.

A bit more deliberately this time and I ran my fingers over her hip, my cock deciding that it was time to get her out of her *wet* clothes. And anyway, Ryan was already slipping his arms beneath Veronica's body and Joel was opening the door and Bailey was taking my hand, tugging me toward the stairs.

Yeah, my cock had the right idea.

Definitely.

Forty

Bailey

"More wine, wench," Dessie demanded.

I glared at her, even though I was in the process of opening the bottle of wine to make a round of refills.

I wasn't buzzed enough for the collective Girl's Night that was Brit and Dessie and Billie Rose, but after our last Girl's Night had hit the rails (arrests and panic attacks and cancer diagnosis sharing hadn't made for all that fond of memories), I'd wanted to keep the circle tight, even while expanding on V and me.

I'd just...underestimated the collective force of this trio.

Or, as Veronica was proving, the quad.

V was quiet on first meeting, but she had an inner strength that shone through, and add in a shyness that faded with a glass or two of wine, along with getting to know someone better, and I was in for a wild ride.

Brit had brought *Ticket to Ride.*

Bad reality TV about people seeking sister wives was playing on the television and making me cringe even as I couldn't look away.

And we were all sharing.

And by sharing, I meant *sharing.*

I'd learned far too much about my aunt that evening.

Including, that those handcuffs—*both* of the pairs she'd used to keep Axel on my porch—had been used.

"Serving wenches in this tavern are slow," Dessie called.

My friend knew plenty about serving. She was a bartender at Monroe's—one of the restaurants (well, bar *and* restaurants) that had recently reopened. She was still being annoying...and I couldn't wait to copiously use the word *wench* the next time I was up in River's Bend.

"I'm trying to drink enough to burn the memory of my *aunt* and her enjoyment of being handcuffed from my mind," I yelled over the din.

Veronica tossed me a smile over her shoulder, her brightly patterned scarf tied in place on her head. "Don't knock cuffs until you try them."

I groaned. "Don't side with *her*," I accused. "She'll be unbearable now."

V's smile didn't fade and her response was nonverbal—holding up her empty glass.

I shoved in the bottle opener. "Okay, okay," I muttered, yanking out the cork. "This wench is getting to work."

"Just saying," Billie Rose said, coming over and plucking the bottle from my hand. She topped off glasses as she studied the board of *Ticket to Ride* with laser focus, no doubt planning her next move that would take them all out. "Sometimes the best type of sex is when you're able to give up control to a partner you trust."

I knew all about *that*.

Just that morning Axel had bent me into a position I hadn't thought was going to possible to hold, let alone be pleasurable, but, swear to fuck, the orgasm he'd given me as he'd pounded oh so slow and deep might have been the strongest one ever.

"Can we talk about anything that isn't sex-related?" I groused, grabbing one of the beers Axel and I had picked up from the microbrewery in town.

The boos came from all around on the heels of my statement and, ignoring them, I popped the top, rounded the island and headed back to my recliner.

Yup. I'd licked it.

It was mine.

Smothering my grin, because that licking had been the result of an accident. I'd been trying to lick my way up a certain big, broody hockey player's body, and I'd overshot.

Big dick problems.

Heh.

"Did you hear back about enrollment for the fall semester?" V asked, and boos aside, I appreciated her throwing me a bone.

"Yes," I said, nerves prickling in my belly. "I got into the program."

For teaching.

My prerequisites were in order for the most part. I had two more courses that I needed to complete, but I had wanted to do them concurrently. One tough year to get my training. Pass the CBEST. Complete my student teaching.

And then...

A dream I'd thought wouldn't ever happen would be within my grasp.

Because of Axel and Billie and Brit and Dessie and so many other people who'd stepped in and shown me the value of *me.*

And because *I'd* finally realized I was deserving of it.

Veronica grinned widely and put her glass down, reaching over the table (and jostling the pieces on the game board, much to Billie's consternation) to hug me tight. "I'm so happy for you!"

"Thanks," I said, hugging her back.

Then the conversation turned toward other things—TV, team gossip that Brit was somehow still keeping apprised of, despite her retired state, *town* gossip that Billie Rose was definitely on top of because she always knew everything about everyone. We talked about Veronica's job and how her boss had finally approved her for a full remote position and then briefly about the next steps for her treatment. It was good news and a step in the right direction—the doctors were pleased that they'd managed to stop the cancer from growing, and the next round would be focused on getting it to shrink. So, the right direction, but not necessarily easy.

No surprise, I was knocked out of the game early.

I'd like to blame it on all my daydreaming about Axel and the orgasms he gave me, but really, the other women were just much better than me.

Well, that, and I was also all in on seeking those sister wives.

There was much drama and much disbelief (how could they think of sharing their man?) and then there was much teasing from Billie, Brit, and Dessie about V and I being sister wives ourselves.

Which, I had to admit, made me reconsider.

Not sharing Axel, but our living arrangements and what those women on the screen must be seeking.

Look at me, taking off my judgy hat.

Eventually, we changed to a cooking show, and started doing the normal thing that people do when partaking in cooking challenges—talked about how much better we could make that particular dish. Judgy hat right back on.

Our disapproval aside, it was getting late, and pretty soon Billie and Dessie headed up.

They'd originally been planning on staying the night, but Billie had a meeting early in the morning, so they'd decided to just go home tonight.

I walked them to their car, got a hug from Dessie, a palm on my cheek from my aunt and a soft, "I'm proud of you about school," that had my eyes tearing up. By then Brit came strolling out, all long lines and bright smile.

She bleeped the locks on her car, squeezed me tight as Dessie backed out of my driveway, and declared that next Girl's Night was at her place...

And with the rest of the crew.

And that Dessie and Billie were invited.

Heaven help Veronica and me.

Grinning with that thought—because it would be fun, no matter how many people were there—I moved back into the house. Time for a soak in the tub, a fresh beer, and a fresh book. I was in the middle of a spicy romance series that had both been keeping me up late at night and also serving as inspiration for me with my man.

More orgasms, muahaha!

After letting Spock out to the back yard to do his business, I came back inside and checked the living room for anything left to clean, not finding anything because the girls had already cleared up before they'd taken off, and then was heading for the stairs when the doorbell rang.

Thinking one of those knuckleheads had left something behind, I tugged open the front door.

And sighed.

It had all been going so perfectly—wine and teasing, junk food and trash TV, hanging out and talking about important things (and plenty of non-important ones).

But now, looking at fucking *Candi* standing on my doorstep, I knew that I'd relaxed too soon.

I gripped the door, started to step outside, hoping to keep her away from Veronica...

Who chose that exact moment to walk into the hall, asking, "Who was there—?"

Candi lifted her arm.

Pointed her gun at me.

Fucking Girls' Nights.

Forty-One

Axel

The lights were on in the family room when I stepped through the door from the garage, using my foot to push the door wide.

Because Alex had passed out on the way home.

His head was nestled into my neck, limp arms hanging down over my chest, his trusting, relaxed body taking up the rest of my arms.

I caught the door with my toe.

The kid would sleep through a lot, but I wasn't sure about slamming doors, so I let it shut softly, nudged it closed with my hip, and then did some more of the shifting that had enabled me to get in the house to lock the door.

A flick turned off the lights in the family room, and then I was carrying him down the hall, to the bedroom he had in the main house—this one was decorated with horses, his one in the guest house plastered with merch from his favorite YouTubers.

He slept in both equally, though, he always slept in this one if Veronica was sleeping in the main house.

Tonight, I helped him use the bathroom, tugged off his shoes, then tucked him in the bed, seeing that the door to Veronica's room was open. Her bed was empty, the lights out, so she must be in the guest house.

Unless Girl's Night had devolved to mani-pedis upstairs.

Unlikely, since Bailey wasn't much of a mani-pedi girl and she was heading up to Cole and Olivia's tomorrow to ride with Alex.

But Brit and Billie Rose together?

Bailey liked to joke about *my* corrupting influence, but those two women were menaces.

Still, when I went upstairs, our bedroom was empty, as was the bath, and the chair she liked to sit in while she was reading—its twin in the family room downstairs.

Her chairs, she'd declared with a smile when she sat in them the first time.

Like I gave a shit.

She could have every single chair in the house, if only she kept giving me that cat ate the canary smile, kept sucking me off as "payment."

My lips curving, I toed off my shoes, changed into sweats, and tugged on a hoodie.

They must be down in the guest house and I was going to crash their party.

I needed Bailey—in my arms, her body against mine, her lips tangling with mine, her body...I needed every single part of her.

My steps were quiet as I headed back downstairs, moving through the darkened hallway, out the back door, into the night air.

Spock greeted me, which was weird because he was usually glued to Bailey's side. But if she'd fallen asleep, she could have accidentally left him out. I scratched his head and together, we rounded the pool we'd had fenced so there was no risk of Alex getting hurt on his treks between main house and guest house.

Heading to Veronica's place, frowning when I saw that it was dark.

Maybe Bailey had passed out on the couch—it certainly wouldn't be the first time I'd retrieved her, carrying her back into the house, back into our bed.

A curl of heat through my middle, stroking down, wrapping around my cock like her fingers always instinctively did when we were in bed, when I woke her slowly with gentle kisses, slow and deep caresses.

Yeah, I wanted to do that.

But when I pushed into the guest house, using the code on the keypad that we'd set up, Bailey wasn't on the couch.

Now that curl of head had become a curl of worry.

Spock whined.

And, yeah, this was weird. He was usually right there inside with her, napping on her feet.

Quietly, I moved down the hall, maybe they were in Veronica's room? Not out of the question if she wasn't feeling well. Maybe—

The door was open and I peeked inside.

That curl became a tangled knot of worry.

Veronica's bed was empty. The bathroom the same. Alex's bedroom also unoccupied. They weren't in the back yard or the guest rooms in the main house.

"Come on, bud," I called, patting my leg, knowing Spock would follow as I continued looking.

But Veronica and Bailey weren't out front.

They...weren't *anywhere.*

"What the fuck?" I whispered, but then I remembered Billie Rose and Brit. Maybe the terrible twosome had convinced the women to go somewhere—out for a drink or desserts or—

I realized I was being stupid and tugged out my cell, dialed Bailey.

The call connected.

Rang.

And I heard her phone ringing down the hall.

Rushing to the front door, I saw that it was sitting on the little table there, my name on the screen.

That wasn't anything bad, I knew. She could have forgotten it.

But a sick feeling had settled in my stomach. The last time I'd felt this, she'd been trapped in a fucking wildfire and had nearly died.

My fingers rushing over the screen, I dialed Veronica.

Her phone rang from the kitchen.

"Fuck," I whispered.

I dialed another number and Billie Rose picked up, but worry filled her tone and replaced the confusion from my initial questions of asking where Bailey and Veronica were. "No," she said. "Brit was behind us, but she and Veronica were both planning to head off to bed when we left."

Pulse thundering in my veins, I called Brit.

There was still the option that they'd gone off together.

Except...

Brit hadn't seen them since she'd left Bailey waving at her on the driveway before she'd turned and returned to the house.

"Where are you?" I asked after I'd hung up, trying to think through the panic.

Alex was here, so I couldn't race off, couldn't jump in my car and start driving through the empty streets.

My phone rang and I jumped for it, hoping it was Bailey, that there was some explanation and she was going to be totally fine.

But it wasn't Bailey.

It was Brit.

"They're not at the Dairy," she said.

Fuck.

Where else? Where else could they be?

I inhaled, exhaled, tried to think this through, tried to reason it out.

But...where the fuck did I start?

"Did you check the Ring?"

"What?" I asked, the words not processing, not making any sense.

"Did you check your front door camera?"

No, I hadn't, but I put her on speaker, scrambled to open up the app, scrolling back through my search of the driveway, me and Alex pulling into the driveway. I saw her and Brit waving to Billie Rose and Dessie, realized I'd gone too far back.

Scrolled forward.

And then stopped, my heart pounding against my rib cage.

"Fuck."

"What?" Brit asked, her voice crackling through the speakers.

I watched the clip again, not quite able to acknowledge what I was seeing.

Then I processed what was on the video feed.

Processed what I was seeing.

And terror gripped me from head to toe.

"Call Pascal," I demanded. "Get him here."

And then I hung up on her and dialed 9-1-1.

Forty-Two

Bailey

I really didn't like guns.

I really did not like them. I really did not the shiny silver death-bringers.

And great, now I sounded like a reject Dr. Seuss book.

But, bad sentence structure and missing rhymes aside, I had to use guns in the past and Gramps had made certain I was more than comfortable with them. But...I still didn't like them. Or maybe it was that I really didn't like that there was an object that could kill me in Candi's possession and I *really*, really didn't like it when it was pointed at Veronica.

Like now.

She waved the gun, drawing the barrel from me over toward Veronica, and shaking it vigorously in a way that sent a shiver down my spine.

If her finger slipped—

"Tie her up," Candi ordered V, now jerking the gun toward the chair that was rusty enough to look like it was going to give me tetanus...if I didn't get shot first.

When Veronica hesitated, the look that filled Candi's face scared me even more than the perpetual state of fear that I'd been existing in since I'd opened the front door to find this psycho standing on my porch. Quickly, not wanting to give Candi a chance for that finger to slip, I moved to the chair, sat down in it.

But though V followed me, she didn't immediately tie me up.

I looked over my shoulder at her, widened my eyes, silently telling her to listen to the psycho. Tie me the fuck up.

Like *now.*

Cooperation was important because I was trying to buy us some time, trying to come up with a plan. Veronica stalling and not following Candi's orders and getting herself—and in all likelihood me—shot was not the plan I was hoping to formulate.

My plan—which was, admittedly, still in process—had one key point.

Getting out of this alive.

Okay, two key points.

Because I was also hoping to get us away from Candi without getting shot.

Now, however, I wasn't sure that either of those were going to work out, especially if Veronica didn't get her ass out of the crosshairs.

"Do it," Candi ordered.

"I—"

"*Do it!*" Candi screeched.

Veronica's hands clenched on my shoulders, and I watched her teeth press into her bottom lip. "But..." she whispered. "With what?"

Ah.

Right.

It wasn't like there was a coil of rope, or a set of Billie's handcuffs at the ready.

The gun went off.

I screamed, and Veronica did too. Pain sliced through me, and for a second, I thought I'd been shot, that my plan was fucked and we were going to die then and there. But then I realized that it wasn't actually a bullet that had hit me. It was shards of concrete, the bullet having hit the wall all of a few feet in front of me.

V wavered behind me, her fingers clinging to my shoulders. "A-are you okay?"

"Yeah." I wiped a stinging spot on my temple, saw that my fingers came away with blood. Not an obscene amount, so that was something, but enough that I knew we were running out of time, plan or not. "You?"

"Fine."

"Think. *Think!*"

My eyes darted back to Candi and it was to see the other woman had begun pacing back and forth, the gun waving around, sometimes pointed at us, sometimes at the floor, sometimes perilously close to her own head as she stomped across the heavy concrete, yelling at herself.

"I need to do this," she said. "I need to do it and get out of here because they'll find me. Like they almost found me before."

They being Pascal, presumably.

Almost tracking Candi down, however, not being quite good enough, considering she was here with her gun and—

"Do it, Candi," she said, going full third person. "Do it. You need to take care of this because the fire didn't. She should have been ash by now. Ash and bone and—" She shook the gun violently. "She should have been *burned!*"

I glanced back to Veronica, my eyes wide.

Had she just said...

"So much burned, but not her! Why not *her?*"

"Shit," Veronica whispered.

And no, I hadn't heard wrong.

"The fire in River's Bend," I whispered back.

"Shit," V said again.

"Think!" Candi screamed, her hands coming to her head, fingers clawing into her hair.

Yeah, she'd totally lost it.

Only, maybe her losing it meant that we could use the time while she was stomping across the concrete floor, yelling into the ether to formulate a plan. Of course, I wasn't a fucking superhero and couldn't use sticky spiderwebs to shoot us toward the ceiling, couldn't teleport us out, couldn't fly through the air or shoot lightning bolts to knock Candi out. I just had me and V.

But neither of us were hurt.

No, we didn't have phones and I was presuming here, since I didn't know where we were, but I also thought it was safe to presume that Veronica also had no idea where we were. Candi had forced blindfolds on us on the drive over and had pulled her car into this warehouse.

Where there was nothing to see except concrete floors and walls.

A few bare lightbulbs turned on overhead.

A narrow strip of windows showing only darkness through the glass.

"Think!" Candi yelled again.

Yeah, seriously. *I* needed to think.

Because this was going to devolve sooner rather than later.

My vision had adjusted to the dark, and I scanned the large open room, spotting the rolling door she'd clearly opened and closed because her car was inside, a smaller steel door next to it. To the left of that I spotted a small office on the far side of the space. A rolling chair. A desk. Another of those small rectangular windows.

Was there a computer inside? Maybe a phone? A landline we could use to call for help?

I quietly pushed out of the seat.

"What are you doing?" V hissed, her hands sliding free of my shoulders.

"Shh." I waved her off, took a few silent steps to the side, trying to get a good look at that desk. If there *was* a phone, I could send V in to make a call, or maybe there was either exit through that room.

Candi was still yelling about burning me alive, acting totally unhinged...or more unhinged, anyway, so I took a chance and crept farther from the chair, peeking into the office.

And felt utter disappointment.

Because the desk was empty.

There was no extra exit.

It was just an almost empty room with a large L-shaped desk and a battered office chair, another of those narrow rectangular windows far above our heads.

Spinning back around, I nearly took out Veronica.

"What?"

V had the chair in her hand, the rusting halves having been

folded against each other. Her eyes were a little wild, but she nudged me back into the office, closed the door, and then tucked the chair beneath the knob, angling it so the door couldn't be easily pushed in.

"V—"

She reached up, tugged off her scarf.

"Wh—"

Fingers in her pocket, brandishing something that had my heart skipping a bit, *my* eyes going wide.

She balled up the fabric, nodded determinedly.

"Shut up and listen to me. I have a plan."

Forty-Three

Axel

There were two police cars in the driveway, another two had taken off just a few minutes before, joining the others that were currently searching through the city.

Pascal had managed to get a license plate number from the video.

It was registered to one of Candi's aliases.

Now he was beating himself up, apologizing to me while dispatching his team, taking responsibility even though the only one they needed to blame was Candi.

She was the bitch who was obsessed with me for no good reason, the insane person who'd shown up and bundled Veronica and Bailey in her car like a fucking psychopath and now had taken them somewhere and—

"I fucked up," Pascal said quietly, his jaw tight enough that it looked ready to snap. "I put looking for her on the back burner with everything else that was going on. I didn't think she'd—"

He broke off and his eyes...fuck, they were filled with darkness. With agony.

"We all thought she'd finally had enough," I said. "None of us thought she would turn violent."

Showing up naked and trying to seduce me was leaps and

bounds away from threatening my woman, from threatening Veronica with a weapon, from kidnapping both of them.

Apparently, it wasn't that evening.

"I fucked up," Pascal said again and his eyes...*fuck*.

The darkness that was in them, the horror and grief and *shadows* in his dark brown eyes threatened to take me to my knees.

I knew he'd been through something heavy, something dark.

I hadn't realized it was something like *this*.

I wanted his help. V and Bailey needed it.

But...I knew this was tearing him apart.

"I'll find them," he said and the quiet determination in his voice eased some of the worry. I had faith in him. I knew that he would come through.

At what cost to himself?

And yeah, I knew it was selfish, and maybe it added to my column of assholeness, but I wasn't going to let him to back out, wasn't going to save him that cost.

Because I'd do absolutely anything to save them.

Even if that meant putting a good man through something that was digging its fingers into the edges of a deep, painful wound, that was pulling on it and tearing it wide open and causing him even more pain.

I clamped a hand onto his shoulder. "I need you to focus."

His head jerked up, those agonized eyes locked with mine.

"I need you to help me find them." A beat. "Alive and whole. *I* need them. *Alex* needs them."

His throat worked.

His nostrils flared.

His hand came down on top of mine, clenching tightly.

Then he nodded. "I'll find them."

He broke my hold in a smooth move that told me I'd never be able to hold my own with this man—at least not in a physical sense—even though I was bigger and heavier than him. He could kick my ass without a second thought.

A moment later, he was gone, melting into the shadows, and I knew that his disappearing skills would have made Bailey smile.

A thought that had agony blooming in my chest and slicing

through my legs. I staggered backward, knees giving way, the thought of never getting to see her smile again sending me to my ass on the concrete. I dropped my head into my hands, trying to block out the fear, what might be a real possibility, trying to pretend there weren't cop cars in my driveway with flashing lights, Pascal and his team out searching.

Trying to pretend that Bailey and Veronica were just inside and asleep and—

The sound of an engine.

Jerking up, I expected to see another police car, or maybe to see one of Pascal's men pulling into the drive.

Instead, it was an older dark gray model that looked familiar, though I couldn't place it.

I didn't know where I'd seen the sedan that was stained with mud and dirt and—

The car slid to a halt and the doors flew open.

And...

My eyes didn't process wasn't what I was seeing.

Couldn't.

But my body felt the touch.

Felt *Bailey's* touch—her arms coming around me, her body slamming into mine.

She smelled like smoke and ash and there was blood on her face, a combination that immediately had terror gripping my insides and slicing deeply.

"I'm okay," she murmured. "I promise."

Her words didn't process, not at first.

Not until she pulled back and cupped my face and stared deep into my eyes.

"I'm okay, honey."

"You're bleeding," I rasped.

"Bailey!"

Pascal ran out of the shadows, skidding to a stop next to us. Bailey jerked back, tugging herself out of my arms.

I growled, started to reach for her, wanting to hold her, needing to make sure she was really okay.

Because—

That was when I realized that Veronica was still at the door.

She looked like she was okay. No blood, though her face was streaked with ash. But she wasn't wearing her scarf. I frowned. She hadn't lost all of her hair, and I thought she still looked beautiful, even with the closely cropped curls. But I knew she was insecure about it, and she wouldn't willingly take it off.

Stupid to be fixated on a scarf.

But my brain was moving slowly. It had been whipping around in a frenzy since the moment I'd seen the clip on the Ring camera. Now, it was barely able to process that Bailey had just driven up, that Veronica was there and okay too.

"You're okay," Pascal said, jerking my mind to the side again, yanking me to focus.

She *was* okay.

They were okay.

"Yeah," Bailey said softly, no doubt seeing that darkness in his eyes. She squeezed Pascal's hand. "We're both okay."

"What happened?" I asked, stepping close, wanting to tug her back into my arms but trying to control myself.

"Where's Candi?" he asked, and yeah, that was the more prudent of questions.

"Um..." Bailey said and fuck, why was there guilt on her face?

Why had happened that she would feel guilty about?

"What?" Pascal asked sharply.

And yeah, I thought that tone was prudent as well.

"Yeah, well"—she cleared her throat—"Candi was going a little crazy. She was waving the gun around and shot at us and so..." Her gaze drifted to the side. "We kind of burned down a warehouse."

"*What?*" Pascal and I snapped.

The officers who'd stayed behind had split up, two coming toward us, two approaching Veronica.

Who was moving.

To the trunk.

"Candi was being crazy, and we were able to lock ourselves into the office, but there was no way out. But V had that lighter"—she'd found that some medicinal marijuana helped with the pain—"and so we used her scarf thinking that we could sneak out in the smoke."

A wince.

"Turns out the walls in the office weren't concrete like the other ones and once the desk caught fire..."

Sweet Jesus.

Pascal rubbed his head.

The officers had reached us, and I saw their brows lift.

"We couldn't fit out the windows, but there was a lot of smoke, so we had to go out into the main area and—" She cleared her throat, voice dropping. "I freaked out a little bit when the smoke came in. Because"—teeth in her bottom lip—"well," she whispered. I took her hand, squeezing it tight. "You know. Veronica was...hell, she was *amazing.*"

Veronica had come over and she slid close to Bailey, wrapping her arm around Bailey's shoulders. "*You* were amazing. *I* was an idiot. The fire got out of control in seconds. We couldn't breathe or see and then Candi came out of nowhere—"

"You're the one who hit her with the chair."

"Wait, what?" one of the officers said.

"She had a gun," Veronica said quickly. "And tried to kidnap us." A shake of her head. "Well, she *did* kidnap us. But then she wanted to kill Bailey because she'd failed in the fire."

"The fire at the warehouse?" the officer asked, making notes on their pad.

"No," Bailey said, her fingers tightening. "The fire she started in River's Bend."

I inhaled.

So did the people around us.

"I always wondered why it started by my ranch." Her eyes came to mine, tears in sad brown depths. "She was trying to get rid of me so that—"

Thudding.

And yelling.

And more ridiculously loud *thudding.*

"What the fuck?" one of the officers asked.

The pair that had gone to Veronica first had moved to the car's trunk.

"Um," the other officer said.

Bailey bit her lip. "Veronica knocked her unconscious with the chair," she whispered. "But we couldn't leave her there, even though Veronica's plan was working way too well."

"*Your* plan?" I asked V archly.

"I didn't say it was a *good* plan." Veronica shrugged. "And in fairness," she muttered, showing a bloodthirstiness that I wouldn't have expected from her, a savage streak that I appreciated, "before you ask, I was all for leaving Candi behind. Bailey was the one who wanted to save her."

I glanced at the woman I loved, my fury surely written on my face. What the fuck had she been *thinking?*

"I couldn't leave her to burn up," she whispered. "I just couldn't. Not after—"

Not after all she'd been through.

Even though the woman had been happy to do the same to Bailey.

Hell.

I loved my crazy, kind, lovely woman.

"She was still unconscious," she whispered. "I didn't want to put her in the trunk, but we didn't have time to think of anything different, and we couldn't risk her free in the car..."

Veronica squeezed her shoulders. "The trunk was all we had."

The thudding got louder.

Was joined by intense screaming.

"Right," the shorter of the officers said. "We should probably deal with that"—a nod to the trunk—"and come back for your statements later."

The other office nodded.

And then they were moving off.

Joining their coworkers at the trunk.

Candi's screams grew louder when the police popped the trunk a few minutes later, guns out and at the ready. There was a scramble of movement, intense orders from the officers, and then Candi was in handcuffs and being shoved into the back of the police cruiser.

"Why do our stories always start with handcuffs?" Bailey whispered.

"Start?" I asked, running out of patience and tugging her into my arms, holding her tight again. "I thought this was the happy ending."

She cupped my jaw. "No," she whispered. "This is just the beginning of our story."

I inhaled sharply, eyes stinging. "Fuck, buttercup."

"I'm okay," she said again.

"I know," I whispered into her ear and then, because I still needed to reassure myself. "You survived." And then because she was okay, because she was here, I bent, kissed her hard and long, needing to know she was here and okay and still my Bailey, still the woman I loved, still the person that was the other half of my soul. I pulled back, chest heaving, hands going to her cheeks, forcing her to hold my gaze. "And I am never *ever* letting you go."

"Of course not." Her other hand holding my face, her eyes on mine. "I won't ever leave you," she vowed. "Not when I have one ounce of fight left in me."

"No," I said, finally, *finally* able to breathe. Finally able to smirk at her in the way I knew she loved. Able to tease because I knew she needed a moment of light. "Because we have that story to build."

"Exactly." A beat, her lush lips turning up. "And it involves lots and lots of handcuffs."

Epilogue

Bailey, a year later

It had taken too fucking long.

But the houses were done.

I wasn't cut out for construction.

I especially wasn't cut out for the construction of two houses and a barn while simultaneously going to school and helping take care of a newly turned six-year-old with a boyfriend who was an assistant captain for a professional hockey team and—

"Bailey! Look at me!"

I grinned at Alex.

That new six-year-old.

He was still horse crazy, and yeah, I'd gone a little crazy for his last birthday, buying him a lovely mare with a gentle disposition.

Who he'd named Chewy.

Chewy!

Mixing up the *Wars* and the *Trek* and stabbing at my nerdy little heart.

I was never going to forgive Axel for showing him those movies.

He was a traitor, waltzing in and undoing my nerdy prep, getting him hooked on all things *Star Wars.*

Worse?

Veronica now had a horse named Han.

Han and Chewy.

Shoot me now.

I shivered, the memories of a year ago threatening to be called forth. Axel and Veronica and Alex and Brit and Billie Rose and Dessie and...a whole host of people had helped me put the trauma of my previous summer behind me. Well, they'd helped along with therapy, but both had enabled me to continue looking forward.

Along with Candi being in jail.

She'd admitted to starting the blaze in River's Bend to Veronica and me in the warehouse, but she'd also screamed it at the officers during their interrogation and hadn't tried to deny it when they'd managed to calm her down.

As a result, she was on trial for multiple counts of murder.

People had died in the fire.

She'd set it.

Add in charges for kidnapping...

And the case had been stacked against her.

Luckily for us, for the town, for the surviving members of Tom, Hank, and Eli's families, we hadn't been subjected to a trial.

She'd pleaded guilty in exchange for life in prison, in exchange for skipping out on a long, drawn-out trial.

I didn't have to worry about opening the door and finding her there.

Not now. Not ever.

Add in the gate and fences and extra security that Pascal had insisted on installing, I was safe.

My family was safe.

So, we'd been able to live.

Alex had started school *and* hockey (and no surprise, he was a natural at the latter and still a good student in the former).

Veronica had finished her treatment—three rounds of chemo, two of immune therapy.

Her last scan had been a month before and there was no sign of cancer.

The ranch had been in good hands, thanks to the manager that Axel had hired, and now I found that I could truly enjoy being up at Russet Ranch, riding Data, hearing the whoosh of the grass, feeling the sun, getting Picard and Data back up here, bringing Spock when we came on our regular visits.

This was now a place of happiness, rather than a heavy burden I would never dig my way out of.

Because of Axel and Veronica and Alex.

Because of Billie Rose and Dessie and Brit.

Because of school and a future job at River's Bend High.

Because of a town that looked after each other and a hockey family I could rely on and...

I belonged.

I'd found my place and my people and it was more than I could have ever dreamed about.

"It's great, isn't it?" Axel murmured, his arm snaking around my middle, tugging me against his side.

"I haven't forgiven you."

He smirked down at me, kissed the tip of my nose. "You love having a full barn, even if the new horses are messing up your naming convention."

"Just saying," I grumbled. "If you'd showed him the Chris Pine *Star Trek* movies he would have been hooked on those instead of all that *Wars* nonsense."

"You like that *Wars* nonsense."

I did.

Which was the worst of it. Because *I* was a traitor, too.

Not copping to that, though.

Nope. No freaking way.

Instead, I flounced over to our porch—with plenty of posts for handcuffs to be used—and scooped up the bag I'd brought.

The most important belonging that needed to be here.

Gramps's horseshoe.

Axel had saved it from the ashes...just like he'd saved me.

Smiling, I gently tugged it from the bag, turning to mock glare at the man who held my heart. "Put your lazy hockey butt to good use and help me hang this."

"My buttercup is so into butts."

Because he had a great one.

But I wasn't going to let him get away with that.

"No," I said, picking up the hammer and small box of nails I'd also brought with me, "that's you."

A nip to the top of my ear. "True," he murmured, smoothing his hand down my back, over my ass, squeezing the round globe.

I held up the horseshoe, positioned it just so. "Help me nail this."

A rough chuckle. "I thought I did that last night."

How did this man always make me melt?

Probably because that rough chuckle reminded me exactly *how* he made me melt, how good it felt, how—

Focus.

"Axel," I warned, glaring at him over my shoulder.

"Fine," he grumbled, bending and snatching up the hammer and nails.

"I ordered one for Alex and Veronica's place," I murmured as he positioned the first nail, tapping it in so that the horseshoe wouldn't fall. "It's not the same as this one." He went to work on the second nail. "But it's made by the same local artist," I said, voice softening. "I wanted them to be able to have something from Gramps and Gran too."

Axel kissed the back of my neck. "They're going to love it."

I knew they were.

Because we were family and Veronica and Alex had never made me feel like an outsider, even though I wasn't connected to them by biology.

I was Alex's second mom.

Hands down.

No qualifications.

People who were kidnapped together...

Grinning, I know that it was more to do with the fact that I loved them both without reservations and they returned the affection. Our family was far from traditional.

But it was ours.

And I couldn't wait to add to it, to expand it, through biology or not—through friends big and small and kids who weren't of my womb (and maybe, someday, those that were) and plenty of annoying, pesky hockey players.

All would be welcome.

Because I'd found a place I belonged, and I wanted to make sure there was plenty of room for all those who didn't have that.

Realizing Axel hadn't finished with the last couple of nails, I spun to face him.

And froze.

Because Axel was kneeling behind me.

Ring box in hand.

I inhaled sharply.

"I love you to distraction, buttercup," he murmured, his eyes so fucking warm that I wanted to dive into them like warm ocean water. "Marry me?"

My lips parted, breath sliding out, head feeling a little fuzzy.

Another tie.

Another connection.

Another way to belong.

"Axel," I murmured, tears gathering on my lashes.

"I had a big speech planned," he said, the giant diamond glinting in the late afternoon sunlight. "With all sorts of fluffy words and heartfelt declarations. But"—he set the ring box down—"I know that you already know I'm in this for life."

I nodded.

Because I did know that.

"So," he went on, "I'll just go with what makes you smile, buttercup, because seeing you grin at me is the best part of my day. *Always.*" He lifted his other hand, the one that had been behind his back.

When I saw what he held, I *did* smile.

And I also laughed.

He rose, clicking one half of the cuffs around my wrist, securing the other around his.

The metal ring was cool on my skin.

But my heart was beyond warm in my chest.

"I'm keeping you," I said, leaning close and pressing my lips to his. "For always."

He kissed me long and deep and slow.

Then I had another ring on.

This one on my finger.

"For always."

BILLIE ROSE

Fire clung to the air, to my lungs, my hair, to the soot on my cheeks, making it hard to breathe, leaving the world looking alien, dystopian, *wrecked*.

And eerily quiet.

My busy, happy town was gone.

Gone.

Tears blurred my vision, choked me, threatened to escape the cage of my lashes.

Fuck.

There was no holding in the sobs. They were too big, too overwhelming, too—

I needed to get in my car.

I needed to get away.

I needed a few moments to just...cry without anyone seeing.

Except, I didn't have time to lose it. I needed to help my town, my people, my—

"*Oof!*"

Warm hands came to my shoulders, steadied me as I bounced off a big, strong chest (a big, strong chest that was part of a big, strong body...that was, incidentally, part of a big, strong man).

A man I *hated*.

Joel Marshall.

Sexy, smart, funny, kind...to everyone but me.

To *me* he was an asshole.

And I heard it in the lazy drawl of his voice even though. Felt it in the way he quickly set me away from him, as though he couldn't stand to be within five feet of me, as though I was so disgusting that my body touching his was enough to send him running for the toilet.

"Slow down there, harpy." A caustic order that sliced as deeply as the disgust.

Because...yup. *Harpy.*

That was me.

The unwanted daughter.

The annoying, bitchy woman who filled men with disgust.

The *harpy* who—

All at once, my control of those sobs splintered.

They erupted out of me, tears pouring down my cheeks, my breath hitching, my body bending in half as I shattered into pieces and completely lost it.

In front of the man I hated.

Thank you for reading! I hope you loved meeting Axel and Bailey! The next book in the Rush Hockey series is book one of Billie Rose and Joel's love story. LOVE, PUCKS, AND OTHER STORIES NOW>. **I hated hockey players. But I especially hated that I wanted one...**

CLICK HERE TO GET LOVE, PUCKS, AND OTHER STORIES NOW>

And if you enjoyed SO PUCKING OVER IT, you'll love the sexy, sweet, and close-knit Breakers Hockey crew. The first book in the series, BROKEN, is now live!

It is sexy, hot, adorable and such a fun read. You will not be able to put this down!" —Amazon Reviewer

---

I so appreciate your help in spreading the word about my books, including sharing with friends! Please leave a review on your favorite book site!

You can also join my Facebook group, the Fabinators, for exclusive giveaways and sneak peeks of future books.

SIGN UP FOR ELISE FABER'S NEWSLETTER HERE: https://www.elisefaber.com/newsletter

Rush Hockey

Big Puck Energy
Filthy Puckboy
So Pucking Over It
Love, Pucks, and Other Stories

Hate missing Elise's new releases? Love contests, exclusive excerpts and giveaways?

Then signup for Elise's newsletter here!

www.elisefaber.com/newsletter

And join Elise's fan group, the Fabinators (https://www.facebook.com/groups/fabinators) for insider information, sneak peaks at new releases, and fun freebies! Hope to see you there!

Also by Elise Faber

Billionaire's Club **(all stand alone)**

Bad Night Stand

Bad Breakup

Bad Husband

Bad Hookup

Bad Divorce

Bad Fiancé

Bad Boyfriend

Bad Blind Date

Bad Wedding

Bad Engagement

Bad Bridesmaid

Bad Swipe

Bad Girlfriend

Bad Best Friend

Bad Billionaire's Quickies

Gold Hockey **(all stand alone)**

Blocked

Backhand

Boarding

Benched

Breakaway

Breakout

Checked

Coasting

Centered

Charging

Caged

Crashed

A Gold Christmas

Cycled

Caught

Cap

Covered

Breakers Hockey (all stand alone)

Broken

Boldly

Breathless

Ballsy

Rush Hockey

Big Puck Energy

Filthy Puckboy

So Pucking Over It

Love, Pucks, and Other Stories

Love, Action, Camera (all stand alone)

Dotted Line

Action Shot

Close-Up

End Scene

Meet Cute

***Love After Midnight* (all stand alone)**

Rum And Notes

Virgin Daiquiri

On The Rocks

Sex On The Seats

***Life Sucks Series* (all stand alone)**

Train Wreck

Hot Mess

Dumpster Fire

Clusterf*@k

FUBAR

***Roosevelt Ranch Series* (all stand alone, series complete)**

Disaster at Roosevelt Ranch

Heartbreak at Roosevelt Ranch

Collision at Roosevelt Ranch

Regret at Roosevelt Ranch

Desire at Roosevelt Ranch

***Phoenix Series* (read in order)**

Phoenix Rising

Dark Phoenix

Phoenix Freed

***Phoenix: LexTal Chronicles* (rereleasing soon, stand alone, Phoenix world)**

From Ashes

In Flames

To Smoke

KTS Series (all stand alone, series complete)

Riding The Edge

Crossing The Line

Leveling The Field

Scorching The Earth

Cocky Heroes World

Tattooed Troublemaker

About the Author

USA Today bestselling author, Elise Faber, loves chocolate, Star Wars, Harry Potter, and hockey (the order depending on the day and how well her team -- the Sharks! -- are playing). She and her husband also play as much hockey as they can squeeze into their schedules, so much so that their typical date night is spent on the ice. Elise is the mom to two exuberant boys and lives in Northern California. Connect with her in her Facebook group, the Fabinators or find more information about her books at www.elisefaber.com.

facebook.com/elisefaberauthor
amazon.com/author/elisefaber
bookbub.com/profile/elise-faber
instagram.com/elisefaber
tiktok.com/@elisefaberauthor
goodreads.com/elisefaber

www.ingramcontent.com/pod-product-compliance
Lightning Source LLC
Chambersburg PA
CBHW031016030726
47497CB00004B/887

* 9 7 8 1 6 3 7 4 9 1 0 7 2 *